She brok… e distracted by a blue … ly, she saw a dragonf… gossamer in the rapid… ve dragon-flies to b… many times had Wu C… told her that, pretending it was her daughter she was instructing in the old ways, but also secretly hoping to turn this foreign devil woman into a more civilized person, someone more worthy of the Ki family's friendship.

Trudie smiled at the memory. The dragonfly's wings trembled in a passing breeze and, as suddenly as it had appeared, it disappeared, apparently into the tomb itself.

Trudie turned away, satisfied that she had had her answer, and, with a lightened heart, she walked down the hillside again to where the man she loved stood waiting for her . . .

By the same author

Dance of the Peacocks

ELIZABETH DE GUISE

Flight of the Dragonfly

PARRAGON

A Grafton Paperback Original 1990

This edition published 1993 by
Diamond Books
77-85 Fulham Palace Road
Hammersmith, London, W6 8JB

Printed and bound in Great Britain by
BPCC Hazells Ltd
Member of BPCC Ltd

For Lucien, who drove from Singapore to the Thai border and on to Penang with never a wrong turning.

And for Ho Peck Choo, to whom I owe much for the information she gave me. The errors are all my own.

And in gratitude for the favourable answer received from Goddess Kuan Yin, Malacca, December 1986.

Author's Note

The local-born Straits Chinese of Malacca are the Babas, the males, and the Nonyas, the females. South Chinese traders arriving as early as the fifteenth century frequently married local brides. The children of these marriages frequently married each other, or *sinkehs*, new arrivals from the South Chinese mainland, which is how they managed to retain their Chinese surnames and customs. Their *lingua franca* is Malay, interlaced with many words of a dialect of their own. Despite having sunk their roots in the Malay Peninsula, the Babas and Nonyas have retained many of their original Chinese customs and traditions, though many local customs have also been assimilated into their distinctive culture. An example of this is that most married Nonyas wear the *sarong* and *kebaya* with decorative brooches rather than *cheongsams* or *samfoos*. The unmarried Nonyas of olden times, none the less, frequently dressed in *samfoos* and sported the two hair buns. The rich Babas frequently employed domestics who did wear *samfoos*, black trousers and white blouse. As most of these servants were Cantonese (they often wore the pigtail imposed on them by the Manchu Dynasty as a symbol of their submission), most Babas and Nonyas could converse in the Cantonese dialect as well as in their own brand of fluent Malay.

Whampoa

Whampoa was, of course, a real person who has his own unassailable niche in the history of Singapore. For the purposes of this story, however, except for his house and garden and magnificent collection of Chinese jades, he appears entirely as a creature of my imagination and cannot be held responsible for any of my character's actions.

Prologue

The silence of the cemetery of Bukit China was almost tangible. The evening sun beat down on the side of the hill bleaching the curved, weathered tombstones still further, as they stood, silent spectators of the life of the city below. According to ancient Chinese geomancy, the graveyard is perfectly aligned to bring happiness and prosperity to both the living and the dead. Certainly, no one that Gertrude knew would have the courage to disturb this, the largest Chinese cemetery outside of mainland China.

Anxiously, she sought the tomb of her dead friend, pausing now and again before one or other of the latest graves, shaped to resemble the womb of a woman, from which one came into this life, and through which one passes again into the next.

At last, she found what she was seeking, the spot where the Nonya woman, Ki Wu Chao, lay buried. Wu Chao whom she had come to love as a friend, and respect as an astute business partner; Wu Chao, for whom she had wept bitter tears and whose death she had resented for so long, only now coming to terms with her loss.

The curved line of the stone was already streaked in different shades of grey by the heavy rains that had fallen recently, followed by the baking heat of the midday sun. Gertrude ran her hand along it, before laying the flowers she had brought in the shade it afforded to the small paved area between the arms of granite.

'Do you already know the news I've brought you, Wu Chao? Do the dead know what happens to the living, I wonder? Will Goddess Kuan Yin bring me an answer from you? Be happy, dear friend, wherever you are, as I am happy at last. See the flowers I've brought you – '

She broke off from what she was saying, her eye distracted by a blue glint by her feet. Looking more closely, she saw a dragonfly flitting across the tomb, a touch of gossamer in the rapidly fading sunshine. The Chinese believe dragonflies to be the messengers of the dead. How many times had Wu Chao told her that, pretending it was her daughter she was instructing in the old ways, but also secretly hoping to turn this foreign devil woman into a more civilized person, someone more worthy of the Ki family's friendship.

Trudie smiled at the memory. The dragonfly's wings trembled in a passing breeze and, as suddenly as it had appeared, it disappeared, apparently into the tomb itself.

Trudie turned away, satisfied that she had had her answer, and, with a lightened heart, she walked down the hillside again to where the man she loved stood waiting for her.

BOOK ONE

Chapter One

Trudie was the youngest of the Reverend Mr Grant's ten children, seven of whom had been boys. Nearest to her in age was Septimus, the seventh son, and her favourite amongst her siblings. She herself had been an afterthought, unwelcome to both parents, a fact of which she had been well aware since before she could walk or talk. Perhaps she was being partial in that she blamed her father exclusively for this state of affairs for, at an early age, she had determined that her mother was as frightened of the stern, distant man who was her husband as was everyone else.

It was on the first Day of National Fasting and Humiliation that distinguished the decade of the 1850s in Victorian England, which had been called in answer to the cholera epidemic of 1853, that Trudie had informed her father he was welcome to dislike and despise her all he wanted, that he couldn't dislike her more than she did him.

The second Day of National Fasting and Humiliation had come a year later on the outbreak of the Crimean War. Trudie and Septimus had discussed its ramifications between them endlessly. It had been Trudie who had pointed out that there was one good thing about it as the mere thought of fasting put their father in a good mood for days before it.

'I must be very bad,' Trudie had confessed to her brother, 'but I *cannot* come to terms with Father's God. I don't believe in him. Have you noticed, Septimus, that Father *prefers* fasting to feasting and punishments to praise? Can you imagine a loving God who would enjoy having someone like Father in his service?'

'He's a hypocrite!' Septimus had growled in response. 'If it's true that one gets what one really wants in the end, he'll end up in hell.'

Trudie had been deeply shocked. 'Father?' She had marvelled over the thought for several minutes. 'I don't think God would dare send Father to hell.'

'Nor do I,' Septimus had admitted reluctantly. 'And don't you go telling anyone that I said such a thing, Gertrude Grant!'

'Who would I tell?' Trudie had sighed. 'I'll tell you a secret in exchange, if you like, and then you can tell if I do.'

'All right.'

Her brother's lordly lack of interest didn't deceive her for an instant. Trudie was even amused by it. Ever since her brother had come home, expelled from his second school, she had done most of his thinking for him, knowing he allowed it only because she was far better than he at covering her tracks; at living her own, secret, private life well away from the prying eyes of the rest of the family.

Trudie was the servants' favourite as well, as Septimus very well knew. He had long envied her her easy relationship with Bates, the butler, and even more with Betty, the parlour maid, both of whom shamelessly protected the youngest Grant from her father's retribution, declaring her to be the sweetest young lady imaginable and one, moreover, who repaid her debts in kind, covering up for their misdeeds, often by calling down Jonathan Grant's disapproval on her own head. It was exactly as she had claimed, she refused to give him the satisfaction of seeing that she was afraid of him.

Which was more than her mother was able to do.

Trudie had leaned forward and almost whispered the words into her brother's ear. 'Father does something dreadful to Mama every Sunday night. I can hear her crying and pleading with him. He says it is her duty to obey him and she cries all the more. On Mondays she looks positively ill!'

Septimus had shrugged. 'Nothing we can do,' he had said.

'No,' Trudie had agreed. 'But I despise them both! That's my secret! I despise Father for making a woman cry and plead with him, and I despise Mama for allowing him to reduce her to a jelly like that! It's what he most enjoys, to have us all quivering with fear of him!'

Septimus was less sure than his sister that his father could be faulted on that score. He might have agreed with her more if he had been her sister and not her brother. If the husband and father wasn't the acknowledged and respected head of his family, there would be anarchy throughout the land, for everyone knew that women were incapable of governing themselves, let alone others, being prey to the excesses of their emotions in a way that men were not. It was a biological fact.

However, he hadn't bothered to argue the point with Trudie. He had been uncomfortably aware that she could almost always defeat him in any argument between them. Besides, it was their father who was given to ungovernable fits of rage, beyond all reason or logic, as was their eldest brother Edward, whereas both their elder sisters were as calm and cool under fire as was Trudie herself, though both of them had taken the first opportunity of escape from the parental home, each marrying whilst still in their teens and neither returning home even for visits if they could possibly avoid it and still conform to prevailing notions of good manners.

On this, the third Day of Fasting and National Humiliation of the decade, Septimus was away. It was a pity that he was, in Trudie's opinion, for she would have liked to have had him explain to her what had caused this Indian Mutiny that everyone was talking about. People shuddered as they whispered to each other about something called the Black Hole of Calcutta, but nobody would explain to her exactly what it was, or why it had been such a terrible thing.

'Let's hope we can expiate some of the terrible guilt of these Indian sepoys by punishing our own feeble frames!' her father had intoned in church when he had made the announcement that the whole country, led by Queen Victoria herself, was going to fast, yet again, in the national interest.

Jonathan Grant had stood up in the pulpit, lit by a ray of sunshine, his pale face wreathed in an ecstatic smile of enjoyment at his congregation's inward breath of dismay.

'I know that this congregation will respond with full hearts to the urgent needs of these pagan peoples who can't help their savagery, knowing no better. We must pray for them, plead to God for them, and work ceaselessly for their conversion to the truth and that they be shown the errors of their ways in rebelling against their lawful governors.'

Trudie's attention had wandered after that. She had been busy wondering if it were true that the whole insurrection had been caused because the Indian soldiers had believed they were being tricked into eating the fat of one of their holy cows. It was hard to believe that anyone would have been stupid enough to have greased the gunpowder papers with lard, knowing the sepoys had to pull them open with their teeth to get the gunpowder out with which to prime their guns, but then people often were stupid, especially when it came to a subject people's beliefs.

'My own family,' Mr Grant had intoned, 'will welcome the fast as the chastisement of a loving father.'

Indeed, she would not! Trudie had felt hungry already, the memory of the previous National Fasts taking possession of her mind in the most unpleasant way.

I don't believe one word of it, she said to herself. I don't believe the sepoys stand in need of our prayers and I don't believe my going hungry will make God look on the dead or their murderers with any greater favour. If I were He, people could starve themselves all they chose, it wouldn't make any difference to me.

She had managed most of the day by sneaking down the back stairs and sharing Mr Bates's breakfast with him. Fortunately, her father never noticed any of the servants unless they were to miss morning prayers. Consequently, he didn't care whether they kept the fast or not.

'It's all very well, miss,' Bates had told her, 'but I can't help you tonight! Your father says *everyone* must go without tonight. Dry bread and sea-kale upstairs and downstairs!'

Trudie had made a face at him. 'Cook won't stand for that!'

'Cook will do as she's told!'

He had looked so severe that Trudie had given up trying to persuade him that she would very likely die of starvation in the night, making them all sorry that they hadn't smuggled her a little something extra to eat after she went up to bed. Somehow or other, her father had got to them first, telling them such tales of horror that the scullery maid, seeing a dark gentleman in the street, had fainted clean away, quite sure he was about to murder them all in their beds. Probably it had been her mother who had carried the tale to her husband, in the idle hope that he wouldn't rant and rave at her for not being able to maintain proper discipline amongst the servants.

Trudie had the children's playroom to herself that evening. At seventeen, she was the only one who was still technically in the schoolroom, though it had been more than a year since her last governess had thankfully left the gloomy Grant household, hoping for better things from her new employers. Six months earlier, Trudie had decided to treat the room as her own private sitting-room. She had searched the house for the pieces of furniture that most appealed to her, stealthily removing a circular table from one room, a couple of comfortable upright chairs with cabriole legs from another, and the two most efficient moderator lamps from her father's study, replacing them with the worst ones she could find, gleeful in the knowledge that, whilst he would have declared them adequate for his family, he would soon purchase two of the very latest design for himself.

She had been particularly pleased to have the moderator lamps for her own use. They were so named because the oil fuel was moderated by being forced up a small central tube to the wick by means of a spring-operated piston, and were vastly more efficient than the old-fashioned lamps they replaced.

Trudie's other triumphs were the deep crimson upholstery and the black-fringed pelmets, which were the very latest in fashionable living and which were quite different from the lighter colours her mothers still favoured downstairs.

Septimus had remarked when he had first seen the transformed room, 'You've turned it into one of the smartest rooms in the borough! What would Father say if he knew?'

Trudie had felt quite safe and more than a little smug. 'He never comes up here,' she had said simply. 'Besides, he has no taste and probably wouldn't notice how nice it looks if he did!'

Her mother had noticed what she had done, however. 'Oh, Trudie, it does look fine!' she had exclaimed. And then, pathetically, she had begged that she might be allowed to do her needlework in there sometimes, it being so much more welcoming than her own small sitting-room that led off her husband's study.

Trudie had tried to be kind, noting her mother's quivering chin and the tears in her pale eyes. 'It's your house,' she had said aloud. 'Of course you may sit in any room you wish to – except Father's study,' she had added, feeling that that was going too far.

'It's your father's house,' her mother had retorted dryly. 'It was part of my dowry, if you must know, but it's the greatest mistake to think women own anything in this world.'

Trudie had never thought of her mother before she had been Mrs Jonathan Grant. 'Your dowry?' she had said blankly.

For a fleeting instant, her mother had looked quite pretty. 'I was very handsomely provided for by my father or we wouldn't live half so well as we do today! Though if there is one thing I can never understand, it is why it is so much more expensive to fast than to have our normal meals! Your father will never believe it, but so it is!'

Trudie had come nearer to liking her mother in that one moment than she had in years. 'When I get married I'll never fast again!' she had declared.

'Let's hope you're right!' her mother had said, looking tearful and defeated once again. 'It's best, though, not to make too much fuss at anything one's husband decrees –

I've learned that the hard way.' She laughed harshly. 'You're lucky, Trudie. Nobody is going to marry you for your money!'

Trudie lit the lamps as a small act of defiance against her father downstairs. She hated the twilight, when the whole of London descended under a gloomy half-light. It was different in the country, when the sky came right down to the horizon, but in the narrow street in which they lived, there were few beautiful sunsets to be admired and only the lamplighter to watch, as he made his round of the new streetlights that were supposed to make the streets so much safer for both pedestrians and the passing traffic.

The dinner gong sounded down below just as she had got a good flame going on the second wick. She hesitated over the extravagance of leaving them lighted in an empty room, shrugging her shoulders at her nagging conscience. It would be more trouble than it was worth to have to light them again, and Betty had more than enough to do without being asked to come up here and light them for her after she had gone downstairs.

Trudie glanced at herself in the ill-lit glass, pulling at her second-best dinner dress. If sea-kale and dry bread were all they were going to get to eat, surely it hadn't been worth the trouble of changing at all. But they always did change for dinner. Her father insisted on it. None of her brothers would have dared to present themselves in the dining-room except in their full evening rig, so she and her mother always changed also, cold as they found the low neckline in winter. Trudie's own dresses had the higher, rising waistline that was fashionable, though she wouldn't have dared to wear her bodice open down to the waist, showing a lace or muslin chemisette, as many of her friends did. Her mother had kept to the lower waistline that had been fashionable in the forties, for she had few new dresses in her wardrobe, Mr Grant being convinced that vanity was a peculiarly female sin and should be indulged as seldom as possible.

The glass was not so dull that Trudie couldn't see the dowdy, badly stitched seams of the dress. It was something she couldn't explain even to Septimus, how badly it hurt not to have the well-fitting, fashionable clothes that she saw in her friends' fashion magazines and which cost so little more than the ones her father deemed fitting for the daughter of the devoted man of God he saw himself to be.

She stuck out her tongue at herself, disliking her image so much that she could feel the beginning of a headache at the back of her eyes.

'Sea-kale!' she muttered, hating that too. 'No wonder Father went out earlier! He probably ate his fill somewhere else, before coming home to say grace for us!'

The gong rang again and she hurried down the stairs, taking her place in the line of those of her family who were eating dinner at home that evening. Her brothers made room for her in silence. She wondered if they ever talked to her elder sisters as she and Septimus talked to one another, but she doubted it. Their faces were all set in the same cast as her father's, round and polished, with mean, furtive eyes that glanced first one way and then the other, as if the whole world were their enemy.

No use looking for amusement there –

A tinkling laugh broke the silence, causing the line of men to look in outraged astonishment for its source. Trudie suppressed a giggle. She would have known that laugh anywhere as being her cousin Hermione's! Her pretty, silly cousin wasn't going to relish having sea-kale and dry bread and nothing else for dinner! Trudie's eyes sparkled at the thought of how her cousin would whimper and plead with her Uncle Jonathan, twisting him around her foolish finger, for, if she had no other talent worthy of the name, Hermione could manipulate any man into giving her her own way, no matter how determined they were to resist her blandishments. Trudie was offended by her, but she didn't dislike her. Her contempt was reserved for her father, who couldn't see his niece as the baggage she was, fondling her and kissing her on the mouth, openly wishing she was his daughter instead of Trudie, whom he had never been able to like and who would have died rather than simper over him and flatter him to get her own way about anything.

Ignoring his waiting family, Mr Grant swept his niece in to dinner on his arm, seating her next to himself with such a flourish that the poor girl nearly landed on the floor. There was no need to look at her to know she was flushed, her eyes too bright, and that strange, sweet smell that hung around Mr Grant's study was clinging to her dress and shawl.

'My dearest niece, you bring joy to an old man's heart with your pretty ways! How I wish my own daughter had one-tenth of your femininity and sweetness!'

Hermione batted her eyelashes. 'You're just saying that, Uncle! We all know Cousin Gertrude is much, much cleverer than I could ever hope to be!'

'The last thing a woman should be is clever!' Jonathan Grant answered heavily.

Hermione bowed her fair head. 'I am for ever telling everyone how fortunate I am to have a clever uncle like you, Uncle Jonathan. If *you* were the one to have the management of my affairs, I shouldn't have to worry about anything ever again, should I?'

From which remark Trudie concluded she had been the recipient of another half-guinea from her doting uncle. She stared at Hermione across the table, knowing that, for once, her brothers were as outraged as she that such largesse never came their way.

'No niece of mine will ever starve, my dear. I think I may safely promise you that!' Mr Grant beamed at the bent golden head.

'Yes, well, that is why I came to call on you this evening.' Trudie, watching her cousin carefully, noted that, although she looked breathless and overcome by her uncle's attention, she was as hard-eyed as ever as she glanced round the table to see the effect she was having on her male cousins. 'I have received an offer of marriage! My father wants me to accept, of course, but I told him I wasn't going to do anything until I had talked to my darling Uncle Jonathan about it!'

'And what did your father say to that?' Mr Grant asked, much pleased at the thought of his elder brother having to take second place to himself in the opinion of his own daughter.

'He said I was a clever puss!' Hermione giggled.

Trudie's eyes opened wide. Would her father swallow that? It seemed he would.

Jonathan Grant twirled his moustache thoughtfully. 'And so you are! I shall look into the terms of this marriage myself and advise you accordingly. Your father never did understand that what a woman needs before all else is security in her future life. That's what comes of being the elder son and having no acquaintance with the ravages poverty can bring to the best-run household! Never was a truer word spoken than when poverty comes in the door, love flies out of the window!'

Trudie saw her mother's miserable face and wished she would stand up for herself for once. Curling her lip, she muttered, 'All younger sons should marry money as you did, Father – '

Mr Grant glowered at her, disliking his youngest daughter even more than usual. 'I suppose it was your mother who told you I married her for her imagined fortune? I thought so. Well, let me tell you, young lady, that I am the servant of the Lord, not of mammon.' His mouth snapped shut into an angry line. 'Not that it is your place to offer any opinion on the matter! If we weren't already fasting, I'd send you to your room on a diet of bread and water until you saw fit to apologize for your impertinence!'

Hermione leaned prettily up against him. 'Please don't be so stern and unforgiving with Trudie, uncle dear,' she whispered. 'I can't bear scenes and – and Cousin Gertrude has such a loud voice when she's upset about anything. It – it quite frightens me!'

Her uncle put a finger under her chin and raised her face to him. 'Now don't you worry your pretty head about that wilful daughter of mine. Being the youngest she is sadly spoilt and needs discipline in a way you wouldn't understand, being such a loving, sweet little thing yourself. Trudie could learn a great deal from you, my dear, if she would! Now tell me your news, child! It's good news, I take it?'

'Oh yes, uncle! At least, I think it is! I am to be married! To such a fine man! Of course, I don't know him very well, but Father says he will take every care of me and that I'm a lucky girl to have attracted his attention.' A shadow crossed her face. 'I may be lonely so far away from my parents, but no doubt I shall get used to it. He is a very rich man, uncle, one of the richest in the whole Empire.' Her chin quivered. 'Father says I must marry him because he doesn't know how he'll manage unless I come up with a rich son-in-law for him! That's why I've come to you,' she rushed on. 'Being a man of God, you won't care if he's rich or not, will you? *You* will only want my happiness, won't you? Of course, I wouldn't presume to criticize Father's judgement – women should never set themselves up against their fathers' and husbands' judgement, should they? – but I should be so much happier in my own mind if *you* approve the match also. You've always been so much more than a father to me and I feel so safe in your hands!'

Trudie found it better not to look at her cousin during this long speech. As it was she could scarcely contain herself. She longed for Septimus to laugh with, for he would have found this blatant flattery as much of an affront as she did. She wriggled on her chair, waiting for it to occur to her father that Hermione's wedding plans were his brother's business rather than his. She would have liked to have seen his face if she were ever to approach Hermione's father with such a speech! However, her father saw nothing wrong in his niece's attitude. He knew his brother to be a profligate simpleton with no idea of money management, or anything else. The fact that his sister-in-law was as fat as butter and as cheerful as his own wife was miserable was a matter of total indifference to him. Money in the bank was the measure by which he judged a man! He was pleasantly surprised that, for once, his brother seemed to be in agreement with him.

'Naturally I shall want to inspect your fiancé before I allow him to marry my favourite niece!' he comforted Hermione. 'I shall want to speak to you *both* before you come before me to make your vows.'

How typical, Trudie thought, that they were to go before him rather than before God. She sucked in her cheeks to stop herself from laughing, looking round the table hopefully. Her brothers were all intent on the empty plates set down in front of them. She doubted her mother was listening at all.

Jonathan Grant breathed deeply. 'We must celebrate!' he

barked down the table. 'Bates! Tell cook to send up something fit for us all to eat, except for Mrs Grant and Miss Trudie. Someone must maintain the fast, mustn't they?' His eye caught Trudie's, returning her dislike with interest. '*All wickedness is but little to the wickedness of a woman*, as the writer of Ecclesiastes tells us, and it's a matter for regret that this applies to my own daughter more than to most. As a loving father, I must see she learns to chastise the body that the soul may live – '

He fell into a deep silence, pretending to pray. No one dared to interrupt him, not even Trudie, burning with resentment as she was. There had been a time when she would have challenged her father's dictum, quoting the Scriptures as easily as he, but over the years she had learned to hold her tongue, if only for her mother's sake. If there was one thing she couldn't bear, it was to see her mother cringing before her husband as if she were his slave instead of his wife.

Septimus said the family's fortune was built on slavery. From time to time, Trudie had heard her father and uncle bemoaning the loss of some of their estates in the West Indies. One of her brothers had once been sent out to Trinidad many years before, almost before she had been old enough to walk by herself, and he had died out there in circumstances which no one had ever explained to her. There had been much talk from her mother of his lonely, unkempt grave, so much so that the little girl had had frequent nightmares in which a large, crumbling sepulchre had figured, out of which a black shape had emerged seeking to take her back inside with him. As she couldn't remember anything about her dead brother, not even what he had looked like, she had been glad when the dreams had finally gone away, leaving her in peace. Only, sometimes, when she saw the great sacks of sugar being offloaded in the docks, her family's name stamped upon them, she would shudder away from the sight, reflecting that the sacks looked like so many dead bodies being brought ashore.

On the rare occasions when her uncle came with Hermione to visit her cousins, the West Indies were the only subject the two brothers ever talked about. As the elder brother, Uncle Henry was supposed to be the one who appointed the overseers and decided the policy of the estates, but, in actual fact, he had long ago allowed Jonathan to outmanoeuvre him and to take the management into his own hands. Henry, his brother declared, besides being a fool, was tainted by radical ideas that were contrary to the will of God. Jonathan suspected him of wanting to free the slaves and had worked quickly to get the rest of the family behind him in deposing Henry from his rightful position. Trudie could remember the row that had rocked the whole family when her younger uncles had woken up to what had happened. It wasn't that they objected to Henry's demotion; that they could have accepted with equanimity, especially if one of them had been promoted in his place. No, what stuck in their craw was Jonathan's resulting supremacy when he had already taken possession of one of the richest livings in London, entering the Church at exactly the right moment to do so. That, in their opinion, should have been enough for him. A man of the cloth had no business making money hand over fist at their expense. They were not so dull that they couldn't see how one son after another had been taken into their business, whilst their own children had had to make do with a small part of their fathers' shares.

All except Hermione. Jonathan's excuse was that as Henry's only child she was entitled to the best of everything – on the clear understanding that his was the hand that fed her and that his brother thanked him publicly, often and long. Trudie wondered if she were the only one to observe that, if Henry failed in this duty, Hermione hurried to fulfil it for him. Hermione was like a cat, always falling on her feet, prepared to purr and fawn against anyone who would provide her with cream in her milk.

Trudie was busy studying the almost sensual pleasure with which her father touched his niece – with his eyes all the time, with his hands whenever he was near enough to her to do so – when Bates, his face totally expressionless, laid the first of the covers on the table, lifting the highly polished silver domes to reveal the meagre helpings of sea-kale and dry bread beneath.

As she helped herself, Trudie felt her father looking at her for the first time since he had ordered Bates to bring something better for the others to eat. It gave her a *frisson* of distaste to know how much he was enjoying humiliating her in front of her cousin. She lifted her chin, pretending the sea-kale was the finest dish in the world. She would have died sooner than allow him to know how much it hurt to see her cousin receiving all the affection and more that rightly belonged to her as Jonathan's daughter. It especially revolted her to see Hermione's plate piled high with all her favourite foods. What were they eating downstairs now, she asked herself sourly, when they had been unexpectedly obliged to send all these dishes upstairs? She might have known Bates had been lying when he had said it would be dry bread and sea-kale upstairs and down!

To hide the raging fire of hatred that threatened to consume her, Trudie took a small bite of bread and turned to her cousin. 'My sisters will love to know more of your plans, Cousin Hermione! If there is one thing that unites the distaff side of this family, it is a marriage! How exciting to be the cause of such a dither! If I know them, they will both be calling on you before you can say knife, but I want to be the first with the news for once! Is he terribly handsome?'

Hermione lifted a bare shoulder. 'He is well enough,' she answered. 'Nothing like as handsome as Uncle Jonathan, but well enough!'

Her eyes flirted with her uncle's. Disgusted, Trudie took another mouthful of sea-kale. So he was ugly, she thought, but undoubtedly rich. 'And where shall you live?'

It was a moment before Hermione answered. 'Somewhere abroad. I forget where exactly. I think it is in India. Oh yes, I remember, it is called Singapore!'

The men looked at one another, none the wiser. Trudie sucked in her cheeks again, longing for Septimus. If anyone knew where Singapore was, it would be he.

Then, almost as if in answer to her prayer, the door opened, admitting a draught that caused the dormant fire to flare into life for a few seconds, and there stood Septimus, immaculate in his evening clothes, a smile on his face.

'Good evening, Father. Good evening all. Is that food I smell? How splendid! I thought we should all be fasting as is everyone else! Ah, Cousin Hermione is here and so we feast instead!'

Jonathan Grant watched his youngest son kiss his mother's cheek with a disapproving frown. He knew his wife well enough to know that none of her other sons would have brought that blush of delight to her face. Well, Septimus was far from being *his* favourite son and he would have been far better pleased by his absence. He had been upset enough to hear of his niece's projected marriage to have to suffer any more bad news.

'To what do we owe the pleasure of your company, Septimus?'

His son sat down on the chair Bates had hastily brought for him. 'I may be mistaken, Father, but I rather thought I lived here,' Septimus drawled.

The sharp intake of breath from everyone present was enough to arouse Trudie's every protective instinct. She put a warning hand on her brother's wrist. 'Septimus, where is Singapore? Is it in India? Cousin Hermione thinks it might be.'

'Then Cousin Hermione is wrong!'

'Manners, Septimus!' his father roared at him. 'It isn't good manners to contradict your cousin!'

'No, sir.' He thought for a moment. 'Singapore is in India, Cousin Hermione, inasmuch as I believe it is governed from there. It is an island at the foot of the Malay Peninsula – '

'And where, pray, is that?' Hermione giggled, pleased that her ignorance should make her cousin sound like a prosy bore – at least to her own ears.

'You may have heard of Malacca?' Septimus returned indifferently.

Much of the charm fell away from Hermione's expression. Something in her cousin's voice told her she ought to have heard of Malacca. She cast a spiteful glance in Trudie's direction. 'Have you ever heard of Malacca, cousin?' she enquired sweetly.

Trudie hid her smile. 'Father has a malacca cane, I believe, haven't you, Father?'

'You're right, he has,' Septimus confirmed before his parent could speak. 'A cane made from the wood of the malacca tree, after which the city is called. It was one of the greatest ports of the East, belonging first to the Portuguese and then to the Dutch. It is ours now, of course, though it lost much of its previous splendour when Raffles created Singapore out of nothing. Singapore has one of the greatest natural harbours in the world – one of the jewels of the Empire!'

As he spoke, Septimus's voice took on an enthusiasm seldom heard in the Grant household. With five living elder brothers, his father had declared his youngest son to be destined for the Church and had already spoken to several of the great landowners of his acquaintance, seeking a living for the boy. What Septimus wanted, however, was to travel and see the world. At one time, Trudie had thought he would run away to sea but Septimus was also possessed of an ambitious streak that his father might have approved of if he had ever taken the trouble to get to know his youngest son. Septimus meant to make more money than his father had ever seen!

'Anyway, what's all this about Singapore?' Septimus went on, carefully concealing his enthusiasm in case it was no more than a passing interest of his father's.

'My – my fiancé lives there.' Nothing could have been more modest than Hermione's lowered eyes and her fluttering lashes. 'That is, I think he may be my fiancé, if dear Uncle Jonathan approves of him!'

'I see,' said Septimus. He looked completely flattened. 'Singapore!' he exclaimed. 'Is he in business there? Who is this paragon who means to marry our cousin?'

Hermione giggled happily, pleased to have everyone's attention centred on herself. 'Christopher Horton. Father says he's a nabob.' Her wrinkled brow showed how carefully she had learned the term even while it meant little to her. 'Yes, that's right! He made his money in India and hopes to increase it in Singapore! That's why I thought Singapore was in India!'

Hermione was making a very good meal. Like her uncle, she was enjoying it all the more because Cousin Trudie, whom she disliked, and her aunt, who didn't figure in her consciousness at all, were watching her every mouthful while they themselves were having to eat that horrible kale, which was every bit as nasty as the spinach she had been forced to eat in the nursery. What fools they were! Still, it served Trudie right for looking down on her in that superior way just because Hermoine knew how to manage Uncle Jonathan and *she* didn't! It would be fun to be rich and married while poor Trudie was still waiting for someone to offer for her.

She looked at her cousin across the table, feeling suddenly sorry for her. Kind as her uncle was to her, and much as she enjoyed being made to feel special in the way that was a secret between the two of them, she was glad she didn't have to live in this freezing house and eat the plain meals that were usually served in her uncle's household. This was quite the best meal she ever remembered eating at his table. If Trudie had some pretty dresses, and weren't so abominably thin, she might be made quite presentable. She thought happily of her cousin's gratitude if she were to give her some of her cast-offs after she was married. Yes, she would do it, because she didn't want Mr Horton to think her family as poor and downtrodden as Trudie and her mother looked. Better, she would tell Uncle Jonathan that Mr Horton might think Mr Grant to be absolutely poverty-stricken if they didn't have new dresses and a lavish table the night she brought her intended to dine there!

She was about to prepare her uncle for the shocking expense this would involve him in, when her aunt cut across her thoughts. Mrs Grant's anxious expression was normal with her, though perhaps her chin was trembling a little more than usual.

'You poor dear!' she said suddenly. 'If Mr Horton lives in Singapore, *you* will have to live there, too! How can you bear to? So far away from all your family and friends! What will you do for servants?'

'I don't know,' Hermione admitted.

'You'll have Chinese, or Malay servants,' Septimus supplied.

'Are they – are they Christian?'

'Shouldn't think so.'

'Oh dear!' Hermione was genuinely horrified. 'Why don't we send out missionaries to convert them all? I should be afraid to be in my own house with nothing but pagans about me!'

'Other people manage,' Septimus said with remarkably little feeling. 'It's too hot for English servants.'

'Then I won't go! I don't like foreigners! I met a Frenchman and he was for ever kissing Mama's hand! She said he had wet lips!'

'That's just their way,' her uncle put in. 'Servants are different. No danger of them kissing your hand!'

'No,' Septimus added with relish, 'you'll be just another foreign devil as far as they're concerned!'

Hermione looked at him with wide-eyed horror. 'I'm not a foreigner and I'm not a devil! How can I be? Singapore is British!'

'The Chinese think they're the only civilized people on earth! I'm sorry, Cousin Hermione, but you'll never be anything else except a barbarian to them. I was reading about them the other day. They believe there is an Upper Kingdom, inhabited by the gods and saints; the Middle Kingdom, which is China; and the Lower Kingdom, the domain of the devils and worse!'

Hermione's eyes filled with tears. 'I don't like Chinamen! I won't go and live anywhere near them! I won't have them for my servants, thinking me a devil! *Everybody* knows how kind and Christian I always try to be!'

Septimus, delighted by his cousin's reaction, flung back his head and laughed. Mr Grant took the opportunity to take possession of his niece's hand, patting it affectionately. 'It's clear you can't be expected to go to such a place alone!' he declared fervently. 'I must speak to Henry! A female companion – '

To everybody's surprise, Mrs Grant's voice could be heard cutting through her husband's. Her children stared at her, astonished, none of them able to remember any previous occasion when she had done so. 'I can tell you one thing, Mr Grant, *no* daughter of mine will ever be enticed into marriage with a man who would take her so far away from her parental home! It's unnatural. Chinese servants – '

'Or Malays,' Septimus put in. 'They're all Mohammedans!' He drew a finger across his throat with dramatic intensity. 'That's what they'd all like to do to us!'

His father pushed his chair away from the table, pointing to his youngest son. 'Go to your room, Septimus, and stay there until you can find the grace to apologize to your cousin for frightening her and your mother out of their wits!'

Septimus rose slowly to his feet. 'And Trudie? Am I to apologize to her also?' he murmured.

His father's dislike spilled over. 'No, not Trudie! She is as unnatural as you are! I dare say your sister could watch us all being murdered in our beds and never shed a tear for us! Not only is she the most insensitive female of my acquaintance, I sometimes wonder how I, a man of God, came to have such an unChristian child to mock my faith and all I hold dear to me! Leave us, both of you!'

Septimus gave his weeping cousin a scornful look, straightening his shoulders. 'Pleasure, Father.' He waited just long enough to make sure that none of his brothers were going to come to his, or Trudie's, defence, before offering his young sister his arm. 'Is there a fire in the schoolroom?'

Trudie raised amused brows. 'On a National Day of Fasting and Humiliation?'

He grinned back at her, squeezing her hand. As soon as they were out of earshot, he shot off ahead of her, mounting the stairs two at a time.

'Is there a fire, Trudie? I know Lily will light one for you, if anyone! Fancy some poor fool actually wanting to marry Cousin Hermione!'

'She's very pretty,' Trudie pointed out.

'If you like that washed-out look. Father certainly seems to! Do you think our parent is unnaturally fond of that silly piece!'

'Septimus!'

He gave her a mocking look. 'Don't say you haven't noticed, sister dear?'

Trudie swallowed. 'He is – fond of her, yes. One can't be surprised at that! Since when have any of us sat beside him, drinking in his every word? It's just what Father likes!'

She opened the schoolroom door, blinking at the bright pools of light that came from the moderator lamps. A fire burned brightly in the grate, the contrast with the room they had just been ordered out of making the whole room seem warm and cheerful. Trudie sighed with content.

'What brought you home today of all days?' she asked her brother. 'I thought you'd decided to stay with a friend for the whole holidays?'

'I had. The thing is, Trudie, I can never bring myself to believe it's as bad here as it really is when I'm away from it. I thought I'd have another go at changing Father's mind about my taking Holy Orders. Tell me truly, do you see me as a parson?'

'You wouldn't be any worse than most of the others.'

Trudie fiddled with the curtains, pretending to peer out into the dark street below. Somewhere a cat yowled and another answered. There were too many stray cats nowadays for her to be able to feed them all with the few scraps that Cook had over. Somehow they seemed to know that there was a free feed waiting for them at the Grant household. Cook said charity towards people ought to come before that for cats. 'If we had as many people as you have cats knocking on our door, I'd believe this to be a Christian household!' Cook hadn't a good word to say for any parson of the Church of England. Cook considered Christianity to be largely a matter of singing long, doleful hymns at the top of one's voice all day every Sunday. Those who preferred a little ritual to the hour-long sermons of her favourite preacher were all 'whited sepulchres'. It was nice, Trudie thought, to be so certain that those one disliked were all consigned to everlasting hell – especially when her father was included in their number.

'I'm not sure I believe in God,' Septimus blurted out.

Trudie merely shrugged her thin shoulders. 'God is easy to believe in. It's Father's deity that I find hard to swallow. He is so like Father that it's very easy to confuse the two. Father frequently does so.'

Septimus's jaw dropped. 'How long have you been thinking like that?'

Trudie turned and smiled at him. 'A long time. Don't worry, it isn't something I'm likely to discuss with anyone else!'

Septimus shook his head at her. 'I hope you don't! Father would never forgive you!'

'He's never forgiven me for being born! Are you as hungry as I am?'

'Hungry as a hunter!' he admitted.

They were both experienced at creeping down the back stairs. They knew which steps creaked and which were slightly uneven, and had not the least difficulty in going down them in almost total blackness. From the first floor they could smell the food from the kitchen below, where Bates and Cook sat at either end of the long, freshly scrubbed table, the two maids, Betty and Lily, sitting one on either side.

They were just starting down the last flight when the baize door, that separated the servants' quarters from those of the family, was thrust open just beside them, catching them in a shaft of light from the lamp in the hall.

'Ah, I thought so!' Mr Grant cried in triumph. 'I knew it wouldn't take you long before you were trying to undermine my servants to get them to give you something to eat! How dare you, sir? As for you, Gertrude, I have given strict instructions that *no one* is to offer you anything other than bread and water until I say so! Is that understood?'

'Yes, Father.'

'Go at once to your mother! She has something to say to you!'

Trudie was too surprised to answer. Mrs Grant seldom had anything to say to any of her children. She stood in total awe of her husband and left all such things to him, seldom even venturing an opinion on anything as unexceptional as the weather.

When Trudie found her mother, seated in acute discomfort in the darkest corner of the drawing-room, she saw at once that she had been crying.

'Oh, Mama, you shouldn't let him see you mind anything he chooses to say to you!'

'Yes, but I do, dear. The very thought of poor little Hermione all on her own in Singapore, in the midst of all those nasty people, must have affected anyone, I'm sure! Think what the sun will do to her complexion! It's very nice that her future husband should have so much money. I rejoice for her, I really do! But I shouldn't have *said* anything, should I? I might have known it would be the wrong thing – '

Trudie's heart stood still. 'What did you say, Mama?'

'Only that I wouldn't permit any daughter of mine to travel so far away from home, married or not! There are the children! First you bear them, one after another, and then so many of them die – and that's in this country! It's much, much worse in India! And very likely in Singapore too! The thought of Hermione having to suffer all that completely alone was too much for me! I shouldn't wish it on my worst enemy!'

She broke off, starting to cry again. Looking down at her huddled figure, Trudie could feel only surprise that this tired, timid woman had anything to do with her. She had cried so many tears and was always dressed in mourning for one reason or another, that it was hard to imagine her as a person with dreams and thoughts of her own.

'I'm sure you would not, Mama,' Trudie said gently.

'Yes, but the minute *I* said so, I knew what it would mean. Oh Trudie, I can't bear it! Your father has decided you will accompany your cousin to Singapore and – '

Trudie gasped. 'And?' she prompted.

'It's worse! I said how terrible it was that she should be leaving her parents' nest with such finality and at such a tender age! We probably shan't even see her again! I knew I shouldn't have said it! I might have known how your father would pick on it and – and – if only you could pretend to hang on his every word as your cousin does, but you don't! And now he means to find you a husband in Singapore, too! I can't bear it! It's wicked not to care if your own daughter dies within the year!'

Mrs Grant stopped crying, an anxious hand covering her mouth. 'Oh dear!' she breathed, her eyes as round as small, pale pebbles in her pale, smooth face. 'Oh dear, he'll never forgive me for giving birth to you, let alone for liking you! Yet it isn't such a terrible thing to like one's own daughter, is it?'

Trudie went down on her knees and took her mother into her arms. 'The terrible thing is to hate one's own child,' she said. 'Or to hate one's parent,' she added softly. 'Never mind, Mama, none of it is your fault. We will all have to pay for our own sins – even Father!'

Chapter Two

Her father was as smug as he was self-righteous. With his Adam's apple bobbing up and down in his throat, he earnestly explained to his daughter that he had only her interests at heart in decreeing that she should be punished, yet again, by being locked up in her bedroom.

'Ever since Eve brought about Adam's downfall, it has been held to be essential for loving fathers to do what they can to control their daughters' fallen nature. It is for your own good, my dear Gertrude. If it were not for your encouragement, Septimus would come to see that the career I have dedicated him for since birth is the right one for him. It has always been the same! There's no doubt but it was woman who brought evil into the world! How much better off we men would be without you!'

Trudie was at least as stubborn as her father. Confined to her room, except for Sundays when she was ceremonially freed to attend her father's services, she organized her resources as best she could. Lily and Betty were her most faithful allies, bringing her forbidden dishes and any letters that came for her, taking out with them her own for posting. Betty, who could read a little, even offered to change her library books for her, an offer Trudie was glad to accept, for reading was one of her greatest pleasures.

Not once did she beg her father's pardon, as he had demanded, nor would she change her mind that Septimus should bow to his wishes and become a parson, for she really couldn't think he would be happy in such a role – not Septimus! He was far too busy sinning to relish having to preach against it. Besides, whatever he wanted to do, she couldn't see that it was any business of hers to dissuade him. In fact, she flatly refused to do so. Her father could lock her up for the rest of her life, she *still* would not apologize to him, or to anyone else, merely for not agreeing with him. She seldom did, no matter what punishments he thought up to curb her wilful nature. She might be a female and therefore more prone to sin than her brother, but she was far better able to stand up to their parent than he had ever been.

Her incarceration on this occasion bothered the rest of the household not at all, with the possible exception of Mrs Grant who, not daring to appeal to her husband, nevertheless spent some time every day pleading with her daughter to do what every woman had to do sooner or later, submit her judgement to that of those whom Almighty God had placed in authority over her. Trudie tried very hard to be patient with her mother, quite sure in her own mind that the poor woman was being daily lectured on her imagined sins which had brought about the unacceptable characteristics of their youngest child.

'Tell Father there is only one favour that he may do me,' Trudie had finally said to her, 'and that is to lock me up on Sundays also so that I don't have to listen to his sermons for hours together!'

'Trudie! I'll tell him no such thing! How can you speak so?'

'I haven't the least difficulty, Mama. The only difficulty I have is in reconciling Father's sermons with anything I read for myself in the Gospels.'

Shattered, her mother had abandoned her efforts, agonizing over her daughter's unnatural arrogance. 'So unfeminine! Oh dear, what is to become of her?'

Trudie's faith in God must have been greater than she

would admit for she never had the least doubt that, as soon as she could make her escape from her father's roof, her life would be both interesting and rewarding.

This opinion was fully shared by her brother Septimus. Older than her by two years, he nevertheless depended on her in ways he never fully understood. It was largely her ideas that he repeated and moulded for his own purposes at Oxford, and, in his more truthful moments, he would admit to himself that it was her courage that rubbed off on him when it came to dealing with their unfeeling parent. He prided himself on understanding their father better than she did, if only because he was a man himself and better placed to see the dangers of allowing women to think for themselves. They simply did not have the capacity to make the greater decisions that affected their lives. The Queen, herself, was the first to admit this self-evident truth, yet Trudie seemed to expect some quite unreasonable dispensation from the general rule when it came to herself and her own interests. Why, she had even declared that she would have made much better use of the year he had just spent at Oxford than he had himself! An unworthy sentiment in any woman! What on earth would she do with herself at a university, without her female cronies to gossip with and pull to shreds, as even the best of women found the best of all sports?

When she had the opportunity, however, she did ask him what else he knew about Singapore. It proved to be very little. He could tell her something about the Opium Wars and how the British had sent their warships to enforce the sale of opium from India to the reluctant Chinese – who had already banned its smoking amongst their people – in exchange for their tea, for which the British had developed an insatiable appetite. The Chinese preferred to be paid in silver, as Japan had always paid through the centuries, but the British didn't have sufficient silver. What they did have was an endless supply of opium, grown in India, for which they required a market.

'We won the war!' he exulted. 'It means we can trade at will in a place called Shanghai, and Nanking, I think it is, and we took an island called Hong Kong. All Europeans can trade in Shanghai, thanks to us!'

He refused to be drawn on the subject after that and Trudie rightly suspected that he knew nothing more about the Far East and had only dredged up that much because of her insistent questioning.

Trudie missed her brother's company sadly. Sometimes, when he was away and she herself was not in disgrace, she would look round the dinner table and wonder why none of her other remaining brothers held any interest for her. They were pompous and self-satisfied, as much disliked by her married sisters as they were by herself. Indeed, if it were not for the occasional visits to see the progress her nephews and nieces were making, Trudie would have been lonely indeed.

She was making a drawing of a newcomer amongst the cats whom Cook had assured her she was feeding in her place, when word was brought that she was wanted downstairs.

'Your cousin has brought her fiancé to tea, miss,' Lily warned her. 'She particularly asked for you!'

'I wonder why!' Trudie responded tartly. She had little faith in her cousin's goodwill towards herself.

'Oh, miss! I'm sure Miss Hermione is very fond of all her cousins and you are the nearest to her in age – '

'Septimus is.'

Lily didn't bother to answer that. There was no need. She knew Miss Trudie was joking because everyone knew Miss Hermione didn't enjoy the society of her youngest male cousin, who never lost an opportunity to make fun of her! Indeed, apart from her uncle, Lily had heard from the maids of Henry Grant's household, Miss Hermione was known to be shy and almost too retiring in the company of men. Lily didn't give much credence to that, as she had seen Miss Hermione flirting with a man in the street with her own eyes! Bold as brass, she had been, when she had thought nobody was watching her! Still, it didn't do to repeat such things to Miss Trudie. She didn't like her cousin, but neither did she gossip about her, as so many in her position would have done. Not much escaped the servants and they had all seen the way Miss Trudie was treated by her father, resenting that their favourite should be locked away in her room for days and weeks together, whilst Miss Hermione could do no wrong where the master was concerned. Even Mr Bates had so far unbent as to say he considered it nothing short of a scandal the way Mr Grant treated his daughter. Still, what could any of them do about it? They had their own lives to live, and who would listen to such as they if they were to take it into their heads to criticize the doings of their elders and betters? Even Mr Bates would find himself shown the door if he were to attempt any such thing. And Lily spent the greater part of her life in trying to avoid attracting Mr Bates's attention to herself, she stood in such awe of his high position and strict ways of disciplining such as herself.

Surprisingly, Trudie found she rather resented the summons to appear downstairs. She should have welcomed it with open arms as a break in the boring schedule she had devised for herself to fill the hours she was being forced to spend by herself, but she didn't. She had no ambition to spend the next hour being sneered at by her father and patronized by her cousin.

Lily flung open the drawing-room door, bobbing a

curtsey as Trudie walked past her, head held high, looking like a pert sparrow beside her pretty, expensively garbed cousin. 'You sent for me, Father?'

Jonathan Grant repressed the spasm of irritation that seized him at the sound of his daughter's husky voice. She was as plain as her cousin was pretty, and she had no business looking him in the eye as if she considered herself to be every bit his equal. What more did God require of him to bring her to a proper sense of her own sinfulness and frailty? He pursed his lips together, reminding himself that it was no more than his duty to chastise her flesh so that her spirit might be made more pleasing to the Lord.

He sighed heavily. 'Your pride will be your undoing, Gertrude. It grieves me how often you set yourself up against my loving care for you. Go and greet your cousin – and try to learn something from her example as to how a young woman should behave in the midst of her family.'

'Yes, Father.'

Trudie admitted to herself a certain curiosity about the man who stood by Cousin Hermione's side. He looked as old, or older, than her own father, or Hermione's either. He was tall, burned a curious red by the sun, with thinning sandy hair and green eyes that were constantly moist with tears. She uttered a quick thanksgiving in her heart that he was not to be her husband! Without touching him, she already knew the palms of his hands were damp with perspiration, the smell of which was soon assaulting her nostrils.

Returning Hermione's embrace, she curtseyed to her cousin's fiancé, head modestly bowed. Christopher Horton bowed in return. 'We were talking of you before you came in, Miss Trudie, your father and I. Believe me, I am very glad to make your acquaintance because I have heard so much about you from my sweet Hermione! She tells me she has always looked to you to solve all her problems for her, as she might her own sister if she had had one, bless her pretty face!'

Trudie bit her lip. 'She flatters me, sir.'

'I'm sure she does not! The thing is, Miss Gertrude, she is faced with quite a little problem right now, which we are all hoping you will solve for her, if you are willing! Neither of you has ever been abroad before, I believe?'

'I certainly have not. I seem to remember Uncle Henry once took my Cousin Hermione to Paris with him – '

Hermione's breathless laugh interrupted her. 'Oh, you know I don't count that, Cousin Trudie! I was ill all the time we were away, as well as being frightened of all those horrid French people. I was only a child at the time. All I can remember is wanting to get home again as quickly as possible!'

'Er, quite, my love! Singapore is much further away from your home than France, however. It'll be years and years before we shall be seeing England once again.'

Hermione looked as if she might cry. 'Oh dear! Cousin Septimus says – '

'You'd do better to ignore anything that young puppy tells you!' her uncle advised her. 'You know Henry and I would never let you go anywhere where you might be unhappy. You're far too dear to your family for that!'

Hermione smiled, hoping Christopher Horton would notice how brave she was being. She half expected him to comment, as another admirer once had, that when she smiled through her tears it was like the sun coming out after rain. Unfortunately, none of her audience were of a poetical turn of mind, their thoughts being engaged by other, much more uncomfortable thoughts.

'I shall be so lonely!' Hermione sighed.

'But, my love, you haven't been listening! Your uncle

proposes your cousin should accompany us as your companion. If you are as fond of her as you have led me to believe, you surely won't be lonely while she is with you?'

'N-no.'

'Then what are you worrying about, my dear?'

Trudie was as angry as she had ever been in her whole life. She put her head on one side, smiling an unamused smile.

'I think Cousin Hermione knows that I have no wish to visit Singapore,' she said quietly. 'Even if I were to travel out with you both,' she appealed to Mr Horton, 'how should I ever get home? I can scarcely travel all that way by myself, can I?'

Christopher Horton scratched his chin thoughtfully. 'No one would expect you to do any such thing! My future wife and I very much hope you will make your home with us once we reach Singapore – '

'Quite impossible!' Trudie said with decision.

She tried not to wince as her father's voice thundered about her ears. 'Be quiet, you ungrateful child! If your cousin has need of your support, you should be proud to give it to her! Anyway, your feelings in the matter are immaterial. I have already decided the matter for you! It is not as if your mother and I hold out any hope of finding a husband for you here, in England, and Mr Horton assures me there are far greater opportunities East of Suez. He has promised to treat you as if you were one of his own family. What more can you want? Tell me that!'

'To be left alone!' Trudie retorted, quite as angry as he was. 'I have no wish to go to Singapore, nor to live for ever as Cousin Hermione's poor relation, beholden to her for everything I eat and wear!' She lifted her chin, giving her father look for look. 'Perhaps, if you will settle an allowance on me, Father, I may reconsider.'

Mrs Grant shut her eyes, her lips moving in silent prayer. The two men were at first shocked by her temerity, as well as being completely nonplussed as to why she should require funds of her own.

'Whatever next!' Mr Horton exclaimed.

Mr Grant preferred to see himself as martyr in the face of a totally unreasonable and disobedient daughter. He sighed long and gustily. 'I despair of you, Gertrude. I have always known you to be a mannerless ingrate, with an arrogance beyond belief in your own importance that another man, less long-suffering than I, would have beaten out of you whilst you were still young enough to be moulded in the way you should go. God knows, I have spent much time before His Throne of Mercy, entreating Him on your behalf, to pardon you for your disobedience to me. You shall surely burn in hell if you continue to flout the commandment that you should honour your father – '

'And my mother,' Trudie put in before she could stop herself.

'Your mother knows better than to have any ideas contrary to mine!'

Trudie was silent. She might have liked to go to Singapore, if only to escape her father, if it hadn't been for Cousin Hermione. How soon would it be forgotten that Trudie was her cousin, to become something little better than a lady's maid? Hermione was both shallow and selfish, and she had frequently been spiteful in the past when Trudie had done something to displease her.

'Miss Trudie is very young,' Mr Horton began hopefully. 'She probably doesn't realize what a grand opportunity this is for her.'

'She is seventeen,' Hermione hastened to tell him. 'She's only eighteen months younger than I am!'

'Old enough to know where her duty lies!' Mr Grant grunted. He wrung his hands together, finding it harder and harder to hide his dislike for his daughter from his visitors. 'The best thing for us to do is to leave the cousins together for a while, Mr Horton. If anyone can persuade Trudie it will be dear little Hermione! So much more pleasant if she goes with you willingly, don't you agree?'

'By whatever means you think best,' Christopher Horton murmured through tight lips. 'As long as my fiancée has the companionship she craves. I hadn't realized how young she is!'

'All the better! I could have wished you'd set your heart on Gertrude rather than her cousin though. Hermione has always been such a frail little thing! Always so obliging and loving, but not strong, you understand. You will have to watch her health in a place like that! Now Gertrude has never had a day's illness in her life and would very likely flourish in the heat, making pets out of the flies and snakes. I never met a female who had less sensibility!'

Christopher Horton's expression didn't change. 'I am only interested in my Hermione's happiness. It may not be easy to find a suitable husband for her cousin, though I shall do my best, you may be sure of that!'

The two men understood each other exactly. Watching them, Trudie thought she understood them all too well herself. Mr Horton was perfectly willing to accept her father's assessment of her own character and worth. All they both wanted was someone to run round after Hermione and keep her sweet. Neither of them had the slightest intention of furthering Trudie's cause one jot! His best would have to be abysmal if he couldn't introduce her to some eligible young men so far away from home. Even Trudie knew that India and such places were the last refuge of the unmarriageable female of even the most dubious breeding. Her social betters, also, frightened at the prospect of one-third of womankind never finding a husband at all, so greatly did women now outnumber the available men, were often sent on 'fishing' expeditions in any part of the world where the British flag flew – and that was now nearly a fifth of the whole globe.

'I am not a man to expect miracles!' Mr Grant sighed. 'It would be a brave man who takes my daughter to wife! A very brave man!'

Hermione followed her cousin upstairs to the old schoolroom, a room to which she had never been invited before. Her narrowed, envious eyes took in the crimson and black colour scheme and the comfort of the furniture that Trudie had spirited away from the other rooms of the house.

'I don't see why you have a room like this of your very own!' she declared.

'It isn't mine alone,' Trudie told her. 'We're all too old for a schoolroom nowadays, and so Septimus and I thought we would have a sitting-room instead, just for ourselves. Of course, I use it more than he does because he is away at Oxford for half the year at least!'

Without waiting to be asked, Hermione seated herself in front of the fire, removing her pretty hat as she did so.

'Then you're not half so miserable as you pretend, living in this house?' she said sweetly. 'I always thought nothing would keep you here if you could only find some respectable means of escape. It must be lovely to be Uncle Jonathan's daughter! *My* father is for ever complaining his younger brother is a much richer man than he is. It isn't fair!'

If her father had money, Trudie thought, there was precious little of it spent on his home and family! 'Never mind, you're going to be very rich yourself now,' she encouraged her cousin.

Hermione pursed up her lips, her eyes suddenly hard. 'I am going to *marry* a very rich man,' she corrected carefully. 'And I certainly don't mean to be living in poverty after his death! You may be sure I shall do all in my power to prevent that!' She shrugged her shoulders, dismissing the matter. 'You'll think me terrible, mentioning such things before I even have his ring on my finger, but, let's face it, he is an old man and everybody says that life in the tropics is far less certain than it is at home. It is in the nature of things that I shall survive him. I am only being what Uncle Jonathan calls a "wise virgin", thinking of the future of – of my unborn children as much as myself!'

'Of course.' The words were automatic; the admiring look only slightly less so. 'Only I've always felt sorry for the "foolish virgins", poor dears. I always think they fell asleep because someone like Father had bored them half to death before the bridegroom finally came!'

'You shouldn't say such things!' Hermione rebuked her.

'You ought to know by now I don't mean the half of what I say,' Trudie answered. 'I never did learn to guard my tongue properly, a first essential in our family, wouldn't you agree?'

Hermione sniffed. 'Why won't you come to Singapore with me?' she asked abruptly. 'Not that you have any choice, you little stupid! Uncle Jonathan will see to that!'

'I don't know,' Trudie admitted honestly.

'If you ask me,' Hermione stated, shrewd as always where her own interest was concerned, 'it's because Uncle Jonathan likes me better than he does you, and wants me to feel comfortable by having you with me! You never want to do anything to oblige Uncle Jonathan! But it's *me* who needs you, Trudie. I should be afraid going all that way by myself!'

'You'll have Mr Horton to look after you.'

Hermione turned drenched blue eyes on her. 'I'm a little bit afraid of him, too. Mama says he won't expect too much at first, but he's so old and – and he has a way of looking through me as if he were expecting to see someone else! It will seem dreadfully odd to be married and – and everything, with no one I know to talk to and advise me!'

Trudie blinked. 'Do you *want* to marry Mr Horton?'

Hermione threw up her hands. 'What does it matter what I *want*? What does it matter what any female wants? Our lives are arranged for us and we have to go along with it. It's a very good match for me – everyone says so! Mama says so! Papa is rubbing his hands with glee! Even Uncle Jonathan thinks I've done well for myself. He told me so. I thought he might persuade Papa how miserable everybody would be with me so far away, but not even he can resist the thought of all Mr Horton's gold!'

Especially not him, Trudie thought, feeling quite sorry for her cousin, an emotion she had never expected to experience. Almost, she was tempted to give way and go to Singapore with her, but other memories made her cautious, memories of the many barbs and slights her cousin had offered her from their nursery days onwards. Common sense told her that nothing had really changed, that, once the white cliffs of Dover had disappeared behind them, she would have more than enough time to regret being manipulated by her cousin.

'You'll soon make friends amongst the other ladies,' she murmured. 'You'll have everyone buzzing round you as soon as they see you, the prettiest bride of the year!'

'Oh, do you really think so?' Hermione preened herself. 'I am pretty, aren't I?'

'The prettiest member of the family!'

'Then why won't you come with me? You'll meet far more interesting people with me than you ever could on your own. You know how everyone overlooks you in society unless Septimus is there to rescue you. Even being married to an old man is better than never getting married at all!'

Trudie had a vision of herself imprisoned in her father's gloomy house until she was an old, old lady, and shuddered. 'We'll see,' she said aloud.

It was her father who decided her. Seated behind his large, polished desk, the lamp strategically placed between them so that her face was in the full light, his in shadow, he lectured her on her good fortune in having such a pretty, charming, *loving* cousin who was prepared to put up with her in return for her doubtful companionship.

'I should be little better than her lady's maid, despite being her cousin, the daughter of her favourite Uncle Jonathan – '

'*Enough!* She is a pretty, affectionate child who isn't afraid to show her fondness for her relations! Whereas you, miss, care only about your own selfish wants, without a thought for anyone else, unless it is for your brother Septimus, who is as graceless as you are!' He smiled a thin smile. 'He'll have a lot less time for you when he finally comes down from Oxford and has a living to care for! What will you do then, eh?'

'I may marry – '

'I doubt it, Gertrude. I don't think you worthy of the estate of marriage and, without my assistance, I fail to see how you will find this grand husband of your dreams.'

'Septimus will help me! I shall go and live with him!'

'Septimus won't be making enough money to keep himself for many years to come.'

Trudie shut her eyes, revolted. 'All my older brothers receive an allowance – '

'Your other brothers have seen fit to obey my wishes when it came to choosing their careers. Septimus is a rebel like yourself.'

Trudie stared at her father's shadowed face. 'Why do you hate Septimus and me? Why us? What have we ever done to you?'

Mr Grant moved the millefleurs paperweight from one side of his desk to the other.

'Nothing. Nothing at all.'

Trudie heard the faint noise and turned over in bed, instantly wide awake. Lily had spent a lot of time telling her about the latest gruesome murder her policeman friend had been dealing with. Tom had been on duty when they had first found the Headless Corpse down by the railway. Tom had spent the whole week helping in the search for the missing head. Tom was ever so brave! It hadn't disturbed his sleep, not for a single night, but Lily hadn't been able to close her eyes since he had described every gruesome detail. Nobody was safe these days! Tom had said the man was a gentleman, as they had been able to tell by his clothes, and he thought he'd been thrown off the train, or he wouldn't have been in such an area, not on his own. What did Miss think?

Trudie hadn't thought about it at all – not then! Now she was certain her hour had come as her window slid upwards and a dark shape eased its way into her room, first one foot and then the other, followed by a lean body and finally a head, grinning at her in the moonlight.

'Septimus! What are you doing?'

He closed the window behind him. 'Everything's shut

up downstairs and the last thing I wanted was to wake up the parents!'

Seeing him all in one piece and unbearably cheerful with it, Trudie naturally lost her temper.

'You could have been killed! You frightened me!'

'Nonsense. Since when were you afraid of anything?'

'Since Lily's Tom's latest murder.'

'Oh?'

'The Headless Corpse,' she said.

Her brother chuckled. 'Really? I'll bet he invented the whole thing to give her a fright!'

Trudie lay back against her pillows, overcome with joy at seeing her favourite brother, and just when she least expected him. 'Why should he do that?' she asked him.

'Frightened females are much freer with their kisses – Lord, Trudie, I shouldn't have said that! Not to you! Wouldn't have done if my mind had been on what I was saying. Thing is, I'm in the devil of a fix! I've been sent down – '

'Father will be furious! Can't you just stay away until you can go back up again?'

'I've been sent down for good.'

Trudie thought how strange men were. If anything as awful as that had happened to her she would be contemplating suicide, not laughing at the Headless Corpse as though nothing much had happened at all! 'What did you do?'

Septimus laughed again. 'Nothing! At least nothing much! It was Father's fault, trying to make a parson of me and letting me in for all those abominable theological lectures? I was bored!'

'Father will be furious!' Trudie whispered with a sinking heart.

'Let him be! I only came home to tell you, because I knew you'd worry yourself sick about me if I didn't. The thing is, Trudie, that I think I've fallen on my feet in all this. You know how Father is always warning us against falling prey to the wiles of socially ambitious females? Well, no, I suppose you wouldn't, come to think about it! Only, he always gives the impression that Mama was on the catch for him and, being a true Daughter of Eve, knew exactly how to go about seducing him into asking her father if he might pay his addresses to her. Poor Mama! If she'd known what he was like, she might have preferred to have stayed in her lower drawer – '

'There's nothing wrong with Mama socially!' Trudie interrupted fiercely.

'I never said there was! It's Father who is always wondering if she is properly appreciative at being elevated to his lonely pinnacle of grace! Haven't you ever wondered why she has no visible relatives around?'

Trudie shook her head. 'Have you?'

'Never occurred to me!' Septimus admitted cheerfully. 'Only I met someone the other day who said he was Mama's cousin. Devil of a fellow! He happened to be in Oxford and thought he'd look me up as a friend of his was marrying my cousin.'

'He's a friend of Christopher Horton?'

'More of an acquaintance. Jeremy Maddock worked for an import/export business in Singapore for some years, putting away a bit of money for himself until he could afford to buy a coffee plantation of his own near to Malacca. However, that's all by the way! The thing is that he's given me an introduction to the London end of the business he used to work for.' He stood up and gave his sister a sweeping bow. 'I'm going into business, Miss Gertrude Grant, and I shall make more money than all my brothers put together. What do you think of that?'

'Oh, Septimus, how splendid!'

'Yes, it is. Father isn't going to be pleased, though. He may not allow me to visit you, Trudie, not until I've made a success of things, and I can't afford to take you with me quite yet!'

Trudie was touched he should have thought of her at all. 'I may be going to Singapore with Cousin Hermione – to keep her company,' she began tentatively. 'Mr Horton is older than Father – '

'And what will you get out of it?'

'I haven't agreed to go yet. I'm locked in my room until I do.' She caught her lower lip between her teeth. 'If you're never going to be here, I think I may quite like to go to Singapore. You see, Father says I'm unworthy to be any man's wife and I don't think I could bear to go on living here for ever!'

'It wouldn't be for ever! As soon as I'm on my feet, you can come and live with me!'

'Your wife may have something to say about that!'

Septimus grinned lazily. 'If you're going to make difficulties, I'll have to see what I can do about finding you a husband myself! Whatever you do, don't agree to go to Singapore yet, will you? I have something else in mind for you, but I'm not sure yet if I can bring it off!'

Trudie's heart flooded with grateful affection for him. 'I expect I can hold out for another few weeks. Tell me about your proposed business career!'

Septimus was quick to oblige. His talk was full of Jeremy Maddock and how they meant to go into partnership. 'We're full of plans! Maddock has a fancy to open an Emporium in Regent Street that would sell all the latest things from the East: wallpapers, silks, satins, ornaments, all kinds of things such as haven't been seen in England since Regency days. We'll have a lot of Japanese stuff as well, now that they've opened their doors to the West again. We'll make a fortune!'

'And what will your part be in all this?' Trudie enquired.

'I shall manage the Emporium, of course. It would be better if I could reinforce my relationship with Mr Maddock before I started to work for him though. I shall have to learn about it as I go along.'

Trudie was hard put to it not to laugh. 'You? Will you learn?'

'I'll do whatever Cousin Jeremy suggests I should! He was in London for the Great Exhibition in '51, soaking up all the ideas he could with just this in view. I tell you, Trudie, everybody will be buying the things we mean to sell in a year or so! Just you wait and see!'

Trudie listened in growing wonderment to all the things her brother and his friend meant to sell, knowing even as she did so how easy it would be to be carried away on Septimus's dreams of the future, a future which didn't really include herself, no matter how kindly he felt towards her.

'It's going to be wonderful!' Septimus enthused. 'I can't wait to get started!'

'Wonderful!' Trudie echoed, her eyes shining. Under the bedclothes, she crossed her fingers to keep the ill luck away from her brother's plans, as Lily had taught her to do. It wouldn't need much bad luck to ruin everything – only their father, if he came to hear of Septimus's plans too soon.

Jonathan Grant noted with satisfaction the shadows under his daughter's eyes, accentuating the thinness of her face. It was unnatural that a young girl of seventeen should stand in his presence, apparently as cool as a cucumber, never moving a muscle no matter what he threatened her with. He found nothing to admire in such resolution. He found it unfeminine and a challenge to himself. He would break her spirit if it was the last thing he did! It was his duty as her father, a duty laid on him by God Himself.

Trudie's thoughts were otherwise engaged. She had realized as soon as Septimus had been telling her about his own hopes for the future that, however optimistic he might be of taking her into his household and caring for her, there was no way that she could allow it. It would be years before he would be in a position to support anyone else but himself and by that time he would most likely have found the woman he wished to make his wife, and neither of them then would want his sister hanging on his sleeve while they set up house together. It was nice of him to think of her – nicer still that he should want her with him! – but she couldn't possibly accept such a sacrifice on his part. No, she must steel herself into going to Singapore with her cousin and, who knew, she might find some way of making her own way in life once she was there. She might even do very well for herself away from her father and his narrow ideas. She could even feel quite cheerful at the prospect.

'I have forbidden Septimus to set foot over the threshold of this house until he is prepared to admit his fault and take up the profession for which he has been marked out.'

'But he says he has no vocation to be a clergyman, Father,' Trudie ventured. 'He'll be far happier – '

'It is not his immediate happiness with which I am concerned! It is a matter of supreme unimportance that he does not wish to be a parson! When God calls, one makes haste to answer. What would have happened to Israel if Samuel had refused to answer when his name was called? Tell me that!'

Trudie opened her mouth, quite prepared to tell him

that Septimus was more likely to model himself on David, a man of action and with an eye for the ladies, than on Samuel, who must have have led a very dull life because she could remember hardly anything about him at all. Her father, whose question had been purely rhetorical, ignored her.

'I sent for you in order to inform you that I am gravely displeased by your behaviour recently. I have long ago resigned myself that God has chosen you and your brother to be the rod with which he chastises his faithful servant, for I can recall no instance when you have afforded me the least pleasure as a daughter of my household. My elder children have been the blessing they should be to a man's married life; even Septimus I could forgive for the disappointment he affords me; but you, Gertrude, have brought me nothing but grief and regret that I should have been in any way responsible for bringing you into the world. Indeed, if I were not convinced of your mother's purity and obedience to me as my wife, I should doubt that I could possibly have fathered one so perverse, so set up in her own conceit, so unloving of her parents as you have proved to be.'

Trudie's attention began to wander. She wound her fingers together behind her back, wondering how to broach the subject of Singapore. She hated the fact that she was going to have to give in to her father about anything: it was worse that he would conclude he had won the battle between them by confining her to her room for weeks on end. She would have liked him to know that it was nothing *he* had done which had caused her to change her mind.

She waited for her father to end his lecture, but he showed no signs of doing so. Shifting her weight from one foot to the other, she wondered briefly what the sickly, sweet smell was that always seemed to be present in her parent's room.

'Father, I am not so undutiful as you imagine,' she said wryly. 'I will go to Singapore – if that is what you still wish?'

At any other time the ludicrous expression on his face would have made her laugh. She was not laughing now. 'It is what you wish me to do, isn't it?'

She could have sworn it was disappointment at the back of his eyes, had it not been that she was finally giving him his own way.

'*My* wishes are of no account!' he snapped. 'Nor am I convinced I am doing your cousin a favour by sending you with her. Poor child, how strange everything will seem to her so far away from home! To one of her sensibilities, it will be almost unbearable, I have no doubt, to be deprived of the loving care of her family – of my care, also, I venture to say! Henry was wise to choose an older man for the child, one who can be father as well as husband, and who will appreciate her gentle, loving nature.'

'Cousin Hermione says he is rich – '

For an instant, her father's face relaxed into a beatific smile. 'He could buy and sell most men in the City of London, Henry tells me. A very useful connection! Very useful, indeed!'

Trudie remembered only that Christopher Horton was known to this strange cousin of Mama's who had taken Septimus up and that he might be useful there also. How gratifying it would be if she could put in a good word with him for her brother as a thank you for all that he had meant to do for her. She considered the best way to approach him and decided it would have to be through Hermione. Would a discount on her purchases at the new Emporium be a sufficient inducement? Trudie wasn't sure.

She had no idea how people set about furnishing their houses, or dressing themselves, in either India or Singapore.

She began to think it would be quite exciting to see this mysterious Orient for herself after all! She made a picture in her mind of a map of an area about the size of the County of Kent, and placed within it, in a haphazard way, the names of China, India, Japan, and, finally, Singapore. Naturally, she thought, her cousin would still continue to make most of her serious purchases in London, and so why not in Septimus's Emporium? Knowing Hermione, she would insist on only the best and the most expensive, and Septimus would grow rich on the proceeds, and it would all be thanks to the efforts of his sister!

'Gertrude, I asked you a question!'

Trudie returned reluctantly to the present moment. 'I'm sorry, Father. I – I didn't hear what you said.'

'Because you weren't listening! Is it surprising that one hesitates to compliment you even when you do finally decide to do your duty? I was saying, daughter, that I feel it to be no more than my duty to warn Mr Horton that, despite the meek face you are wearing this morning, you are stiff-necked and disobedient by nature. He may yet decide Hermione to be better off without your constant society. You have proved yourself a very bad influence on your brother, as I shall tell him, though I fancy Hermione is of a sufficiently saintly disposition not to be corrupted by your selfishness and natural indolence.'

Trudie lowered her gaze. 'I shall be just as happy to stay at home in London, with you and Mama,' she said.

'Yes, well, let's hope it doesn't come to that! With any luck you will find yourself a husband out East and will make something of your life!'

His lack of conviction that she should do any such thing

was obvious. It hurt to know that she was so unwanted, unloved, he didn't ever want her home again.

'Perhaps Mama will miss me a little,' she said, fighting the unwanted tears that seemed to have gathered at the back of her throat despite her determination never to cry in front of her father.

'Your mother will do as I tell her!'

Trudie swallowed. 'Yes, Father. Will – will it be all right for me to go out to the library if Lily can spare the time to go with me?'

'I don't see why not.'

'I thought I'd like to read something about Singapore.'

Her father stared at her, his face unreadable. 'Time enough to find out what it's like when you get there!' he said. 'Oh, and Gertrude, the library, you said! I shall question Lily as to where else you have been when you get home. I will not have my servants used to carry messages back and forth between you and Septimus, nor do you have my permission to visit him wherever it is he is staying. Is that clear enough for you, miss?'

'Yes, Father.'

Trudie bobbed a curtsey and made for the door, already excitedly thinking of ways and means of getting in touch with her brother, preferably without getting anyone else into trouble. Septimus would be as pleased as Punch she was going to Singapore! It would be a joy to see his face when she told him!

Chapter Three

Trudie looked her elder sister over with disapproval. It was one thing not to be fashionable, especially if one was starved of money, it was quite another to insist on wearing outmoded garments as if it were somehow more worthy to do so.

'Really, Letty, *piped* seams is what you need with that gown. I told you so when you were first discussing it with your seamstress.'

'Did you, love?'

Trudie's dismay softened into affection. 'I wish I thought you cared a rap for my opinion – '

'Oh, I do, I do! It's just that I always end up looking a bundle no matter what I wear, so I might as well do it as cheaply as possible! Sam always says he thinks I look charming and that's all that really matters to me.'

'Samuel must be remarkably near-sighted!'

'He is,' Letitia agreed comfortably. 'As blind as a bat.' A small smile disturbed her bland features for a moment. 'You're looking thin, Trudie, and pulled down. What has Father been doing to you this time?'

'We had a slight disagreement – '

'As always!'

'Yes,' Trudie sighed, 'as always. How well you know me!'

'How well I know you both!' Her sister suppressed a shudder. 'What I should have done if Sam hadn't rescued me from my father's household I dread to think, and I never had half as much to bear as you have. Edward – no,

Geoffrey, told me Septimus has been forbidden the house. I hope you haven't been taking his part again? He can fend for himself, my dear, and all it does is give Father another handle to beat you with!' A thought struck her, disturbing her equanimity. 'He hasn't *literally* been beating you, has he?'

Trudie shook her head. 'Oh no, he can't bring himself to come near enough to me for that! No, Letty, what I wanted to talk about was Septimus! He is going into business with a friend of his, Mr Maddock, who is also some kind of a cousin to Mama, and they are going to set up an Emporium in Regent Street – '

'Septimus is? Trudie, I don't believe a word of it! What does Septimus know about business?'

'Not very much, I suspect,' Trudie admitted readily. 'The thing is, darling Letty, he'll be much happier doing almost anything than going into the Church and, now he's been sent down from Oxford – '

'He hasn't?'

'On my honour!'

Letty shut her eyes. 'Expelled from two schools and now sent down from Oxford! Oh well, one can't be surprised he isn't Father's *favourite* son, pet, one really can't.' She opened her eyes again, very much on her guard. '*No*, Trudie, I will not ask Sam – '

'Of course you shan't! I wouldn't ask it of you! What I did think was that you wouldn't mind Septimus and me meeting from time to time in your house in the next few weeks, now that he's not allowed to visit me at home. You see, Septimus is only half my news. The other half is that I am to go to Singapore! Did you know Cousin Hermione is to be married to a nabob?'

'I had heard some such nonsense. The man is older than her own father, I believe?'

'But much richer!'

'That certainly explains it,' Letty said with every bit as much disapproval as Trudie had shown towards her dress. 'What I fail to see is why you are going with her to Singapore. Does she plan to marry the man out there?'

'Oh no! Father will marry her, crying real tears all through the ceremony at the thought of losing her! I am to go with her to give her some female company on the voyage out – '

'You mean she is afraid to go all that way by herself, without someone to fetch and carry for her! Father's idea, I suppose? My dear girl, you won't be able to call your soul your own! Is she taking a lady's maid with her? Or is that to be another of your functions?'

Trudie wound her fingers together, wishing her sister had been a little less forthright. 'That's what I thought at first. I refused to go. Father shut me up in my room for – well, anyway, Septimus came to tell me about being sent down and everything. He broke in through my bedroom window. Father was most displeased when he heard about it and – and I was afraid I might not be allowed to see any of you ever again! Septimus said he would look after me, that I could go and live with him, but that may be years away, and it won't do, will it? He'll want to marry – '

'Oh dear!' said Letty. 'My dear, if it's as bad as that, I might be able to persuade Sam to have you come and live with us.'

'No, that wouldn't do either!' Trudie exclaimed. 'You know Sam doesn't like any of your relatives, and who can blame him? No, I've decided I want to go to Singapore. I have been reading some books about it, and it is one of the greatest trading centres in the whole of the East. Once Hermione is settled, I plan to buy things and send them home to Septimus for him to sell in his Emporium. You see Japanese and Chinese things everywhere now – '

'Oh!' Letty cut her off. 'If I weren't so angry with that miserable parent of ours, I'd scream with laughter at the very idea! What do you know about buying and selling Chinese ornaments, pray?'

'Not very much – as yet, but I shall.'

'Nothing at all!'

'Yes, but I am very good at decorating rooms and knowing what things are coming into fashion, and so on. It will be much better than having to go on living in the same house as Father, especially as he doubts he will ever be able to find a husband for me! I don't know why it is, but he hates me more than the rest of you all put together!'

Letty knew that to be true. It was something which had concerned both her and her other sister from time to time. The age difference between herself and Trudie was such, however, that on her few visits home she had been quite easily able to convince herself that it was only because Trudie was still a schoolgirl that she spent so much time by herself, confined to her room. Her conscience smote her. They both should have done much more for their little sister in the past, no matter what the inconvenience. Oh well, Sam or no Sam, she would do what she could to help her now! If only she had some flesh on her bones and would be just a little less quick to take one up on a half-truth, or a well-meaning generalization, she would be quite an appealing little thing. Hatty said she was too clever to appeal to any of the young men she knew, but then Hatty, being the most selfish creature imaginable, always said something like that if she thought her peace was going to be cut up by one of her siblings!

'Singapore is so far away!' Letty said faintly.

Trudie nodded importantly. 'I know. It's further away than India, even. Septimus told me.'

Letty became more worried than ever. 'What else do you know about this mysterious cousin of whom no one has ever heard? Have you met him?'

Trudie turned on the charm, beginning with a warm smile of affection for the only one of her siblings who had ever bothered about her, apart from Septimus

'Letty, would you invite him here? With Septimus? I'm dying to meet him, to find out if he really will be good for our little brother. I worry about him so, because he never gives the least thought to the consequences of his actions! And you must admit to some curiosity about Mama's cousin! He may be the first of many – all rich and presentable! Think how grateful Sam would be to discover his wife had a whole set of relations he didn't have to dodge across the road to avoid meeting!'

Letty laughed out loud. 'Baggage! I'm sure he doesn't cross the road to avoid you!'

'N-no, but then he never meets me outside of this house, does he?'

Letty bridled. 'It isn't his fault he feels unwelcome in our father's house!'

'No, of course it isn't!' Trudie agreed warmly. 'I feel decidedly unwelcome there myself every day. Besides, as he had practically to abduct you from under Father's nose when he married you, he's bound to be a bit prejudiced against the dragon he had to defeat to win you! Dragons, by definition, are not the sort of people one *wants* to associate with.'

'Is that why you are going to Singapore?'

Trudie blinked first and then grinned. 'It was at first but, do you know, Letty, I think it will be the most exciting thing ever to have happened to me! I've never been anywhere! Septimus says Chinamen regard all Europeans as barbarians, uncivilized people, unworthy of being called proper human beings. Doesn't it all sound familiar to you, somehow? I'm sure it's how the average gentleman regards all the females of his acquaintance! I don't think I shall feel nearly as strange there as any of our brothers would be!'

Letty held her tongue. There were any number of things she might have said, but she knew, as few others did, what Trudie suffered at home. There was little doubt in her own mind that almost anything would be better than the life her sister was being forced to live at home.

'I hope you may be right,' she said aloud, and went on to lay her own plans for her placid, much-loved spouse to make enquiries about this supposed new cousin of theirs. Only then, when she was assured of her husband's approval at least, would she expose Trudie to his society. Sam would know exactly what to do! How glad she was, she could leave it all to him and would not have to take the whole responsibility on to her own shoulders, for she was very well aware that, once Trudie made up her mind to anything, neither she nor Hatty had ever been able to dissuade her from it.

In the event, Trudie was to meet the mysterious Mr Maddock sooner than she had expected. Seated in her sitting-room one day, a newly lit fire burning brightly in the grate, a flustered Lily had come upstairs, her face tight with disapproval and fright as to what her employer would do if he should ever come to hear of it.

'Miss Trudie! Miss Trudie! Mr Septimus is below and says he must see you at once. He has a friend of his with him. An older friend, if I may say so. Oh, miss! What are we to do? Your father is gone out for the afternoon, and your mother is visiting Miss Hatty! What are we to do, with Mr Septimus forbidden the house? I don't think he'll go without seeing you!'

'No, of course he won't!' Trudie cast a quick look round the room to make sure everything was in order. 'Show them both up, Lily, and then bring some tea, please – '

Lily stiffened. 'Quite the little madam you are, and no mistake! And what is your father going to say to such carryings-on?'

'He won't know,' Trudie assured her with a great deal more confidence than she was feeling.'You're not going to tell him, are you?'

Lily disdained to answer. She went slowly down the stairs with a heavy footstep and returned, panting with fright more than with the exertion involved, opening the door for the two men, and announcing them in stentorian tones. Trudie considered reminding her that she was not deaf, but Lily was away down the stairs before she could say anything at all. Instead her young mistress rose to her feet, smiling at her favourite brother.

'What trouble are you in now?' she greeted him.

He grinned. 'Stuff it, Trudie! I wanted you to meet our cousin Mr Jeremy Maddock and I couldn't wait for Sam's invitation a moment longer – you know how long it takes for him to make up his mind about anything! Cousin Jeremy, may I present my youngest sister, Miss Gertrude Grant?'

Mr Maddock bowed over her hand, a twinkle at the back of his eyes that made her like him very much. She noted the yellow-brown colour of his face that came from being in the sun too much, and that his clothes were fashionable enough, without being in the first stare. He was not what she would have called handsome, but his face had a comfortable, lived-in appearance that made her think he might be easy to confide in. Septimus was completely at home in his company and, whilst he had never been as shy and as cautious as she was with strangers, she thought the better of their cousin that he allowed such familiarity from a much younger man.

'I am sorry my father is not here to receive you,' she began. His raised eyebrows made her want to giggle. Trudie dearly loved anyone who was able to make her laugh. 'No, I'm not sorry at all! Septimus wouldn't have been allowed to bring you to see me if he had been here and I very much wanted to meet you! Are you really going to include Septimus in your plans for a London Emporium?'

'Possibly,' he responded.

How like Septimus to think everything cut and dried when it was only a possibility, Trudie thought, casting her brother a cross look.

'You won't regret employing him,' she said abruptly.

'You think not?'

Mr Maddock wandered round Trudie's sitting-room, a slight frown between his eyes. 'Is this your own room, Miss Gertrude?'

Trudie stood with her hands clasped behind her back like a guilty schoolgirl. 'Yes, it is, sir. This room used to be the schoolroom and nobody else had any use for it. Don't – don't you like it?'

'I like it very much! You have excellent taste.'

Trudie sat down, visibly pleased by his compliment. She was beginning to understand how Septimus found their new cousin so easy to get along with. She didn't hesitate to answer all his questions as to where she had found all her treasures, her enthusiasm bringing a flush to her pale cheeks as she enlarged on her ideas of the importance of design in everyday living. 'I like nice things about me,' she ended abruptly, aware that she had been speaking far too much and too freely. How was it she could never remember she was a mere female and keep a still tongue in her head?

She glanced at her brother, seeking his support, and saw only disapproval in his eyes.

'It's a nice room,' Septimus muttered. 'But you don't know anything about real interior design, Trudie. Cousin Jeremy is an expert!'

Trudie bowed her head, accepting the rebuke. Mr Maddock put a hand on Septimus's shoulder, smiling down at Trudie. 'I acquired my expertise the hard way, Septimus. Your sister has flair and natural good taste. It might be interesting to take her to some of the sales we have been attending and see what she makes of them, don't you think?'

'But Trudie's only a woman!'

'Yes, I'd noticed, young man. Women, too, have their uses!'

Trudie positively glowed. She was unused to admiration of any sort and, although she mentally reminded herself not to allow it to go to her head, she knew she wanted to see more of this remarkable man, learning all that she could from him, more than she wanted anything else in the world.

She blinked. 'I know I can't be of any use to you – as Septimus is! – but please say I may accompany you both to some of the galleries and sales. I'd love to see them for myself!'

'And so you shall,' her new cousin assured her firmly. 'I mean to see a great deal more of you, if you'll allow me?'

Trudie went scarlet in the face. 'Yes, please. There's nothing I'd like better!' She giggled happily, looking younger than her years. 'I'm so glad you came!' she said.

* * *

Trudie sat on the very edge of her chair, unpicking the seam of her glove with nervous fingers. Excitement had been building up in her all day at the thought of going out with her brand-new relation. She had been tempted to whisper it to her mother where she was going and why, belatedly remembering that she might be interested in this cousin also. Only the thought of her father's rage deterred her. Her mother's life was miserable enough without adding to her troubles.

And now here she was, with Septimus seated beside her, watching every movement Mr Jeremy Maddock made as he assessed the various articles that were on sale. 'What do you really think of him?' Septimus whispered to her.

'He's quite old,' she observed.

'In his prime!' Septimus declared. 'Did anyone tell you, sister dear, that Jeremy Maddock is a bachelor and in need of a wife to take back with him to Singapore? Think about it! If he should take a shine to you, that would be one in the eye for Cousin Hermione, would it not?'

It would, indeed. Trudie's mouth went dry. She felt quite faint at the mere thought. Not that she could believe that any gentleman as worldly and experienced as Mr Maddock would ever look twice in her direction.

When, a few minutes later, Mr Maddock ousted Septimus's position beside her and asked her opinion on the various articles he had decided to bid for, she immediately forgot her embarrassment that he was a man and she was a woman in the excitement of deciding how much she would give for each object, always supposing she had the money to make a bid at all.

He listened carefully to her assessments and, after a while, suggested she should buy something for herself. 'Something you really like!' he invited her.

That her choice was the right one in his eyes gave her

almost as much pleasure as did the battle of wills between herself and the seller to agree a fair price. That she had done well brought her satisfaction she had never known before: that she had done better than her mentor had expected was sheer bliss.

'But you are entrancing!' he exclaimed. 'When your brother told me you were going all the way to Singapore, I decided you must be a woman of courage, indeed! But you are better than that! You're sensational, my dear!'

Trudie gave him look for look. 'I'm glad if I can please you, Mr Maddock, and not just because you are being very kind to me. You hold my brother's future in your hands and that matters very much to me. Septimus is my favourite brother, you see.'

'You are a firm favourite with him, too. But you don't need me to tell you that! From all that he tells me about your home life, I can see why you wish to escape to Singapore. If I may be of any service to you whilst you are making your preparations, you have only to let me know. I, too, shall eventually be returning to the East.' He looked at her long and hard. 'I could wish your brother had one-half your aptitude for the task I've set him. He will always need someone to keep an eye on him, to tell the truth. Must you leave London just now?'

It was the beginning of a friendship between them that met with Septimus's complete approval. 'Didn't I tell you he's a splendid fellow?' he asked her. 'If you could just bring yourself to flatter him a little, I'm sure you could make him fall headlong in love with you and then we could all be comfortable for the rest of our lives.'

Meaning that he could be, Trudie thought with a sigh. But she had to agree that she would rather like the independence marriage would give her and not only because it would be one in the eye for Hermione! Mr

Jeremy Maddock was the kindest man she had ever met, and quite the nicest. He was not at all like the heroes she read about in books, who were considerably more dashing where women were concerned, but then she doubted Mr Maddock saw her as much of a woman at all. His manners were always impeccable. When he handed her up into a hansom he, as nobody else had ever done, went out of his way to protect her skirts from the dirty wheels. He treated her with as much care and deference as if she had been one of her elder sisters, and that could only endear him to her. She was starved for someone to take her seriously as an adult and she blossomed under his obvious approval of what she was rapidly becoming, a grown woman of taste and wit.

'Will you marry him if he asks you?' Septimus pressed her. 'It'd be a devil of a lark! Imagine Father's face when he asks to pay his addresses to you! I'd give a monkey to be there!'

'I don't think he means to ask me and, if he does, I doubt Father would give his consent,' Trudie cautioned him.

Septimus's expression sobered. 'He must do so! It's desperately important to me that he should! Cousin Jeremy likes me, I know he does, and he knows I'll work myself into an early grave setting up this Emporium of his. But it doesn't give me much security. I'm not as good at buying and selling as you are, Trudie. I'd be much better placed as his brother-in-law! You do see that, don't you?'

Trudie kept her own counsel about that. She found herself curiously unwilling to discuss her feelings for Mr Maddock with her brother, but she was already quite sure of one thing, though she would hardly admit it even to herself. If he were ever to ask her to be his wife, she would accept him then and there, before he could change his mind and find someone else to marry. 'If he asks me, I'll certainly give it some thought,' she promised, 'but he's much older than we are. He probably wants more in a wife than I have to offer.' She sighed heavily at the thought. 'And you're not to try and act the matchmaker, Septimus! I forbid it absolutely, do you understand?'

'As long as you like him,' her brother answered uncomfortably, colouring up with embarrassment. 'You have to marry someone after all!' he burst out. 'You don't dislike him, do you?'

'No, I certainly don't dislike him,' Trudie confessed. 'I sometimes wish we knew more about him, that's all. Septimus, do you suppose he's had a great deal to do with women? In Singapore, I mean?'

'All the better if he has,' her brother responded gruffly. 'Bound to make things easier between you if he knows what he's about. *You* don't know anything at all!'

So Trudie scarcely turned a hair when Mr Maddock spoke to her sister about arranging a picnic to Richmond, not noticing the meaningful look he gave her. 'Gather your father may be a bit difficult,' he added.

Letty raised an enquiring brow. 'She's very young,' she said at last.

Mr Maddock flung himself into the chair next to hers, his eyes still watching Trudie as he always did these days. 'You're not against my offering for your sister, are you, Lady Craddock?'

'I'd be happier if I didn't think Septimus's enthusiasm for the match wasn't considerably greater than Trudie's,' Letty said in a flurry. 'He could always persuade her black is white, especially when the alternative is more of what the poor child has always had to put up with.' Her vague gaze suddenly focused on Mr Maddock and he began to wonder if she weren't more of a power behind her husband's throne than he had let himself believe. 'Can you make her happy, Mr Maddock? If I help you fix your interest in her, will she find any skeletons buried away in some cupboard in Singapore?'

She hoped it was not too soon to speak so frankly and was reassured when he flushed up in the most absurd way, saying hastily, 'Oh no, nothing like that! She is too young for me, I'm not denying that! I'd have set her up in her brother's place had she been a man!' He laughed shortly. 'Skeletons, Lady Craddock? Do you doubt the affection I have for her?'

Indeed, he sounded so appalled that Letty was satisfied. She was of the opinion that it was no bad thing for a husband to be several years older than his bride, the more so if the couple were to make their home in some far-flung part of the Empire, where there were even fewer restraints on an errant husband than there were in the metropolis, not that there were many there.

'Have you met our Cousin Hermione?' she enquired thoughtfully.

'The one who wishes to make Miss Gertrude her companion on the voyage out?'

'You know her husband-to-be, I believe?'

'We all know each other in Singapore. Christopher Horton is as well known as anyone else out there.'

Letty noted his dry tone. 'Have you had many business dealings with him?'

Mr Maddock managed a reluctant laugh. 'I worked for him some years ago, until I found it much better, and vastly more profitable, to start up my own business after a while. I didn't make a very good employee, Lady Craddock, but I pride myself on being an excellent employer! I bought land, whenever and wherever I could, and it has paid off handsomely. Now, when I want something sent from one side of the world to the other, it is I who employ the Christopher Hortons of this world. Your sister won't want for anything as my wife!'

Letty smiled, delighted with his answer. 'As long as you make her happy, Mr Maddock, I shall be more than content.' Her eyes lit with naughty laughter and, for the first time, he was able to see a likeness between the elder sister and the younger. 'Speaking personally, of course, it would give me some pleasure to see my little sister wipe our cousin Hermione's eye for once, only you are not to tell anyone I said so, for my husband would not approve such sentiments and I would flatly deny telling you any such thing!'

'I shouldn't mind myself,' Mr Maddock responded with a quiet smile. 'I shouldn't mind at all!'

The same could not be said of the rest of Trudie's family. Once they had overcome their first surprise that anyone should have made an offer for the youngest Grant, they were outraged that the whole thing had been arranged behind their father's back – and largely by the disgraced Septimus, with help from Letty of all people, who should have known better!

'What do you know of the fellow?' Trudie's brothers asked one another. 'He's a complete commoner! Must be, to set up in trade as a glorified shopkeeper! Father will soon send him about his business!'

That was Mr Jonathan Grant's firm intention when Mr Maddock first sent in his card, asking permission to call on him. He didn't like the idea of his youngest daughter making a better marriage than her cousin. It bothered him considerably, for he knew in his heart of hearts that Trudie was the least deserving of all his children. Her only hope of salvation was to be made to suffer in this life such privations as would curb her rebellious spirit and bring her into the paths of virtue. Up until this time, it had been his sad duty to try to bring her to a realization of her sinfulness and disobedience, and he was afraid for her if she were to have money, and servants, and all the temptations such wealth would inevitably bring in its train.

That had been before Mr Maddock had happened to mention he had been at school with Mr Grant's bishop, a friendship he still maintained, because, as he had had the impertinence to put it, one never knew when an advocate with the Almighty might come in useful.

Mr Grant knew a sinner when he saw one. He had looked Mr Maddock straight in the eye and had accused him of practically every sin in the book. Mr Maddock had returned the look with a sour smile.

'Oh quite! One doesn't make money these days without cutting a few corners, and I'm as guilty as the next man of doing what I have to to put a better profit into my pocket. I plan to be a millionaire before I'm finished, Mr Grant, and a millionaire might well choose to have his parson father-in-law made a bishop, or even an archbishop. Money talks, even in the Church, does it not?'

Mr Grant had been rendered completely speechless. 'I'll speak to my daughter,' he had offered at last. 'Mind, the final choice must be hers!'

Mr Maddock had grinned, whirling his watch round in a complete circle on the end of its chain. 'It will probably be Septimus who will have the last say, if I know anything about that scamp! He inherited all his mother's charm and your determination, sir! Septimus also means to make money and he sees me as his ticket to having a Regent Street Emporium of his very own. Please don't discourage him. It will keep Miss Gertrude happily occupied as my wife searching for the numerous artefacts he means to sell to fashionable London, probably with great success. Boredom is the great enemy of all European women who venture East of Suez, Mr Grant, leading to every vice under the sun. My wife, however, will be above suspicion, as the saying goes, making me the envy of every man – including Mr Christopher Horton!'

Mr Grant had come to a much better opinion of Trudie's suitor than he had thought possible. Drumming his fingers on the arm of his chair, a smile touched his lips. His young daughter would be in safe hands with that one. He would know exactly what to do at the first sign of rebellion. How odd that Gertrude should have found someone so wise in the ways of women and the world. He closed his eyes. Without doubt, it was a sign of the loving care their Heavenly Father extended towards even the least of His Creation.

It was a strange courtship, not that that seemed to disturb Trudie in the slightest. Betty and Lily might shake their heads as they discussed Miss Gertrude's coming marriage; Trudie was happier than she had ever been, enjoying all the attention that was being showered on her for the first time in her life. She didn't mind in the least that Mr Maddock's first concern was that she should learn the principles of what he called 'good taste', in her clothes, in her surroundings, in her manners and the way she comported herself, and, above all, in learning to distinguish between the good, the bad, and the indifferent in all matters of design. It became a game between them, played with real money, to see who could find the more impressive articles with which to stock his new Emporium and, if at first she made some mistakes, she quickly learned to make a very decent profit, sometimes outwitting even her future husband in her deals, which seemed to please him as much as it did her.

Indeed, so engrossed was Trudie in her new skills, she never stopped to wonder at the contrast between the proposal she had received from her business idol and those she had frequently read about in the books she borrowed from the commercial library and read aloud to her mother in the evenings. Mr Maddock hadn't gone on one knee, nor, so far as she knew, had he ever considered that she might reject his offer. On the contrary, he had held out his hand to her, kissed her on the cheek, and with a murmured: 'Brave girl! Between us, we'll turn first me and then Septimus into rich men! That's what you want, isn't it?' he had settled the matter once and for all.

'Yes, it is,' she had agreed. Belatedly, she had remembered that he might require more of her than he would of any of his other employees and she had managed to add that, of course, her *first* consideration would always be to do her best to please him as his future wife, but he had cut her off with a laugh.

'You can please me best, child, by allowing me to bring out the beauty of your bonework and to cultivate your natural good taste. Beautiful things are the greatest consolation one can find in this vale of tears, don't you agree?'

Trudie had been so overcome that anyone should think her the possessor of even potential beauty that she had hardly heard the rest of the sentence. It mattered remarkably little to her as to why he should want to marry her, to tell the truth. She was enjoying herself far too much to think much beyond the immediate future. For once, she was completely happy and she was grateful. If Mr Maddock wasn't as deeply in love with her as Letty seemed to think he should be, Trudie herself didn't think she had anything to complain about in his attitude towards her.

Business, in her opinion, was a far more exciting affair than any amount of romance.

She particularly enjoyed the trips Mr Maddock took her on to the major collections that were on display in London. Like Septimus, who was probably only repeating his cousin's views anyway, Mr Maddock was of the opinion that the whole of Europe was about to go mad for artefacts from the Far East. 'The opening up of Japan is the clue to the next great fashion which will sweep Paris and London,' he said.

Trudie didn't need anyone's enthusiasm to fire her own once she had seen for herself the silks, the bamboo wallpapers, the mythical birds, and the strange outlined drawings that all Orientals seem to go in for. She loved everything she saw and her confidence in her own judgement grew by leaps and bounds.

Nor did she mind that Mr Maddock proved a hard taskmaster. After a few weeks of his tuition, she could infallibly distinguish real ivory from its counterpart, jade from the cheaper stones which were often passed off as the real thing, and could even make a tolerable guess as to whether some Chinese bowl was genuine or had been fashioned in the same style in Birmingham, or some other such factory in England. Always the possessor of flair, she was now able to bring the necessary knowledge to what she would choose or what she would reject if she were ever to be in the position to buy and, for the moment, that was more rewarding to her than any amount of male attention. She was quite simply in her element.

Letty's pride in her refurbished drawing-room was unbounded. Hesitating for the third time as she led Trudie up the stairs, she said over her shoulder, 'I had it done ready for your wedding! I hope you won't mind, dear, but our mother feels the arrangements are too much for her and so I have offered to act as hostess. Sam says Father is bound to think I'm shouldering my way in where I'm not wanted, but I told him how cold and miserable that dreadful house always is, and how much I wanted to give you the kind of send-off into married life you are entitled to! He's well acquainted with the stories I've told him of my own girlhood and, when I told him how much worse it has been in every way for you, he gave in at once.' A worried look crossed her normally placid face. 'I suppose you couldn't see your way to asking him to give you away? Would Edward mind very much, do you think?'

Trudie was startled into missing her step. 'Is that what Lord Craddock wants?'

'Yes, it is.' Letty smiled a conspiratorial smile. 'Ridiculous, isn't it? But with our own children still in the nursery it will be a good many years before anyone else is likely to ask him to fulfil such a role. He's such a family man at heart, bless him!'

Trudie followed her elder sister up the remainder of the stairs. 'Has anyone ever told you how lucky you were to find Sam? After Father, it must have been sheer bliss to find yourself married to him!'

'So I tell myself every day!' Letty affirmed solemnly. 'Marriage is so important to any woman! You know, dear, I'm sure it's right that women should keep well away from public life and dealing with things like that, but you'll never persuade me that *every* man has a natural understanding of how to govern, any more than every woman has it in her naturally to submit to her husband's decrees. There's no going back after the marriage ceremony, you know!'

Trudie was scarcely listening. She was very well content with what she knew of her own future. She was the first to realize that she wasn't as much in love with Jeremy Maddock as Letty seemed to be with her Sam, but the excitements of her coming wedding and the intensive training he was giving her in the arts were enough for her to digest at the moment. She would worry about being a married lady when she was one. All she knew was that the whole world had suddenly been transformed into the most exciting place imaginable and, if Mr Maddock never gave her anything else, it would still be enough for her.

'Well, what do you think of it?'

It was hard to recognize the room without its slip-covers, made to match the curtains and the acres of carpets which were her sister's pride and joy. The furniture underneath had been largely inherited from Lord Craddock's parents and was more old-fashioned than Letty would have chosen for herself. Nevertheless, the needlework was remarkably fine still, and the unwashable upholstery, though shabby, had once been the very finest that money could buy.

Letty watched her sister's reaction with increasing anxiety. 'Don't stare at those old pieces of furniture!' she commanded. 'What I want you to look at is the whole effect! Have you any idea what that new marble fireplace cost? And I'm told it's the very latest thing to have a continuous upper drapery to unite the windows. Isn't it beautiful? And what do you think of the new colour scheme? Do you like the white ceiling? Should I have chosen a more definite colour than pale rose pink for the walls?' She whirled about the room, never pausing for an answer. 'You know, Trudie, I really like this room much better when the slip-covers are on! They are the same pink and apple-green as the curtains and carpets. I wish you would tell me what you think?'

'I think it suits you,' Trudie answered.

'You don't like it?'

'Of course I like it, silly! You had led me to expect something more in the forefront of fashion – '

Letty gave her sister an exasperated look. 'I don't wish to be in the forefront of fashion!' she declared crossly. 'None of my friends have the least ambition to return to Chinese walls and uncomfortable, straight-backed chairs. We like to be comfortable! Besides, if one is in the fashion and not leading it, one's friends are not afraid to like one much more than if they find one extraordinary in any way.' She frowned. 'What do you think of that swag with the fringed valance looped over a pole like that? I can't make up my mind if it isn't too heavy for the rest?'

Trudie patiently admired each feature in turn. She thought the pastel colour scheme to be out of date by at least ten years, but then so were her sister and most of her sister's friends. Given the allowance of the least expensive of Letty's friends, Trudie would have transformed herself into a veritable butterfly, or would she? She put her head on one side and looked round her sister's room again.

'It *does* suit you!' she reiterated. 'It's gentle and kind, like you, Letty. Are you sure you want to take on all the trouble of my wedding? Neither Mr Maddock nor I were expecting anything other than a quiet ceremony and a reception for our families and close friends.'

Letty hugged her. 'That reminds me, love, give me a list of Mr Maddock's guests, will you. Do we know any of his immediate family?'

Trudie returned the hug, her thoughts elsewhere. 'Didn't Septimus tell you? Mr Maddock is some kind of cousin of Mama's.'

'No, he didn't tell me. Are you sure?'

'Oh yes,' said Trudie. 'Actually,' she added, 'I don't think Mama knows. Do you think we ought to tell her?'

Her sister, proud of her social *savoir-faire*, struggled in vain with the feeling of sheer exasperation that seized her. Being the eldest of ten children had not been easy, especially as she had had to watch her brothers being given everything that she was not, merely because they were boys and she an insignificant girl. Until Hatty had grown up sufficiently to be some kind of ally against this male bias, she had looked hopefully to her mother to supply the affection and interest her father had denied her. Her mother, however, had never lived up to her expectations in this respect, being far too frightened to stand up to her husband in any way at all.

'No, I don't think we should tell her anything!' Letty said firmly. 'That's one thing we may safely leave to Father. We're not asking anything else of him, are we?'

Trudie merely grinned. 'I never knew it before,' she said cheerfully, 'but you're quite as secretive as Septimus and I, where the parents are concerned, aren't you? As if any one of us would dare to tell them anything! Not me, and not Septimus, and not Mr Maddock either, if I know anything!' She stretched, still smiling, and looked round her sister's room once again. 'I love your decorations, Letty. They really are as kind and gentle as you are. If I am one-half as happy with Mr Maddock as you are with your Sam, I shall think myself a fortunate woman!'

'I am sure you will be!' Letty returned warmly, hiding her own doubts in the matter. Of one thing she could be certain, she told herself comfortably, Trudie would manage to be happy with very little and, given her circumstances, that was probably the best gift that life could have given her.

Chapter Four

It was a soap-bubble of an existence. Somewhere, deep down inside, Trudie knew it couldn't and wouldn't last, and waited, breathlessly, for the bubble to burst. She was frankly enjoying the unusual sense of importance being a bride gave her. It was true her mother asked her frequently and with increasing anxiety whether Jeremy Maddock was an entirely respectable person; Trudie cared not a jot. He was, as she pointed out, a friend and employer to Septimus, as well as being one of her mother's own cousins.

It had come as a shock to Mrs Grant that one of her family should have come back into her life in this way. She had been even more affronted when Mr Maddock hadn't recognized her at first as the charming, bright girl she had been in her youth.

'Whatever has he done to you?' he had asked her, horrified.

'We all of us grow older,' she had parried. But she had been hurt all the same.

She had been even more hurt when she had overheard her cousin say to Trudie that, whilst he would never make the sort of husband most girls dream about, he would be kinder to her than her father had been to her mother. 'I can't believe she would allow any man to murder her spirit in that way!'

Trudie had put that look on her face that her mother particularly disliked, knowing she was about to say something outrageous and uncomfortable.

'Father's sins customarily cry aloud to heaven for vengeance!'

And her cousin had *laughed*! 'Let's hope mine don't do the same! I'm a selfish devil,' he had said. To which Trudie had paid no attention at all.

'You should have insisted on seeing your own family!' Trudie told her mother, 'then they wouldn't come as such a shock to you.'

She did her best to suppress the irritation she frequently felt for her mother's dithering distress. It was very wearing, she had discovered long ago, feeling sorry for someone as close to one as a parent, perhaps because it mattered too much how they felt about themselves – and others.

'You don't understand, dear,' her mother responded tearfully. 'Your father would never have looked at me if it hadn't been for the dowry I brought with me.' She wrung her hands together, sniffing back yet more tears. 'Darling, marriage for a woman can be a lifelong martyrdom. It has been for me. We are not all as fortunate as your sister Letty!'

Trudie merely shrugged her shoulders. She didn't want to hear about marriage from her mother, or anything else for that matter. She much preferred Letty's unpredictable instructions – dear Letty! – who considered marriage to be the ultimate test of one's good manners. 'It's the only thing that matters in the end, love.' She had smiled slowly, a look of remembered glory on her face. 'Sam has beautiful manners!'

It was her second sister Hatty, however, who came to call one afternoon, clearly come to do her duty for she, too, visited her parents' establishment as seldom as she could manage it. She looked round the schoolroom, astonished by its transformation, and said in grudging tones, 'I wish I had your good taste, Trudie. People keep saying one can acquire it if one educates oneself carefully enough, but it comes naturally to you! Self-help is my husband's creed, as it should be for all of us. What does your Mr Maddock believe in?'

Trudie was forced to admit she hadn't the faintest idea. 'Well, let's hope his creed is a little more enlightened than Father's! Letty and I have discussed your wedding and we agreed that I should be the one to make sure you are prepared for – everything Mr Maddock will ask of you. It ought to be Mother's job, of course, but if she told you as little as she did me, you'd get a fine shock when you first find yourselves alone together!'

Trudie looked at her sister wondering what she was getting so fussed about. What could possibly be so special about a single night?

'Don't you enjoy being married?' she demanded. '*You* may have been shocked,' she added thoughtfully, 'but you'll never persuade me that Sam ever succeeded in shocking Letty – '

'Possibly not,' Hatty answered dryly. 'So you know all about that side of things, do you?' She looked surprised. 'I never thought Mother could bring herself to speak of such things – she never did to Letty or me, which is why I thought it my duty to explain things to you myself. Ah well, that's that! I won't pretend not to be relieved because, although we are sisters, the age difference between us is such that I often feel us to be more strangers than close relations.'

'I see more of Letty,' Trudie admitted.

Hatty managed a wry smile. 'Of course you do! We all see more of Letty than anyone else in the family, which isn't at all surprising, as she is by far the most likeable one in the family! I wouldn't have offered to have your wedding breakfast in my house, let me tell you! What is she planning to give us to eat?'

'A feast!' Trudie assured her happily. 'Sandwiches of all sorts, from smoked salmon to egg and cress; *petits fours*, and other little cakes and biscuits; and all sorts of frozen creams with various flavours of chocolate and different fruits. She means it to rival the most fashionable menu of the year! Mama says Father will be most displeased at such a display of ostentation!'

'Nonsense! He'll enjoy it extremely as he isn't having to pay a penny piece towards it! Oh well, my dear, I wish you joy of your Mr Maddock and that he will turn out to be one-half as open-handed as Letty's Sam Craddock!'

And with that she was gone, reporting back to Letty that their little sister was as knowing about the marriage act as the two of them had been ignorant. 'There must be some advantage in being the youngest after all!'

Letty had laughed and nodded. 'You know, Hatty, I can't believe Mama brought herself to tell her much though, it was far more likely to have been young Septimus!'

Which so shocked her sister that Letty wished she had held her tongue, only feeling comfortable again after her husband assured her that she was very likely right and that he, for one, was glad of it, as he had always had a soft spot for her younger sister and still bore his mother-in-law a lasting grudge for having put his darling Letty's happiness at peril by leaving her in total ignorance of everything to do with the marriage bed.

'But dearest, you made me feel so loved and happy – '

'All the same,' her spouse informed her with unusual grimness, 'no daughter of mine will go to her husband until she has had the facts of life explained to her, and so I am telling you now!'

To which Letty had very properly responded that it would be her *first* consideration when either of their little girls was old enough to have need of such knowledge. 'Though it won't be half as much fun for them as having you to instruct one was to me!' she had added with a naughty smile.

He had grinned, also. 'It's their husbands' feelings I am concerned about!' And then he had kissed her and, for half an hour or so, all else was forgotten by both of them.

Of far more consequence to Trudie was the projected opening of the Regent Street Emporium. It was rumoured, so Septimus told her, that various members of the Royal Family meant to be there. 'Nobody very important, but a compliment to Maddock all the same. Think what it would mean if the Queen, herself, were to come!'

Trudie had repeated this to Mr Maddock when he next came to call, offering to drive her round Richmond Park. Mr Maddock had squeezed her hand and kissed her cheek. 'Did I tell you how pleased I am with your progress recently? Sometimes I think you have more flair for the art world than has your brother!'

Trudie had been thrilled by the compliment. 'Is Singapore as exciting a market place as it says in the books? Do you have godowns of your own, with Chinese coolies carrying all your goods in and out of them, loading and unloading your ships?'

He had laughed shortly. 'You have a vivid imagination, my dear, which is probably why you understand the sort of goods I wish to sell my foolish, untravelled compatriots. For the most part, we lack taste in this country, preferring the cheap bargain every time. Prince Albert may have hoped to change that with the Great Exhibition, but it's my belief you need to lead the public by the hand and show them the things they must have in their houses if they mean to keep in the swim of things. I wonder if Septimus is sufficiently sure of himself to be left to his own devices quite yet. This has been a most expensive business and I don't want there to be any possibility of it failing now. What do you think?'

Trudie had licked her lips, agitated by the question. She hadn't wanted to seem to lack enthusiasm for her brother's abilities, but she did think him slipshod and over-optimistic about his business abilities. That was his character, after all, to take such things lightly and to laugh in the face of fate. It was what she loved him for. 'What alternative is there?' she asked.

'I was thinking that after our wedding I might leave you in England for a while, just until Septimus finds his feet. Would you mind very much?'

Trudie hadn't minded at all, but had thought it unkind to say as much. 'Where would I live?' she had asked him abruptly.

'In the house I am leasing for you as a wedding present! You'll scarcely have time to miss me before I shall send for you – it's Septimus I am thinking of, you know. The poor boy is still very young!'

Trudie had had to admit the truth of that. She forgot that she was even younger. Her one, consuming thought had been that for a short time she would know total freedom, without either parent or husband to interfere with her. She had reached up and kissed Mr Maddock on the fleshy line of his jaw, her eyes shining with pleasure and excitement.

'I'll do everything as you tell me!' she had promised. 'By the time I come to you in Singapore, the Emporium will be a great success, patronized by the Queen herself, I shouldn't wonder!'

Mr Maddock had stroked her cheek. 'There will be time enough for – other things, Gertrude. You're still a child, far too young to have children of your own!'

Trudie hadn't known what he was talking about. She couldn't have been more pleased with herself – and with him. 'More than anything else,' she had said, 'I want to see Septimus settled, because Father won't help him at all now he's decided not to take Holy Orders. We shall both always be grateful to you, Mr Maddock, all our life long, because of the fine opportunity you've given him to make something of himself.'

The man beside her had given her a thoughtful look. 'Is that why you're marrying me?'

Trudie had looked up at him through her lashes. 'I like you very well for yourself, of course,' she said, 'but it's such a relief to me to know Septimus is settled. You don't mind my being pleased for him, do you?'

He had barked a short, unexpected laugh. 'No, I don't mind at all,' he had said. 'Always believe that the last thing in the world I want is to hurt you, though, when you know the whole, I doubt you'll ever believe me!'

Which was quite the most ridiculous thing she had ever heard!

The day of the wedding came and went. Letty complained audibly that, as far as she could see, it meant much more to her than it did to Trudie.

'My dear love,' she protested gently as she helped her young sister dress for going away with her brand-new husband, 'must you talk of Septimus and the new Emporium all the time? No man likes to have to share his bride's attention on his wedding day, you know.'

'But, Letty, you don't understand! Mr Maddock is just as interested as I am in setting up the new Emporium. He said so. In fact, he's going back to Singapore on his own, leaving me to help Septimus for a while. I can travel out later.'

'He's leaving you in England *on your own*? *At your age?*'

'Of course not on my own, silly! He's leasing a small house where Septimus and I can live together – just until he's settled! – then I shall join Mr Maddock in Singapore as his wife. I shall be older then and better able to cope with all that will be expected of me out there. He says he's an important man out there, so I shall be important too! More important than Cousin Hermione, I dare say.'

Letty felt quite faint at the idea. Sam, she knew, would be equally horrified to know these two children were to be let loose on London on their own, without anyone of sense to keep an eye on them. It was too bad of Mr Maddock to slough off his responsibilities in this way! Indeed, she quivered with indignation as she thought of how she would never have a moment's peace if she didn't take a lively interest in their welfare herself, which was the very last thing she wanted now that her own family was increasing year by year and would probably continue to do so because she could never summon up enough resolution to keep Sam out of her bed for two nights put together.

'I see,' she said aloud. Then, noticing how very pleased with herself her young sister was, her usual good nature reasserted itself, and she added with some amusement, 'Though what use *you* are going to be to our little brother, I simply can't imagine!'

'A lot of use,' Trudie assured her. 'Mr Maddock says I have a much better eye for Oriental artefacts than Septimus has. Besides, I'm much better at thinking up ways of making extra sales. It was my idea to box up one of those lovely scarves and ask Lady Eden to present it to the Queen. Next time, the Queen may come in person, or at least ask us to send a selection to the Palace for her to see, because she loves to be given things. She wrote personally to Mr Maddock to say how pleased she was with the gift and how she meant to wear it often to encourage others to take an interest in the artefacts of the Empire.'

'Heaven spare us!' Letty exclaimed. 'If you ask me, the sooner you are packed off to Singapore the better!'

But that day was still a long way off.

Returning from her supposed honeymoon as innocent as the day she had departed on it, Trudie accompanied her husband to Tilbury from where he was to depart on the long voyage to Singapore.

'It's a pity Cousin Hermione and Mr Horton aren't travelling on the same ship,' she remarked, 'they would have been company for you.'

'Ah, but would it have been company I should have enjoyed?'

Trudie giggled. 'You may have done. Most gentlemen seem to approve of Cousin Hermione in every way. Even Father. Father would have much preferred to have had a daughter like her instead of any of us.'

Mr Maddock put a finger under Trudie's chin, turning her face up to his. 'I prefer my own little bride. You have more character in your little finger than your pretty cousin has in her whole body!'

Trudie's eyes filled with tears. She blinked them back with determination. 'You're far too good to me, sir!'

'I wish that were the case,' Mr Maddock said more to himself than to her. 'Never mind, I'll make it up to you when you join me in Malacca.'

'Malacca? I thought you lived in Singapore.'

'That was before,' Mr Maddock said gently. 'Now I shall be living in Malacca.'

Trudie knew so little about either place, it made very

little difference to her where he was going. 'Malacca!' she ran the word slowly over her tongue. 'It sounds much nicer than Singapore. I'm glad you're going to live there!'

'I hope you'll always think that,' said her husband.

The Emporium went from strength to strength. Everywhere one went in London people were talking about the variety and scope of the luxury articles that were to be obtained there. Trudie had never enjoyed herself more. She, who had spent most of her life being bored by the regime of needlework and reading such improving literature as her father could bring himself to approve, interfered happily in every aspect of the Emporium, quite unaware of Septimus's increasing frustration at finding his own orders countermanded and her presence everywhere. He couldn't even escape her at home. There, she had installed Lily, borrowed from her parents' establishment, who had always adored the youngest Grant and readily set about making life as easy for her young charge as she could. Septimus soon found he had no more say at home than he had in the Emporium. Worse still, Trudie was almost invariably *right* in all the things she did, thus undermining any confidence in himself he might otherwise have had. It seemed to him to be more than time that Trudie should join her husband in Malacca, where she could concentrate on his career and home as a woman should.

'I won't go until Cousin Hermione has safely arrived in Singapore!' Trudie said with decision. 'I won't travel with them under any circumstances, no matter what!'

Septimus eyed his sister with a mixture of respect and exasperation. 'Christopher Horton could be very useful to us,' he basely reminded her. 'Cousin Hermione would drive a saint into the arms of the Devil himself, but you're a married woman yourself now, so you don't have to stand any nonsense from her. I should have thought travelling all that way with them would be a small price to pay for all the advantages that might come of it. Dash it all, Trudie, Mr Horton doesn't patronize you nearly as much as Hermione does and you must be used to her by this time!'

Trudie looked glumly back at her favourite brother. 'I don't like her. I never did.'

Septimus grinned. All women, even Trudie, were the same under the skin. They couldn't bear any competition from their own sex. He felt much better about Trudie's greater flair in the business world as he dwelt on her jealousy for her pretty cousin. What she needed was a husband to make much of her and give her something else to do but interfere in a man's world. He might even mention to their father how much happier he would feel if his young sister were to have company on the long voyage out to her husband's home. Not even Trudie would be a match for their father joined in action with Christopher Horton, both of whom were still bemoaning the prospect of poor little Hermione having to travel all that way without any reliable person of her own sex in attendance.

It didn't seem possible that it had been two years since the opening of the Emporium and his sister's marriage. In all that time, the Hortons had been leaving for Singapore on practically every ship which had set sail for India and further east. First Uncle Henry had died and Cousin Hermione had declared that nothing would induce her to leave her afflicted mother until a proper period of mourning had intervened. No sooner had she been out of black than Horton's elder sister had been carried off by some fever, and that had delayed them still further.

Christopher Horton had hated every moment of his enforced stay in England, worrying about the state of his business in Singapore and how the Chinese overseer would be fleecing him left, right and sideways. 'The sooner I get back to see what they've left me the better!' he told his wife bitterly.

'Surely you're rich enough to be able to spend a little time away from the heat and everything else? I wish we never had to go! Why don't you leave me behind, here in England, as Mr Maddock has Trudie? *She* hasn't a care in the world! I'm sure I shall look like a haggard old woman beside her by the time she finally does join that husband of hers!'

'Never, my dear! Your cousin doesn't know her husband if she thinks she can behave with such unbecoming independence when she joins him out East. Mr Maddock is a strange man, but he will be horrified to hear of the freedom she has had living in that young scamp's establishment and running every moment of his life. Septimus, for one, will be heartily glad to be rid of her!'

Hermione's eyes hardened. Now she was comfortably established, she took less trouble to hide the calculation that lay behind her bright blue eyes. 'I wonder if the Emporium will make as much money without her?'

Christopher Horton exploded into laughter. 'Since when has any woman understood anything of business, my dear? Oh, Septimus may indulge his favourite sister by letting her think she has the running of everything, but no woman can really come to grips with the intricacies of buying and selling. She can't run the staff to begin with. That takes a man's hand if they are not to take advantage every moment one turns one's back. No, no, little Miss Trudie will soon be where she properly belongs, in her husband's home with a child at her knee!'

Hermione became thoughtful. 'Shall we take her up when we're all in Singapore?'

'I doubt we'll see much of her. If you'll take my advice,

you'll take your time before you bestow your friendship, my love. We have our own ways in the Colonies and you don't want to do the wrong thing, do you? I've been away for too long to be able to help you at first as to who is in and who is out at the moment. Your cousin will undoubtedly rush her welcome! I shouldn't like you to do likewise!'

'No, no, of course not,' Hermione agreed hastily. 'Still, I shouldn't like to offend Mr Maddock, you know. He is supposed to be one of the richest men East of Suez.'

'No, you're right! That wouldn't do at all.' Mr Horton rubbed his chin through his beard, making a scratching noise that recently had begun to irritate his wife's nerves, putting her teeth on edge. 'We must all compromise at times, I suppose. It will be enough for now for you to befriend her on board, my love, introducing her as your companion. If anyone comments on your tolerance, you may always point out that she is your first cousin. Never was there a truer *bon mot* than that our relations are given to us, it is our friends we choose for ourselves. Then, however she behaves in Singapore, you will have shown a proper womanly feeling towards her for which no possible blame could attach to yourself.'

Hermione's fair face smiled prettily back at him and he was satisfied she would do exactly as she was told. Hermione, however, was already thinking of all the ways she could make use of Trudie on the long voyage out. It would be so much more comfortable to have someone on hand to fetch and carry, to brush her long blonde locks, and to bathe her forehead with eau de cologne if the seas should be rough. What was more, as she would frequently point out to anyone who would listen, she was doing her cousin a kindness by allowing her to do these little services for her in exchange for her chaperonage, and for the untold benefits of having Mr Horton's help, getting on and off the ship, and protecting her from the many mistakes a woman would inevitably make travelling on her own. Really, there was no doubt about it, her cousin was getting the best of the bargain, though she had her doubts that Trudie would ever be brought to acknowledge as much.

Trudie would have put off her own departure if she could have done so. She wrote an agonized letter to her husband, begging him to be allowed to stay on in England a little longer. She had written to him before from time to time, relating her doings with an impulsive intimacy that had received little encouragement from his replies.

Dear Mr Maddock, she wrote, ending up, *Your devoted and obedient wife, Gertrude Maddock*. The middle part was taken up by a whole lot of facts and figures to do with the Emporium. It was only after that that she summoned up the courage to explain she had no fancy to travel on the same ship as her cousin. She spent a long time trying to conjure up the likeness of her spouse in her mind, sighing over the vague picture she had of a man whom she had liked well enough, but whom she had been equally pleased to wave goodbye to so long before.

His reply was even shorter than her own missive. Septimus was of the opinion that the Hortons might be useful to their future financial ventures and she would do well to be guided by her brother in this as in everything else. When she read Mr Maddock's brief, formal note, Trudie began to have doubts about her future with her unknown husband for the very first time.

The whole Grant family came to see them off. For one, heart-stopping moment, Trudie thought it was because they were sorry to see her go, but it was soon made clear to her that it was Hermione's departure that concerned them, especially her father.

'Don't take it to heart, love,' Letty advised comfortably. 'He's always been more fond of our cousin than of any of us.'

'But why, Letty?' For once Trudie allowed the agony she had always felt where her father was concerned to emerge.

Letty took her hand in hers. 'I've always thought it better not to dwell on the whys and wherefores of such things. Poor Mama!'

Trudie cast her parent a contemptuous look. 'I wish she'd answer him back sometimes!'

Letty laughed lightly. 'As you would, no doubt?' She patted her sister's hand. 'If you only won't fire up at me, my love, I have a word of advice for you, which I only offer because I, at least, love you the best of all the family. It's a strange marriage you've had so far, with your husband so far away and Septimus quite useless when it comes to stopping you from managing all his affairs for him! Mr Maddock won't like it if you argue with him over every suggestion he makes to you as you do with our brother. Remember, there won't be anyone out there to take your part if you quarrel with him, you know!'

Trudie kissed Letty's plump cheek. 'What do you know of quarrelling?' she scoffed. 'You and Sam are like a couple of comfortable cushions together!'

Letty sighed. 'Even Sam expects to be master of his own household! He wouldn't like it if I presumed to tell him what to do!'

Trudie's eyes filled with laughter. 'Letty! You tell him what to do every day, you know you do!'

Her exasperated sister slapped the hand she was holding. 'But *he* doesn't know it! That's the art of being a good wife, you silly girl! That's what I'm trying to explain to you!'

'Darling Letty!' Trudie said fondly. 'Mr Maddock likes

me very well as I am. He especially likes it that I'm interested in his business matters. I doubt he would have married me otherwise, if I hadn't shown at least as much flair as Septimus in buying and selling Oriental artefacts.'

Letty accompanied her young sister down the narrow companionway to her cabin. It was not as well positioned as her cousins,' but it was quite large enough for one person, having a bed, fastened to the floor by great bolts, and a washstand of a kind, and even a press in which she could put some of her clothes, the greater part of which were packed away in her tin trunk, painted with her name and destination and already disposed of somewhere in one of the great holds below.

'Trudie, tell me to mind my own business if you like, but I have the oddest feeling that Mr Maddock never really made you his wife at all. Did nothing happen on your wedding night?'

'Nothing that I can remember now,' Trudie responded cheerfully.

'Oh dear! No wonder you came home so – unchanged!'

'What on earth should change me in a single night?'

Letty saw clearly that she had done her younger sister a great wrong by allowing Hatty to have her way and be the one to instruct her in the duties of the married state. What she couldn't understand was how Trudie had managed to pull the wool over Hatty's eyes and convince her that Septimus had already told her all she needed to know. She was extremely vexed with herself for not seeing how unlikely it was that Septimus should soil his sister's ears with any such information, vexed with Sam for agreeing so easily that that was how it must have been, and positively furious with Hatty for making such a mull of the task she had volunteered to take on her own shoulders.

'Trudie, marriage is a very close relationship – '

'I know that! I'm looking forward to it, to tell you the truth. I mean to learn everything I can from Mr Maddock about the Orient.'

'Trudie! I'm talking about your life with him as his wife. He may want children – '

'He said I'm too young to have children of my own yet. I was only seventeen then, Letty. I'm much more grown up now, don't you think?'

Letty did think so. She also saw that in her present mood there was no telling Trudie anything she didn't wish to hear. 'Look, love,' she said at last, 'I know you don't like Hermione very much – I don't much myself – but if you ever find yourself in difficulties, she is a member of your family and I'm sure she'll do everything she can to help you. There are some things that come better from another woman than even from the most loving man, as I can tell you! Oh dear, I do wish you weren't going so far away!'

'You can't wish it more than I do! But only because Septimus will never spend sixpence to make a pound. Sometimes I think he takes after Father more than any of us have allowed! Oh Letty, love, don't worry about me. To tell you the truth, I am pleased to be going at last, though I could have done without having to dance round Cousin Hermione on board for weeks on end.' She hugged her sister, as exuberant as ever. 'I have a fancy to see the Orient for myself, you know. One of these days, I mean to be a trader in my own right, even if I have to wait to be a widow to begin, for I'm much better at it than Septimus is. Won't it be fun to have a whole fortune to spend exactly as I please? Wouldn't you like to have a competence all of your own so that not even Sam could tell you what to buy, or when? I shall give it to you.' Her brow darkened. 'I shan't give one penny to Father, however, so you had better not tell him of my plans!'

There was little danger of that, for Letty didn't believe that such an impossible dream could ever come true. Instead, it served to add to her worries about her sister, making her seem more of a child than ever.

'Oh, Trudie, dear, foolish Trudie, I wish you could hear yourself babbling on about nothing when there is so much I should be saying to you! Look after yourself, love, and come safely home again!'

Trudie was fascinated by the great Port of London. The great masts that towered overhead; the bare-footed men who ran up and down the ropes, setting the sails and making fast; the small boats, rowed by grey-faced men with straining muscles, that pushed and pulled the great ships into position to load or unload, or even into the channel from which they would make their way out into the open sea beyond.

All of it was exciting. Hermione sent a message that she was overcome with her grief at being wrenched from her mother and all those who were dear to her, and had taken refuge in her cabin until she should feel better. Trudie cared not one jot. She stood on deck, watching the bustle going on all round her, thinking that if she had been a boy and had seen all this, she would have run away to sea many years before. She sniffed at the salt in the air and longed to be gone.

The passengers were carefully arranged as to class, the deck on which she was standing being reserved for the first-class passengers, who also ate together and had a saloon to themselves. The other passengers were huddled further forward, some children amongst them, and several young women laughing and talking among themselves.

She was intrigued to see two of the latter wearing the most outlandish clothes, so that they didn't look English at all. They had striped skirts, checked aprons, and weird top hats, taller than most men would have worn on horseback, that made them look a little like the illustrations of witches one saw in children's books. Trudie wondered who they were. She would have made her way down to them to find out had Mr Horton not come out to find her just then.

'Mrs Horton hates being so confined!' he fussed. 'Perhaps a little female company – '

Trudie saw the strange ladies looking in her direction and waved to them. They waved back, their glowing cheeks turned towards her. 'Who are they, do you think?'

Mr Horton cleared his throat. 'I was saying your cousin – '

'Cousin Hermione always fusses over nothing,' Trudie answered him. 'She would do better out here, seeing everything that's going on, instead of worrying about how she will feel shortly.'

'A little unfeeling, Miss Trudie, but you may be right.'

'I'm sure I am! Look, they're not speaking English so they must be foreigners. Oh dear, I was so hoping to talk to them!'

'They're Welsh,' Mr Horton supplied. 'I imagine they are army wives going out to join their husbands. Are you hoping to employ one of them as your maid?'

Trudie shook her head. 'They look more interesting than anyone on our deck.'

'You could do worse, my dear. I'm told they make good domestics, if you can stop them jabbering away in their own language. It's forbidden to them in the schools now, but they will keep on with it at home. Uncivilized lot!'

'They look charming!' Trudie insisted, more to annoy him than because she really thought so. She found their costume eccentric in the extreme, but she couldn't help thinking them a jolly couple all the same.

Mr Horton primped up his mouth. 'If you don't intend to employ them, stay away from them, my dear. One never knows what they're talking about in that outlandish tongue of theirs – probably dissension and rebellion, or they would be speaking English like the rest of us!'

Had he known it, nothing could have made Trudie more determined to make the Welsh ladies' acquaintance. She watched them covertly the whole time they moved slowly down the Thames and out into the open sea. They laughed a lot and they were excited by the same things that excited her. She thought them a great deal more fun than her disapproving cousins and vowed to herself she would find out all about them just as soon as she could.

Trudie was confirmed in this resolution by the first formal meal they made, seated at the captain's table, she and Hermione both splendid in their dinner dresses and trying to pretend the swell of the sea under the ship was not making them nervous.

Mr Horton had already made the captain's acquaintance and he made haste to introduce his wife to him, adding, 'My wife's cousin and companion for the voyage, Miss Trudie.'

Trudie looked the captain in the eye, liking the firm grip of his hand. 'I am Mrs Jeremy Maddock. Perhaps you know my husband?'

'I know of him, Mrs Maddock. I didn't know he had married.'

Trudie smiled one of her most engaging smiles. 'He hardly knows it himself! He left for Singapore almost immediately and it is only now that I am to join him. It wasn't convenient before for a number of reasons.'

The captain's keen glance took in her clear, smiling face and he blinked. 'I hope you'll find everything ready for you when you do arrive.'

Which was a mighty odd thing to say, Trudie thought. She tried to explain the delays had been at her end, what with setting up the Emporium and so on, but Mr Horton cut her off with a bilious glance and monopolized the conversation thereafter.

Trudie finally relapsed into total silence, ignoring both the lowering glances of her cousin and the more flattering openings offered her by the captain. She had much to think about and there was so much to look at! The high polish of the mahogany table was pleasing to her eye, especially when she saw the way each glass had a place bored into the surface to hold it in rough weather. They were served with an excellent meal, almost as though they had been on land, the wines served from flat-bottomed decanters that would also be very hard to spill.

'How neat everything is!' she exclaimed at last.

The captain, relieved to see his young passenger feeling more at home, bent his head towards her. 'Shipshape and Bristol fashion, Mrs Maddock! I come from Bristol myself, ma'am, and so the saying has a special meaning for me.'

When the ladies rose to leave the gentlemen alone together, Hermione's stormy expression warned Trudie her cousin was determined to have it established once and for all that she was the senior lady on board.

'Really, Trudie, must you flirt like that with the captain! I didn't know where to look! I shall wish I'd never acknowledged you to be my cousin if you have to behave so badly! What came over you? You know Mr Horton and I promised Uncle Jonathan we would look after you during the voyage, but I didn't expect to have to apologize for you on the very first evening! I could tell how embarrassed both men were! Christopher hates what he calls "female wiles" at the best of times! If you can't be more circumspect, I think it would be better if you kept to your cabin!'

Trudie glared at her. 'Whilst we are discussing manners, may I remind you that I'm every bit as much a married lady as you are. It was my husband who paid for my passage – as *his wife*, not as your companion!'

'Well really!' Hermione exclaimed angrily. 'Surely it isn't too much to ask you to do one or two little things for me? Uncle Jonathan insisted I should make good use of you as you were lucky enough to be travelling with us! You know how easily overset by the least thing I am and you have always had the strength of ten!'

Trudie began to feel guilty, though why she should was beyond her. 'Of course I shall do what I can to make things more pleasant for you, but as Mrs Maddock, not as little Cousin Trudie!' She owed that much to her husband, she thought, to bear his name with pride and not to allow it to be forgotten. She only wished she could remember the man who had given it to her with the same clarity as she could most other things.

'Oh, very well!' Hermione muttered crossly. Her mouth took on a sulky curve as she flounced down the narrow corridor that led to her cabin. Cousin Trudie had a great deal to learn if she thought her marriage made her the social equal of Mrs Christopher Horton. Uncle Jonathan should have made it clear to her that she owed Hermione a vast debt of gratitude in return for her condescension in knowing her at all! How many others in her position, who dabbled in *trade*, expected to be recognized by their less commercially minded relations? Not many, she'd be bound!

It was a week or two before Hermione found her sea legs. Trudie, on the other hand, spent as little time as she could manage confined in the minute cabin that had been allotted to her. She was everywhere. Invited by the captain up on to the bridge, she was soon demanding to be shown the navigation instruments and could shortly make a tolerable job of working out their longitude and latitude, as excited as a child with a brand-new toy.

She also ventured on to the lower decks, coming across the two Welsh ladies almost immediately, for they, like herself, much preferred the open air to the crowded conditions down below.

'Are you really Welsh?' she asked them.

They dropped her a curtsey, shy to be thus greeted by a stranger. '*Bora da,*' they whispered.

Trudie's face fell. 'Don't you speak any English?' she demanded.

'Oh yes!'

'Well, that's good, because I speak no Welsh at all. Where are you from and where are you going?'

The two exchanged glances, the braver of the two answering for both of them. 'I am Gwennant Jones, and my friend is Glynis Jones – no relation really. There are many of us named Jones in Wales. I used to be Gwennant John and she was Glynis Evans. Our husbands are soldiers in the Welsh Fusiliers, stationed out in Singapore. We are on our way to join them there.'

Trudie stumbled over the names, gaining confidence at their evident pleasure that she should take the trouble to make the attempt. 'I'm going out to join my husband also,' she told them. 'He used to be in Singapore, but now he has a coffee plantation, I think, near Malacca. His name is Jeremy Maddock.'

Glynis Jones bit her lower lip. 'I had no idea Singapore could be so far away, had you, madam?'

Trudie tried to explain to them where they were and how far they had to go, drawing a map of the world for them in the spray on the deck. Baffled, they stared at the shapes she was making, refusing to believe that Great

Britain, let alone the Principality of Wales, could possibly be so small in comparison with the enormous shapes of Africa, India, even the Straits Settlements for which they were headed.

'This morning,' said Trudie firmly, 'we were approximately here.' She pointed near to where she had marked Gibraltar, already disappearing as it dried in the sunshine.

'We shall be on board for ever!' Gwennant exclaimed.

Trudie nodded her head. 'I'm afraid it will be several weeks before we see our husbands.' Her eyes glinted and she tossed her head. 'I never thought to have such a splendid adventure as to travel round the world on a ship though, did you?'

The Welsh women thought they could well do without such a treat. They spoke long and often of their homeland, bemoaning their fate at ever having to leave it.

'There's beautiful it is!' Gwennant sighed. 'I miss the strong stone and the changing greens of the pastures. There are sheep cropping the hills all round where I live, and the birds overhead, great eagles, some of them, they can carry off a new-born lamb in their talons. Then there is the chapel where we go on Sundays. 'Twas not long before we left that a famous preacher came to Maenclochog and we all went to hear him, didn't we, Glynis?'

Trudie thought of her father's sermons and felt nothing but relief that she didn't have to listen to him again for a long, long time to come. 'Did he preach in Welsh?' she asked.

A certain excitement surrounded them as they spoke to each other with their eyes. Finally, Gwennant shrugged her shoulders. 'He spoke with the glory of the true poet! If they'd known he was going to speak in Welsh though, I think he might have been arrested and carried off to prison – '

'For speaking in Welsh?' Trudie was shocked.

'We are supposed to be speaking the English. We are punished if we speak Welsh in school, or anywhere else.'

'Why?'

'Because we can't be understood. At least, that's what my Da says. Have you ever travelled to Wales, madam?'

'Never,' Trudie admitted. 'I've never been anywhere before this.' She hesitated, then she went on, 'Do you mind if I come and talk to you from time to time? There's only my cousin and her husband travelling in my part of the ship and she spends most of the time being ill.'

'You are not at all like her! *She* wouldn't want to talk to us!'

Trudie wondered how they knew. 'Do you always dress in those strange clothes?' she burst out.

'Oh yes! How else would you know we come from Pembrokeshire?' They giggled, only knowing that, at home, everyone was dressed much the same. It was only since they had left Wales that they had become aware of English fashions and had marvelled at the numbers of changes of clothes Trudie and her cousin indulged in on board ship.

'I've never seen hats like yours before!' Trudie told them.

'Beaver hats. They were new to come away with. I spent five guineas on mine. Idris never told me no one wears hats like these away from Wales, so my Mam said I must have one to show I wasn't penniless but came from a respectable farming family. At least nobody will think me anything but Welsh in these clothes!'

'No, indeed,' Trudie agreed.

Glynis, who preferred to leave most of the conversation to her friend, suddenly broke into speech. 'It's easy to see why we wear clothes like these. We make them ourselves, you see, from the things we find around us. The red comes from cockles, so if one lives by the sea, it's easy to have scarlet shawls and whittles. We all wear red wraps near where we came from. When the French came and tried to land at Fishguard in 1798, they say it was seeing all the women wrapped in red that frightened them into giving up. Squire Cambel – '

'Lord Cawdor,' Gwennant supplied.

'He saw there were some four hundred women gathered and asked them if they were to fight, and they said they were. They soon sent the French about their business, with pitchforks as their only weapons. It must have been a brave sight to see them!'

Trudie had never heard of such an invasion. She imagined it must have had something to do with the Napoleonic Wars which had already receded into history as far as she was concerned. What impudence to try and attack through the back door, as it were!

'Did only women fight?' she asked.

Neither of the Welsh girls really knew. 'It might have been,' they compromised. 'They say the French had an American admiral – and he had been a Scotsman once upon a time!'

Trudie looked down her nose in disdain. 'Then he should have known better!' she declared firmly, her eyes sparkling. One thing was quite certain, she would never have had such an interesting conversation with anyone else on board! She grinned happily at her new friends. 'The Welsh are obviously a force to be reckoned with!' she said.

'Maybe, maybe not!'

And they laughed together like three happy children who had managed to escape their adult keepers for a while.

Chapter Five

Singapore!

Trudie rose so early that the edge of the sky was still silver with that unearthly light that betokened the dawn. Hurrying down to the lower deck, she found the only other passengers to be stirring were the Welsh women.

'I was beginning to think we'd never reach Journey's End!' she greeted them. 'Are you being met by your husbands?'

Neither of them knew. 'They will have made some arrangements for us,' they comforted each other. Now that they were here, they were both wishing they were safely back home in Wales. Their husbands had the familiarity of the Army, no matter where they were stationed; the few wives that were allowed to accompany them overseas had no such prop and stay. More often than not, their husbands would be gone on duty for weeks on end and they had only each other to make their lonely lives worth while. 'Who is meeting you, Mrs Maddock?'

'I really don't know,' Trudie confessed.

She saw the captain making his way towards them and moved forward to save him a few steps. He took her hand in his, his eyes glinting at her through his bushy brows.

'So, we reach the end of the voyage!' he said. 'I come to say goodbye, Mrs Maddock. I am on my way ashore to present my papers to the authorities and I expect you will be gone by the time I get back. Your cousins were telling me they are expecting to stay with the Governor and his Lady; are those your plans also?'

Trudie was unprepared for the question. She wished she had thought to ask someone, but who would know? Doubtless a message would be brought to her from Mr Maddock sooner or later and, until then, she could wait.

'My husband – ' she began.

The captain's eyes sparkled a more vivid shade of green. 'Ah yes, of course, your husband will have made arrangements for you. I hope he appreciates you, my dear, for you have a lively way with you. A pity you're not a man, ma'am, for you'd have made a fine sailor, if you don't mind my saying so. Bless my soul, I hadn't looked for such entertainment from my passengers though, not on this voyage, for I've travelled with Mr Horton before – and his like! A worthy gentleman, I'm sure, but you, ma'am, have an eye for detail, which might make you uncomfortable company for your relations, but has endeared you for ever with my officers and with myself! May I wish you very happy in your new home when you finally reach it! You will always be welcome on my ship, I hope you know that, whenever you wish to travel back to England again!'

Trudie thanked him gravely. She stood aside so that he could say his farewells to his Welsh passengers, which he did, calling them both by name with the same ease and dignity with which he had addressed her. When he had done, the three of them stood on the deck and watched him climb down into the tiny rowing-boat that was to take him ashore.

'I hope we won't have to go down a ladder like that!' one of the Welsh girls exclaimed.

'Surely not!' Trudie answered firmly.

She was reluctant to leave her two companions but she still had the odds and ends of her packing to do and, if she knew anything about it, she would very likely have to cope with Cousin Hermione's as well. Reluctantly, she went down below, marvelling at how perverse human nature could be for, now that she was leaving the ship, she was quite sorry to lose the familiarity of her minute cabin and leave behind the swaying sensation beneath her feet that by now seemed like second nature to her.

Cousin Hermione had a great deal to say about her not having put in an appearance earlier. 'I did tell you Mr Horton and I are to stay with the Governor and I shall never be ready if you don't help me, Trudie! What a selfish creature you are, to be sure, never to be here when I need you!'

'Well, I'm here now,' Trudie returned, determined not to quarrel with her cousin on this last morning, as from now on she would have Mr Maddock beside her to lend her a dignity and position which she was certain was every bit as important in the Colony as that of her cousin's.

She wondered if she had been included in the Governor's invitation to the Hortons, not much concerned either way. Her own husband would make her arrangements for her in future, she reminded herself, and then she would have nothing more to worry about. More, he would be here in all probability before she could turn round and it would be much better if she were not still engaged in packing up her cousin's belongings when he did.

Judging by the disarray all about her, Hermione had pulled every garment she had out of her trunks, looking for something suitable to wear as a guest of the Governor himself.

'He's by far the most important person outside of India!' she told Trudie, rummaging through her jewel-case one last time. 'Singapore is the capital of the Straits Settlements now and the Residence of the Governor. There's a garrison here as well, and plenty of warships in the harbour, which is why there are so many military gentlemen about. Of course, there are the commercial expatriates, too, like your husband I dare say,' she added, conveniently forgetting her own husband's interest in trade, as was her way. 'A lot of people hope to make their fortunes out here and then go home to England pretending they are better than they really are. Mr Horton has been telling me all about such people, though I can't think they will bother you much, hidden away in Malacca, or wherever it is you're going to live. Malacca has only a Lieutenant-Governor, as does Penang, both of them subordinate to Singapore. The rest of the peninsula is made up of various native states, ruled by some of the richest princes in the East. I don't suppose they shall be independent, though, for much longer if the British have their way, do you?'

Trudie sat on the last of the trunks, forcing it shut. She could have told Hermione the names of some of the native states, having learned them carefully from one of the books she had brought with her. Names like Sungei-Ujong, Selangor, and Perak; magic names which she and the Welsh girls had rolled round their tongues, quite sure in their own minds that they were full of romance.

'And very likely dragons, too!' Trudie had said.

The Welsh girls had giggled. 'Wales is the land of the dragon, but we've yet to see one!'

Trudie took a last look round Hermione's cabin, making sure nothing was left behind, before saying, 'Do you mind if I go on deck, cousin? Singapore must be one of the largest harbours in the world and I may never have a chance to see it again. Besides, I want to be up where I can see when Mr Maddock comes for me!'

Hermione yawned. 'As long as you don't expect me to hang over the side in that common way! I shall very likely be sick of the sight of Singapore before long, so I think I shall stay here and rest. It's like an oven outside, not that I expect you to notice such a detail! You'll ruin your complexion in a trice, going out in the sun as you do!'

'I'm wearing a hat.'

'Much good that may do you! I can't think why I perspire so much more than you do. I feel like a sponge, though I do nothing but sit here quietly. How you can rush around like you do, I really don't know!'

Trudie was only too glad to get away by herself on deck. A sailor brought her a chair and set it up for her in a shady corner from where she could see everything that was going on all round her. It was certainly hot, especially now they were still, the sails furled instead of cracking over their heads as they filled with the wind. She would miss the sights and sounds of being at sea, she thought, but really her mind was already dancing before her on to the next adventure. How exciting it was to be in the East at last, thousands of miles away from the familiar grey drizzle that had been her last sight of England. Singapore was so unexpected, with the sun beating down on everything like a heavy weight from above, and the greenery which came right down to the water's edge, a tangle of plants, none of which she could recall ever having seen before.

Gwennant and Glynis were already ashore. They were dressed in their Sunday best, their tall hats gleaming in the sunshine. With them was a dark-haired giant of a man, plainly as Welsh as they were themselves, his attention divided as he tried to sort out their luggage as well as answer all their numerous questions. Trudie eyed him with interest, wondering how he dared to go about dressed in no more than a flimsy shirt and a pair of trousers that would better have graced one of the natives rather than a European. He didn't look a military man to her, neither in his bearing nor in the quiet way he addressed the Chinese coolies who were vying with one another to do his bidding.

She could have laughed out loud to see them thronging about him in vain, whilst others shouted and swore at the few who remained, without any visible results at all.

Then, quite suddenly, he looked up at her, to where Gwennant was pointing her out to him, and their eyes met. Such was the impact he made on her that a curl of excitement trembled within her. Hastily, she averted her gaze as she had been taught and missed his light-hearted salute and the last cries for her to look after herself from the two girls.

Instead, she was in time to see the rather grand carriage drawing up down below and her cousin, leaning heavily on her husband's arm, walking towards it. For once Trudie was glad she was not a blonde, for Hermione's face, scarlet in the heat, was already dripping with perspiration, whilst she, although she was equally unused to the sultry atmosphere, still had the strength to be interested in all that was going on about her without too much discomfort.

The Hortons were driven off without a backward look. How like Hermione! No doubt if things failed to go her way, she would remember Trudie and make a great fuss of her for a while, but there was little enough affection there, little enough for anyone other than her own self and her immediate needs as she saw them, then and there.

Once the carriage had moved away out of sight, Trudie turned her attention to the crowd that had gathered on the side of the harbour. The population seemed to be predominantly Chinese, which surprised her. Surely the Malays ought to be better represented, yet those few natives who were not Chinese seemed to be mainly Indian. Perhaps things were different up country, she told herself. Whichever race they came from, she noticed, they seemed to be more at home than the occasional European who came into her view, the men half hidden beneath their pith helmets and the even fewer women determinedly protecting themselves from the ravages of the sun with parasols, sometimes held by themselves and sometimes by a servant who ran alongside the rickshaws, which were hauled by other, thinner scraps of humanity, their ribs sticking out under their shirts so that she could almost count them from where she was sitting.

Trudie waited as patiently as she could for Mr Maddock to come and seek her out. More than two hours went by and all the other passengers had long ago gone their several ways, when she began to consider just what she would do if her husband delayed much longer. She remembered her father telling her that one of his classmates – a hopeless fellow, without the push of a mouse – had been sent to Singapore as a missionary. Another half-hour and she had remembered his name, Cecil Eliot. She went up on the bridge and asked the young officer she found there if a message could be sent ashore on her behalf.

There followed another long wait before Mr Eliot arrived, white-haired, pink-faced, and flustered. 'My dear Miss Grant, however long have you been waiting? What an ordeal for you in this heat! You should have sent a message to me earlier, indeed you should!'

Trudie smiled prettily at him. 'Alas, not Miss Grant any longer. I should have told you in my note that I am now Mrs Jeremy Maddock. I was expecting my husband to meet me, but I expect he has been delayed in Malacca, or somewhere along the road. I can only apologize for imposing myself on you, Mr Eliot, but I really didn't know what else to do. My cousin is staying with the Governor – '

'Enough said, Mrs Maddock! One does not go there without an invitation! Please say no more, you are doing my wife and me a favour, if you only knew it! You can't know how we long for news from home! My wife would meet every ship in the hopes of letters if I would let her, I'm sure, and talks of little else than the time when we shall retire to a small place of our own back in the Mother Country.' He sighed heavily. 'I must confess I long for the time myself when I shall live again amongst proper Christian folk in a country where the seasons come and go. My word, what wouldn't I give for one of those sparkling days of winter – but there, you have just left all that and I mustn't say a word to make you regret coming out here amongst us.'

He was silent for a long while, leaving her to marvel inwardly at the mangrove swamps, the coconut palms, the banana palms, and all manner of tropical fruits and strangling plants, all of them fighting for space in their green and gold surroundings.

When he spoke again, she was busy wondering why it was that the few European women she could see were all so inelegant. They dressed as if they were still living in the temperate climes of the British Isles, with none of the flair and comfort of the Indian women in their saris, for example. The European ladies were rigidly corseted, flounced and frilled, and one and all looked about to expire with heat.

'Maddock,' Mr Eliot murmured to himself. 'I did hear something about a Mr Maddock recently. Mr Jeremy Maddock, you say?'

Trudie nodded. 'He used to live in Singapore, but he's been in Malacca for about two years now.'

'Ah yes, I remember now, he didn't come to church. Bad that! Sets a bad example, you see, to those we are trying to convert – a losing battle at the best of times.' He frowned. 'Perhaps we should have tried harder to encourage him, Mrs Maddock, for I can't believe your father would have allowed you to marry one who had turned his back on the Lord Jesus. No, sir, there must be a lot I don't know about your husband. You must take him by the hand and bring him back to his duties every Sunday now that you're here. I'm sorry to say that many gentlemen grow slack when they don't have their womenfolk beside them to show them the way.'

'I shall do my best,' Trudie promised, though she couldn't imagine herself leading the Mr Maddock she remembered anywhere he didn't wish to go.

Mrs Eliot was beside herself with joy at having a visitor as a house guest, especially one who could tell her all the secrets of the latest London fashions.

'You travelled out with your cousin, Mrs Maddock? Would that be the new Mrs Horton? How odd that she should have abandoned you to your own devices without assuring herself your husband was there to meet you! Mr Horton, at least, must know that anything can happen in this place to delay one, or otherwise inconvenience those who wish for nothing more than to be left in peace! I should know all about that! I'm a martyr to my husband's calling, as I'm for ever telling him, because it doesn't do for a man of the cloth to put himself first, does it?'

Trudie raised a disbelieving brow. 'I can only speak of my father, Mrs Eliot, and I assure you he never does anything other than put himself first. He has very strong opinions on the subject.'

Mrs Eliot's jaw dropped, then her mouth quivered with suppressed laughter. 'My dear! I can't believe you're serious! Though it's very true! I remember your father well, and he never could abide anyone to contradict him! Between you and me, my husband was more than a little bit scared of him, though I believe him to be the better scholar – '

'And by far the better Christian!' Trudie finished for her.

'Well, yes, that too. Oh dear, how dreadful of us to speak so of your poor father!'

Trudie shook her head. 'He says much worse of me! If I shall never be grateful to him for anything else, I shall always be grateful to Mr Maddock for marrying me and taking me away from my father's house.'

Mrs Eliot swallowed. 'Have you been married long?'

'Two years.'

'Oh, I thought you still a bride – '

'It's hard to know what I am,' Trudie confessed cheerfully. 'My husband returned to Malacca almost immediately after we were wed, whilst I remained in London with my youngest brother to help him set up a new Emporium in Regent Street in London. My husband and my brother are partners in the venture.'

'I see,' Mrs Eliot said faintly.

Trudie smiled across at her. 'I don't suppose you do. I didn't myself, because I had no idea how fascinating it is to buy and sell things until my husband made it possible for me to try it for myself. To tell you the truth, I was sorry to leave it all in Septimus's hands. For the first few weeks, I worried myself to death about him, but Mr Maddock said he never would learn with me to make the decisions for him, and Septimus couldn't wait for me to be gone, having no very high opinion of women in business, or so he said. He wouldn't have got very far without me, let me tell you!'

'Buying and selling? My dear, however did you find the courage – '

'That was the easy part! It was learning how to do it that was hard. I was lucky enough to be trained by an expert – my husband!'

Mrs Eliot sniffed, sure that her young guest had been a player in a great romance. She leaned forward breathlessly. 'No wonder you fell in love with him!' she breathed.

Trudie knew very little about love or marriage, but she saw it wouldn't do to say as much. Try as she would, she could not see herself as a romantic figure. Regretfully, she abandoned the role, though only because she was reasonably sure it wouldn't take her hostess long to find her out.

'I suppose so,' she said doubtfully.

'How much you must be looking forward to seeing your dear husband again! Mr Eliot will ask about tomorrow you may be sure, my dear, and we shall soon know exactly where he is and what has delayed him! Meanwhile we shall do our poor best to entertain you amongst our friends in Singapore.'

Left alone in the small, neat bedroom that had been allotted to her, Trudie lay down for a moment on the bed, trying to sort out the welter of impressions that had come her way since leaving the ship. She had been lucky, she knew, to be taken in by the Eliots, obviously kind people, though she doubted they would ever be more than acquaintances in the normal way.

Nor, she was to discover later, was Mrs Eliot much of a hostess. Her welcome had been eager enough, but Trudie soon learned she had no conversation at all that did not revolve around the mail to and from England. Every time a ship was due, Mrs Eliot would brighten, eager for news of her sisters and English friends. In return, she wrote long and carping letters about her own life in Singapore, in which she took no interest at all. After a week of her society, Trudie came rapidly to the conclusion that hers was a wasted life, lived vicariously in her imagination of how life was lived in England, a life which she probably would have detested quite as much as she did her present one.

Mr Eliot had arrived in Singapore already a disappointed man. As a young man he had believed that faith would conquer all, that it was the only thing necessary to lead the perfect life. Yet his peers had refused to recognize the shining example he had offered them, preferring more worldly men to fill the plum jobs in the Church. In despair, he had considered giving up his vocation altogether and would have done so had it not come to him like a flash of lightning that he was, after all, being saved for the best of all. He was to go to a foreign land, where he would win many souls for Jesus; the harvest was ripe, all that was lacking was the labourers to bring it safely in. He had had a picture of himself, standing tall, almost as tall as the Cross he had held up to the many pagans seeking conversion who had bowed before it and him.

How different had been the reality. He had been hoping to be sent to India and to find himself in Singapore had been but the first of many disappointments. It had not taken him long to discover that the Moslem Malays were contemptuous of his efforts; the Chinese, with their effrontery in considering themselves to be the only truly civilized people in the world, wondered openly what the red-faced foreign devil could be wittering on about; even the Europeans, who were all nominally Christian, were too busy making money to bother to live up to the promises of their baptism, or too busy arguing over the finer theological points that divided them one from another. Only the Catholics, the ones the Chinese called the 'skirted devils', had made any real impression on the local populace. For some reason that Mr Eliot couldn't understand, these foreign priests – for even the most English of them were not true Englishmen with undivided loyalties such as he was himself – could outface the Chinese, as confident in their superstitions bred in Rome as any Malay bowing down five times a day in the direction of Mecca.

Even so, he might have found a measure of contentment had it not been for his wife's lack of fervour for the cause. In agony he had prayed that he might lead her to a better understanding of how pleasing his work was to the Lord they both served. Sometimes he had even been tempted to doubt that she was one of the chosen, for wasn't it written that Christ would spew out the lukewarm? Mrs Eliot had never been the recipient of those flashes of intuition when one knew the rightness of one's cause and the certainty of one's own salvation. She was a prey to doubts, going so far as to insist that the local peoples would never be induced to submit to the yoke of Christ in any meaningful way.

'One visit to a Chinese temple convinced me of that!' she would claim in loud, ringing tones. 'Jesus cleared the Temple in Jerusalem, declaring it to be a den of thieves. He wouldn't have been able to make Himself heard amongst the gambling and feasting and the playing of games that goes on out here! I'm sure He would have done what I did, shake the dust from my feet and vow never to go near such a place again! If they wanted to be Christians, it would only be because they thought they could turn a penny making a fool of one of their betters!'

Mr Eliot shook his head in remembered dismay. Hatred, he thought, could sometimes be turned to love; a fastidious dislike was more difficult to deal with, especially when one often felt the same way oneself, wondering what those blank, narrowed stares concealed, hoping one was wrong in one's instinctive conviction that every other enigmatic face was secretly plotting one's downfall, even one's death.

He wouldn't have believed the presence of another person in his house could have made such a difference to him. Mrs Maddock never complained about the heat in his hearing, nor did she fall silent every time a servant came into the room. By the time a week had passed by he had completely fallen under her spell. He was particularly pleased to discover that she shared his own fear of being held in dislike by most of their friends, openly sympathizing when she had confessed to him that, as none of her family had ever liked her very much, she failed to see why anyone else should, either. He thought she showed a modesty of which he could only approve, all the time liking her himself more and more every hour he spent in her company.

'How sorry we shall be to lose you to your own household!' he told her daily, meaning every word of it and heaving a sigh of sheer pleasure to have someone else to talk to other than his complaining wife.

Dutifully, he enquired as to the present whereabouts of Mr Maddock, but nobody seemed to know anything about the man who had once been one of the most prosperous traders of Singapore. 'He went to Malacca,' he was told again and again, but nobody seemed to know any more than that.

Mr Eliot waited until they were at the dinner table before he finally declared himself beaten. 'Few people have been travelling here from Malacca recently. It happens from time to time, Mrs Maddock. We must resign ourselves to a longer wait than we thought, that's all.'

'You mean nobody has any news of Malacca?' Trudie asked him.

'None.'

Trudie ate the food put before her without interest. The blandness of the flavours was a matter of indifference to her. Living in her father's household had taught her to eat almost anything and so it didn't occur to her to wonder why her hosts made no use of the many local exotic fruits and vegetables that were on offer in the market. Rather did they bemoan the lack of apples: how the cabbages never firmed up without a good frost to put heart into them; and how the meat was often in the process of going off before they could even get it home.

'Some people keep live chickens running about in their yards,' Mrs Eliot told Trudie. 'That I can't and won't do! I'd never know a moment's peace wondering if they weren't being exchanged for something I'd prefer not to know about!' She shuddered delicately. 'My dear, the Chinese will eat *anything*! Even ducks' feet!'

'I'm told they spit in the food too,' Trudie returned calmly. 'They probably don't enjoy cooking for barbarians who don't appreciate their own food.'

Mrs Eliot went white, her breath coming in gasps. 'Have you seen them spit?' she managed to enquire faintly.

'Only out in the street,' Trudie reassured her.

Mrs Eliot pushed her plate away. 'This abominable place! Surely it isn't too much to ask that we should be able to eat proper meals at our own table?' She burst into noisy sobs. 'How you must be missing England! When I think of the pleasant green fields, the fruit and vegetables, and, above all, the pleasure of having proper servants, I can't wait to see it all again!'

Trudie felt sorry for her. She, herself, was fascinated by the brighter, richer greens of Singapore. Never had she seen anything like the green of a banana leaf with the sun shining through it. The energy of both the people and the plants was a constant marvel to her. Even the elderly, old ladies dressed in black trousers and shirts, hauled heavy loads along the streets, refusing to lie down and prepare for death. Trudie had exchanged an occasional, shy smile with some of them, and she wondered why she heard on every side that the Chinese and the Malays all looked alike, for they didn't to her, any more than did the Europeans she met.

'I think' she said at last, returning to Mr Eliot's lack of news for her, 'I shall go and call on my cousin at Government House and find out what they know about Malacca and my husband there.' She put a hand on Mr Eliot's arm, smiling at him through her lashes. 'I'm sure nobody could have done more than you have for a virtual stranger, and I thank you for all your trouble! It's a debt I shall be hard put to it to repay. However, I can't believe that Government circles don't know what's going on in Malacca, even if the Church has temporarily lost touch! Will you come with me?' she applied to her hostess, secretly hoping to be refused, for not even the proverbial penny-pinching of the Church Missions could explain Mrs Eliot's choice of attire on Sundays, or when she went out visiting.

'Oh no, dear, I couldn't go to Government House! Your cousin will be there to chaperon you, won't she?'

'I hope so,' Trudie said comfortably. 'I should be obliged, however, if I might borrow your maid to escort me there?'

Mrs Eliot looked relieved. 'If you can explain what it is you want of her, you're more than welcome! The stupid girl can barely say good morning and she's been with me above two years.'

But then neither could Mrs Eliot say good morning in Malay, let alone Chinese, and she had been living in Singapore for all of five years.

Trudie set forth the following morning in a mood of optimism. Her enjoyment of being hauled through the streets in a rickshaw was lessened by the ill appearance of the young man between the shafts. He had no shoes, the soles of his feet as hard as treated leather from padding mile after mile at a steady run, uphill and downhill, wherever his customer bade him go. Trudie had thought to take the maid up with her but, unable to bring herself to add to his load, she opened negotiations on the price of two rickshaws, ignoring the girl's open delight. Having agreed a sum, she stepped into the better of the two vehicles and gave the word for them to start.

To counterbalance her weight, the man had to jump into the air, bringing the shafts down parallel with the ground only with the greatest of difficulty. The drag on his shoulders made his neck muscles stand forth like ropes then, a second later, he had the rickshaw under control, and was running at an even pace up the slight incline that led eventually to Government House.

Trudie had her cards ready as she mounted the brief flight of steps behind the guards and waited for the footman to enquire her business. In the hall beyond, she saw her cousin and stepped forward for her embrace.

'I wondered when you'd come to see us,' Hermione greeted her reproachfully. 'You've left it rather late to be civil, you know!'

'Have I?' Trudie was surprised by her cousin's indignation for she hadn't imagined she would be looking for her at all. 'Did you make enquiries for me?'

'Of course not! How could I know where you are staying, whereas *you* knew where I am!'

Trudie managed a tired smile. 'I didn't know where I was staying myself when Mr Maddock didn't turn up. Fortunately, I remembered an acquaintance of Father's is a missionary out here and I'm staying with him and his wife until I can find out where my husband has got to.'

'Is he missing?'

'Oh no! I expect *he* knows where he is, only he isn't in Singapore where I expected him to be, and there doesn't seem to be any news coming through from Malacca. Poor Mr Eliot has been making enquiries all week without result – '

Hermione frowned. 'Did Mr Maddock know you were coming?'

Trudie suppressed a sigh. 'You know as well as I that he arranged and paid for my passage here. I am sure he has merely been delayed either in Malacca, or on the road here. That's why I'm here.'

'But, Trudie dear, what makes you think I can help you? I have to do as my dear Christopher tells me, until I find my feet, you know, and I'm only just finding out how important he is out here. *Everybody* respects him, as I find they don't your husband. Really, I don't know what I'm doing speaking with you now, for I have to be most careful only to know the right people, even if you are my cousin!'

Trudie gave her an exasperated look. 'I thought you might present me to the Governor. I refuse to believe that there are no government channels between Singapore and Malacca. If anyone can get a message through to my husband, it has to be His Excellency, don't you agree?'

'I suppose so,' Hermione was far from being convinced it was a good idea to approach him, however. 'As long as you remember I am a guest here! I shouldn't want him to think I would allow any of my family to impose on him just because I'm staying at Government House!'

'I shan't mention our relationship at all, as you seem to prefer it that way,' Trudie retorted, annoyed despite her best intentions not to allow her cousin to irritate her until she had got what she wanted.

'Well, I should prefer it!' Hermione snapped. 'I haven't forgotten how difficult you were on board ship, putting me in the worst possible light to the captain whenever you could!'

Trudie's temper, ever held on a tight rein where her cousin was concerned, brought her up with a jerk. 'I don't remember mentioning you above half a dozen times!' she said with devastating clarity. 'You flatter yourself, Hermione, if you think yourself an interesting topic of conversation to any except the most partial of your relations – '

'You've always been jealous of me!' Hermione complained.

Trudie took refuge in a smouldering silence, remembering belatedly that she had come to ask a favour, not to quarrel with her cousin. What she would have liked to have done was to turn on her heel and walk out into the hot sunshine again until she could regain control over her heated emotions. Instead, she took a deep breath, and made herself remember why she was there.

'Yes,' she said at last, 'I've always been jealous of you.'

Hermione gave her a dazzling smile, her grievance against her cousin forgotten. 'I knew it! Only you never would admit it before!'

Trudie was saved from having to answer by the arrival of one of the Governor's aides, a young man in full military uniform who looked as if he were about to expire on the spot from heat. He took one look at Trudie and came straight over. 'I say ma'am, do you happen to be Mrs Maddock? I have been searching for you all over Singapore!'

Trudie extended her hand to him, only to be interrupted by an impatient Hermione. She frowned at the scarlet-faced young man. 'I was about to introduce my cousin to – '

'Their Excellencies have an engagement.'

Hermione gave a crestfallen *miaou* of disappointment which the aide ignored.

'His Excellency has only just heard you arrived on the

same ship as your cousins. He hopes you will accept his profound apologies that no one was sent to meet you. It was a doubly unfortunate occurrence as he had wished to tell you personally about the state of affairs in Malacca – as much as we know ourselves, that is.'

'Oh yes, do tell me at once!' Trudie begged him. 'I feel sure something must have happened there to prevent my husband coming to meet me in person as he promised!'

'A very good reason!' the young man said. 'There's been an outbreak of cholera round Malacca.' He paused thoughtfully. 'I trust you know what such an epidemic can mean?'

Trudie presented him with a white face. 'We have had cholera in England recently. It came on a ship from India, or so it is believed. Are there many dead?'

'Our information is a bit sparse at the moment, ma'am. His Excellency may be able to tell you more, if you care to wait – why don't you visit with your cousin for a while until he returns?'

Trudie made herself relax her fists, aware that her nails had been biting into the palms of her hands, so tightly had she been holding them. 'Thank you, but I must start for Malacca just as soon as I can make the necessary arrangements – '

'Ma'am, you can't do anything on your own!'

Trudie lifted her chin. 'Why not?' she asked coldly.

'Don't be silly, Trudie,' her cousin interposed, 'you can't go gadding about the country on your own!'

'Then what do you suggest I do?'

'Well, I would wait until the epidemic were over,' Hermione answered with undoubted truth. 'Sooner or later, someone will be going that way and you can travel with them. If you go now, you may catch it yourself and that wouldn't help anyone; in fact it would be a confounded nuisance, for someone would have to nurse you better, and then they would get it, and so on! You'd much better wait here, in Singapore, which everyone says is much more lively than Malacca nowadays. If your husband could wait two years for your company, surely he can wait a few weeks longer!'

'I don't know that his estate has the cholera at all!' Trudie pointed out. 'It may be some way outside Malacca, which is why he hasn't been able to get a message to me.'

'Very true, Mrs Maddock,' the aide chimed in. 'I think I should tell you, however, that you would have to go through Malacca to reach your husband's estate. There's no avoiding it! If I were you, I'd wait at least until after the Governor's Ball in honour of the Queen's Birthday. That will be a very grand affair, with parades all day, Beating the Retreat, bands playing, just about everything to please the ladies!'

Trudie wondered if Mr and Mrs Eliot would receive an invitation to such an event. From what she had seen of their establishment, she very much doubted that they were in the first front of society, even in such a small place as Singapore. Nothing could be more awkward! If she were to receive an invitation on her own account, she couldn't possibly accept it unless they were to be included, and the likelihood of that was practically nil. She had already discovered that there were several circles within the European community and that they met as seldom as possible, the men only a little more often than the women, and that only when they had business together.

There were a couple of chairs placed by the wall where people who had business with the Governor could wait until he was free to see them. Determined that her cousin shouldn't overhear what she had to say, Trudie took the aide's arm and led him over to the chairs, sitting down on the one furthest from Hermione. 'You have the advantage of me, Mr – ?'

With her head on one side, he thought she looked even younger than her actual age and he wondered what manner of circumstances had induced her to marry a man of whom he knew the Governor disapproved. Indeed, if all the stories of him were true, about his cost-cutting exercises and his womanizing amongst the Chinese ladies, he knew he wouldn't have allowed any sister of his anywhere near him. 'Mr Allison, ma'am.'

'Yes, well, Mr Allison, I am staying with the Reverend Mr Eliot and his wife – he studied with my father before he came on the Missions – and I don't wish to impose on them a single moment longer than necessary.'

The young man began to look flustered. 'I am sure invitations for them could be arranged,' he began.

'I'm sure they could be,' Trudie agreed doubtfully, 'but I wonder if either they, or I, would feel quite comfortable about that?'

Mr Allison swallowed, his Adam's apple pushing against the tightness of his military collar. 'Malacca really isn't safe.' He swallowed again. 'No Europeans are travelling there at the moment.'

'But it is possible to travel there?'

'His Excellency won't allow it, I assure you of that!'

Trudie smiled at him. He was such a very proper young man, no older than Septimus, and so very hot in his scarlet coat and his gold braid. 'Forgive my asking, but is yours a Welsh regiment?' she asked him.

He shook his head. 'No, ma'am! I am with the Queen's Own. Singapore is garrisoned by the Welsh Fusiliers at the moment, but I have been personally seconded to His Excellency's staff.' He lowered his voice, grimacing.

'Ah, that accounts for it,' Trudie said. 'I travelled out with two Welsh army wives. We became good friends on the journey out.'

Mr Allison looked askance, deciding it must be her father's influence that had led her to make such eccentric friends, let alone choose to stay with people like the Eliots when she might have been staying at Government House, as was her cousin. He wondered if she would take it amiss if he offered her a word of advice.

'If you must leave for Malacca straight away, perhaps your cousin could accompany you?' he began, knowing as well as Trudie did that nothing would induce Hermione to leave Government House a moment before she had to.

Trudie opened her eyes wide. 'Will you suggest it to her?'

'No, ma'am!'

'Nor I! Cousin Hermione – '

Hermione moved smoothly across the hall to join them. 'What about me, cousin?'

Trudie returned her false smile with one of her own. 'I was saying that the last thing you would wish would be to accompany me to Malacca right now,' she said.

'I should think not!' Hermione exclaimed. 'No one is going there. They have the cholera, you know. Indeed, now I come to think about it, I heard some people discussing your husband yesterday – or was it the day before! They said they had heard he had caught the cholera himself and was most unlikely to survive. I had meant to tell you before but it slipped my mind.'

'Slipped your mind! How could you, Hermione! You know I never would have applied for your help unless I'd been desperate for news of my husband!'

Hermione clamped her mouth shut, her blue eyes hard and cold. 'I see, first you admit you're jealous of me, and now you're implying it's me who lacks family feeling! Well, you're wrong! I may not approve of the man you married, but I hope I should always do my cousinly duty by you, or I should have sent you away long ago! As a matter of fact, even if I had remembered, I might not have told you until I'd talked it over with Mr Horton. If you have any sense at all, you'll go home now and wait until Mr Horton considers the matter and tells you what to do. You're very fortunate to have him to advise you, let me tell you, for no one will want to know you if you do anything as harebrained as leaving for Malacca on your own! I wish you'd remember that your actions are bound to reflect on me as your cousin, much as we both might wish it otherwise!'

Trudie's own temper snapped. 'I prefer to answer to my own husband for my actions!' she declared hotly.

'If he's still alive! You may find youself a widow by the time you get there!'

Trudie slumped in her chair as her cousin's words hit home. She was not one easily to admit defeat, however, and almost immediately she had risen to her feet, her head thrown back and a fixed smile on her lips. 'If he is ill, I must go to him immediately! Even His Excellency will admit that my place is by his side! Who else has a better right to nurse him well again?'

Mr Allison nervously cleared his throat. 'Your husband must have half a dozen people to nurse him, Mrs Maddock. I think you can only add to his worries if you were to travel to Malacca in the immediate future.'

'Yes, indeed,' Hermione chimed in with a self-righteous flounce, 'if all the rumours are to be believed, he will hardly feel your absence at all!'

But Trudie's mind was already made up. Long experience of dealing with her family had inured her to their more pointed remarks. She easily discounted the thought that Hermione knew any more about Jeremy Maddock's chosen lifestyle than she did herself. True, she had probably heard some rumour that he was ill but, if Mr Eliot had been unable to discover anything about him, it was unlikely that Hermione's sources had really known what they were talking about.

'I shall leave on the next ship going to Malacca,' Trudie determined. 'And you, Mr Allison, will use all your influence to get me the best cabin possible. Will you do that for me? I don't suppose His Excellency will mind if you mention his name once or twice just in case they are a little reluctant to take me.' She put a gentle hand on the sleeve of his coat. 'I hope you won't mind my making such shameless use of you, but you do so remind me of my favourite brother and I can't think you would countenance my buying my own ticket, as I should have to if you refuse me, you know?'

'Certainly not!' he agreed hoarsely, his head spinning. 'But, ma'am, have you thought – '

'There's only one thing to be thought about,' Trudie returned calmly. 'If my husband is ill and has need of me, I must go to him at once, don't you agree?'

Mr Allison looked hopefully for some support from Hermione, but she was examining one perfectly manicured nail with a thoughtful air. Finally, she said, 'Oh, let her go! If it doesn't matter to her that she may catch the cholera, I'm sure it doesn't matter to me, or to anyone else!'

Trudie, her good humour restored to see her cousin so put out, came out with one of her deep chuckles. 'You see what a lovely family we are, Mr Allison? Don't let it worry you, for I am quite set on going to Malacca whatever my cousin may say to keep me here!'

Mr Allison's lips twitched into a nervous smile. He was

a conventional young man and had found it shocking that Mrs Maddock had not been included in the Governor's invitation in the first place. He found it even more shocking that Mrs Horton should make her dislike for her unusual cousin so obvious and thought the less of her for it.

He stood to attention and muttered that he was proud to be of service and it said something for his confused state of mind that he didn't even consider what the Governor would have to say about his helping Mrs Maddock on her way to Malacca and an epidemic of cholera until a long time later.

Chapter Six

Mrs Eliot could not approve her young guest's plans. 'Really, my dear, I think even you must admit that this time you must bow to my husband's superior knowledge of the country and stay in Singapore until your husband is ready to make other arrangements for you.'

'Well, I won't!' Trudie tossed over her shoulder.

Mrs Eliot pounced on her. 'Won't go to Malacca, I hope!'

Trudie laughed. 'Won't stay in Singapore – not if I have to *walk* to Malacca.' She saw her hostess's crestfallen face and hastened to reassure her. '*Dear* Mrs Eliot! You've done everything to make me welcome ever since I pushed myself on to you, but, admit it, you would like to have your house free of house guests again, and I would like to be sure my husband has the best nursing possible – if he's still alive – and that means my getting to Malacca.'

'What difference can a short delay make now?' Mrs Eliot moaned. 'Make up your mind to it, Mrs Maddock, we can't allow you to travel all on your own, on a Chinese ship – ' She shuddered. '*Anything* might happen to you!'

Trudie set her mouth in a firm line, determined not to give way to the doubts her hostess's words had conjured up. Although the British were the most important people in Singapore, if only because they were the rulers, no one could ignore that it was largely a Chinese city. True, there were the Malays, the Parsee traders, and the Javanese who were reputed to make excellent servants, as well as the Indians who had come with their British overlords to work in the Straits Settlements, but the city remained predominantly Chinese in character and population.

It hadn't taken Trudie long to discover that almost everyone was afraid of the Chinese. Nobody said anything, of course, unless it were to bewail their habit of spitting and making disgusting noises in their throats, but there was a look on their faces when the Chinese were mentioned that was unmistakable. Most people professed to despise them. A lot of coolies, good for nothing else but to collect what was politely called the 'night-soil' and to work until they dropped, loading and unloading the increasing number of ships that plied their trade in the splendid harbour. What they refused to acknowledge was that the Chinese were equally contemptuous of the British. In their own opinion, the citizens of the Middle Kingdom, situated between the abode of the gods above, and the abode of the devils below, were the only civilized people on earth and all the rest were barbarians, foreign devils, to be done down with impunity whenever possible. In that Septimus had been perfectly right. What bothered Trudie far more was that neither side in this battle of the barbarians ever seemed to find it in the least bit funny, or anything other than a deliberate assault on their own dignity. She, on the contrary, was often amused by the ignorant barbs that passed back and forth, neither side taking the least trouble to find out anything about the other.

Most Europeans, Trudie knew, would think her mad to travel on a Chinese ship, unescorted by anyone of her own kind, but what choice did she have? It might not be desirable, but as it was the only possible way open to her she would have to take it.

In this plan, her best ally proved to be her cousin Hermione. Hermione was quite simply sick to death of all the enquiries she had received about Trudie. She recognized it to have been a mistake not to have insisted on having her included in the Governor's invitation to stay at Government House in the first place. Christopher had been annoyed by the comment it had caused that Trudie had had to apply to an old friend of her father's for shelter. This story had grown with the telling and, before any of them knew it, it was all over Singapore that the two cousins had quarrelled before they had even left England and that the Hortons had done precious little to put matters right. Hermione might have shrugged her shoulders at this tittle-tattle, but Christopher was appalled. It was swiftly borne in on him that most people were taking Trudie's part and that their own reputation in Singapore could be impaired unless he were to put an end to it. Consequently, he bought Trudie's ticket to Malacca with his own money and made quite sure that Hermione accompanied him to the dock to see her off.

Trudie, blissfully unaware of the gossip, was surprised by Mr Horton's generosity, but even that took second place to her interest in the ticket itself, covered in Chinese characters and without anything on it that she could discover to tell her the number of her cabin, or even that she was to be conveyed to Malacca.

'Surely, it would pay them to have English on one side?' she suggested, puzzling over the pretty characters and wishing she could read them.

'Whatever for?' Hermione's grimace spoke volumes for her distaste for the whole venture. 'I can't imagine any sensible person venturing on board such a dirty-looking vessel. You always were a glutton for punishment!'

Trudie sniffed thoughtfully. 'It smells clean enough.'

'Everybody knows the Chinese are a dirty people – '

Trudie frowned. 'Do they?'

Hermione was launched. 'My dear, don't you listen to anything that's said to you? Haven't you heard how they sleep out on the streets, without any proper facilities for washing and cooking?'

'I imagine we'd have to do likewise if we came here with only the clothes we stand up in.'

'They don't have to be poor! Some of them have been here as long as we have!'

'Oh well,' Trudie retorted carelessly, 'some of us are richer than others too.'

'You'll be telling me you like them next!' Hermione snapped.

Trudie blinked. 'I'm not sure if I do or not. To tell you the truth I'm quite nervous enough of what lies before me without being told any more horrors about the Chinese!'

'They eat pet animals,' Hermione put in with deliberate malice. 'Are you going to find some reason to excuse that too?'

'I'm going to put it right out of my mind – if I can!'

Hermione balked at actually going on board with her cousin. She perched herself on the seat of the rickshaw she had arrived in, fanning herself from time to time with an expensive Chinese silk fan. It was left to her husband to see her cousin to her cabin, his eyes darting from side to side as he tried to ignore the bland stares of the Chinese crew. Only with the captain could he bring himself to exchange a few words.

'The *mem*'s husband will meet her at Malacca,' he muttered.

'We hope. We hope.' The captain waggled his head from side to side.

Christopher Horton looked at him with acute dislike, 'You'd better look after her!' he growled. 'You'll never sail a ship in these waters again if you don't!'

'Missee safe with me!'

Trudie went on deck to wave goodbye to her cousins. Hermione was looking the other way, eager to be gone, but Christopher waved to her, smiling graciously about him just in case anyone who mattered was around to see. Left alone, Trudie pulled her shawl more closely about her shoulders, wondering what to do next. Common sense told her she would be a nervous wreck by the time she reached Malacca unless she was able to put her worst fears about the Chinese crew at rest. With determination she approached the captain.

'When do you expect us to be in Malacca?' she asked him.

He waggled his head in silence.

'You must have some idea!' Trudie insisted.

The almond-shaped eyes darted in her direction and away again. 'Maybe tomorrow, maybe next day, who can tell? Five rupees says we arrive tomorrow afternoon.'

Trudie managed to look equally nonchalant. 'Ten rupees says we arrive tomorrow morning!' she responded. They shook hands solemnly. The captain spat accurately into the water, nodding his head.

Trudie delayed going to her cabin for as long as she thought wise. She rather enjoyed standing on the tiny bridge, watching everything that was going on in the harbour around them. She had thought most of the ships would be European, such as the one which had brought her from England, but that was far from being the case. Malay prahus, sharp at both ends and with eyes painted on their prows so that they could see where they were going, were everywhere, mixed up with Cantonese and Cochin China boats, swaying under their heavy mat sails, and rowing-boats darting to and fro, rowed by the handsome Klings, as the Indian immigrants were known.

Only when she realized that they were about to set sail did she reluctantly leave the bridge. Her cabin was even smaller than she had first thought it. Standing in the middle, she could easily touch all four walls, and the narrow bunk was far shorter than she was herself and probably every bit as uncomfortable as it looked.

It was a relief to her to be called up on deck to eat her dinner. It had been spread out on to the roof of the cabin, a mass of tiny dishes filled with strange-smelling mixtures that made her mouth water. Nothing would have induced her to ruin her appetite by asking what they consisted of, it was enough to know that it tasted good and, following the captain's example, she piled her plateful of rice with bits of this and that and proceeded to eat it with the help of a spoon.

Somehow or other, quite how she could never afterwards remember, the captain had ascertained the year of her birth and introduced her to the twelve animals that make up the Chinese astrological years.

'*Ming Shu* very important to Chinese peoples!' he assured her. He went on to tell her she had been born in the Year of the Rat and, seeing her shudder, laughed and said it could just as well be called the year of the mouse, or the hamster, or mole. 'Rat people are very charming, very sociable, very quick-witted!' he told her.

'Oh?'

He grinned, showing blackened teeth. 'You manipulate people and love to gossip,' he added. 'Rats make the very best planners. But always remember you need a good partner to help you make real money. In which year was your husband born?'

Trudie confessed that she didn't know. 'You find out,' he told her. 'Yes, you find out and consult with a good Chinese person who understands *Ming Shu*, yes?'

'I may do,' she said. 'We have a quite different astrological chart in Europe.'

To please her, he invited her to tell him about it, but Trudie knew very little about the stars and their signs. 'My father doesn't approve of such things,' she tried to explain. 'He's a clergyman.'

'Ah so!' He frowned. 'The skirted ones have no children. Your father is one of those?'

She was as confused as he was. 'The skirted ones?'

'Jes-u-its.'

'They're Roman Catholics. My father is Church of England.'

'Not Catholic?'

'No.'

The captain shrugged, showing his blackened teeth again. 'All foreign devils much the same.' He swore fluently under his breath in a language Trudie fortunately didn't understand. He obviously felt better when he had done and managed another toothy smile.

'Aren't you a Christian?'

'Me?' He was so startled she almost laughed. 'I am a civilized person!' he claimed. He waggled his head angrily. 'What makes you think I am foreign Christian devil?'

Trudie wiped her face clear of any expression. 'Me, I'm a civilized person, also,' she said.

Outraged, he glared at her for a long moment, and then he began to laugh. He put his finger and thumb practically together. 'You very small foreign devil,' he conceded. 'Hardly uncivilized at all – just this much!'

They laughed together. The curry was hotter than Trudie had expected; not that she minded, it was the best meal she had had since she had last eaten in her sister Letty's house. 'Civilized enough to enjoy your food,' she said with satisfaction.

'Good Nonya food,' he agreed. She didn't know what he meant, but neither did she want to betray her ignorance to him by questioning him further.

It was late when she retired. She wasn't looking forward to a night spent in that tiny cabin. It was worse than she had thought in the airless atmosphere, with the thermometer mounting minute by minute until she was sure that it had reached the hundred mark, but it was the cockroaches that wholly disgusted her, even while she was uncertain as to what they were at first. There was nothing, she told herself, intrinsically horrible about a cockroach rather than any other insect, but she couldn't make herself believe it. The idea that these creatures should crawl over her bed made her feel sick to her stomach. With the light on, they disappeared, but every time she settled down to sleep they came out into the open again until she could imagine them wherever she looked and was becoming quite hysterical.

Never had she been more glad to greet the dawn. With shaking fingers, she dressed herself and went out on deck, taking great gasps of air into her lungs, uncaring at the already damp, overheated atmosphere. She fanned herself in a desultory way, watching a Chinese coolie wash down the decks with sea water dragged up over the side in a canvas bucket.

Breakfast consisted of coffee, locally grown, she was assured, and a choice of breads all of which she pronounced excellent. There was a kind of porridge also, which she declined to sample, but which the captain ate with gusto. How odd it was, she considered, that these working men seemed to eat vastly better than the greater part of her own acquaintance, however much money was spent on the household bills. She tried to imagine her own parents eating fresh bread and drinking coffee first thing in the morning on a deck such as this one and was obliged to admit they would sooner starve than do such a thing. What a lot they had missed in life!

A school of fish danced just below the surface of the water. For an instant she longed to join them and feel the cool water against her flesh, but the impossibility of such a thing was forcibly brought to her mind by the reappearance of the captain at her side.

'Malacca this morning,' he grunted, pushing ten rupees into her hand. 'You have good joss! You make another bet?'

Now Trudie had been brought up to believe that all gambling was sinful, the means by which the Devil tempted his victims away from the straight and narrow path that leads to salvation. Her eyes glinted with excitement.

'What kind of a bet?' she asked.

His gaze narrowed, refusing to meet hers. 'You make bet!' he said.

Feeling delightfully wicked, she considered the matter. She looked wildly about her, ignoring the packed Chinese passengers on the foredeck, making their way to the tin mines of the north, ignoring everything except the odd little Chinese man beside her. On the horizon she sighted land and decided on her bet.

'Ten rupees says that's Malacca!'

He looked over his shoulder, spitting into the water. 'You think that's Malacca?'

'Isn't it?' He handed over the ten rupees. 'I thought so!' she exclaimed in triumph.

She looked towards the land again, her whole attention on the edging of coco palms, the rolling forests behind, the hills behind leading upwards to Mount Ophir, the mountain of gold. Was it the same Mount Ophir that is mentioned in the Bible? Trudie didn't know. She could have made her bet on that, but how would she have found out the answer? Certainly the Chinese captain could not have told her.

'Malacca,' she whispered. 'Is it as beautiful as it looks?'

He shrugged his shoulders. 'Blitish city. Before that Dutch; before that Portuguese; before that Malay.' His teeth showed briefly. 'Many Babas and Nonyas there now.'

'Oh! Who – who are they?'

'Straits Chinese you call them. Chinese people who live here long time, speak Malay – '

'Are they civilized or barbarians?' Trudie enquired, wrinkling up her nose.

He took the question seriously. 'Civilized people. Chinese people.'

He stomped away from her, muttering under his breath. A little while later, Trudie could make out the red-tiled roofs of the houses, many of them built on piles, and the ruined cathedral that surmounted the central hill and which is probably the oldest Christian building in the Far East. A long, deserted jetty ran far out into the shallow sea. Chinese junks lay at anchor and Malay fishing-boats slumbered in the hot sun. Nothing moved as they sailed in closer and then, suddenly, a number of small Malay boats surrounded them, their heavy sails of matting as silent as the men who sailed them.

Trudie found a man who spoke a little English and sent her card ashore in his care, hoping for a better reception than she had had in Singapore. She had no need to worry; long before she had packed her few things, she was told the Lieutenant-Governor had himself come out to meet her and she went in search of the captain to wish him goodbye and thank him for his care of her.

It was easier than she had expected to climb down into the European boat, manned by six smartly uniformed Malays who proceeded to row her ashore.

'Was it a horrendous journey?'

Trudie started at the question. She thought it might be better not to admit how much she had enjoyed everything except the cockroaches; she didn't feel that many people would understand her interest in the native peoples she had met. Most of the Europeans she had met in Singapore hugged their culture around them as if they were afraid of being contaminated by some dread disease of which every native was a suspected carrier.

'I wanted to be with my husband,' she answered.

'Oh, quite!'

Mr Beresford, the Lieutenant-Governor, tugged uncomfortably at his side whiskers. His uniform, which had been freshly laundered when he had donned it that morning, was already damp with sweat and sagging round his ankles. He wished himself anywhere but in this boat with this determined young woman.

Trudie, quite unaware of her lack of welcome, leaned forward eagerly to get her first good look at Malacca. 'It's such a beautiful name!' she enthused. 'I wonder how it came by it?'

'Some prince named it when he was resting under a malacca tree. A long time ago of course, before we Europeans arrived here.'

Trudie was delighted with the answer. 'Of course! Malacca canes! It has a timber that varies from black to pale, isn't that right?'

'I believe so. I'm surprised you should have heard of it though.'

'Mr Maddock and my youngest brother set up an Emporium in London,' Trudie explained. 'We import many things from out here – my husband sees to that!'

'Ah yes, Jeremy Maddock. Interesting fellow, I believe. Haven't seen much of him, to tell the truth.'

Trudie was unconcerned. 'I suppose he's been out on his plantation?'

'Er – some of the time.'

Trudie favoured him with a closer look. He looked hot and embarrassed and longing to be rid of her. 'Is the cholera over?' she asked abruptly.

'Except for a few small pockets of resistance which only time will sort out, I think we've seen the back of it for the moment. It's endemic here, which means it can reappear any time and probably will. You catch us at a bad time, Mrs Maddock, as we're still recovering from all the extra work the last lot involved us in. My wife, particularly, is very tired. She takes our responsibilities very seriously and doesn't rest enough.'

Trudie didn't need telling twice. 'I'll try not to add to her burdens for long,' she promised. 'As soon as my husband knows I am here, I'm sure he'll send for me.'

For some reason, Mr Beresford seemed far less convinced of that than she was. 'Are you sure he is expecting you, Mrs Maddock?'

'Well, yes, of course! He left me behind in England to help my brother get started, you know. I think Septimus must have told him he was heartily sick of my interference, because I'm much better at buying and selling than Septimus ever will be, though of course nothing would induce him to admit it, and so Jeremy decided it was time I joined him out here and booked my passage for me. So he has to know I'm coming, don't you think?'

Mr Beresford blew out his cheeks thoughtfully. 'Nothing was said to any of us, Mrs Maddock. I don't suppose you know why not, though, do you?'

'Perhaps my husband couldn't see the necessity to tell anyone,' Trudie suggested, unperturbed.

'Perhaps. There are people he would have done better to

tell, if you don't mind my saying so! I'm told your father is a clergyman. What has he to say to your coming out here to live?'

'He thinks I should be at my husband's side, what else?' she returned gravely. She could have added that he had been even more glad to be rid of her than Septimus had been, though for different reasons, but she didn't. She was more concerned at the moment at what he was implying about Jeremy Maddock, something which she couldn't understand but felt might be important to her. 'What do you know about my husband, Mr Beresford?'

The Lieutenant-Governor turned a beetroot red. 'My dear Mrs Maddock, I was not implying – ' He broke off as they reached the shore. 'Allow me to help you!' He was younger than he looked, she noted, as he sprang ashore, holding out a hand for her to follow him more soberly on to the muddy bank of the river.

Something stirred in the water beside her and she was alarmed to see some animal move in the water. 'What's that?' she cried out. 'It looks like a dragon, or a giant lizard!'

'It's harmless enough,' Mr Beresford sought to reassure her. 'There are lots of them around here. You'll soon be as used to them as we are!'

Trudie didn't believe it, but she saw no reason to say so. She was glad to see the creature swimming away in the brown waters, making for a rock that protruded above the surface further up the river. 'Are they sea creatures?' she asked.

'No. Like any other lizard they get their heat from the sun, I'm told,' Mr Beresford answered. 'Snakes do the same. Beware of snakes, Mrs Maddock! They are for ever sunning themselves in strange places and *they* are not always as harmless as the lizards.'

Having got that sorted out, he drew her swiftly up on to firmer ground where his wife waited to greet their unwelcome guest. Mrs Beresford was a kind woman, however, and she would have died sooner than have the young woman before her guess how little she wanted to get herself involved in anything to do with the Maddocks, husband or wife.

'You poor dear,' she said in a soft, faded voice, which somehow made Trudie think of the scent of lavender and the way her mother was always clutching a damp handkerchief in one hand. Yet Mrs Beresford was nothing like her mother in actual fact. To begin with she was a much younger woman, though her looks were already faded by the tropics and the endless battle to keep up a respectable front in a climate that fought one at every turn. 'I wish we'd been told you had arrived in Singapore and we might have delayed your journey here until you could have made it in greater comfort. How brave you must be to have come on that Chinese vessel! What an adventure!'

'I rather enjoyed it,' Trudie confessed.

Her hostess shuddered. 'That shows you haven't been out here very long, if you don't mind my saying so. It does my eyes good to see anyone looking as young and fresh as you do, but I must warn you that it doesn't last. The mould, and the insects, and the endless heat!'

'Never mind that now, dear,' her husband sighed. 'Mrs Maddock must be longing to get out of the sun. Come along, ladies, the Stadthaus awaits you!'

As soon as he had successfully transported Trudie, Trudie's baggage, and his wife, from the riverside to the square in the centre of the city, which, he explained, had been painted a dark red by the Dutch in imitation of the reddish buildings of Rotterdam – though they may originally have been white – Mr Beresford excused himself, saying he had business to attend to. He shouted inside for a servant to come and fetch the luggage, and then he was gone, disappearing down a flight of steps to the square below which they had just come through.

'I hope you won't mind being in such an un-English place as Malacca!' Mrs Beresford fussed. 'I never have got used to it myself! Nothing ever happens here, it is perpetual afternoon, with everyone drowsing in their own rooms. What do the Spanish call it? The time of *siesta*, isn't that right? I dare say the Portuguese use the same word – '

'But this building was built by the Dutch, wasn't it?' Trudie interrupted, puzzled.

'Oh yes. The church was built then too, in 1753. You'll see it on Sunday. I always used to think the Dutch to be very much like ourselves, before coming here, I mean, but now I'm not so sure. They are Protestants, of course – '

'It's a beautiful house!' Trudie exclaimed.

'Yes, it is,' her hostess acknowledged. 'It's quite beautiful and very old, the oldest Dutch building in South-East Asia because it must be all of two hundred years old, but it isn't at all practical to live in.'

Trudie thought that may have been because it had been designed as the Town Hall and not as a residence, but she said nothing, not until her hostess had taken her in person to her room and they had duly admired it together.

'Those must be the original Dutch red tiles on the floor,' Trudie remarked. 'It's marvellous to think of them being brought all this way, isn't it? One would think there would be so many other things – '

'Wait until you see the Portuguese tiles, my dear. Even the humblest houses around there have steps leading up to the main door and the best of them are always covered with Portuguese tiles. Have you ever visited Lisbon, or Oporto?'

Trudie had to confess that she had not. 'Then you won't have seen the houses there, completely covered in tiles, some of them making up the most splendid pictures. They say it's because the Portuguese cities are so damp, which they are, but never inside their houses, so far as I know. However it is, the results are original and charming. The Portuguese, even more than the Dutch, take their comforts with them wherever they go. By comparison, we are positively modest, though I have seen some very fine houses in India.' She sighed heavily. 'We are always back and forth to India as we are ruled from there. If we could move there altogether, I'm sure my husband would soon be promoted to something better than this backwater.'

'A very pretty backwater,' Trudie put in.

'Yes, it is,' Mrs Beresford agreed. 'We're happy enough here most of the time, I must admit, but this last bout of cholera makes me wonder if I shouldn't send my three girls home to their grandparents. This is a terrible climate for children!'

So far, Trudie had never felt better, despite the heat, made more oppressive by the humidity, and the dust that whirled about the streets and the square below no matter how often they were neatly swept during the day. She spent a lot of time looking out of her window at the feathery green of the malacca trees, the flowering trees in the garden and, in the distance, the masts of the Indonesian boats, carrying thousands of staves for who knew what purpose, which rode at anchor in the wide mouth of the river.

She became used to the blue painted walls and the German shutters that replaced the more usual glass of windows at home. Even the extrordinarily high bed seemed a mere commonplace after she had spent three nights perched up on its giddy heights, trying not to mind that the servants, all of them men, seemed to appear and disappear at will without ever knocking on her door.

Her days were spent in the company of Mrs Beresford and her three small daughters. The little girls had that grey look of children who are brought up in the tropics, but otherwise seemed unharmed by their unusual life. They spent much of their time at their mother's knee, learning from her the first rudiments of needlework, an art in which Mrs Beresford excelled, having been educated at a convent school in France in the days of her own youth. 'Not that I'm a Catholic, or anything like that,' she explained hastily. 'My parents thought it most important we should all speak French well, though I can't say it's much use to me out here!'

After three days, Trudie thought she had presumed on the Beresfords' good nature for long enough. She sought out her host, finding him standing in his office in full uniform about to go out on some official engagement. 'Have you had any news of my husband yet?' she asked him.

He hummed and hawed until her patience was exhausted. 'Is he dead? Is that what you're trying to tell me?'

'I don't know for sure, Mrs Maddock.'

'Well, I can't stay here for ever, can I?' she retorted. 'If he doesn't come for me tomorrow, I'll make my own way to him!'

'You're welcome to stay on here, Mrs Maddock, as I'm sure Mrs Beresford will have told you. What's the hurry?'

'The hurry is that my husband may be dying and nobody seems to want to help me to get to him. What are you all trying to hide?'

Mr Beresford wiped his face with a large white handkerchief. 'It takes time to arrange these things – '

Trudie gave him look for look. 'I expect I can find someone to take me out to the plantation in a few hours – '

'I trust you won't make the attempt! If you insist, I'll send for your husband's manager and he'll escort you out there tomorrow. How's that?'

'Thank you,' Trudie responded stiffly.

Mr Beresford tugged at his whiskers. 'I hope you'll still be thanking me when you find yourself miles from anywhere, without a soul to turn to if you should run into any trouble.'

Trudie managed a jaunty smile. 'That's my business! Besides, I can hardly believe my husband lives all alone on his plantation, Mr Beresford. There must be plenty of people about, growing the coffee, and so on!'

'I believe your husband employs Tamils on the lines.'

'Oh,' said Trudie, feeling suddenly very ignorant and nervous of the future. Almost, she wanted to change her mind and stay on in Malacca in the safety of the Beresford household. She stiffened her back, forcing herself to dwell on her husband's need and less on her own comfort. 'Is it very far away?' she asked.

'The better part of a day's journey.'

Trudie blinked. 'I must go. Jeremy expects me!'

Mr Beresford looked rather less certain of that. 'Quite so. However, if you find things are not quite as you like, Mrs Beresford will be glad to receive you back here in Malacca. It's a lonely life for any woman to be posted out here and she's been glad to have your company. The girls, too!'

Trudie thanked him gravely, telling herself how glad she was to have something finally settled. But she was not glad. She had never felt more alone in her whole life. She couldn't even be sure that Jeremy Maddock would be particularly glad to see her. It had taken him a mighty long time to send for her and he hadn't sounded particularly enthusiastic about her joining him when he had sent the money for her passage out. Her eyes filled with tears. Nobody really wanted her. For a while she had thought Mr Maddock had – why else had he married her? – but he couldn't have wanted her very much after all, so perhaps it had been no more than a passing whim to marry and settle down. She had an idea that things might have looked different to him as soon as he got back to Malacca and his old life. But she was here now and they would both have to make the best of things because she wasn't going to go away again.

She lifted her chin, frowning slightly. 'I don't see why one should be more lonely here than anywhere else. I mean to enjoy my life out here very much!'

Mr Beresford smiled at her. 'I hope you do,' he said.

The following day Trudie was in her room when Mr Maddock's manager arrived. Through her window she saw him ride up and thought how familiar he looked. She hurried downstairs, anxious not to lose another minute, and found him, hat in hand, standing in the hallway, staring out of the still-open door. 'Are you looking for me?' she asked him.

He turned and looked her over, bringing the colour flying up into her cheeks. She knew now where she had seen him before! It had been with the two Welsh army brides she had travelled out with, a great black Welshman who spoke their barbarous tongue as easily as he did the English language. She had wondered about him then and she wondered about him again now.

'Mrs Maddock? Mrs Jeremy Maddock?'

She nodded, holding out her hand to him. 'Are you my

husband's manager? What were you doing in Singapore meeting my Welsh friends? I thought they're army brides?'

He tipped his hat to her. 'We were brought up in the same small area of Wales,' he answered reluctantly, plainly not wishing to discuss his private affairs with her. 'Caradoc Rhys is my name.'

She took her cue from him, changing the subject. 'Perhaps you can tell me how my husband is?'

'He died two days ago.' His eyes didn't quite meet hers. 'I'm sorry, ma'am.'

Trudie sat down on the nearest chair. The roaring in her ears slowly subsided and she realized with relief that she wasn't going to faint after all. She shut her eyes instead, recalling the image of Mr Maddock and all he had meant to her. Two tears trickled down her cheeks betraying a weakness she could only despise. She might be a widow instead of a wife, but nothing else had changed. There was no going back now, if only because there was nothing to go back to. She couldn't imagine Septimus being pleased to see her. She sniffed pathetically. What would Mr Maddock have wanted her to do next?

'Dead?' she said aloud. 'I suppose it was the cholera?'

He didn't bother to answer directly. 'I came to tell you to go back to Singapore. I don't know how you got to Malacca – '

His awkwardness made her sniff again. She had never met anyone less sympathetic than this Welshman. Well, she would show him that, although her husband might be dead, he still had a Maddock to deal with!

'I came on a Chinese ship.'

'Alone?'

'Do you see anyone else here?'

'No, ma'am. Isn't there some woman who could keep

you company for a while – until you feel better and can make arrangements for your return to your own relatives?'

'The Beresfords are gone out – '

He shrugged massive shoulders. 'You should have gone with them, Mrs Maddock. The Lieutenant-Governor is a good man. He'll see you get back to Singapore and find a ship home to England. You'll be all right once you're back with your family and friends.'

Trudie stood up again. 'No,' she said, quietly and distinctly. 'I was brought up to believe that one's duty comes before everything. Mr Maddock would have expected nothing less from me.'

'Then what are you going to do?'

'I'm going to live on my husband's plantation.'

There was a long, long silence. 'I wouldn't be in too much of a hurry to do that, Mrs Maddock. It would be different if Mr Maddock were still alive and able to protect you from those aspects of our life there that must be displeasing to a lady such as yourself. As it is, I must advise you to stay away – '

'No,' Trudie said again.

His eyes met hers. His were dark brown with laughter lines in the corners. Looking at him, she became aware that he was wearing only a shirt and that was open practically to the waist. Swiftly, she averted her gaze, half turning away. He wasn't at all like the men she normally mixed with, not that she minded that exactly, but she thought it would be as well to remember that she knew nothing at all about him, not even whether she liked him or not.

'Then on your own head be it,' he said quietly.

'Of course. How soon can we leave, Mr Rhys?'

'Just as soon as we can get your luggage stowed away on the cart. Do you ride, Mrs Maddock, or shall I leave a place for you with the luggage?'

She wished she could have told him she would ride. What she would have liked better than anything would have been to have raced him over a mile or so, leaving him far behind as he deserved. She looked down her nose, regretting that she might never have that satisfaction.

'I'm an indifferent horsewoman,' she confessed. 'I prefer to travel in as much comfort as you can contrive for me on the cart, if that is the only conveyance available? I can't believe my husband ever rode such distances on the back of a horse.'

'No, he didn't.' The man sounded bitter. 'If I'd known you were going to insist on coming back with me, I'd have brought his dogcart with me. As it is, I have nothing suitable for a lady like yourself. I'm taking a whole lot of supplies back with me.'

She inclined her head. If he thought her a lady it had to give her some kind of advantage in their dealings. 'That was going to be my next question,' she said. 'I was wondering what I should need to take with me from Malacca, but if you've already arranged all that, all the better.'

'There are few luxuries – '

Trudie gurgled with sudden laughter. 'Believe me, Mr Rhys, if I could survive life in my father's household, I can live anywhere! At least one isn't cold out here, nor very often hungry, I should imagine?'

'No,' he agreed slowly, 'we suffer from heat here more than cold. You can die of the heat if you're not used to it,' he added.

'I don't mean to die at all quite yet,' she assured him. 'I haven't come this far for nothing!'

Her heart sank when she saw the cart, however. It was a wonder the wheels hadn't fallen off long ago and the boards were riddled with the depredations of insects and the damp atmosphere. Not for worlds was she going to let him see her despair, though. She put off the evil moment for as long as she dared, pretending to be waiting to bid a fond farewell to Mrs Beresford, who was not expected back until nightfall and whom she had already thanked again and again for all her kindness to her.

She put up her parasol and twirled it around a couple of times, dismayed by the small amount of shade it offered. She felt quick sick with shock and heat already.

'Right, up you go!'

She started at the Welsh voice close behind her, only to have the breath knocked right out of her as he lifted her feet clear of the ground and deposited her, not ungently, on the bare boards of the cart.

'Want to drive?' he asked her.

Still breathless, she shook her head, still saying nothing when a young Malay boy sprang up beside her, clicking his tongue to get the beasts moving slowly down the hill.

She had not known that a man could be so strong. Covertly, she watched Mr Rhys walk away from the cart and mount his own ugly-looking animal. They looked two of a kind, she thought, ill bred and good only for their brute strength. He had the loose-limbed movements of a man who had walked long distances all his life. Nor had he done up his shirt, which was flapping about his broad chest, and it was impossible to ignore the deep tan of his unexpectedly hairy skin. It came as a shock to realize that she didn't like the Welshman very much and didn't want to have to depend on him for anything to do with her future. It would all have been so much easier if Jeremy had still been alive to receive her.

The narrow streets of Malacca were fascinating to her. Mrs Beresford had refused to allow her to venture into them by herself, and had refused just as adamantly to accompany her. Indeed, there were very few Europeans to be seen and Trudie could only suppose they were all, like her hostess, confined by custom to the inside of their houses. Even the men never walked anywhere, travelling between their homes and their place of business in closed carriages, leaving the streets free for the dark brown, gentle Malays and the scurrying Chinese, their pigtails hanging down their backs and their thin, white legs looking thinner than ever in their black pyjama trousers.

She peered into the shops, full of strange foods and even stranger objects; she stared with disbelief at the outside of a Chinese temple, decorated with dragons and magnificent carved stone lions; and she marvelled at the children of all hues who tumbled in and out of the traffic. She envied the children their freedom; at their age her life had consisted of endless visits to her father's freezing church, constant hunger pangs from the many fasts her father had imposed on the whole family, and the loneliness that came from being so much younger than either of her sisters and discouraged from having any friends of her own age.

At last, they left the town behind and were almost immediately engulfed in the jungle, a mass of tangled bushes and trees where everything looked exactly the same no matter where she looked. 'How do you know which path to take?' she asked Mr Rhys.

'We all have our own landmarks after a while. Me, I follow that creek over there to the next village.'

The creek was what she would have called a stream. She didn't know how long they had been going along beside it, but now it had been pointed out to her, she watched the dirty brown waters slowly widen until it was a shallow river. Shortly afterwards, they came to the outskirts of a village, and the mouth of the river filled up with fishing-boats, as brown in colour as the water they floated in.

Mr Rhys urged his animal closer to the cart. 'I have friends here. I'll get the woman of the house to bring you out some tea.'

'I'd rather have a cold drink,' she told him.

'Tea is safer.'

The men sat under a tree, talking together in some strange language. Trudie's tea was brought to her in a gaudily painted glass by one of the women of the village. She and the cart had been left in a circle of would-be shade, but the heat was stifling. The tea tasted good to her, being flavoured with lemon instead of milk, a change she approved of as the sharpness was refreshing and more thirst-quenching than she would have imagined. None of the other women stopped to speak to her and the men ignored her, so she spent the interval drowsing and wishing the journey over.

Then, across the village, came the sound of a man's voice, rising and falling as he chanted some command. Within seconds, the men had risen to their feet and, all facing the same way, bowed low, holding their hands up to their heads, shortly afterwards prostrating themselves on the ground and rising again. Trudie was entranced. Septimus had told her the Mohammedans prayed five times each day, but she had never expected it to be such a public event as this. Her eyes darted over to where Mr Rhys was standing a little away from the others, his hands by his side, his whole being motionless in respect for the villagers' devotions.

'We'll be on our way now,' he muttered as soon as the prayers were over. 'Ready?'

Trudie automatically rated most of the men she met in terms of her various brothers, but Mr Rhys wasn't in the least bit like any of them. She didn't like him, but he interested her.

'Taffy was a Welshman, Taffy was a thief;
Taffy came to my house and stole a leg of beef:
I went to Taffy's house, Taffy was not at home:
Taffy came to my house and stole a marrow-bone.'

She smiled to herself. She didn't know if he was a thief, though it wouldn't surprise her to find he ran her husband's plantation largely for his own benefit, but he certainly wasn't a gentleman. No, by no stretch of the imagination could he be called a gentleman!

Chapter Seven

The jungle closed in round them once again. It should have been cooler in the dark cave under the trees, but it wasn't. It was like being baked alive in a black oven. It should have been silent, but it wasn't. From time to time a bird sang, the insects kept up a constant background of noise, or there was a movement in the undergrowth that reminded Trudie that this was the land of snakes and other nasties which, no matter how hard she tried to discipline her imagination, were constantly at the back of her mind. She made a conscious effort to remember Mr Maddock as she had known him and gave silent thanks for all that he had taught her, and given her, even while it was getting increasingly hard to remember exactly how he had looked. He had been kind, and that was a virtue she would always appreciate in any man. She looked about her, telling herself she would soon get used to her new surroundings and not believing a word of it. She certainly couldn't imagine the Mr Jeremy Maddock she had known living in a place like this!

'You should have gone back to Singapore!'

The sound of Mr Rhys's voice made her straighten her back. 'What's so wonderful about Singapore?' she retorted. 'The Eliots, with whom I was staying, were for ever telling me tales of the Bugi pirates lying in wait in Johore to slit one's throat, and of the tigers who eat a native every day, and the prickly heat that can turn a sane man into a raging lunatic in no time, let alone the mildew that destroys all one's clothes – ' She broke off, her eyes wide. 'I'm not going back to Singapore and that's that, Mr Rhys!'

'What makes you think things will be any better at your husband's place?'

'He wanted me to be close to Malacca. Malacca is the key to the China trade and the Emporium we started in London is making a lot of money out of Chinese and Japanese *objets d'art*. I hope to buy a lot of stock out here – much cheaper than we ever could in Europe. My husband's death makes no difference to that!'

'Perhaps you should have stayed in Malacca!'

'How?'

Mr Rhys pushed his horse on ahead, then fell back again beside the cart. 'You do realize you'll be the only European woman on the plantation, don't you? You'll be *on your own*. You come from a large family. Have you ever been completely alone before?'

'Often.'

He was startled by her vehemence. 'Often?'

Trudie put her hands in her lap. She had given up trying to hold the parasol over her head and was relying on a broad-brimmed straw hat instead. What she couldn't know was that it gave her a rather mysterious air, the brim drooping over one eye and hiding her thoughts from the man on horseback.

'I may be the youngest of ten children, Mr Rhys, but my sisters were both married and having children of their own before I was out of the nursery and my brothers were interested in their own affairs. Also, my father holds very strong ideas on original sin, of which, apparently, I have more than anyone else in my family. I have spent many, many weeks completely alone in my room, with only bread and water to sustain me. I can assure you I have no fears of my own society. I rather like myself as a matter of fact.'

He shrugged his shoulders. 'You'll find out!' he muttered.

She spent a lot of time looking at his back after that. It was ridiculous to mind, but she would have preferred him to have had some sympathy for her. What was it about her that made people wish her somewhere else? It was hurtful, even when the person concerned was a Welsh peasant, no better than he should be. Did he think she would welcome his company with open arms? Well, she wouldn't. It was his job to run the plantation, hers was to make Septimus's fortune one way or another, and that was sufficiently important to her to make anything she had to suffer in the cause worth while.

Caradoc Rhys rode his horse as he did everything else. She had a wild memory of him greeting the two Welsh girls who had travelled out with her, sweeping them off their feet with the same easy movements with which he rode, or walked, or even stood, his legs a little apart, looking about him with lazy eyes. What had he done in Wales? One day, perhaps she would ask him, but not today. Today, it was important to her to be on her dignity and bring it home to him that, with Jeremy's death, *she* was now his employer and he would do well to remember it.

They passed a waterfall, but he refused to allow them to stop. Trudie would have liked to have bathed her face in the cool water and spend a little while there, but she was too proud to argue with him about it and she rightly suspected that if she had ordered him to rest there for a while he wouldn't have listened to her.

It was five o'clock when Mr Rhys next spoke to her. 'We're on the plantation now,' he said. He pointed at some scrawny bushes with his whip. 'Those are some of your coffee bushes, Mrs Maddock.'

'They look sick,' she observed.

'They are sick. It's too hot for them at this altitude. They look better than the tea though. Tea needs mountain slopes and cool evenings. I told your husband as much every day I worked for him, but he was determined to have his own way. What are you going to grow here?'

Trudie swallowed. 'What do you suggest?'

'I suggest you cut your losses and go home!'

'Leaving the property to you, I suppose?' she retorted sweetly.

'You could do worse,' he grunted. 'When I find something that will grow here, or some tin to mine, I'd pay you royalties on anything I made out of it. How about it?'

Trudie was beginning to think he had a point. She was hot and tired and wishing herself anywhere else but there.

'We could cut down some of those trees and sell the timber,' she suggested. 'Is any of it mahogany? Everybody in England is buying mahogany furniture nowadays.'

'It's an idea,' he admitted. 'Have you heard of rubber, Mrs Maddock?'

'What's it used for?'

'It comes from South America. It has a sticky resin that some people think will make all our fortunes. I have my doubts. I like to see a need for something before I put any sweat and tears into it.'

'It sounds useless to me!' Trudie decided.

'Maybe.'

'There has to be something else!' she exclaimed.

He grinned suddenly. 'There will be! As long as you back me up when I find it!'

There was no harm in promising that, she thought. She might not like the Welshman much, but he seemed to know his job. If there was money to be made, it would be good to get in first! She rather liked the idea of making her fortune and being fêted and courted by her brothers and sisters, let alone her parents!

'It's a bargain,' she said.

She was surprised to see that all the labour on the plantation had been brought over from the Indian sub-continent. Mostly they was Tamils, dark-skinned and mysterious. The young women all looked beautiful, wrapped in their multi-coloured saris, but there didn't seem to be any old women and she wondered why not.

'Where are all the Malays?'

'They don't like regular work,' Mr Rhys told her. 'I first came out here to work in the mines around Perak. The Malays are good at finding new seams of ore, but they won't work as miners. They go back to their compounds and leave it to others to do the hard work.'

'Is that why the Chinese came here?'

He shook his head. 'The Chinese live mostly in the towns. Some of them have lived here so long they even speak Malay amongst themselves. Often, you'll find the men were Chinese immigrants who married the local women and never went home. Babas, we call the men. The women are known as Nonyas. They own a lot of the mines and some of the plantations too, but they don't work them themselves, any more than we do.'

'They seem a very strange people to me. I want to know everything I can about them because they're the main traders in Malacca. They may sell me things for the Emporium, which will be good for Septimus. That's what my husband wanted more than anything else, too. He trained me himself to recognize good Oriental artefacts.'

'He'd have done better to have taught you to be a wife!

It seems to me he treated you more like a daughter than the woman he wanted to share his life with!'

'He said he was waiting for me to grow up.'

Trudie regretted the words as soon as she had spoken them. Her relationship with her husband was *her* business and nobody else's, certainly not this rough Welshman's! She puckered up her mouth and lowered her eyes, hoping he would go away.

Mr Rhys dismounted and walked along beside the cart, the reins dangling in the fingers of one hand. The big, ugly animal followed him, snuffling down its nostrils now and again as if inviting his attention. It was almost as if man and horse were friends, as two men might be friends. Trudie would have been impressed had she not been inclined to be cautious of anything as large and as loose-limbed as the piebald stallion.

'Were you so desperate to marry that you couldn't wait for anyone better than Jeremy Maddock to come along?'

Trudie was truly outraged. Her mouth went dry with shock. 'He was a fine man!'

'Is that so? What makes you think so?'

Trudie straightened her back. 'My father thought so!'

'Did he know him well?'

'No.'

'Even ministers of the Church can make mistakes.'

But not about Jeremy Maddock! 'I was very proud he chose me to be his wife,' she informed him coldly.

'He made you very happy, I suppose?'

It occurred to her that this was a most unsuitable conversation. Letty would have known exactly how to put this upstart in his place, she thought. Even Hatty would have made a better job of it than she seemed able to.

'Is that any business of yours?' she demanded.

He shrugged. 'Women make bad employers, unhappy women worse ones – '

'I'm not going away, Mr Rhys!'

'So it seems, Mrs Maddock.'

'I mean to get to know all the Chinese traders in Malacca – '

'And how do you mean to do that?'

'I thought you might introduce me to them?' she suggested hopefully.

Mr Rhys stood still for a pace, allowing his horse to catch up with him. He put a foot in the stirrup and mounted as easily as if the beast had been half its size.

'The European and Chinese communities don't mix socially, Mrs Maddock. You're going to be lonely enough without depriving yourself of the friendship of your own kind. My advice to you is to go carefully at first, if you insist on staying. You have a lot to learn, don't you realize that? The British don't consider any other people capable of governing themselves, that's why they make such splendid rulers, and, if you don't conform to local custom they can make your life impossible – '

'Aren't you British?' she shot at him.

'I'm *Welsh*, Mrs Maddock. I'm not even allowed to speak my own language in my own home in my own land. I do as I like out here. It's different for you. You can be one of them – if you want to be!'

He rode off ahead of the cart, digging his heels into his horse's sides. Trudie drooped, feeling like a piece of chewed string. It irritated her that he should speak of such a grand enterprise as the British Empire as if it were a thing of no moment, nothing more than a group of busybodying women telling other people what to do, when it was the men who did the ruling and the women merely suffered the heat and the flies – and the contempt of their menfolk every time they opened their mouths!

Well, she wouldn't accept that! If Mr Rhys could do as he liked, why shouldn't she?

Her spirits were further depressed by her first sight of her future home. The house was only half built, the newly cut palm fronds that made up the roof still loose and falling untidily on to the surrounding verandahs.

She jumped down from the cart, her knees shaking. 'Where's your house, Mr Rhys?'

He pointed across the compound in silence into the jungle, lowering her luggage piece by piece on to the ground beside her.

'If you don't live in that other house over there, who does?' she demanded, gesturing towards the only other dwelling around.

'That's where your husband died. You wouldn't want to live there. We can't have you dying of the cholera, can we?'

Trudie sniffed. 'You may despise the Empire, Mr Rhys, but you seem to be doing as well as anybody out of it! I presume your house is as well built as the one you're expecting me to live in?'

'There have been problems with yours,' he acknowledged. 'I'll see to it in the morning. You'll be all right as long as you stick to the part which is finished. The *jagger* will sleep across your doorway. You'll be perfectly safe.'

'*Jagger?*'

'A native guard.'

At least it was a human being and not an animal. 'I'll bid you goodnight then,' she said bravely.

He tipped his hat to her. A gentleman would have taken it right off and may have kissed her hand as well. 'I'll see you in the morning.'

She suppressed an inward shiver. There were strange noises all about her and she was afraid, but there was nobody she could tell of her fears. She was, as he had prophesied, completely alone.

It was morning at last and Trudie could only thank God for it. She washed herself in the bowl of water that a servant had left outside her door, and dressed herself in clothes that should have been clean, but which were already grubby with the tell-tale signs of mould that attacked everything in the tropics.

It had rained in the night. She watched forlornly as a bent Malay tried to brush the remains of the water out of doors, cursing the leaking roof under his breath. At intervals, she looked across the compound at the other house where Jeremy Maddock had succumbed and died of cholera. Did that mean that nobody could ever live there again? She went inside her own house again, hating everything about it. The raw wood was rough to her touch and left a splinter in her unwary finger. Anxiously, she poked at it, pulling it out and sucking at the small spot of blood that followed it. The other house looked more and more attractive to her.

The thing to do, she decided, was to go and look round the other bungalow before the sun got up too high and the enervating heat prevented her from doing anything. It wasn't far to walk. Children peered out at her from behind the flowering bushes that she imagined Jeremy must have planted, hoping to start a garden. None of them spoke to her, just looked and hid and then ran away giggling.

Trudie had expected to find the house empty but, as she approached the steps that led up to the surrounding verandah, she saw that it was very much occupied. The Portuguese tiles that decorated the steps had been scrubbed and polished. They were the cleanest thing Trudie had seen so far. She stood at the bottom, admiring them, only slowly becoming aware of the tiny Chinese lady looking down at her.

'Good morning!' she said briskly.

The Chinese lady hobbled across the verandah towards her on the tiniest feet Trudie had ever seen. They couldn't have been more than three inches long and were encased in embroidered damask slippers of such beauty that Trudie couldn't tear her eyes away from them.

'*Nai-nai!*' The words were softly uttered, as if the speaker couldn't quite believe her eyes.

Trudie blinked. The woman was like a little doll, her hair beautifully arranged in the Chinese style, her face powdered white, without any expression at all. She was also large with child.

'Do you speak English?' Trudie asked her, raising her voice as she did so.

'Supleme Rady!' the other replied readily.

'I'm afraid I don't understand,' Trudie said firmly.

The Chinese lady beckoned her up on to the verandah. She crossed her arms over her breasts and bowed low.

'Supreme Lady,' she said again, very carefully.

'Me?' said Trudie, much astonished.

'Honoured you visit here.'

Trudie looked about her, thinking how much better this house was than her own. She wanted it. She could be as comfortable in this house as she was uncomfortable in her own.

'How long have you been living here?' she enquired with deceptive calm.

'Since one and a half years. Since I first came here.'

'In this house?'

The Chinese lady bowed. 'In this house. This house good house. Your house no good.'

'You're right!' said Trudie.

'Of course I am right. Other house fall down. I not live in such a house!'

'Nor will I!' Trudie confirmed.

Far from being upset by this declaration, the Chinese lady nodded approvingly. She burst into a flood of words in which the expression *Feng Shui* occurred several times, while she pointed to all points of the compass in increasing agitation.

'I'm sorry, I don't understand.'

Contrasting with the gentle babble coming from the Chinese woman, her own tones were strident. Trudie fell into a self-conscious silence. She looked at the mask-like face through her lashes, but could detect no expression at all in the smooth, delicate face and the enigmatic almond-shaped eyes. Annoyed that she should feel red and bloated as well as loud-mouthed, she began again, almost whispering the question.

'What is *Feng Shui*?'

An imp of mischief appeared in the back of the black eyes. '*Nai-nai* sit. I tell *Nai-nai* what is *Feng Shui*.'

'Thank you.'

Trudie sank thankfully into a rattan chair on one side of the steps. From there she could admire the Portuguese tiles, making out different scenes of the Spice Islands in which she remembered Mr Maddock had once expressed a warm interest. This had been his house, she was sure of that, so why had she been relegated to the half-built monstrosity down the road?

She pointed to herself. 'My name is Mrs Maddock.' She pointed to the Chinese lady. 'What is your name?'

'Ki Wu Chao.'

Trudie stumbled over the strange name. Whatever she attempted in front of this strange woman seemed to find her making a fool of herself. 'Ki,' she tried again.

The woman shook her head. 'Wu Chao. Ki is family name.'

Trudie tried again. The woman laughed. 'You take tea wiz me?'

'Thank you,' Trudie assented. She hoped the glass would be clean and the water boiled.

Wu Chao flicked her fingers and a small figure in black pyjamas rushed into the kitchen to do her bidding. Wu Chao went on standing beside Trudie's chair, saying nothing.

It was a few moments before Trudie realized she was waiting for her to ask her to sit down. She jumped to her own feet and gestured to the pregnant woman to take her place.

'Do please sit! How soon will your baby be born?'

'Soon.'

'Then do please sit down!'

'*Nai-nai* sit on chair. I sit on steps.'

Puzzled, Trudie sat down again. 'Why do you call me *Nai-nai*?' she asked.

'*Nai-nai*, Supreme Lady. You Jelemy's *Nai-nai*.'

'Oh! His *wife*! I see!'

It didn't tell her who Wu Chao was, however. Then enlightenment came as the only possible answer. Of course Wu Chao had to be something to do with the Welshman! He had probably brought her out here from Malacca, poor girl, and had lost little time getting her with child. Trudie supposed she ought to object to such goings on, but she hadn't the strength and, truth to tell, she had no ambition to expose her own ignorance on the subject to those enigmatic black eyes.

Tea came, flavoured with ginger, and served on the most delightful silver tray. Trudie admired it with a quick smile and was rewarded by a nod of the head and a shy smile from her hostess. 'In Malacca many antique objects, some from Middle Kingdom, some from elsewhere.'

Trudie was glad she knew the Middle Kingdom to be China. 'Were you born in China?' she asked.

'No. I Nonya, born in Malacca.' Wu Chao hesitated, searching her mind for the right words. 'Straits Chinese,' she said at last. 'Nonyas in Singapore and Penang too.'

Much elated by this information, Trudie proceeded to tell her all about the antiques she was hoping to acquire for the Emporium in London. She told her about Septimus; about the visit of the Royal Princess to the Regent Street store and, most of all, she talked of the importance of getting the right objects to send back to her brother in England.

'That's what Mr Maddock wanted,' she explained kindly. 'That's really why I'm here.'

The Chinese lady was frankly baffled. 'You good wife to Mr Maddock?' she asked.

'I hope so,' Trudie sighed.

The Chinese lady pressed her further. 'Your Mama teach you good things, yes. How to cook? How to make cakes? Fine embroidery?'

Trudie shook her head. 'None of those things,' she admitted.

This was plainly a disaster to the Chinese way of thinking. Wu Chao simply couldn't think that this newcomer was a real woman at all. She strove valiantly to find some point they might have in common. She primped up her mouth. 'What she teach you?'

Trudie thought of her mother with mild contempt. What had she taught her? She thought of her, clutching her damp handkerchief, hoping against hope her husband wouldn't hold her to blame for whatever it was that had displeased him now. It was a memory that distressed Trudie, knowing that she had learned to be afraid almost before she had learned to walk.

'I had a governess,' she said aloud.

Wu Chao didn't understand. What she did know was that this extraordinary wife, who had come from nowhere and knew nothing, was completely lost in this strange world she had come to. She probably couldn't help her lack of manners and the loud way she spoke, just like a man, with no respect for anything. She was untaught and, it was exactly as Wu Chao had always been told, these pink, overheated Europeans had no idea how offensive they were being to others and were too arrogant to care.

'You like tea?' she asked hopefully.

Trudie nodded, draining her glass. 'I didn't know how to ask anyone to bring me a drink this morning,' she confessed. 'I was hoping Mr Rhys would visit later and tell me what to do.'

'Mr Rhys tell you?' she asked in horror.

It was Trudie's turn to be baffled. 'He is the manager of the plantation, isn't he?' she said.

Wu Chao raised fine eyebrows. 'I t'ink it better I tell servants all t'ings, yes?'

Trudie cast her a grateful look. 'Would you? I must admit I don't know where to begin in that horrible house!'

'Bad house! You tell Rhys man to see about house!'

'I will!'

'You understand what must be done?'

'It would help,' Trudie said, 'if it were to be properly finished. The roof keeps falling down.'

'House falling down. Not built according to *Feng Shui*. You understand?'

Trudie shook her head. 'No,' she said.

Wu Chao sat in silence for a moment, then she began. 'Spirits everywhere. You understand that?'

Trudie wondered if she should insist that her Christian faith didn't allow her to believe in other spirits but, as she wasn't sure of her theological ground, she decided to let the Chinese lady finish and then make up her mind whether she believed her or not. She certainly sounded as if she knew what she was talking about.

'I think so,' Trudie answered cautiously.

'Good spirits, bad spirits, all spirits live somewhere. Prefer different places. This place has many spirits. Best not to make spirits angry by building house looking wrong way, or making others uncomfortable. Maybe house built on the eye of a dragon, yes? Dragon shake head and house fall down. You understand now?'

Trudie was completely fascinated by this mythical dragon. She was about to dismiss the whole business as nonsense when she remembered the curious creaking noises of the night that had frightened her half to death. It might as well have been a dragon shaking his head as anything else. In fact, she thought it preferable to the tigers, or the murderous intruders of her imagination. Why not a dragon?

'Who understands where these dragons live?' she asked.

Wu Chao smiled encouragingly at her. 'Rhys man must find expert in reading principles of *Feng Shui*. This man very venerable, very wise. He will draw plan telling you how to build house. Must have right proportions; must be right with compass: otherwise no good!'

'I see,' said Trudie, wondering where such a wizard could be found locally. 'Why haven't you spoken to Mr Rhys about all this?'

Wu Chao spread her hands in despair. 'No listen,' she said sadly.

Her hands were not as tiny as her feet, Trudie noticed. But they were the most beautifully shaped hands she had ever seen. The fingers were perfectly in proportion with the palms, and beautifully kept. However, it was the way Wu Chao used them to punctuate her conversation that fascinated Trudie most. She was like a beautifully dressed porcelain doll, her black hair drawn to either side of a single parting and arranged in two buns held in place by jewelled hairpins. Her face had been painted an unnatural white, touched with colour on the high cheekbones. It took some getting used to, especially as Trudie had been taught to believe that a powdered and painted woman and a fallen woman were one and the same thing.

'He'll listen to me!' Trudie declared grimly and saw again the glimmer of amusement in the back of the black eyes.

'You *Nai-nai*,' Wu Chao acknowledged. 'Even Rhys man know that!'

He also knew her to be an arrogant newcomer and a female to boot, Trudie told herself with an inward grimace. If he didn't want to follow her orders, she had no idea how she would go about enforcing them. She could dismiss him from her service, she supposed, if the worst came to the worst, but, as she had never read his contract of employment, she might find even that power to be beyond her.

'I suppose you know Mr Rhys very well?' she said aloud.

Wu Chao shrugged. 'I see him many times,' she answered elliptically.

Trudie wished she were on such terms with her hostess as to be able to ask for more tea. 'Tell me more about your life here,' she suggested instead.

But Wu Chao hadn't missed the way Trudie was playing with her glass. It was the first time she had ever spoken to a European lady, or even been close enough to exchange the most ordinary greeting. She had heard much about them, of course, as had everyone who lived in the Straits Settlements of Penang, Malacca, and Singapore. Some people thought there was little difference between the Portuguese, the Dutch, and now the British, all of whom had ruled Malacca in turn. She knew better than that. Many Portuguese people had stayed behind in Malacca, long after the Dutch had forced them to give up their sovereignty over the area. These Portuguese lived in a little enclave of their own nowadays, intermarrying with the local people, as had her own forebears, and keeping their own customs and religion, even their own language, though it was more a dialect these days, as incomprehensible to the few Portuguese sailors who called at Malacca as it was to everyone else.

The Portuguese had been followed by the Dutch. They had come with their Dutch East India Company, making treaties with the local Mohammedan rulers, claiming that their only motive for turning out the Portuguese was trade. They had been jealous of the Portuguese for many years, plundering their ships and their possessions whenever and wherever they could, and having Malacca for themselves had been more than they could resist.

Wu Chao's family had not liked the Dutch. They were stiff and ugly, making much of their own civic virtues and despising those of everyone else. The Hollanders had had an inordinate respect for law, even the law of the Portuguese, and had enforced the tolls and licences for cruising in the Straits, most of which had never been paid before by the Chinese sailors, who swarmed all over the southern seas. Wu Chao's grandfather had once known a Dutchman, an unwashed barbarian who had smoked a clay pipe and had claimed himself to be a Christian. He had declared the Portuguese churches to be unholy places, however, their worshippers destined for a terrible afterlife. Wu Chao's grandfather had said that nothing better could be expected from any of the barbarian peoples. How could it be, when none of them really understood even the most basic principles of how the world was really organized?

The British had taken Malacca from the Dutch by trickery, or so it was said. No Chinese would condemn his new masters for that. Gambling was something he understood and the British were right to make the most of their joss for, as surely as it was working for them now, it would work against them one of these days. Let them make their laws, and pay their servants, it made little difference to the Babas and the Nonyas, or to the Malays either.

Wu Chao looked again at the British woman who had come to visit her at a time of the day when her peers would most certainly be in their own houses. She looked hot and uncomfortable in the strange clothes she wore, and she had huge, ugly feet, which were probably the reason Mr Maddock had decided to leave her behind in England. Wu Chao shuddered inwardly at the thought of any civilized man having to take such a person into his bed. Plainly, Trudie's parents had neglected her from childhood, teaching her nothing of the things a wife should know. How thankful she was that her own parents had schooled her long and hard to make herself agreeable in the sight of the man she should ultimately have the good fortune to marry.

'Have you eaten yet today?' she asked Trudie gently.

'There isn't anything to eat in that horrible house!'

Wu Chao suppressed a smile. 'You ask servant?'

'What servant?' Trudie demanded. 'Everyone ran away

as soon as it got really dark. I'm not surprised. I was expecting to be eaten by a tiger myself!'

Wu Chao uttered an unexpected, tinkling laugh. 'You hungry? You feel better when you eat good food cooked in my kitchen, yes?'

Trudie looked down her nose, telling herself she ought to refuse. She had no reason to suppose the last of the cholera had been banished from the house where Jeremy had finally succumbed and died. Goodness knows, enough people had told her how dirty all the natives were for her to believe it must be true.

'If I might have some more tea?' she began unsteadily.

Wu Chao merely heaved herself up on to her tiny feet and tottered across the verandah, disappearing into the shadows of the house. Curious, Trudie followed her more slowly, astonished by the beauty of the furnishings and the high polish on the elaborately carved antique furniture, much of it Chinese in origin. She was particularly taken by a screen lacquered in black and gold, with splashes of scarlet, that she knew would sell for a small fortune in London.

'What lovely things!' she exclaimed.

'Poor Chinese furniture,' Wu Chao murmured, not meaning a word of it. Trudie listened to the words and saw the meekly bowed head, and might have been deceived had she not also seen the appreciative snap of satisfaction in the Chinese woman's black eyes. 'My family give me few old things nobody has space to have in house.'

Trudie rubbed her fingers against the intricate carving on the sideboard. 'Is it easy to buy such furniture in Malacca?' she asked.

'Babas bring from China many years. You want?'

Trudie nodded. Some of these pieces were so beautiful

she doubted she could bring herself to part with them for Septimus's shop. She wanted to surround herself with their beauty, just as she had wanted to create an oasis of taste for herself in the schoolroom of her father's house in London.

'You eat now,' Wu Chao changed the subject.

She made a rice dish, with chicken and spices and a mixture of vegetables such as Trudie had never seen before. When she had that cooking to her satisfaction, she took four or five different kinds of cakes out of a cupboard and laid them on the table, finishing up with a cream of some sort in a folded banana leaf instead of a bowl.

She gestured to Trudie to sit down at the table, surrounding her with all these good things, pressing some chopsticks into her hand. Helplessly, Trudie looked from the rice to the decorated sticks in her hand and wondered what to do next.

'Eat!' Wu Chao bade her.

Trudie swallowed. 'Have you a spoon?' she asked humbly.

It took the Nonya woman a moment or so to see her guest's dilemma, then that tinkling laugh came again, followed by a quick hand placed over her mouth in case Trudie should be offended. She picked up the chopsticks and demonstrated their use. 'Like this you eat!'

Trudie took the chopsticks into her own hand, dropping one of them on the floor. She felt first foolish and then furious, determined to conquer the stupid things! 'Show me again!' she commanded.

Wu Chao hid her astonishment at the angry, arrogant tone, for she was beginning to understand Trudie better than she had at first sight. Patiently, she showed her again how to hold the chopsticks, keeping one still in the palm of her hand, and manipulating the other with two fingers.

After a while, Trudie managed to transfer a little bit of food from the bowl to her mouth and crowed in triumph.

'I can do it!'

'Even children can feed themselves, *Kak* Tludie!'

'*Kak?* What does this *Kak* mean?' Trudie managed another mouthful and grinned over the bowl at the Chinese lady.

'Elder sister. The whole word is *kakak*, but we just say *kak*. It is respect. I call you this because you young woman. If you old woman I call you *wak*, which means *wawak*.'

'Elder sister! You're older than I am!'

'But you *Nai-nai*.'

Trudie went on eating. She found it all delicious and was tempted to try everything on hand. After a while she became aware of Wu Chao watching her every movement, just as she would have watched a greedy child. Trudie flushed, putting the chopsticks down and folding her hands into her lap.

'I know, I'm a barbarian!' she sighed. 'A starving barbarian, before you took pity on me and gave me something to eat.'

Amused, Wu Chao asked her, 'You like Nonya cooking?'

Trudie sighed. 'I must do. Our food has far less taste because we boil all the vegetables. I don't know much about cooking,' she added, thinking she was stating no more than the obvious.

'You have cook to cook food?'

'We always did at home.'

'Never mind cook. Best to know cooking yourself, then you have better cook because know you not fool. I find you good cook.'

Trudie wondered if she wanted to be under such an obligation to someone who was not a European and who might ask goodness knows what favours in return. Her doubts were clearly reflected on her face.

'Never mind now. We soon understand each other much better, no? Even though you barbarian and I civilized person,' said Wu Chao, marvelling that anyone could display their feelings so plainly to anyone else as Trudie did. No wonder Europeans were such bad gamblers! 'You play *cher kee*?'

'No.'

The Chinese woman sighed. She obviously thought Trudie good for very little. 'Never mind,' she said sadly. 'I find cook and someone to wash clothes. You talk to Rhys man about *Feng Shui*.'

It took even longer for Trudie to walk back to her own house, there were so many distractions on the way. The house, when she reached it, was even worse than she remembered it, especially when she compared it to the one she had just come from. She stood back from it, shading her eyes with one hand as she stared up at the disintegrating roof.

'Anything the matter?'

Trudie turned with dignity, opening her parasol slowly. 'The house is falling down,' she said.

The Welshman shrugged his shoulders. 'It isn't finished, that's all that's wrong with it.'

'Then why don't you live in it?' she asked him sweetly.

'Me?'

She inclined her head, looking up once again at the roof. 'Why not?'

'I have my own house!' he protested.

'There's always my husband's house,' she suggested. The idea grew on her as yet another palm frond fell on to the ground from the roof. Then she remembered that Wu

Chao was nearing her time. It would hardly be a Christian act to turn her out of her comfortable dwelling before she was safely delivered of her child.

The Welshman glared at her. 'What do you want done about the house?' he demanded.

Trudie gave him look for look. 'I'm told it may be sited on a dragon's eye, or something equally uncomfortable – '

'What happened to your spirit of adventure?' he retorted, amused.

'It isn't equal to the house descending round my ears in the middle of the night because the dragon feels it must shake its head! How would you feel with that thing poking you in the eye?'

Mr Rhys groaned. 'Not you, too! How can you believe such nonsense?'

'Very easily,' she assured him. 'At any event, I believe it enough to much prefer your house to mine! So what are you going to do about it?'

'You'll be quite comfortable once it's finished,' he assured her. 'I'll put the men on to putting a proper roof on for you. You have everything you need inside, haven't you?'

'I don't know,' she answered frankly. 'I'm not experienced in such matters. I expected to find my husband's household running as smoothly as it would have been had he still been alive. Who cooked and cleaned for him? You can't tell me he did it all himself?'

The Welshman changed colour, going an ugly brick red. His eyes didn't look away from hers, however. He looked more sorry for her than anything else. 'I'll see you're made more comfortable,' he muttered. 'The cholera took its toll on more than your husband, Mrs Maddock. It'll take a day or two before everything gets back to normal.'

Trudie's suspicions were aroused. 'That reminds me,'

she said. 'Has my husband been buried yet? Should I – should I – ?'

'No, ma'am. Your husband was buried within the half-hour, as is usual out here. If you want to visit the grave, I'll be glad to show you the way, but don't expect too much, will you? The jungle takes back any ground one turns one's back on for two days put together and, although I marked it with a wooden cross, even a stone marker will flake away in a year or two unless it's looked after.'

Trudie, unlike so many others of her generation, had no particular feeling for the graveyard monuments that were so popular in Europe. Worse still, she felt a hypocrite as she asked, 'I suppose someone read the burial service for him?'

'I read some prayers.'

She wondered what her father would have said to that, and then whether it mattered who said the prayers as long as they were said – and meant.

'Thank you,' she said simply.

He looked more uncomfortable than ever. 'I doubt you will approve, but some of the Tamils have left offerings to their gods beside the grave. I can have them cleared away if you like?'

She shook her head. 'Have many of them died from the cholera also?'

'A few. Some of the children.'

She sagged a little, thinking of them. 'Is it over?'

'Mr Maddock was the last to die. I thought for a while he might pull through as one or two of the others had, but he hadn't the will to live at the end.'

'I expect he was lonely,' Trudie commented. 'He should have sent for me to come to him long ago. He would have done, if he hadn't wanted the Emporium to succeed so much! I wanted that too. Perhaps I wanted it too much! I don't know, I hadn't realized how far away from everyone else one is out here.'

'Perhaps you should go back to the Emporium?'

Trudie lifted her chin, facing facts as she always did. 'When I was on hand for Septimus to ask what he should do, he never did anything else, and he came to resent me always being there, looking over his shoulder. I can't go back until the Emporium is really his.' She bit her lower lip. 'Septimus is my favourite brother, you see. I don't want to lose him.'

'Did you tell that to your husband?'

'I didn't have to. Mr Maddock understood most things without having to be told. He would expect me to take over here, I'm sure.'

Mr Rhys went on looking at her. 'What do you know about growing things in the tropics? What do you know about the kind of life we live out here? You won't find it easy, ma'am.'

'I can learn.'

'It isn't a proper life for a lady such as yourself. If you went back to England – or even to Singapore – you'd soon marry again. Mr Maddock won't have left you penniless!'

But Trudie had already made up her mind. 'You don't know what it means to be a woman, Mr Rhys. If I went back to England, I should be subject to my father's authority again. Here, the worst that can happen to me is that some dragon will shake its head and bring my house down. Which would you choose?'

He was silent for a long moment, then he said, 'I understand better than you think. I was born into servitude just as much as is any woman. Children shouldn't be forced down into the mines almost before they can walk as I was. I won't go back either.'

Her brow cleared, thankful that they seemed to have come to some sort of agreement. 'Are you sure we ought to be growing coffee here?' she asked him.

'We've already discussed that, ma'am. What else do you want us to grow until I find something better?'

'I don't know,' she admitted. 'I've heard there's too much coffee in the world. Is that true?'

He nodded briefly. 'Your husband wasn't interested in the plantation, Mrs Maddock. He came here because the land is cheap and he was near enough to Malacca to carry on with his other interests, antiques and the like.'

'Why not Singapore?' Trudie wondered.

'Too many rules and regulations. Singapore was a British city from the very beginning. Malacca is a backwater and easily overlooked. At least, that's the way I look at it.'

'I see,' said Trudie. She thought of Wu Chao and was more than ever convinced that she was this man's mistress. 'Well, Mr Rhys, if my husband could make a living out here, so can we! Perhaps we can look over the books together sometime?'

He went back to looking at the roof of her house. 'Anything you say, Mrs Maddock,' he said at last. 'The first thing is to make you more comfortable though, don't you think, dragons or no dragons?'

Her lips twitched into a saucy smile. 'I never thought of St George as being a Welshman before,' she said.

'As long as the job gets done, why should you care?' he retorted. And he grinned back at her, forgetting for the moment what a nuisance to him she was likely to be.

Chapter Eight

Caradoc Rhys sat astride the roof, checking the last of the primitive thatching. Today he had on no shirt at all. His voice rose and fell in a song Trudie had never heard before and couldn't understand. The subversive Welsh! She laughed to herself, averting her eyes from his naked torso. Members of the lower orders were so much more physical than were the young men she was accustomed to. She had never met anyone who rejoiced in his own strength as the Welshman did.

'Gwlad! Gwlad!
Pleidiol wyf i'm gwlad.
Tra mor yn fur i'r bur hoff bau,
O bydded i'r hen iaith barhau.'

He raised his fist high above his head. '*Cymru Rydd, Cymru Gymraeg* – there you are! Didn't I tell you the house would be just fine with a little attention?'

'I still prefer the other house,' she maintained. 'Why don't you offer me yours?'

'You've not seen my house.'

'Of course I have!' she muttered to herself. She was quite sure in her own mind that he was living in the same house as the Chinese woman, for it was the only other house in the compound that was of any stature. The others, standing at a distance from the two main ones, were probably for servants and the workers on the estate. She shaded her eyes as she looked up at him again. 'What's the song you were singing?'

'Ah, better for you not to know. Some of us call it our national anthem – '

She licked her lips. 'Are you a republican?' she demanded.

'I am not. I'm a nationalist, wanting freedom for my little country, but the Queen, God bless her, is scarcely an English woman herself, now is she?'

'I'm English!'

He patted the roof with one hand. 'Doubtless it'll be forgiven you, as long as it doesn't make you think you're better than the rest of us!'

She tapped an impatient toe, unconsciously taking up the rhythm of the song he had been singing. She thought herself very much better than her manager if the truth were told. In London, she probably wouldn't even have noticed him, certainly they never would have met socially, it was only because he was the only other European on the plantation that she seemed to be constantly tripping over him out here. She knew exactly what her brothers would have said about him: that he had ideas far above his station in life! And she agreed with them. She knew him to be both pretentious and over-familiar and, if she hadn't been so lonely, she wouldn't have exchanged more than a casual good morning with him, just to put him in his place.

'I'd have thought Wales would be proud to be united with England,' she said as he climbed down the makeshift ladder to stand beside her.

'We might be – if it were on equal terms. It's no good telling people all the time what they should be doing and never asking them what they want to do.'

This was so much how Trudie, herself, felt about life in general and her own life in particular that she felt quite friendly towards him. Perhaps, she thought, she might offer him a cup of tea and some of Wu Chao's delicious little cakes? Then she thought he would recognize the source of the cakes and might even guess that she was having to rely on his mistress's good nature for almost everything she had to eat.

'It's still a woebegone, sad-looking house!' she exclaimed. 'I'm sure you still haven't got it right!'

'You're not still going on about *Feng Shui*, are you?'

She sniffed. 'I'm living in the house, you're not!'

'It'll stand up for as long as you're likely to want it,' he retorted.

Trudie wished she could think of something crushing of her own to say. She wondered what Letty would have said to him. Her eldest sister was the kindest and gentlest person imaginable, but she wouldn't put up with impertinent servants about her. Perhaps a manager wasn't precisely a servant, but it was just as necessary to keep him at a proper distance and let him know when he had gone too far.

'I shall probably be here for years and years,' she said.

'I doubt it.'

Angered, she turned away from him. 'And I wish you wouldn't walk about half naked! It may not mean anything to you, but I find it offensive – '

'And you a married woman!'

She took a deep breath, knowing she was very close to losing her temper entirely. 'That has nothing to do with it! You shouldn't need telling to be properly dressed when there are members of the female sex about! In future I shall expect you to be decently covered – '

'You want me to wear a coat?'

'A shirt. Properly buttoned!'

He threw back his head and laughed. She tried not to look at him, but the sight of his bronzed chest and the great column of his neck reminded her of illustrations she had seen in Septimus's Greek primer, the only pictures of naked men she had ever seen. She found herself blushing at the memory.

'Why don't you visit with the other women on the neighbouring plantation?' he asked her gently.

'I prefer not to.'

Well, she herself had said it, she was English! He gave her an exasperated glance, wondering what kind of a marriage it had been between this girl and Jeremy Maddock. In many ways she was still a child, pretending to be grown up, but that wouldn't last long, it never did in this climate. Her cousins would claim her and carry her off to Singapore before long and he would probably never see her again. Perhaps it wouldn't hurt him to wear a shirt in her presence until then, if that was what she wanted. He saw it as no more than a ruse to prop up an authority they both knew she didn't possess. She'd do better to unbutton a little herself, as he would have told her if she hadn't made it plain that his advice was unwelcome to her. Poor little thing! What would she have made of things if Maddock had still been alive when she had got here? He had an idea she would find loneliness easier to bear than dishonour. If she only knew it, she had had a lucky escape when Mr Maddock had succumbed to the cholera. This one was a lady for sure, and Caradoc Rhys had a low opinion of the fortitude of the upper classes. If she could only be persuaded to return to Singapore, she need never find out anything of what had gone on out here. Even if she stayed she was not going to hear one word about it from him. It was better she didn't know.

'Are you settling in better now, ma'am?' he asked awkwardly.

Trudie cast a last look over the new house. 'I have a cook and so on, but I still hate this house!'

He shrugged, the muscles rippling down his back. 'If you stay, I'll have another built for you one of these days, according to the principles of *Feng Shui*, if that's the only way you'll be satisfied.'

'I'm staying,' she said again.

She found her new life unbearably lonely, however, and could think of no way of filling her time profitably as everyone should. She could, of course, have taken Wu Chao up on her offer and visited with her every other day, perhaps even learning from her the rudiments of running a house in Malaya, but she didn't like to. Mrs Eliot had told her more times than she could remember, during her stay in Singapore, that it was *fatal* to be too friendly with the native peoples – they always took advantage of such condescension – and every one of them was a traitor in his heart, a hotbed of sedition waiting for the careless word to set alight a whole rebellion against the established order.

'It isn't as though they can rule themselves, my dear!' Mrs Eliot had insisted. 'Just look at the native states all round the Settlements! Their people are for ever making their way into British rule if they can possibly get away with it because they know they'll get *fair treatment* from us, not the slavery which is all they know at home!'

Trudie had heard of the existence of slavery from other sources as well. Everyone spoke with horror of the conditions under which the people lived. Only she seemed to have wondered why they should have been so horrified. Didn't her own family's money come from the work of slaves in the West Indies? And that was considered perfectly respectable by everyone she knew, even the sanctimonious Eliots. She wished she had asked more questions about the sugar plantations when she had had the chance, not that her brothers would have answered her. Not for the first time, she cursed the way nobody took women seriously. Why did her gender make her less able to know something, to run her own business, or even to handle money? She was not a child, so why did all her male compatriots conspire to treat her as one?

Trudie was asking the same questions of herself again later that day. She had been sitting on the verandah, sipping tea flavoured with ginger that was the only way her new cook knew how to make it, when a letter from Christopher Horton had been delivered to her. She had written to him, or rather to her cousin Hermione, when she had first arrived on the plantation and had discovered her husband to be dead. She had expected a reply, of course, a black-rimmed note of sympathy perhaps, but nothing more. This letter was pages long, however, written in Mr Horton's spidery hand, and as pompous as the man himself.

Trudie read it through the first time with mounting anger. Then she forced herself to read it again, coming to the reluctant conclusion that if her cousins were determined to take a hand in her affairs there was nothing she could do about it.

Her rage smouldered inside her for the rest of the day. She had thought herself safe from meddling relatives so far away from her own family in England. How could she possibly have overlooked the connection between herself and the Hortons? Christopher Horton, oozing sympathy for the young widow, had hastened to assure her that he and Cousin Hermione would be putting themselves to the trouble of travelling to her new home as soon as they could arrange their passage satisfactorily. Meanwhile, she was to spend her time recovering from her loss as best she could, leaving all her husband's affairs for Christopher to deal with on her behalf.

'What does he know about growing coffee?' she stormed at the empty air. 'What does he know about *anything*?'

There was no answer to that and she knew it. He was entitled to take all her finances into his own hands and make of them what he wanted. The only way he could be held accountable for his actions would be if she were to marry again, then her new husband would be entitled to treat her property as his own in his turn, and Mr Horton would be obliged to relinquish the reins to him, explaining his stewardship as he did so.

Worse, though, than knowing herself to be helpless in the face of the law, was to know how Cousin Hermione would enjoy the situation. Hermione would think of a dozen reasons why Trudie's profits should be diverted into her cousin's pockets. Trudie could feel her dislike for her cousin as a bad taste in her mouth, destroying her, as hatred always did. Forget her, she advised herself, but she could not. She could feel those pale blue eyes watching and enjoying every moment of her distress as she tried to calm herself and find some defence against having to submit her whole way of life once again to someone she despised.

She was glad to see Mr Rhys when next he called. Silently she handed him the offending letter. 'What am I to do?' she moaned.

The Welshman tipped his hat on to the back of his head. 'I warned you I didn't think you'd be staying here long,' he reminded her, somewhat smugly. 'If your cousin has any sense he'll take you back to live with them in Singapore until another husband can be found for you – '

'Heavens above! I'm only just widowed!' she protested.

He stood over her, glaring down at her. 'You were hardly married at all, woman!'

She was on her own feet in an instant. 'What do you mean by that?'

He shrugged. 'Forget it. Suffice it to say, I'll be glad when your cousin comes for you. There's nothing here for a woman of your quality, Mrs Maddock, whatever you may be thinking you'll find to do here.'

'Indeed? Well, one of the things I intend to do is rebuild this house!' she informed him at a shout. 'And, if you won't help me, I'll do it myself!'

He shut his eyes, praying for patience. 'You'll do as you think best,' he said at last, 'but, if you'll take my advice – '

'You haven't met Mr Christopher Horton!' she snapped.

'I feel sorry for the man!' Mr Rhys shouted back at her. 'I feel sorry for anyone who tries to bring you to heel, ma'am. You're everything I've always known about the English! You're bossy, with far too good an opinion of yourself, and you make no effort at all to get along with those you consider to be your inferiors! If Mr Horton can make anything of you, he's welcome to you!'

Trudie watched him walk away from the house, hating him almost as much as she hated Christopher and Hermione Horton. He didn't even look back! On the contrary, just down the track he met his Chinese mistress and put a friendly hand on her shoulder, obviously asking her where she was going. The answer was soon obvious as behind Wu Chao came an army of workmen led by a tiny Chinese man, a small black pill-box hat on his head, pressing down on the queue of silvered hair that fell down his back.

Wu Chao should not have been out in the full heat of the sun, not when she was so near her time, Trudie thought. If Mr Rhys had any sense he would send her straight home, but no men had the sense they were born with when it came to dealing with women! He turned around and came back, the Chinese lady leaning on his arm, her tiny feet completely inadequate to the task of carrying her any distance without support.

Trudie went down to greet her, a little put out when Wu Chao bowed several times to her with exaggerated respect.

It was all so unnecessary. Besides, it destroyed her own intention to show Mr Rhys that she could be as civil as anyone else to a woman even he had to admit should never have been brought to her notice in the first place.

'It's too hot for you to be out, Wu Chao,' she smiled at the Chinese woman.

A gabble from all the men, accompanied by much gesticulation, was her only answer. One and all pointed up to her roof. There, a monkey sat alternately scratching himself and pulling out pieces of her roof. In a matter of seconds, Trudie was transformed from being the well-bred gentlewoman to a virago, screaming at the monkey.

Wu Chao put a gentle, timid hand on her arm. 'Ssshh!' she begged. 'Animal not listen. House fall down anyway.'

'And you should be resting in the shade!' Trudie insisted. She marched the reluctant Chinese woman towards the verandah, forgetting for the moment the difficulty the other had in walking.

Wu Chao made an effort to gain her full attention. '*Feng Shui!*' she cried out.

Trudie looked from her to the tiny Chinaman. 'That man?'

Wu Chao nodded eagerly. 'Pull down house. Build again, yes?'

Trudie hesitated. If the Hortons really intended to descend on her, she had to have a house to put them in. Any house was better than none under the circumstances. 'I don't know.' She looked round for help and found it in the form of Mr Rhys striding towards her, his face thunderous as he observed the gathering.

'Did you arrange this?' he demanded of Trudie.

Wu Chao took a faltering step towards him. She bowed several times, folding her hands into her sleeves. 'It is necessary change house,' she told him. 'Some calamity come to *Nai-nai* else.'

'Rubbish!'

'But it isn't rubbish,' Trudie felt moved to say. 'Sooner or later the house *is* going to fall down!'

'Because it was badly put up in the first place! In a hurry! For you! *Not* because it's poking out a dragon's eye!'

'How do you know?'

Wu Chao clapped her hands, hastily covering her mouth as Mr Rhys turned his rage on her. The Malays, brought in to rebuild the house, stood around and grinned, waiting for the entertainment to continue.

'Well?' Trudie insisted.

He made an exasperated, explosive sound, turning on his heel. 'Get rid of them!' he ordered.

'I will not! This gentleman is an exponent of *Feng Shui* and I want to hear from him what is wrong with my house!'

'Gentleman?'

Trudie's eyebrows rose. 'Loosely speaking,' she said with dignity.

Wu Chao nodded agreement. 'Velly tlue!'

Trudie thought the Chinese woman looked quite awful. Forgetting all about the house, she helped her up her own poorly tiled steps and on to the verandah, easing her into the nearest chair. 'Would you like to lie down? The sun's far too hot for you to have walked all that way!'

'Not sun. Baby come.'

For a stunned instant, Trudie stared at her. She thought she might faint, and rather hoped that she would because she hadn't the least idea what to do next. Black and scarlet alternated behind her eyes.

'Baby,' she repeated foolishly.

Wu Chao folded her hands over her stomach. 'You not notice I have baby coming?' she asked.

'Well, yes,' Trudie admitted.

'Husband not tell you?'

'No.'

Wu Chao shook her head. 'Never mind, not matter now.'

'Yes, that's all very well,' Trudie retorted, 'but what are we going to do now?'

Wu Chao managed a small laugh, cut short by a labour pain. 'My family coming. *Nai-nai* do nothing. I bling baby for you see later.'

Trudie was horrified by the thought. She went to the edge of the verandah and beckoned to Mr Rhys. She knew herself to be close to hysteria, wondering how it was that other women could accept birth and death as being strictly their business, while she hadn't the first inkling of what to do next.

'The baby's coming,' she announced baldly. Yes, and *he* was the father, she remembered belatedly. '*Do* something!'

'You won't be any help to her if you panic,' he said.

She blinked. 'Me?'

He grinned. 'Cheer up, Mrs Maddock. Her family are coming from Malacca today – '

'You'd better go and meet them! I don't know what to do!' His look told her how useless he thought her to be. It wasn't fair! She flushed, close to tears. 'I'm afraid,' she said.

'It'll be all right,' Mr Rhys comforted her awkwardly. 'It'll be a long time yet. Stay with her, will you? Let's hope her sisters arrive soon. Meanwhile, Wu Chao will know what to do.'

That was all very well for him to say! She hadn't the remotest idea of what to expect should the baby arrive earlier than Mr Rhys thought it would. And how did he know anyway?

She stood there, picking at her fingers, trying to force her panic down to manageable proportions. 'I'm a Rat,' she said. 'What will the baby be?'

'This Year of Monkey,' Wu Chao put in.

Trudie gave her a wan smile. 'The monkey on the roof?'

Wu Chao shook her head. 'Monkey people very quick, very curious. Invent many t'ings. Velly nice people, but like drunk men if too successful. How you know you Rat, *Kak* Tludie?'

Trudie looked down her nose. 'Someone told me.' She was oddly reluctant to tell anyone of the Chinese captain of the ship that had brought her to Malacca, or of the bet they had made between them.

'Rhys man is Tiger.'

Trudie could imagine the qualities of the Tiger. He would be a born leader, full of animal magnetism, rash and impetuous. If she hadn't been so worried about Wu Chao, she would have laughed at the thought.

'What are you, Wu Chao?'

The Chinese woman gasped. 'I Dog. Good friend. Royal.'

'Royal?'

Wu Chao tried again. 'Loyal,' she said carefully.

Mr Rhys looked from one woman to the other. 'I can see you two'll have plenty to talk about while I'm gone!' He grinned cheerfully. 'And to think I was worried in case Wu Chao thought you loud-mouthed and arrogant! Rat! More like a Rooster!'

Trudie eyed him steadily. 'Hens don't crow,' she observed.

'Remember that when your cousins come!' he advised her.

Trudie was glad to see the back of him until she found herself once more alone with his mistress. Anxiously, she stood over Wu Chao, wringing her hands, until even she could hear that she was beginning to sound like her mother and desisted abruptly.

'I think we will have that tea,' she said.

Wu Chao looked back at her, her enigmatic eyes bright. 'Who told you 'bout *Ming Shu*?'

'That I'm a Rat? I know very little about it. In Europe we have signs for the month, but my father's a parson and wouldn't allow any of us to even talk about such things.'

'What signs?'

Because it was easier to talk about something that seemed to interest the Chinese woman, Trudie did her best to remember which sign was applicable to which month and what their main characteristics were said to be. Some of them she invented, preferring to mislead than to be faced by the agonized silence that was interrupted at intervals by another bout of pain. Happily, she knew herself to be Taurus, the Bull, and admitted she could sometimes behave like one.

'You have loud voice,' Wu Chao agreed. 'Rhys man has loud voice too. Maybe all Europeans like that?'

'What about you?' Trudie countered.

'Only when angry – like 'bout your house!'

Trudie was glad of the tea, though Wu Chao left most of hers untouched It gave her something to do if nothing else. She could never remember feeling so inadequate as she did now. She longed for Letty's gentle encouragement, wishing that either her mother, or her sisters, could have told her more about such things as childbirth. Ignorance was all very well, she thought, but it was too easy for her compatriots to confuse it with innocence, and that was something she herself would never do again. It was better to know, even if one never had to make use of that knowledge.

'Why don't you lie down on my bed?' she suggested. 'You seem to be in pain now more often than not.'

'Yes, baby soon come.'

Trudie went out on to the verandah, scanning the path that led to the house every few seconds, willing Wu Chao's sisters to arrive.

When they did so it was almost an anti-climax. They came on the same kind of cart that had transported her and her luggage all the way from Malacca. It was slow, but a more comfortable way of travelling than the more elegant carriages most of the Europeans preferred. It was all too easy to lose a wheel on the rough ground, or even to break one of the shafts miles from anywhere with no one to repair it.

A small woman, younger than Wu Chao, but so like her that she had to be her sister, dismounted with difficulty, balancing herself on her own tiny feet.

'I Swee Neo.' She bowed solemnly several times, her eyes lowered to a spot a couple of feet in front of where Trudie was standing. 'Wu Chao here with you?'

Trudie couldn't usher her into the bedroom fast enough. The two sisters looked at one another and began to speak in what she thought first of all was Chinese, but it was not. Later she was to discover that most of the Babas and Nonyas spoke a dialect of Malay between themselves, mixed in with a variety of Cantonese which most of the *sinkehs*, or new arrivals, spoke, coming as they did from South China. Eventually, other women emerged from under the woven cover of the cart, all of them smiling and respectful, and each of them apparently knowing exactly what to do and where to go, despite never having been inside Trudie's house before.

Swee Neo spoke better English than her sister. It was she who put a chair to one side of the bed in Trudie's bedroom and ushered Trudie into it as if it were a position of honour. It was she who introduced the other women to Trudie, pointing out the midwife and the midwife's assistant, both of whom were always used by all her family.

'No trouble now,' she promised blithely.

Trudie sat in silence, watching the bustle all about her and wishing herself anywhere but where she was. She felt the whole weight of her own culture on her shoulders as she wondered how other European women coped with the strange life they were forced to participate in, always as outsiders because they were members of the ruling nation, even while they, as women, held none of the political power in their own hands as their menfolk did. Did none of them ever rebel? Would she?

Her spirits became lower and lower as she realized that she wouldn't. She was caught in the trap that lay in wait for all her kind. If she treated the Nonyas and the Malay women as her friends, she would be an outcast from her own society; if she kept herself apart from them, she faced the loneliness she had known ever since her arrival for the rest of her stay in the country. It was hard to know which was preferable, but her whole upbringing militated against her acknowledging that these native women were anything other than her inferiors in life. It came all the harder to know that they could cope with a crisis which had caused her nothing but panic and distress. She should be the one in charge, dignified and unflappable, not a young girl deeply distressed by her first experience of the way a baby comes into the world.

Swee Neo had no such doubts. She smiled more than her sister and her English came more readily to her tongue.

'What that man do?' she enquired, spotting the Chinaman outside.

Trudie muttered something about Wu Chao and *Feng Shui*. 'We plan to rebuild the whole house,' she added, knowing she could never do so without Mr Rhys's help.

Swee Neo's eyes rounded in horror. 'This house bad luck?'

'More badly built, I think,' Trudie told her.

'Bad luck!' She savoured the words. 'Bad luck for baby! I go ask, yes? You never mind, you wait here!'

Swee Neo was gone only a few moments. When she came back some of her sister's implacable determination was written on her face. 'We move Wu Chao and baby to other house! We do so chop chop, before baby born!'

It all turned out to be much easier than Trudie had imagined. The women, their voices sharp and constant like baby birds waiting for food, ordered all that they needed from the Malays outside. Soon they had a makeshift palanquin made and were transferring Wu Chao from the bed, first on to it, and then to the other house down the track. Willingly, the men carried their light burden, though they, like Trudie, thought *Feng Shui* to be no more than an idle superstition. They, too, were people of the Book, having a Bible of sorts of their own, as Mr Rhys had explained to her on their way from Malacca.

She followed the small procession down the track and into the house she was still determined to make her own one day. Her thoughts travelled far more quickly than her feet, which had to accommodate themselves to Swee Neo's much slower pace. Should she, or should she not, offer to stand as godmother to the new baby? In similar circumstances in England, she thought it might be expected of her, but here, with a pagan baby, governed not by Christ but by superstitions, she was less sure of her position.

The midwife and her assistant stood around Wu Chao, patting her at intervals to give her encouragement. Wu Chao made no sound at all. A light sweat had broken through what was left of her immaculate make-up, but otherwise she gave no sign of the pain she was suffering.

Trudie rapidly came to the conclusion that she was not necessary to the proceedings. Too much had happened to her too quickly recently for her to be able to cope with much more. Yet even she could see it was too much to expect these extraordinary Chinese women to cope with her hysterics as well as everything else. Once or twice, she moved nearer to the doorway, only to return almost at once, intrigued by an event that nothing had prepared her for. How strange that babies should be born in this way and how stupid of her never to have realized it before! Was that what her mother had suffered when she and her siblings had been born? No wonder she burst into tears when anyone mentioned the pains of motherhood!

Wu Chao uttered a sharp cry. Trudie crept closer to the door. 'I – I – ' she began.

Swee Neo smiled kindly at her over her shoulder. 'Not long now, never mind. Please not to go away until we know if boy or girl.'

Trudie sat down hard on the chair nearest the door, her mouth dry. She was obsessed by the lowering conviction that more was going to be asked of her than she was going to be able to give. Worse than that: *she was frightened!*

She licked her lips. 'How will we know?' she heard herself asking.

'Never mind, we know!' Swee Neo soothed her.

It was Wu Chao who laughed, the laughter breaking into a sharp scream of pain, followed by silence. Almost immediately there was a triumphant chatter of approval as the baby's head appeared, followed by the baby itself. Swee Neo executed a quick step, holding the blood-smeared child out to Trudie. 'You want to see? Pity, but it girl.'

Trudie made no comment. Indeed, she could not. She had never been so shocked about anything as she was about what she had just witnessed.

There was a lengthy, strained silence around the bed, followed by a flutter of anxious whispers. Trudie strained her ears, even though she couldn't understand a word of what they were saying. She put an anxious hand out to Swee Neo. 'Is anything the matter?'

This time there was no smile from the Chinese girl. She looked as strained as if she had just given birth herself. 'The baby is a girl!'

Trudie was pleased. 'How nice!' she exclaimed.

Swee Neo bent towards her earnestly. 'No, no, no good! Chinese saying that a boy is a great happiness, because boy is future of whole family; girl is only small happiness, because bling up girl for 'nother family. This girl no happiness in life because never find husband in father's people. Better dead!'

The midwife nodded in agreement, guessing what was being said.

'What an outrageous thing to say!' Trudie exclaimed.

Swee Neo shrugged. 'What person marry this girl?'

Trudie was scandalized. 'Marriage isn't the only thing in life!'

'You think not? What else cheap native girl do?'

Trudie felt cold inside. She went over to the bed, taking Wu Chao's hand in hers. 'Don't you love your baby? Don't you want her?'

'Too many girls in family already,' Wu Chao whispered. 'Too many to find husbands for all of them. Good Nonya girls with Baba fathers to find them husbands.' She turned her face away. 'Who find husband for this baby, never mind?'

Trudie took her first look at the baby herself. She had never seen anything so perfect as the golden-hued child with strongly growing damp black hair on her head. Somehow or other, this little mite had to be given a future.

She set her mouth in a determined line. If she had wanted any proof that the Chinese were a barbaric people, this was it! Then an uncomfortable memory of her own father's attitude towards herself and her sisters came to mind, destroying her momentary feeling of superiority. Her father would willingly have strangled her at birth, if he had not been a Christian parson and afraid of the consequences for himself. The knowledge made her all the more determined to save this little girl's life, no matter what her future. Why should being female be such a terrible handicap, even at the moment of birth? If there were a God, it couldn't be what He intended, she told herself, no matter what anyone else thought!

She picked the baby off the bed and cuddled the tiny form to her. At another time, she might have been afraid of hurting such a tiny person, but now she felt completely at one with her. She smiled down at the child, cooing gently to her. It was as if a great peace had descended over her with the certainty that she was right and that only she could do anything about it.

'I will not be a party to murder!' she said softly.

Wu Chao relaxed on the bed like a pricked balloon. Her exterior might have been stoical, but she felt like any other woman, Trudie realized. Swee Neo merely bowed. Trudie thought she would have argued further, only Wu Chao pulled at her sleeve, speaking earnestly to her.

Swee Neo listened, then bowed again. 'Wu Chao says you Supreme Lady. Your decision final.' She snapped off the words as if she disapproved of the whole business and would have nothing more to do with it. Then she put a finger under her niece's chin and smiled at her. 'Girl baby,' she said sadly. 'Very bad thing, never mind.'

'Good thing!' Trudie retorted. 'Would you rather be a man?'

The two sisters giggled together at the thought. They looked at one another, both of them thinking that Trudie was rather mannish, with her decided ways, her loud voice and her enormous feet. And yet there was something very vulnerable about her, almost as if she didn't know how important it was to please the man in one's life and make the most of the few assets one had as a female. Why hadn't she given her husband children as a good wife should? It was all a great mystery to them, but then it was well known that European ladies were incomprehensible to all civilized people and why should this one be any different?

With a rush of affection for them both, Trudie placed the baby in her mother's arms and watched as Wu Chao held her close to her, her eyes tight shut to hide the tears of gratitude that it had been decided her child should live. It was a moment Trudie was to remember all her life long. It was the moment when she realized all humanity to be one, and that Wu Chao was already more her friend than were any of the English girls she had left behind in England. For the first time since she had arrived in Singapore, she had a purpose in life.

'She'll be as beautiful as her mother when she grows up!' she said aloud.

Swee Neo shook her head. 'Baby have ugly nose. Round eyes.'

Which put her in her place, Trudie thought with a chuckle. But, as she had never thought of herself as being anything remarkable to look at, she didn't mind a jot. The baby would live and that was all that mattered to her!

Chapter Nine

With her new-found confidence, Trudie took to visiting Wu Chao more and more in the next few days. Besides, she was in despair over her own house which was rapidly being taken apart and put up again in accordance with the instructions of the strange Chinaman, and she was no nearer finding a good reason as to why she should evict Wu Chao and take possession of the other house, though she was still working on the problem.

It was, she told herself, no more than her Christian duty to visit the mother and child and make sure they were progressing satisfactorily. This wasn't as easy at it seemed, for the *anuk dukun*, the midwife's assistant, had taken up residence in Wu Chao's house, planning to stay there for a full month after the birthing, and her disapproval of Trudie was plain to them all. Once, Wu Chao had tried to apologize for the other woman.

'She not knowing Eulopean woman. So solly, *Kak* Tludie.'

'It doesn't matter,' Trudie had assured her. 'I don't know your customs, either.'

She rapidly came to the conclusion that she would have been much better off if she had remained ignorant of the extraordinary things the Chinese did. How glad she was that nobody need ever know she had witnessed such primitive, superstitious customs for, not even to Letty, could she ever have explained how she had seen such things without making a single protest! She had searched her conscience with increasing anxiety, wondering if she should put her foot down once and for all but, as she had no idea what good Christian women did in the same circumstances, she held her tongue and pretended not to notice the worst of the superstitious excesses that surrounded Wu Chao's every movement.

It was a relief when the midwife departed back to Malacca in a haze of last-minute instructions, all of which the *anuk dukun* seemed to know perfectly well for herself. It was she, after all, who did all the work, as she pointed out to anyone who would listen to her. Who else washed all the soiled linen? Who else saw to the 'smoking' of the patient, she would like to know, let alone the tying of the cloth girdle round Wu Chao's waist to restore her figure? It was a disgrace the way she was treated! It was a disgrace the way that uncivilized barbarian female devil came and went, poking her nose in where it wasn't wanted! It meant trouble, as Wu Chao should have known without being told!

Wu Chao listened and smiled, saying nothing at all. It was Swee Neo who told the old woman to shut up. She knew how grateful her sister was that Trudie had insisted her child should live, but in her heart she agreed with the midwife; barbarians remained barbarians and couldn't help making trouble for everyone else. Look at the trouble the dead Jeremy Maddock had been, and women were always more dangerous than men, as anyone could tell you.

Trudie strode up the tiled steps with even more determination than usual a couple of days after the birth. They were taking the roof off the other house, a fact which gave her a certain satisfaction for it seemed to her an excellent excuse for putting off her cousins' visit. The tiles always attracted her and she stopped to admire them as usual, noticing all over again the quaint curved lines of the steps and the way the tiles had been fashioned to fit them exactly. She wondered why similar tiles hadn't been found for the other house. There was little that was valuable or attractive in the other house. In fact, she couldn't think of a single feature that recommended it to her. *This* was the house she wanted!

She was still standing on the verandah, looking down at the blue Portuguese ships sailing across an endless sea on the steps, when she heard Wu Chao's voice inside raised in anger.

'What's the matter?' she demanded loudly from the doorway.

Neither woman paid any heed to her. The assistant midwife was cringing away from the furious Wu Chao, who was standing over her baby as though she was in fear that she would be taken away from her after all.

'I came to see – ' Trudie began.

Wu Chao straightened her dress. 'You not understand. This nothing to do with you!'

Trudie went straight to the baby's cot. Ever since she had been born a pot containing the placenta had been put beside her head – another of the repulsive customs that Trudie had pretended to ignore. It was this pot to which Wu Chao now pointed.

'No father to take to river to throw away. No fortune for baby.'

Trudie almost laughed. Was that all? What did it matter what became of the placenta? 'Is that all?'

'*All?* What you mean, is that all? I tell you no father – '

'Why don't you apply to Mr Rhys?' Trudie asked her.

'Rhys man? Rhys man not father! You know Rhys man not father of baby!'

Trudie rocked back on to her heels. If Mr Rhys wasn't the father, who was? He was the only possible European man around, as far as she knew, who would have married

Wu Chao and brought her out here. Mr Rhys, being a Welsh radical, didn't think like the other Europeans she knew. He was the only one she knew who would even contemplate having a relationship with a Straits Chinese woman. Everybody else was far too respectable to go outside their own circle of friends for a wife. Maybe a mistress was different, she thought it probably was, though she was honest enough to admit she knew very little about such things, but mistresses weren't often introduced to respectable women as far as she knew, or left around for such women to discover for themselves.

'Not the father?' she repeated.

Wu Chao was as puzzled as was Trudie. 'You know he is not father.' Understanding flared at the back of her eyes. 'Oh, I see. Never mind. Rhys man do very well.'

Trudie went to fetch him, trying not to let the problem of the father seize her mind to the exclusion of all else. She found him arguing with the Malay housebuilders who now wanted to pull the whole house down and start again. Together, they were poring over the plans the *Feng Shui* expert had left with them, all of them infuriated by the superstitious interference they were being subjected to and none of them really wanting to make the changes the little Chinese had demanded.

'What do you want?' Mr Rhys snapped at Trudie. 'Haven't you and the Ki sisters been enough trouble?'

'What trouble have I been?' Trudie demanded. 'I can't think of anyone who could live happily in that house as it was!'

He looked helplessly at her. If she didn't know, he certainly wasn't going to be the one to explain it to her. 'What do you want?' he asked again more gently.

'It's to do with the baby,' she began to explain. 'There's

some ceremony the father has to attend to. I thought you might do it?'

'You did, did you?'

Trudie watched him carefully for any sign of guilt. There was none. Nevertheless, if Mr Rhys wasn't the father, who was? If he wouldn't fetch the man to carry out his own responsibilities, he shouldn't be surprised if she expected him to take the unknown father's place.

'I wouldn't have bothered you if it hadn't seemed important!'

He was as angry as she for a brief moment, before the absurdity of the whole situation struck him.

'It isn't a Christian ceremony,' he reminded her. 'What do I have to do?'

Trudie was struck dumb. 'I don't know,' she admitted after a while. Her conscience smote her, making her go on, 'I don't want to ask you to do something you don't like – '

He sighed. 'I suppose you know the Chinese have a saying that if you save someone's life you're responsible for them thereafter? Don't get too involved with these people's lives, Mrs Maddock. You'll get hurt if you do.'

'I already have a responsibility. This is all Maddock land, Mr Rhys.'

'Until your relations relieve you of your inheritance! You can be sure that *he* won't let you stay here a moment longer than it takes him to look round the place!'

Trudie shut her mouth in a mutinous line. He was a fool, this man, if he thought she would go quietly back to Singapore. 'There's another Chinese saying,' she said, 'that women hold up half the sky! I don't see why I shouldn't have some say in the matter!'

He was surprised by her knowing that. 'It only means

that women do half the world's work, not make the decisions – '

Which brought her back to the baby. 'And bring the children into the world. I think they deserve better from men for that.'

Again he was surprised. She had been a child when she had arrived, he thought, but she was growing up fast.

'Very well, Mrs Maddock. I'll act as stand-in for the father just this once, but I want it clearly understood that I'm employed as manager here, not as general dogsbody according to your whim!'

Trudie straightened her spine, her head well back to give her the sensation of looking down on him, even if he was nearly a couple of feet taller than she. It was a gesture she had borrowed from Queen Victoria.

'Of course, Mr Rhys.'

He gave her back look for look. 'Manager,' he repeated.

To his surprise she gave him one of her sudden, unexpected smiles. 'I'll do my very best to remember,' she promised.

Swee Neo came to the very edge of the verandah as soon as she saw Mr Rhys. She was happy to relapse into her own tongue as she told him of the importance to the child's future of what he was about to do.

'The *periok uri*, the pot containing the placenta, must be thrown into the nearest river, but first you must crack the pot with the handle of this knife so that it sinks straight away and doesn't float. Then you must walk home, without looking back at the pot once, or the child will develop a squint.'

'Is that all?' Mr Rhys asked bitterly.

Swee Neo looked unhappy. 'Should be father,' she said in English. She looked from Mr Rhys to Trudie. 'Better she go to Wu Chao, no?'

'Yes.'

Trudie turned from the Chinese girl to Mr Rhys, anxious not to lose the advantage she thought she had won from him earlier. She resented it that they should decide between them what she should do. 'I'm sure you're just the man for the job!' she told him flatly.

His look made her wish the words unsaid. She still suspected him of being the baby's father, but if he wanted to deny it it was really none of her business. Unconsciously, she wove her fingers together, feeling guilty. If she hadn't been so bored and lonely in her own house, she thought, she wouldn't have become involved in all these wretched pagan customs. Her father might be right when he had told her she would surely end up in hell, as would every female he knew except Hermione, but the child was alive because of her and she wouldn't be if Trudie had looked the other way and she was sure that that would have God's approval and surely that was far more important than what any *man* thought of her?

She walked away with all the dignity she could command, wondering why Mr Rhys disapproved of her so strongly. It was true she had an unfortunate manner sometimes, a trifle overbearing, though only because she was really, deep down, unsure of herself, but she suspected it was something more than that he held against her. He had disapproved of her before he had ever met her.

Wu Chao looked up when she came into the bedroom. She was feeding her baby, a fact she tried to hide from Trudie at first, until she realized that, far from being upset by it, Trudie was obviously thinking about something quite different.

'Rhys man take *periok uri*?' she asked timidly.

Trudie nodded. 'Are you sure he isn't the father of your baby?' she demanded crossly.

Wu Chao winced. 'You know Rhys man not father.'

Trudie sat down on the nearest chair, fanning herself with a banana leaf she had brought in with her. 'If Mr Rhys isn't the father, who is?'

Wu Chao's only answer was silence. She went on feeding the baby, glancing at Trudie at intervals through her lashes. She was getting used to Trudie's strange ways: the way she raised her voice to get her own way, never having learned to please a man; and the way she pretended that she knew all about everything, though Wu Chao secretly suspected she knew much less than any Chinese girl of her age.

'How long you married to Mr Maddock?' she asked her gently.

'Two years. We were married in the spring of 1858. It was such a lovely day! I was truly happy that day!'

'But no baby come?'

Trudie had worried over that at first, until Letty had told her that it frequently took longer than a few short weeks to make a baby. Trudie had felt exactly as she had always felt when she came home from her honeymoon, although everyone seemed to have expected to find her different. Her old inadequacy in the face of her family's expectations overwhelmed her.

'It wasn't my fault! It takes time, doesn't it, and there was no time!'

'You wanted baby?'

'I don't know,' Trudie admitted. 'At the time I was more interested in Septimus's Emporium. It was terribly important to us both that he should make a success of it. It was important to Mr Maddock, too, of course, otherwise he wouldn't have left me behind in England to help Septimus get started.'

Wu Chao nodded thoughtfully. 'Mr Maddock, he say you have mind like man in business. Is true?'

'I'm better at it than my brother,' Trudie acknowledged. 'When did Mr Maddock tell you that?' She was flattered and it showed.

'Never mind. I t'ink 'bout that. You t'ink also.'

What a strange conversation, Trudie thought. She felt very grown up, discussing marriage with the Chinese woman under such circumstances, almost as though it was a shared experience, which it wasn't. She might be ignorant of most aspects of married life, but even she had known there was more to it than had passed between herself and Mr Maddock. Watching Wu Chao nursing her baby, Trudie wondered if Mr Maddock had ever really seen her as a wife at all. She had felt more like his favourite ward, guarding his interests in England while he increased his wealth abroad. Looking at Wu Chao, though, Trudie was beginning to think that if that was the only reason he had married her, he couldn't have thought very highly of her as a woman, and the knowledge hurt.

'I think I'll go and meet Mr Rhys,' she said abruptly. 'He didn't want to go. He doesn't like me and still less does he like taking orders from me.'

Wu Chao patted her baby on the back, bringing up the wind. 'Why you mind what Rhys man t'ink?'

'I can't imagine!' Trudie answered dryly. 'I employ him, after all, not the other way round.'

Wu Chao laughed. She shook her head. 'I t'ink you employ no one. You woman. Same England, same here, men have all money, women have none.'

Thinking of her cousins, Trudie gave her a disgruntled look. 'It's more than time all that was changed!' she said firmly.

Wu Chao shook her head again. 'Never change. Only way is make man t'ink he number one. Better you have Rhys man as ally than enemy.'

Trudie was in no mood to listen, however. Whenever she thought of her cousins coming to take charge of what was rightfully hers, she burned with rage and it seemed to her that Mr Rhys was Mr Horton's ally in depriving her of her inheritance. It was probably that he didn't like taking orders from a woman rather than that he actively disliked her – look how tiresome he had been over her wanting to live in the house of her choosing and not in the ramshackle place he had organized for her! – or it may have been merely because he felt threatened by her, as she did by him most of the time – she had no means of knowing, but she knew better than to rely on his support against Mr Horton's legal rights over *her* property. She was sure they would be as thick as thieves, which was no more than what they both were in her opinion.

She had seen the grim expression on Mr Rhys's face as he had departed, pot in hand, and she had felt like a cat on hot bricks ever since. She didn't stop to ask herself why she should worry that she might have pushed him too far, but she went to meet him all the same, her long skirts drooping in the dust and the hot sun bringing a glow of perspiration to her face.

She met him more than a mile down the track, about halfway to the river. It was the longest walk she had attempted and she was hot and tired when she at last saw him coming towards her. Worse still, her guilt had had time to build up within her and not even the singing of various hymns, such as 'The Church's one foundation is Jesus Christ, her Lord Christ is Made the Sure Foundation', had had any effect on her certainty that she had failed Mr Rhys, failed herself, and failed her God, and all because she hadn't had the courage to denounce a pagan custom that she didn't even understand, let alone appreciate what it was all about.

She was prodding at a termites' castle with her closed

parasol and watching the strange white ants run backwards and forwards, trying to escape her, when the first thought that she might be being watched by a tiger first occurred to her. She turned her head very slowly, just in time to catch sight of a small procession of people backing off into the jungle, as horrified by the sight of her as she was of them. Terror lifted the hair on the back of her neck and she wished she hadn't come. To her relief she saw Mr Rhys walking towards her and, picking up her skirts, she ran towards him, babbling some nonsense as she went.

He caught her to him, calming her and putting her away from him again. The shock of finding herself clasped against the wall of his chest, even briefly, sent everything else out of her head.

'What scared you?' he asked her, concern in his dark eyes.

'Some men. I thought it was a tiger,' she admitted with a shaky smile. 'I remember that the Buddha, in one of his existences, gave up his life so that a starving tigress could feed her cub. I must be a better Christian than I thought!'

He stared down at her, thinking that perhaps he could like this strange woman after all. 'Who told you about Buddha?' he asked, teasing her to help her get over her fright.

'Mr Maddock. It's very important to know about all sorts of things like that if one is going to buy and sell Oriental *objets d'art*.'

'I see. What else did the two of you talk about?'

'Japanese painting, Chinese porcelain, things like that.'

'Didn't you ever discuss your own future with him?'

Trudie looked away. 'There wasn't time. I knew I would come out here and live with him sooner or later, meanwhile Septimus's Emporium was to be my first concern.' She gave him an ironic look. 'Septimus didn't entirely appreciate my interest, but he wouldn't have done half as well without me beside him. Not all women are fools, you know.'

He began to walk back towards the compound. 'You're pretty proud of that Emporium, aren't you?'

'Yes. You'll think me immodest to say so, but I really am better than almost anyone else when it comes to assessing what will sell and what won't. Mr Maddock taught me, you see, and *he* was a splendid teacher because it really interested him to know about such things. Septimus makes the mistake of being more interested in the money than in the commodities he's selling.'

'Is that why you married Mr Maddock?'

Trudie retreated into herself. 'Not entirely,' she said.

She found the heat more enervating than she had expected when she had set out to meet him. She tried to remember how important it had been to her to make him some kind of apology for forcing him to participate in a ceremony he didn't like.

'I'm sorry you had to take the pot to the river,' she began. 'It wasn't my place to order you to do such a thing, but I thought you were the baby's father. If you're not, who is?'

Mr Rhys was completely taken aback by this attack. 'Can't you guess?' he asked her.

'I wouldn't ask if I knew,' she answered irritably. '*Someone* must have brought Wu Chao out here to the compound!'

'You're right there, *bach*.' Mr Rhys took out a handkerchief and wiped the sweat off his face and the back of his neck. 'There's no easy way of telling you this, Mrs Maddock. You were married to the man after all, so you probably knew him better than anyone – almost anyone,' he amended. 'He was a man who took a lot of knowing – '

'You mean Wu Chao was his mistress!'

'Look you, Mrs Maddock, why don't you ask Wu Chao yourself what she was? She won't hold it against you!'

'That isn't the point,' Trudie responded soberly. 'It isn't easy for me to discuss such things with – with a man, but you are the only other European here, Mr Rhys. Doesn't that mean anything to you?'

He shrugged his shoulders. 'Not just at this moment it doesn't.'

She flushed angrily. 'No! Because you're Welsh and have no allegiance to anyone or anything! I should have known better than to think you might help me! Well, I shan't lower myself to ask Wu Chao anything at all – '

He put his hands on her shoulders and turned her to face him. 'She's a better woman than you'll ever be, Gertrude Maddock, Chinese or not! You'll be the fool I first took you for if you look down on her because she isn't a narrow-minded Christian like yourself! The Chinese are a quarter of the world's population! Who are you to decide that their gods and virtues are beneath your notice?'

It was irresistible not to tease her a little. She asked for it with every breath she drew, sticking her nose in the air and pretending to know all about life when she was nothing but an ignorant young girl. He glared at her, relishing the task ahead of him.

'All right, Mrs Maddock! Your husband *married* Wu Chao according to her own rites. He took her to wife, brought her out here, and lived with her as a man does live with the woman of his choice!'

Her white face betrayed the shock he had dealt her. 'I don't believe you!' she whispered.

'What else was he to do when you chose to linger in

England minding your brother's business instead of your own?'

'You mean Mr Maddock's the father of the baby?'

He wished he had been less brutal. Her eyes had a bruised look and the heat of the sun had caught the end of her nose. She looked very young and vulnerable. 'It's better you should know,' he said roughly.

She stood still, putting up her parasol with trembling fingers to give herself time to think. What a fool she had been! Why had it never occurred to her that Mr Maddock was the father? She wished yet again that innocence in women was not confused with ignorance in her society; life was hard enough to deal with without being handicapped in that particular way.

'It's bigamy!' she said aloud.

'Not really,' the Welshman told her. 'English law doesn't apply exclusively out here. The Chinese follow their own ways, as we do, and the Tamils, and the Malays follow their Islamic customs. No one will bring a charge against him.'

'Of course they won't! He's dead!'

'True. Wu Chao and the baby are your responsibility if they're anybody's now.'

Trudie knew then what it meant to be frightened. Surprisingly, she wasn't immediately concerned about her own feelings; she was overwhelmed by her own inadequacy in the face of a situation that would have been inconceivable days, *hours* ago. It was so unfair that Mr Maddock should have placed her in such a quandary! She would have liked to have known what *he* would have done to resolve matters. She would have liked to have known what she was going to do also! She straightened her back, feeling very young and afraid and, at the back of her mind, like the refrain of a song she never wished to hear again, she couldn't help going over and over the puzzle of what could have happened between the Mr Maddock she knew and Wu Chao that he should be the father of her baby.

'Mr Horton won't see that it has anything to do with me,' she said dryly. 'What am I to do?' She hesitated, making a decision, then she faced him with that characteristic lift of her chin. 'You'll have to help me!'

He was startled. 'Me?'

'You're my manager, aren't you? Why shouldn't you have a mistress and child? Don't you see that *that* wouldn't be any business of mine – or of Mr Horton's?'

Mr Rhys eyed her with naked dislike. 'Not me, Mrs Maddock! If I'd wanted to be stifled by your English respectability and your English laws, I'd have stayed at home in Wales. I came to be free of servitude and pretence and to make a fortune for Welsh people to enjoy – my own family! It's no concern of mine what your cousin sees fit to do with your inheritance! If it doesn't please me to work for him, I'll move on elsewhere. Now, tell me how I'd do that if I saddled myself with a Chinese mistress and a girl-child, who wouldn't be a problem at all if you hadn't chosen to meddle in things you don't understand!'

'I suppose you'd have allowed the child to be murdered just because she's a girl?' Trudie roared back at him.

'All I'm saying is that my money goes home to my own mother, to feed and clothe my own brothers and sisters, before I take on any more responsibilities, even a wife of my own choosing!'

'Then you won't help?'

'I can't help!'

Her contemptuous scorn cut him to the quick. She had a way of getting under his guard that was particularly irritating, especially as he suspected she had no idea of how people like his own family were forced to live. He knew her father to be a parson with private means and, if Trudie didn't seem to have much money of her own, he was sure she had never gone hungry, or known any of the depredations that were an everyday affair amongst his own people.

'Mr Horton is a man of the world,' he tried to defend himself. 'Why should he condemn your husband for doing something he'd probably like to do himself?'

Trudie uttered a hollow laugh. 'I assure you Mr Horton would take no joy in a Chinese mistress – '

'A Chinese *wife*, Mrs Maddock!'

Trudie was effectively silenced. Mistress or wife, there was no way she could ever explain Wu Chao's presence to Mr Horton, or to Cousin Hermione. Neither of them would ever accept that because a few Chinese rites had been performed over the union Wu Chao had any rights on Jeremy Maddock's estate. Good heavens, they would pare her own rights down to a bare minimum and there was no doubt that she was his legal widow in the sight of God and society. They would push her back to England and her father's care as fast as they decently could, dividing her husband's property to suit themselves. What none of them would ever admit was that she was entitled to make her own decisions about her own inheritance. She was as much a chattel as were any of the slaves on her family's estate in the West Indies.

'A female, Mr Rhys,' she said sadly. 'There isn't a lot of difference between a wife and a mistress in the last resort, is there? Both Wu Chao and I will be forced to do what some man decides for us unless I can think of some way out for us! And don't think I won't, because I will. And if you won't help me, I'll find somebody else who will! Someone with more courage than a Welshman who's only good for singing songs in a language no one else understands!'

He stood watching her rigid back as she walked away

from him for a long time, thinking what a proud piece she was. Then, suddenly, he threw his hat up into the air and caught it again. 'So what are you going to do about that, me boyo?' he asked himself, not liking any of the answers that immediately occurred to him. 'Women are the very devil, no matter what the colour of their skins, and that's the truth! But where does that leave you?'

Mr Horton came alone.

'You couldn't expect me to expose my dear Hermione to cholera, or to make do in this shack you call a house,' he explained to Trudie. 'You were fortunate I could come myself at a moment's notice, but there, we all have a duty to our families or there would be anarchy in the world!'

His sympathy, if he felt any for her on the loss of her husband, was kept strictly under control. 'Does this place make any money?' he asked her.

Trudie didn't answer directly. She asked after Cousin Hermione, expressing her pleasure in her relative's social successes in Singapore, putting off the moment for as long as she could when she would be obliged to summon Mr Rhys to turn over the books to her unwelcome visitor.

'I am not sure coffee is the right crop to grow here,' she murmured. 'You must tell me what you think, Cousin Christopher.' It was the first time she had ever addressed him as such and she saw at once that it had been a mistake. He didn't relish the connection any more than she did.

'What can you possibly know about such things?' he retorted.

'Nothing,' she answered frankly, 'but I hope to learn. Mr Maddock must have had something in mind when he acquired all this land and I mean to find out what it was.'

'No, no.' Mr Horton waved all such notions away. 'Your cousin Hermione and I have discussed your future together, my dear, and we can see no other course open to you other than returning to England. Your parents will be glad to have you home again. Your mother hasn't been in the best of health these last months and it will be a comfort to her, no doubt, to have her youngest daughter to fetch and carry for her.'

Trudie clenched her fists. 'Mama has always suffered from her nerves,' she agreed. 'However, I think I should tell you at once that nothing is going to induce me to go back to England!'

Christopher Horton's jaw dropped. 'I've bought your passage on the next ship!'

'How kind, but you really shouldn't have gone to so much trouble before we had an opportunity to discuss the matter. You see, my marriage to my husband was an unusual one in that we were business partners as well as man and wife. I should be failing in my duty if I were to let all his good work go for nothing because of the cholera!'

For a few triumphant moments she thought he was going to let her have her way, but one look round the half-built house where she was living was enough to strengthen his faltering resolution.

'I can't allow it!' he said at last. 'If anyone were to discover how you were living, what would they think of me for allowing it? No, no, the best I can offer you is that you set up an establishment in Singapore, with some respectable female to keep you company, and even that will depend on my being able to find sufficient funds from your inheritance to make it possible. You can't expect your cousin and me to support you, you know, not when you have a perfectly good family of your own willing and waiting to do so!'

'I think,' Trudie said thoughtfully, 'I should prefer to

live in Malacca. The Beresfords were very kind to me the short time I was there – '

'I'm sure. However, I can only tell you what they told me, that Jeremy Maddock had a very peculiar reputation, from which, in such a small place, you'd be bound to suffer as his widow – '

'Whatever did the poor man do?' Surely, Trudie thought, they couldn't have heard about Wu Chao in Malacca, though, as the Chinese woman came from there, she supposed it was possible that they had and had disapproved.

'I won't sully your ears with the details,' Mr Horton answered quickly. 'Suffice it to say I shouldn't want any scandal to be attached to Hermione through her family.'

'Certainly not!' Trudie agreed robustly. 'That would never do! It makes me all the more certain that Malacca would be a much more suitable place for me to live than Singapore.'

Mr Horton blew out his cheeks and glanced round the uncomfortable house once again. 'I really ought to consult your father before I come to any final decision. He has more right than I to advise you, being your natural guardian, even while he is so far away.'

'My father's only emotion where I am concerned is one of acute dislike,' she told him. 'Am I to have no say in my own future, Mr Horton?'

He had looked embarrassed for a moment by that. 'We'll think about Malacca again when I've had a chance to look into your finances, Miss Trudie,' he promised.

'Mrs Maddock, if we must be formal,' she corrected him, smiling through her teeth.

'Mrs Maddock,' he confirmed. But the reminder had made him angry, because neither he nor Hermione liked to acknowledge Trudie's dignity as a married woman. 'I'll see you in the morning,' he added. 'Your manager is going to give me a bed tonight.'

There was no opportunity to discuss anything with him in the morning, however. One night away from the comforts of civilization was more than enough for Mr Horton to tolerate. As soon as the sun was up, he had his horse brought round and, taking the plantation's accounts with him, he set off for Malacca and a few nights in the old Stadthuys as a guest of the Lieutenant-Governor and Mrs Beresford.

Trudie was more angry than she had ever been in her life. 'How could you let him go?' she demanded of the luckless Mr Rhys, stamping her foot. 'I will not go back to England and he'll find it much easier to say that I should when he doesn't have to tell me so face to face!'

Mr Rhys's eyes creased with reluctant amusement. 'I'll tell you one thing, he doesn't want you in Singapore!' he told her.

'I know that!'

'Then what will you do?' he asked, intrigued. He tried not to notice the forlorn look in her eyes. He hadn't cared much for Mr Horton, but he had seemed a decent enough man in all conscience.

'I don't know,' Trudie said. 'But whatever I do it will be as the result of my own decision! I may even take it into my head to manage my own plantation!' she warned him.

He tipped his hat to her and grinned. 'If you say so, ma'am.' His smile grew even wider. 'Your husband kept two lots of accounts, Mrs Maddock. It might interest you to compare them before you make your final decision. I gave your cousin the more public version to keep him quiet. The second version isn't for anybody's eyes but our own. That was our agreement together, and I take it that is the way you still want it?'

'Yes, it is,' she said.

Amen to that, she added to herself in triumph. Oh yes, indeed. Amen to that!

Chapter Ten

Wu Chao held her baby close. The small bundle was all the more precious to her because she had nearly been snatched away from her. It probably would have been the wise thing to do, she reflected. Swee Neo had been quite right about that, for what kind of life could the girl-child expect? The British were a strange kind of barbarian people, as everyone knew. Despite her father's blood, not one of them would consider the child to be British and so it was far better that she be considered Nonya from the very beginning! But there were difficulties there, also, for then she would have no father to call her own, no one would take responsibility for her future as her own father should have done.

Never mind. Perhaps the loud foreign devil woman with the huge feet would bring the baby good luck. *Kak* Trudie was not like the other foreign women Wu Chao had come across. She had seen these others travelling around Malacca in their horse-drawn carriages, wearing clothes that would be far better suited to their own damp, chilly climate, with terrible, arrogant manners that meant they were unaware of anyone else's existence. They made such remarks as that there were very few people in Malacca, ignoring those who were not the same as themselves. In the same way, they spoke of the many temples and mosques as sources of superstition and shut their ears when anyone tried to explain their beliefs to them, even though those beliefs had a far older pedigree than their own belief in the Man Jesus, about whom the Europeans quarrelled endlessly, for the

British had their own English priests and wouldn't attend the churches run by the skirted men who had first come with the Portuguese. Wu Chao thought them all mad, for what could any human being know of the life of the gods? One took the good things they offered and gave thanks. The good and the bad would be rewarded for their deeds in future lives – maybe they would even be gods themselves! – it mattered little when it came to making decisions in the here and now.

Never mind. *Kak* Trudie had one quality she understood very well, and could admire with a full heart. The English woman accepted her fate with a stoical courage that was almost Chinese. Wu Chao also believed that a wise person gave their luck a helping hand whenever the opportunity occurred. If they had to be bound together for life because they had each married Jeremy Maddock, it would have been far worse for her if Mr Maddock's *Nai-nai* had been a less determined woman. Wu Chao had already heard she had refused to return to England and had refused to be ordered to Singapore also.

The future still looked bad to Wu Chao, never mind. She examined the baby carefully, looking for anything that might remind her of the foreign devil she had married; she could find nothing; the child seemed wholly hers. She sighed with relief, feeling again the bitterness she had known when her anxious parents had first told her she was to be married to a foreign devil to safeguard the future of the rest of her family. He was strong and powerful, they had told her, an Englishman recently returned from securing his fortune in a new venture in that land. Even more important was his appetite for owning land. He had already bought one plantation, and he had let it be known he was in the market for others. The Straits Chinese had always known the value of owning land. They already owned a great deal of it themselves, together with the tin mines up north. They imported their own cousins, indentured for the price of their passage, and put them to work to gain still more land and wealth for their extended families. Marriage, too, was an easy way of gaining title to future wealth. If her family were careful and wise, no thieving government would ever be strong enough to take away from them what was rightfully theirs. Her distaste for the Englishman was a small price to pay for all that.

Not that Wu Chao had disliked Mr Maddock any more than any other foreign devil she had met. His scent was unpleasant, but she had grown used to it after a time. On the whole, he had been a kindly man, asking little of her, and she had tried to be contented with her lot.

Never mind. She would not go over the ceremonies that had given her to him again in her mind. She could still feel the horror she had felt when she had been taken from the dancing and the other ceremonies to learn to pay obeisance, *belajar sohjar*, as it was in her own language. The *sangkek um*, a woman of great experience, had given her tuition on how to be the perfect traditional bride, severely pinching her for every mistake she had made as she had learned to pay her obeisance to man and God, and was coached in the swaying gait that every bride was expected to perfect. If it had been for another husband, one who could appreciate her virtues, Wu Chao wouldn't have minded the agony with which she had rehearsed taking her groom his first meal as her husband. At the time, she had been filled with fear that she would do something wrong and humiliate herself before the foreign stranger. What had actually happened had been far worse. 'Never mind about all that,' he had told her. 'What I want is you here, in my bed!' She had been his wife, but he had treated her from the start as if she were a whore taken from the streets, without any dignity or pride.

She could barely remember the vowing ceremony, which both groom and bride performed in their own establishments. She doubted Mr Maddock had made his vows at all. What she could remember – indeed, would never be able to forget! – was his whoop of joy as he had carried her off to his house, shrugging his shoulders at her parents' protests as if they were of as little account as their daughter. She had known then that it was all true, that Europeans were a vulgar people, with no manners or respect, and that she would have to put up with him for the rest of her life.

Never mind, the cholera had put an end to his existence, despite the careful nursing she had given him. She had been afraid of the cholera, all the time she had been afraid, but it had been her duty and so she had nursed him, laying him out with her own hands when he had finally breathed his last. It was only then she had learned about his *Nai-nai* coming, and had wondered why she hadn't come sooner so that *she* could have nursed him and put up with his groans and ill temper.

Worse, had been to learn that the whole marriage had been for nothing. Jeremy Maddock had made no acknowledgement of her existence in his will. She might just as well not have been his wife at all. Her family's anger had been fierce and terrible. Why, they had demanded, should they do anything for Jeremy Maddock's daughter?

Yet *Kak* Trudie had chosen to save the child of her husband. Wu Chao had soon discovered that Trudie was almost as helpless as she was herself. It had come as a shock that English women were no more in charge of their own affairs than if they had been children. Trudie had had to wait for her cousin's husband to tell her what to do, a man it was obvious she disliked and distrusted. Now he had ridden away again and, if the two women didn't make some plan to take their future into their own hands, there would be nothing left for either of them.

Wu Chao screwed up her eyes and thought about Trudie. When she had first seen her she had felt the fear inside her as her own. She was a foreign devil, of course, she couldn't help that, but, unlike her barbarian husband, she had respect for the customs of others. The Rhys man wouldn't have taken the *periok uri* if she hadn't insisted on it. Better still, she had courage and she appreciated beautiful things – Chinese things. With a little help, she might become a civilized person. Yes, Wu Chao decided, that was the best thing for her to do: she would throw in her lot with the foreign woman and, together, they would make a fine future for themselves – and for the baby too!

Trudie arrived at Wu Chao's house in a thoroughly bad frame of mind. She walked up the tiled steps, trembling with indignation. 'May I come in?'

'Oh yes!' Wu Chao bowed low. 'Please to come in! Many t'ings for you and I speak together, no?'

'What things?' Trudie asked. Wu Chao was not usually so direct as she seemed prepared to be today.

'What your man-cousin like?'

'Awful!'

Wu Chao hid her mouth behind her hand. She thought him 'awful' too, but she wouldn't have dreamed of saying so. 'He bad man?'

Trudie gave her parasol a grumpy twirl. 'No, he isn't a bad man; at least, I don't think he is. He's doing what he thinks is right!'

'Ah!'

'Exactly. He hates everything to do with the plantation, but he sees it as his duty to interfere in everything Mr Rhys is trying to do. The last time Mr Horton visited us he threatened to dismiss Mr Rhys and take the management of the plantation into his own hands! I know more about growing coffee than he does! He'll bankrupt me! The only thing he's interested in is growing opium, or some such nonsense!'

Wu Chao's bland expression never changed. 'Not'ing you can do. He say I not wife, no money. You wife, still no money!'

Trudie lifted her chin. 'I am not going back to England!'

Wu Chao ushered her visitor into a chair, putting a glass of tea beside her, together with a pile of Trudie's favourite little cakes. It was important to put her in a receptive mood before she made her suggestion as to how they should manage their own future.

'There is Chinese saying, *moh ching, moh meng*. Velly wise saying.'

'What does it mean?' Trudie asked.

'No money, no life. Very true, no?'

'Yes,' Trudie agreed dryly. If Christopher Horton had much more to do with the plantation, there would be very little of either commodity for her, she thought. He was a fool!

'So, we make much money together, yes?'

Trudie jumped, not really taking in her hostess's remark. 'How?' she demanded as Wu Chao repeated herself.

Wu Chao tittered, nonplussed by this reaction. She would have preferred to skirt round the subject for a few minutes before committing herself. Her Chinese love of gambling made her chary of revealing all her cards at once. Trudie's reactions seemed childish to her, as immediate as the first thought that came into her head. How could she be successful in business when she didn't take the trouble to hide her thoughts from her inferiors, let alone those she considered to be her equals? Wu Chao had heard how she had stormed at Mr Horton, practically accusing him of theft, when any civilized person would have swallowed her anger and charmed her cousin into leaving her alone, if that was what she wanted. Wu Chao had watched her mother manage her father too often not to have learned the valuable lesson of how a mere female could manage to get her own way with a man.

'How much you like Mr Maddock?' Wu Chao countered carefully.

'I don't know. It's two years since I last saw him.'

Wu Chao inclined her head. 'You marry Mr Maddock same reason I do? Mr Maddock rich man, much property. Your blother poor man.'

Trudie bridled angrily. 'There were other reasons!'

'But you want blother successful man, with fine business, no? How much you want for blother and how much you want for you?'

Trudie was as surprised and shocked as if she had been caught naked in public. She had never troubled about her motives in marrying Mr Maddock. It had seemed a good idea, if only because it provided her with an escape route from her father's house. Had she done it for Septimus? She had told herself she had, but she knew now what she had known inside all along, she had been fascinated by the Emporium and had enjoyed every moment of its beginnings, choosing the right artefacts that would appeal to the discerning public, and bargaining for a good price that would bring the profits rolling in, thus pleasing both her brother and her husband but, most of all, herself.

She shut her eyes and opened them again. Slowly, she smiled a conspiratorial smile. It never occurred to her to deny it; she had wanted success for herself and she saw no harm in admitting as much to this discerning woman.

'My brother didn't like it that I'm a better business-woman than he is,' she confessed.

Wu Chao accepted that. 'All men t'ink women stupid. We show them different!'

Trudie chuckled. 'I'd love to see the back of Mr Horton!'

'Yes, but better not get angry. Never mind man-cousin. Never mind he take everything. Nothing you can do!'

'It isn't Mr Horton who will take everything, it's Cousin Hermione!' She grinned, looking like the child Wu Chao thought her. 'We have a saying in English that the female is deadlier than the male! Wait until you meet dear Hermione!'

'She want your money?'

Trudie nodded. 'Mr Horton has just finished telling me he can't spend all this time here for nothing; the estate must pay his expenses. His expenses come to more than ours put together!'

Her indignation amused Wu Chao. She wondered if Trudie knew that Mr Horton had told her to pack her bags and leave the plantation earlier that day. She slanted her an enigmatic look. 'He say I not wife, I whore,' she said finally.

Trudie's outrage made her feel good. She was sure now she had made the right decision. With the faintest smile of her own, she began to lay her cards on the table. 'Your blother sell many Chinese t'ings in his Emporium, yes?'

'Yes,' said Trudie.

'Malacca good place to find many such t'ings. My family go China all the time. Many contacts. We buy many t'ings. Your blother sell t'ings London. You agree?'

To Trudie it sounded like a dream come true. 'It's a bargain. We'll divide the profits three ways; one-third for Septimus, one for you, and one for me.'

Wu Chao looked doubtful. 'And baby?'

Trudie would have enjoyed seeing if she could get the better of Wu Chao if she held out for a while. Her regret showed clearly on her face as she gave up the idea. The baby was entitled to her share. 'The baby's expenses will come out of our two shares equally. When she gets older, we can talk about it again.'

It was better than Wu Chao had expected. She wouldn't have given away so much to a wife who was little better than a concubine. She found herself liking the barbarian lady as much as one could a foreign devil. Alone amongst her kind, she was acknowledging the baby to be Mr Maddock's legitimate daughter and herself a wife according to her own customs. It must be a hard thing for an ignorant barbarian to do, when everyone knew they thought their own ways to be always right and everybody else wrong.

'You speak for blother?'

A touch of steel came into Trudie's face. 'I speak for us all,' she said firmly. She meant it too. She might be a woman, but she knew herself to be the head of this particular family. The fate of them all rested fairly and squarely on her shoulders and on no one else's.

Hermione came unannounced. She came in a hired carriage and arrived in a flaming temper. She was hot and tired and she found it completely incomprehensible that anyone should actually live in such a place by choice.

'Good God, Trudie, you must have run mad to want to stay here!'

Trudie knew better than to argue with her cousin. 'Come inside,' she invited her. 'You'll feel better when you're rested and have had some of the ginger tea everyone drinks around here.'

Hermione managed a smile. 'I wouldn't have come but I realized that Christopher would never finish here unless I did. You've had him to yourself long enough, Cousin Gertrude! If I don't reclaim him, I may lose him to you altogether!'

Trudie knew a moment's complete disbelief. 'He'd finish a good deal sooner if he didn't travel back and forth from Malacca all the time!'

The caustic comment was lost on her cousin. 'It's very difficult socially in Singapore not to have a man on hand. You have no idea how many invitations I have lost because I've been on my own! I came to the conclusion I may as well be here as there. That was before I saw it, of course! I can't believe Christopher can be right when he says there's a whole fortune tied up in this place, if only he could find the key to it!'

'I doubt it,' said Trudie.

Hermione smiled. 'You've nothing to spend it on anyway.'

Trudie gave her an odd look. 'Mr Maddock's estate has more than just me to support.'

'Oh certainly! Christopher deserves his share for having to run the place for you. I've already written to Uncle Jonathan explaining why most of the ready capital should come to us – you'd find it impossible to manage if we *weren't* here, wouldn't you?'

'What makes you think so? Mr Rhys does all that's necessary for me, as he did for my husband.'

'Is he the Welshman Christopher has taken in such dislike?' Hermione asked lazily.

'He is Welsh, yes.'

'A dangerous radical! The sooner you are parted from his influence the better, my dear. You must admit I am far more experienced than you when it comes to men, and I dislike him!'

'Have you met him?' Trudie asked, startled.

'I don't need to. I'm told he actually speaks Welsh.'

'Mr Rhys is certainly unmistakable,' Trudie assured her. 'He is so large for one thing, and he's much browner than any other European I've seen because he is for ever going out and about in the full sun.'

Hermione's eyes narrowed. 'Are you in love with the man?' she demanded.

Trudie was astonished that she should ask. 'Oh really!' she said, losing all patience. 'He's a Welsh miner, not a gentleman! Of course I'm not in love with him!'

'I never thought you to be in love with Mr Maddock either,' Hermione pointed out thoughtfully. 'Don't be surprised if Uncle Jonathan insists you return to England, cousin. He knows better than anyone that you're your own worst enemy and will do anything to spite your family! You're fortunate Christopher is willing to manage your affairs, because you wouldn't like it to devolve on your father, would you?'

Trudie digested the implied threat. She thought it unlikely her father would come so far from his parish on her behalf, but then she remembered that Mr Horton had taken it into his head that there was some kind of a fortune tied up in the plantation. Her father would come for that. Or, failing him coming himself, he would send one of her older brothers, which would be equally disastrous to her own plans.

She made one final appeal to her cousin. 'Don't you ever wish, Cousin Hermione, that you could run your own affairs, without having to have some man to do it for you?'

Hermione uttered a brittle laugh. 'Good heavens, no! I wouldn't know where to begin! I am perfectly content with things as they are! It seems to me to have every advantage for us women. If you go about it the right way, any woman worthy of the name can get what she wants from her man! I know I can!'

'It's a little more difficult when your man is dead and buried,' Trudie pointed out.

Hermione didn't even blink. 'There's always a price to everything! You always were a greedy little thing. Look how you used to complain on fast days that you were hungry! Surely you don't resent Christopher and me taking our fair share?'

'I have to consider others besides myself,' Trudie began to explain. 'Mr Horton won't discuss such things with me, but somebody has to make proper arrangements for Mr Maddock's – other dependants!'

Hermione looked down at her perfectly manicured nails. 'Are you referring to the Chinese concubine?'

'And her baby.'

Hermione shrugged. 'I don't see that either of them are any business of yours. I can understand Uncle Jonathan's despair that you would ever learn to behave properly – no nice woman could have brought herself to mention their existence! Don't give them another thought, cousin. Christopher will send them packing and make sure they never make any claim on you. No wonder anyone who's anyone out here had reservations about asking that husband of yours to their homes! You can be glad you have us to support you, or you may have found yourself tarred with the same brush!'

Hermione refused to continue the conversation after that. She demanded to be shown into Trudie's bedroom where she lay down for an hour or so, saying she would stay to lunch and would return to Malacca later on with her husband.

'Why don't you stay the night and save yourself a long drive?' Trudie invited her, feeling it her duty to do so.

'Here? My dear girl, if Christopher found it too uncomfortable for him, what on earth makes you think I could survive a night here?'

And, indeed, after the disaster that luncheon turned out to be, Trudie was heartily glad to see the back of her. She had forgotten how much she had come to rely on Wu Chao providing her meals until Hermione refused even to try any of the Nonya dishes that were put before her. Mr Horton, too, who had joined them by that time, and who had never seen fit to complain before, refused the spicy food with a gesture of distaste. Trudie found them a selection of cold meats and pickled vegetables, hoping they wouldn't realize the source of the latter to be the same as the food they had already rejected.

'I think you should come to Malacca with us,' Hermione said with a shiver of distaste as she watched her husband carve her a massive helping of meat. 'Mrs Beresford seems to be quite fond of you, which only goes to show that you do know how to behave quite prettily when you want to, and she will welcome you as a guest for the next few weeks, I'm sure.'

'I prefer to stay under my own roof,' Trudie insisted, sounding as stubborn and as ungrateful as her family thought her to be.

'Until it falls around your head, I suppose?' Hermione said, exasperated.

'I shall move into the other house if that happens,' Trudie retorted.

Husband and wife exchanged glances. 'Isn't it – er – occupied?' Mr Horton murmured.

Some devil made Trudie want to laugh. 'The only thing wrong with this house is that it isn't built in accordance with the principles of *Feng Shui*,' she said with the utmost seriousness. 'That's why it's being pulled down, bit by bit, and put up again.'

'You're joking, aren't you?' Hermione retorted uncertainly.

'Certainly not,' said Trudie. 'I have it on the very best authority that it may be poking some dragon in the eye. It only takes one shake of the beast's head and the whole structure will come tumbling down!'

'Now I know you're mad!' Hermione said. 'You're not fit to be allowed out by yourself! I'm ashamed to be related to you!'

'That's easily answered,' Trudie said with a smile. 'All you have to do is go back to Singapore and forget all about me.'

Christopher Horton cleared his throat, casting a warning look at his wife. 'There's no need for you cousins to quarrel, Miss Gertrude, no need at all. Hermione is an excellent woman in every way, but, like most of her sex, I may say, she has little sense of humour. You shouldn't tease her, you know! You'd have found yourself in a fine mess if we hadn't been on hand to rescue you.'

Trudie lifted an eyebrow, despising them both. 'I wonder,' she said.

Trudie had more to worry about later that day. Her cousins had long since departed, leaving her to contemplate the damage they had already done to her modest inheritance. She was tempted to walk across to Wu Chao's house, a temptation she was doing her best to resist. There had to be a reason why her family disliked her, she thought. Whatever she did was wrong in their eyes. She felt quite different in Wu Chao's company, despite the vast differences between the two of them. For some reason, she had never felt the Chinese woman disliked her. She might find her incomprehensible and ugly, but she didn't dislike her, or, if she did, she didn't allow it to show.

'Mrs Maddock.'

Trudie came out of her reverie to see Mr Rhys's grim face looking at her over the verandah rail. She sighed. 'What's the matter now?'

'I think you should ride round the plantation and see the state it's in for yourself, ma'am. If that cousin of yours has his way we may as well give the whole place back to the jungle now as later. What's he trying to do?'

'He's searching for the fortune he thinks Mr Maddock hid out here.'

Mr Rhys looked at her furious face and wondered what she had been thinking about when he had disturbed her. Mr Horton was all very well in his way, but he knew nothing of growing coffee, or any other plant.

She put her head back and looked him straight in the eye. 'Mr Rhys, why did my husband buy this plantation? Do you know?'

He nodded slowly. 'There's tin up on the northern boundary. More than that, he was happy to grow coffee until the bottom dropped out of the market because he wanted the land. The Babas will always buy land around these parts, and he knew them to be the key to his artistic interests. I think you've come to much the same conclusion yourself, haven't you? It had another advantage that most commodities could be stored here and sent on to Malacca and Singapore when it was convenient. That's one of the things that doesn't figure in your cousin's set of accounts, but he'll have to know it sooner or later.'

'Much good that will do us! What shall I do when Mr Horton has rendered me penniless? One needs capital to trade.'

Mr Rhys gave her a wicked smile. She could believe him

to be a dangerous radical when he looked like that. 'It'll not be long before your cousins decide your husband came here in a fit of foolishness. They'll leave you alone after that.'

'But will my father?'

'Won't that depend on what he's told? If I were you, Mrs Maddock, I'd do some of the telling. Now, are you going to come and look at your poor diseased bushes and tell me if you want to go on growing coffee at all just now?'

Trudie stood up, wondering if she wouldn't do better to put this man in his place rather than go gadding with him on horseback all over the plantation. She wished she knew how far she could trust him, if at all.

'If I go and live in Malacca, what will you do?' she asked him.

'I'll keep the jungle from taking your grand fortune away from you until I can think of something better to do. Between us, we ought to make some kind of living, until we find something to grow that'll make all our fortunes!'

'I doubt it'll be rubber,' she told him. 'Mr Horton says there's no demand for that, any more than there is for his opium.'

'Not yet there isn't, Mrs Maddock. Not yet. Don't dismiss the money the opium trade can make too easily, though. It's the basis of a good many fortunes out here.'

She frowned. 'I have yet to have it explained to me why we should force it on the Chinese if their Emperor doesn't wish it,' she said.

'There's money in it, ma'am. As someone in Parliament said, isn't it better for the Chinese to smoke themselves silly on opium than that the producers in the British Empire should lose their main market?'

Trudie heaved a sigh. 'I don't know. I wish I did! A lot

of Englishmen smoke opium now and again for the good of their health as well as the Chinese!'

'Perhaps they can afford to,' he retorted, leaving her with the uncomfortable feeling that she had somehow disappointed him.

Wu Chao had Swee Neo with her. The two sisters folded their hands into their sleeves and bowed, their tiny feet rocking dangerously beneath them. It was Swee Neo who spoke.

'I blought you plesent from Malacca!' she said. She picked up a strange lacquered basket, decorated in black, scarlet, and gold. Carefully, she unpacked it, showing off each layer as she did so, the top ones with minute holes in them and the whole held together by the handle. 'Tiffin box!' she exclaimed.

In its way it was beautiful. Trudie handled it carefully, wondering what on earth it could be for. It looked newly made rather than antique, and the lacquer had been rather inexpertly applied at the bottom.

'For tiffin,' Swee Neo repeated.

'Tiffin?'

'Lunch. Wu Chao cook lunch and servant bring it to you, piping hot.' She gave Trudie a teasing smile. 'You like Nonya food, no?'

'Yes.'

Wu Chao laughed slyly. 'No Nonya food, no eat!' she summed it up neatly.

Trudie managed an uneasy smile of her own. 'I really do like all your food! I've never taken much interest in preparing things to eat before I came here. Our food doesn't taste much,' she added gloomily.

Wu Chao said something in Malay and both the Chinese girls laughed.

'You like Nonya cakes too!' Swee Neo teased Trudie.

'Yes, I do. I hate having to fast if there is no reason for it. I always have. Though it's much worse in the cold weather such as we have back in England.'

Swee Neo put the tiffin box into her hand. 'And now you have Nonya lunch every day! Wu Chao say you cook nothing, eat nothing. Very important you keep good health now!'

Feeling a little like a goose being fattened for the Christmas table, Trudie wondered what else the sisters had in store for her. They were plainly much excited by something, though Wu Chao's immaculate make-up betrayed very little of what she was thinking.

'You have money in England, *Kak* Tludie? Share in Emporium?'

'How do you know?' Trudie retorted.

For an instant, a sympathetic gleam shone in the Chinese woman's black eyes. 'Mr Maddock talk when we pillow sometime. Never mind. Blother guard your share, not man-cousin. Blother pay rent on house in Malacca, you t'ink?'

Trudie swallowed. 'What house?'

A wave of excitement passed through her. If only Septimus would agree! Could he possibly refuse her?

'Family house,' Wu Chao told her. 'B'long family long time. All right we live there, next door to house of childhood.'

Trudie's doubts surfaced, drowning her brief hopes. 'I couldn't live in the Chinese quarter,' she said regretfully. 'Even Septimus would put his foot down. No European would ever visit me there.'

'No tlouble. You have beautiful house which many people want. You live there alone. You tell Mrs Beresford you have Nonya maid because you not cook, not keep house. Mrs Beresford very envious of house! You see!'

Trudie looked stricken. 'But you're not my maid!' she objected.

'Better she t'ink maid, not partner. I no' worry. Nonya women stay in house all the time, you see. We make much money. Remember, *moh ching, moh meng*?'

'No money, no life,' Trudie repeated. 'If only Septimus will agree!' She thought for a moment, half smiling to herself. 'Do you know, I think he might,' she said at last, 'if only to keep me away from England and interfering with the Emporium. He was very glad to see the back of me, if the truth be known!'

The two Chinese ladies exchanged triumphant glances. 'You write blother straightaway!' they said in unison.

Colour touched Trudie's cheeks as she thought of what she would say to her brother. Anxiously, she crossed her fingers. 'Even Rats have to be lucky sometimes,' she reassured herself.

Wu Chao thought what a child she was. 'Rats first of the twelve animals, make very good beginnings, yes, no?'

'Yes,' said Trudie, not knowing the first thing about it. She knew Wu Chao looked on her as a child, easily pleased by little things most adults had long ago grown out of. At another time, she might have minded, but not now. Now, she was completely happy at the thought of being free of her cousins, her father, her whole family. It was something to be relished slowly and at leisure; something she was enjoying all the more because she liked the Chinese women very much indeed, even if Wu Chao had been her husband's concubine. At that moment, she couldn't have cared less about that!

* * *

Trudie had never seen another house quite like it. From the street, she had thought it small, though Wu Chao had explained that it went back a long way, the most private rooms being at the rear, protected from the eyes of strangers. The whole Ki family had been present the first time Trudie had seen it. The men had glowered at her, peering over each other's shoulders and hissing through their teeth. Trudie had pretended not to notice them and had been rewarded by an approving look from Wu Chao.

The women had been overcome by their curiosity. They were all dressed exactly the same, in Malay dress, with a tailored, elaborately embroidered coat over a narrow skirt. And they all had the same tiny feet, enclosed in minute embroidered slippers of brocade, on which they hobbled round the house, giving orders to the unfortunate servants as they went.

Most of the servants had only just arrived in Malacca. They were addressed in Cantonese for the most part and were dressed in the black pyjamas of all their kind. Trudie felt something in common with them when she realized that they, too, were despised for their large, unbound feet and their lack of those accomplishments which were considered essential for ladies of good breeding. Explosive sounds had accompanied their astonishment at finding a European amongst them. Trudie was probably the first one they had ever seen close up and they had been noisy in their derisory comments until Wu Chao had clapped her hands at them and sent them scurrying about their business.

Trudie had taken the trouble to call on Mrs Beresford that same day. She had been touched by the welcome she had received from the kindly woman. 'My dear, my husband and I have been so concerned for you ever since you left us! What a terrible ordeal you have been through!'

Trudie had thanked her, feeling rather a fraud. 'My cousins make it sound worse than it is, ma'am.'

'But to leave you penniless!'

'Oh, not penniless,' Trudie had denied. 'I have more than enough to be able to live here in Malacca, not in the best district, it's true, but I am relying on you to lend me countenance amongst the other Europeans here.'

'Willingly! Your cousins were of the opinion they couldn't do much for you, which worried my husband and me not a little! Are you sure you wouldn't be more comfortable with your family in England?'

'No,' Trudie had assured her bluntly. 'Comfort is not something I associate with my father's household. I much prefer life in the tropics.'

'Do you, dear?' Mrs Beresford had been quite unable to understand it. She herself had fond memories of her home in Hampshire and the pleasantly mild climate she had left behind her.

Trudie had smiled a naughty smile. 'I love it here,' she had said simply.

Now, as she looked around her very own house, she gave a little skip of pleasure. It was beautiful. She ran her fingers over a lacquered cabinet that took up one side of the sitting-room, admiring the elegant lines of the black and gold dragon that decorated it. Vases that she was sure were genuine Ming stood on either side of the door, and jade ornaments had been placed about the room, each one more beautiful than the last. To Trudie, it was sheer bliss to be in a place of her own, surrounded by beautiful things, and she knew she would never be able to thank Wu Chao enough for making it possible for her.

Beyond her own apartments, situated in the front of the house, and on the other side of the staircase and well, was where Wu Chao and her baby had already taken up residence. The Chinese woman was able to receive a constant stream of visitors from the rear where there was access out to a covered pathway shared by the whole terrace of houses. She had already turned part of her downstairs into a warehouse to store the brocades and jades they would import from China, exchanging them for incense, Indian cottons and vermillion.

'Our only difficulty,' Wu Chao had ventured when she had first shown Trudie round the household, 'is to find a man – an English man – to smooth our way with the authorities in Malacca. That way, no tlouble with customs, no tlouble with anyone!'

Trudie's spirits had sunk. She could think of no one she wanted to take on such a task. '*Not* my cousin!' she had exclaimed.

Wu Chao, too, had little time for Mr Horton, and even less for Mrs Horton, who had succeeded in confirming her every prejudice about European women. Hermione had not only ignored her, except to look her over with a glacial stare from her invisible eyes, but had deliberately and loudly cast aspersions on the whole Chinese people as being dirty, uncivilized, and totally without any morals. This last she had accentuated meaningfully and often. If she had not been *Kak* Trudie's cousin, Wu Chao would have put her in her place with a single, pithy sentence. She had thought long and hard what she would have said to the barbarian bitch, enjoying the exercise, but good manners forbade repeating any of this to Trudie. To insult any member of a person's family was to insult them.

'Man Rhys best choice!'

Trudie had been shocked at the idea. 'The Welshman! What does he know about antiques? He's a miner!'

'Not matter. He man.'

Trudie had recovered herself, turning the idea over in

her mind. 'It's ridiculous!' she had said finally. 'It's *we* who'll be doing everything, why won't they ever understand that?'

Wu Chao had shrugged. 'Custom. Rhys man understand velly well! Better than cousin. Better than anyone! Crever man, that one! You notice your man-cousin losing interest in plantation? Soon he go away, leave you in peace!'

Trudie had noticed, not that she had admitted it had anything to do with the Welshman. She had told herself that Septimus had had something to do with it, especially when he had written so enthusiastically about her plans for living in Malacca. She had poured out her heart to her brother, telling him everything that had happened to her. She had told him, as she could not tell anyone else, how much she disliked and despised the Hortons. She had even told him of her suspicions that if Christopher Horton had his way, he would fleece her of every penny piece Mr Maddock had left to her. Surely, it had been Septimus who had come to her aid?

'That's my brother's doing!' she had claimed.

Wu Chao had only looked at her. 'You b'lieve that?'

'Of course,' she said with dignity. After all, the Rhys man, as Wu Chao called him wasn't even a gentleman, so how could it be he?

Once she had moved into the house in Tun Tan Cheng Lock Street, which was still sometimes referred to as Heeren Street, as it had been when the Dutch were the lords of Malacca, she put the plantation to the back of her mind. Life had a new momentum and she was very well satisfied with everything about her new abode.

Most surprising amongst these new arrangements were the Hokkien servants she found she was employing. They were all *sinkehs*, newly arrived in Malaya, speaking only their own dialect of Chinese, and both she and they found themselves submitting to Wu Chao's patient tutelage in the mixture of various Chinese dialects and Malay that is the *lingua franca* for the whole area. Indeed, after a week or two, Trudie gave up the pretence of running her own household and left it to Wu Chao to organize the shopping and the cooking, leaving her free to poke about the Chinese shops as much as she liked, looking for antiques and other objects for resale in the Emporium in London.

Led by Mrs Beresford, she was soon accepted by the tight European circle who lived in Malacca. Most of them enjoyed the Nonya cuisine which was all she had to offer them when they called on her in her new house, though they wouldn't have dreamed of eating such things in their own home. Trudie soon found herself the butt of their jokes over living in the Chinese area, as well as having a Nonya personal maid, but the jokes were good-humoured and mostly envious, as her guests compared the smooth running of Trudie's household with the chaos and misunderstandings that mostly inspired their own homes.

Only when she was alone did Trudie indulge her curiosity by visiting Wu Chao's part of the house. She soon became accustomed to seeing the other Nonya women, intent on their game of *cher kee*, which they all claimed to be an innocent card game, but which Trudie had already discovered was an endless gambling session much loved by all. The women played for small old Chinese coins with holes in their centres, thus laughing away Trudie's accusations that they were inveterate gamblers and ought to be ashamed of themselves. At the end of every session, however, they would change their money for the real thing, their almond-shaped eyes glinting with satisfaction as they counted their winnings.

'Why you pull face over us play *cher kee*? Velly good game!' Wu Chao demanded of Trudie one day.

Trudie carefully crossed her fingers in her lap. 'Christians don't approve of gambling,' she said with her nose in the air.

Wu Chao shook her head sadly. 'Po' *Kak* Tludie, no good Christian! Velly solly!'

And the two women laughed happily together. They both knew it wouldn't be long before Trudie learned to play the game herself.

Trudie had been living in Malacca for three months when Septimus arrived. Her delight at seeing her brother was enough to put her in a good mood for several days as she questioned him closely about everything to do with the Emporium in London.

'It's managing very well without you, if you want to know!' he said at last. '*I* am managing very well without you! Look, Trudie, I came to get you out of trouble, not the other way round!'

'And what trouble am I in?' she demanded.

He looked about him. 'The parents wouldn't approve of the way you're living, my girl. If you don't want me to tell them how you've pulled the wool over Cousin Christopher's eyes, you'd better remember that *I'm* the one who controls the business, not you.'

Trudie lowered her gaze meekly. 'Very well,' she murmured.

Septimus grinned, pleased with himself for putting her in her place so easily. 'I'm not like Father,' he reminded her more kindly. He put his arms about her and lifted her clear off the floor. 'We're going to be rich, Miss Gertrude Grant! Between us, we're going to be as rich as Midas!'

Trudie had never heard of the mythical king whose touch turned everything to gold and, if she had, she wouldn't have given a row of pins for his gift. It was the excitement of making money she craved, not the money itself. And, at that particular moment, even that had little attraction for her. It seemed to her that, for the first time in her life, she had everything to make her happy, and that was the best feeling in the whole wide world.

BOOK TWO

Chapter Eleven

Trudie awoke on her birthday in 1863 feeling very well satisfied with life. She was twenty-three years old, a widow, and with a business of her own. It was the business that gave her the most pleasure. She and Wu Chao had been successful beyond their dreams, buying precious silks and brocades and the most expensive of Chinese teas, and selling vanilla, spices, and some manufactured articles from Birmingham that were beginning to gain in popularity in China. At first, Trudie had kept the accounts in her hands, working over them endlessly at night in her own laborious way. Then she had discovered that Wu Chao could do the same calculations in a flash, using an ancient abacus as she had been taught as a child, the beads flowing through her fingers with the greatest of ease.

'I shall grow lazy doing nothing while you do all the work!' she had said one day, enjoying the sight of Wu Chao, as immaculate as ever, whizzing the beads from one end of the frame to the other as she did her sums.

'We do well!' Wu Chao had triumphed. 'I t'ink better we keep gold in Chinese bank. What you t'ink?'

A Chinese bank? Trudie had hesitated. She had quickly learned that the Straits Chinese used their wealth to reinforce their family ties. She was fortunate, she supposed, that she had been accepted by the Ki family almost as if she had been one of them. It was only because she had had doubts about the safety of their money, transformed into neat ingots for easy transport, that her share of the gold hadn't been used for the benefit of the whole Ki family as was everyone else's. She had no doubt that Wu Chao had been instructed to convert her to their Chinese ways if she could and, left to herself, she wouldn't have had any objection. That she worried as to what her brother would say about their having so little control over it themselves was something she didn't like to mention – not even to Wu Chao, who understood how constricting one's male relations could be much better than most.

'Blother not like Chinese bank?' Wu Chao asked sympathetically.

Septimus hadn't even been able to see that his sister had a problem. He had written in his last letter that he thought all her money should be transferred to London where he could look after it for her, ignoring the Ki family's interest altogether, just as if they didn't exist. He had learned a great deal about stocks and shares recently, he had reported, and he was sure it would give her added satisfaction if she knew her money was going to build up the Home Country and the whole Empire. Septimus's letters had become very dull recently. He had been entranced by the advantages of the new limited companies which he said would transform the whole business world. Before their arrival, directors had risked everything they owned in their companies and could be made bankrupt for no good reason. Now, with the limited companies, they risked only their venture capital, limiting their risks on all else. If their companies failed, their liabilities to their creditors were limited, protecting their families and homes. It had meant a whole injection of capital into the new industries, money making money, and the whole wealth of the nation expanding accordingly. Trudie had felt torn both ways from the very beginning. Her interest in building up the British Empire was not great – like the Kis, her interests were far more personal and immediate, and related to those around her – but nor did she want to antagonize her brother, who had always been her first concern ever since she could remember.

Because it was her birthday, there would soon be another letter from Septimus. For some reason she didn't like to identify to herself, she had never revealed to her brother exactly how well she and Wu Chao were doing. She sent him accounts, of course, she was obliged to do that, but they were the official accounts that she declared to the Colonial Government and on which she paid taxes. Wu Chao kept the other accounts, out of which she paid their rent and all their household expenses. Trudie never asked her the exact figures of their earnings, feeling it was better not to know. They both preferred it that way because Trudie hated lying, especially did she hate lying to Septimus, who, every bit as much as their father, thought of women as children, unable to do anything in business for themselves.

'I'll think about it,' Trudie had said to Wu Chao. Septimus was thousands of miles away, although he liked to think he ran her business as well as his own. There had been a time when it had been the other way round, she remembered, when she had thought herself the mainstay of the Emporium. How much Septimus had resented her then, though he never would have thought up all the ploys she had to make the Emporium popular at the very beginning.

Well, today, she was surely old enough to decide for herself and she thought her money to be safer with Wu Chao. Septimus might be a man, but he was far more impulsive than any female she knew.

'It's my birthday!' she announced as she went downstairs.

'So solly, forgotten birt'day,' Wu Chao answered with complete indifference.

Trudie grinned. 'Any letters?'

Wu Chao handed them over, adding a small package of her own to the pile. 'You still child, Tludie.'

'So Septimus keeps telling me.' She flashed a look at the Nonya woman. 'Wu Chao, how would it be if we sent our "profits" to London and put the rest into the Chinese bank?'

'Good.'

Trudie turned her letters over, opening the one from Septimus first. She scanned it eagerly, wanting to know what he thought about her latest consignment of malacca canes and bowls, which she had sent off to him on a wave of enthusiasm, without even telling him they were coming.

Her breakfast, the Nonya version of porridge, was put in front of her as she went on reading her brother's letter.

'Where's Black Jade?' she asked. She and Wu Chao's baby had a very special relationship and she missed her when she wasn't there.

'Baby with aunt. What blother say?'

Trudie stared down at the pages of writing in front of her. 'He's sold everything we sent him. There's been a most successful Japanese Exhibition in Paris, which has had a terrific spin-off in London. Everybody is pouring into Regent Street in search of Oriental shawls and Chinese and Japanese *objets d'art*.'

'Which sell best?'

'Anything and everything, if he's to be believed.'

Trudie went on reading, a thoughtful frown between her eyes. She looked up. 'He wants more Japanese things. He said that last time, too. I told him to save those paintings they wrap everything in because they get a good price in the European galleries these days. It's exciting to them, you see, because Japan was shut off from trade for all those years. Do you think I should suggest Septimus should visit Yokohama? I never told him that we're trading with them directly now. There are so many things I don't tell him.'

'Best that way. Blother t'ink he run everyt'ing, but never like that. Best he not know, yes?'

Trudie thought how wonderful it was to have a partner who understood the realities of life so well. 'Much better,' she agreed fervently.

She went back to her letter, looking for her birthday wishes, but there were none. Instead, Septimus had written something which truly shocked her.

'Septimus has become involved with a family up North in England and he is thinking of going to work for them. He wants to *leave* the Emporium, have less responsibility and more time to do what he wants to do! Needless to say, Father doesn't like the family because they're Roman Catholic.'

Wu Chao shook her head. 'Cat'olics not Christian?'

'My father doesn't think so.'

'All same to me,' said Wu Chao.

Trudie was more doubtful. 'I don't think I know any,' she said.

Wu Chao choked on a giggle. 'Many Cat'olics in Malacca, with skirted priests like St Francis Xavier. He Jes-u-it.'

Trudie gave her a bewildered look. 'Oh well,' she said, 'let's hope we can persuade Septimus to visit Japan before he abandons us. He might come to his senses and realize he'll never make much money working for somebody else. How could he want less responsibility than he has now?'

'Many Cat'olics in Nagasaki,' Wu Chao observed. 'Jes-u-it Francis Xavier there, too.' Her eyes laughed at Trudie. 'Japans do most trade in Nagasaki, so permit foreign customs not allowed elsewhere. Very strange t'ing they not want foreign devils making all the plofits!'

Aware she was being laughed at, Trudie put her worries about her brother at the back of her mind and changed the subject. 'Are you going to cook something special for dinner tonight?' she asked.

'What you like?' Wu Chao asked, amused. There had been a time when she had thought Trudie's lack of guile was because all foreign devils lacked self-discipline, but she had learned that this wasn't entirely true. Trudie's enthusiasms were many, and she never did without unless there was a very good reason for it; once she had made up her mind to something she would never give up, working endlessly towards her goal, no matter what the cost to herself.

'You choose!' Trudie bade her. 'I have to call on Mrs Beresford this morning and I may stay and eat luncheon with her. Is Mr Rhys coming?'

'Does Rhys man ever forget birthday?'

'There's always a first time!'

Trudie chose to walk the short distance to the Stadthuys. She knew it was frowned upon by her European friends, but she couldn't resist the sights and sounds of the narrow Malacca streets, much of which she felt to be lost if she summoned a rickshaw as others did. If she were tired, she didn't hesitate to beckon one of the creaking, padded two-wheeled seats that were pulled along by a man, running between the shafts, a shade pulled up over the passenger's head; but if she were fresh, she much preferred peering into the small shops, peeping into the many temples, and watching the black-pyjamaed old ladies who acted as porters for their merchant sons, pushing and pulling huge loads in cardboard boxes, earning their living the hard way, only occasionally stopping to exchange toothless smiles with their peers, spiced with the gossip of the day.

Trudie walked first to the river, where she now had a godown of her own as they had long ago outgrown the part of the house Wu Chao had put aside to hold their goods. The name 'godown' came from the Portuguese, but everyone used the term to mean one of the warehouses that edged the mouth of the river. Once upon a time, the Portuguese had held a virtual monopoly of European trade with the Far East and, in those days, Malacca had been one of their key possessions, along with Macao and Manila in the Philippines. Malacca was a comparative backwater nowadays, ever since the Englishman Stamford Raffles had discovered the natural harbour of Singapore and had claimed it for the British. Ships still came and went to the older port, however, and these were the ships that mattered to Trudie, for they were the Chinese junks, now that the English and French gave it a wide berth. There were the two Chinese mail ships as well, causing a flutter of interest amongst the few Europeans, but mostly Malacca was a secret city, a Chinese city, which the English ruled but didn't know at all.

A flight of steps led directly up to the Stadthuys from the Square below. Trudie folded her parasol and mounted them with ease, making light of the steep climb. Mrs Beresford was waiting for her at the top, her smiling face giving no clue to the envy she felt for the younger woman who never seemed to feel the heat and, more remarkably, had never been heard to complain of the mosquitoes which made everybody else's life a misery every dusk.

'Happy birthday, Gertrude!' She kissed Trudie lightly on either cheek. 'My dear, I hope you can bear it, the girls have chosen to celebrate by going for a picnic?'

'How perfectly lovely!' Trudie exclaimed.

'Well, I hope it may be! You will have to help me control my darling daughters from going out into the sun! They're as brown as berries and it *is* so unattractive!'

'You can't keep them inside all the time,' Trudie returned easily. Mrs Beresford was an indulgent mother, much given to fussing over her offspring and husband alike, all of whom returned her concern with a devotion Trudie would not have believed had she not seen it with her own eyes. There was none of the dark underside of fear that had been such a feature of her own childhood. Even their family prayers were a hit or miss affair, frequently forgotten, but none the less sincere when they did take place.

'I suppose I can't,' Mrs Beresford sighed. 'I did think of locking them in their rooms for a while, but Mr Beresford pointed out they would soon learn to climb out on to the roof through their window and, up there, there is no shelter from the sun whatsoever!'

Trudie thoroughly enjoyed her day. It was always a pleasure to her to be driven out in the Beresfords' comfortable carriage, passing under the coco, betel, and sago palms, processing down the avenues of trees of enormous girth, which bore yellow flowers of delicious fragrance. Once, she asked that they might pause while she examined some sugar cane, explaining that Mr Rhys was still looking for exactly the right crop for them to grow up country.

'Doesn't your cousin see to all that?' Mrs Beresford asked.

Trudie made no attempt to hide her dislike for her cousins from her hostess. 'My only hope of ever making the plantation pay its way is if they stay away!'

'Oh, my love, never say so! It isn't becoming in you to speak of Mr Horton like that, let alone your Cousin Hermione!'

'Especially Cousin Hermione!' Trudie agreed dryly.

Mrs Beresford shot her a warning look. '*Pas devant les enfants!*'

Trudie obligingly pointed out to the girls a mass of lianas, their stems as thick as a man's arm, knotted and tangled into extraordinary shapes, their red blossoms as large as bread-and-butter plates. When this had been commented on, some remarks were exchanged on the strange pineapples for which Trudie had developed a passion, much to the amusement of the Beresford daughters who, following the example of their mother flatly refused to taste the fruit for themselves. Mrs Beresford, like so many English women in the tropics, agonized over the lack of apples and pears without ever bothering to sample the many exotic tropical fruits all about them. Before Trudie had practically forced a papaya on to her, Mrs Beresford had eschewed even the succulent flesh of this fruit, but no longer! Slowly but surely, all sorts of new foods were making their appearance on the Stadthuys table and, when complimented on her open-minded hospitality by their occasional visitors, Mrs Beresford was always generous in her praises of her young friend's interest in the local fauna and flora. 'The rest of us can never keep up with her!' she would say. 'Every fruit and every flower is of interest to Mrs Maddock. One would almost think her to be a botanist, if she didn't insist she's nothing of the sort!'

Trudie did, indeed, love the extraordinary plants that grew everywhere. Much of her enjoyment in the drive was in seeing the huge trees that edged the jungle, their branches nearly hidden by orchids and epiphytes, her favourite of which was the aptly named Flower of the Holy Ghost, an orchid whose likeness to a hovering dove had given it its name, together with its unbelievable fragrance that scents the air for a brief day at most.

Here and there, they came across a clearing, one of the *kampongs* of the Malays. Each would have its own graveyard, the stones like so many turbans, each one facing Mecca and shaded by the exquisite white flowers of the frangipani, known as the Temple Flower to many Buddhists who plant it freely in their temple grounds so that every pilgrim, no matter how poor, will have something to offer before the image of the Enlightened One. Here, to the Malays, it was the Grave Flower, shedding its petals with beneficent impartiality amongst the tombs.

They stopped for their picnic beside one of the muddy streams in sight of one of the Malay *kampongs*. The young girls were set to draw the distinctive houses, which were all of the same architecture whether rich or poor, with a high, steep roof over a platform supported by posts, approached by a flight of tiled steps, the lowest of which was nearly twice as wide as the top one.

Mrs Beresford heaved a sigh of satisfaction. 'Now we can have a comfortable coze together before the girls grow bored again! How does it feel to be a whole year older and wiser, my love?'

'Exactly as yesterday,' Trudie answered. 'I have never enjoyed life more! And why not? I have everything in life to make me happy!'

Mrs Beresford wondered if this were the moment to bring up a subject which had frequently been on her mind of late. Mr and Mrs Horton, much as she disliked them, had first asked her to raise the subject with Trudie a year ago, but she had put it off, not liking to interfere in something she felt to be none of her affair.

'Have you thought of marrying again?' she said aloud.

'No, once was quite enough!'

Mrs Beresford made a quick sound of sympathy with her tongue. 'You were hardly a wife at all, living apart all that time, and Mr Maddock was – how shall I put it – a little out of the usual run? But marriage can be a sharing and a delight – '

'I'm sure it can be! But I'm quite content as I am, ma'am. I don't want another husband!'

Mrs Beresford opened her eyes very wide. 'I trust it isn't because of the Welshman who is in and out of your house?' she said tartly.

'Mr Rhys?' Trudie started to laugh. 'He's my manager – a Welsh miner! If he's interested in marrying anyone, he would probably choose my Nonya maid. He dotes on her little girl, almost as if she were his own.'

Mrs Beresford winced, wishing she had minded her own business as her husband had advised her to do. 'Oh yes, the little girl,' she said in hollow tones.

Trudie was busy with her own thoughts. 'He *says* he isn't the father, and so does Wu Chao, but I've never known whether to believe them or not.'

Mrs Beresford coughed. 'It was rumoured that Mr Maddock – '

'But he was married to me!' Trudie said simply.

For a long time there was silence between them, then Mrs Beresford said, 'I think we might eat now, don't you?'

The girls unpacked the food, making a great deal of noise about it. Trudie, quite as eager to eat as they were, joined in the excitement of unwrapping the packets of sandwiches and stringy pieces of chicken, and pouring out glasses of bottled lemonade for them all. Trudie quelled the thought that Wu Chao would have supplied them with something vastly more tasty, and tucked in with a will. Any food was better than none when one was hungry.

It wasn't until she was in bed that night that Mrs Beresford allowed herself to dwell on that strange remark of Trudie's.

'You know,' she remarked to her husband, 'I'm convinced that child is as innocent as the day she was born. Jeremy Maddock may have given her his name but, if you ask me, that was all there was to that marriage! Oh dear, do you think I ought to tell the Hortons?'

'They wouldn't believe you!' her husband snorted. 'Not sure I do myself, come to that.'

'If I trusted the Hortons – '

'Don't like them. Either of them!' her husband averred.

'Nor do I,' Mrs Beresford sighed. 'Oh well, at the moment she is very happy as she is and who am I to spoil it all for her?'

'Did you talk to her about Mr Rhys?'

Mrs Beresford gulped at the memory. 'I tried to. She thinks he's Black Jade's father. The Hortons are perfectly right in their concern for her. I wouldn't allow any daughter, or cousin of mine, to live in such a household for a moment! It's most unsuitable, whatever she may say! The devil of it is that she's having the time of her life living what she calls "independent of her family", and how can one possibly explain to her why she can't go on doing it!'

'Why not leave her alone?' Mr Beresford asked sleepily.

'Because it simply won't do!' his wife informed him in exasperated tones. 'And those Hortons are the last people I'd choose to tell her so. They aren't kind, for one thing, and they don't wish her well! I can't think what she does for money, because that man has allowed the Maddock plantation to revert to jungle, and it isn't only Mr Rhys who says so, so what I am to do?'

Mr Beresford wriggled himself into a more comfortable position. 'I'm not saying it isn't an unusual household, but nobody will turn their back on her all the time she has your friendship. The wife of the Lieutenant-Governor is not a nobody, my dear, and you grace the position as no one else could. Let the Hortons do their worst, I say, she'll be all right all the time you choose to lend her your contenance. I'm glad. Nice little thing. The girls like her too, don't they? The only thing I ask is that we don't have the Hortons to stay again for a long, long time, if we can possible help it!'

With which sentiment Mrs Beresford heartily concurred.

Wu Chao was alone when Trudie returned home. 'Gold gone to *kongsi*. Better so, yes?'

Trudie didn't know. She presumed the *kongsi* was a kind of Chinese bank. Then she thought that the money was as much Wu Chao's as hers and, if that was what Wu Chao wanted, who was she to object? She hadn't wasted any time getting it out of the house if it was already gone.

'You'll have to explain it to me sometime,' she said aloud.

'Yes. Better not talk too much to blother?' Wu Chao responded.

Trudie couldn't have agreed more. 'Certainly not! I don't think I shall tell Mr Rhys more than he has to know, either. The fewer people who know about our business, the better!'

Wu Chao laughed. 'You become like good Chinese, Tludie!'

Trudie laughed also. 'The English enjoy a gamble just as much as any Chinese!'

But this Wu Chao wouldn't allow. 'Too tlansparent! You much too tlansparent to make good gambler. Tlansparent as glass!'

Trudie laughed again without resentment. 'You think that because you know what I'm thinking. I'm sure Mrs Beresford doesn't think anything of the sort!'

'Not about business. Mrs Beresford not interested in business. I t'ink she know 'bout Mr Maddock.'

'There's nothing to know!'

'Much to know!' Wu Chao insisted. 'Maybe she guess you no' ploper wife to Mr Maddock. Once she know that, she agree with man-cousin better you go Singapore. She t'ink you married woman, not young girl.'

Trudie found the idea preposterous. 'I'll show her my marriage lines.'

'She no' fool!'

Trudie frowned. 'Wu Chao, I'm not sure I know about marriage.' She felt suddenly uncertain, as well as a fool. 'He did marry me!'

'Yes, you not know,' Wu Chao agreed. 'Rhys man, he tell me you not know 'bout men. Good, I tell you now.'

'Now?'

Wu Chao was at her most stubborn. 'Now!'

By the time the Nonya woman had finished her explanation, Trudie was in a state of shock. Never in her wildest fantasies had she imagined that she had unthinkingly given Mr Maddock such intimate rights over her body when she had consented to be his wife.

'Then he really is Black Jade's father?'

'Yes, he father. I consort of Mr Maddock.'

Trudie shut her eyes, trying to shut out the memories that crowded in of her mother weeping and her fears of her father. Poor Mama!

She opened her eyes again, a new thought occurring to her. 'Did you enjoy all that? I don't think I should.'

Wu Chao's black eyes snapped with amusement. 'I not like Mr Maddock velly much,' she confessed. 'But with other man – maybe I like velly well!'

Trudie looked down her nose. 'I don't think I should!'

But Wu Chao was adamant. 'Yes, you liking very much

also with light man. Mr Maddock not light man for you. Not love you enough. He choose you to make money in England. He choose me 'cause he want woman on plantation, woman who no' make tlouble. Nonya women blought up no' make tlouble. You understand?'

Trudie thought she did. Most of all, she saw that Wu Chao was her ally in her flesh as well as in their business. She had seen a side of Jeremy Maddock Trudie had thought that only she knew. Indeed, Wu Chao had seen that side far more intimately than she, had felt his selfishness in her own body. It was strange, but it drew them even closer together.

'Why did you put up with such a marriage? At least I was handsomely paid for taking his name!'

'Family chose husband.' Wu Chao shrugged. 'I velly happy now.'

Trudie grinned. 'I know! *Moh ching, moh meng*!'

Wu Chao nodded happily. 'Velly tlue!'

By the time Mr Rhys knocked on Wu Chao's door things were back to normal. Wu Chao had made Trudie's favourite chicken curry, *ayam* curry, which she served with numerous side dishes. It was followed by *kueh chuchi mulot*, cakes to melt the mouth with, *kueh koo*, a glutinous, rice-flour cake with green-pea paste, and *kueh keledek*, a sweet potato cake, two of Trudie's especial favourites.

Mr Rhys brought no gift with him. He stood over Trudie, looking larger even than usual. In his best clothes and with his hair slicked down with pomade, he looked more like the evil villain of a morality play than the loose-limbed man she had grown accustomed to.

'Happy birthday,' he said curtly.

She inclined her head. 'Thank you.'

He sat at the table, opposite her, a little awkward with his cutlery, though not at all, Trudie noticed, with the chopsticks that Wu Chao silently put by his side. With those, he was as adept as any Baba, whereas she was still a novice with them, infinitely preferring her own knife, fork and spoon.

'How's the business going?' he asked her.

She winced, not wanting to discuss such matters at table. No matter how much she valued Mr Rhys, even liked him, his manners were as uncouth as ever.

He sat on long after they had finished eating. He had joined in Wu Chao's deft teasing with a heavier hand. Wu Chao was amused by Trudie's frank enjoyment of her food; Mr Rhys went further, telling her he had always thought ladies had ladylike appetites.

Trudie had taken the implication seriously. 'I have done all the fasting I mean to in my life. You forget my father is a parson.'

'Rich men don't fast!' Mr Rhys had pointed out.

'No, *they* don't, but their womenfolk do.'

There had been a shocked silence. 'I don't believe you've ever been really hungry!' Mr Rhys had declared at last.

It had been Wu Chao who had answered him. 'I believe. *Kak* Tludie is like deep pool, simple on surface, many t'ings underneath.'

Trudie had flushed with pleasure, liking the Nonya woman very much in that moment. 'Things that I don't even know about!' she had laughed it off.

'Maybe,' Mr Rhys had grunted. Trudie hadn't known what he really thought, but then there had been nothing new in that. He, like every man, had suddenly grown a new dimension for her, a dimension that was still a mystery to her and was ever likely to remain so.

Now, with Wu Chao gone to her own rooms to put her little daughter to bed, she had other things to discuss with her manager. She pushed the dishes aside, leaning her elbows on the table as she addressed him.

'I had a letter from my brother this morning. I'm worried about him. He – he wants to give up the Emporium and go and work for someone else. It will make me even more dependent on someone I know nothing about. I don't even know if he'll take our stuff, or allow us the same margins of profit we are making now.'

'Maybe your brother has already discussed all that with him,' Mr Rhys pointed out.

'Without saying a word to me? I wouldn't put it past him.' She shrugged her shoulders. 'What worries me is that we'll find London a much more difficult market without him, especially if someone is put in charge of the Emporium who has a prejudice against Oriental *objets d'art*, which is more than possible. It's bad enough having to deal with the Hortons out here over the plantation!' Her expression softened. 'I've been meaning to thank you for a long time for leading Cousin Christopher out of his depth!'

'We haven't got rid of him yet,' he warned her. 'He's found his own use for the plantation, a use your husband turned a blind eye to, but in which your cousin is an eager participant.'

'Is it illegal?'

'Would you mind if it were?'

'No, the less I know about his doings the better, however. I am embarrassed enough by their constant visits. Thankfully, the Beresfords don't care for them much either and are making difficulties about their staying at the Stadthuys for weeks together at their expense. I don't see either of them staying for long right out in the jungle, do you?'

He grinned, shaking his head. 'Mr Horton thinks every sound is a tiger roaring, as you used to do, and your cousin is afraid of rats, mice, snakes, as well as the mosquitoes and other insects. They're still siphoning what profits there are from your coffee into their own pockets, however.'

Trudie shrugged again. 'It's a small price to pay!' She grinned also. 'I'm glad she's afraid of rats!'

She sobered abruptly, her brow creasing in a frown. Mr Rhys never complained but he must sometimes be lonely, living amongst the rack and ruin of a plantation rapidly returning to the jungle. Her newly gained knowledge made her feel very wise.

'Have you thought of marriage, Mr Rhys?' she asked him abruptly.

'I send my money home to Wales. My mother and I want the young ones to have a better chance in life than I had. It isn't easy to bring up children without a husband bringing in a wage every week.'

'I didn't know your father had died.'

'You didn't ask.' Mr Rhys wriggled, uncomfortable in his Sunday clothes. 'He isn't dead. He was crippled down the mines – another mouth for my mother to feed, and one who will never grow up and leave home as the rest of us will. The youngest children are still at school!'

Trudie felt as if she had been slapped. She might have known hunger, but she had never had to wonder where her next meal was coming from.

'Still, you must often be lonely, living on the plantation all alone,' she said to cover up the silence between them.

'Sometimes,' he admitted.

She chewed on her lower lip. 'You could do as Mr Maddock did, marry a Nonya woman,' she suggested.

His suntanned faced reddened. 'Look you, I know you mean well, ma'am, but you don't know what you're talking about.'

'No, I probably don't,' she admitted frankly. 'I was

thinking about Black Jade too. You could be a father to her if you were to marry Wu Chao.' The idea seemed the more attractive to her, the more she thought of it. 'And the plantation wouldn't be new to Wu Chao. She's lived out there before.'

'Marriage means more than that to me,' he maintained stiffly.

Trudie sighed. 'I thought it might help Wu Chao – '

'Did you, now? Hasn't one marriage outside her own community been more than enough for Wu Chao? He made no effort to understand her ways and customs. He was far too much in love with himself as a man of good taste! Wu Chao was just another beautiful object for him to acquire and enjoy. What you were to him only you can know.'

Trudie straightened her back. 'Her family agreed to the marriage!'

'And lived to regret it!' he snorted. 'Do you think they don't know what she suffered, married to a foreign devil who had no care for her, or for the child she was bearing, other than that he wanted a woman in his bed?'

Trudie was offended. Nobody had the right to speak to her like that, certainly not about her husband! 'Mr Maddock was not a loving man, but he was not a *bad* man, Mr Rhys.'

'Was he not? And what would you know about such things, Mrs Maddock?' he mocked her.

Trudie gave him look for look and it was he who backed down. She primped up her mouth, remembering her mother's tears and her perpetually damp handkerchief. 'I know,' she said softly. 'I know more than you, or any other man, could ever know. My mother is afraid of my father *all the time*. I was never afraid of Mr Maddock – '

'You had no cause to be!'

She was back in control of herself again. Her glance mocked him. 'You think not?' She reminded herself that this was her employee she was talking to, a Welsh miner who had none of the finer feelings she had perceived in her own husband. 'No, I had no cause to be. He was a gentleman, a lover of the finer things in life. He taught me to appreciate art, Oriental and European, and many other things, and he never raised his voice to me once.'

The Welshman could make nothing of what she was saying. His own father had shouted at his family as lustily as he had sung the new Welsh patriotic songs that sounded all the better for being written in their own language. A man could roar like a lion, drink the other men under the table, and carry more coal on his back than any other man in the neighbourhood, it didn't mean he was unkind to his wife.

'Does your father shout much?' he asked the young woman before him.

'No, only when he's preaching.'

'Then I don't see why Mr Maddock's not raising his voice should matter to you?'

Trudie shivered. 'You would if you knew my father. He doesn't shout, but nobody else speaks either. I talked to Mr Maddock all the time and he never made me feel foolish, or in the way. He was a gentleman! He didn't go around half naked – '

Mr Rhys rocked back in his chair. 'He was a gentleman right enough! He didn't care what any lesser beings thought of him. He'd go in to Wu Chao unwashed and smelling of his own sweat and thought it only right and proper for her to pretend not to notice! Do you think Wu Chao wants another stinking barbarian in her bed? She found Mr Maddock as distasteful as you would a real man, only it wouldn't occur to you to marry outside your own narrow circle, now would it?'

Trudie rose to her feet. 'No, it wouldn't!' She pressed her fingers together. 'I think you'd better go, Mr Rhys. We've both said more than we meant to – '

'And I'm sorry for it,' he interrupted her. He looked as though he might say something else, but he didn't.

Trudie swallowed, wishing she wasn't so conscious of the sheer stature of the man. He made her feel small in every way. 'I think we'd better pretend this conversation never happened,' she said in frozen tones.'It will be best that way as – if we have to go on working together. Please don't mention my husband to me ever again!'

She went on standing there for a long time after he had gone. She never saw Mr Rhys without that unexpected curl of excitement exploding within her. It was unsettling, something to be avoided at all costs. What she might have told him was that she wouldn't look outside her own circle for a husband, because she wasn't looking for a husband at all! She would never, never marry again. She was far too happy exactly as she was.

Chapter Twelve

Mrs Beresford was asking ruefully if Trudie didn't feel able to put up her own cousins on their next threatened visit to Malacca.

'It is too bad of you to wish them on to me all the time,' she complained good-naturedly. 'It's more than your turn.'

Trudie was unable to hide her dismay. 'Oh, ma'am, do you think my household quite suitable for them?'

'I don't think it suitable for anyone, my dear, as you very well know! I'm beginning to think you chose it deliberately, however, just so I should have to entertain your cousins for you! Very understandable, if I may say so, but I should be happier if my girls didn't see too much of Mrs Horton. She has the most curious habits, as I expect you must be aware?'

Trudie chuckled 'I always disliked Cousin Hermione. My father dotes on her!'

Mrs Beresford tried not to show her disapproval. 'The least said about *that* the better!' She held Mr Jonathan Grant almost entirely responsible for the more eccentric aspects of his daughter's life.

The last thing Trudie felt, however, was sorry for herself at that moment. 'I might quite like Mr Horton under other circumstances,' she confessed. 'Being married to dear Hermione is a handicap for any man.'

'Wretched for him!' Mrs Beresford agreed. And wretched for Trudie, too, she added silently. She had seldom met a greedier couple, openly lining their own pockets at her young friend's expense. 'Well, I won't wish him on to you if you don't want me to, but a word to the wise, Gertrude. Don't let it be seen that you're too friendly with either that maid of yours, *or* with your manager. Not only will it not do out here, but if someone should see fit to tell your family how you are living, there is very little either my husband or I could do to help you.'

Trudie was silent for a long moment. 'You're very kind, ma'am,' she said at last. 'I'll remember what you say.'

'Do, my dear. I've grown very fond of you since you came to live in Malacca – as have my girls, I may say. We should miss you very much if you were forced to return to England.'

Long after she was gone, Trudie sat thoughtfully on. How unfair life was! How could it be considered just in this day and age that women were not allowed to hold property in their name, or enter into legal contracts? How was it that more than half the population had no right to live their own lives without the consent of some male? And what males! She had depended on Septimus more than she had any idea until he had decided he had a better future working for someone else. That showed such an alarming lack of judgement in her opinion, that her confidence was sadly shaken, but he was still better than the Hortons.

She was quite pleased, therefore, when she heard from her brother that he was sending a friend of his out to see her, even while she was disappointed that he wasn't coming himself. There always seemed to be something to hold him fast in England just when she needed him most! If anybody could, her brother could have dealt with the pretensions of the Hortons, but would he want to now, even if he were to see the deprivation of the plantation and realize it was affecting his pocket as much as his sister's? Writing to her, he was convinced she would look favourably on Jack Taviton, who might, indeed, be the ideal person to go to

Yokohama on their behalf. Septimus would leave it to her as to how much business she chose to put in his hands, remembering that it was impossible for her brother to come himself just now with his new commitments. Jack Taviton might be able to do them all a bit of good all round.

He certainly made a very good impression on everyone from the moment of his arrival. The Beresfords were quite happy to have him as their guest at the Stadthuys, enjoying the fund of stories he had to tell them about the London fashions and personages, reviving their own nostalgia for the social life Mrs Beresford, in particular, had enjoyed in the capital. Used to mixing with all kinds of people, they found no difficulty with Mr Taviton's lack of interest in anything else but himself. With Trudie it was otherwise. When she first met him, she was astonished to find him so much like her brother, full of himself and his own future, and delighted to have a ready-made audience in herself. He spoke about the same things, in much the same accents, and was as romantic about the building of Empire as ever Septimus had been, knowing just as little about it.

'Tell me about Septimus,' she begged him, as soon as she could have a word alone with him.

'What do you want to know about him, ma'am?'

'I thought he was as keen as I to make our fortunes,' she said sadly. 'He seems so changed in his letters.'

Mr Taviton looked suitably grave. 'I suppose he is changed,' he acknowledged. 'But it wouldn't be right for you to remain a charge on him for the rest of his life, would it? He had the idea you might like to get married again.'

'Whatever made him think that?'

Mr Taviton looked uncomfortable. 'It can't have been easy for you alone out here. I know Septimus has always done his best to help you, but that isn't like having a man of your own.' He cleared his throat doubtfully. 'I'm sure that's his thinking on the matter, ma'am. You don't want to take it too seriously, if you don't want to.'

Trudie rapidly came to the conclusion that Jack Taviton took very little seriously. He was more like Septimus than she had first thought. It reminded her of the early days of the Emporium when she had sometimes been at her wits' end to make Septimus concentrate on business when he had only wanted to enjoy his new independence.

'I take everything seriously when it comes to business,' she said, 'which is more than can be said for that brother of mine!'

Mr Taviton smiled a charming, if superior smile. 'He's managed to make a lot of money, however he did it. Not many people would have had the foresight to see how popular everything Oriental is now in Europe, or made such a success of a complicated import/export business – '

'My husband, Mr Maddock, had something to do with that,' Trudie interposed dryly.

'Oh come, ma'am! The only thing I know about your husband is that he ran that worthless plantation your cousin is trying to put into shape for you! You're very fortunate in your relations that they should all come to your rescue. Not many of us can claim to have such protective families!'

Trudie wondered how anyone could be so blind. 'If you say so,' she said lightly, dismissing the need to defend Jeremy Maddock from such a trivial, ill-thought-out criticism.

'You probably don't realize how fortunately placed you are,' Mr Taviton went on cheerfully. 'Women never understand business, even if you do say you take it seriously. They don't have to, bless them! If ever they change the laws governing women's property it would lead to anarchy! I've never yet met a woman who could count up her change from a pound note, let alone make sense of a column of figures!'

'They seem to manage,' Trudie said.

'But do they? It must be the duty of every man to find himself a wife these days when so many of our sisters never have the opportunity to find a husband. Don't you agree?'

'Let's hope your future wife agrees with you!' Trudie retorted.

'I haven't met her yet!'

'Just as well! Women sometimes have ideas of their own, you know.'

His cheerful grin reminded her of her brother's insouciance. 'I'll take your word for it!' he said.

Trudie kept meeting Mr Taviton after that. Mrs Beresford gave the friendship her blessing, shamefully throwing the two of them together whenever she could.

'I like him so much better than that Mr Horton,' she explained frankly, 'and he does come from a good family. That means a great deal back home, you know.'

Trudie knew it all to be true. She considered telling the older woman that she was perfectly happy as she was, but hadn't the heart to do so when she saw the pleasure Mrs Beresford was getting from encouraging what she was convinced was going to be the romance of the year. Besides, she was enjoying being courted for once, her jokes laughed at, and being complimented on her looks.

She was glad, therefore, when Jack Taviton asked if he might escort her to the party at the Stadthuys in honour of the Beresfords' wedding anniversary. The only drawback to the evening was that the Hortons were expected to arrive that day: these days Hermione always came with her husband, unwilling to allow him out of her sight for a minute.

'She's being ridiculous!' Trudie had remarked to Wu Chao. 'What mischief could he possibly get into here?'

Wu Chao had looked amused. 'You are here, Tludie.'

Trudie wasn't thinking of her cousins, however, as she squashed herself into the rickshaw seat beside Mr Taviton. Given the choice, she would have preferred to have a rickshaw to herself, but she didn't like to say so, especially as she knew Jack Taviton to be nervous of his own shadow every time he ventured into the Chinese quarter of the town. Again and again, he said to her how much he wished she lived on the hill, closer to the Beresfords, or at least in one of the other better areas, where her neighbours would be European and her servants more carefully chosen. All Trudie wished was that Mr Taviton could have protected her from the Hortons as Septimus could have done had he been there. How dare he send someone so superficial when she had specifically asked him to come himself?

'You're in very good looks this evening. I don't know how you always manage to look so cool in this oven!' Mr Taviton pulled down the corners of his eyes and put a silly smile on his face. 'If you're not careful you'll turn into a Chinaman yourself, yes, no?'

Trudie didn't answer. She wished she could look one half as cool and tranquil as Wu Chao had when she had left her, already seated at the card table in expectation of the game of *cher kee* she was going to play with her sisters. Nonya women seldom ventured out, except to scuttle from one house to the next on a visit to a close female friend, but that didn't stop them from knowing exactly what was going on all over town.

'I enjoy life in Malacca,' Trudie answered at last, 'more than I ever did in England, if the truth be told.'

'I can't believe that! Wouldn't you prefer to live somewhere in the English countryside? Have you forgotten the soft green of the grass and the leaves, and the soft rain that gives our women their beautiful complexions?'

'I believe not,' Trudie returned firmly. She had no wish to be uncivil, but what she had not forgotten was the grey drizzle and the leaden skies over London in the winter, a feature she inevitably associated with the long Lenten fasts her father had insisted on every year.

'You can't live in Malacca for ever!' Jack Taviton protested. He slapped the side of the rickshaw and gestured to the man between the shafts to get going. Grumbling under his breath, the scrawny Chinaman jumped high into the air to bring the vehicle level with the road and began to run, slowly at first, increasing his speed as he approached the river.

'Why not?' Trudie was hardly listening as she grew increasingly concerned as they started up the hill to the Stadthuys.

'A woman like you will soon feel the need to marry again – a friend of your brother's as likely as not! It would be the perfect answer to everything.'

Trudie uttered a sharp command. She slipped out of the rickshaw, glancing up at the feathery leaves of the malacca trees that stood sentry on either side of the road.

'We must walk,' she told Mr Taviton. 'We're too heavy for that poor man to pull us up the hill.'

'If he finds it too hard, he shouldn't hire out his rickshaw!' Jack Taviton snorted angrily. He got out, however, his mood changing as he saw Trudie was already walking easily up the steep slope. He paid off the man and ran after her, putting a familiar hand on her arm to slow her down. 'My dear, you are far too soft-hearted for your own good. He could probably pull a dozen of us up the hill if he put his back into it. I'm told these Chinamen are far stronger than they look!'

'I'm sure they are.' Trudie made her voice agreeable.

She was totally unprepared for what happened next. Part of the reason why she had alighted from the rickshaw was because she had found herself too close to Mr Taviton. To her astonishment, she had found herself assessing his body in terms she found distressing, having always been brought up to think that any such thoughts were sinful and should be put away from one as speedily as possible.

She was doubly unprepared, therefore, when he made a grab for her and turning her into the circle of his arms, lowered his head and kissed her with a thoroughness that sent her already racing heart pounding against her ribs. It was only when he thrust his tongue right into her mouth that she began to protest, not caring for the taste of him. Nothing, however, could destroy the shaft of self-knowledge he had given her, leaving her breathless and shattered. How could one feel such things in the arms of a man who meant less than nothing in the ordinary way? Was it always like that when a man kissed a woman? She had no means of telling.

'Mr Taviton!' she exclaimed.

He was far less affected by the embrace than she. 'Mrs Maddock!' he responded. 'Don't you think it's more than time we reached this point in our courtship?'

'Courtship?' she said blankly.

'Why else did you suppose your brother sent me here? Don't you like my kisses?'

'No!' she said. 'No, I do not! And we are *not* courting, Mr Taviton! I can assure you of that!'

His face tightened angrily. 'That isn't what I understood. I didn't come here for the good of my health! If it weren't in order to meet you, why do you suppose I came?'

'Because we need someone to go to Yokohama! Didn't Septimus tell you that?'

'He thought we could go together – '

'Oh, he did, did he?'

Mr Taviton began to lose his temper. 'He thought you'd be pleased, Miss Gertrude. You don't like the way Mr Horton is managing your plantation; you think you can run Septimus's import/export business as if it were your own, without reference to him, as often as not! What *do* you want?'

Trudie saw the trap in the question. There were all sorts of things she didn't want Septimus to know. She raised her chin. 'I may be a widow, Mr Taviton, but my name is still Mrs Jeremy Maddock. It is years since anyone addressed me as Miss Gertrude. As for what I want, I really can't see that as being any business of yours, can you?'

'But Septimus said – '

She looked the other way. Thankfully, they had gained the Stadthuys front door where the Beresfords were waiting to greet their guests. Mrs Beresford kissed Trudie fondly, accepting her congratulations on their anniversary with a smiling face.

'Yes, but, my dear, I don't know what you will think of me when I tell you there is absolutely no room for your cousins to stay here tonight. I have sent instructions down to your house that a room must be made ready for them.' She made a slight face. 'I didn't do it deliberately, I promise you, but, with so many people staying, I had no bedrooms available and nothing else would do for them, I fear, for nobody, not their best friends, could say your cousins are *adaptable* in their needs.'

Trudie belatedly remembered her manners, still feeling prickly from her encounter with Jack Taviton. 'Don't give it another thought, ma'am. Of course they must come to me. If they find my hospitality less than they're used to, they will have to put up with it.'

Mrs Beresford leaned forward confidentially. 'Well, I wish you joy of them, my dear. If only they weren't so particular – but there, I mustn't criticize them to you. They are your cousins after all!'

Trudie's dislike for her cousins could only increase over the next few days. That they should find her household bizarre in the extreme and had no compunction in saying so went without saying. They refused to eat what they termed 'Chink' cuisine, appealing to the good-natured Mrs Beresford to allow them to have their meals at the Stadthuys, even if they couldn't sleep there. Every time they saw Wu Chao a silence would fall and they would exchange meaning glances, until Trudie longed to send them about their business if they couldn't bring themselves to be polite to the Nonya woman and her friends.

It was all made the more difficult because, while Wu Chao didn't give a rap what the Horton barbarians thought of her, she chose the second day of their visit to approach Trudie about the binding of Black Jade's feet.

'She is still young,' she admitted. 'It is easier when one is young.'

Trudie swallowed down her horror, making an effort to understand a custom that seemed abhorrent to her. The bile rose in the back of her throat. 'I won't allow it!'

Wu Chao was startled. 'Arrow?'

'Oh, Wu Chao, I didn't mean that. What I mean is that it must be wrong to deliberately cripple another human being. Look at you, and how difficult you find it to walk any distance. I can see you're in pain – '

'No matter!'

'But it does matter!'

Wu Chao grew increasingly stubborn. 'Important have husband. Who marry Black Jade with huge, ugly feet? No one! Who marry you?'

Trudie blinked and swallowed. 'She may marry one of her father's people, have you thought of that? No European would want a wife with crippled feet!'

Wu Chao had not thought of that. 'You think Black Jade English?'

Trudie became more doubtful. 'She's half English.'

'I think Black Jade Nonya – all Nonya!'

Trudie gave her a troubled glance. She knew Wu Chao's assessment to be far more realistic than her own. *She* might consider Black Jade to be half English, her cousins certainly didn't. Their dislike for her made them shudder whenever they saw her, exactly as they did if there was any danger of them coming into physical contact with the little girl's mother.

'How can you wear clothes that woman has touched?' Hermione had asked her the evening before.

'Why ever not?' Trudie had retorted.

'I couldn't! It gives me the creeps to know she's shuffling about the house all the time! The Chinese are all the same, no one can tell what they're thinking! For all you know, she's planning your murder this very moment!'

'I like her,' Trudie had said.

Hermione hadn't troubled to hide her contempt. 'You always were your own worst enemy, Cousin Gertrude. Instead of playing the heartbroken little widow, why don't you find yourself a new husband and save Christopher and me the trouble of having to do anything further for you. You may not know it, cousin dear, but we've had about enough of your affairs! I don't believe your husband ever had a fortune out on that plantation of yours, or Christopher would have found it by now! To tell the truth, I don't know how you live so well when you're practically penniless!'

'I manage,' Trudie had retorted.

'At *our* expense!' her cousin had insisted. 'We scrimp and economize all the time in Singapore and for what? So that you can spend it on that sly Chinese whore and her child! Well, it won't do! Either you find yourself a husband, or I'll do it for you!'

That had been enough for one day, she thought, without Wu Chao wanting to bind Black Jade's feet as well! Trudie sat down, feeling defeated. 'Wu Chao, Black Jade is far too young either way, isn't she? Do we have to discuss it today?'

Wu Chao bowed. 'Never mind. I mention now because you child yoursel', Tludie. Take you long time to face inevitable, no? Better you be prepared.'

Trudie buried her face in her hands, wondering if it were true. Was marriage to Jack Taviton inevitable?

'I'm no child!' she insisted. 'I'm a grown woman! I just wish somebody would treat me as such!'

'Somebody like who?'

'Somebody like you!'

Wu Chao had covered her mouth with her hand, smothering a laugh. 'You never mind, *Kak* Tludie! Someday everyone t'ink you glown woman and then you be happy, no?'

'If only I could get rid of those cousins of mine!' Trudie sighed. '*That* would make me happier than anything else!'

'Why not tell them go?' Wu Chao suggested.

If only she could! There must be some way of making them think she was penniless and better left alone.

In that, however, she had reckoned without Christopher Horton's sense of duty. He arrived back from the plantation dispirited and beginning to wish he had never heard of the place. Nothing had worked out as he wanted. More, he hated having to bring Hermione with him every time he came. He was more worried about her than he was about the wilting coffee bushes that were being overtaken by the jungle quicker than he could force that seditious-minded manager to have them cleared, which he wouldn't do until Christopher produced their wages. It was easy to see that the Tamil workers were growing more sullen and dangerous every day. Caradoc Rhys, who should have stayed down his Welsh mine with all his fellows, was obviously quite unable to control them, bleating on that it was lucky they stayed at all and that it wasn't his job to see that anyone worked without payment, just as if their wages could be summoned up out of thin air! Far from being the source of any wealth, Mr Horton reckoned it to be a dying liability and had begun to wonder how best he could rid himself of its management – and of his wife's cousin! Hermione would object when she was deprived of her visits to Malacca, but that, too, would be one less worry for him to have to bother about.

His temper was not better improved when he saw Wu Chao and Trudie in earnest discussion, their heads close together, so intent on their conversation that neither of them had heard him come in.

'Where's Mrs Horton?' he demanded of Trudie, ignoring the Nonya woman as if she weren't there. She had a way of looking at him out of those black almond-shaped eyes that bothered him. She looked at him as if she knew him to be stealing from her mistress and, sooner or later, she would put the idea into Trudie's mind also and then where would he be?

'She went to her room,' Trudie answered.

Mr Horton jerked his head towards Wu Chao. 'Get rid

of the maid,' he commanded. 'It's time we talked about your future, Cousin Gertrude.'

Wu Chao was gone before Trudie could turn round. Trudie saw her stumble in her haste in the doorway and hurried to help her, only to be gestured away by one doll-like hand. The contrast between the sheer elegance of the Nonya and the overheated, fleshy appearance of her cousin's husband was almost too much for Trudie.

She sat in silence, one eyebrow raised in enquiry. 'You should have a shower and a rest first, Mr Horton. You press yourself too hard.'

'I trust I do my duty,' he grunted.

'More than your duty,' Trudie agreed with conscious irony.

Mr Horton looked down at her bent head, wondering what it was about Gertrude Grant, or Maddock, as he ought to call her, that made Hermione so dislike her. He thought of her as a poor dab of a creature, himself, when he thought of her at all.

'I do my best. I doubt that plantation of your husband's can ever be made to pay, Mrs Maddock. Your labour is close to mutiny, and your overseer isn't of the right stuff to manage anything, certainly not out here! You'd do better to be rid of it *and him*, my dear.'

Trudie took a deep breath, determined to keep her temper. 'My husband bought the land as a long-term investment, not for any immediate gain. He and Mr Rhys seem to have understood each other very well and he was promised employment out there for as long as he needs it. I don't like to interfere with my husband's promises to a valued employee, Mr Horton. It isn't as if I need much to keep me going here in Malacca.'

'It isn't a life I would choose for any relation of mine!'

'Perhaps not, but it suits me.'

Christopher Horton put a hand on her arm, rubbing it up and down her sleeve. 'It isn't your decision to make, Gertrude. Nobody wants you to be unhappy, of course, but it's obvious you can't go on as you have been doing. Don't worry about it! Anyone can see how you came to be placed as you are – it could have happened to any woman! And that's the point, my dear. No woman can expect to manage her own life to her family's satisfaction, she isn't capable of it. Her nature is against her. You've done your best – goodness knows, we all admire your courage, my dear, but courage isn't enough, is it? Women can't help it that they're incapable of logical thought, or a proper understanding of public affairs and making money. We all know it! If you ask me, that's why Cousin Septimus has sent Jack Taviton to take over from you out here. Things not going too well, are they? Only being your brother, he doesn't like to say so. You could do much worse and do as your brother wants and marry young Taviton. He seems to be a fine young fellow and will allow you more freedom than most.'

Trudie forced all emotion from her expression. She had learned more from Wu Chao than she knew, living in the same house with her. 'You're very kind,' she said gently.

For an instant his eyes met hers, before darting away again. 'I hope I am. It's a pity you and your cousin are not better friends. I know very well it isn't all your fault, so don't go blaming yourself entirely! I have frequently mentioned it to Hermione that your life out here would be much easier if she were to invite you to Singapore and introduce you to our own circle of friends – '

'I'm very happy as I am,' Trudie ventured.

Christopher Horton heaved a sigh. 'It won't do! If you'll take my advice, Cousin Gertrude, you'll think seriously about Taviton's offer. I can't hold out any hope of getting a proper income for you from the plantation, good manager as you are. I expect you find it cheaper living amongst the Chinese, but it won't do. Ask Mrs Beresford if you don't believe me!'

'Oh, I know she doesn't approve!' Trudie exclaimed, laughing a little. 'She does allow her daughters to visit me here, though, and frequently comes herself. She and Wu Chao share a love for intricate embroidery, did you know that?'

She could see him think *another foolish woman*, and wished she'd held her tongue. 'Please don't worry about me, Mr Horton. I'm really very contented with my lot!'

'That may be so, but the way you're living reflects on your cousin, my dear, and we can't have that, can we?'

Trudie's eyes twinkled back at him. 'Can't you persuade her to disown me?'

He patted her hand awkwardly. 'It would make my life easier if she were sometimes a little more like you!' He hesitated, thinking his own thoughts. 'Don't you think you should call me Cousin Christopher after all this time?' he complained at last. 'Mr Horton is rather formal – '

'Cousin Hermione insists on it, however.'

'Yes,' he agreed with unusual bitterness. 'She's jealous of you – always has been!'

'*Of me?*'

He nodded his head. 'Your father is everything she wanted in her own: kind, generous, and never short of an admiring word for her. Her own father was a weak man who depended on his younger brother for everything. Hermione doesn't tolerate weakness in a man – as I should know!'

Trudie had never considered what it might be like to be married to her cousin. How strange if Hermione really was jealous of her being her father's daughter. How awkward it was going to be, too, if everyone expected her to marry Jack Taviton. Could she do it? She thought again of the moment when he had kissed her and shuddered inwardly. If all Wu Chao had told her about marriage was true, she knew she could never share her body with anyone like Mr Taviton. She told herself it was because he was a Catholic. Never trust a Catholic! Even her father would agree with that; even, she thought, her jealous cousin wouldn't wish a papist on her, or would she? *Dear* Hermione! How much Trudie wished she'd go back to Singapore and leave her alone!

She would have liked to have discussed the whole interview with Wu Chao. They were no longer merely business partners, though quite when the change had come about, Trudie didn't know. It was something they both took for granted, though Trudie soon found she was telling Wu Chao far more about her life than she heard about the Nonya's intimate doubts and fears. Wu Chao was naturally reticent and her upbringing had made her more so. Besides, she had her parents and her sisters living next door and saw them most days, if only for one of their endless card games. Perhaps she didn't need an outlet as much as did Trudie, who was alone and vulnerable to the social pressures that were put on her.

'I won't marry him! I won't!' Trudie stormed, her temper rising like a geyser now that she had relaxed her control over it. 'Why can't people mind their own business? And as for the suggestion that we're not managing our part of the business to Septimus's satisfaction and need a man to do it for us! Well!'

Wu Chao barely looked up. 'Why you all hot over not'ing? Better you tell me 'bout Maddock ancestors. If Black Jade half English, you tell me 'bout her ancestors.'

Trudie couldn't believe her ears. 'Her *ancestors*? What ancestors?'

Wu Chao plucked her sleeve with an anxious hand. 'All families having ancestors.' She pointed towards her own household shrine, clicking her tongue in exasperation at the bare look it presented. 'Come!' she commanded imperiously.

She led the way out the back door and teetered down the covered passage that led to her parents' house next door. A shout outside the back door was enough for it to be flung open to allow the two women to enter. An excited conversation followed, during which Wu Chao bowed low before the household shrine and then began pointing out to Trudie the names of the Ki family who had done such deeds in their lifetime as to make them worthy to be ancestors.

'Now, who Maddock ancestors?' she demanded.

The Ki women all turned reproachful eyes on Trudie, waiting for her answer. None of them could understand her silence.

'Better take you temple,' Wu Chao said in exasperation. 'You see all Ki ancestors in temple. Where Maddock ancestors?'

'Mr Maddock was a Christian,' Trudie tried to explain. 'I don't know who his ancestors were.'

Wu Chao turned on her in triumph. 'No ancestors! Foreign devils uncivilized people! Better Black Jade be Nonya!'

Trudie was dismayed by the attack. She was impressed despite herself at the small altar, with the pictures of dead members of the Ki family, all of them painted in exactly the same pose. The most revered ancestor was the first Ki who had come to Malacca, alone and without any money at all, and who had died one of the richest of the Babas in the Straits Settlements.

'He civilized person!' Wu Chao informed Trudie, her black eyes gleaming with pride. She bowed low before the altar. 'He come from Middle Kingdom with blessings of gods. Much good joss! He worthy ancestor!'

Trudie tried to remember if Mr Maddock had ever mentioned his parents to her let alone any of his other relatives. They had never had time to discuss such things! It might have been different if his family had come to England in William the Conqueror's train but, as far as Trudie knew there had been nothing to distinguish them from any other English middle-class family who much preferred to keep their own ancestors out of sight as they had probably made their money in trade, or had even come from the artisan class, which nobody would admit to nowadays – nobody from the professions at all events.

'Why do you call China the Middle Kingdom?' she asked instead.

The Ki women were appalled by her ignorance. 'Well known China on'y country, only one civilized. Upper Kingdom abode of gods, especially Jade Emperor, head of all gods. Lower Kingdom bad place, full of devils. China Middle Kingdom. Civilized!'

Trudie was scandalized. 'What about England? Aren't we civilized? What do you think we're doing in India, in Malaya, in Africa? We're doing our best to civilize half the world! How could we do that if we're not civilized ourselves?'

The Ki women tittered and bowed as one person. 'So solly, Tludie.'

Slowly it was borne in on Trudie that to these Nonyas she was the barbarian, the uncivilized person, someone who didn't even acknowledge her own ancestors, let alone pay them the respect that was their undoubted due. She began to laugh.

'I have ancestors!' she claimed.

'Ah!' They were impressed. 'What about your ancestors?'

'They took slaves from Africa and grew sugar in the West Indies. They made a great deal of money.'

Wu Chao breathed out noisily through her teeth. Neither Africa nor the West Indies meant anything to her at all. 'Perhaps this place near Japans?' she asked hopefully.

'On the other side of the world!' Trudie claimed expansively. 'The world is like a ball – '

But the women were already shaking their heads, smiling politely. 'Everybody know Middle Kingdom centre of earth,' they said. And when, later on, Trudie showed Wu Chao an atlas of the world with all the British possessions coloured a pretty pink, the Nonya had remained completely unimpressed by the sight. 'Blitain small place. Middle Kingdom huge. In heart, in mind, on'y just below the abode of gods. Better Black Jade Nonya, yes?'

'Better Black Jade Nonya, no!' Trudie had retorted.

Nor was Wu Chao any more understanding when Trudie tried to explain her reservations about marrying again. Wu Chao only shrugged and went on with her embroidery, her face expressionless. 'What woman ever have say in man to mally?'

'We do in England!' Trudie declared angrily.

'Then tell blother not mally blother's friend.'

For once in her life Trudie dithered. She didn't want to marry Jack Taviton, it was true, but she knew Hermione would never rest until she saw her married to someone. It had been different at first, when her cousin had thought the plantation spelled untold riches which the Hortons would naturally share, Christopher Horton being Trudie's only male connection in the Straits Settlements. Now, she was convinced Trudie had been left a pauper and bitterly resented the time her husband spent on her cousin's affairs. It was as well she was also a stupid woman or it might have occurred to her to wonder how Trudie lived as well as she did, even if it was in the Chinese quarter, away from her own kind.

Trudie plumped herself down on a chair beside Wu Chao. 'You don't understand! Septimus can do anything he likes to our business – and probably will, if he ever guesses that he's only getting the official version of our profits! What are we going to do then?'

Wu Chao remained calm. 'If no' liking blother's fliend, better choose 'nother way. Change joss. You t'ink some-t'ing, Tludie.'

Trudie could only hope she was right.

Where Hermione was concerned, Mrs Beresford's hospitality was wearing thinner by the day, so Trudie wasn't completely surprised when she received an urgent message from the Lieutenant-Governor's wife that she herself would be unavailable that day for lunch and tea and would Trudie please do what she could to entertain her cousin in her stead.

Trudie knew this to be a perfectly reasonable request as, officially, her cousins were still staying with her and there was no reason why Mrs Beresford had been called upon to feed them all this time, even if they did object to the mixture of Chinese, Malay, and English cuisine that Wu Chao organized in Trudie's household. Wu Chao had been astonished by their bad manners, doing her best to save Trudie's face by never mentioning such uncivilized persons in her presence. Inwardly though, she shuddered to think what the rest of Trudie's family must be like. Very probably, they were even more unmannerly than the barbarian Hortons, for Trudie had said herself they had no respect for the things that matter in this life, only for their strange god who, for some incomprehensible reason, had determined that Trudie should spend most of her childhood alone in her room, existing on a fast of bread and water.

To Wu Chao, religion meant colour and excitement. There was the Chinese New Year, the Cheng Beng, when they all visited the graves of their ancestors and shared a great feast with their whole family in the temple; there was the Dragon Boat festival in honour of a Minister of the State of Chu, who had committed suicide after a disagreement with his King, when there were dragon-boat races held wherever there were Chinese people to witness them; there was the Moon-cake festival, a female occasion when little moon cakes were offered first to the moon and then to relatives and friends; and, best of all, was the month of the Wandering Ghosts, when the Hungry Ghosts of Hell were let loose to wander the world and had to be fed with offerings in the temples, market places, and even in private homes. Yes, this was the festival Wu Chao liked best, as there were sometimes Chinese operas performed in specially constructed open-air theatres near the temples. Also, it was a time when everyone burned large quantities of joss paper which would re-emerge as real money in the spirit world, thus keeping the living free from any mischief the spirits might otherwise visit on them.

Soon would be another festival, the 24th day of the 12th moon, when the household gods would go up to heaven, to report the doings of the people in their charge on earth. Everything had to be cleaned and polished inside the house for this particular day, and the gods were sent off to the sound of firecrackers exploding all about them, to remind them not to tell tales on those who cultivated their shrines and gave them worship all the year long. Wu Chao was doubtful what the household gods would report this year, no matter how carefully Wu Chao had explained to them that Trudie had her own Christian God and meant no disrespect to them when she passed them by without so much as a nod of the head. Wu Chao had done her best to appease their anger, the rest was how it would be. Joss was joss.

Trudie, as unaware of Wu Chao's worries about her lack of respect for the gods as Wu Chao often was of Hermione's honeyed barbs whenever the two cousins met, sped her way up the hill to the Stadthuys, comforting herself with the thought that several of the European women would be there, making the most of each other's company while their husbands were otherwise engaged.

Hermione behaved abominably as always, patronizing the insecure and making far too much of those few Malaccan residents whom she felt would be socially useful to her. Trudie was ashamed for her, and ashamed that she should be her cousin. She felt she had more than done her duty by the time Mrs Beresford returned and relieved her of her responsibilities as substitute hostess.

'When are they going back to Singapore?' the older woman hissed in her ear, as she escorted her out to the hall to say goodbye.

'Perhaps you could get your husband to banish them?' Trudie retorted hopefully.

'If only he would!'

Trudie was still laughing as she stepped into the waiting rickshaw. The Chinese coolie turned round and really looked at her, seeing her for the first time, when she gave her address. He, too, was a member of the Ki clan, he told her, and would one day be as rich as Wu Chao's branch of the family.

It was difficult to understand much of what he was saying. His English was poor and the faster he ran, the less intelligible he became. When they came to a halt outside Trudie's house, he helped her out of the rickshaw with as much refinement as if he had already achieved his aim, refusing her proffered fare as if he could afford it as easily as could any European. It didn't matter that he was dressed only in a few rags and that his feet were bare because he couldn't afford any shoes.

There was silence when Trudie entered the house, an unnatural silence at that time of day. Anxiously, she went into Wu Chao's part of the house, calling her name. An upstairs door slammed, but there was no other answer.

Trudie rushed up the narrow, wooden steps, going straight to the room where Wu Chao slept, Black Jade in a tiny cot by her side. 'Wu Chao – '

'Tludie, help!'

Trudie pushed open the door and went inside, her stomach heaving in shock. She wasn't even surprised to find Christopher Horton standing over Wu Chao, his trousers about his ankles.

'Go away!' he ordered Trudie over his shoulder. 'It has nothing to do with you!'

Her fury lent her a strength she never would have possessed otherwise. Trudie hurled herself against Mr Horton, inserting herself between the astonished man and Wu Chao's cowering figure on the bed.

'Out! Get out!' she screamed at him. 'This time you've gone too far! I want you and Cousin Hermione out of my house tonight. Is that clear?'

She thought he looked more pathetic than alarming as he tried to fasten his trousers, his face scarlet and his breath coming in great gasps. Trudie opened her eyes wide, refusing to look away.

'It's your fault,' he whispered. 'All your fault, Gertrude! You don't understand! Your woman invited me – '

'Liar!' Trudie went on looking at him, thinking how easy it was to despise men who had no control over their baser instincts. She was ashamed that Wu Chao should have seen him like this. She turned on her heel. 'I'll see you downstairs!'

She could still taste her fury on her tongue when he finally came down the stairs.

'You can't turn us out at a moment's notice! What am I to tell dear Hermione?'

'Tell her what you please,' Trudie returned shortly.

Christopher Horton came a couple of steps nearer. 'My God, Gertrude, these things happen all the time! Women like that expect it! A few coins change hands and nothing more is said! What did you expect when you asked me into this house? I wanted it to be you, someone warm and affectionate! You don't know what it's like, married to Hermione.'

'No, but I can imagine – '

'You mean we can stay?'

His eagerness made him the more pitiful. 'This is Wu Chao's house. It belongs to the Ki family, not to me. You can never enter this house again. Never! Ki Wu Chao is a virtuous woman, as anyone around here will testify. She is right to call us barbarians, foreign devils, with no face to lose in front of civilized people because we look on them as dirt!'

She saw the anger light in Mr Horton's eyes, but she didn't care.

'Virtuous, is she?' he spat across the room at her. 'What do you suppose happened between her and your sainted husband? He was married to you, wasn't he? I tell you again, it's all your fault for giving houseroom to such a female in a supposedly Christian household! What else did you expect? She's *Chinese*!'

The words refused to come. Trudie went on staring at Mr Horton, unable to say a word. What she wanted to shout was, *Maybe she is Chinese, she's also the best friend I've ever had!* But she didn't say it, because she knew he would never be able to understand it. She wasn't sure she understood it herself, but if it came to a choice between Wu Chao and her cousins, she knew she would choose Wu Chao every time.

Chapter Thirteen

Hannah Beresford wished she were a wiser woman. She was appalled by what had happened, but she was also a woman of the world and knew it to be inevitable. How did one begin to explain all that to Trudie? It was quite beyond her.

'My love, you have every reason to think me disloyal for taking in your cousins last night, but what else was I to do?'

'I don't know,' Trudie said wearily. 'I still can't believe it really happened. How could he do such a thing to Wu Chao?'

'I imagine any woman would have done,' Mrs Beresford said dryly. 'I agree it's very shocking, but you're making all too much of it. Wu Chao was unharmed, thanks to your timely arrival, and *she* isn't making a fuss, is she?'

Trudie lifted her chin in an all too characteristic gesture. 'Wu Chao is a friend of mine.'

'Yes, and therein lies the trouble,' Mrs Beresford said with unusual bitterness. 'I'm sorry, Trudie, but someone must say it! It's all very well to have a Chinese woman as your maid, but *not* as your friend. I'm sure she's very nice, nicer than most of the Europeans you know out here, but that isn't the point. No, listen to me, if you please, because somebody *must* tell you this. It ought to be Mrs Horton, she is your cousin after all, though one can't help understanding your reservations about that young madam! She really is the most tiresome creature alive! I trust you won't feel that about me, however?'

'Of course not, ma'am.'

Mrs Beresford relaxed a trifle. 'Good, because I've become very fond of you and I've no ambition to trespass where I'm not wanted; indeed, I wouldn't be speaking to you now if I didn't feel it to be my duty, for I can imagine few things more likely to cause trouble than minding someone else's business for them!'

Trudie's anger died down a little as she acknowledged the justice of that. 'Am I giving you a bad time, ma'am? I apologize for making you uncomfortable in my behalf, but I shall not have either of them under my roof again!'

'I should hope not!'

Trudie sat down again, casting a puzzled look at her hostess. 'Then what do you want of me?'

'A little discretion, my dear. No more than that! You realize what the Hortons will be writing home to your father, don't you?'

Trudie did. Some of her confidence deserted her. 'What am I going to do?'

'If you'll take my advice, you'll do nothing. *I* will write to your mother, I think, explaining exactly what happened. I shall also explain how you have no choice but to live where you do, and how you do, and that your parents aren't to believe one word of anything Christopher Horton may imply to your disadvantage. I shall leave them in no doubt as to what actually happened – '

'They won't believe you, ma'am.'

Mrs Beresford was not accustomed to having her word doubted. 'What makes you say that?' she demanded.

Trudie sat perfectly still, the colour drained from her face. She looked much younger than her years and Mrs Beresford's first reaction was to put her arms about her and give her some of the affection she had plainly never known from her own parents.

'My father won't hear a word against Cousin Hermione.'

'I see.'

'I don't think you do, ma'am. He also hates me!'

Mrs Beresford was shocked. 'But why?'

'I think he despises all females – except for Hermione! My sisters both say he does. They say his particular dislike for me is because I'm the youngest. My – mother can't have any more children. She – she cries a lot. I used to wonder why, but Wu Chao – ' She broke off, not liking to confess her former ignorance, quite sure in her own mind that nobody could ever have suspected that she hadn't known.

Mrs Beresford, not deceived for a moment, was only glad that *someone* had taken the trouble to explain the facts of life to her young friend. 'You need say no more, dear. I understand exactly. No wonder you were so irate that Mr Horton should try to force your maid under your own roof, if that's the way your father treats your mother! Thankfully, most men are not at all like that, but there have always been the few, and there probably always will be. I'm afraid Mrs Horton is exactly the sort of silly woman who would exploit such a situation to her own advantage – if I read her aright! She must know that you can't possibly be living on the profits from your late husband's plantation and would love to make even more trouble for you.' She frowned, a new thought crossing her mind. 'How *do* you manage?'

'Wu Chao's family in China send all kinds of antiques and Chinese artefacts to us here in Malacca and then I sell them through my late husband's Emporium in London which my brother has always managed until now.'

Mrs Beresford's jaw dropped. 'You're in *partnership* with Wu Chao? My dear child! I hope the Hortons don't know that?'

Trudie shook her head. A mischievous smile lit her face. 'Nobody knows, not even Septimus! Women are at a shocking disadvantage in business, not being allowed to make our own contracts and so on, though I have discovered that being a widow has certain advantages over having a husband when it comes to dealing with one's own possessions and, as I have no ambition to starve, I decided to do something to make some money – something which didn't involve my family. I thought it better to keep it to myself – '

'I should think so!'

Trudie bit her lip. 'Oh dear, I've made things awkward for you now, haven't I? I'm so very sorry. I didn't think – I do apologize! How could I have had the bad manners – ? Mrs Beresford, please forget I said anything at all!'

To her surprise, the other woman was far from being embarrassed by her revelation, however. She was looking at Trudie with new eyes. 'I can't think why I never guessed before!' she said at last. 'Do you – do you make much money? I know I shouldn't ask – '

'A great deal.'

'All by yourself?'

'Oh no,' Trudie corrected her. 'Wu Chao is an excellent businesswoman as well as my friend. I couldn't do anything at all if it weren't for her family's help. *My* family wouldn't care if I starved, as long as nobody could point a finger at them, of course!'

'I hope you're not right about that,' Mrs Beresford rejoined, very much afraid that she was. 'Better not to chance your arm, however, by telling anyone else – not even my husband! Though I'm sure he'd admire you as much as I do if he *did* know! No, my love, discretion is undoubtedly the better part of valour. I shall explain to your cousin that shock made you hasty in your condemnation of her husband,' she decided, 'and I shall most certainly write to your mother, explaining how fond of you I have become and how much I hope you will be allowed to stay on in Malacca all the while that we are here.'

Trudie put her hand over the older woman's in real gratitude. 'You are much too kind, ma'am!'

'I like you, Trudie. Won't you call me Hannah after all this time? I have been meaning to ask you these last few weeks but never seemed to have the opportunity somehow.'

'Thank you.' Trudie looked as complimented as she felt. 'And what should I do?'

'As little as possible,' her hostess answered her quickly. 'I should wait and see what your cousin has to say. It might be a shrewd move to return to Singapore with her for a while, if you're determined not to go home to England. The poor dear doesn't exactly shine in your company and that will be bound to occur to her after a while. I think, when it does, she will be only too glad for you to return to Malacca.'

Trudie laughed. 'I'm afraid it's the other way about! My cousin, and my sisters, too, have always outshone me in society! Not even my brother likes me very much – and he is quite the nicest of us all.'

Mrs Beresford reminded herself how important it was to give one's daughters the confidence and pride in themselves that would see them safely launched when they came to be adults, whilst at the same time swallowing down her anger that none of Trudie's family had seen fit to do the same for her. No wonder the child consorted with the Chinese in preference to her own kind! Wu Chao was obviously a sensible and kindly woman who, in other circumstances, might have done wonders for the young Mrs Maddock. As things were, however, the sooner Trudie forgot all about her the better, and Singapore might very well be the answer to that.

But would Trudie forget about the Chinese woman? 'You didn't tell me how you met this . . . Wu Chao, did you say her name is?'

'No,' Trudie said.

Mrs Beresford sighed. 'I don't want to press you if you don't want to tell me, but there were some rumours going about at one time that your husband – '

'He married her,' Trudie said bluntly.

Mrs Beresford felt quite faint. 'Married her, dear? I thought he was married to you?'

'Yes, he was. He married her according to Chinese custom. She was his consort – '

'His mistress?'

Trudie shook her head. She wrinkled her nose thoughtfully. 'I don't know if we would consider it a legal marriage exactly, but as far as the Ki family is concerned, it was perfectly legal. Black Jade is my husband's daughter. I found it rather awkward at first, especially as Mr Horton wasn't prepared to admit that either of them had any claim on Mr Maddock's estate, but there was no point in making a great fuss about it. Jeremy was dead, and Wu Chao and Black Jade were very much alive. As Jeremy's widow, they became my responsibility, whether I wanted it or not.'

It was at this precise moment that Mrs Beresford admitted to herself that the whole situation was quite beyond her. 'Why you?' she asked.

'I'm not sure,' Trudie admitted. 'I think it's a matter of honour. Anyway, the long and the short of it is that I can't just abandon them, can I?' She preferred on the whole not to rehearse the details of Black Jade's birth, realizing that Mrs Beresford would never understand why she had acted as she had. 'Nor should I want to,' she added quietly. 'Wu Chao is the best friend I've ever had. I know I ought to like Cousin Hermione more than I do, but one can't like people to order, can one? Surely friendship ought to mean more than making use of other people for one's own ends?'

'I suppose so. What would your father say about it? He's a clergyman, after all. He should know what's what, if anyone does.'

'Yes, he is. He doesn't like people much though. We'll never agree, he and I. He judges men by the length of their purses and his religion is cold, a matter of law and avoiding anything that might condemn one to hell. I can't be like that! People and religion should be shot through with the beauty of truth and compassion, and as much joy as one can find in both God and man, otherwise it doesn't seem to be worth very much, does it?'

'My dear, don't expect too much from life!' Mrs Beresford exclaimed, seriously alarmed. 'There is a thing called duty, too!'

Trudie smiled and deliberately twisted the other woman's words. 'I was brought up to do my duty! No one ever mentioned love, or joy, believe me! It's my duty to make provision for all Mr Maddock's dependants, and I will, but I also mean to enjoy myself as much as I possibly can while I'm doing it, Cousin Hermione or no Cousin Hermione!'

Mrs Beresford saw she was being managed, but she didn't resent it. 'I hope you do, my dear,' she said gently. 'But go carefully! Neither of the Hortons wishes you well and you are very vulnerable as a woman on her own out here.'

Trudie, if she had not already known the truth of this, had ample opportunity to find out when her cousin came to call, battering at the door of the house in Tun Tan

Cheng Lock Street with the handle of her parasol. Trudie herself went to the door, determined to spare Wu Chao what embarrassment she could.

'Cousin Hermione! Won't you come in?'

Hermione sniffed. 'I thought you had forbidden us to enter your establishment, though what all the fuss is about I really don't know! Your behaviour towards Christopher and myself leaves a lot to be desired, Gertrude Grant!'

'Shall we have some tea?' Trudie suggested calmly.

'Not until you've apologized for misjudging my husband! I couldn't believe it when he told me what you'd accused him of! I don't know how you've managed to persuade everyone in Malacca that you're so innocent, when you choose to live with a Chinese whore, and then imagine that my husband should want to rape her! Ugh! Imagine it! A dirty Chinese woman! You ought to know by now that none of them have any morals, hiding themselves away in their houses and getting up to God knows what! If anyone was in any danger, it was poor Christopher!'

'Wu Chao – '

'She isn't even Christian! Uncle Jonathan will have something to say about that! And, as for the child! Well, words fail me! Of course we can all guess who the father is! You should have seen to it that that Welshman was shown the door along with his harlot! *That's* what any proper Christian would have done. You, more than any of us, should be setting these heathens a good example, not condoning their sinful ways!'

'Mr Rhys is not the father.'

Hermione made the most of her superior height, shaking out her skirts and arranging her parasol to its very best advantage. Trudie thought it a shame that her only audience should have been a despised female cousin, for she certainly looked very pretty.

A bland stare from the pale blue eyes completed the picture. 'You'd know, wouldn't you? Oh, don't pretend to me, my dear! As if we don't all know perfectly well that you were never a wife to Mr Maddock, no matter what you pretend!'

Trudie forced an amused expression on to her face. 'Do you?'

Hermione was suddenly less than sure. There was something different about Gertrude which she couldn't quite put her finger on. Was it possible that she really did know what she was talking about? Surely not!

'How's the romance with Cousin Septimus's silly young friend going?' She deliberately accentuated the 'silly' to make it more pointed.

Trudie raised a brow. 'Romance?'

Hermione raised her parasol and arranged it across her knee. It was made of sheer silk and was beautiful. She would have liked it less if she had known that it had been Wu Chao who had sold it to her husband – not directly, of course, but through one of the Hokkien maids who thought nothing of bargaining with the foreign devil, laughing at him behind his back because he was so easily parted from his money.

'Wasn't that the idea of his coming?'

'Septimus was hoping he would make the voyage to Yokohama in his place. Apparently, Japanese goods are all the rage just now in London.'

'Christopher says they're a lot of murdering devils!'

Trudie sucked in her cheeks, her eyes dancing with laughter. 'Exactly what they say about us!'

Hermione was genuinely appalled. Was this creature the same person as the dowdy sparrow her uncle had taken such a delight in bullying? For the first time in an age, perhaps as long ago as when they had all sailed out from

England together, she really looked at her cousin and was astonished by what she saw. Where had this elegant young lady come from? Her dress was not only beautifully cut, it was embroidered with real jewels and, even in London, would have cost a fortune! Hermione was used to being fêted for her fashionable appearance and her cool beauty: she was angered to realize that Trudie was far better turned out than she could ever hope to be! Why, the material of her dress alone cost more than Hermione's whole allowance for a year!

'I hope you won't make such a ridiculous assertion to anyone else!' She eyed her cousin thoughtfully. 'I'm ashamed of you, I really am. I'm ashamed to be connected to you! What Uncle Jonathan would think of his daughter now, I really can't imagine!'

'Who cares?' Trudie muttered. She put her head on one side. 'You'll never persuade me to return to London, Cousin Hermione, so don't waste your time trying, please. I don't want to quarrel with you, but we could easily fall out over that, and so I warn you!'

Hermione's mind was still on her cousin's dress. She wanted one like it, wanted it so badly that she could hardly contain herself.

'Why don't you come and stay with us for a while in Singapore? You could visit with Mrs – I really forget her name? – Eliot, wasn't it? You could even spend a few weeks with us, if you've a mind to, replenish your wardrobe, and so on. I should be glad to lend you a hand. It would do you good to get out and about and forget about the havey-cavey way you've been living here.'

'I like it here in Malacca!'

A shadow crossed Hermione's fair features. 'Yes, but you have to get away for a while whether you like it or not! The incident with Christopher really made me very angry, you know. I said more than I should have done – as anyone would have done in the same place, I'm sure, for I was sorely tried, having to stay here in this terrible house instead of with the Beresfords at the Stadthuys. You always were insensitive and thoughtless of others, Cousin Gertrude, so you won't begin to understand how ordinary people might feel to know those horrible Chinese are always about, and that half-caste child! That woman's part of the house is little better than a gambling den, did you know that? Christopher told me! *And* you make a terrible hostess, cousin dear! Refusing to supply us with ordinary food, or indeed with anything fit to eat, smugly expecting us to treat your *maid* as if she were our social equal, just as if she were a decent Christian person and not a savage!'

Trudie sat very still for a long moment, then she said, 'Who have you been talking to, Cousin Hermione? Mrs Beresford – '

'Not to her! She wouldn't listen! But there are plenty of people who feel threatened by the way you live here, exactly as Christopher and I do! Good Christian people who try to give a good example to these benighted heathen, wearing themselves out to bring them a little civilization in exchange for trade – ' Her blue eyes were two chips of ice. 'Do you trade with your maid's people? Do you?'

'I? Surely Cousin Christopher – '

'Mr Horton to you!' Hermione snapped. 'He isn't your cousin!'

'He's your husband,' Trudie pointed out carefully. She wanted time to think, time to decide for herself what would be the best thing to do.

'Is that how you make your money?' Hermione insisted.

'I have no money!' Trudie retorted, committing herself to the lie almost with relish.

'What about that dress you're wearing? Such garments don't come free, my dear!'

Trudie looked down at herself, seeing herself through her cousin's eyes. She smiled a sweet smile. 'Not free, but they're not as expensive as you might imagine if one has a Nonya maid. Their embroidery is famous throughout the Straits Settlements – like their cuisine.'

'Is that why you keep her?'

Trudie went on smiling. 'It could be.'

'I see. I wonder if you shouldn't bring her to Singapore with you, what do you think?'

'I think not.'

Hermione flounced round the room in silence, fingering this and that as she went. Everything, she noticed, was in the best of taste, even though she wouldn't have wanted half the objects in any house of hers. She could have wept when she thought how little Christopher had been able to wring out of the plantation, when Trudie had all this! She had to have another source of income! Whoever had thought up that stupid saying that two could live as cheaply as one had never tried it. Hermione needed more, and more, and more! There weren't enough jewels and fine materials in the whole of Singapore to satisfy her, even had Christopher been willing to pay for them, which he was more and more reluctant to do, and all the time Trudie had been feathering her own nest, the deceitful minx!

She thought back to all she had heard about Mr Jeremy Maddock when Trudie had married him. Few people had known anything about him, except that he was rich, rich, rich! He had put up the capital for Septimus's Emporium, agreeing to be the sleeping partner in the venture, and he had left Trudie behind in England while he had returned to the East to make yet more money. Why the plantation? There was no money in the bedraggled coffee bushes out there! So where was it all coming from? She knew for a fact that Trudie knew nothing about anything else that went on out at the plantation and she most certainly didn't benefit from her husband's little sideline there.

'Does Septimus know about everything you buy and sell?' she asked, whirling round to face her cousin.

'Of course he does! I send him accounts every month. You're making too much of a small hobby, Cousin Hermione. What Septimus allows me to keep for myself wouldn't keep you in pin-money. In his opinion of women he is very like our father, though I wouldn't dare tell him so!'

'You seem to do yourself very well all the same!' Hermione spat out.

Trudie went on smiling. She thought her face would never be the same again – or her conscience! 'I hire this house from the Ki family. Fortunately, it never occurred to them to ask a European an economic rent in case they brought themselves to the notice of the Foreign Devil Government, which no Chinese wants to do even when they have nothing to hide. I couldn't live like this anywhere else – as your husband would be the first to tell you!'

Somewhat mollified, Hermione sat down again. 'All the more reason for you to come to Singapore for a while,' she said. 'It would be hateful if it were to get out that you're in debt to the Chinese! I'd never live it down!'

With her cousin gone, Trudie sat on by herself for a long, long time, her hands folded on her knee, thinking. It had been a mistake to wear this dress when her cousin was in Malacca, and even more of a mistake to let Hermione see too much behind the scenes of the way she lived.

The door opened and she looked up with a sudden lightening of her spirits. She was sure it was going to be Mr Rhys, who never waited for anyone to open the door to him, but came stamping in, often whistling or singing one of his Welsh songs. Trudie enjoyed his visits with a fierce enjoyment, although she would never admit as much to anyone, least of all herself, for he was always cheerful, and seemed to have the strength of ten, riding back and forth from the plantation as though it were a mere afternoon's stroll.

But this time it was not Mr Rhys who stood in the doorway, but Mr Taviton, hat in hand, smiling nervously at her across the room.

'The door was open,' he explained, 'almost as if you were expecting me! Were you, by any chance?'

Trudie returned the smile, as she shook her head. 'You just missed my cousin.'

'Ah!'

'She's invited me to stay with her for a while in Singapore,' Trudie went on smoothly.

That wiped the smile off Mr Taviton's face. 'Has she, by jove! Did she tell you why?'

Trudie stretched lazily. 'Does there have to be a reason? We are cousins! I expect she feels the need of a little female company. Cousin Hermione always has hundreds of male admirers, but she doesn't easily make friends among their wives.'

Mr Taviton blinked down at her, a look of disapproval on his face. 'You don't much like your cousin, do you?'

'She doesn't care for me either,' Trudie responded.

'Indeed? She and Mr Horton seem to be doing everything possible to rescue you from the disastrous position your husband left you in! Are you going to Singapore?'

'Yes, I think I shall.'

Mr Taviton sat down opposite her, on the very edge of his chair, frowning at a spot on the floor somewhere between his knees. 'What about the import/export business you run for Septimus? You can't run that from Singapore!'

'Oh, there's nothing much happening at the moment,' Trudie said with indifference. 'Japan is the coming place! For two pins I'd go myself to Yokohama!'

Mr Taviton was aghast. 'That's no place for a woman!' He cleared his throat angrily. 'This isn't either!' He pulled at his too tight collar. 'There isn't any chance for me with you, is there?'

'I'm sorry,' Trudie answered uncomfortably.

'You're not at all as Septimus led me to expect,' he went on. 'Oh, please don't misunderstand me! You see, he said you were easily managed, with few ideas of your own. You're not like that, are you?'

'No.'

'No, you're better than that, but I didn't know. I wish I had – before I met you, I mean.'

'It wouldn't have made any difference,' she said. 'I'm sorry.'

'So you say. Forgive me, but I can see why Septimus is anxious about you. He and I thought we had the answer to that. We were wrong. But the basic situation hasn't changed. Your cousins, no matter how much you may dislike them, are right about that!'

Trudie flashed him a look from beneath her lashes. 'I am very well as I am,' she repeated. 'What's wrong with the way I live here?'

'Nothing, if you were a man. Septimus said that running the Malaccan end of his business was a nice little hobby for you while you were getting over the death of your husband, but it will hardly do for the rest of your life. Now don't flare up when I say this, for it can only be the truth, and that is that women were not meant to earn their own living and play at being businessmen like their brothers!

That's for men, not women! Only bad can come out of a woman presuming she's as good as her brothers, you know! Women are biologically incapable of thinking clearly about their dealings with other folk – look at the way you have allowed that Chinese woman to make rings round you, taking advantage of you in every way! I know, I know, you think it a great piece of impertinence on my part to be saying all this to you. I can only excuse it by reminding you that Septimus is my friend and he did me the honour to take me into his confidence long before I left England. He had little good to say about either your father or Christopher Horton, as a matter of fact, the only two male connections you have who *do* have the right to rein in your activities, and I know he'd think me failing in my duty to him if I didn't speak out to you now.'

Trudie clenched her fists, striving for calm. 'I see. You blame Wu Chao for Cousin Christopher's attack on her?'

'That's neither here nor there – '

'It is to me! Common justice – '

'My dear Miss Gertrude – if I may presume to call you that? – it's precisely because you don't see why I must take the word of a respectable European gentleman before that of a serving woman, brought up to lie and cheat, that it's obvious that I am right!' He paused significantly. 'I am sure she misunderstood your cousin's intentions,' he added at last.

Trudie could only stare at him in disbelief. How was it possible that he, and Septimus, and all the rest of them, not only could bring themselves to believe such an obvious untruth, but also that they couldn't be wrong? They were all so certain of their own superiority in every way, when they were moral pygmies! And hypocrites! She felt ashamed to be associated with them!

She wouldn't help Wu Chao by quarrelling with Jack

Taviton, however. 'You think Septimus would want me to go to Singapore with my cousins?'

'I think it would be the wise thing to do. Forget Yokohama! Forget all about business for a while, that's my advice to you.'

'Septimus will feel the draught in London, even if I only go for a few weeks. I wonder if he's thought of that?'

Mr Taviton managed not to laugh. 'He won't notice the loss of what you manage to send him! He's been running a whole Emporium, not a street stall! That's what I love about you ladies, you do exaggerate your own importance, don't you? Septimus told me you could hardly bear to tear yourself away from London, thinking he couldn't manage without you then, but he did, didn't he?'

'His profits fell,' Trudie observed dryly.

'And you thought that had something to do with you? Never, my dear! You think that because you didn't understand all the different strands that went to make up the business. He had to keep an eye on more departments than you have fingers to count on. Bless you, he didn't only buy and sell Oriental goods.'

'No, but they made up more than half his profits. More, after the success of the Japanese Exhibition in Paris. I'll have to see what new lines I can put his way while I'm in Singapore. Malacca is a bit of a backwater in some ways these days, though it suits our purpose better for the moment.'

Mr Taviton smiled kindly. 'To hear you talk, one might think you knew what you're talking about! Who actually runs the business for you? I dare say Septimus wouldn't object to my keeping an eye on it for you for a while – better than Christopher Horton, eh?'

'Much better! I'd love it if you'd go to Yokohama, Mr

Taviton, but there's nothing to interest you here. A woman's hobby, as you say!'

'People say the Japanese are worse than the Chinese!' He shuddered, then he sighed. 'I wonder what your husband would have made of all these changes in the world, Mrs Maddock. Would he have gone to Yokohama, I ask myself, and I answer, probably not. He'd lost his touch before he died, hadn't he? It was his money that opened the Emporium in the first place, wasn't it? I wonder why he left it that none of the profits should come to you – that is the position, isn't it? How few of us will admit our own mortality! He can hardly have thought he'd be dead before he even saw you again, leaving you with so little to live on. He must have had some plan, though not even Septimus knows what it was.'

Trudie hesitated, then she said, 'He was a very long-sighted man. I think he did have a plan, and I'm sure Yokohama would have been part of it!'

'But not for me,' Mr Taviton answered sadly. 'I'll have to seek my fortune elsewhere – and my wife also, isn't that so?'

Trudie bit her lip, liking him better than she ever had. 'I'm so sorry, yes, it is,' she said.

Wu Chao placed the dish of duck in front of Trudie, bowing slightly as she did so. 'Plenty for two, Tludie. I tell Rhys man he eat with you, yes?'

Trudie felt her tiredness recede into the background. A little company was exactly what she needed just then and who better than Mr Rhys, who might be as scornful of women's abilities as were any of the other men, but who wouldn't dare show it because he knew himself to be little better than a manual worker, even though he called himself the manager of her plantation, almost as if he were a gentleman.

She felt a warmth and a sparkle come to life inside her as he walked into the room, but no one else would have known of it. He sat down, folding his large body into the chair with practised ease. He looked what he was, his large hands dwarfing the spoon and fork Wu Chao put beside his place.

'Eat!' she bade him, ignoring Trudie for once. 'Eat much, Rhys man. Better you keep up strength, no?'

Mr Rhys did as he was bidden. When he was on his third helping of rice, manipulating the chopsticks as dexterously as any Chinese, for it was only when he used the European implements that he looked clumsy and unsure of himself, he looked up and saw Trudie's amused eyes watching his every movement.

'What's the joke?' he asked her. 'I expected to find you in tears at the prospect of going to Singapore!'

She lifted her chin. 'I'm not so chicken-hearted!'

He looked down at his food. 'Was I eating too fast? I wasn't taught the sort of manners you're accustomed to – '

'You weren't taught any manners!' she teased him. 'If you had been, you'd know it's customary to see that I have everything I want before you tuck in to your share!'

He reddened. 'My mother always makes my father eat his fill before she helps herself. Is that wrong?'

Trudie shook her head. 'It's not right or wrong, it's different from the way I was brought up.' She grinned. 'Wu Chao would probably approve! I'm beginning to think the manners of the gentlemen are as hypocritical as everything else about them! They pretend to defer to the weaker sex, while actually ruling them with a rod of iron!'

He went back to eating his rice. 'As bad as that?'

'Worse!' She watched him shake with laughter and hated him for it. 'I thought *you* would understand!' she exclaimed.

'I do. The Welsh have been dealing with such things ever since King Edgar forbade them to cross Offa's Dyke into England on pain of death! The Welsh, they keep telling us, sing well, but they don't understand how to govern themselves.'

She nodded, her resentment ebbing away. 'Like women!'

'Are you going to Singapore?'

'I think I must.'

His eyes met hers across the table, but she had no way of telling what he was thinking.

'Good,' he said. 'Singapore should be very good for you. There's someone there I should like you to meet.' He leaned back, putting his bowl back on the table. 'Have you ever heard of a Chinese gentleman known as Whampoa?' he asked her.

Chapter Fourteen

Wu Chao pushed her chair a little away from the table, her expression as carefully blank as ever. She had explained to Trudie many times before that, amongst her people, it was the height of bad manners to embarrass other people with an undignified display of emotion. She, herself, never did so, unless it was when she was overcome with excitement at one of her interminable card games.

She had already chided Trudie for railing against her relations, especially for trying to push her into marriage with Jack Taviton, who might have been a good friend to Septimus, but who had little else to recommend him.

'What woman ever choose husband?' Wu Chao had asked her. 'Better obey palents. Palents take good being of whole family into consideration. Why you not do what blother want?'

Trudie's explanation that he would be bad for business had almost convinced her. 'Worse than cousins?' she had asked in sudden anxiety.

'He would be my *husband*!' Trudie had reminded her forcefully.

Now, seated in the background as she was, Wu Chao nevertheless seemed to dominate the whole discussion without saying anything unless she was directly appealed to by one of the others.

'Better Tludie go Singapore, why not? Never mind not rike man-cousin, woman-cousin. Never mind liking. Not important. Important make good business, no? Important not to anger family. Much better dutiful daughter, no?'

Trudie sought Mr Rhys's support. '*You* know better than anyone how Christopher Horton has tried to use the plantation to enrich himself. I don't want *either* of them having any say in our future!'

'No,' Mr Rhys agreed fervently. 'Take the advice of a Welshman, Mrs Maddock, and do what we've always done when the English threatened. Make the terrain as unattractive as possible; pretend you have nothing they want, that you're poor and defenceless. If they believe you, they'll go away again and leave you alone.'

'Is that what you did in the Welsh mines?' Trudie asked, hoping to find out more about the large Welshman.

'Less in the mines. The mine-owners have always known the coal is there.'

'And they're all English, I suppose?' Trudie asked innocently.

'Not all. We've been living side by side for a long time now. England forgets all about us when it comes to lawmaking, however. They know nothing about us.'

'It seems to me you're doing pretty well out of that law!' Trudie told him flatly. 'You're still living under the Union Flag, as well as all the Scots and the Irish who are making their fortunes in its shadow.'

He looked at her, his eyes lazy and watchful. 'The Welsh flag isn't represented in the Union Flag.'

How strange, she thought. What a strange people the Welsh must be, and how few gentlemen there must be amongst them for she could never recollect having met any in her father's parish, or anywhere in London. Perhaps one couldn't tell them apart from other people once they had lived away from their homeland for some time.

'Yes, well,' she said aloud, 'we'll none of us make our fortunes under any flag if the Hortons get to know about our true profits. I'll have to pretend I have nothing to lose by going to Singapore. That means Wu Chao will have an awful lot to do here in Malacca.'

Wu Chao never even looked up. 'When you go Singapore?'

'I'll leave with my cousins.'

A faint sigh came from the Nonya. 'You miss wedding of Swee Neo. So solly. Never mind, you saying much work. Rhys man help, no?'

Caradoc Rhys shook his head. 'I shall go to Singapore also.' He grinned at Trudie and, although she didn't mind his familiar manner precisely, she wished she understood him better. Far more than Wu Chao, he made her feel that in the last resort he would go his own way, rather than hers. She hoped it would never come to a battle between them because her heart wouldn't be in the winning of it. How much more difficult it was to deal with one's inferiors than with one's own kind.

'Never mind, I help Swee Neo marry,' Wu Chao interspersed gently.

That brought Trudie's attention back to her. 'You won't be able to manage that and all the extra work in the business, will you?'

'Oh yes, not worry, Tludie. I do much work before wedding. Never mind business for month of wedding. Swee Neo have beautiful wedding, much good joss for whole family. You never mind. You go Singapore. Rhys man, also.'

The Chinese woman and the Welshman exchanged glances. They understood each other very well, Trudie decided, better than she did either of them. They both treated her as a child, still seeing the world in black and white, and full of the prejudices of youth they would both indulge to bring her round to their own way of thinking. Mostly, she accepted their judgement, as she accepted that

Swee Neo should be marrying a man she had not even met yet, but every now and then she took it into her head to surprise them. Whose business was it, after all?

Could Wu Chao manage? 'How much do you have to do towards your sister's wedding?' Trudie asked her cautiously.

Wu Chao was amused. 'Much.' She launched into a detailed résumé of the many days a Baba/Nonya marriage took, with its days of feasting, its peculiar customs and the involvement of the whole families of the bride and groom in every little detail.

'Big wedding, never mind,' Wu Chao added with satisfaction. She drooped her eyelids, her expression as opaque as always. 'Maybe good for business. Many families come. Some coming flom Middle Kingdom.'

Trudie felt Mr Rhys stiffen with excitement. What did they know that she didn't? 'Do you want me to go to Singapore?' she asked the other woman bluntly.

Wu Chao smiled faintly. 'Oh yes, if you please, Tludie. Need whole house for wedding. If you guest, Europeans not understanding; if you no' guest, what you do? Better go Singapore.' She rose to her feet, bowing slightly first to Mr Rhys and then to Trudie. 'Rhys man explain *kongsi*, yes?' She broke into the mixture of Malay and Chinese dialect the Babas and Nonyas used between themselves, and Mr Rhys laughed and nodded.

'Are you sure, Wu Chao, you want her to know that?' he teased the Nonya. 'Mrs Maddock's an English woman through and through.'

'Tludie fliend!'

His eyes were shadowed in the uncertain light from the lamps. 'She's no friend of mine!'

Wu Chao turned on him, as angry as Trudie had ever seen her. 'Tludie *my* fliend! You man, you not understand!'

Mr Rhys stared at her for a long moment. 'You really mean that, don't you?' he said at last. 'And you're right. I'll never understand women!'

'Not have to,' Wu Chao rebuked him, frowning. 'Tludie and I understand.' She sniffed. 'You tell her 'bout *kongsi*. Tell her gold in Ki *kongsi*, velly safe. Time Tludie know, no?'

'If you say so,' he grunted.

'Ki family say so!' Wu Chao told him contentedly. And, for her, that was the end of the matter.

Trudie gave Mr Rhys a covert look from beneath her lashes. How was it that he knew so much? And why did she know so little?

She said the first thing that came into her head. 'Why am I no friend of yours? I've never done you any harm.'

'I don't believe in friendship between a man and a woman, and between us there can be nothing else. You're gentry, I'm not!' The suppressed violence behind the statement made her open her eyes wide. Why should he care? She hardly behaved like a member of the gentry these days.

Which didn't solve the problem of why it had to be he who was to explain to her what a *kongsi* was? Why couldn't it have been Wu Chao?

'I don't know what to make of you, and that's the truth!' she sighed.

'It's little you need to know about me. It's probably better if you don't know too much. I'm not a gentleman, but I'm still a man, look you!' The Welsh intonation underlined his lack of breeding to her ears. She didn't listen to the words at all.

'Did Mr Maddock have something to do with this

kongsi? I suppose it was his idea?' His wry disbelief made her less certain of her ground. 'I don't understand!'

'No, you don't,' he agreed. 'The *kongsis* are what hold the Straits Chinese together. They were formed by the first immigrants who came to Malaya, as long ago as Lee Kap, Lee Wei King, Kap being short for Kapitan China, a title created by the Dutch for the Chieftain of the Malaccan Chinese community. Lee Kap was a fugitive from China after the fall of the Ming Dynasty, when the Manchus ascended the Imperial throne. He died in 1688, so they've been here a long, long time. When they first arrived here as immigrants, they felt lost, estranged from their families left behind in the Middle Kingdom. It was almost as if they had lost their identity, away from their homeland. So they built their own temples and some of them became ancestors themselves – '

'Don't we all?' Trudie interrupted him.

'The Chinese worship their ancestors, remember?'

'Well, yes.' Trudie didn't want to dwell on that. For some obscure reason it made her feel guilty, as if she ought to be on her knees, praying for their conversion –

'You mind that?'

She chewed on her lower lip. 'I'm trying not to. I am a parson's daughter after all!'

'Is that all it is? I thought you were a businesswoman before you were anything else? So are the local Chinese, and the reason for their success is the *kongsis*. The temples don't only store their ancestral memorials, they're also able to lay their hands on capital at a moment's notice and with the minimum of trouble. Each *kongsi* is a co-operative of Chinese who come from the same area and speak the same dialect. The Malays don't have this advantage. No matter how successful and rich an individual Malay becomes, he never has the same resources at his disposal as does his

Chinese competitor. I learned that when I was working in the tin mines up north. They're mainly Chinese-owned – and Chinese-worked as well. They bring in their own people, distant cousins, neighbours' sons from the same village, and they keep everybody else out. The Malays, no matter how rich they may be as individuals, don't have these advantages. I doubt the British have either. One day the Chinese will own the whole country.'

'Isn't that what we're here to stop?' Trudie asked him. 'British law protects all the different communities equally, doesn't it?'

'As far as it goes. When I was working in the mines, the Malays would find the tin for us in the jungle, then back they'd go to their *kampongs*. It was always the Chinese who provided the capital to open up the mine, and the Chinese who worked the mine too.'

'Not the Europeans?'

'Sometimes the Europeans will own a mine, but they don't work it themselves. They employ yet more Chinese to work it for them.'

Trudie frowned, trying to understand the point he was trying to make. 'You met my husband in the mines, didn't you?'

He nodded soberly. 'He couldn't raise the capital for all he wanted to do, and I didn't have any. That's when he decided to go to London to raise it there. The opportunity to start up the Emporium in Regent Street as an outlet for trade was too good to be missed, but it was expensive. He had a lot of trouble convincing the City to back his tin mines without losing his independence to a lot of shareholders. In the end, he abandoned that part of his plan and came back here. That was when it occurred to him that if he could marry Wu Chao, he could gain access to the Ki *kongsi* and his troubles would be over.'

Trudie felt hurt on her Chinese friend's behalf. 'I thought he must have fallen in love with her,' she said.

'He'd never met her! Nonyas seldom go out and never in the company of men. She would have been far too closely guarded for a foreigner to get so much as a glance of her.'

'Poor Wu Chao!'

'There isn't much love lost in the average Chinese marriage.'

That might, or might not be true, Trudie had no means of knowing. She thought back to her own wedding day and how reluctant Mr Maddock had been to touch her, even to help her in and out of the coach. With her new knowledge about the ways of men, she didn't think he had ever liked women very much, yet he had managed to father Black Jade so he must have felt something for Wu Chao after all.

'I still don't understand,' she said aloud. 'If he wanted to raise Chinese capital for the tin mines, why did he buy the plantation?'

'The *kongsi* insisted on it. The Babas believe in owning the land. They know the British and the Malays will combine to keep them out if they can. The more land they acquire now, the better placed they'll be when Britain takes over the independent Malay States, as they're bound to do sooner or later.'

'You think so? Why should we be interested in them?'

He pulled a face at her. 'We'll tell ourselves it's our duty to bring civilization to the whole peninsula. The runaway slaves who come flocking into the Straits Settlements will help convince us of our duty. What we really want is to build up our own wealth and trade in the whole area.'

His tone of voice rattled Trudie, who was already uncertain of her own role in her husband's plans. She felt that at any moment the Welshman would tell her that Jeremy Maddock had forgotten all about her!

'What's wrong with that?' she asked sharply. 'It's more than time that all slavery was done away with! I can't bear to think of men owning people as if they were animals!'

'Doesn't your own family own slaves?'

She bent her head. 'That doesn't make it any better!'

He put his hand over hers. 'It isn't your fault,' he said awkwardly. 'Nothing's your fault! You're probably the only innocent party in all this.'

She shook her head. Her hand felt very small beneath his. Small and feminine. She swallowed the thought down in case it led somewhere she didn't want to go. She pulled her hand away.

'I think I should have been told all this before,' she said in a voice not quite her own. 'I don't know whether I'm coming or going! Does anything belong to me, or not?'

'Quite a bit belongs to you.'

'Not to the Ki *kongsi*?'

'Wu Chao transferred a number of gold ingots to the *kongsi* the other day. It's possible you may even be in credit. You've done well with your import/export business, haven't you? The Ki family are proud of their connection with you, they wouldn't allow Wu Chao to live here with you otherwise.'

Trudie managed a shaky smile. 'You forget I'm Mr Maddock's *Nai-nai*, Supreme Lady. Isn't that why?'

'Possibly, at the beginning. It's as nothing to their respect for you for the money you make! They're Chinese, don't forget!'

She shook her head, a little shy of the look in his eyes. 'If they like me at all, it's because I'm Mr Maddock's widow. I wish I'd known him better. He seems to have been everybody's friend; a good man, don't you think so?'

The Welshman gritted his teeth. 'A good man by whose reckoning? I never knew him be anyone's friend, Mrs Maddock, not unless there was some advantage in it for him. If I may say so, I prefer working for his widow.'

She coloured up in complete disbelief that he should say such a thing. 'Are you sure it isn't my gold you like?' she taunted him, then wished she hadn't because he hadn't done anything to deserve the accusation. 'I didn't mean that,' she went on quickly. 'Oh dear, I wish I didn't have to go to Singapore!'

'It'll be good for you to have some time to yourself,' he answered gruffly. 'You'll meet new people, go to parties, do all the things all young ladies like to do.'

'Maybe.'

He grinned wickedly at her, reading her thoughts. 'You won't be having the time to be bored, Mrs Maddock! Do you remember the two Welsh army wives you travelled out with? Gwennant was widowed within a few weeks of her arrival. She married the regiment's colour sergeant shortly after that. She'll always say you were visiting her if you want to look round Singapore on your own – '

'I'd love to see her again! And Glynis too!'

'They'll be honoured that you remember them. Don't forget now, Gwennant will accompany you anywhere you want to go and no questions asked! She's a good girl, that one, always was, even though she's my cousin!'

'And what about you?' Trudie thought to ask him. 'Do you visit with her and her husband often when I think you're out at the plantation?'

'Not often. But I'll see you in Singapore this time, Mrs Maddock. By the way, you didn't say whether the name Whampoa meant anything to you?'

She yawned, not wanting him to know that she was

more interested in him than any Chinese. 'Should it? Is he another Chinese?'

'A rather special Chinese.'

Her interest was caught, but she didn't want him to know it. She liked to be in charge of herself and her own affairs and this Welshman was far too knowing altogether!

'I can't believe he's really called Whampoa!'

'No, it's his nickname, you might say. He was born there. His real name is Hoo Ah Kay. A most interesting man! I'd say he was one of the very few who has crossed the barrier into European society – even your cousins receive him! He represents the interests of the Russian Imperial Court in Singapore, among other things. A *most* interesting man!'

She blinked several times, uncertain of what was expected of her. 'I can't think such a person would be interested in me,' she murmured.

'Oh, but he is!' said Mr Rhys.

Hermione was vastly relieved to be back in Singapore. It was just as hot as it had been in Malacca, but the faces were more friendly, much, much more friendly, and they were her own kind, which meant that she could relax for a while, until the next time the craving came upon her, a craving Christopher insisted she should only satisfy in Malacca. He was insisting now that she pretend to an affection for her cousin, no matter how she really felt about her.

'People will comment if you are less than civil to her. Remember how it was when we first arrived? Don't put me in the position of having to explain why you should be cold-shouldering her again!'

Hermione had heard the roughness under his tone of voice and had winced. She didn't like being threatened. It was something else for which she blamed Trudie and which added to her hatred for her. She comforted herself that Uncle Jonathan disliked his daughter as much as she did. Uncle Jonathan never thought that anything Hermione did was contemptible, not as Christopher sometimes did. She and her uncle had always understood one another, always, ever since she had been a tiny child and had first been left alone with him.

Trudie was remarking on the greenness of Singapore, an innocuous remark in itself if only Mr Horton hadn't leaned towards her in that confidential way.

'They say it only rains here two hundred days in the year, but it seems like every day,' he answered. 'That's why it's so green, of course. Keeps the dust down, too, though it's still too hot to go out in the streets. Never see a European out in the streets, any more than you do in Malacca.'

Trudie listened in silence. She felt as though she were seated in a warm bath for, although it wasn't outrageously hot, the humidity was far more than she was accustomed to, Malacca being on the west coast, away from the influence of the monsoons. It was all of two miles from the pier where they had alighted from the Chinese steamer to the centre of the city, and she felt sorry for the horses that were being encouraged to keep up a brisk trot all the way to Bukit Timor, the Hill of Tin, which was the highest point on the island at 525 feet. From the top, one could look down into Singapore's famous harbour, the prize which had caused Sir Stamford Raffles to start bargaining with the local ruler to bring it under British control, and see the rows and rows of visiting ships from every nation in the world. No wonder the trade had slipped away from sleepy Malacca to join the bustling excitement of the new port. Perhaps she would find more to interest her here than she had thought.

What she had forgotten was the boredom all the ladies suffered from in Singapore. Hardly had she entered her house than Hermione was already demanding that her husband should rush off and collect any letters that might be waiting for them.

'We all live for the news from "home",' she explained languidly. 'Not that I expect there to be anything for you, cousin. Uncle Jonathan is always saying that if it were not for my letters to him he wouldn't know you were still alive, he hears from you so seldom! I suppose you write to Cousin Septimus when you do write? Much good that may do you!'

'We do business together,' Trudie responded lightly. 'I'm very grateful to Septimus because, as Mr Horton will have told you, Mr Maddock left me with scarcely a feather to fly with. Septimus was always the kindest of my brothers.'

Hermione was incensed. 'You mean *Septimus* has been supporting you all this time? Why didn't you tell us before?'

Trudie shrugged a shoulder. 'Septimus helps. He likes the Oriental pieces I send him to sell in the Emporium. Surely you knew that, cousin?'

'Yes, I did,' Hermione admitted. 'I hadn't thought it so profitable!'

Trudie looked round her cousin's room. It was bare and cold, without any discernible character, as though it were a temporary residence without any interest for its owner. Perhaps that's what it was, she thought, a place to eat and sleep until the magic day when Hermione should return to England, fortune made and honours assured. Poor Hermione, how terrible to live such an empty existence in such an empty place.

'My needs are few,' she said out loud, hoping her cousin's attention would soon be diverted on to something other than herself.

Hermione gave her only a passing glance. 'Are you trying to tell me that Christopher will never see any recompense for all the trouble he's taken to make that plantation of yours into something more than a patch of jungle?'

'I suppose I am,' Trudie admitted.

'You should have told him so at once! I suppose you thought Christopher should do it for nothing?'

'Oh, hardly for nothing, cousin! He had his share of the price Mr Rhys obtained for this year's coffee.'

'His share? It barely paid his expenses!'

Trudie smiled. 'It hardly paid mine either!'

'You can always show that Chinese whore the door!'

Trudie went on smiling. 'Never!' she said sweetly.

If she had ever considered she had anything in common with her cousin, she learned otherwise in the next few days. Hermione chose to breakfast in her own room, seldom rising much before noon. The servants crept about the house, wincing at the quarrels between husband and wife that they were forced to witness, as also did Trudie. The only thing she could discover that gave Hermione any joy was when she was shredding the reputation of one of her friends, or when she received a letter from her beloved Uncle Jonathan. How odd it was, she thought, that her father could find the time to write so frequently to his niece and to his daughter not at all. Nor did he receive much response from Hermione in return for his efforts. Mrs Horton received far more letters from England than she ever bothered to answer.

'What have we got to tell them about our doings out here?' she would moan at length. 'Uncle Jonathan would think me wanting in my wits if I were to tell him every time a tiger eats some wretched Malay, or that it rained again today, or even about our stupid attempts at holding parties to keep ourselves amused! The food wouldn't suit him at all!'

'Too rich?' Trudie was moved to ask.

'Don't be ridiculous!' her cousin snapped. 'You should know that Uncle Jonathan always likes the best of everything! I'd be ashamed to offer him the poor little dishes that are all I can get our servants to produce!'

To which Trudie answered not a word. Her father was not a subject on which she wished to dwell.

The times she enjoyed most were when she escaped her cousins' house. The first time, mentioning that she was going to visit Mrs Eliot, whom she was guiltily aware was not on her cousin's visiting list, she had summoned a rickshaw and given him the address of the colour sergeant's wife, hurrying him all the way down the hill to the barracks where Gwennant had been given married quarters by her husband's regiment.

She was wearing her second-best day dress as a compliment to the Welsh woman. Her best dress she felt was too elaborate for the occasion as she had no ambition to overwhelm Mr Rhys's friend. The frothy sea-green silk she had chosen was rich and rare, but she didn't expect Gwennant to assess its cost with the same ease as Hermione had done.

Her cousin had looked decidedly knowing when she had visited her briefly in her room to tell her she probably wouldn't be back until sunset. 'I'm still wondering if you are as innocent as you look,' Hermione had observed. 'Your "dear friend", Mrs Beresford, must be wondering also. I asked her where she thought you got your clothes and she had no more idea than I! That maid of yours may be the best in the whole world, that silk still cost more than my year's allowance!'

Trudie had remained calm. 'It's nice, isn't it? That's the best of living in a place like Malacca, one's good clothes last for ever because one never has the occasion to wear them. I'm so glad you like it!'

Hermione hadn't been convinced. 'I asked Mrs Beresford if you didn't have a man friend somewhere in the offing – '

Trudie had laughed. 'In Malacca?'

'That silk looks Chinese. He doesn't have to be a European! In fact, knowing you, it's just the kind of caper you would cut just to spite me – and Uncle Jonathan, because he would just die with the shame of it, if it were ever to come to his ears!' Hermione had retorted.

'Then let's hope no one is foolish enough to put such a silly idea into his head,' Trudie had murmured. 'He would be bound to discover it to be untrue and he never forgives anyone who upsets his view of himself as the perfect father and servant of God.' And she had laughed to herself, wondering how her father would explain away God's visiting such a terrible punishment upon him – if he still thought of Trudie as having anything to do with him at all!

'What's the joke?' Hermione had asked her sourly.

'I was thinking how horrified Father would be that such a thought could cross his darling niece's mind. He really thinks you love him.'

Hermione patted her curls into place with a complacence Trudie found quite unbearable. 'He never liked you,' she said. 'I consider I've earned any love he has for me! I've always been kind to him – *always*!'

Trudie had stopped laughing. 'You don't really love him at all, do you?'

Hermione had shrugged. 'He loves me and he doesn't love you!'

Trudie wondered why she didn't mind more. 'Love that has to be bribed and pampered isn't love at all in my book!' she had declared roundly.

She hadn't waited to see what her cousin had made of that. All she knew was that she had found it an oddly satisfying exchange and her triumph lasted the whole way down the hill and along the road that wandered through the orchards where most of the fruit was grown that was on sale all day and every day in every street market in the city.

It was rumoured that the British community were beginning to think of building a cathedral amongst the public buildings, such as the justice buildings, and others where the government of the Straits Settlements was carried on: Penang, Malacca, and Singapore itself. Trudie thought they should start on it as soon as possible before Singapore, too, fell under the influence of the Catholics as had so much of Malacca. Of course Malacca had once been a Portuguese possession, in the days when they and the Spanish had divided the world between them with the blessing of their terrible Pope. *That* couldn't happen today, and a very good thing too!

Gwennant was exactly as Trudie had remembered her. She was no longer dressed in her Welsh beaver hat, preferring a neat cap that suited her far better if the truth be told.

'What news do you have of Caradoc Rhys?' she asked at once.

'He'll be in Singapore himself soon,' Trudie responded. She sobered her expression. 'Oh, but I was sorry to hear about your husband – '

'And I yours!'

'You married again?'

'I did – the first man who would have me! It's quite a step up to be the colour sergeant's wife, rather than that of an ordinary private. Not that that would have persuaded me! He's a lovely fellow, my Idris! I bless the day when we got together and decided to be man and wife. I'm happier now than I've ever been!'

She looked it. She ushered Trudie into her living-room, full of noise and children and other wives who could always be sure of a welcome from her. It was a cheerful apartment, plainly furnished with wooden chairs and a much-washed mat on the floor. Gwennant showed Trudie her double-bedded bedroom, proud of the washstand that was squashed in beside the bed in the tiny space that was all that was available.

'Where do you cook?' Trudie asked her.

'The men eat over at the mess.' The Welsh woman's eyes danced. 'Mine goes to the sergeants' mess, the best of them all, he says! The food is better there than it is for the officers as often as not! We none of us starve in this posting!'

Gwennant made tea for her guest, carefully putting before her the plateful of Scotch pancakes (which she called pikelets) she had made earlier. She sat down on one of the wooden chairs, opposite Trudie, sipping her own tea. 'Now, how may I serve you, Mrs Maddock?'

Trudie thought how different the married quarters were from her cousins' fashionable house. It was shabby and poor, but people were living real lives there, not sheltering in a lifelong envy of other people's possessions.

'It's doing me good just to be here,' she told Gwennant.

The Welsh woman's sympathy was balm to her lacerated feelings. 'Caradoc told me you'd be staying with your cousins and that you'd be the readier for a change now and then. We have little to offer you, but all that we have is yours. You'll always find a welcome here, ma'am.'

'You're much too kind. The truth is I'm bored in Singapore. I wondered if I could presume on you and Glynis to accompany me round the Chinese shops now and then, looking for bargains for my business?'

Gwennant flushed with pleasure. 'We'll *both* come – whenever you say!' She slapped her hands on her aproned knee. 'We both love Singapore and can never see enough of it! The Chinese women are so dainty and their temples so extraordinary! We'd never dare mention all we've seen at home, they wouldn't understand! I nearly died when I first saw the horrible things the Chinese use for medicines! Most of them are quite unmentionable! Indeed, I didn't know what most of them were, but my husband did all right – he's never at a loss about that sort of thing! He swears they work, too, though none of us women dare try them for ourselves. My husband let them stick needles into him for the headaches he gets and he's never had another one since. If I told the minister that back home, he'd tell me to wash my mouth out with soap and water for telling lies!'

Trudie shut her eyes and said a brief prayer of thanksgiving. For the first time in days, she wasn't bored at all.

Hermione smothered a yawn. Letters from home had come that day, causing a flutter of excitement round the colony. Trudie could understand the importance of letters to parents whose children had been sent back to England for their health and for their schooling but, in Hermione's case, with her husband and friends mostly in Singapore, this insatiable appetite for the minutiae of life in England seemed unhealthy.

'I hope you're not expecting me to entertain that Welsh manager of yours here! My friends wouldn't understand.'

Trudie was startled out of her reverie. 'Mr Rhys?'

'Christopher saw him in the street this morning.' Hermione gave a scream of artificial amusement. 'He was *walking*. I've never seen a European walking in the street, have you?'

Trudie hoped she didn't look as guilty as she felt. 'Well, not often,' she admitted.

'I should hope not! *Think* of all the things one might catch from those filthy Chinese! I heard of a case of smallpox – '

'Amongst the Chinese?' Trudie was surprised. Wu Chao had told her the Chinese of the Middle Kingdom had armoured themselves against the disease by rubbing a cloth against the pustules the disease produced, pushing it up their nostrils, and breathing in. Apparently this caused a mild version of the dread disease that rendered one immune from the real thing.

' – or cholera just today!' Hermione finished, annoyed at being interrupted. 'Someone is always dying of one or the other out here.'

'Mr Rhys says we should wash more,' Trudie murmured, enjoying provoking her cousin. 'And wash our clothes more often,' she added.

The spiteful look she received in reply made her want to laugh. Hermione's preference for scents rather than soap and water had always been a joke between Trudie and her sisters. In that respect, living in tropical Singapore hadn't changed her at all!

'I refuse to have him in my house!' Hermione said awfully. 'The impertinence of the man discussing such things with you! Where did your husband find him? You should have allowed Christopher to get rid of him for you when he first offered to do so!'

'Oh, I don't know,' Trudie answered. 'In some ways he suits me very well.'

When, one day, she received a note from Gwennant to say that Mr Rhys was waiting for her at her convenience at the barracks, in their married quarters, she couldn't understand her pleasure in the thought of seeing him and being in his company for a while. Had she been so impossibly lonely all the time she had been staying with her cousins? She, who had always been accustomed to spending most of her time alone?

Please wear your best dress, the Welsh woman had written, *because he plans you should call on Mr Whampoa, a heathen gentleman of very good taste*.

That was an exciting prospect in itself and, when she came face to face with Mr Rhys, such was her excitement that she could as easily have kissed him as shake him by the hand. He had one of Gwennant's children perched on his shoulder and was laughing at something Gwennant had said to him in Welsh.

'How do you do?' Trudie greeted him with a calm she was far from feeling.

He looked her over with masculine appreciation. Hermione was right about his impertinence, Trudie told herself, but she didn't care. She was pleased to see him anyway.

'Just right!' he congratulated her. 'Whampoa will love you! He's always called Whampoa,' he reminded her, 'the name of the place in China from which he came. His real name is Hoo.'

He didn't attempt to share a rickshaw with her. Apparently he had already engaged two, speaking an easy mixture of Chinese and Malay to the coolies who dragged them through the streets. They nodded obsequiously when he told them where to go, accepting the fee he suggested immediately, almost as if he were one of themselves. Trudie had waited for hours in the hot sun while Christopher Horton had argued over a few miserable pence, and she greatly appreciated Mr Rhys's approach. Even more did she enjoy the leisurely route beside the sea while he pointed out various sights he thought she ought to see, all of them connected with the early history of the Colony.

Nothing he told her had prepared Trudie for the surprise that was Whampoa, however. His house was by far the most beautiful she had seen in Singapore, surrounded by lawns of *lallang*, a tough, quick-growing grass that offered the green, if not the delicacy, of the fashionable lawns back in England.

An *amah*, a Chinese woman servant, opened the heavy front door to them and beckoned them into the magnificent open hall. A few minutes later, Whampoa himself appeared in Chinese dress of such magnificence that Trudie thought he would have outshone the Emperor himself if the occupant of the Dragon Throne had been present. She made a slightly deeper curtsey than she had intended, noting that Mr Rhys was as much at home in these splendid surroundings as he had been in Gwennant's married quarters.

'Will you deign to take tea in my poor house?' Whampoa invited her. His English was every bit as perfect as her own and she wondered where he had learned it.

'Thank you, Mr Hoo.'

The tea was delicate and fragrant. Whampoa observed her interest in his careful preparation of the drink, which he refused to delegate to any servants. 'Tea-drinking was first observed in Southern China at the time of the Three Kingdoms, 220–265 A.D. A little earlier than you began to drink tea in England.'

'Just a little!' Trudie agreed with a laugh.

Whampoa was large for a Chinese. He sat back on a throne-like chair, watching her sip her tea through his black button, almond-shaped eyes. 'Unfortunately, tea has meant war between our countries. It is much better drunk in peace, don't you think?'

Trudie thanked God for Wu Chao's instruction in all things Chinese. 'The drink of the gods should be drunk in peace and tranquillity,' she agreed carefully.

'You are very wise,' he congratulated her.

Trudie tried to remember why the British had first traded opium with the Chinese in return for tea, and wondered what the educated Chinese thought of their tactics. With a lowering feeling, she remembered hearing that the British had stolen the precious bushes in the end, planting them in the most suitable terrain that could be found in India, hoping they would soon produce enough to supply the whole Empire.

'Most women must prefer trade to war!' she claimed, refusing to take responsibility for the actions of her compatriots.

'Ah yes, trading with the Orient is your business, Mrs Maddock?'

She flushed with pleasure that he should know about her interest in his country's products. 'China is the source of so many beautiful things,' she said simply.

'How interesting,' he commented. 'Not many Europeans admit China to be the oldest civilization in the world. It is not our time – perhaps it is the time of the British just now – but our achievements are many and to be admired, I think.'

Trudie chuckled, her initial shyness gone. 'I can only apologize, Mr Hoo, that so many of my compatriots think the Chinese to be the barbarians you think us!'

He laughed also, his ample stomach heaving beneath his

silk tunic. 'I will allow you to be a foreign devil, ma'am, but not a barbarian! How much do you know of our history?'

'Not nearly enough!'

'The first Chinese State evolved between the twenty-first and sixteenth centuries B.C. under the Xia Dynasty. That was when silk was first produced, and when we devised the first calendar. You trade in silks, Mrs Maddock?'

She nodded. Then, daring a little more, 'My personal love is Chinese jade. I have only a few pieces, none of them worthy of your consideration, but one doesn't have to own something to appreciate its great beauty.'

'You want to see my collection?'

Her enthusiasm pleased him. His collection, destined to be one of the greatest in the world, was magnificent. Politely, almost as if he were asking her for the information, he showed her the two different semi-precious stones which commonly come under the umbrella term of jade. He pointed out the varying shades and what produced the greens, the creams, and even the blacks and yellows.

He showed her the *congs* he had obtained from his homeland, telling her he thought they had once been memorial flasks containing the ashes of the dead. 'Some people say they were merely decorative, but I don't believe it. We Chinese only make articles that are useful – we consider that to be a part of the beauty of any object.'

That met with Trudie's complete approval. The *congs* were interesting, but her own taste ran to the small carved animals and birds. Jade, she knew, was considered a symbol of immortality. Wasn't the Jade Emperor the chief of the Chinese gods? And Wu Chao had whispered to her that the Chinese referred to a woman's private parts as her jade gate because of the pleasure that men could find there.

She cleared her throat, thoughtfully staring at a white

jade box, embellished with rubies and emeralds set in gold, and the most exquisite Moghul inlay work.

'That is one of the most beautiful things I have ever seen,' she said.

'A good choice,' Whampoa approved. 'Does your brother sell much jade in London?'

'Only what I send him.' She sighed, peering at a delightful carved grotto. 'Nothing of this quality! I wouldn't know where to begin to find such pieces!'

'Quite so,' the Chinese agreed. 'If you would like it, Mrs Maddock, I would be honoured to put some jade pieces in your way. Not such exquisite examples as you see here, because they are very few and far between, but some nice pieces that would sell well in London.'

Trudie's excitement showed clearly in her face. 'That would be marvellous!' she breathed.

Whampoa smiled. 'The Ki family are known to me. They will bring the pieces to you as they already bring many things to you in Malacca – '

'But how shall I pay you?' Trudie wondered. 'I haven't much capital with which to try out new markets.'

'There's no need for you to concern yourself. The Ki *kongsi* already holds a great deal of gold in your name. Your credit is good with me and those I deal with in the Middle Kingdom.'

She thanked him prettily, but she couldn't help wondering why he should be prepared to do so much for her. 'Did you know my husband, Mr Hoo?'

'No, I'm sorry I never had that honour.'

'Then why – ?'

'I knew of your husband, Mrs Maddock. It was Caradoc here who recommended you to my attention, however. He has proved himself to be my friend in the past and so his woman naturally has a very special claim on me. Feel free to ask whatever you want of me and mine.'

Trudie's mouth went dry. Anxiously, she licked her lips, seeking inspiration as to how she should answer him. *Mr Rhys!* What on earth could the Welshman ever have done for Whampoa – *his woman*? *That* she was not, nor would she ever be!

'I don't think I quite understand,' she began feebly.

'No,' Whampoa answered, silencing Mr Rhys with a look. 'To your people, mine must always remain mysterious, isn't that so? The Ki family have introduced you to our *kongsis*, Mrs Maddock. We have also our secret societies, our *hui*, of which most Europeans never know anything at all. Caradoc will tell you all about them and then you can make up your own mind if you want to do business with me.'

Still bewildered, Trudie thanked him again, knowing perfectly well that she would trade with him no matter what, for no better reason than because he shared her passion for the semi-precious stone known as jade.

Chapter Fifteen

Whampoa bowed them out the door himself, a great compliment to his visitors. 'Please walk round the gardens before you depart.' He sounded genuinely sorry to see them go, looking sadly after them as he prepared for his next appointment which, he had told them, was in his role as Russian vice-consul.

'I was proud of you,' Mr Rhys said. 'It was very important you should make a good impression, and that you did, a magnificent impression!'

'I'm glad you're pleased,' she said dryly. 'May I ask you why it was so important?'

He was immediately serious. 'I'm not sure. Come, look at these beautiful orchids, and the canna lilies.'

She did as she was bid, wishing she had Mrs Beresford's daughters with her. 'They draw all the strange flowers they see,' she explained. 'Some of them are most exotic. I wish you could see them.' She bent to take a closer look at one particularly beautiful pink orchid, laughing at him over her shoulder.

The expression on his face gave her pause. She steadied herself, taking a quick step away from him, annoyed with herself for forgetting, even for a moment, the great gulf that lay between them. He was a *miner*, she reminded herself. A *Welsh miner!* If she were to encourage friendship between them, it could only lead to trouble. She, herself, might know it for what it was, but it would be unforgivable in her to give him a bruised heart for no better reason than that she *liked* him – and was bored by the life she was being forced to lead in Singapore!

She straightened herself, brushing down her skirts to hide the sharp regret she felt. 'How did you come to be a friend of Mr Hoo?' she asked, still not looking at him.

'Hoo Ah Kay knows everyone, some better than others.'

'I imagine he might,' Trudie conceded. 'I don't suppose they are all his friends, however. My cousins, for instance.'

'They wouldn't want to know a Chinese, no matter how eminent!' he sneered.

Trudie ignored the insult to her family, considering it to be more than justified. 'I shouldn't be too sure of that. If one can meet the great Whampoa at Government House, my cousins will most certainly do their best possible to get an introduction to him.'

He was silent. For a moment she thought he was sulking, but he wasn't. He was standing where she had left him, maybe a couple of paces away from her, his head slightly on one side as he regarded her thoughtfully. It was hardly the way a man looks at a woman to whom he is attracted, but it brought the colour zinging into her cheeks all the same.

'Tell me about these *hui*, or whatever you call them!' she said to give herself time to calm down. She simply couldn't imagine why seeing Caradoc Rhys so much at home in Whampoa's house should have had such an effect on her. She had a horrid feeling that it would have been better for both of them if she had been able to go on regarding him as a clumsy miner and nothing more. Mr Rhys was so much more her ideal man than any other she had ever met.

'That's a lovely dress. I was thinking, Mrs Maddock, you're no longer the poor little dab of a creature you were when I first set eyes on you!'

Her eyes opened wide. She forgot all her good intentions. 'You're still the same mannerless giant!'

'Mannerless, is it? Now what are you meaning by that, I wonder?'

She refused to answer. 'The *hui*!' she commanded him.

He bowed. It was a very elegant bow despite his size. Oh, she was sure she could make a gentleman of him – if she had to! But did she want to? She pulled her mind back from such forbidden thoughts, and solemnly curtseyed. She felt better as they both broke into a shared laughter. Wu Chao said laughter was a gift from the gods, and so it was!

'The *hui*,' he began. 'Have you ever heard of the Chinese Triads?'

She shook her head. Then thought again about it. 'Secret societies!' she exclaimed. Excitement gleamed in her eyes. 'Surely, Whampoa – ?'

'No, no, nothing like that! At least, I don't think so! No, I just thought it would make it easier to explain the *hui* to you. They're much the same thing, and yet they aren't! There are three main *hui* in Singapore, so I'm told, and goodness knows how many smaller ones built up around the local *kongsi*, or the particular dialect its members speak. It's a dangerous place for the Chinese immigrant when he first arrives in the Straits Settlements. Nobody, except his own family, is going to put out a welcome mat for him. They're all too busy making their own fortunes to welcome any more competition. Most of them join a *hui* as well as a *kongsi*.'

'Yes, I can see why they would,' she said. 'But what do such things have to do with you?'

He grinned. 'Why not a Welsh *kongsi*, speaking our own language and helping each other to make a fortune! The Welsh are as good as any Chinese!'

She was amused. 'More subversion! I'm beginning to think that those who want to ban your language from the length and breadth of Wales have good reason to do so!'

'Give a little, gain a little,' he replied. 'People in power should remember that sometimes, instead of looking down their noses at anyone different from themselves!'

Surely he didn't mean her? 'What power do I have?' she retorted.

'You come here knowing all the right people, most of us don't.'

She digested that in silence. In some ways, she supposed, that was true. She might have no power of her own, but she did, in theory, have access to those who made the laws and passed judgement on their fellows in the courts. She spoke their language and her brothers had been to the same kind of schools and had been nurtured in the same culture.

'What would this Welsh *kongsi* or *hui* have done?'

'I never got beyond looking into them when I first got here. There weren't enough of us to make the system work for us,' Mr Rhys admitted. 'When the Dutch controlled Malacca, they kept them all under very strict control, but the British never understood their potential as a focus for rebellion until they'd grown big enough to look after themselves. What good ever came from the dirty Chinese? Well, now, I may want to speak my own language freely, but Queen Victoria is my sovereign too, and so I told the authorities what I knew about the *hui*. They weren't much interested, truth to tell, but, in the telling of it, I realized what a valuable thing they could be to someone like me who means to die a rich man, no matter where I started. Nor was I the only one to think that. I discovered some *hui* had Malay, and even Portuguese, members. I got quite friendly with them, as a matter of fact.'

Trudie grew thoughtful. 'Are you a member?' she demanded.

'No.'

'Then what have you got to do with Whampoa?'

'I learned one of the *hui* was in sworn opposition to the Hoo family and I thought it better to warn him of the danger he was in. I like the man, and he's a good person to know if one's going to make one's fortune.'

'Properly grateful, was he?' Trudie said aloud, but her mind was on other things. She was wondering what other European she knew out here who would have been in the position to do such a thing. How strange that this mountainous Welshman should know so much more about what was going on under the surface of the Colony than his betters, who shuddered every time they came in contact with a Chinese or a Malay, not wanting to understand anything about them, or allow them too close, in case they were contaminated by their heathen ways.

'He puts a bit of business my way,' Mr Rhys admitted.

Trudie laughed out loud, suddenly very happy and not caring that he should know it because she was liking him very much. 'I'm glad you're working for me and not for anyone else!' Then another thought occurred to her. 'I suppose you *are* working for me?'

But he only shrugged his shoulders and refused to answer.

Trudie sat on a stool on the very edge of the verandah. Her needle flashed back and forth as she accomplished some of the embroidery that Wu Chao had shown her how to do. She found it a soothing occupation as she half listened to Hermione and two acquaintances discussing another of their friends.

'What a fool she is! *Everyone* knew he had a native

woman tucked away somewhere. They'd all do the same if they thought they could get away with it! But to go back to England and say she'll have nothing more to do with him, that's taking things too far, don't you agree?'

Hermione cast a meaningful glance in her cousin's direction. 'She's probably afraid of catching something. *I* should be! As if we didn't have enough to contend with – people dropping like flies from cholera and smallpox, and the sheer dirt, I shouldn't wonder! The mosquitoes are too depressing, don't you find? *I* shouldn't want to share my husband with a native on the top of everything else! Though if you want to know about that sort of thing, you should ask my cousin Gertrude. She has very strong ideas on the subject!'

Trudie made a mistake in her embroidery and carefully unpicked the last few stitches. It wasn't only embroidery that Wu Chao had taught her. She had taught her the value of saying little and showing that she minded even less when Hermione's constant pinpricks threatened to destroy her peace of mind. 'Velly bad manners to lose temper. More, velly sirry!' she had added, smiling a little. 'Very silly,' she had said again carefully, pronouncing the words perfectly as she could when she took the trouble to do so.

'Mrs Maddock?'

Trudie half turned, a little shocked by the malevolence on the woman's face. 'Yes?'

'What can your cousin mean?'

'I haven't the least idea!' Trudie answered.

'What about that Chinese maid of yours?' Hermione said with a tinkling laugh.

'What about her?' Trudie countered comfortably. 'She's a Nonya – '

'With an illegitimate brat by a European father!'

Trudie went on stitching, swallowing down her anger.

'Really, Cousin Hermione, you shouldn't say such things! You must get Ki Wu Chao to show you her marriage lines sometime. Her family would have had something to say to her otherwise!'

'You mean they care about things like that?' another woman wanted to know.

Trudie smiled warmly at her bewilderment. 'Far more than we do, I believe. The girls are very strictly brought up. They're marvellous cooks and needlewomen. I know less about the Babas, the men, of course, than of the Nonyas, but I do know that they consider us all to be barbarians – with some justice, as their civilization is so much older.'

'That can't be true!'

'Oh yes!' Trudie managed to sound astonished by their ignorance. 'They had a nation state of some sort in the twenty-first century B.C., and a form of writing in the Shang Dynasty, which was about the sixteenth to the eleventh centuries B.C. I'm not sure we had even arrived in Britain.'

'I don't believe a word of it!' Hermione exclaimed, hating the thought.

'They invented paper around the time when Jesus Christ was alive, and had invented printing and a paper currency a thousand years later. Gunpowder came along in the Tang Dynasty just before that – '

'Enough!' commanded Hermione. 'You're making it all up! I know you, Gertrude Grant! Why else would we all be here if not to civilize the native peoples?'

'To make our fortunes,' Trudie answered dryly.

Her cousin's furious face told her she had hit home. She tried to regret it, failed, and took some pleasure in listening to the new argument that had broken out amongst the ladies. None of them could believe the Chinese to be superior in anything.

'They can't do anything nowadays without smoking opium until they're half asleep all day long! I don't believe they ever achieved so much!'

'My husband says they won't work unless you stand over them every moment of the day. Only the Malays are lazier. They won't work at all!'

That was something about which they could all agree. Soothed by cups of tea served by a Chinese *amah*, they soon forgot anything they didn't wish to remember and went back to discussing each other.

It was unfortunate that Mr Rhys should have chosen this moment to call on the Horton household wanting to consult Mrs Maddock about a deal he was engaged in on her behalf.

Hermione was furious. Hardly had he set foot on the verandah than she had started berating him for leaving Malacca without her husband's permission. She was further annoyed by the wide-eyed excitement of her friends at the sight of the broad-shouldered Welshman. They whispered to each other from behind their fans, eyelids drooping and knowing smiles only barely repressed.

Trudie rose to her feet, putting her embroidery away in the needlepoint bag she kept for the purpose.

'Are you sure it isn't Mr Horton you wish to see?' she murmured. 'You know how little I know about plantation affairs.'

'Yes, ma'am.'

She sucked in her cheeks, trying not to laugh. 'Well,' she went on, 'as Mr Horton isn't here at the moment, perhaps you can tell me while we take a turn about the garden?'

'Yes, ma'am.'

'I hope you know,' she said to him as soon as they were out of earshot, 'that all Singapore will know every detail of your visit long before the gates shut behind you?'

'The gates? You make it sound like a prison!'

'It feels remarkably like one – to me. Well, what was so important that you had to seek me out here?'

'Whampoa has some pieces of jade for you. I shall need two thousand dollars to complete the deal. Can you find as much as that in Singapore?'

Trudie nodded. 'Wu Chao insisted I bring a small chest of gold with me – ' She broke off, pretending to bend down to look more closely at a dragonfly that was seated on a flower, drying its wings in the afternoon sunshine. 'Someone's coming!'

Hermione came towards them across the patchy lawn. 'Cousin Gertrude, I need you to help me dress to go to Government House this evening. Tell that man of yours to come back later when Mr Horton can deal with him! He's presumed on your time quite enough already.'

Trudie reminded herself that she was her cousin's guest, no matter how reluctant a one. The rules of hospitality forbade her to ignore her cousin altogether.

'I'm coming,' she said quietly. 'Mr Rhys has business of his own in Singapore, cousin, so he won't need to bother your husband. This is no more than a courtesy call. Mr Rhys, you know my cousin Mrs Horton, don't you?'

He stepped forward, hand outstretched, only to be pointedly ignored. Hermione turned away, pulling Trudie after her. 'I wouldn't have believed you could be so brazen, Cousin Gertrude! My friends are horrified that you should carry on so! Tell him to go at once!'

'We are discussing business, cousin.'

'Then he should be consulting Mr Horton, not you! What do you know about business? You didn't even have enough sense not to marry that improvident creature who was foolish enough to saddle you with that plantation! Goodness knows, poor Christopher has tried to wring a penny out of the place for you – and without any help from your fool of a manager! You'd be better off without him! Tell him now that you never want to see him again and have done!'

Trudie looked her cousin directly in the eyes. 'Certainly not!'

'I suppose you want to have it spread all over Singapore that he's your lover? Because that's what all my friends are already thinking! Jumping up like that, as if you couldn't wait to be alone with him! Uncle Jonathan was right about you when he called you a true daughter of Eve. Wanton! Even he would be shocked to know you prefer servants to real men!'

Trudie's temper flared and burned brightly. The cloud of depression that had encircled her ever since coming to Singapore lifted to be replaced by a new zest for life which made her feel as if she had the strength of ten. She was invincible! She could even afford to feel pity for her malicious cousin and her vapid friends! If they wanted to talk about her, what did she care? Metaphorically speaking, she flicked her fingers under their noses and laughed in their faces. She was *glad* Mr Rhys had come to call on her!

'My father should look to his own morals!'

Hermione's shock showed in her face. She was grey with it, sweating profusely. 'Why do you hate Uncle Jonathan so? It's sinful to hate your own father!'

'And for a father to hate his child,' Trudie responded more gently.

'Uncle Jonathan – ' Hermione gasped.

'Let's say he loves you too much, and me too little,' Trudie interrupted her smoothly. Her anger was under better control now and she was already regretting losing her temper. Pride goeth before a fall, she castigated herself mentally. Where was her still tongue now? How stupid to allow Hermione to goad her into saying much more than she had intended.

She turned back to Mr Rhys, her back very straight, and her eyes very black with the strength of her emotions. 'I apologize if we have embarrassed you, Mr Rhys. Please put it down to the boring existence we women have to put up with in Singapore. If you wouldn't mind coming back some other time, we could finish our conversation then. I am taking tea with Gwennant tomorrow – '

'Of course, Mrs Maddock. I shall see you there.'

Hermione's nostrils were white with temper. Always pale, she looked downright ugly without any colour in her face at all. By contrast, Mr Rhys looked totally at ease and the picture of male health in its prime. Trudie turned her eyes away from him.

'You're not going anywhere tomorrow!' Hermione shouted at her cousin. 'You're going to help me scotch these evil rumours about a member of my family. You owe me that much, surely?'

Mr Rhys managed to find a spot somewhere over Hermione's head on which to fix his gaze. Trudie had the uncomfortable feeling that he was trying not to laugh and felt a new exasperation with her cousin that she knew to be unreasonable. He was laughing at her quite as much as he was at Hermione. No doubt he thought their concerns to be foolish and unworthy, completely beneath the notice of any sensible man, but then a man's reputation could survive much that would make a social pariah of any woman. That was the way of the world. Much as she resented it, she would have to do as her cousin wanted.

'Very well, cousin.'

Mr Rhys frowned. 'Perhaps you could visit Gwennant tomorrow morning?' he suggested.

'I'll try.'

Hermione's friends had departed when she and Trudie walked back to the house. Both women were silent, busy with their own thoughts. Trudie was trying to persuade herself there was no necessity for her to apologize to Hermione, thus giving her a quite undeserved victory. Hermione was excited, over-eager, because at last she thought she had her cousin totally in her power and she meant to make the most of it. Trudie had been a thorn in her flesh for quite long enough, making a figure of fun of herself in Malacca, befriending that ghastly maid of hers, and now this!

She cast her a glance through slitted eyelids. The sun was very strong at this time of day and she hated having to be out in it. It was all very well for Trudie to rush about in the heat, she always had been as strong as a horse and, more to the point, she didn't look like a boiled tomato after a mere couple of minutes' exposure to the fresh air. She was as brown as any gypsy – just like that tiresome Welshman, who ought to know better than to come calling on respectable women! How dare he consult Trudie on business matters, when he knew her husband had expressly forbidden him to consult with her cousin over the plantation and when he could barely summon up a civil answer to any of the questions Christopher had thought to ask him. Both he and Trudie badly needed putting down a peg or two, and who better to do it but herself! How Uncle Jonathan would enjoy hearing all about it when she wrote and told him. Uncle Jonathan had always loved her more than anyone else in the world and the secret that lay between them had been a small price to pay for his preference for herself rather than any of his own daughters.

The thought of her uncle made her tremble inside. She missed his affection far more than she had ever thought she would. It was evil of Trudie to belittle something which meant so much to her! Ever since she could remember, Uncle Jonathan had presented her with little gifts, asking nothing in exchange except a few kisses. She couldn't have been more than three years old when she had first discovered that, in exchange for sitting on his knee and pulling on his whiskers, she could have a bright new shiny coin, or some of the peppermints he always kept in his pocket. As she had grown older, he had kissed her more often and had fondled her golden ringlets, but there had been nothing wrong in that! Half of Hermione's pleasure in her uncle had been because of the stricken look in her cousin's eyes as she had watched them together. She had liked to think of herself as the apple of his eye, while Trudie was beaten and starved every time she opened her mouth. Stupid little thing! What else could she ever have expected when she made no secret that she despised her parent for his little weaknesses? What man didn't have them? Uncle Jonathan, or Christopher Horton, they were both as easy as pie to manage if one knew when to give, and when to refuse to give anything at all. It wasn't her fault if Trudie was her own worst enemy!

She waited until Trudie had taken out her embroidery again. 'Your behaviour has been completely disgusting ever since you learned you were widowed! I've made every allowance for you, because my worst friend couldn't accuse me of not having every proper feeling for *every* member of my family, whatever you may think! Do you think Christopher *wanted* to have to deal with your affairs? He did it for me! I didn't believe him when he first told me how primitive the place was. I even felt sorry for you! I overlooked your doing your best to seduce my husband because I didn't really believe it, no matter what people said!'

'I should hope not!'

'Well, Christopher believed it!'

'Rubbish!' Trudie said roundly. 'I saw as little of him as I possibly could every time he came to Malacca!'

Hermione sniffed. '*He* couldn't believe you'd stoop to that – that Welsh miner! That's what made him think you might have your eye on him! It's a good thing he wasn't here to see you carrying on with the only man in sight this afternoon! He'll probably hear the gossip, however, and how am I to explain that I allowed you to do such a thing in front of all my friends?'

Trudie carefully put her needle away. 'Not even Mr Horton could be ridiculous enough to think that Mr Rhys and I could have got up to anything improper in full view of you all! Do strive to show a little common sense, Cousin Hermione!'

Hermione changed tack. 'I wouldn't say anything to you, dear, if it weren't for my cousinly concern for you. You may have been a married woman, but poor Mr Maddock couldn't have been very – exciting, shall we say? I do understand, my love, truly I do! Christopher isn't the most exciting man in the world either, if the truth be known, but one has to be *discreet* in a place like this. I'm sure every one of us would have enjoyed a toss in the hay with your Welshman if the opportunity presented itself – which made it all the more enjoyable for them to tear you to pieces for having a soft spot for him. You may not have done anything this afternoon, but we could all see the way you looked at him!'

'He's my manager – '

'Tush! Nobody's going to believe that's all there is between you! If you'd wanted us to believe that, you wouldn't have looked so pleased to see him!'

Trudie blinked. 'But there isn't anything else between us,' she said.

But Hermione wasn't even listening. 'I shall have to tell Christopher how Mr Rhys's visit was interpreted, as he'll be bound to hear about it from someone else if I don't. You do see that, don't you? I should be failing in my duty – '

Trudie refused to lose her temper with her cousin twice in one afternoon. 'Your imagination is running away with you, Cousin Hermione. Mr Rhys is a man of the most radical ideas, but he would hardly presume to have a love affair with his employer's widow. He knows, or he should do if he doesn't, that someone of my background doesn't see him as a man in that sense – any more than one thinks of your Chinese gardener as a man!'

'But you *do* think of the Chinese as men!' Hermione pointed out in triumph. 'You were quick enough to lecture me and my friends on the grand history of the Chinese, quite as if you admired them more than your own people. What you said probably isn't even true, because how should you know anything about it when none of the rest of us do? You might have known it would cause comment and that someone will wonder why you should make such extraordinary claims on their behalf. Well, let me tell you, Cousin Gertrude, none of the women here this afternoon will think anything other than badly of you and I, for one, don't blame them!'

The gardener, in his conical hat and short, baggy trousers, came into sight at that moment, as stooped in his walk as were any of the monkeys that played catch as catch can, up and down the trees, snatching at the flowers and generally making a nuisance of themselves.

Oh, Mr Rhys, Trudie apologized silently to the Welshman, how could I have compared you as a man to that? Even to deceive her cousin, it seemed a petty thing to say! She wished she did feel as little for the Welshman as she did for the gardener, because nothing could ever come of it. She wished even more that she had sat still and refused to see him that afternoon. And more, much more than anything else, she wished she weren't so bored all the time with every aspect of her life in Singapore as her cousin's guest.

She rose to her feet, her back straight, and lifted her jaw. 'You and your friends must do as you all think fit,' she said calmly. 'As shall I, Cousin Hermione, as shall I!'

Christopher Horton felt a great weariness as he sat beside his wife in the carriage coming home from Government House. It had been a far from pleasant evening, with everyone enquiring for his wife's cousin and exchanging meaningful glances with one another, just as though they thought that he and Hermione had deliberately kept her at home. He had smiled and nodded his way through half a dozen such enquiries before Hermione had whispered in his ear that she wanted to speak to him about Trudie's behaviour that afternoon. In vain had he reminded her that Gertrude was *her* cousin and nothing to do with him!

There had never been a time when he had felt other than bored by his wife's society. He had married her because it was expected of him and because he knew of no one better suited to helping him achieve wealth and fame. It hadn't turned out that way. Hermione had hated Singapore from the first moment she had stepped off the ship on to the green, palm-fringed island. She had been horrified to discover Government House to be provincial in its manners and dress when she had expected something of the gloss of the Court of Queen Victoria herself. She had despised the faded British wives, endlessly in mourning for a child or a husband, and had taken a perverse pleasure in flirting with their husbands, not because she cared for any of them, but for the fancied power she derived from making them do things for her they wouldn't do for their wives.

Christopher considered Hermione to be spoilt and petulant. He knew her to be greedy also, which had been one of the reasons he had married her, but he had soon discovered hers to be a selfish greed which saw no need to ally itself to his. This wife of his didn't want fame on his terms, she hadn't the concentration to want anything for long enough to be of any help to him. She wanted what she wanted, at the very moment she first conceived a desire for it, and was totally undisciplined in her means of acquiring it, moving on to the next desirable bauble if her appetite for the first was not immediately satisfied.

Her husband might be aware that Hermione was not universally liked or admired by the British residents of Singapore. Hermione had no inkling that she was not the most popular person in the whole Colony. She was convinced that only her presence was sufficient to make the difference between the success or failure of any social event, and showed a quite remarkable lack of taste in the way she spoke of anybody whose consequence was greater than her own. Her Uncle Jonathan was her sole arbiter of fashion, virtue, or a suitable menu for a dinner party in the tropics. Christopher had come to hate his very name. Indeed her father's dislike for Gertrude had been the first thing to recommend Hermione's cousin to him and the only reason why he had agreed to try to rescue something of her fortune for her.

She was an uncomplaining little thing for the most part. Sometimes, when she looked at him with that clear, expectant look in her brown eyes, he felt quite guilty that he allowed her so little from the plantation. He took no more than his fair share, considering all the time and effort he had put into her well-being, nevertheless he was uncomfortably aware that more of the profits had gone on Hermione's back than ever had on Gertrude's. He would have washed his hands of the business long since if it hadn't presented him with an opportunity to remove Hermione from Singapore from time to time. That, lately, had become more and more necessary and it was hard to forgive her for having so little control over her own nature. Mr Grant had a great deal to answer for, but it would be less than honest to blame Gertrude for that! It was a pity she didn't stand up for herself more and make it less easy for him to steal what profits there were from her inheritance from her. Anyone as easy to dupe as she was had to take some responsibility for the wretchedness of her own fate! And if she didn't stand up to him a bit more, why didn't she turn on her cousin from time to time? He knew what he would have done in the same circumstances!

With all this going through his mind, it didn't give him any pleasure to hear Hermione's whining, high-pitched voice rehearsing her cousin's latest indiscretion.

'There is nothing for it, Christopher dear, you must persuade her to return to England. Uncle Jonathan has always known exactly how to handle her. Why should we have to suffer for her wild ways?'

'Wild?' It was not an adjective that Christopher would have chosen.

'I'm sure she's having an affair with that Welsh manager of hers!'

'I doubt it!' Christopher responded, not without bitterness. He still remembered Trudie's burning contempt for him when he had thought to pleasure himself with that Nonya maid of hers.

'Well, everybody else in Singapore believes it!'

'Doubtless because you have told them so.' His weariness overcame his native caution. 'Your Cousin Gertrude behaves more like an outraged virgin than a wanton in my experience!'

'And you'd know, I suppose?'

He sighed. 'What do you want me to do, dear?'

'Get her out of my hair!'

He sighed again. 'Very well, I'll do what I can. But I won't have it said she was driven out of the Straits by her own family, Hermione, not even for you! There are enough people already who take her part against us whenever her name is mentioned – '

Hermione smiled sweetly up at her husband. 'You do talk a lot of rubbish, my dear love!' she said, her voice no more than a thin thread. Inwardly, she was already considering how to punish him for not immediately bowing to her wishes. What was worse was that she thought he might be right and that her friends didn't quite understand how thoroughly undesirable a person her cousin was, despite the hints she had dropped from time to time. Her eyes narrowed, giving her an ugly look. If Christopher Horton didn't understand the necessity of making Gertrude a pariah on the island, Uncle Jonathan would only applaud her for bringing it about. Who knew Trudie to be one of the greatest sinners in the world if it were not her own father?

When the Hortons had first moved into their bungalow, Christopher had chosen one of the rooms for his own use, furnishing it with two comfortable leather chairs and a Chinese lacquered desk which he used only when he was writing personal letters because it was as fragile as it was beautiful.

He waved Trudie into the chair opposite his own, not bothering to hide his appreciation of the sight of her in her pretty dress. She smelt of gardenias and her own woman smell, and not at all of perspiration as did every other European woman of his acquaintance.

'Who are these people you visit so frequently on your own?' he asked her, taking a kumquat from a dish of fruit at his elbow and offering one to her as he did so. Trudie bit into the small orange-like fruit with relish. That was another thing about this woman, he thought, aggrieved, she enjoyed everything she did far too much. It wasn't comely in a young widow! He could understand why Hermione should resent her presence in Singapore.

'We travelled out on the same ship. Don't you remember?'

'No, I don't. As far as I remember you and Hermione were the only two ladies travelling first class.'

Trudie took pity on him, hiding her amusement at his obvious chagrin at the task his wife had set him. 'Two Welsh army wives. You can't have forgotten their national costumes, with those high hats and striped and squared skirts and aprons. They both wore bright red shawls, which are apparently only attainable if you live by the sea. I'm sorry to say they dress as everyone else does nowadays.'

'Army wives? You mean wives of ordinary soldiers?'

'Well,' Trudie considered, 'Gwennant is married to the colour sergeant, on whom the whole regiment depends, if she is to be believed.'

Mr Horton shifted uncomfortably in his chair, wondering if he might light up a cigar, or whether his cousin would object as strongly as did his wife to the smell of tobacco. 'Most unsuitable friends for you, I should have said, cousin.'

Trudie's expression was bland, apart from the characteristic lift to her chin. 'It amuses me to visit them. They are very kind to me, always making me feel most welcome whenever I go there. I can't say the same for some of the other homes I have visited in Singapore.'

'Perhaps you don't try to please hard enough!' Christopher snapped.

'Very likely!'

'Your cousin has made you welcome! Done everything she could to introduce you to her circle of friends here, hasn't she? What more do you want?'

She considered the question for a moment. 'Since you ask me, I'd like to go home,' she said simply.

'Ah! Very wise! England at this time of year is always delightful! How much one misses the change of season when it is always hot and humid outside – and frequently raining!'

'England!' Trudie was startled out of her calm. 'Nothing would induce me to return to England! I meant I'd like to go home to Malacca!'

Mr Horton was aghast. 'You can't regard Malacca as your home, Cousin Gertrude! You might as well say you want to return to that dilapidated hovel in which you lived on the plantation!'

'I'd prefer that to here,' she said frankly.

'Because that Welshman is there?'

Trudie managed a laugh. 'You don't need me to tell you that Hermione always has some bee in her bonnet about something or other! Mr Rhys was a miner before he came out here – '

'He's still a man!'

'Cousin Christopher! You forget I was married to Jeremy Maddock, an art-lover and a true gentleman. I'd hardly replace him in my affections with a man who earned his living grubbing coal out of some Welsh valley! I've probably exchanged one word with him for every ten that you have! What on earth are we supposed to have in common? It's true he offered to introduce me to some Chinese person known as Whampoa, but as I'd never met him in your house – '

'*Mr Rhys* offered to introduce you to Mr Hoo Ah Kay? But of course you should have agreed, cousin! One can meet him anywhere – he's the Russian vice-consul and speaks English as well as you and I! How does Mr Rhys come to know him?'

Trudie shrugged. 'I didn't ask him. I know what Cousin Hermione feels about the Chinese – '

'Oh quite,' said Mr Horton, swallowing his anger. 'But Hoo Ah Kay is not an ordinary Chinese.' He brooded on the stupidity of all women for a moment, wondering how he could retrieve the situation best to his own advantage. 'Maybe Mr Rhys would introduce me to him as you don't care to meet him yourself?'

Trudie raised her brows thoughtfully. 'I can't speak for Mr Rhys, or for Whampoa, but I don't think so, cousin. I couldn't ask Mr Rhys for any favours after the way Cousin Hermione spoke to him this afternoon. Besides, I believe Whampoa is a friend of Wu Chao's, too, and I know how you and Hermione feel about my being over-friendly with her and her family. You do understand the difficulty, don't you?' she added brightly.

Mr Horton tried to keep some kind of control over his emotions, and failed. In that moment he hated Gertrude, but not as much as he hated his bungling, whining wife! Didn't she know how valuable it would be to him to be befriended by Whampoa?

He saw the laughter in Trudie's eyes and lost his temper entirely. 'The sooner you get out of my house and back to your *friends* in Malacca the better!' he said. 'I wish you joy of them! But don't expect me to rescue you when you get in over your head with your Chinese acquaintances! You'll never be anything but a foreign devil to them, no matter how they make up to you for their own ends!'

Trudie laughed. 'Do you know, Cousin Christopher, I mind being a *yang kwei*, a foreign devil, far less than I minded being the despised Miss Gertrude Grant. Mrs Maddock has a far more enjoyable life than her former self ever had in England. Thank you for agreeing to my going back to Malacca. I'm sure it's the right decision for all of us. It can't be at all comfortable for you to have your wife permanently at odds with her cousin under your roof. It's a pity we can't agree together better, but I'm sorry to say we never did!' And she smiled at him, both of them well aware that she had been the winner of the battle between them, and that, if he could, he would one day make her pay for that victory, and pay dearly. It was up to her to see that he never had the opportunity.

Chapter Sixteen

Caradoc Rhys took off his coat and spread his arms to greet the sun and the spray. Beneath his feet, the deck heaved as the ship met the open seas and left Singapore Harbour. Trudie stood beside him, thanking God they were going home. Her eyes glinted with pleasure and excitement, emotions she knew to be not entirely unconnected with the man beside her.

'Gwennant made us up a basket of food for the journey,' she told him, one side of her wishing he would put his coat back on, as was only decent, and the other side of her glad that it wouldn't occur to him. 'It's a modest little picnic – '

That caught his attention. 'That's not like Gwennant! Isn't she the one that's always saying the way to a man's heart is through his stomach?'

'Is she? Perhaps she only says that to her cousins.'

He checked on the basket for himself, relieved to see it packed with all his favourite goodies. 'It's obvious she doesn't know about your appetite. Perhaps you didn't like to eat her out of house and home when you visited her?'

Her eyes flashed. 'There's nothing wrong with my appetite!'

His face softened. 'No, nothing. I've known other young ones who went hungry. If ever I meet your father, he'll have a piece of my mind for the way he treated you. It's all right to take it out of a lad, but not a bit of a girl.'

Trudie looked up at him, liking him very much. 'It's

because I'm a girl he doesn't like me. It doesn't matter to me any more.'

'It matters to your cousin. Does she always carry on like that when you do something to displease her? Does your father really favour her so much?'

Trudie choked on a laugh. 'He *dotes* on her! He must write to her twenty times for every once he does to me. I'd rather he went on disliking me than smothered me with that particular kind of love, however. If you ask me, there is something unhealthy about it.'

'Very likely.' She was relieved he made no more of it than that, but then he went on. 'Look out for her, *bach*, she's a dangerous woman, and she more than dislikes you, she hates you.'

'But why should she?'

'Perhaps because she's not your father's daughter. Mr Christopher Horton isn't your father either and I dare say she can't forgive him that either.'

This was so nearly what Trudie had thought herself and had tried to put out of her mind ever since, that she was startled into clutching at his arm. 'That's a terrible thing to say!'

'Isn't it though? I wish you didn't have to have anything more to do with the Hortons. Neither of them wish you well!'

Trudie put her head on one side, giving some thought to the matter. 'That's true of Cousin Hermione. Poor Mr Horton isn't bad, just easily led. I feel sorry for him most of the time.'

'You have no need to. He's pocketed most of your revenues from the plantation – everything I couldn't hide away from him. Your cousin may have led him on, but his lack of integrity is all his own. The man is supposed to be the head of his household, not his wife.'

Trudie hung over the side of the deck, letting the spray cool her face. It was all true, of course, every word he had said, but she couldn't see that things would ever change until women had control over their own property. How fortunate she was to be able to do business on her own account for, left to the mercies of her cousins, or even of Septimus, she would never have been allowed to do it. How strange it was that Caradoc Rhys, the Welsh miner, had done so much more for her than her own relations, yet even he thought the man should have the final say. Was that truly the way it had been meant to be? The women she knew were so much wiser than their male counterparts, or so she thought. Didn't Wu Chao have a better head for business than Septimus would ever have?

The captain of the ship recognized Trudie at once. His button eyes snapped with amusement when he saw the man she was with.

'What time do we arrive Malacca this time?' he tempted her.

She thought about it. 'Twenty dollars says before lunch tomorrow.'

'Done.'

Mr Rhys shouted with laughter. He slapped hands with the Chinese captain. 'Double or nothing if Mrs Maddock can name the hour.'

'You are hard man!' the captain told him.

Mr Rhys looked at Trudie. She was very conscious of his easy stance and the laughter lines round his eyes. It was useless telling herself he had hardly washed the coal dust off his face and hands; he was still the best-looking man she had ever seen.

'Are you going to name the hour?' he asked her.

She shook her head. 'Twenty dollars is my limit.'

The captain waggled a finger at her. 'No, no, missie. You name hour, bet between Rhys man and me.'

'Oh well, in that case, I'll say between eleven and twelve noon.'

'Never do it,' the captain insisted. 'Never do that time. I bet forty dollars against that time.'

Mr Rhys smiled slowly. 'I'll back the lady's judgement.'

They slapped hands again, the captain spitting accurately over the side into the sea. 'I hope you have good joss, my frien'. Velly pletty lady!'

'I work for her.'

The captain's shoulders shook with laughter. 'Oh, Rhys man, I know you better than that. You never work for anyone but yourself! Since when you work for missie?'

'Since her husband died.'

The captain cackled with laughter. 'Ah, that man! Now I know who you work for!'

Mr Rhys's look was a warning not to say anything more and, Trudie noticed, the captain immediately backed down. Once again, she was struck by how much more at home in his surroundings was the Welshman than any of the other Europeans in the Colony. He spoke their language in more ways than one; he actually seemed to understand the way they thought and he was far from disapproving of them all the time.

When the captain had gone about his business, she told Mr Rhys of the time she had sailed with him before.

'This time,' Trudie decided, 'nothing will induce me to sleep down below!'

Mr Rhys grinned at her. 'I'll guard you with my life, pletty lady!'

'Thank you.' She was dismayed by the gush of pleasure his words brought her. At that moment she had no higher ambition but that he should find her pretty.

He was amused by her demure expression, knowing how relieved she was to put Singapore and her relations behind her. She might excuse her cousins' attitude towards her, but they both knew how precarious her situation would be if her family were ever to insist she returned to England, or that she should give up her home in Malacca.

He put out a hand, lifting a lock of her hair away from her face. 'I mean that, Gertrude Maddock. You grow more beautiful in my eyes every day!'

His use of her name surprised her. 'My friends call me Trudie,' she murmured. 'But I forgot, you said you weren't my friend, didn't you?'

He undid the top button of his shirt, pulling at the collar. Trudie frowned at the gesture, reading it to mean that he was nervous and wondering why he should be. Surely he knew her well enough to know there was nothing she could do to harm him?

'You'll never be my friend, Trudie, all the while I want to kiss you more than shake you by the hand,' he said dryly.

Her heart missed a beat before she found herself saying, 'Then why don't you?'

He bent his head and, for a moment, she really thought he was going to kiss her. She braced herself. Her heart felt like a painful vacuum in her chest and then rushed into life again, pounding against her ribs. Then he took a step away from her, searching through Gwennant's basket for a sandwich.

Her head a little on one side, she watched him as he found what he was looking for and bit into the bread. She tried to make her mind a blank, but she wasn't very successful. *She didn't want to be his friend either!*

'What are we going to do?' she asked him, knowing him better than to think he would ask her what she was talking about. He *knew* – just as she did – and he knew the impossibility of it all – just as she did.

He was silent for a very long time, biting into his sandwich with strong, white teeth that were all the more noticeable in a time when most people's teeth were discoloured and often decayed.

'Nothing, Mrs Maddock. We're going to do nothing. Nothing at all. Imagine what your relations would make of your having anything to do with me! Your fate would be sealed!'

'They can't force me back to England!' she exclaimed proudly.

His eyes were sad. 'Can't they?'

'Haven't we paid Mr Horton enough for his silence?' she demanded bitterly.

'He was taking no more than his due. If he can persuade himself of that, he can persuade others just as easily,' Mr Rhys reminded her. 'He's entitled to his expenses for running the plantation on your behalf. Anyone will tell you that.'

She burned with indignation that it should be so. 'Do I have no rights?' she cried out.

'You could go to law to have his trusteeship enquired into, but we'd both be in our graves before any judgement would be given. It's the same in the mines, when a widow demands compensation for her husband's death. More often it's she who finds herself working for the mine-owners to fulfil her dead husband's quota. I've always found it best not to call the law's attention to oneself. It's law for the rich and order for the poor, and that's the way it'll always be!'

'You're nothing but a Welsh radical!' she accused him.

'And you're nothing but a poor widow, ready for the fleecing by your respectable relations. It's a pity your

Cousin Hermione hates you for being your father's daughter, or she might have chosen to forget all about you. Be warned, my dear Mrs Maddock, she means no good to come your way!'

Trudie shivered. 'In England we were told that Mr Horton was a rich man – far richer than Mr Maddock. I wonder what he does with his money. I saw no sign of his investing it in anything out here. He works for a London company, mostly in spices, or so we were told when they married. I suspect him of dealing in opium.'

'That wouldn't surprise me. What makes you think he's not a successful businessman?'

'I don't know,' she admitted. 'He'd give his right arm for an introduction to Whampoa – '

'So would many men!'

She shut her eyes. 'I know. I didn't thank you then, but I will now.'

'Not now,' he answered very gently. 'One day, if we're very lucky, if our joss is good, I'll ask you to return the favour, but now isn't the time. I'm just an ex-Welsh miner, remember?'

How could she have forgotten? She turned away, heaving a sigh. When she next looked at Mr Rhys, she was smiling again. 'I ought to go to my cabin,' she said, with obvious reluctance.

He jumped to his feet, laughing down at her. 'I'll make you a bed up here on deck and we'll watch the stars move round the heavens together! After we've eaten Gwennant's feast, of course.'

'Of course,' she said gravely.

When she woke, her makeshift bedding on the deck was still in shadow. Mr Rhys, on the other hand, was in the full sun, his sleeping face lit and rendered beautiful to her.

For a while she allowed herself to commit every detail of every plane of that face to memory, remarking the way his brows slanted towards his nose and the small lines that had etched themselves into his skin that were not all laughter lines. He seldom spoke of his life in Wales, but she knew he had suffered in ways she could never comprehend, having no knowledge of the kind of life he and his family had always lived.

He stirred and she turned her face away, knowing the moment to be ended. Perhaps, one day, she would tell Wu Chao how she had looked on the Welshman and found him pleasing, or perhaps she would never tell anyone, keeping the moment buried away in the depths of her heart. It didn't matter. She still had a great deal of living to do, and that was good because she enjoyed the unexpected and her life had certainly brought her a full measure of that so far.

A rivulet of dirty water passed close by her nose. She lifted her head, dismayed, and found a furious Chinese deckhand cursing her under his breath as he tried to wash down the deck all round her.

'Good morning,' she said to him in the strange words that Wu Chao had taught her everyone would understand.

The little man danced with rage, his bare feet drubbing on the deck in time to his curses. Mr Rhys groaned and turned over to see what was happening. The next instant he had lifted her, bedding and all, and had placed her on a stack of life-rafts high above where the man was working. Trudie had known he was strong, but she was astonished, nevertheless, at the ease with which he had borne her weight – as if she were a sack of coal and just about as interesting!

She put her hand on his shoulder, feeling it as hard as if

it were made of marble. 'The sensible thing would be for you to marry Wu Chao,' she said.

'Sensible for whom?'

She faltered. 'For all of us.'

'Wu Chao will marry a Baba – if she marries again at all. Like to like. It's best that way. It's always best that way!'

His eyes burned into hers, but she refused to look away. He kissed her then and it wasn't at all as it had been when Jack Taviton had kissed her. She felt nothing but delight and a warmth in her middle like melting butter. Gasping for breath, she opened her mouth to him, wanting more. Then she was alone again and he was walking away from her, rubbing his fingers over the light stubble on his cheeks. Was he going to shave? But no, he turned again and blew her another kiss, walking right back to within feet of where he had left her.

'It isn't like to like; it's man to woman!' she challenged him fiercely. 'Even Baba to Nonya is man to woman.'

His hands tightened on her arms. 'How much do you know about it?' He read the answer in her eyes and said something in Welsh that she was glad she didn't understand. 'Who else knows you've never made love with a man?'

He shook her when she didn't answer. 'Does your cousin know?'

'No. Only Wu Chao knows.'

He released her and she rubbed her upper arms, knowing he had bruised her and not caring if he had.

'Are you sure? Are you sure you haven't told anyone else?'

'Of course not,' she said. 'Whom would I tell?'

'You told me!'

'I did not! You guessed!' She turned on him in sudden anger. 'How did you guess?'

He spread his hands. 'Maybe it was what I wanted to believe. Maybe it was your reaction when I kissed you. How can I tell how I know? It's obvious that no man has ever touched you – obvious to me, who would like to do a great deal more than touch you!'

Trudie stared at him, biting her lip. She would like it, too. She would like it more than anything, but she knew that it could never be.

Mr Rhys helped her ashore by the bridge near the square. 'You are in a hurry, aren't you?'

She acknowledged that she was. 'I'm longing to see Wu Chao,' she admitted. Her face shone with excitement. 'She's my real family.' She paused, helpless to explain. 'She's taught me so much more than my mother and sisters ever did!'

'She's a good friend to you,' he acknowledged. 'Don't repay her by putting her in jeopardy with the authorities here. Your cousins would be the only ones to benefit from that. You'll repay her friendship best by your discretion!'

'It's all so silly!' she retorted abruptly.

'Weren't you ever afraid of the Chinese – before you knew any?'

'*Everybody* in Singapore fears them!'

'So, if your Cousin Hermione uses Wu Chao to get at you, everybody will be on her side!' he said, his tone sharp. 'Remember that!'

Trudie sighed, impatient with him for pointing out the obvious. She couldn't imagine why Hermione should ever meet Wu Chao, or get to know anything more about her than she did already. She tapped her foot against the ground, looking about her for a rickshaw, and was further irritated when one appeared in answer to Mr Rhys's lifted finger. How unfair life was! Her money was just as good, if not better, than the Welshman's, yet not one man there had come to her bidding when there was a man present to do her bargaining for her.

Only when she was safely seated in the rattletrap of a conveyance that Mr Rhys had helped her into, did she allow herself to lean back and let the peace of Malacca seep into her. In the short time she had been away she had already forgotten the tranquil beauty of the centre of the city. It wasn't at all English, as so many Colonial towns were. Somehow or other it had remained itself, different from anywhere else in the world. She took a deep breath, glad of the velvety green that came right down the slope of the hill, crowned with the old cathedral and the Stadthuys. The feathery green of the malaccas was broken by the scarlet flowers of the flamboyant trees. It was magnificent in its proud antiquity, with only the ravages of the mosquitoes to spoil its peace.

When she arrived at the house its shuttered windows gave it a gloomy aspect. She flung them open, welcoming in the sunshine in a way that Wu Chao could never understand. No sound answered her. She knocked on Wu Chao's door, opening it and walking through into the Nonya's private quarters.

'Wu Chao!'

A breathless Swee Neo came running in from the covered passage at the rear. 'Ah, you are home! I'll fetch Black Jade to greet you! So much news! So sorry no one here to greet you!'

Trudie concealed her impatience as best she could. 'How was the wedding? Are you happy, Swee Neo?'

'Happy, yes. Wu Chao was married too – '

Trudie sat down on the nearest chair. 'Wu Chao? Married?'

Swee Neo nodded violently. 'Married to *sinkeh* from

South China. Living next door. Black Jade stay with you, with Younger Sister to look after her.' Swee Neo bowed low, her eyes shining with pleasure at Trudie's return. 'Wu Chao come quickly, not worry! She say you eat nothin' if she no cook, so bling your food every day, just like before. On'y difference she live next door now with honourable husband.'

Trudie tried to take it in that Wu Chao had married again. 'Had she ever met this man?' she asked helplessly.

'No, never meet. Good husband. Wu Chao very grateful to parents for finding such good man.'

Black Jade was walking all by herself now. She staggered across the room, reaching out for Trudie's skirts, chuckling with glee at her own cleverness. It was flattering not to have been forgotten by so young a child. Trudie picked her up and sat her in state on her knee, tickling the small body until the child squirmed with glee.

When she looked up again from the child, Wu Chao was there. She was the only person Trudie knew who could stand perfectly still for minutes together. She never fidgeted, or looked impatient, or even touched her hair. She stood and waited.

Trudie yelped with joy at the sight of her, jumping to her feet and transferring the child on to one hip.

'*Married*, Wu Chao? How could you get married without me?'

Wu Chao's black eyes snapped with amusement. 'Velly sorry, Tludie, but you not necessary to malliage!'

'I shall miss you!' Trudie exclaimed.

Wu Chao pooh-poohed such an idea. 'I am living next door, no' far. Leave Black Jade with you for company. Also husband no' liking girl-chil' flom other malliage.'

'Black Jade is welcome to stay with me,' Trudie confirmed.

'Yes, no hope Black Jade,' Wu Chao agreed with resignation. 'No bind feet, no good t'ing when older. Elder Sister, *Nai-nai*, Supreme Lady, now responsible for girl-chil'. You Black Jade's mother, no?'

Trudie wondered what she was taking on. She was rather amused that Wu Chao had it all worked out and, with her mother living next door, she didn't think she'd find the responsibility of looking after the child too much for her.

'One day I'll take Black Jade to England,' she promised. 'She ought to see her father's land, don't you think?'

'T'ink England cold. Relations not wanting Black Jade.'

'Not want her? She's a perfect darling!'

Wu Chao bowed gravely. '*Nai-nai*'s daughter, no' mine. *Nai-nai* do as t'ink best.'

Trudie felt cold inside at the thought. All Wu Chao's family thought the child to be bad joss, only Trudie wouldn't admit it! One made one's own fortune, good or bad, she had always thought that and she always would. She would do what she could for Black Jade, but only the little girl herself could make that multitude of choices that would add up to her ultimate fate.

Wu Chao bowed again, dismissing her daughter from her mind for the moment. She had no fear that Trudie would ever reject the child. Between the two of them they ought to be able to push a little good joss her way. Trudie's joss would always be good even if she was a barbarian still in many ways. Her heart was good.

'I make tea, yes? You tell me 'bout Singapore?'

'Yes.'

Wu Chao gave Trudie a sharp look. 'Never mind cousins, Tludie. Tell me 'bout Rhys man. You enjoy his visit, no? Good man?'

Trudie felt herself blushing. It was no good hoping Wu Chao hadn't noticed, so she came straight to the point.

'I like Mr Rhys, but only as a friend. Anything else would be frowned on by both our families. It isn't only mine, Wu Chao! These Welsh mining families are very close knit. What would his mother think of someone like me for a daughter-in-law?'

'You no' bad wife now, Tludie. Cook. Sew. You learn well, no? What more Rhys mother want?'

'I don't know,' Trudie admitted. 'She probably wants him to marry the girl next door. Besides, if they're Chapel, they wouldn't want him to marry the daughter of a Church of England parson.'

Wu Chao's bewilderment was only too obvious. 'Right for parents to arrange marriage, but Rhys family so far away!'

Trudie shrugged. 'I'm not sure I want to marry him anyway. We have nothing in common! What would we find to talk about?'

Wu Chao crowed with laughter. 'Talk to husband? Husband no' want talk!'

They both sipped the green tea Wu Chao had made. Trudie inhaled the delicate aroma and wondered how it was that it was always black tea that the Europeans drank, frequently served with milk and sugar. She liked both, learning from Wu Chao that the secret was in the boiling water and always using fresh tea. Cousin Hermione insisted that the tea leaves be used several times over as an economy measure. She liked it stewed and with a strong bitter taste. How very good it was to be home!

Wu Chao sipped her tea again. 'You make good business in Singapore?'

Trudie leaned forward to tell her all about her visit to Whampoa and his promise to put some of his trade in jade her way. There seemed to be so much to say and so little time to say it all, for she was very conscious that Wu Chao had a husband to look after now and that his calls on her time would take precedence over Trudie's.

'I visited with Mr Rhys's cousin Gwennant several times. Together, we looked round the shops. I have a whole case of things to be unpacked and sent on to London. I think I did well.'

Wu Chao looked down and all Trudie could see of her eyes were her beautifully lacquered lashes against her white make-up.

'And cousin? Did cousin see purchases?'

Trudie shook her head. 'I saw as little of Cousin Hermione as I could but, even then, we managed to quarrel. Cousin Hermione accused me of having an affair with Mr Rhys.'

Wu Chao looked concerned. 'I see. Bad.' She put a gentle hand on Trudie's. 'Never mind cousin. Joss. What man-cousin do?'

All the bitterness Trudie had felt at the Hortons' treatment of her welled up inside her. 'He was very surprised that Mr Rhys should have introduced me to Whampoa. He's a very important man in Singapore. Apart from being the Russian vice-consul, one may meet him everywhere, in the drawing-rooms of all the ruling classes, military and civil. He speaks the most beautiful English, which, I suppose, helps them to forget he is Chinese.'

Wu Chao nodded. 'Whampoa very great man. You like?'

'He was most gracious,' Trudie said. 'He showed me his jade collection. Wu Chao, you should see it! If he sends us even a few such pieces for sale in London, we'll be rich!'

'Then what you do?' Wu Chao asked.

'Do? I'll go on living here in Malacca!'

'What if cousin say you marry?'

Trudie smiled sadly. 'I'll never marry again.'

Wu Chao was unimpressed. 'Why not you marry? Mr

Maddock bad husband. But you woman, Tludie! You need good man. Not worry Mr Maddock no' like you for wife. Never mind.' She sniffed. 'Mr Maddock no' good at pillow with woman. Too quick, no enjoy.' She smiled suddenly, a smile that lit her black, almond-shaped eyes with laughter. 'New husband pillow good. Good pillow talk. Good everyt'ing!'

Trudie was afraid she was going to burst into tears. 'I'm so glad for you!'

'Yes. No tell Swee Neo, Tludie. Husband beat her twice now. Joss.'

'But that's dreadful! Won't your parents help her?'

'Maybe. Maybe no'. Woman b'long man, no?'

They talked for a long time about men and marriage, Wu Chao mocking Trudie for wanting to change the whole world in her favour.

'Did mother tell father what to do?' she demanded. 'Does sister tell blother how to run business?'

'Sometimes she does!' Trudie said dryly.

Wu Chao laughed. 'Yes, I remember. Blother send her out here to Mr Maddock!'

A new worry came to Trudie. 'Will your husband interfere in our business, Wu Chao?'

The blank look descended over Wu Chao's face. 'Honourable husband not interest himself in barbarian business. He no' Ki. B'long other *kongsi*, understand?'

'I understand that I hate changes!' Trudie retorted. 'You know the whole business depends far more on you than it does on me!'

'Husband understand velly well. Never mind husband, Tludie. I manage everyt'ing, only glad married, you understand?'

Trudie thought she did. 'I'm glad for you too,' she said.

'Yes, better you marry also. Have children to come after you. Become ancestor!'

'I'm a Christian. I don't believe in ancestors,' Trudie objected.

'Ancestors are ancestors whether you b'lieve or no'. Much better be great ancestor than forgotten on face of earth. Foreign devils very ignorant 'bout t'ings that matter. You have good joss knowing civilized people. One day you ancestor!'

As far as she was concerned that settled the argument. Trudie wondered what her father would have said to such an idea, and shivered, almost feeling the lash on her flesh in her imagination. Oh yes, that was his answer to everything. Punish the child for the good of her soul; starve her of food and affection and she would learn to love God: only Trudie didn't believe any of it. Why not be an ancestor?

'How Cousin Hermione would hate that!' she said aloud. 'She thinks I'm a barbarian too. I think she's in love with my father.'

'Cousin stupid person,' Wu Chao answered flatly. 'What Rhys man t'ink?'

Trudie bit her lip, lifting Black Jade more securely on to her knee. 'Mr Rhys guessed before I did. My father and she write endless letters to one another. Do you think that's why they both hate me, Wu Chao?'

'Yes, t'ink so.'

Trudie saw that the Nonya was not at all surprised. Oh, wise Wu Chao! She would make a worthy ancestress in her time!

There was a long silence between them. Wu Chao collected up their cups and put them carefully on one side. Trudie watched her careful movements, noting the beauty of the porcelain. They were Wu Chao's cups, imported by her family from China, and of a delicacy that had never been achieved in Europe, no matter how hard they had tried to copy the eggshell, translucent quality of the fragile china.

'I'm so glad to be home!' she said.

'I glad also.' Wu Chao's brow creased with the seriousness of what she was about to say. 'Tludie, forgive me say bad t'ing? Better marry good man or man-cousin take everything from you. Plantation now, later everything! No law ever stop man take money from woman wit'out man. Not'ing anyone can do.'

'Joss,' said Trudie.

'Never mind joss. We consider business now!'

Trudie felt a certain triumph at Wu Chao's cross tones. She began to laugh. 'That's what you always say! Joss!'

'Good joss, yes. Bad joss, no. Better change bad joss, no? Much better you marry Rhys man, or 'nother good man. If not, you tell blother to come quick and make man-cousin give account of what he do. Bad man make bad joss! I 'fraid for you, Tludie!'

'Christopher Horton isn't a bad man, he's weak and greedy. When I thought it was all I had, I worried about what he was taking from the plantation, but we can afford it, Wu Chao. The plantation doesn't matter to *us*!'

'Yes, *matter*!' Wu Chao insisted. 'Cousin not know why Mr Maddock buy plantation. Decided mistake. But woman-cousin know you make money, Tludie. I seen her look at you. She want that money for herself, just like she want your father, your whole life!'

Trudie laughed again. 'She's decided I'm a disgrace to the family, carrying on, as she puts it, with Mr Rhys. She was very glad to see the back of me. It'll be a long, long time before we see either of them again in Malacca!'

'I hope so. She like to do you harm, Tludie.'

Trudie knew the other woman was right.

'Joss,' she said again, but this time she wasn't laughing.

'Much better change bad joss!' Wu Chao maintained stubbornly.

Trudie thought so too, but there was nothing she could do to change the way her cousins felt about her. All her life it had been the same. She had been useful to one or other of her relatives from time to time, but none of them had ever liked her. She no longer expected to be liked. Wu Chao was the first real friend she had ever had. And, as for Mr Rhys, she didn't know how he felt about her, but she suspected it was not liking he felt for her, not as she liked him, as well as wanting him as a woman will want a man. Joss, she thought. Even when she was a great ancestor, she doubted if her descendants would find her likeable; no one ever had.

'I'll think about it,' she promised. Perhaps Septimus would come and rescue her from her cousins. It would be good to see him again. Of them all, Septimus had come the closest to liking her. She'd write to him first thing in the morning and ask him to come, completely forgetting for the moment that Septimus was more interested in the Catholic Church than he was in their business. By the time she had remembered that, she had already written her letter and had sent it up to the Stadthuys for franking. It didn't matter, because she didn't really think her brother would come, not for her, not even if the Hortons were to dispose of her altogether. She was as much alone as she had ever been, only now she wanted more than that. Damn Caradoc Rhys! He had no right to show her what love between a man and a woman could be and then walk away from her! Joss? No, that she would never believe! Joss was joss only because people believed it to be so. She, if anyone did, ought to know better.

Chapter Seventeen

Mrs Beresford reminded herself to keep calm. There was no good reason why she should take sides or express any opinion at all. In fact, as her husband kept telling her, it would be much better if she were to keep a still tongue in her head and remember that people were entitled to work out their own problems without her help. Of course, a man would say that, especially about Trudie Maddock, who was as awkward a person as she was ever likely to meet. Then she remembered Trudie's disbelief in any display of affection towards herself, even from the girls, and she vowed that she would do everything in her power to protect her from those insufferable, presumptuous cousins of hers.

'That poor girl should have children of her own!' she declared robustly. 'If only Mr Rhys – '

Mr Beresford's only response was a quizzical look over the paper he was reading.

'Yes, I know he's *quite* unsuitable on the face of things. Her family would be absolutely appalled – and quite rightly! But whom else is she ever going to marry?'

Her husband, who was fond of his wife, gave the matter his consideration. 'Jack Taviton,' he suggested.

'She won't have him because she says they have no interests in common. Though why she should be so choosy all of a sudden is beyond me, for she doesn't turn a hair at people who visit mosques and Chinese temples and places like that, thinking them quite normal and not in the least strange! Do you know, she actually told me the temples were rather jolly places – *as if she'd been there herself?*'

'I hardly think she'll start worshipping her ancestors,' the Lieutenant-Governor responded. 'I met a fellow the other day who knew her father. A bigoted monster of a man was the mildest thing he had to say about him. Apparently there are some nasty rumours about the way he treats his wife. Nothing anyone can do – a man can treat his wife as he chooses as far as the law is concerned – but it makes one wonder about Mrs Maddock's childhood. *You* like her well enough, don't you?'

'Oh, bless you, yes! And the children positively dote on her! But that doesn't help her find a good husband – '

'Jack Taviton,' her husband said again.

'I suppose so,' Mrs Beresford conceded with marked reluctance. 'He's better than nothing and I suspect the trouble is more that he hasn't any interests than that she finds them incompatible with her own.'

Her husband uttered a bark of laughter. 'My dear, if you can think of anyone better, you have my full permission to act as broker between them, but I fear it's Jack Taviton or nobody.'

His wife made a face at him. 'I confess I find him rather boring myself. Perhaps he's a man's man?' she added more hopefully.

'He's a man out of place,' her husband observed. 'If you ask me the fellow should have stayed at home in England – '

Mrs Beresford bridled with indignation. 'And you want to wish him on to my Trudie, who never knew a moment's happiness until she came to Malacca?'

'Who else is there, my dear?'

'Mr Rhys – '

Silently, Mr Beresford shook his head from side to side.

'You'd better forget all about him as a candidate. However rich he grows, he'll never be considered good enough for someone of her quality, my love, sad though it is – '

'He speaks well!'

'With a Welsh lilt! Can you imagine the Hortons inviting him to their home, or making him welcome? He told me once his mother sent him to a dame school until he was eleven years old. After that he had to go down the mines with his father – a boy of that age! – and he's earned his own living ever since.'

'Surely that is admirable, not something to be sneered at?'

'My dear, sweet woman, the Hortons sneer at me, let alone a Welsh miner, and, whatever you think of them, they are the girl's cousins. They'd never give their consent to such a match!'

All of which Mrs Beresford knew to be only too true, and which was all the more irritating as, try as she would, she knew nothing would persuade Trudie into accepting Jack Taviton, and she really didn't blame her. It was such a terrible waste, for Trudie needed children. It was only with them that she relaxed her guard and showed her true self, a girl with an appetite to experience all there was in life.

'How cruel life can be sometimes!' she said to herself. Her own marriage had brought her much happiness and children she adored. To her mind, there was nothing sadder than to live and die an old maid, and she was determined this shouldn't happen to Trudie. Even Jack Taviton would be better than that, and so she would tell her the very next time she saw her. It was more than time that somebody took the young Mrs Maddock in hand and, if the Hortons couldn't do it in Singapore, when they had had every opportunity, as Trudie had had nothing better to do there than heed their advice, it could be nothing less than her duty to see what she could do for her in Malacca, despite the silly girl's devotion to that Nonya family she lived amongst, and despite Trudie's own lack of interest in her own future. She just wished there were somebody other than Mr Jack Taviton to dangle before the silly girl for, being a woman herself, she couldn't imagine anyone falling in love with him, not all the while there was that Welsh miner in the offing – so much more of a man in every way!

Mr Taviton had been in Malacca far too long. That morning, when a Malay servant entered his room to awaken him, it had come to him that he had been more or less in a state of fear ever since he had arrived out East. The servant was completely silent as he padded round the room in his bare feet. He could tell the man was a devout Moslem, for he had that mark on his forehead that was brought about by the frequency he bowed his head to the floor when he was praying. Jack Taviton tried to pretend he hadn't noticed his arrival, putting off the moment when he would have to acknowledge him and his surroundings. When Septimus had suggested he should come out here, he had thought it a devil of a lark, but it hadn't turned out to be anything like he had expected. When he thought of how Septimus had lauded his sister to the skies, he could only wonder if he had been talking about the same female as the eccentric Mrs Maddock, a lady possessed of the strangest ideas he had ever encountered.

The manservant lifted the mosquito net, putting a tea-tray on the bedside table where he could reach it easily. The Malay was wearing a kind of uniform, one of the native knives attached to his belt. It was said they never drew the *kris* without drawing blood, a thought to make one shiver when one saw the evil-looking blade, sharpened to a wicked edge and as wavy as the ripples on water to make it the more deadly.

'Good morning,' Mr Taviton remembered to say. To thank him for his service might be going too far.

'*Tuan*.'

'Is my bath ready?'

The man merely looked at him. After a while, he made a gesture in the direction of the bathroom and walked away.

Insolent blighter! Jack Taviton levered himself out of bed and wandered down the steps to the brick-floored room below that contained a large high tub of Shanghai pottery. When he had first seen this remarkable article, he had tried to squash himself into it, but now he knew better. He took the dipper firmly in one hand and poured some of the water over himself from a great height. The water was much the same temperature as the surrounding air, which was already up in the eighties. Mr Taviton had been brought up to believe that too much bathing was weakening to the body. It was the reason, his father had informed him at an early age, that the Roman Empire had crumbled into anarchy and worse. One had little choice in the tropics, however, if life was to be bearable at all. Each morning he longed a little more for home and comfort in England.

His distaste for his surroundings was exacerbated by the sight of his waiting breakfast. It had probably been cooked an hour before, the bacon burned and the egg standing in a ring of congealed fat on the plate. Beside the plate was a letter. Mr Taviton poured himself a cup of lukewarm coffee and used his knife to cut the envelope open. It was wrong to feel a lowering of the spirits at the sight of a letter from a friend, but Septimus had gone too far, in his opinion, sending him on a fool's errand out to this wretched place.

He flipped over the single page of writing, checking

automatically on the signature, then he started to read, grunting with approval as he took in Septimus's news that he was to marry the daughter of his new employer and that his future was finally settled. Less inviting was the charge that Jack should break the news to Mrs Maddock, as he would know better than anyone the best way to cheer her up and make her see it was all for the best.

So taken up was Mr Taviton with Septimus's decision that, for once, he barely noticed the strange smells of the narrow streets as he made his way to the Chinese quarter, or the disgusting way the Chinese had of spitting, often as close as they dared to his highly polished boots. Even the heat seemed to have lost its edge that morning.

'Here, this is the house here!' he called out to the rickshaw coolie. The man came to an obedient stop, clearing his throat of a load of phlegm as he did so. Mr Taviton ignored him, searching his pockets for the smallest coin he could find, before the man could spit in his direction again.

Trudie came to the door herself. She often did, he had noticed, apparently not minding that her maid was a cripple, with those ridiculous, tiny feet of hers. A barbarous custom if you like!

'Come in, Mr Taviton!'

She smelt as fresh and as sweet as an English summer's day. He wondered how she managed it, when everyone else he knew, male or female, smelt permanently of perspiration no matter how often they changed their clothes and washed themselves from top to toe.

'I've had a letter from Septimus.'

Trudie swallowed her disappointment that she had not received one also. It was natural that her brother should write to his friend before he wrote to his sister. Most of the letters she did get from him were to do with buying and selling, saying nothing of what he was doing and what was the latest gossip in London. She knew hardly anything nowadays of his doings.

Trudie asked Mr Taviton to sit down. He had obviously received good news from Septimus for his whole face glowed. 'Is he coming out here?' she asked.

'No, no, nothing like that. He is to be married! He asked me to be the bearer of his good news because I know the young woman concerned and can reassure you that she comes of a good family. He's done pretty well for himself, despite her religion.'

'Oh? Who is she?'

'Her family's name is Walmsley. An old recusant family – '

'A what?'

Mr Taviton consulted Septimus's letter. 'One of the old Catholic families who stuck to their faith right through penal times. She comes from Lancashire. Her father is well known up there.'

Trudie blenched. 'Father will never forgive him!'

'I don't suppose he gives a brass farthing for that! He never did care what anyone thought of him! Splendid chap in that way! He says it's all settled that he should go to work for his new father-in-law and he'll let you know what he decides to do about the Regent Street Emporium.'

'I see,' said Trudie. She was annoyed to find her hands were shaking. To give herself something to do, she deliberately smiled at him. 'Would you care for some tea?' she asked.

He accepted at once. 'You do realize that if he puts in a manager, you may lose your best market for your little hobby?' he asked her. 'Don't you care?'

'Very much.'

'Septimus was always a thoughtless kind of a person,'

Mr Taviton went on more slowly. 'The best friend a fellow could have, but it can't always be easy to be his sister. What will you do?'

Trudie refused to give him the satisfaction of admitting to the desperate anxiety that filled her whole being. Carefully, she made her face a blank. 'I will think of something. The demand for Oriental objects won't disappear overnight. There will be other outlets.'

Jack Taviton wondered if she already had something in mind. A light sweat broke out on his face. He wiped it away with an already damp handkerchief.

'I'll remind him you do have an interest in the outcome of what happens to the business, even if only as a junior partner. He – he'll probably arrange something – if he thinks of it in all the excitement. Will you go home for the wedding?'

Trudie pursed up her mouth, hating every minute of this interview. 'No,' she said.

'Very wise! It'll probably be over and done with long before you can get to Cape Town. What did you think of the Cape Colony, by the way? It would be a vast improvement as a place to live to being here, to my way of thinking! Did you go ashore when you were there?'

'Yes, I did,' Trudie admitted. She wished she could think of something to say that would put him at his ease, but all that would come out of her mouth were these strange, stiff sentences in the same, wooden voice with which she had always addressed other members of her family.

'Didn't you think the climate – '

'I didn't care for the Dutch.' Trudie forced a smile. 'That isn't quite true, because of course I don't know anything about them, but none of them seemed to like us very much.'

Mr Taviton visibly swelled with pride. 'They'll never

dislodge *us* from such a harbour! Where else would we find that'd be as good to provision our ships on the Indian run?'

'They talk about cutting a canal from the Mediterranean to the Red Sea. The French – '

'It'll never happen! Nobody but a lunatic would put money into such a scheme!'

'Disraeli – '

'Another foreigner! We've far too many of them in the Empire, if you ask me!'

Trudie raised her brows in distaste. How had it come about, she wondered, that British pride in their Empire stopped short at most of the people in it? Not that she considered Disraeli to be a foreigner herself. Indeed, she knew next to nothing about him, but it seemed churlish to say the least to accept the Old Testament and reject the people who had written it. And she knew he was one of the Queen's favourites, of course.

'Even the Straits Chinese and our Malays are British citizens now!'

It was remarks like that that made him glad he had never actually asked her to marry him. He had come so close to it once or twice, thinking she must be more like the reckless, rue-nothing man who was her brother, and whom he had always liked and admired. It had been what Septimus had hoped for, but it had been a long time since her brother had last seen her and he probably didn't know about the kind of life she was living out here. Mr Taviton had even thought that he might ask her today, but now he was glad he hadn't. He could imagine his family's reaction if she were to come out with one of her strange opinions in their presence. It wasn't as if one could rely on her to keep a decent silence, as a woman should when she couldn't agree with her menfolk. Even Septimus said his sister was like a dog with a bone once she got an idea into her head.

'That isn't the same thing,' he said aloud. He said it gently, not wanting to argue with her. Now that he had finally made up his mind not to marry her, he even found himself quite liking her.

She left him for a moment, clapping her hands to summon the latest Hokkien maid, unsurprised when she made her appearance from next door, a sheepish grin on her broad, rather featureless face. When Wu Chao had lived in the same house, the maids had always been clean and tidy; now, even though she was only next door, Trudie was for ever having to speak to them about washing their hands before they touched the food, let alone to keep their clothes clean and tidy. At least the girl was willing, as her mistress asked her to bring tea and some of Wu Chao's little cakes for her visitor.

The tea was black and strong, because she knew Mr Taviton didn't appreciate being offered anything else. 'I suppose I should be glad about Septimus's marriage,' she said when the tea was finally poured and milk and sugar added to Mr Taviton's cup. 'He never goes home these days. He doesn't even visit his sisters, or so Letty tells me, which is sad, because she has always had a fondness for us both.'

Jack Taviton took a quick sip of tea, burning his mouth in his haste. Annoyed, he banged his cup down into its saucer, spilling some of the tea as he did so. To cover his embarrassment, he took a quick bite out of his cake, trying to hide his dismay as it disintegrated on his tongue, a mixture of sweet and sour that took him by surprise.

'Don't you long to see them all?' he asked her.

'Not really. I feel at home out here, you see, far more than I ever did in London.'

The bleakness of her tone made him wince. He swallowed. 'What are you going to do? Septimus provided most of your income, didn't he?'

She gave him a thoughtful look. 'Most of it,' she admitted. Actually, it had been a long time since Septimus had provided her with much except a cover for her activities, but that was a secret between herself and Wu Chao. If anyone else were to know of it, she would soon lose her freedom to trade in her own right!

'I wonder if Septimus has given it any thought,' he went on. 'Hasn't he talked it over with you at all?'

Trudie struggled to retain her iron control over herself. 'He did tell me he had some plan or other to help me. I dare say he'll remember to tell me what it is, sooner or later. Why couldn't he have waited until we had all made our fortunes to find someone he wanted to marry?'

He felt a sneaking sympathy with her over that. 'As a matter of fact, I wondered if I could be of service to you in Septimus's stead?'

Trudie's face was a study. Surely he was not going to propose to her after all? She hoped against hope that he wouldn't or that, if he did, she would find the courage to refuse him. Poor Mr Taviton most certainly didn't want a wife that bore any resemblance to herself. He'd be completely miserable long before they had even tied the knot!

A gleam of humour lurked in the back of her eyes. 'What did you have in mind, Mr Taviton?'

He reddened, looking much younger than his years. 'You may feel at home out here, Mrs Maddock, but I long for England and sanity! What would you say if I were to set up as your partner in England in your brother's place? They may not take me on at the Emporium, of course, though with Septimus on the board, he could put in a good word for me. I can't think they want to lose your trade, can you?'

She sat for a moment, looking at him and trying to make up her mind what to do. He saw her hesitating and grew redder than ever. 'You won't regret it! I'll do everything for you that Septimus ever has!'

Her smile took him unawares. It softened her face, making her almost desirable. 'I'm not worried that I might regret it, but I think you could – very easily! I've always been better at trade than Septimus and it's only because the law won't allow me to buy and sell in my own name that it was necessary for him to be my senior partner. It's *my* business, Mr Taviton, and I run it. Septimus signs the ledgers and appears as the proprietor on our notepaper, but *that's all*. You wouldn't really like to be employed by a woman, even if nobody else knew about it, would you?'

'No.'

He felt her amusement and wondered if that was what Septimus had meant when he had said his sister had no sense of what was fitting. 'I thought not,' she said gently.

He pulled at his collar. 'You've misunderstood me, Mrs Maddock!' he exclaimed, his voice rising perilously. 'It isn't that I mind a woman being the presence behind the throne, as it were, but I have my own future to consider and, at the moment, it isn't a very rosy prospect. I should tell you that my father has had several reverses recently and my brother and I have scarcely a feather to fly with.' He swallowed convulsively. 'It was pointed out to me that my duty lay with caring for my family first of all,' he went on, knowing that this woman was never going to understand anything of what he was about to tell her. 'My parents are used to having only the best, and I have two unmarried sisters – I must find myself some real work to do.'

Trudie went on looking at him. 'You could still go to Yokohama on our behalf. I'm convinced there's a fortune waiting for anyone who can get a stake in the Japanese trade.'

'I've heard that Yokohama is even worse than Singapore! They hate all foreigners there!'

'There are great riches to be gained in Japan,' Trudie told him, 'and the climate is more like England's, being in much the same latitude. You'd probably feel quite at home there.'

His hands shook as he wiped them on the sides of the trousers he had had made specially for himself. 'Please don't ask me to go anywhere except home to England.' He forced a small smile. 'I'd sooner marry money than venture abroad again!'

Trudie hadn't got the heart to point out to him again how it could be the answer to all his problems. 'Was it to look me over that Septimus sent you out here? Mr Maddock was reputed to be a rich man, but he left me scarcely sufficient to keep me – let alone all your hopeful relations! Septimus was always the most impractical one of our family!'

He looked so horrified that she almost burst out laughing. She had very little use for him, but she could have wished he had thought it worth while to court her because he liked her a little. What was wrong with her that no man wanted to make her his wife?

'I don't know how you live out here!' he burst out. 'They all hate us, all of them! The Japanese more than anyone, or so I've heard!'

'If they're anything like the Chinese it's because we smell to them,' Trudie informed him, having long ago accepted Wu Chao's dictum that most Europeans would be a great deal happier in the tropics if they would only bathe more often.

Mr Taviton gave her a scandalized look. 'That's ridiculous!' he exclaimed. He'd never heard such nonsense!

Trudie considered him carefully, seeing him as a way out of her own difficulties. 'I'll write to Septimus – ' she began, breaking off as the door opened and a small, laughing face peered round it at her. 'Come in, Black Jade!' she bade the child. 'Where have you been hiding yourself away?'

A giggle was her only answer. The face disappeared, only to reappear. 'Boo!' said the child.

'Not "boo",' Trudie laughed back at her. 'Peep, po!'

'Boo!'

Trudie held out her arms to her. The little girl let go her hold on the door and came towards her at a run, clinging to her skirts in triumph as she made it known that she wanted to be lifted up on to Trudie's knee.

Trudie turned a laughing face towards the watching man as she cuddled the child against her, and was dismayed to see the fascinated horror reflected in his eyes.

'How can you touch her?' Mr Taviton asked her, unable to stop himself.

'Very easily. My husband was her father.'

'Your husband, ma'am?'

'Well, yes. You see, Mr Taviton, it isn't only for myself that I went into trade with Septimus. At first, it was because Mr Maddock wanted me to learn a little about his business, though I enjoyed it far more than anything else that had ever come my way! Far more than Septimus did! It seems hard to believe now, but I was rather reluctant to leave London and come out here. I suspected Septimus of writing to my husband and asking to be given a freer hand without my telling him what to do all the time! I still think I may have been right about that, but, by the time I arrived here, Mr Maddock had already succumbed to the cholera and I had to do the best I could for us all as the plantation produced practically nothing.'

'Trading with London?'

'That and other things. I didn't only have myself to consider, you see. Mr Maddock had other dependants I had to provide for – '

'You didn't have to make yourself responsible for his child!'

Trudie kissed the top of Black Jade's head. 'What else could I do? Her mother – '

Jack Taviton stared at her in horror. 'There are orphanages for such children. If your husband made no provision for his illegitimate – '

'Oh, but she isn't illegitimate!' Trudie interrupted, frowning at him. 'He married her mother quite legally. She was just as much his wife as I was.'

'Impossible!'

'No, truly, he married her according to her own customs. If he hadn't, she never would have gone to live with him!'

'My dear woman, her family have been making a fool of you, that's all I can say! One doesn't marry a Chinese whore, no matter what ceremonies one may go through! As for the child – '

'She's my husband's daughter!'

Mr Taviton leaned forward, wringing his hands excitedly together. 'No wonder your cousins wanted you in Singapore where they could keep an eye on you! Do you realize what you're saying?' He jumped to his feet. 'No, of course you don't! Your innocence of the ways of the world does you credit, but I couldn't look Septimus in the face if I didn't try to make you understand what a terrible thing it is you're doing!'

Trudie looked as stubborn as he. 'Septimus has nothing to do with how I deal with my husband's legacy to me!'

'Then who has? Somebody must explain it to you! Good God, as a Christian, your husband couldn't possibly have intended to marry anyone other than yourself! It's no more than your duty to put the woman out of your house as the sinner she is, and make her take her child with her! Believe me, if your husband had lived, the last thing he would have wanted was for you to find out the woman even existed! She's no responsibility of yours!'

Trudie sat up very straight, looking straight ahead of her. 'That's where we differ, Mr Taviton, for I see it as my Christian duty to provide for them both to the best of my ability. What life would the child have if I put her in an orphanage? She might eventually find work as a servant, but I consider she deserves much better than that! When she's older, I shall take her to England – '

Mr Taviton shut his eyes and groaned aloud. 'You're out there, ma'am, if you think your father, or any of your family, will receive her. Your husband's bastard?'

Trudie had some doubts about that herself. 'I keep telling you! Mr Maddock *married* Wu Chao. Black Jade is as much his legitimate daughter as any child of mine would have been!'

'And what does Mrs Horton have to say to that?'

'I've never asked her,' Trudie confessed. 'She doesn't really like Chinese people. I don't think she'd like them even if they were Christian like ourselves.'

Mr Taviton laughed shortly. 'I'm not surprised Septimus couldn't deal with you in London, or that your cousins wish to be rid of you from the Settlements! It's unbelievable! Don't you ever consider anyone else's point of view but your own?'

Trudie thought about it. 'I do what I consider to be right.'

'When your own relations tell you that you don't know right from wrong?'

Trudie set her teeth. 'Yes.'

He flung up his hands in horror. There wasn't much difference between this man and any other, she thought sadly. They all thought that she, or any other woman, was incapable of having any ideas or beliefs of her own.

'I don't know what to say to make you understand!' he said at last. 'I've tried not to listen to the gossip that goes round Malacca, but I feel it's my duty to tell you that most of the Europeans think that Chinese woman – your Nonya maid, as you describe her – is manipulating you in a clever, Chinese way, just to get money out of you. I dare say the whole family is living off your bounty, if you did but know it! One never hears of them making much money on their own account, do you?'

'Oh yes, indeed, one does!' Trudie was glad to enlighten him. 'There are more Chinese millionaires in Singapore – '

'You don't believe such a ridiculous story as that, do you? If there are, it can only be because they don't have any morals to hold them back! Have you heard about their secret societies? You're a fool to get involved with such people!'

Was she? For a moment, Trudie was uncertain that she had done the right thing after all. What did she really know about the *kongsis* or the *hui*?

'None of this has anything to do with Black Jade,' she insisted. 'It doesn't make her any less the daughter of Jeremy Maddock, does it?'

'She'll never be a European!'

'Her father was a European and a Christian! If she isn't of her father's race, what is she?'

He shrugged. 'Chinese, I suppose.'

Trudie hugged the child to her. 'If her mother had her way, she'd bind her feet and cripple her for life, as her parents did to her! Is that what you want for her?'

Jack Taviton looked down at her angry face and sighed. 'No, I suggested you put her in an orphanage, remember. She'd be all right in one of those. The people who run them are every bit as Christian as you are! They wouldn't bind her feet!'

But Trudie was no longer listening to him. She shut her ears, wishing he would go away. 'Nor would they give her any love! All children need to be loved, Mr Taviton.'

She looked so proud and so *stubborn*, that he could admire her, especially as he would never have to take responsibility for any of her actions. 'I'll do my best to forget this conversation,' he promised her awkwardly. 'Septimus will never know from me about the Chinese woman – or the child.'

Trudie said nothing at all. She didn't even go to the door with him as she would normally have done, and she was crying as though her heart was broken when Wu Chao came in and found her, still with the child on her knee, for once not knowing what she should do next.

'What am I to do, Wu Chao?' she asked her.

The Chinese woman touched her lightly on the cheek. 'Never mind now, Tludie. Tomorrow 'nother day, never mind. Maybe next day you know what to do, no?'

'Maybe,' said Trudie. But she had no faith in it. Indeed, she thought she had been a fool to confide in Mr Taviton at all. She could only hope he would be too embarrassed to rehearse all the details of her life to her brother. It would be the end of everything if he did, for she couldn't believe that Septimus would ignore his sister taking responsibility for Black Jade, even with his mind more or less wholly taken up with his own coming nuptials. What a fool she had been! Surely, after all these years of making her own way in the world, she should have learned better than to confide in a man of straw such as Jack Taviton, when she had never even told her brother one half of what she was up to!

Chapter Eighteen

'Where's Mr Rhys?'

'Where would he be but out at the plantation,' Trudie answered placidly. In the sea of troubles that surrounded her, only Mr Rhys remained a warm, honey-tasting memory. She didn't care that it was also a forbidden one.

'You're getting to sound like him!' Mrs Beresford said with a warning look. 'You're not seeing too much of him for your own good, are you?'

'I'm not seeing him at all. He's far too busy trying to retrieve my fortune from the hands of my cousins. Oh, he'd dearly like to take that man to court for the way he's stripped the place of anything that would raise a little money for him to pocket! The only thing that stops him is that I won't allow it.'

Mrs Beresford maintained an uncomfortable silence.

'So far I've succeeded in persuading him that women can't expect any justice – ' Trudie continued fiercely.

'My dear, I'm sure that's not true! You have to admit the circumstances to be extraordinary – and what would you have done without your cousin's help, answer me that!'

'I'd have a small but continuing income. As far as I can understand, Mr Rhys has been working for nothing all this time because Cousin Christopher never paid him! And, as for my needs, my cousin shares my father's conviction that women don't need to eat, or clothe themselves decently – '

'I wouldn't have said your Cousin Hermione goes short of anything!' Mrs Beresford observed dryly.

'She never did!' Trudie said on a sigh. 'I don't know how it is, for she isn't at all clever in the normal way, but there isn't a man born alive who doesn't immediately think she needs cherishing and all kinds of special indulgences!'

'I can think of one man who doesn't!'

Trudie smiled slowly. 'Mr Rhys,' she agreed with certainty.

Mrs Beresford hadn't been thinking of the Welshman at all, but of her own husband, and she was considerably startled by her young friend's tone of voice. Alarmed, she made haste to change the subject before Trudie could say anything else about her manager that either of them might regret.

'What news do you have of your brother? Mr Taviton told me he had received a letter from him in his mail, so you must have done so, too?'

Trudie managed another smile. 'I expect mine has been delayed. You know how it is!'

'That's the first thing I learned out here,' Mrs Beresford assured her. '*Never* depend on the mails. There's no rhyme or reason to them. I often think they're just like that passage in the Bible: one is taken and the other left behind! My mother once posted me two letters on the same day and they arrived six weeks apart!' Unconsciously, she added an indignant cluck of her tongue, for she would dearly have liked to have a word with some responsible member of Trudie's family so that she could tell them exactly what she thought of them, an indulgence her husband would have frowned on severely, she knew, but which would give her a great deal of satisfaction, for she could not approve their continued neglect of the young Mrs Maddock, apparently not caring how she survived, if at all.

On this occasion, however, it seemed that Trudie had

been right about her brother's good intentions, for, by the time she returned home, Septimus's letter was there waiting for her. She ripped it open, astonished at its great length, and settled herself down to read it.

He began by confirming that he was about to marry and there followed a eulogy on his proposed bride. The only salient facts Trudie was able to elicit was that she was far from beautiful, and that her brother adored her, finding in her a warmth he had never known in any other female. Indeed, Trudie was beginning to think that she might do very well for Septimus after all, when she went on to read that Teresa, for such was her name, had effected a reconciliation between Septimus and his father.

I am so much happier now Father and I are friends again. To see Teresa is to love her, so I wasn't surprised that Father should have been bewitched by her also. Better still, Trudie, my darling has suggested you should return to England in the near future and she will do her best to reconcile you to our parents, despite all we have heard of your way of life in Malacca. Teresa has no doubt that all you need is a husband and children of your own to give up your wild ways and take up a normal life again at home.

'I don't believe it!' Trudie exclaimed to herself. 'How can he suggest any such thing? And who does she think she is? She doesn't even know me!'

Septimus went on to say that his duty to his new family definitely meant that he was resigning his position at the Emporium, *such as it was*, for he had never been the master of his own fate there, having to carry out his brother-in-law's stated instructions to give priority to the artefacts Trudie had sent him for sale in London.

Since your widowhood, I have had serious misgivings that you should be forced into trade on your own account, being conscious that you were reared for gentler pursuits, and every report of you I have heard from our cousin has stressed how unfit you are to be left in the Colonies with no proper guidance as to how you should comport yourself in such surroundings. Father has told me several times how willingly he would welcome you home to take your place in the parish as his daughter once again.

'Has he, indeed?'

She flung the letter down on the table, trying to calm herself. It was only to be expected, she thought, now that Septimus had someone else to provide him with the backbone he had always lacked. If she could have met and known Teresa for herself, she might have been able to put her side of things to her but, as it was, her father and brother had already presented her as a rebellious, wild creature, with no manners and less wit. She could have wept when she thought about it! But she would not cry again, she vowed to herself. She had done too much of that already.

It wasn't often that she went out the back door and down the covered passageway to the house next door. On the rare occasions that she did so, she was always made welcome but, although she knew Wu Chao to be always pleased to see her, she was still shy with the other members of the Ki family, very conscious that to them she was a foreign devil, without benefit of civilization or proper upbringing.

'Wu Chao!' she called, knocking on the door of her friend's house.

It was Swee Neo who came to the door. 'Please to come in! Do you look for Black Jade?'

Trudie shook her head. Belatedly, she remembered to bow and to enquire after the various members of the family who might, or might not, be present. 'Swee Neo, will you tell Wu Chao I've had a letter from my brother. It's much worse than I thought! I may have to go to England.'

'Oh, bad!' Swee Neo exclaimed. 'Never mind! I send Wu Chao to see you and between you, you t'ink of somet'ing, no?'

'I hope so.'

'Yes, never mind! You go home, Tludie, and Wu Chao come now.'

It was with relief that Trudie saw Wu Chao stumbling along towards her. She had never discovered if it was actively painful to walk on her tiny, crippled feet, but she imagined that it must be, for Wu Chao seldom walked any distance from her own house, though she was immensely proud of what she considered to be her most beautiful feature.

The Nonya immediately made tea, settling herself on one of the wooden chairs. She was immaculate as always, without a hair out of place, her high Malay collar encrusted with heavy embroidery, and her long tunic as fresh as if it had been brand new instead of at least two years old.

'Tell me what blother say,' she suggested comfortably.

Trudie did so, adding her own graphic comments as the full horror of her first reading of it came back to her. 'I won't go back to England! I won't!' she reiterated.

'Maybe best t'ing,' Wu Chao said doubtfully.

'*I won't!*'

'No, then we must do somet'ing else, no?'

Trudie marvelled that Wu Chao should be so unmoved as their whole world crashed about their ears. 'You don't understand! Septimus was the perfect cover because he never asked awkward questions about the stuff we sent him, never took any interest at all in what we did, or didn't do, out here. Can you imagine anyone else showing such a lack of curiosity that he wouldn't wonder where we were getting our best pieces from? Or how we managed to find the capital to buy where we choose, without reference to the person who is supposed to be holding the financial reins in London? Have you thought what will happen to *us* when whoever takes over from Septimus decides he can do without us and wants to deal directly with *our* contacts?'

'Never happen. The *kongsi* have somet'ing to say 'bout that.'

'Exactly,' said Trudie. 'And what will happen then? *We* have precious few rights in law as women. How will you feel when Cousin Christopher pockets all our profits, as he already has anything that the plantation produces?'

Wu Chao was stirred to a fleeting anger. 'Better not that man! Better marry Rhys man, no?'

'Oh yes!' Trudie turned away. 'But it isn't possible, Wu Chao. I did wonder for a while – '

'Why?'

Trudie looked at the Nonya's frowning face and wondered how to explain it. 'Your family wouldn't allow you to marry a Hokkien *sinkeh*, of bad blood and with no education or prospects, would they?'

Wu Chao looked bemused. The Hokkien lower classes were known to be whores and the sons of whores, who wouldn't think of binding their daughters' feet to form the Golden Lilies that made Chinese ladies the more pleasing to the men they married. They cared nothing for such things, knowing nothing of the elegancies of life. Trudie was right! Nothing would have induced the Ki family to turn their carefully reared daughter over to such a man, unless he was as wealthy as the barbarian who had bought her from them only to die before he could fulfil his part of the bargain they had made with him. What she couldn't understand was why the Rhys man didn't buy Trudie from her brother and put an end to all their troubles? The foreign devils, even the best of them, had remarkably little understanding of life. Aloud, she said, 'Rhys man like t'at? You sure, Tludie? Rhys man friend of Whampoa, not of servant people!'

'Ask Mrs Beresford, if you don't believe me.'

Wu Chao had always liked what she had heard of Mrs Beresford. Trudie had no idea if the two women had ever met, but she knew they respected one another in a way that was unusual across the cultural divide that lay between the Europeans and the rest. It was a divide that was deeper between the women than between the men, who met and mingled in the course of their work, if not at other times. The women never met and were accordingly much more suspicious of each other's customs than they would have been otherwise.

'Very well, we ask Goddess Kuan Yin to help humble servants. Come now to Temple of the Green Clouds and we ask if business survive without blother's help. She tell us if you find happiness, no? You come, yes?'

Trudie hardly hesitated. Of course it was outrageous for a Christian to go to a heathen temple on such a mission, but what harm could it do if she merely escorted Wu Chao? She didn't have to believe in the goddess: indeed she knew nothing about her! And she had always wanted to step over the wooden bar that guarded the temple doors to see what went on on the other side. 'Yes,' she said.

Wu Chao found the walk to the temple difficult to manage. She dismissed the idea of taking a rickshaw, however, making light of the pain she suffered.

Only when they reached the temple did she begin to worry that Trudie might show her ignorance and not behave in a worthy manner. The responsibility was very great and it took all Wu Chao's affection for her to encourage her first look inside the temple from the street.

'You see entrance guarded by "Fo" lion and lioness. One on left has cub to show she hand that rocks the cradle; one on right has ball of Chinese coins to show he breadwinner of family: mother, father, understand? We offspring inherit sacred inheritance from parents and show respect. Without father, mother, we no' see sun or moon. When we see lion and lioness we remember filial respect.'

Trudie's eyes darted about her, looking at the elaborately carved dragon on the roof and the magnificent doors that stood open to receive them. In vain, did she strive to put herself in a proper state of mind to step over the plank of wood that stood in the doorway, forcing everyone who came in to automatically bow their heads as they entered. She could feel nothing for her own father, and very little for her grandparents.

Anxiously, she consulted Wu Chao about this quandary she found herself in. 'I don't even like my father!' she said baldly.

'No' worry, Tludie. Father, mother give life. 'Tis 'nough, no?'

Oh yes, Trudie thought, she was passionately grateful to them for giving her life, for enabling her to see all these strange things. She was beginning to see what Wu Chao had meant when she had said that without the benefit of her parents she never would have seen the sun or the moon.

She put a hand on the lion's head as Wu Chao did before her, a little amused when the Nonya gave a push to the ball of money in the beast's mouth. 'More money, more life,' she said to herself, and stepped over the wooden barrier.

The temple was like nothing she had ever seen before.

There were people everywhere, all busy with their apparently unrelated activities. To Trudie, accustomed to groaning a few hymns in a dim, religious light, the whole atmosphere seemed a rich tapestry of life put on display for her personal delight. Men were eating picnics in the corners; women stood before the ancestral altars, muttering prayers and incantations under their breath and placing the favourite foods of the departed on the altar tables in the belief that the *manes*, or spirits, will come and enjoy the delicacies; and children rushed back and forth, playing games and calling out to one another, just as if they weren't in a religious building at all.

Wu Chao told her that on festivals such as Ching Ming, all souls' day, whole families will show up and share a banquet with their ancestors, thus cementing their particular clan together in this life. She showed her, too, the huge furnace where the lately bereaved burned the paper replicas of houses, carriages, foods, everything that might make the next life easier for the loved dead one.

'What do you want burned for you?' Trudie asked her, expecting her friend to join in the joke.

But Wu Chao's face grew solemn at the thought, her eyes wide as she reviewed the choices open to her. She lowered her gaze to the burning wood, a little self-conscious.

'Many dress,' she said, in a small, breathless voice. 'Many, many dress. Nice house. Much money. All usual t'ings.' Her voice changed as she lost her seriousness. 'Chinese b'lieve dlagonflies bring messages from dead.' She nodded her head with complete conviction. 'I b'lieve that! I b'lieve that very strongly!'

Trudie recalled sitting in the family pew at home when the sun was shining, and watching the specks of dust dance in a sunbeam from the stained-glass window. In her imagination, she had thought of each speck as an angel taking prayers up to God. Dragonflies were better, she thought, much better with their iridescent gossamer wings!

'Show me Kuan Yin,' she said.

The statue was very white, the goddess's hair done up in a top-knot on her head. She wore a dress of crimson embroidered brocade, and carried a small bottle in one hand, the equivalent of a cornucopia showering her gifts on humanity.

Trudie looked carefully at the doll-like face, but could see very little character written there. The brows were plucked and arched, the eyes slanted in the Oriental way, the nose small, and the mouth a scarlet bow that almost smiled but not quite. It was hard to believe her to be interested in the happenings in the bustle of humanity that went on all around her.

'Please to kowtow,' said Wu Chao, bowing low herself.

Trudie did so, keeping her reservations to herself. This wasn't a goddess, she insisted silently. Kuan Yin was a saint of her day, much as the lives of Christian saints are held up for the admiration of the faithful. She stifled the knowledge that her father would have preached for hours against such excesses. How many times had she heard him rail against the 'ritualists' and their Catholic worship of the Virgin Mary? He would not have it that any woman had had a part in the great scheme of salvation, no matter how small. Women, he had stormed at his congregation, were merely conveniences in which the man's seed was stored and eventually brought forth. Trudie stared at the representation of the goddess seated in a muddle of candles, bowls of burning joss sticks, fruits, and paper-written messages of all kinds. Her enigmatic expression reminded her of Wu Chao and she felt a warm feeling of affection that she would know and understand the frustrations that every woman was heir to, and which no man could ever know anything about, no matter how kindly his intention. She bowed again, content to linger where she was, especially now an elderly woman had come to stand before the altar, a young woman beside her, and proceeded to carry out a full medical examination on a third woman complaining of a stiff neck that was daily rendering her less and less mobile.

Trudie watched, astonished, as prayers were said, joss sticks lit, the neck massaged and touched with magic pieces of paper. Meanwhile an animated discussion took place, with various passersby joining in with other suggestions as to how the patient might be made more comfortable.

'Come!' Wu Chao bade her, lifting an imperious hand. She went to the side of the altar and picked up two small carved pieces of wood, shaped like boomerangs, one of them with a flat surface, the other rounded. '*Yin* and *yang*,' she explained, holding one out flat on either palm. 'Male and female principle, understand? If in perfect balance *yin* and *yang* lead to perfection!' Her black eyes lit with laughter. 'You not knowing 'bout that, but one day Rhys man show you great tluth, no?'

Trudie refused to answer. She was shocked that Wu Chao should mention such a subject at such a time, but then Wu Chao laughed at her when she said sex was sinful, telling her a man could not be healthy unless he put his jade stem into the jade gate of a woman as frequently as he felt the urge. 'One day you find out!' she had smiled at Trudie. 'Very happy feeling. Very nice.'

Now, she placed the two pieces of wood into Trudie's hand, leading her to a spot in front of the altar and making her kneel down on a leather cushion. If, when she threw them up in the air, they came down on different sides, it would mean that Goddess Kuan Yin would answer her question. The first time, they both fell on the flat side, but the second time they fell one and one, and Wu Chao allowed her to go on to the next stage, shaking a beaker full of spills round and round until, finally, one of the spills fell out on to the floor in front of her.

Each one of the ancient lacquered spills had a Chinese character written on it. Trudie's was seized upon and taken to one of the keepers of the temple, who matched the character against those written on a hundred different little drawers in an antique chest. Finding the one that matched, he opened the drawer and took out the top piece of paper and handed it to her.

Wu Chao snatched it eagerly, reading it avidly, with little crows of delight. The people around read it, also, those of them who were able, comparing notes as to its meaning.

'Very good,' Wu Chao told Trudie at last. 'You must suffer first, but soon content and happy. Much riches too. All made more better because it take time to achieve. Very good! Better you suffer if it make you happy in end, no?'

'Maybe,' Trudie said. She wasn't keen on suffering.

'But yes, Tludie! Now we know that one day you happy. If you happy, I very happy too!'

Trudie saw that she meant what she said. Tears flooded into her eyes. She could not remember that anyone had ever *liked* her before, not as Wu Chao liked her, wanting nothing from her, just enjoying her presence and the way they laughed together, and the multitude of foolish things that had become a part of their everyday existence.

'Does Kuan Yin say how the business is going to succeed?' she asked.

Wu Chao shook her head crossly. 'Always you expect too much! Must goddess do everyt'ing for you?'

Trudie looked at her sideways. 'It would be nice!' she remarked.

Wu Chao's irritation fell away from her. 'Yes, velly nice, but no' good for ordinary peoples. Must be worthy of great ancestors to be ancestor oneself! Must change world, no?'

'That's too much for a mere female to want! All I hope for is to end my days as a rich, eccentric old lady – with lots and lots of friends!' she added with a lift of the chin. 'People I really like!'

Wu Chao nodded complacently. 'And family! Honourable husband and many sons and daughters!'

It took them a long time to walk the short distance home. Wu Chao took Trudie to one of the many shops near the temple that sold the paper representations of this world's goods to be sent by fire into the next. Together they marvelled over the beautiful objects, all made of paper; carriages to ride in; pots and pans to cook with; toys for children to play with; everything that the heart of man could desire.

Next door to the Chinese shop was an Indian flower shop, hung about with necklaces of sweetly smelling flowers, trays of blossoms, and elaborately formed designs being prepared for a local wedding.

'Is beautiful!' Wu Chao exclaimed, breathing in the perfume of the flowers.

Trudie thought of Mr Rhys. 'There's beautiful!' she agreed.

'Ah hah!' Wu Chao laughed at her. 'You t'ink Rhys man beautiful?'

'Him too,' Trudie agreed on a sigh. 'Him too.'

When Trudie got home from visiting Mrs Beresford the next day, she found Wu Chao patiently instructing Black

Jade in how to reverence and greet her elders. The Nonya frequently pretended a dislike for her daughter, but no aspect of her life was neglected by her mother. She taught her all the things she had been taught as a child, seeing to the smooth running of Trudie's household as she did so. Then she would go home again to serve her husband, bringing up his motherless children as if they were her own. The servants respected her high standards, but preferred to deal with the more happy-go-lucky Swee Neo, when they couldn't make Trudie understand what they were talking about. But, as this happened less and less, they took it for granted that the *Nai-nai* had other things on her mind besides their miserable affairs, and even became quite proud of serving the strange, European lady who, just when they would least expect it, would turn on them in their own language, calling all heaven to witness what she had to put up with from such a whoremongering, ill-bred bunch of illiterate nobodies, just as if she were a civilized person and not a barbarian at all. These outbursts would be discussed for days, over their gambling sessions with the other servants of the neighbourhood, and it was probably as well that so few of the European *mems* listened to their servants or it most certainly would have been yet another black mark against Trudie's name.

'Better now with English friends that you no' have Nonya maid?' Wu Chao suggested meekly, her eyes filled with laughter.

It was easier, much easier, but not for worlds would Trudie have admitted it to the smiling Chinese. 'They wouldn't think so if they knew you were teaching me to play *cher kee*! It must be the most expensive game in the world!'

'That because you always lose! Very sad!'

'Not only that!' Trudie exclaimed. 'Look what it costs to feed all the players. Are Nonyas always so greedy?'

Wu Chao refused to answer. 'Rhys man send you message, Tludie. Man bling it from plantation this afternoon.'

'What kind of a man?'

'Him Kling. Tamil Indian. I seen him on plantation. He stay Portuguese Nonya tonight.'

Trudie nodded. There were several Eurasian Nonyas she had come to know through Wu Chao, all of them of Portuguese extraction. It made her feel better about Black Jade's future, especially when her own European friends rejected the little girl outright, never including her in any of the parties they held for their own children.

Wu Chao gave her the sealed envelope, watching anxiously as Trudie slit the envelope open and took out the hand-written message inside.

Come at once, it read, *and bring Wu Chao, Black Jade, and husband with you. Your house has been completely pulled down and Jeremy Maddock's will was found in the rafters. I'll expect you tomorrow afternoon. Caradoc Rhys.*

'Will you come?' Trudie asked Wu Chao.

'Yes, come, if honourable husband permit.'

'Mr Rhys wants you to bring him with you,' Trudie said.

Wu Chao veiled her expression. 'Not possible. Honourable husband stay home. What time we go, Tludie?'

They arranged a time between them, Trudie still trying to explain that Mr Rhys was expecting Wu Chao's husband as well as herself.

'Very well. Ask husband,' Wu Chao conceded at last.

But when the carriage was brought to the door the next day, only Wu Chao and Black Jade were standing on the pavement waiting, their luggage wrapped in two small bundles beside them.

'What about your husband?' Trudie asked, as she climbed inside.

Wu Chao got in beside her. 'Better two fliends go together,' she said firmly. 'Honourable husband t'ink so, too. This Maddock business. You Maddock *Nai-nai*. Better so. You t'ink better, Tludie?'

'Yes. Yes, I suppose I do,' Trudie admitted, though she couldn't have put it into words as to why she thought they would be better off on their own. And it couldn't have come at a better time, she thought, her spirits rising dramatically as she considered the adventure before them. No matter what Mr Rhys had found in Jeremy Maddock's will, no one would be able to take away from her these few days, with just Wu Chao and Mr Rhys for company, her two favourite people in all the world.

Chapter Nineteen

The Kling driver had the handsome good looks of the Southern Indian. He wore an East India Company uniform tunic, which had been washed so often that it was falling apart at the seams. He flashed a smile at the two women, taking the little girl up on the driving seat beside him to give them more room inside.

He spoke to Wu Chao in a mixture of Malay and Tamil. 'Tell the *mem* we must drive fast, stopping only for lunch in the hottest hour. The *tuan* Rhys wants us there before nightfall.'

Wu Chao translated this for Trudie's benefit. 'Never mind hurry, I bling picnic.' She spoke rapidly in the Malay *lingua franca* to the driver, explaining where she knew there was a magnificent waterfall and where she wanted to stop for lunch. When she was satisfied that he knew the spot, she leaned back, sighing with happiness at the joy of the moment. ''Tis nice to be outside, no?' she murmured.

It brought home to Trudie how very restricted the other woman's life was, if largely by choice and custom. She very seldom left the privacy of her own home and, when she did, it was never alone, or with one other chosen person as it was now. She thought how much her European friends missed by never getting to know these private shadows, not that her own kind ventured out into the streets much, considering the city to be too hot, too dirty, and too full of natives to be a proper place for them to do their own shopping. They sent the servants instead, willingly paying the squeeze that every inbetween considered to be their natural right. Trudie had been saved any of this hassle by having Wu Chao organize her household for her. Nor did it stop her from poking about in the dingy shops of her choice, which was one of the joys of her life as she never knew what to expect, or what she might see, and that added a zest to her existence she had never known in London.

She smiled at Wu Chao. 'How much poorer I should have been if I had never known you!' she exclaimed.

Wu Chao was pleased. 'Too kind! Very happy to have served you!'

'You're my friend – '

'Don't Europeans serve their friends?'

'I can't think I have ever served you!' Trudie returned impulsively. 'It's always been the other way round!'

'No, not alway. You give me baby daughter. I no' forget. Never, I forget!'

Trudie watched the child playing with the Kling's driving whip as she proudly sat up on the seat beside him. The Indian seemed to welcome her company, making animals' noises for her delectation. It was seldom one saw any of the native peoples turning their backs on a child, or finding their presence unwelcome. She wondered why it was that Europeans so often did, refusing to admit their children to be people at all until they were much older. Even Mrs Beresford, who doted on her daughters, longed for them to grow older and do something on their own account. Children are such a worry, she would say, regarding them as empty slates waiting for her to write their characters on them. Wu Chao knew Black Jade to be her equal, lacking only the manners that governed the Nonya's life. She had taught her to kowtow almost before she could walk, but she made no effort to educate her views on life. 'Why not she t'ink that?' she would ask with a shrug of her shoulders.

'Maybe she one day change mind.' To Trudie, who had never been supposed capable of thinking for herself at all, the novelty of such an approach had an immediate and immense appeal.

The jungle had a shut-in appearance to Trudie. The tracks, which she remembered as being fairly open, had been reclaimed by the undergrowth since she had last travelled that way and, sometimes, it was quite difficult to pick out the way forward. It was all part of the general neglect that had taken over everything to do with the plantation since the Hortons had taken control. Trudie recognized the village where she and Mr Rhys had stopped once before. She remembered the way all the men had stopped to pray. Was the Kling a Moslem? she wondered.

She found he was not when they stopped for their picnic. Taking Black Jade by the hand, he walked a little away from the waterfall, pushing his way up a narrow path to where someone had created a small, highly painted shrine in a cave. An elderly Indian, dressed in a dirty white dhoti, received them both, took the Kling's gift of fruit and a coin and, in return, placed some coloured ashes on their foreheads.

'Should Black Jade be doing that?' Trudie asked uncertainly.

'She enjoy it,' Wu Chao said simply. 'You come my temple.'

Trudie was still in two minds about her justification in doing that, but she said nothing more. The warmth she had felt when she had knelt before Kuan Yin was still with her, pagan goddess or not, and she had more than half believed the answer she had received, but her Christian self still felt guilty that she hadn't refused point blank to make such a visit.

'Have you ever been inside a church?' she asked Wu Chao.

'Oh yes, when little girl. Seen dead man Christ! Very sorry He die. So sad. Never mind, Him happy now.'

Trudie watched Black Jade coming back down the path, pausing at intervals to ask the Kling to carry her for a while, or to watch the sunshine making rainbows in the waterfall. For a moment she envied her, remembering her own grey childhood and the constant hunger that had run like a thread through her young life. An instant later, the child came running towards her, throwing herself into Trudie's arms, and giggling as her mother wiped the ashes off her brow.

'Did you kowtow properly?' Wu Chao asked her.

She shook her head, unperturbed. 'He wasn't a man,' she explained. 'Only a post – and a man with an elephant's head.' She turned her attention to the food her mother had laid out on a beautifully embroidered cloth. 'I'm hungry!' she declared.

Trudie had never seen Wu Chao so relaxed as she was during their picnic. The Kling took his food a little away from them, preferring to eat alone, and the two women were glad of it, for Wu Chao was in the mood for teaching Trudie more about the Nonya customs that were so dear to her. She told her about Second Brother who had had to have an ear pierced because he was a sickly baby. One would often see a Baba with a single earring, either for that reason or because he was the spitting image of his father. She told her about how she had learned to make the *baju panjang*, the long dress favoured by the Nonyas, from her grandmother, and how she would teach Black Jade in her turn so that people would come from miles around for their best dresses as they did for Wu Chao's work today.

She told how amongst her family she was sometimes

called *Puteh* because of her very fair complexion. It was true that Swee Neo was much darker in colouring because, as the whole family openly admitted, when the first Kis had arrived in Malacca they had intermarried with the local Malays and, sometimes, even with one of the Tamil Indians. Swee Neo bore the nickname *keleng* for that reason.

She explained, too, that it was the distinctive Nonya hairstyle, with the hair combed up into a tight top-knot and kept in place with pins, that caused so many older ladies to have a receding hairline. To hide this, many of them kept a piece of roasted candlenut in their make-up boxes with which to colour the bald patches to disguise them from a distance. Wu Chao's own thick, black hair had been inherited from her Chinese ancestors, as were her white skin and her distinctive eyes. One day, she said, she would visit the Middle Kingdom for herself; maybe they would go together, to Shanghai, the market place of the whole land, where everything had its price to those who wanted to buy.

She told Trudie, too, of the small community known as Chetty Malacca, which was the term by which the Indian Babas were known. Apart from their Hindu religion, their customs and dress, even their language was that of the other Baba/Nonya communities. 'My new husband b'long Chetty Malacca.'

Trudie wasn't as surprised as she might have been for, on the rare occasions when she had seen Wu Chao's new husband, she had noticed he was far darker than any of the others of her family.

'Babas always marry again,' Wu Chao went on in matter-of-fact tones, 'especially if having children. Nonya more virtuous to stay widowed.' She shook her head. 'I not very virtuous woman – not like my friend Tludie,' she added with a gleam of laughter.

Trudie smiled also. 'One day, when we're both doddering old ladies, I'll tell you what true virtue is,' she promised. '*Who can find a virtuous woman?*' she quoted softly, '*for her price is far above rubies. Her children rise up and call her blessed*. That's from our Holy Book.'

Wu Chao nodded her head with complacent satisfaction. 'A virtuous woman become ancestor, no?'

'I'm sure you'll be a great ancestor!' Trudie chuckled, never having read precisely that meaning into the words before. 'Lucky Black Jade!'

'Oh you!' Wu Chao chided her. 'You don' b'lieve anyt'ing!'

But that wasn't quite true. 'I'm beginning to,' Trudie assured her solemnly. 'It isn't quite as I thought it was, that's all.'

The Kling driver told them they would have to approach the plantation by another, slightly longer route because a tiger was prowling round their usual road. The day before a child had been taken, and the day before that a dog had gone missing.

'The *tuan* is hunting the tiger today, but the tiger is old and cunning, that's why he is looking for easy food.'

Neither of the women was eager to meet the tiger, though Black Jade was loud in her protests that Mr Rhys might need their help in bringing the tiger to book. 'Is he a lovely striped tiger?'

'He's old and tired,' Trudie told her. 'Mr Rhys wouldn't want to kill him if he were young and able to feed himself.'

Black Jade was contemptuous of such an idea. 'Why not?' she demanded.

Trudie looked hopefully at Wu Chao for support, but found none. She would never, never understand the Oriental attitude towards death, she told herself. Wu Chao, quite as much as her daughter, was all for Mr Rhys shooting the tiger dead. Wasn't death a part of life? So why should either of them mourn over putting an end to the existence of a magnificent animal?

The change of route meant they had to go by a settlement Trudie had never seen before. It wasn't a Malay *kampong* as she first thought, for the main building seemed to be a secluded European bungalow. 'Who lives there?' she asked the Kling.

'Some people from the city.'

'What kind of people?' Trudie pressed him.

'*Tuan* Maddock know these people,' he answered with even greater reluctance. '*Tuan* Horton like them come. White man's business. Much better know nothing.'

Wu Chao and Trudie exchanged glances. Then, suddenly, Wu Chao uttered a little choking exclamation. 'Better you not go there!' she told Trudie sternly.

Trudie was more intrigued than ever. 'Who lives there?' she asked again. 'Tell me!'

'A Eurasian man live there,' Wu Chao answered uncomfortably. 'No' nice man. Mr Maddock go there sometime to smoke opium.' Her eyes flashed as they were apt to when she was greatly stirred. 'Many people smoke opium, Chinese, European, all peoples, but bad t'ing all the same. You promise me you never take Black Jade to smoke opium? Never!'

'I promise,' Trudie said.

She wasn't thinking of the child, she was thinking of all she had heard about the great opium trade with China and how important it was considered to be for the whole Empire. If the British were prepared to go to war for the privilege of supplying China with Indian opium, surely it couldn't be so very bad. What was it like, she wondered, to smoke the Green Dragon, as she remembered Mr Maddock calling it?

Wu Chao calmed down again, now she had Trudie's promise. 'Very bad, never mind,' she tried to explain her attitude. 'Some people like the dreams too much and want more and more. If you lucky, opium make you sick, and that that. But if the smoke likes someone, that person never free again. You stay away, Tludie.'

'Have you ever tried it?' Trudie asked. 'Wouldn't it be fun to try it, just once, to see what it's like?'

Wu Chao shook her head. 'Mr Maddock like dream all time before he die. Very sad to see man want on'y more and more smoke. If he live, he sell everyt'ing for smoke. He build house and bring bad man here.'

'You mean this place is actually on the plantation?'

'Yes,' Wu Chao conceded reluctantly. 'What you do, Tludie?'

Trudie was in no doubt about the matter. She would go and see the place for herself!

At first, the driver tried to dissuade her from her arrogant command that he draw up outside the compound until she was ready to go on again, but when she pointed out that he worked for her and not for Mr Rhys, whatever he might like to think, he reined in the horses and, keeping up a sharp exchange with Wu Chao at the same time, he jumped down from the box and helped both ladies down the steps.

'Wait here!' Trudie commanded them all, climbing down on to the ground.

Now that she had her way, she wasn't quite sure what to do next. If she had thought of some way she could have retreated back into the carriage without losing face, she would have been delighted. As it was, she felt obliged to walk up the steps on to the bungalow's verandah.

The front door stood ajar, but nobody came in answer to her half-hearted call. A slightly sweet odour hung on the air, a smell she recognized from the short time she had spent with Mr Maddock, for his cigarettes had had that same sickly perfume, one which she hadn't much cared for, though her husband had laughed at her complaints, telling her that every man needed some vice or other to keep him going. There was another, frailer memory she had of the same smell in her father's study, but she thought that could quite well have been her imagination. Her father had never required any substance, narcotics or alcohol, to strengthen his sense of sin, nor could she imagine him compromising with his free will by enslaving it to the poppy. Her brothers were a different matter, though she acquitted Septimus without question. She would have known if Septimus had ever tried smoking opium; it would have been far too exciting an innovation for him to have kept to himself.

She might have turned and gone back to the waiting carriage, if she had not heard a woman's voice coming from inside the house. Cousin Hermione? But no, it couldn't be, for what would her cousin be doing here, without a word to anyone? And where was Mr Horton?

The woman's voice cried out again. Trudie peered through the window, shading her eyes from the light. It was her cousin, right enough, lying on a low bed, dressed only in a silken negligee which displayed quite as much of her as it pretended to hide. Beside her, a young man was kneeling. In his hands, he held a needle and what looked to be an inkpot. He picked out a small smoker's ball of opium on the end of the needle and held it over the naked flame of the lamp, rubbing the needle between his fingers until the opium began to give off a vapour. He then transferred the opium into the silver cup of one of the pipes he had placed beside the bed, kneading the ball of resin down with his thumb.

Impatient for him to finish, Hermione began to berate

him again, moaning as if she were in agony. 'If you don't hurry up, I won't give you any money at all!'

The young man showed his teeth in an attempt at a smile. 'Your husband said to wait for him,' he reminded her smoothly.

'Then he should be here!'

Trudie thought her cousin sounded very old, much older than her years. Was that why Wu Chao didn't want Black Jade to succumb to the habit?

Hermione snatched the pipe, inhaled luxuriously three times and then settled herself back against the pillows, returning the pipe to the young man's outstretched hand. She had put on weight since Trudie had last seen her without her outer garments. Her breasts and stomach protruded from under the silken negligee, very white and soft-looking. Trudie noticed the young man's expression of distaste as he looked down at the sleeping woman and wondered that Hermione should allow herself to be seen in such a state. She was ashamed for her lack of dignity and felt an urge to rush inside and cover her up before her own husband should see her in such a state.

The young man began to prepare tea and the fragrant scent of the blossoms that floated in the hot liquid vied with the decadent sweetness of the opium. Trudie felt slightly sick and wished she had listened to Wu Chao and gone on to the plantation house without stopping. She tried to make her feet obey her and tiptoe away from the window and the bungalow, but they would not. She blinked, trying to concentrate better on what she should do next. The décor of the room was an Oriental fantasy that she found vulgar and unappealing. Dragons had been painted on the walls, and silk hangings were everywhere, discoloured from the constant smoke that rose from the low beds below. It was not Chinese, but an idea of what a

Chinese room ought to look like, seen through the eyes of another culture. Trudie felt sad for her cousin that she should find such a place romantic or exciting, when it was merely trite and ugly. There had to be far better opium dens than this one to be found in Singapore. Why come all the way out here to such a tatty place?

The sound of a horse galloping from the plantation gave Trudie back the use of her limbs. She hurried down the steps, her skirts in a whirl about her and ran across the open ground, leaping up into the carriage just as the driver cracked the whip and the horses pulled away.

Taking one look at Trudie's stricken face, Wu Chao leaned forward, herself worried and far from being as calm as was her usual way. 'Was the Rhys man there?'

'No.' Trudie still looked as though she had seen a ghost. 'Cousin Hermione dressed – dressed as a trollop. I thought she was in Singapore!'

It was obvious that it came as no surprise to Wu Chao though, at that moment, the horse and rider came galloping towards them, hardly reining in at all as they passed each other on the narrow track, the carriage being almost forced into the surrounding jungle. The Kling steadied his horses, his eyes flashing white as he stared after the disappearing horseman.

'Are you all right, ladies?'

'A few bruises,' Wu Chao complained.

'Did you see who it was?' Trudie demanded, made angry by the shaking she had taken.

'Man-cousin.' Wu Chao wrinkled up her nose. 'He there much. Very bad t'ing!'

'It certainly is! I shall ask Mr Beresford what he intends to do about such places when I get back to Malacca.'

'Forbidden in China before. Not now,' Wu Chao said, so sadly that Trudie nearly didn't hear her.

'What I want to know is why isn't it forbidden here, on British soil?'

'Blitish don't think it bad thing. Very bad in Middle Kingdom. You Blitish force trade in opium – '

'I don't understand it! Nobody could think what my cousin is doing is a good thing!'

'Oh yes, Tludie! Make much trouble for Chinese. You want Chinese silk, Chinese tea; China want not'ing in exchange, so you make war and insist Middle Kingdom buy opium from pirates.'

'We don't control the pirates, Wu Chao! I asked Septimus about it, and he said it wasn't anything to do with the British after the opium left Calcutta. The middlemen are pirates, not the British! He was quite definite about it!'

'Yes, your pirates! Pirates defended by Royal Navy gunboats. Everybody know. You make very good trade for Indian Empire. Blitish Government say forbidden in India now. Maybe Blitish say not'ing to do with them once opium leaves Calcutta, but it all go Hong Kong, Shanghai, Nanking. After defeat in war, the Ineffable Dragon, sitting on Celestial T'rone, can do not'ing. Many t'ousand years of civilization, all not'ing when Blitish guns fire on poor Chinese junks. Ki family say after Treaty of Nanking, not'ing save old Empire now. We come Malacca to learn new t'ings from Blitish – new trade. Very sad, no!'

'I think it's outrageous!' Trudie said roundly, deeply shocked by this recital. 'I wonder if we have opium dens in England! I never heard that we have any, but Cousin Hermione must have picked up the habit somewhere!' Surely not from her father! That was an idea that shocked her to the marrow. Not even to Wu Chao could she give voice to such a terrible possibility!

'Everybody smoke now in China. In Fukien Province, eight out of ten mens smoke; in Canton Province, nine out of ten. Also Blitish take much Imperial gold. Much, much! Chinese servant Lin break a £30 chest of opium, Blitish charge six hundred thousand pounds. After Tleaty, China pay over two million pounds. Very bad, no?'

Trudie set her jaw. 'Someone should put an end to it!'

'No good. Too much money. Ki family very wise to come Malacca!'

Trudie was still burning with impotent rage when they drew up just inside the plantation compound. Her own house was no more. It was hard to tell where it had been, so quickly did the jungle reclaim its own. Wu Chao's house, on the other hand, was obviously in use. 'I suppose Mr Rhys is living there,' Trudie remarked.

Wu Chao laughed. 'Why not he live in own house?'

Trudie remembered how she had concluded before that Wu Chao and Mr Rhys were living together. She never had seen Mr Rhys's house, but she presumed he preferred to live out of sight of the rest of them, a feeling with which she had a strong sympathy.

Hardly had they arrived, Wu Chao taking possession of the house in her inimitable way, the servants scurrying hither and yon to do her bidding, than Mr Rhys came walking up the path, his hat pulled well forward over his eyes and his shirt open practically to the waist.

Trudie averted her eyes from the welcome sight he presented. For two pins she would have run to him and thrown herself into his arms, she wanted to touch and feel his strength so much at that moment. 'I wish you'd warned me my cousins were here!' she snapped, put out by the strength of her need for this one man in the whole world and not wanting him to guess the effect he had on her.

'You've met them already?'

'Mr Horton practically ran us off the road, if road one can call it! I prefer not to say what Hermione was doing!'

'Ah.'

'Is that all you have to say?'

He pushed his hat on to the back of his head. 'I hoped you wouldn't find out about that place,' he admitted. 'Since you have, I shouldn't mention it to your cousins – '

'I shall never understand how the most respectable amongst us can turn a blind eye to this pernicious trade – '

'A blind eye?' Mr Rhys choked. 'There's big money involved. India sends nearly five thousand tons of the stuff into China every year. That's real trade, not turning a blind eye!'

'They can't know about it in London!'

He gestured Trudie towards a seat, sitting down himself on the top step of the verandah. 'There's the innocent you still are, Mrs Maddock! Do you think a great many English throats don't swallow the poppy dragon for the dreams it induces? The poppy trade is the only business that thrives on this plantation. Did you not know that?'

'I don't believe it!'

'It isn't such a wicked thing. You've probably felt its benefits yourself. Have you never had a toothache to be soothed, a fever, or needed a tonic to make you feel better? It was most likely opium you were given.'

'As a medicine, yes. Hermione wasn't using it as a medicine!'

'No.'

'Then what are we going to do about it?'

'Nothing.'

Trudie's indignation boiled over. 'Nothing?' she repeated.

'Singapore lives on the trade, as Malacca did before Singapore was opened up. That's what *we* are doing here!'

'But that's terrible!' Trudie exclaimed. 'Do you mean Mr Maddock was involved in the opium trade?'

Mr Rhys traced the pattern on the tiled steps. 'I decided long ago I didn't want to know about that side of his business. I told Mr Horton as much. I'll only take responsibility for my own deals, good or bad. If you're wise, you'll do likewise. The powerful don't like having their thrones shaken by radicals like myself – indeed, they do not!' He cast her a slanting, amused glance. 'There's no hope for a female radical such as yourself!'

'I'm not a radical!'

'Oh? What are your politics?'

'I don't have any!' She looked at him, liking him very much, her anger gone. 'Yes, I do. *Moh ching, moh meng!* No money, no life!'

'Then don't stick your nose where it's not wanted, my dear. You might find a lot more than you bargained for!'

Trudie chewed on her lower lip thoughtfully. 'The thing I disliked most about seeing Cousin Hermione like – like *that*, was that it was so undignified! How could she?'

'It's an addiction. Don't ever start the habit, that's my advice to you!'

Trudie shook her head. 'Wu Chao has forbidden it.'

He smiled. 'You like her, don't you?'

'Yes, I like her,' she admitted.

'That's good. This is going to be a difficult time for you, made worse because your cousins have seen fit to join us. They're not going to like what I have to tell them!'

'Will I?'

He considered her for a moment. 'I think you'll be glad – for Wu Chao.'

Trudie lowered her eyes, trying not to look at the bare skin of his chest. The sight of her cousin, lying in abandonment to her own need on that low bed, had awoken a desire in herself, not for opium, but for the fufilment of her own womanhood. She wanted to put her hands beneath his shirt and tempt him to do the same to her. They were sinful thoughts, she knew; ones she shouldn't indulge for a single moment; but she could find no defence against them.

'Caradoc.' She rolled his name over her tongue, experimenting with it, knowing it to be as forbidden to her as he was himself. 'Do you mind me calling you Caradoc?'

'Not if you've a mind to.'

'What do you do by yourself here? Do you smoke opium, also?'

'No.'

She looked at him solemnly, weighing up the odds of his telling her the truth. Everybody told lies, to themselves or to others, when they couldn't face the truth. Yet she did believe him. She thought he would scorn to lie to her about something which was really none of her business. He would be more likely to refuse to answer.

'Mr Maddock smoked.'

'Did he tell you that?' Mr Rhys countered.

'You know he didn't. He never told me anything except those things he thought would make me more useful to him. I may be the innocent you think me, but I'm not so green as to imagine he had much affection for me. He saw me as a tool to help build up his empire, one who would never renege on him, or cheat him, because a married woman has no rights apart from her husband. Septimus would never have succeeded so well in London without me. Do you believe that?'

'Your husband did.'

'Maybe. He didn't have to like me to believe that much about me. It was the liking he found difficult.'

'Ah, now, that's a different matter,' Mr Rhys said. 'Did you want him to like you?'

She considered the question carefully. 'People don't like me,' she said at last. 'Except Wu Chao. I think she likes me. It's very strange, isn't it? You don't like me much, do you?'

He grinned at her. 'If I were to tell you how I feel about you, Mrs Maddock, you'd take to your heels and run all the way back to Malacca!'

'Would I?'

'You should!'

Her smile was a little shaky. 'It makes me very happy you should say that, Caradoc.'

'Wu Chao is not the only one to be liking you either!' he said suddenly. 'Mrs Beresford has a fondness for you. And Whampoa didn't despise you when he met you.'

She laughed in embarrassment. It was stupid of her to have mentioned anything so trivial, so silly, to a man like him, when she had never spoken of it to anyone else that she could remember. What did it matter if so few found her likeable? She minded; yes, of course, she minded, but she had grown used to it over the years. What mattered was that this Welshman should see the same quality in her that she saw in him, a quality that transcended liking, though she did like him. She liked him very much indeed!

'My own family dislikes me,' she said at last. 'They could be right to do so. I sometimes think they are because, you see, I'm not a very good Christian, if Christian at all. They are right to hate me for that, aren't they?'

'I'm not qualified to speak of such things. Maybe you're too much a Christian for them to understand you – '

'*Me?* I don't even fast willingly. I never have!'

'So what?' he retorted. 'If I remember rightly, Christ himself was accused of much the same. You'll have to do better than that if you want to be a great sinner!'

She laughed with him, oddly comforted, as if she had thrown off a weight that had been wearing her down for far too long. 'What would I do without you and Wu Chao to remind me how unimportant I am in the scheme of things!' she teased him. 'I'll have you know that one day I may like to grow a little conceited without one or other of you bringing me back to earth!'

'You can be as conceited as you like when you've made your first million – unless I make mine first! A rich man has the whole world at his feet and can make all sorts of choices denied to other men. He can go where he likes; *marry* whom he likes – '

She didn't pretend to misunderstand him. 'I didn't tell you about another failing of mine, I hate waiting for anything! I grab at life, everything! And I've never yet regretted anything I've done, only those things I hadn't the courage to do.'

'You're still gentry, my girl!'

'I'm a woman first!'

'Maybe, maybe not. I don't believe in hole-in-the-corner affairs, though, and that's an end to the matter!'

She blinked, afraid that she might cry. 'All right, Mr Rhys, help make me a million, and I'll guarantee to have the Beresfords dance at your wedding – if you think I'm enough of a woman to suit you! Because, I don't mind telling you, an ex-miner is much more romantic to me than just another millionaire!'

'Devil!'

But she refused to let him escape so easily. She gave him a deliberately demure look and tossed her head. 'I wish I could stay with you tonight, instead of with my cousins in this house! When Wu Chao was here, I envied her having the better house, but it seems to have lost its character along with her furniture. How gloomy it is!'

He was amused. 'Don't you like it? Mr Horton spared no expense on its decorations, I assure you. What don't you like about it?'

'All those instruments of death on the walls – '

'The stuffed heads are mine!' he interrupted, his eyes gleaming with laughter.

'Really? And all those knives, and guns, and all those other things?'

'Your cousin has a taste for Malay weapons.'

'Well, I don't share it! They give me the shivers.'

His amusement fell away. 'That isn't like you. You're usually interested in all such strange things!'

She pulled a face. 'It's more Mr Horton I don't like,' she admitted. 'I'd much rather be with you!'

'You'll have Wu Chao with you.'

'My cousins don't like her either,' Trudie said sadly.

Mr Rhys had gone when the Hortons arrived. He had said he would come back later, accepting Wu Chao's invitation to dine with them. Wu Chao was inside lighting the lamps, hobbling round the rooms on her tiny feet, Black Jade pulling at her skirts in her eagerness to help. 'Come inside before the mosquitoes eat you alive!'

'I'm coming.'

Christopher Horton had to practically carry Hermione up the steps. To Trudie's eyes, her cousin looked grey, her eyes vacuous and unseeing. She was fully dressed, though some of the buttons were in the wrong buttonholes, and her hair had slipped out of its usual disciplined style to fall about her shoulders in a tangled disarray.

Trudie rose to greet them. 'Cousin Hermione, Cousin Christopher, what brings you here?'

Hermione wilted, shading her eyes from the beam of light that came from the door. It was Mr Horton who answered. 'We only have your interest at heart, *cousin*. Why else should we be here?'

Trudie looked about her. 'You seem to have made

yourself very much at home here, despite your dislike for the place. I had no idea! I thought you'd decided nothing would make the place pay?'

'Quite right. So why are you here, Gertrude?'

Trudie managed a slow smile. 'Didn't Mr Rhys tell you? When they pulled the other house down, they found Mr Maddock's last will and testament. It seems we may have been taking too much for granted, thinking the place to be mine!'

'Whose else would it be?'

Trudie shrugged. 'I don't know. What's the matter with dear Hermione?'

Mr Horton's fists tightened angrily. 'She should have stayed behind in Singapore – as she usually does. She complains of the hardships of coming up country, but she comes just the same! She never listens to anything I say!'

Trudie's eyebrows rose. 'Perhaps you should have insisted – '

'You, her family, can say that? The damage was done by the time she married me!' His bitterness brought her father back into Trudie's mind. Was it really possible?

Hermione giggled suddenly. 'No good talking to Cousin Gertrude about the pleasures of life! Nobody ever wanted *her* around when they were having a little fun!'

Wu Chao teetered to the door and beckoned to them to come inside. A look of distaste crossed her cousins' faces that Trudie found disturbing. Hermione hadn't cared that the Eurasian man should have seen her half naked and out of control of her own senses, yet she could still hate Wu Chao, who had never been less than polite to her.

Trudie went and stood beside the Nonya. 'Have you forgotten this is Wu Chao's house? She is our hostess here. You're lucky she will receive us because she keeps the best table of anyone I know! Shall we go inside and join her?'

Hermione made a sound of protest, pulling a face at her husband. 'You always were a greedy pig, Cousin Gertrude,' she said.

Chapter Twenty

Dinner was a strained and uncomfortable meal. The only person oblivious of all the currents swirling around the adults at the table was Black Jade. She was thoroughly enjoying the unusual experience of having Wu Chao and Trudie vying with each other for the privilege of pushing little delicacies on to her plate to distract themselves from the Hortons' displeasure at their dinner companions.

Trudie was at first nervous of Mr Rhys's finding himself out of his depth, but this was not so. He chose to eat with chopsticks, it was true, manipulating them with a dexterity that made everyone else except Wu Chao seem clumsy. Trudie could have laughed out loud when Hermione bent forward and asked him how he had acquired the art, suggesting that Europeans should keep to their own implements, as she did. He was more than able to hold his own with her cousins.

Afterwards, seeing that Black Jade was falling asleep over her glass of milk, Trudie picked the child up and slipped away to put her to bed. This was a moment she always looked forward to. She and Black Jade enjoyed a good romp together, something Wu Chao would never indulge in, for, to her, no child was ever too young to be taught to respect her elders. Indeed, one look from her mother was enough to quieten Black Jade, though no one could have said she was afraid of her parent. Far from it, the love between them was beautiful to see, and Trudie never feared that she would come between them, no matter how much time she gave the child, the presents she made her, or even the occasional admonishment she made, for Black Jade knew very well who had given birth to her and, although she kowtowed to them both, she knew Trudie didn't care if she bowed low or not, whereas Wu Chao most certainly did.

She was giving the child a ride on her back when she became aware of Wu Chao standing in the doorway watching them. 'Have they finished dinner?' Trudie asked her.

'Yes. Cousins not pleased that you leave table with child, though. Very bad manners, they say.'

'Phooey!' Trudie retorted. She sat on the floor, looking up at the Nonya and admiring her gentle, feminine appearance. Where she had first thought her enigmatic, she now saw warmth and kindness, made all the more obvious by the icy selfishness of her own cousin.

'Why phooey? You should serve your guests, Tludie.'

'They're no guests of mine!' Trudie's face lit with mischief. 'We're all your guests tonight! Isn't this your house?'

'Maddock house! Cousins not want Nonya in same house. Better Elder Sister do duty by family, no?'

Trudie sighed. 'If you say so.' She got slowly to her feet. 'They wouldn't give you the same consideration, Little Sister! How is it that your manners are so much better than theirs? I apologize for family!' she added with a deep bow.

Wu Chao choked back a laugh. 'Better aporogize Rhys man! Man-cousin tell him no' be friend of Whampoa any more! Rhys man unworthy serving man, on'y fit to mine coal from earth!'

Trudie wasn't surprised. 'I wish I knew what my cousins came here for this time!' she exclaimed. 'And why Mr Rhys sent for us in this secretive way!'

'Why not ask him, Tludie? I finish with Black Jade.'

The Hortons barely looked up when she joined them. Making a determined effort to be pleasant, she offered them tea, and was unsurprised when they refused, adding churlishly that they would have preferred something stronger. 'Cousin Hermione, too?' Trudie murmured.

But she was never answered. Wu Chao came into the room, sitting silently in the corner, busy with her needlework and, at the same moment, there was the sound of someone arriving outside. A few minutes later, Mr Rhys came in from the verandah, a young, earnest Chinese following, a briefcase in one hand.

'This is Ki Thian Heow,' the Welshman introduced him.

Only Wu Chao made any response. She recognized her kinsman at once, though she had only met him once to her knowledge. She greeted him with humility, offering him refreshment and enquiring after the various members of his immediate family that she could recall.

Trudie bowed in her turn, refusing to acknowledge her cousins' distaste at the politeness.

'Who is this Chink?' Hermione asked Mr Rhys, not quite looking at him.

'He is a lawyer, Mrs Horton. Mr Maddock's lawyer. It was he who drew up Jeremy Maddock's final will, made on his deathbed. It is a legal document, I assure you!'

Hermione cold-shouldered him, turning her attention on Trudie. The pupils of her eyes were still enlarged in her pale blue eyes, giving her an unfocused look. Trudie felt her hatred like a body blow although she expected nothing less from her cousin.

'Your ideas of hospitality are decidedly bizarre, cousin! What may we expect next, I wonder?'

Her husband was quick to join in the attack. 'I had a right to be consulted, Cousin Gertrude, before you arranged this charade! I have given up a great deal of time to deal with your affairs – a thankless task, I may say! I think I have earned better from you than to have to suffer being forced to sit down to dinner with a woman who, I believe, was once your maid, and now we are being asked to believe your late husband employed this dressed-up monkey as a lawyer! What trick are you planning to serve us up with next?'

'Mr Ki is a Baba,' Trudie said automatically. 'Shall we listen to what he has to say and then perhaps we'll know why he's here.'

Christopher Horton twirled his moustache between two fingers, trying to gather his own thoughts together. The Chinese had very little body hair which, in his opinion, made them lesser beings. Indeed, he wondered they could procreate at all, as even their old men had the appearance of boys!

'I'm tempted to send him about his business! And Rhys along with him!' he muttered, one eye on Hermione's sculptured features. He didn't like the way her eyes were wandering round the room, focusing now and then on some object and then passing back again to her cousin, as if Trudie were the only other person there, the object of her hatred and discontent in her whole life. He thought her mood uncertain and wished she had stayed behind in Singapore as he had asked her to. Above all, he wished she didn't show her hatred for her cousin quite so clearly when they were in company. Even Mr Rhys made no bones of his disapproval of the way Gertrude Maddock was treated by her in public. It was embarrassing, and not to be borne much longer, and so he would tell her, conveniently forgetting that his own manners left a great deal to be desired, also.

'So sorry, Mr Horton,' the Baba put in quickly. 'I am

sorry to tell you that you have no rights here. It must be a shock for you, especially for Mrs Maddock, what I have to say. I did, of course, inform Mr Rhys of the conditions of Mr Maddock's will on his employer's death but, at that time, the document couldn't be found. I therefore advised him to do nothing until it came to light.' He was pleased with himself for his idiomatic English and the certainty of his pronunciation and it showed in the slight smile that curled his lips.

Trudie responded with a good-natured smile in return. 'I'm sure you did everything that was proper, Mr Ki.'

'One could not foresee that he would place the will in the rafters of the new dwelling place that was being erected for your arrival, madam,' the Baba agreed, clearing his throat as he hoped to clear away the embarrassment these Europeans caused him from clouding his mind.

Trudie's smile changed to one of glee. 'It was the obvious place when you come to think of it,' she said. 'He probably knew Wu Chao's views on *Feng Shui* and that it would have to be pulled down again!'

'Yes, indeed,' the Baba approved.

'But who do you suppose put it there?' Trudie went on, busy with her own thoughts. 'He was too ill to do it himself.'

'I put it there, *Kak* Tludie,' Wu Chao volunteered, her face averted, hating to call attention to herself in this company. 'Mr Maddock tell me it charm to keep away evil spirits from *Nai-nai*. So sorry, I forget. T'ink not important!'

Trudie exchanged a fond look with the Nonya. 'It was probably the only thing that held the place up!' She turned impulsively to her cousins. 'Every day, a bit more of that awful house would collapse. I can't tell you how I envied

Wu Chao this one! I used to plan for hours together how I could persuade her to exchange dwellings with me!'

'It yours, Tludie!'

Trudie shook her head. 'I don't want to live here now. You gave it life, but it's a gloomy-looking place now, don't you think? I can't imagine my husband living happily here now, either. He would have hated all those military objects on the walls and the clutter everywhere – '

'Cousin Gertrude!'

Trudie presented an innocent face to Mr Horton. 'I'm sorry, did I interrupt you, cousin?'

'If you could keep a still tongue in your head for two minutes put together, we might hear what was in this remarkable document!'

'Oh yes, of course.'

The Baba's enigmatic gaze rested on her face but, as soon as he realized she had seen him studying her, he looked down at the paper in his hand and cleared his throat again. 'So sorry, but Mr Maddock was a very determined gentleman who liked to have his own way. Nothing I could say would turn him away from what he wanted to achieve by making this will. I told him the Kis did not expect it and that he would be making things very awkward for his European wife, but he would have it that both women needed an income of their own if they were to fulfil his ambitions for his family. I couldn't argue against this, for on such reasoning are great families founded. It's sad there is only one daughter to come after him, but Mrs Maddock may marry again and give his name to one of her sons – '

'Good Lord!' Mr Horton exclaimed in a strangled gasp. 'What is the fellow talking about?'

Trudie hastened to enlighten him. 'The Babas and

Nonyas frequently change the status of their children by adoption, or other means – '

'Cousin Gertrude!' he choked. 'Your late husband was a member of a civilized nation, even if he did have some pretty odd ideas one way and another! As you were not destined to bear a child of his, we can presume him to be without any other legitimate heir besides yourself! The sooner this pantomime is brought to an end the better!'

'So sorry, but the will is a legal document, Mr Horton.'

The earnest Chinese looked so ill at ease that Trudie took pity on him. 'Why don't you read the will, Mr Ki?'

'Yes, madam.'

'I suppose you can read it?' Christopher Horton asked in lordly tones.

'Yes, sir, I can read it. I drew it up in the first place on Mr Maddock's instructions – '

'Get on with it, man!'

He did so. He was a young man, and not very tall, but he already had an enormous dignity, which was far from being matched by the Europeans, who sat, uninvited, and fiddled with her jewellery, in Hermione's case, and with the rings on his hands in the case of Christopher. The latter had a couple of new rings, Trudie noticed, and was immediately certain that in some way or other they had been paid for by herself.

She looked around for Mr Rhys, feeling the need of his support, but he must have gone out on to the verandah again. It was a tactful move, though she doubted that anyone would appreciate it except herself. The Hortons despised him too much to be concerned if he should be a witness to their humiliation or not. They hated him as they hated her and Trudie was almost sure their dislike was returned with the same stinging intensity as her own contempt for her cousins and the way they chose to live.

She wished the Welshman had stayed, all the same. She had come to rely on his support more than she had thought. Indeed, she doubted now if she would ever be able to do without the comfort of knowing he was there, if only in the background of her life. He was growing in importance for her day by day.

The will was simply drawn up and easy to understand. Jeremy Maddock had left his interest in the London Emporium and what remained of his import/export business to Trudie: the plantation he had left to Wu Chao and their child. Both women he recommended to the care of the Ki family, his partners in everything he had achieved in the Straits Settlements.

Trudie was delighted. 'There, I told you this is your house!' she exclaimed to Wu Chao, laughing. 'Goodness knows, the plantation isn't making much money at the moment, but one day it will!'

The lawyer smiled and nodded. 'The Ki family thinks so, Mrs Maddock. I am glad you aren't too distressed by this turn of events. It was a part of Younger Sister's marriage settlement but, when the will could not be found, she refused to allow me to tell you of your late husband's wishes in her behalf.'

'How like her!' Trudie said warmly. 'I wish I thought the plantation was going to bring her the joy she deserves from it but, as Mr Horton will be the first to tell her, it brings in mighty little!'

It was only then that she turned to include her cousins, sure in her own mind that Christopher, at least, would be as glad to be rid of the place as she was. Who better to have it than the Kis, who had wanted Mr Maddock to buy the land in the first place? The Hortons, however, were livid with anger.

'Let me see that will!' Christopher Horton demanded,

snatching the paper out of the Baba's hand. 'How do we know this is Jeremy Maddock's signature, or that the witnesses are genuine? I doubt this forgery would stand up in any reputable court of law!'

'Disgraceful!' Hermione chimed in.

The Baba bowed. 'The will was registered with the Malaccan authorities yesterday, sir. If you wish to make an objection to its terms, I suggest you take your complaint there.'

Christopher Horton struck out at him. 'Don't you come the uppity lawyer with me! I'll see what a proper lawyer has to say about it, not some dressed-up baboon in the pay of Chinese bandits!'

The Baba barely seemed to move at all, yet in a second Mr Horton had dropped the will on the floor and was nursing his wrist as if he feared it might be broken. 'I'll see you in gaol for this!' he growled, his eyes glittering with frustrated fury.

'Indeed, you won't!' Trudie retorted sharply. 'None of this has anything to do with you – '

He recovered himself a little. 'You forget yourself, Cousin Gertrude! As your closest male relative, of course the matter is of interest to me, and I assure you I won't allow it to be stolen from you and handed over to a half-caste brat whose claim on her father can only ever have been on his charity!'

Trudie stared at him, aghast. 'Don't be ridiculous!' she said sharply.

He forgot his annoyance with the Baba and turned on her instead, slapping her hard on the face with his open hand. One of his rings tore the corner of her nose, making the blood spurt on to her lip. The salt taste of her own blood made her lose her tenuous hold on her temper and she slapped him back, forgetting how much stronger all men are than women, forgetting everything except her own pleasure in doing him a physical hurt, as he had her.

Then, as suddenly as she had wanted to hurt him, she wanted to run away by herself as far away from him, and from Cousin Hermione, as she could get. She wanted to run to Mr Rhys and have him deal with the Hortons for her, as she made no bones he could if he were driven to it. She never wanted to set eyes on either of them again. Her dislike for them was a physical thing.

She tightened the muscles in the small of her back, standing as tall as her inches would allow, her head thrown back. 'How many times do I have to tell you that Black Jade was Jeremy's *legitimate* daughter? And I dislike the term half-caste – '

'How else would you describe her?'

'As Miss Black Jade Maddock.'

His astonishment held him silent for a moment. Then he laughed. 'You poor fool! Hermione and I have put up with all we're going to take from you, Gertrude Grant, because you were never woman enough to be Mrs Maddock in fact, were you? Is that why you make so much of your husband's mistress? Because she relieved you of the necessity of having to warm his bed? You wouldn't demean yourself to be of any use to a man, would you? Think yourself above our animal appetites, isn't that so? Yet you dare to look down on your cousin because *your father* taught her to smoke opium and how to enjoy herself as a woman! Well, let me tell you, madam, that your husband was no better than he should be either! Had his own supply of opium out here, and his own pretty boy to prepare his pipes for him! *He didn't need you! Nobody* needs you! But I'll be damned if I'll allow you to give away anything which is of use to me and Hermione! I want this plantation and I mean to have it!'

'*You* want it?'

'Why not? Neither your father nor your brother wants it – '

'It isn't theirs to want!'

'No, because you want to give it away to this Chinese whore and her bastard half-caste daughter!'

'If you say that once again, I'll ask Mr Ki to escort you back to Malacca,' Trudie shot at him. 'You may be lucky! Mrs Beresford may take you in, but if she does, it will be as a favour to me!'

Hermione came suddenly to stately life. 'Mrs Beresford will be most interested to hear how you put your husband's mistress ahead of your own family! I shall enjoy telling her all the details! She's always been so snooty where I'm concerned, holding you up as an example of the kind of woman we want out here! Well, you can believe me that she won't think so well of you when she hears about this carry-on!'

Trudie stared at her, seeing her cousin not as she was, dressed and coiffured, but lying flat on her back on that low bed, with all that white flesh on display. She felt shamed by what she had seen all over again.

'I'm glad to be rid of the plantation,' she said abruptly. 'I don't like what goes on here!'

Hermione's skin turned a blotchy red, as she realized that, somehow or other, Gertrude must have found out about her coming to the plantation to smoke opium. Briefly, she considered trying to make her cousin realize the acute pleasure she got from the narcotics-induced dreams, as she always had. She would tell her how her uncle had first introduced her to the strange delight, giving her a golden guinea every time she had prepared the opium for him, kneeling between his thighs and rubbing herself up against him. It had been their secret ever since she could remember, her Uncle Jonathan frightening her half to death as to what he would do to her if she were ever to tell anyone else. She had known from the way he treated Gertrude that he meant every word of his threats, and they had added a delicious touch of fear to all the rest.

Nor had she told anyone until long after she had married and come out to Singapore. She had missed the treats her uncle had given her more and more, becoming so homesick and listless that even Christopher had noticed. At first sickened by her story, he had eventually come to enjoy a smoke every now and again himself. For this purpose, the plantation had been a gift from the gods: it was private and no questions were ever asked of either of them. When Gertrude had gone to live in Malacca, he had swallowed down his fears of the jungle and had come out there more and more frequently, mostly for his wife's sake, it was true, but also because he was becoming more and more addicted himself to the poppy-induced dreams.

'It isn't your decision to make!' she hissed. 'Uncle Jonathan – ' Her voice rose to a scream of despair.

Trudie took a step towards her, afraid of what she might say. They had lost sufficient face as a family that evening and she had no mind for the Ki family to despise them more than they did already. But Hermione misunderstood her motives. She turned on her heel and made a rush towards the wall, seizing one of the native Malay knives out of its sheath. Its wavy, razor-sharp blade danced in the lamplight as she brandished it above her head.

A shocked breath escaped Wu Chao's lips as she saw what Hermione meant to do with the knife. She started forward, intent on catching her by the arm, but her tiny feet betrayed her into tottering head first into the path of the blade. 'Run, Tludie! She kill you!' she cried out.

The *kris* slipped between the Nonya's ribs as Hermione

rammed it viciously home. Blood poured out to stain her bodice, and a small amount escaped her lips.

'Tludie, see 'bout Black Jade! You second mother! Remember Kuan Yin plomise. I tell her you good woman!'

Trudie fell to her knees, desperately trying to staunch the blood. It had all happened so quickly that she couldn't believe that she couldn't somehow roll the time back again and do something that would save her friend.

'Caradoc!' The sound of her own voice frightened her half to death. She was already sure there was nothing anybody could do to help – not even the Welshman.

Mr Rhys knelt beside Wu Chao. 'She's dead,' he said quietly.

'Murdered!' Trudie contradicted him.

Hermione flung the *kris* at her cousin, refusing even to look down at Wu Chao. The knife skimmed across the floor, coming to rest in the folds of Trudie's skirt. Trudie threw back her head and espied Mr Ki standing, behind them, a look of horror on his face.

'Mr Ki, you're a witness to how Ki Wu Chao died by my cousin's hand!' Trudie's voice rang through the room. She thought she was in command of herself, that she knew exactly what to do next, and then her control over herself slipped dangerously. She bowed her head and burst into tears.

Mr Rhys put his arm round her, holding her tightly against him. 'Don't look any more, my darling! She thought your cousin was going to kill you and deliberately took your place. I saw it all from the doorway. She chose it that way, Trudie. She loved you very much!'

Trudie buried her face against his chest. He was warm and hard and reassuringly alive. 'I wish it had been me!' she said simply.

'I wish it too!' Hermione spat at her cousin. 'I've always wished it!'

To Trudie, it seemed the sum total of her existence, that she was in some way cursed. She had known Hermione didn't like her, but to hate her so much as to wish to kill her was something she couldn't cope with just then. She should have realized what was coming and done something to protect Wu Chao. Oh, how much she wished she could roll up time and live through those last few moments again. She wouldn't have cared greatly if Hermione's blow had found its mark in her own body. She and her cousin had always been at enmity. But that *Wu Chao* – she couldn't bear it! How would she exist without her?

'Caradoc, what am I going to do?'

'What one always does,' he answered her. 'Go on living, one day at a time, until you forget a little and remember her only with gratitude. Black Jade will have need of you!'

'I bring everyone bad luck. Supposing Black Jade – '

His hands were very gentle as they caressed her. 'Wu Chao trusted her to you. You've always been her second mother. You didn't bring bad luck to her, but life. Remember?'

Trudie felt comforted. She allowed herself a moment longer inside the circle of his arms, relishing the feel of him against her own body. How much she would have liked the right to have gone to him that night to make new life between them.

Then she pulled away from him, recovering a little, and saw that Hermione had watched her every move and would use it against her if she could. Her cousin was shrewd enough to know that attack would probably be her best defence when these events were reported to the authorities in Malacca.

* * *

Mr Ki made arrangements to transport the body back to Malacca. He took the will with him, earnestly promising that Black Jade's interest in the plantation would be protected, come what may.

'The Ki family bought the plantation with their money when Mr Maddock married Wu Chao. They will manage the land for Ki Black Jade. The *kongsi* will arrange everything, Mrs Maddock.'

'Thank you,' she said.

He gave her an odd look. 'The Ki *kongsi* protects its own, even you, Wu Chao's Elder Sister. It is better you go home to Malacca, taking the child with you. Mr Rhys will take you.'

'What will happen to my cousins?' Trudie asked.

He shrugged his shoulders. 'We Straits Chinese think we all write our own fate with our deeds. Your people rule here now, but if such as I were to take two respected British citizens to court for the murder of a Nonya, should we find justice?'

Trudie found herself unable to return his level gaze. 'What if I were to lay a complaint before the Lieutenant-Governor? Mr Beresford is a good man.'

He shrugged again. 'How shall we prove murder, Mrs Maddock?'

'But it was murder!' she protested.

'You and I know that. Mr Rhys knows that. Your cousins, deep in their hearts, know that.'

Trudie lifted her chin. 'It doesn't seem right – ' she began.

Mr Rhys put his hand out to her, deliberately calming her. 'What he means is their equivalent of our *Vengeance is mine: I will repay, saith the Lord.*'

Trudie opened her eyes wide. 'But will even the Lord give them justice?' she demanded.

'Their Jade Emperor will,' he said sadly. 'No one can escape the consequences of their own actions in the end.'

Trudie couldn't bring herself to speak to her cousins before she left. Her feelings of misery and guilt had settled in a lump somewhere inside her. She knew it was only just beginning, that she was still too numb with shock to feel the full cutting edge of her grief. Only Caradoc Rhys seemed real to her, a still centre to her whirling world.

Her cousins showed no signs of wanting to see her, either. Sometime or other, Christopher had taken his wife away to their own bedroom, his face grey with shock. Trudie had heard Hermione cry out, 'Who cares if she is dead? I wish Uncle Jonathan were here! He'd tell you all that it doesn't matter, that I'm still his pretty little niece! He wouldn't have cared if it had been Cousin Gertrude, not if he knew what I know about her!'

'Hush!' her husband had pleaded with her.

'Gertrude is bad!'

Oh yes, Trudie thought, her Uncle Jonathan would have agreed with that. He had always known his youngest daughter to be an evil catalyst, the cause of other people's sins even when she didn't sin herself. There was no escaping the burden of such a responsibility. She had known it all her life. Her own father had been certain she was predestined to everlasting darkness, and had told her so with all the fervour of a Calvinist preacher, despite his own calling to the Church of England.

Wu Chao had never believed that. Wu Chao's stories of the afterlife were always happy ones, full of light and precious fulfilment. There were various tests one had to undergo, though Trudie couldn't remember any one of them. Whatever they were, Wu Chao would surmount them with honour and so she would assure Black Jade –

Black Jade! She must get the child out of here, far away to where her cousins couldn't harm her as they had her mother. Trudie had no illusions that they wouldn't lie and cheat, *anything* to deprive the child of her inheritance.

'Mr Rhys!' she cried out. There was no immediate answer and she went outside to find him. He had already brought her carriage round to the door, his face dark and intent on what he was doing. 'Mr Rhys,' she said more calmly, 'I think I should take Black Jade away from here.'

'Yes, ma'am.'

She swallowed. 'Are you going to drive us to Malacca?'

'Did you think I'd allow anyone else to go with you?'

'No.'

He touched her arm. 'You have blood on your skirt.' He cupped her face in his hand. 'Don't look like that, love. I only told you in case it should frighten the child.'

She looked down, but could see nothing in the darkness except the swell of her skirts about her legs. It would be an uncomfortable journey by night, she thought, so very different from the one they had made earlier, when she had been young and happy and not the old lady she had turned into in the last hour.

'I'm afraid,' she confessed.

'You'll think of some way to protect her. Will you fetch her now?'

Trudie didn't awaken the little girl. She lifted her out of her cot, wrapping the bedclothes more closely about her, and carried her out to the waiting carriage.

'Will the Kis blame me for her death?' she asked when they had left the plantation far behind them.

He put an arm about her shoulders. 'Aren't you one of them?'

Trudie was silent for a long moment, then she said, 'I think I may take Black Jade back to England for a while.'

'Will she be welcome there?'

Trudie didn't know, but her family were good Christians who would surely make any orphaned waif welcome, and who knew what would become of Black Jade in Malacca? The Hortons wouldn't rest until they had deprived her of her inheritance.

'I'm not sure the Kis will be able to protect her. The Hortons will go to law and then she'll be left with nothing!'

'Ki Thian Heow seems a clever young man to me. What makes you think he won't win any suit your cousins may bring?'

Trudie cast him a guilty, but nevertheless determined, look. 'Our law has few attractions for the Chinese. They avoid it whenever they can – and they have good reason to do so! Oh, I know men like Mr Beresford try to be fair, but if a European says something which a Chinese contradicts, whom is he likely to believe? Who would you believe? A well-reasoned argument in your own tongue, or a muddled talk about ancient customs and ways you know nothing about?' Her feelings of guilt turned to exasperation. 'You don't think I have any right to keep Black Jade with me, do you?'

'You're not a Nonya. Hasn't the child a right to her own heritage?'

Trudie closed her mouth in a disapproving line. 'Black Jade's father was a European: *that's* her heritage also! Besides, Wu Chao entrusted her to me. She's been living with me ever since Wu Chao was married and none of the Kis objected once. Nor did you!'

'It wasn't my place to object,' he reminded her sharply. 'Besides, Wu Chao was always on hand to see Black Jade was brought up as one of them. You'll never make a European of her, *cariad*.'

'I can try!'

He looked so miserable that she nearly changed her mind. She would have done if she hadn't been so afraid that Black Jade would follow her mother into an early grave if she didn't take her away and look after her herself. She had saved her once, but she hadn't been able to save Wu Chao, not even the Kis had been able to do that! Black Jade would be safe with her. She might not be happy, but at least she would be alive!

'I'm going, and that's that!' she said aloud.

'What of your business in Malacca?'

'There are the Kis – and you. I need to go to England, Caradoc, about my own affairs, as well as for Black Jade. If I don't, I may not have a business to worry about in Malacca. At one time, I would have left it to Septimus to deal with the Emporium, but he has other interests now that don't include his sister's affairs. To tell you the truth, I don't think he was ever particularly enthusiastic about being a businessman in his own right. I wanted it so badly for myself, you see, that I couldn't believe he could want anything else, but, deep down, I always knew he wasn't as keen as I was. I can't impose on him any longer, for it would be an imposition and, truly, I'd prefer to deal with everything myself!'

'I'm not arguing with you about your need to go, Trudie. I was wondering how pleased your family will be to see you. Will they be good to you? They've hurt you so badly in the past.'

'I could visit your family,' she suggested, touched by his concern.

'Wales is a long, long way from London,' he started to tell her.

'Yes, I know,' she cut him off, 'but will I find a welcome at the other end of my journey?'

He was silent for a long moment. 'Would you really go to Wales for my sake?'

'For both of us. I want to see your home, Caradoc. How else am I ever going to know you better?'

'Are you sure that's what you really want? Wales is far away from anything you've known.'

'So was Malacca – and Wu Chao – once!'

He put his arm about her, tucking the child into the small space between them. 'If you do go,' he said finally, 'will you do something for me?'

'Of course. I'll do anything I can.'

He took her hands in his, rubbing them between his rough fingers. 'My family live a very poor life, *cariad*, such as I hope you will never have to know. You are always finding new things to buy and sell, new ways to make money. Will you see what can be done for them?'

For an instant she forgot Wu Chao, forgot everything except the urgent request of the man in front of her. She felt humbled by his trust in her abilities, a confidence she was far from sharing, knowing how difficult it was for women to do any business for themselves.

'Won't they mind my sticking my nose in their affairs?' she asked him.

He looked up at her. 'You'll find a way if you set your mind to it.'

'Then I'll do it,' she promised. 'But you must keep things going here for me – and for Wu Chao!'

'Ay, you don't want your cousins interfering in that side of things. Between us, the Kis and I will arrange things until you come home again.'

Her lips twisted in the travesty of a smile. She must be the only European in the whole peninsula for whom Malacca really was home – and how much of that she owed to Wu Chao! Nothing, she was convinced, could ever be the same again without her!

[illegible]

[illegible] we ought to have [illegible]

[illegible] really [illegible] 'Well, [illegible]

[illegible] Will Clare [illegible]

[illegible] pushing the children into the small space between them. [illegible] really will you do something for me?'

'Of course I'll do [illegible]'

[illegible] in the [illegible] about [illegible] particularly [illegible] You are always finding new things to try and new ways of [illegible] money. Will you ask [illegible]

[illegible]

[illegible] into the [illegible]

[illegible] home here for me [illegible]

[illegible]

[illegible] the only [illegible]

[illegible]

BOOK THREE

Chapter Twenty-one

It was early Spring, but Winter was refusing to make way for the new life and the longer days that were coming. It wasn't raining, but the very air was damp, penetrating the thin coats that were all Trudie and Black Jade possessed. The child was blue with cold, as she had been ever since she set foot on English soil. Her miniature dress, passed on to her by Letty's youngest, who had more or less outgrown it and grown into something more fashionable, dragged in the mud, ruining the soft suede of her shoes at every step. Her shoes were her own because her feet were smaller than those of even the smallest of Trudie's nephews and nieces. She was four years old and she was miserable.

Nor was Trudie any happier. It was the third time she had pulled the reluctant child up and down Regent Street, trying to find the courage to go inside the Emporium of which she was now the majority shareholder and owner, thanks to the will her husband had concealed before he had died and which, thanks to Caradoc Rhys, had been found that dreadful time when Wu Chao had been killed. It was difficult, Trudie found, to concentrate on anything except the chill and Black Jade's increasing melancholia. Trudie had no doubt that living in an English household had a lot to do with the child's depression. She felt it herself, glad as she was to be reunited with her favourite sister. Had the weather always been so bleak and dismal? Her father seemed smaller than she had remembered; her mother hardly seemed to be there at all. Only once, when they had been visiting her parents, had her father tried to tempt

Black Jade into his study alone with him, but such had been Trudie's outspoken horror that he should so much as look at the child, that he had retired, defeated. Indeed, he was a much milder man than Trudie had remembered. True, he would attempt from time to time to reassert his authority over her, but she was astonished how easy it was to vanquish him with a couple of words and a few well-chosen threats of her own.

'I promised Wu Chao that her daughter would never smoke opium whilst she is in my care. I'm sure you understand that, Father.'

Mr Grant had been inclined to bluster but, when Trudie had said nothing further, merely looking sadly at him, he had admitted himself defeated. 'I didn't know you knew,' he had muttered.

'Cousin Hermione wasn't the best choice of associate,' Trudie had retorted briskly. 'Really, Father!'

And he had said nothing at all. How strange to think him almost timid after all the years she had lived in awe of his every gesture. At first, she felt he had deceived her all through her childhood, but then she had been amused that he had been able to do so. How much she had learned of the ways of the world since she had left his household behind her!

'I am so glad, dear, that you and your father don't find it necessary to quarrel all the time, as you used to do,' Mrs Grant had said to her daughter.

Trudie had said nothing for a long moment, only looking at the pathetic, bent form that was her mother, then she had burst out, 'I don't know why you put up with him, Mother. If you stood up to him for once, he'd collapse like a pack of cards!'

Her mother's glance had been ironic. 'I shouldn't have thought you needed to ask, my dear. You weren't married very long, it's true, but long enough to know that we women have precious little say how we are treated by our husbands in ways that are never mentioned in polite society. I have no ambition to starve in the street, which is what he once threatened me with.'

Trudie had known only anger at that answer. It had been several days before she had brought herself to think over all the implications of what her mother had said. Had Wu Chao had any greater say in the way she lived her life? Trudie didn't know. What she did know was that the other woman had maintained her own identity and pride in herself as a person, whereas her mother had given up the struggle long ago, exchanging life for a drab existence that stretched her as little as possible.

The first, wholly predictable, disaster that had struck Trudie and Black Jade had been when they had attended her father's church the first Sunday after their arrival. The familiar smell of beeswax and hymn books, and the creak of the hand-pumped organ, had taken Trudie straight back to the endless services of her youth. What she had forgotten was that Black Jade had scarcely darkened the door of a Christian church since she had been born. The child had looked about her with questioning eyes, astonished at the neat rows of worshippers, all in their Sunday best, and all facing the same way. The tunes of the hymns grated on her ears, and the hour-long sermon, preached by the man she had already come to dislike because he smelt bad, bored her almost to tears.

'Where are your ancestors?' she had whispered to Trudie.

'Hush!' Trudie had whispered back.

'What are we doing here?'

Trudie had begun to answer, but the question had slowly burned into her soul. What were they doing there?

'I don't know.'

'I don't like it here! I don't like it here at all!' Black Jade's voice had grown louder with every word. 'I want to visit your ancestors and take them some rice cakes. Trudie, they *can't* like the food here! It doesn't taste of anything. Is that why they've all gone away?'

'It's what my ancestors have always eaten,' Trudie had tried to explain, knowing it to be a losing battle immediately she noticed the lack of conviction in her own voice.

Black Jade had tried another tack. 'Doesn't the sun ever shine?'

Everybody in the pew behind had tried to hush the child. A kind, portly gentleman had offered her his watch and chain to play with. Black Jade had thanked him with dignity, refusing the treat. Sensing an audience of her own, she had displayed her milk teeth in her first smile for weeks and had knelt up on the pew the better to talk to him in her piping treble.

'Do your ancestors live in this cold house? Some of mine are in our family temple, some are in my aunt's house. It took us three months to come to England. Have you ever been to my home?'

Mr Grant's sermon had come to a telling halt. He glared at his daughter from the pulpit. 'If you can't control that child, Gertrude, kindly remove her outside!'

Black Jade had been forbidden to attend church after that. Mrs Grant had muttered that she might find Sunday School more suited to her lack of deportment. Trudie had disagreed. The prospect of having to explain to anyone else Black Jade's lack of any Christian background was more than she felt able to deal with. The taste of failure had risen in the back of her throat, as it had so often in her childhood, as she had realized her total inability to explain to the little girl anything of her father's culture and beliefs.

Mr Grant had determined to teach the child a little Christian doctrine, but, met with a blank wall of dislike, mixed with a detached amusement that anyone could believe in a god who punished those he loved, no matter how hard they tried to please him, he had desisted, declaring Black Jade to be the spawn of the Devil, a title that had given the child inordinate pleasure because, as she explained to Trudie, the Devil was the only person Jonathan Grant knew who seemed to enjoy himself.

An elegant carriage passed them, spitting up the mud on to their clothes. Trudie had forgotten the necessary technique of dodging out of the way of approaching traffic; besides, in the last while she had lived in London, there had always seemed to be some man standing between her and the worst of the filth that made even the streets of fashionable Mayfair seem dirty in a way dusty, sleepy Malacca was not. The anxious small boys who earned an honest penny, sweeping a trail whereby one could cross from one side of the street to the other in comparative comfort, were no comfort to Trudie, who was bitterly aware of their ragged clothes and chilblained fingers, and almost preferred to slosh through the ankle-deep mire than count the ribs of some snotty-nosed youngster sweeping the way ahead of her. She was reminded of the thin, tired coolies who pulled the rickshaws in the East, and thought that if one had to be dirt poor, as she prayed she never would be, it would probably be easier to bear in a hot climate rather than a cold one.

The Emporium had grown considerably since she had last seen it. Part of it was housed in an ancient, black and white building that stood shoulder to shoulder with the more modern buildings of the curved Regency terrace which had replaced its fellows. The rest was next door, set out in the most modern manner behind the magnificent Portland stone façade.

Trudie paused for a moment in the entrance, well pleased to see the quality of the customers who drifted about her. One or two of them she recognized from the days when she had pushed Septimus into expanding into the unusual lines that had made their Emporium so different from all the rest. In her muddy skirt and clutching the hand of the small black-haired child beside her, no one gave her a second glance. She could have been invisible for all the attention she aroused.

Then one of the doormen, taking the opportunity to warm himself in the lobby before going out into the street again, came uncertainly towards her. 'Mrs Maddock, isn't it?'

'Arthur,' she smiled at him, more with her eyes than with her lips. 'How are you?'

'It's good to welcome you home again. I'm afraid your brother is no longer with us – '

'No, I know. I'm here to see the new manager on my own account.' She turned to the child. 'Black Jade, may I present to you Arthur, who finds cabs for our customers if they want them, and carries their parcels out to their carriages. Arthur, this is Miss Maddock, my adopted daughter.'

Arthur bowed over the little girl's hand. 'Oh, you're so cold, miss!' he exclaimed. 'What you need is some good, warming soup!'

'Yes, please,' Black Jade answered. She waited while Trudie produced a coin and placed it in the man's hands. 'I'm going with Arthur,' she announced. 'I like him.'

Trudie smiled again at them both. 'Very well,' she agreed. 'Where do I find Mr Ollerton?'

The manager's office was in the older part of the

building. The manager, Mr Ollerton, was a pompous, rotund little man, his twinkling manner hiding a shrewd head for business that had served him well since he had taken Septimus's place at the head of the business. He and Trudie summed each other up in a matter of seconds, each approving of what they saw, though if his respect for her capabilities was somewhat more grudging than hers, it was understandable as he had never previously had any face-to-face business dealings with a member of the fair sex, and he was frankly disgruntled that he hadn't been warned of the hour of her coming as ordinary good manners would have dictated.

'We were all very sorry to hear of the untimely death of your husband,' he said, giving himself time to think. 'All the staff wore black bands for a month, of course, and Mr Septimus had the counters decorated with black crepe for a week. We didn't close as, by the time we heard of his death, we reckoned that you must have been thinking of wearing colours again.'

'Very proper,' Trudie murmured.

Mr Ollerton fussed about her. 'You look pinched, ma'am, if you don't mind my saying so. A nice cup of tea will warm you up, and some of our latest little cakes, which are the talk of London, if I do say so myself.'

'Thank you, that will be very nice. I'd like to take a tour of the store also, if you have the time. I'm impressed by how many different lines we seem to be selling these days.'

Mr Ollerton was pleased by her praise. He remembered her as an awkward young woman, always pushing Septimus further than he was ready to go. She looked as gaunt as ever and as if she had suffered greatly. He wondered what she had been doing these last few years. She couldn't still be grieving for her husband, he thought. She must have realized long since that she was as able a businessman as ever he had been, even while her brother had always maintained his awed respect for his brother-in-law, but then Septimus had never possessed a tenth of his sister's intelligence. A very pleasant young man who would promise you the earth, if he thought that was what you wanted, all the time he was with you, and forget all about you the instant he turned his back. Was it that which had given Mrs Maddock that grey, haunted look? She deserved better, he thought, and hoped they would be able to work amicably together. At the moment she looked fit to drop and he wondered nervously if she might faint before the tea and cakes could be brought upstairs to restore her.

Over tea, Mr Ollerton gave Trudie a brief résumé of his strategy for the Emporium. He was impressed by the quickness of her mind and the speed with which she saw that the whole had been built up around the Oriental trade that she and Wu Chao had provided. Everywhere, there was Wu Chao's unmistakable legacy in her choice of brocades, in the quality of the porcelain, the jade ornaments, the silks and satins.

Trudie looked at the samples Mr Ollerton showed her and her eyes filled with tears. 'You would seem to be managing very well without my brother,' she said at last.

Mr Ollerton twinkled a modest denial, caught the sadness at the back of his new owner's eyes, and said abruptly, 'Truth to tell, ma'am, we are managing better without him than we could without your trade!'

To his dismay, Trudie first bit her lip, and then burst into tears. She cried like no female he had ever seen, not prettily with half an eye on her audience, but in great gulping sobs as if her heart were about to break.

'My dear Mrs Maddock – '

'I'm sorry,' she apologized. 'This is awful of me – quite

unforgivable! I don't know how it may be, but I don't seem able to stop!'

Mr Ollerton forgot she was the new owner, forgot, even, she was a young lady, though a widow it was true, who might – nay, probably would – misunderstand the familiarity of his putting a fatherly hand on her shoulder.

'You go right ahead and cry all you want, Mrs Maddock!' he advised her. 'Don't mind me! Just pretend I'm not here at all, just as my own wife does, God bless her, when life gets on top of her for a while!'

And cry Trudie did. When she had done, her head ached and the rest of her felt like a chewed bit of string. 'I don't know what to say, Mr Ollerton. I *never* cry!'

'Perhaps that's your trouble, ma'am. I've often thought women to be the more sensible sex, not bottling up their emotions like we poor men have to do, but laughing and crying as we were all undoubtedly meant to do. Shall I send for some more tea?'

Trudie refused the offer with as much dignity as she could contrive. She re-pinned her hat and wiped her face with a clean handkerchief, sure that she must still look a mess.

'It was seeing all those things,' she explained lamely. 'They reminded me of Ki Wu Chao. She was accidentally killed by my Cousin Hermione. I asked Arthur to look after her little daughter while I was up here with you.'

Mr Ollerton had never heard of Arthur. Discreet enquiries, carried out in a whisper to one of his underlings, revealed that one of the doormen had taken a little Chinese girl into the staff locker room, where he had introduced her to a member of the female staff, bidding her take time away from her counter, if you please, to help him look after the child.

'Send them all up here to my office,' Mr Ollerton ordered.

He went back to Trudie. 'The Ki family did business with your husband when he was alive, I believe, and also with your good self, isn't that so?'

Trudie nodded. 'Ki Wu Chao was my partner.'

'Your brother never told me that!'

'No. Everyone in my family preferred to think of our import/export business as my little hobby. Without Wu Chao though, there would have been no business. I never could have found all these Oriental objects by myself. Many of them were brought to Malacca by members of her family.'

'The Ki family. They were Chinese?'

'Straits Chinese.' It took a little while to explain how the Straits Chinese differed from those of the Middle Kingdom. 'Wu Chao was a Nonya.'

'She was your friend?'

Trudie nodded eagerly, pleased to find at least one European who seemed to understand how it was possible to love someone from another race and culture as much as if she had been her own sister. 'I miss her very much.'

He nodded gravely. 'We'll miss her trade, too, Mrs Maddock. Forgive me, I don't know what your plans are, but I think I should tell you that the Emporium will not be nearly as profitable without that trade as it has been in the past.'

Trudie heaved a sigh. 'I don't know what I shall do yet. I had hoped to bring Black Jade up in her father's country, but she's miserable here and, to be honest, so am I.'

Mr Ollerton twinkled an encouraging smile. 'Your friend was married to an Englishman?'

The impossibility of telling him that Wu Chao had been

married to her own husband came to Trudie just in time to prevent her from making any such damaging admission.

'Mr Ollerton,' she said instead, 'it isn't for women to do business on their own account in this world. Officially, my brother was my senior partner and signed all my accounts, and so on. I hate to ask you this, but if you were to become a shareholder and a member of the board in your own right, would you be willing to continue with that arrangement, substituting yourself for Septimus?'

Mr Ollerton's twinkling manner fell away from him. 'It would put me in the position of being legally able to line my own pockets at your expense, Mrs Maddock. Don't you think you should know me better before making me such an offer?'

'No. I like you.' She smiled weakly, her tear-streaked face a mess. 'Of course I'm not expecting you to like me, that's not part of the bargain, but you will have to trust me to make all the decisions in Malacca. I don't think the Ki family will deal with anyone else. They may not want to deal with me, but I think they will – because of Black Jade. She lives with me as my daughter. In her interests, they may forget it was my cousin who put an end to her mother's life.'

'Is that the way you did business with your brother?'

Trudie flushed. 'I suppose you think me unwomanly?'

'Why should I, Mrs Maddock? I have always had a great respect for your business acumen, uncomfortable as you often made life for your brother and, therefore, for me, as his assistant. I didn't like you much in the old days, but then I didn't really know you, did I? If you will allow me to say so, I like you much more now that I understand you better. It will be a privilege to serve you in any way I can.'

Almost, she felt she ought to argue with him, to confess her own uncertainties about the future and to admit that, without Wu Chao, she wasn't even sure if she could find the trade on which they all depended. She was knowledgeable, yes, but she would never acquire Wu Chao's instinct for a good bargain. Nor, she thought humbly, would she ever possess Wu Chao's ability to distinguish between the good and the best, or only sometimes when she thought herself into her friend's mind. Lately, she had been able to do that more and more often, but she didn't expect Mr Ollerton to have any faith in such methods.

Instead, she thanked him. The details of how they would operate in future were easily dealt with. Trudie was relieved to find Mr Ollerton more flexible in his ideas than Septimus had ever been. She couldn't have made a better choice of manager if she had brought him into the firm herself, for, although he had never travelled out of England, indeed he had scarcely ever been outside the London borough that contained his place of work and home, he instinctively saw people as individuals, even his most distinguished customers, refusing to categorize them according to class or origin. Much later, she was to discover he had endeared himself to the Queen herself by suggesting Her Majesty should introduce her children to strange foods from all over the world, pointing out that they would be far better prepared to travel her dominions if they were already experienced in such tastes. Queen Victoria had been much taken by the idea: better still, Prince Albert had confirmed her enthusiasm. Mr Ollerton was delighted, seeing it as a first step towards being awarded a Royal Warrant. Trudie, when she heard, danced a short victory dance and then sat down and wrote to him, congratulating him on his perspicacity. Septimus, she knew, would never have thought of such a thing. It reminded her of the time when she had first had the idea of sending complimentary Oriental shawls to members of the Royal Family to bring the

Emporium to their notice. She was very well satisfied with Mr Ollerton.

Black Jade was brought upstairs and introduced to Trudie's manager. The child looked more cheerful and even managed a woeful smile as she kowtowed in the way her mother had taught her. Mr Ollerton picked the small figure off the floor and threw her up in the air, catching her again with an ease that belied his well-rounded stomach and pudgy features. Black Jade crowed with delight and demanded he do it again, which he obligingly did.

Only then did Black Jade turn her attention on to Trudie. 'You've been crying,' she accused her.

Trudie made a hasty effort to repair the damage. 'There, does it still show?'

'A bit.' Black Jade was disapproving. 'It's bad to cry. It's much better to control one's emotions.'

'Quite right,' Trudie agreed, as solemn as the child.

Mr Ollerton patted Black Jade's head, stooping right down to her height. 'Sometimes,' he said, 'tears build up inside us until we are in danger of drowning. It's better then to cry, because afterwards we feel better.'

Black Jade thought about it. 'I understand,' she said firmly. 'Are you Tludie's – Trudie's brother?'

'No.'

'He married someone, like my aunt did. My mother said never mind – '

Trudie made a face over the child's head. 'I haven't yet met my new sister-in-law and I haven't forgiven her yet for taking my brother away from us. I am very glad to have you as his replacement here, though. I am sure we shall deal extremely well together.'

Mr Ollerton was at his most twinkling. 'I hope so, Mrs Maddock. I am delighted to have made your acquaintance properly at last.' He became more confidential, holding her hand between both of his. It was the first time he had shown he was aware of Trudie's sex, as well as the fact that she was his employer. 'If I might make a rather bold suggestion, ma'am, why don't you and the little girl slip through into Warwick Street. Your brother's wife always goes to the church there when they are in London, and I'm told it's very quiet there. It would give you a few moments to yourself before going home to your family.'

Did she look as bad as all that? Trudie looked down at Black Jade. 'Will you be good if we go and look at the church?'

'Yes, very good.'

Already thrown off balance by the tears she had shed, it was like an earthquake going off inside her as they rounded the corner from Golden Square and saw the Church of Our Lady of the Assumption and St Gregory in front of them. Black Jade pressed on eagerly, pulling at Trudie's hand. She smelt the remnants of incense in the atmosphere at once.

'Joss sticks!' she said with satisfaction.

'Oh, I don't think so,' Trudie objected.

But Black Jade had already seen a statue dedicated to the Virgin Mary. 'Ancestor!' she exclaimed, wide-eyed.

Trudie heard a choke of laughter and was deeply embarrassed to find herself being watched by a tiny cleric, dressed wholly in black. 'I'm not a Catholic!' she told him at once.

'Nor the child either,' he acknowledged ruefully. 'It doesn't make you the less welcome. Did you come in to pray?'

'I suppose I did.'

He pointed towards the sanctuary, where a light burned before the altar. 'You'll find Jesus there,' he said simply.

Black Jade pulled at his sleeve. 'Whose ancestress is she? Is she yours?'

The priest took the little girl by the hand, leading her towards the statue. 'She's the Mother of God. In a way, you may say she is the mother of us all.'

'My mother's dead.'

'Is that so? Then why don't you have a talk with Jesus's mother here? Light a candle, or two, and tell her all the things you think she ought to know.'

Nothing could have given the child greater pleasure. One after another, she lit every candle in the box until she had a blaze of light in front of her.

'I'm afraid I'll have to charge you a florin for the candles,' the priest said to Trudie. 'It'll make the poor mite feel more at home in a strange land, though, so it will be money well spent.'

Trudie thought it cheap at the price. She picked a half-crown piece out of her purse and put it in the priest's open palm.

'And now yourself?' he went on calmly, pocketing the coin with an innocent relish that amused Trudie. She doubted the candle-box was ever going to see it. 'Is there any way I can help you?'

Trudie told him she lived in Malacca and was gratified to discover he knew of the city from reading the life of St Francis Xavier. He had so many questions for her as to what the city was like and about the different communities that made it their home, that she found no difficulty in telling him all about her brother going to work for his father-in-law, about her own marriage and widowhood, her friendship with Wu Chao and, finally, the details of the latter's murder exactly as she remembered them.

'It should have been me who died,' she ended. 'If Wu Chao hadn't stumbled because of her tiny feet – '

The priest nodded. 'I have heard that Chinese ladies bind their feet. Isn't it painful for them?'

'Very. Wu Chao's feet were only three inches long. Golden Lilies, they call them. They find our large feet very unattractive!'

'And she fell in the path of the knife, you say?'

'I think she must have done. Cousin Hermione had no reason to kill *her*! It was me she wanted dead.'

'And you feel guilty about that?'

Trudie nodded, her face in shadow. 'It haunts me,' she said. 'I can't forget it for a moment. I feel as though I murdered Wu Chao myself.'

She sat down in one of the pews, hardly noticing when the priest sat down beside her. The silence was soothing, just as Mr Ollerton had suggested it might be. If she had mentioned the load of guilt she had been carrying to anyone else, she knew she would have been told not to be a fool. How could she have known what Hermione had had in mind?

'Forgive me, I shouldn't have bothered you – '

'Why not? Isn't that why you came?'

'I came to see if I could find a clue to my new sister-in-law's appeal for my brother, not on my own account!' If she sounded prickly, she *felt* prickly, she thought with irritation.

'Of course. You are not one of my flock. But, forgive me, do you have to be to accept any help I may be able to give you? Did you never accept anything from your friend Wu Chao? God is far greater than the little limits we try to force him to conform to. It seems to me your friend was wiser than you in that she knew that; loved good wherever she found it; isn't that so?'

It was not a question to be answered lightly. Trudie concentrated so fiercely on it, she forgot the priest beside her, forgot Black Jade, forgot everything except that devastating moment when she knew Wu Chao was mortally wounded.

'She would want me to go on living,' she said at last.

'And what do you want for her?'

'I want her alive again!'

He was very gentle. 'Isn't that rather a childish wish? You know, if you could bring yourself to view her death less personally, more as a part of all things, I think you would find her again. Not as you knew her before, but as a real part of your own life. Consciously, or unconsciously, the whole of creation is summed up in Christ and given its relevance in him. Isn't that our Christian belief?'

Was it? Trudie had no idea. 'You mean she's alive in some kind of afterlife?' she probed.

'Is there a difference? She exists for God, just as she always existed.'

'She's not a Christian. My father says she's in hell.'

'I see. And what do you believe?'

'I believe she's alive, though how, or where, I don't know. I've never understood much about religion. I find sermons boring.'

'Most people do,' he agreed calmly. 'I often think we preach too much and listen too little. We live in time and space and therefore we're apt to imagine that God does too. Ridiculous, really, when you think about it. That's the great danger for all of us, to make God in our own image and condemn everyone else who sees him differently. It's called idolatry.'

She was shocked into silence. It was certainly a novel thought!

Black Jade, her candles all lit, came running up the aisle towards her, climbing happily up on to her knee. 'I feel better now,' she confided. 'When we go home, we can send many things to Mama in the other world, can't we? And I'll tell her about the candles, shall I?'

'If you like.'

Black Jade heaved a sigh of content. 'Let's go home soon,' she said.

As if by magic, the sun was shining the next day and the leaves, which had all been in bud the day before, came out to greet the new warmth, clothing the London trees with a vivid green, quite different from that seen in the tropics. The leaves were shortly followed by the first of the blossom. On Septimus's suggestion, Trudie took Black Jade by train to Liverpool to visit the newly weds and to meet her brother's in-laws.

Mr Walmsley lost no time in inviting his son-in-law's sister to take a look round the grand store he was creating in the centre of the city. Being a blunt man himself, proud of calling a spade a spade, he found Trudie's comments very much to his taste.

'A young woman after my own heart!' he commended her. 'I can understand now how it is that Septimus gives you so much credit for the way that Emporium of yours has prospered in London. Well, I'm not above learning from anyone! If you've a mind to meet my prices, lass, you and I could do some business together in the Oriental field. What do you say to that?'

Trudie saw her brother's face fall and, with unusual tact for her, suggested Mr Walmsley should do his trading with Septimus. 'You are still my partner in the import/export business, aren't you?' she added to her brother.

'I'd like to be,' he admitted.

When she had the two men together, Trudie mentioned her pet project that someone should visit Yokohama and set their seal on the Japanese trade. 'It's going to be more and more important in the future,' she told them earnestly. 'If you will let Septimus go, Mr Walmsley, on both of our behalves, we could split the trade between the London

Emporium and your store in Liverpool on a fifty-fifty basis. All of us would benefit if we kept the trade exclusive to ourselves.'

'I'll think abaht it!'

Septimus waited until he had his sister alone before he mentioned Jack Taviton. 'I thought he was going to Yokohama for you?'

Trudie shook her head. 'He hates the Orient. He wouldn't do at all.'

Her brother gave her an impatient look. 'I'd hoped you'd take to one another. What are you going to do? You can't live on your own out there for ever! You'll have to marry someone!'

Trudie put her head on one side, thinking her own thoughts. 'Maybe,' she said at last. 'But it won't be Jack Taviton!'

Septimus grunted, shrugging his shoulders. 'He *did* like you, you know. He would have married you if you'd said the word!'

'He didn't like me at all!' Trudie laughed. 'He liked Black Jade even less.' She put her hand on his arm and smiled up at him. 'You mustn't feel you have to worry about me any more,' she bade him. 'You have Teresa now. She won't like it if you go running about the world doing your sister's bidding!'

His relief that she should understand his problem was painful to her, but she refused to let herself dwell on it. 'What about Yokohama?' he said.

'That will be as much for your father-in-law as it will be for me. Why don't you ask Teresa if she'd like to go with you? She strikes me as someone who would make a good travelling companion.'

She could not have said anything to please him more, nor her new sister-in-law when her words were repeated to her. 'I'd love to go to Japan!' she confessed to Trudie. 'I'd love to go *anywhere* to tell the truth! Wouldn't it be a good idea if we went as far as Singapore and Malacca with you and Black Jade? Septimus would be so much happier about you if he could renew his acquaintance with some of your friends, especially the Beresfords.'

Trudie agreed that that would be lovely. She knew Septimus would enjoy staying at the Stadthuys in Malacca. It was only when she thought of introducing him to Caradoc Rhys that she wondered if she wouldn't do better to persuade him to stay in Singapore, giving Malacca a miss altogether.

But Teresa, too, was determined to find Trudie a suitable husband. Her brow furrowed as she made lists of all the possible candidates she could lay her hands on at a moment's notice. 'I do wish you were staying longer!' she exclaimed half a dozen times a day to Trudie. 'It would be so lovely to have you for a neighbour!'

That was something that Septimus could very well do without, however, as Trudie knew from past experience. Fond of his sister as he was, he hated being shown up by her in any way. All the time she was in Liverpool, he lived in hourly dread that his father-in-law would discover her to be the better businessman and think less of himself. Happily, he was unaware that Mr Walmsley had made his assessment within the first five minutes of meeting Trudie and that it had made no difference at all to his liking for his young son-in-law. Mr Walmsley wanted no competition from anyone in his own backyard, any more than Trudie did.

'Ee, lass, have you thought it might be best for Septimus and Teresa to go straight to Japan?'

'I've thought about it,' Trudie admitted.

'Well?'

'Why don't you arrange it, Mr Walmsley? I want to make a trip to Wales before I return home, and the sooner Septimus leaves for Yokohama the better for all of us.'

'My sentiments exactly! You're a good girl, Mrs Maddock! Wish you were my own daughter!'

They shook hands solemnly, then Trudie laughed. 'Indeed you don't! I'd be stepping on your toes within the week, exactly as I do on Septimus's! But thank you for the compliment, Mr Walmsley. It means more to me than you can know.'

'Ay, lass, I've heard from Septimus how it was for you at home!' He patted her hand with one of his own. 'So, you plan to visit Wales, do you, my dear? A land of legend, they tell me, a land of heroes!'

Trudie dismissed any such notion as being beneath her notice. 'I wouldn't know about that,' she said, 'but I shouldn't be in the least surprised to find that it is so. A Welsh hero would have to be someone special, wouldn't he?'

Mr Walmsley chuckled. 'Have you one in mind, lass?'

Trudie presented a meek face. 'I don't know yet,' she said with her usual bluntness. 'And if I did, I'm not sure I'd tell you. I don't want Septimus interfering – or anyone else! – not until I've made up my own mind about him.'

'Reet, I'll not tell on you, my dear. You'll know your own mind best, even if you are only a bit of a lass when all's said and done. It'll be our secret, between the two of us. That'll give our Septimus something to think on! Do the lad good to know other people can see your worth, even if your own family can't! He's a good lad, right enough, but no man likes to think his sister is able to run rings round him.' His eyes crinkled into laughter. 'And between the two of you, I'd say you were always the one to have the bright ideas, weren't you? I respect you for that, but you mustn't mind if I tell you that I'd sooner take Septimus into my business than his sister. You're a grand lass and I wouldn't want to clash with you, as we surely should if we were to see too much of each other, but that shouldn't stop us from doing business together, you and me, and Septimus will be useful to both of us for that.'

He held out his hand to her and she put her own in his with a rueful smile. 'I think we understand each other very well, Mr Walmsley,' she said.

Chapter Twenty-two

The sun was shining when they alighted from the train. The railway hadn't long gone beyond Cardiff and it was still new enough for children, and some adults too, to come pouring out of their houses to see the steaming monster pass them by. Sometimes they had waved and Black Jade had waved back, staring out of the window with a fixed concentration on the passing scene.

A breeze caught at their skirts as they stepped on to the platform, making them shiver.

'It's cold here too,' Black Jade complained.

Trudie paid no attention. A small group of ragged children were eyeing her through the fence, waving grimy hands in her direction. Could these be Caradoc Rhys's relations. Then she saw a tall, thin woman, who could only have been Caradoc's mother, waiting beside the ticket-collector. Trudie took a firmer grip on Black Jade's hand and walked towards her.

Apart from her being the image of Caradoc, the first thing she noticed about Mrs Rhys was that she looked freshly laundered from head to foot. Her hair was clean, her face and hands were clean, her clothes, though well-worn, were immaculate. Even her shoes were clean. Trudie felt very conscious of her own travel-stained state. Almost, for one awful second, she wished she hadn't come.

'There now, you must be Mrs Maddock! And the little one will be Black Jade, isn't it? There's beautiful you are, *bach*, and cold by the look of you! Let's hurry away to the fire as quick as we can!'

To Trudie's surprise she found herself warmly embraced and kissed on both cheeks by the tall woman, a greeting she had not received even from her own mother. 'Come away now. There's some miles yet before we can say we're home, but we brought a warm blanket to wrap you in and you'll not notice the nip in the wind once we get started.'

The horse was a retired pit-pony, worn down by age and years of living in total darkness. The carriage was little better than a board of wood balanced between two wooden wheels. When they came to a hill, of which there were many, everybody had to get down and walk, Mrs Rhys encouraging the elderly pony as best she could, taking some of the burden on to her own broad shoulders as often as not.

Despite the hills, the magnificent sky stretched from horizon to horizon just as if the earth was flat. Flocks of birds played in the light breeze, rising, turning, and wheeling in the sky. Trudie marvelled that they never collided with one another, apparently being of one mind as to when to change direction. Then she caught sight of the stupendous Pembrokeshire coastline, some of which she had already seen from the train, but this time she could stop and stare, and marvel at the great stretch of sand before her, the cliffs rising with massive indifference above, their constant battle with the sea fought out twice a day with the movements of the tide.

'Caradoc said it was beautiful.' Some of the tiredness fell away from Trudie as she pointed out some horses exercising on the long stretch of sand. 'We haven't far to go now, have we?'

'Not far. Is it tired you are from your journeyings? You need a good use of your feet to live in these parts.'

Eirlys Rhys could walk ten miles and consider it a stroll. She was of the opinion, however, that London folk, and quality at that, were pampered beings who had never done a day's work in their lives. She was far too well-mannered to say anything of the sort, though her restraint might not last very long for, like every Celt, she considered herself to be as good as anyone else in the kingdom.

She pointed out the Newgale mines, nothing much to see on the surface, as they spread out under the cliffs in the shape of a bell, which gave them their name.

'Is that where Caradoc worked?' Trudie asked, unable to conceal her eagerness to know as much as she could about him.

'With his father.' Eirlys was reluctant to speak of those days and it showed in her face. 'Our house is up on the cliff there. Was Caradoc telling you about that? He and I built it together overnight. A *Tŷ un nos*, we call it in Welsh, an "overnight house". 'Twas built on common land, starting after sunset and completed before sun-up, as is the custom. We had no place to live, you understand, after his father met with his accident.'

'You must have worked terribly hard,' Trudie said.

'Ay, we did, especially the boy. We began cutting the turves and stacking them to make the walls and then we put the previously made roof over the top. Caradoc thatched the roof with his own hands. We miss him sorely when it comes to re-thatching it these days. My, but we worked ourselves close to death that night for, you see, everything had to be done and smoke rising from the chimney at sunrise. We could then lay claim to all the land within a stone's throw of the door.'

'I'm surprised such a house could stand up all these years,' Trudie said, awed.

'He rebuilt the walls before he left, using stone in the place of the *cwlm* we had put up at first.'

Trudie could imagine a younger Caradoc, his shirt open

to the waist, struggling to make his mother and family more comfortable, much as he had tried to patch her house on the plantation. How good it would be if he were to materialize beside her now! She swallowed down the thought, remembering him as she had last seen him, waving her goodbye from the crowded shoreline of Singapore. As much as Black Jade, she longed to be home again; longed for it with such an intensity that the real world slipped away from her for a moment until she had reasserted her control over herself.

The house had only two rooms and one of those was the kitchen. Mr Rhys lay on a truckle-bed beside the coal oven on which they cooked and heated their water. What kind of a man he had been, Trudie could only guess at, for he had been bedridden for so many years that he hardly seemed to be there at all. Children came and went, all of them greeting him in Welsh, their faces grave and concerned. Some were grandchildren, some Caradoc's brothers and sisters, much younger than he, but all of them with the same intensity of purpose. The younger they were, the more rudimentary was their English, which was hard on Black Jade, who was also trying to converse in a language that was not really her own.

Even so, Trudie was shocked by seeing one of the children come home from school, the 'Welsh Not' around his neck, a humiliation earned by speaking his own, forbidden tongue in the playground. He would have to wear this heavy lump of wood until the next child was caught speaking Welsh, and so on, in a determined effort to root out the language once and for all. It seemed to Trudie that nothing could be better calculated to keep Welsh alive than to use such tactics, but she said nothing. She was very conscious of being English, though no one else ever referred to her being the enemy of much that they held dear.

'London is very far away, isn't it?' she said by way of apology to Eirlys.

'It is that. Malacca is even further. There is always something we have to put up with, but life goes on, *bach*, as Caradoc would be the first to tell you. What London doesn't know, London doesn't grieve about.'

'Oh yes, that's exactly what Caradoc would say!' Trudie exclaimed. 'He doesn't care a button for the authorities!'

'Gives you a hard time, does he?'

Trudie caught the mocking humour at the back of the eyes that were so like Caradoc's, and reddened. '*He* doesn't! It's everyone else! Any friendship between us is most unsuitable, isn't it? What could we possibly have in common?'

Eirlys Rhys raised a brow. 'You must think there's something to come traipsing all this way. Sweet on him, are you?'

Trudie didn't even flinch. 'Yes.'

'And he on you?'

'He keeps telling me he's an ex-miner and I'm a lady.'

'True enough.'

Trudie's smile caught them both unawares. 'The trouble is that I'm not enough of a lady. I've never been good enough for my own family, yet he'd have me believe I'm too good for yours!'

'Are you?'

Trudie shook her head. 'The only thing I'm good at is business. He'd be getting a poor bargain in every other way.'

'Maybe.'

It wasn't what Trudie wanted to hear, though she recognized the justice of Mrs Rhys's doubt. How could she think anything else when it rapidly became apparent that Trudie had never peeled potatoes, or fetched water from an outside pump, or struggled to keep a recalcitrant fire in overnight? Even the smallest child was more useful about the house than she was.

Lying in bed that night, a bed that had been pulled out of a cupboard and which she was expected to share with Black Jade, she wondered if she hadn't made a mistake in coming to Wales. She was worn out with the travelling and pretending to take for granted a grinding poverty she had never known. She was sure that if she ate the plateful of stew she was offered, someone else would have to go without, and she took enormous care to make it obvious that she didn't expect to be served by her hostess apart from the others, only to be overcome with anxiety that she might be thought patronizing not to accept what was offered her.

It was morning before she came to any conclusion. At least, she supposed it was morning, for it was still as dark as night outside. She knew she had to get out of bed because, until she did so, there was no room to move and everybody else was already lining up for their breakfast. She put the bed away as best she could, splashed some cold water on to her face, took care of Black Jade as best she could, and felt she had already done a day's work. There was no peace anywhere until the children had set forth for school, some miles away across the fields.

'It's difficult to pay for them all to learn,' Eirlys confessed. Her face took on a stubborn look. 'A proper schooling is the only way they'll ever make something of themselves. I won't have any more of them risking their lives in the mines!'

'Doesn't Caradoc send you any money?'

'Ever since he went away. There's never enough for all

of us, with Levi the way he is, though. After the accident, we owed the mine-owners more than I would admit to Caradoc. We lived in a company house and bought our food at the company store. Then there was the contract Levi had with them to cut so many tons of coal. With him helpless, there was no way of fulfilling it. I would have gone down the mine myself, but there's this law now that prevents women from going underground.'

'Quite right too!' Trudie said, horrified. 'Women can't – '

'They didn't bring it in because we can't do anything! It's hot down there, and the women would strip off as do the men. It was thought shocking that they should display themselves in such a way – as if any of the men had the time to notice!'

'It seems too dreadful to be true!'

'It's the truth, *cariad*, make no mistake about that. That's why I encouraged Caradoc to run away before the company realized he was old enough to fulfil his father's contract and took him by force. It nigh broke my heart to see him go underground with Levi when he was still a bit of a boy. His father had to carry him home, he was so tired that first day. It's no life for any man. Half of them end up coughing up their own lungs, and the other half are killed because the shafts flood, or the tackle breaks because nobody will pay to repair it. What happened to Levi is enough for this family!'

'What other work is there for them around here?'

'Caradoc's dream is to send enough money for us to buy a farm. His brother Sam is going to be a herdsman, just as soon as the debt's paid.' The older woman drew herself up proudly. 'Don't you be saying anything to Caradoc, now! He's done enough for us! He has his own life to lead, as I keep telling him. I won't have him dragged back to where he started!'

Trudie could understand that, she could even admire such an attitude, but she wasn't going to make any promises. Caradoc had a right to know.

'What else is there around here?' she asked.

The children walked her the six miles to St David's, to show her the cathedral and the ruins of the Bishop's Palace, where so many of the medieval kings had stayed when they made their pilgrimages to Wales's patron saint to be confirmed in their right to rule the Principality. They took her to see the place where St Non had given birth to the Welsh saint, and where a spring had miraculously come into being in the thunderstorm that had crashed about them all the time she had been in labour. They showed her the spot where St Patrick had left to convert the Irish, and the house where he had had his school, a school to which St David, himself, had gone many years later.

From time to time, their English deserted them and they would chatter on in Welsh, laughing at her confused expression.

'Black Jade understands more than you do!' one of them told her.

Trudie admitted she was not very clever. She didn't mind their laughing at her. She was too busy looking about her and asking questions about everything she saw. Most interesting to her were the lime-kilns that lined every port they came to. Stopping to talk to the men who were working one of these stone-built round kilns, she found they had been in use in the small port that served St David's since at least 1384.

'What is it all used for?' she asked.

They told her the acid soils of the Pembroke land needed

a great deal of lime to sweeten it up. The culm- and lime-ships came and went to all the ports along the northern coast of the county. Inside the kiln a fire would be lit, with layers of culm and limestone being fed in from the top. The resulting quicklime would be pushed out and, since the fuel used was anthracite and there was no coke mixed with it, it would be slaked nearby and then carted off to the surrounding fields.

'Who owns these kilns and ships?' she asked.

It didn't take her long to find the name of a London-based company whose lack of interest in their far-flung possessions meant they would soon be going cheap on the market if anyone wanted to buy. She made a mental note to have Mr Ollerton enquire into its purchase and then, satisfied, she turned for home.

'Are there any sailors in the family?' she asked Levi that night.

'There's none of them who don't go fishing from time to time – smuggling too, if they get the chance. Wrecking is something else. I don't approve of wrecking – men's lives can be lost, and I wouldn't wish that on my worst enemy!'

'Better than mining?'

'Any time! You're your own master at sea!' He spoke with such longing that she realized how much he hated the half-life he had been forced to lead after his accident.

Trudie sat on a milking-stool, her hands neatly folded on her knee. 'Mr Rhys, I've seen a business that interests me in St David's. I'm a foreigner in these parts and I need someone to advise me. I suppose I couldn't ask you to help me?'

'What use would I be to you?'

She hesitated. 'I'd ask Caradoc, if he were here. It's those lime-kilns at Porthstinian, is it called? There are some at Solva too.'

'I know them.'

'Yes, but what do you *know* about them? Do you know how they work?'

'There's not many around here who don't! Pot-kilns they are, unlined, not like the larger draw-kilns which are lined with fire-bricks – they're kept burning continuously, you see. The pot-kilns need from seven to ten hundred-weight of *cwlm* to produce a ton of lime.'

Trudie grinned broadly. 'I see you know *all* about them!'

'I had a brother who worked the kilns for a while. He was older than me, and our Da wanted to keep him out of the mines. He were drowned at sea. It isn't a business for a woman, though.'

'I don't mean to work the kilns myself.' Trudie clasped her hands tightly together. 'Nor do I want to invest in something that isn't going to bring me a good return. I like making money – it's the only thing I'm really good at. I like buying things and selling things.'

'Make a bob or two, do you? Caradoc says you've a good head on your shoulders.'

'Yes, I make a good living for myself – and others.'

Levi Rhys looked almost cheerful. 'You'd need someone local to keep an eye on the kilns for you!'

'Someone I could trust,' Trudie agreed. 'More than that, someone the local people could trust too, who wouldn't overcharge them, or expect them to work for less than a fair wage.'

'You have someone in mind, haven't you?'

Trudie nodded. She swallowed the lump in her throat. 'You!'

'You're out there, girl. One doesn't manage a business from one's bed! Ask anyone!'

Trudie allowed herself to look crestfallen. 'Well, there is a house that's empty just by the kilns. I thought if you and your wife were to live there, you could oversee things from a trestle-bed on wheels. You'd have your sons to help you.'

'Is this some charity you've cooked up for our benefit?' the man demanded, his suspicions vying with the hope she was offering him.

'I don't believe in charity! I don't give it and I wouldn't take it! If the job is too much for you, I shall find someone else to do it.' She stared back at him, as proud as he, and it was he who backed down.

'We'd best ask Eirlys what she thinks,' he mumbled at last. 'It'll be a surprise for her, for we've both of us got used to thinking me a useless cripple. It would be good not to see her worrying herself to death about where the next penny's coming from.'

Eirlys was cautious, but she was soon as enthusiastic as her husband. 'To get away from that mining company, why, it's my idea of heaven!'

'Yes, but I want a good return on my money,' Trudie insisted. 'If you can't make it pay, I'll have to sell out. I don't believe in keeping any loss-makers going.'

They walked to St David's again the next day, Eirlys going with them and feeling sufficiently at home with Trudie now to laugh at her groans at the distances involved and her aching muscles as they carried her up and down the steep hills. 'Don't you ever use your legs in Malacca?'

Trudie had been taught to refer to her legs as limbs and was rather shocked to hear such frank speaking. 'Never! I use a rickshaw if it isn't far – ' She came to an abrupt halt. 'The very thing! That's exactly what your husband needs! An ordinary carriage-maker could make one for him, I'm sure!' She went on to explain how a rickshaw worked, a man running between the shafts of a very lightweight vehicle.

'A fine sight that would be!' Eirlys laughed at her.

But Trudie wasn't listening. 'If only there weren't so many hills!'

The day after that, she and Black Jade started their journey back to London. Mostly, they travelled in silence but, as they drew in to Paddington Station, Trudie asked the little girl, 'How did you like Wales?'

'It was nicer than London.'

Trudie raised an enquiring brow. Black Jade put her hand deep in hers. 'Let's go home,' she said.

'Don't you like your father's country at all?'

Black Jade shook her head. 'We're strangers here. Don't you want to go home?'

'Yes. Yes, I do,' Trudie admitted. She, too, longed for the warmth and colour and, above all, the people of Malacca. Wales had been beautiful; London was busy and interesting; but she, herself, had been a part of neither. She and Black Jade belonged elsewhere and she couldn't wait to get back there.

The more Trudie thought about going home, the more Caradoc Rhys seemed to take up residence in her mind and heart. She was glad, though, she had made the voyage home to England, if for no other reason than that she had seen his family and had learned so much about him that he never could have told her. It had given them a space apart, a time to consider what they really wanted from one another. She had owed him that time, she thought. And it had been necessary for Black Jade to be out of sight of her cousins for a while, but the thought of home drew her like a magnet. More and more, she wanted to be within sight and sound of Caradoc, as well as being in her own house in Malacca. No matter how much she had liked and respected him before, she realized, she had always seen him through the eyes of others in certain respects. She had seen him as a poor boy, an ex-miner, a man of no education, and, without thought, she had contrasted this with her own gentility, imagining how he would seem to her father and sisters. Now, she had met and seen the worth of his family and she no longer saw herself as quality condescending to a working man: she now wondered if someone of his beginnings would ever look the way of someone like herself, for it seemed that she had remarkably little to offer him, except her ability for making money. It still gave her a warm feeling that he should have asked her and *trusted* her to find some way of providing his family with the living they so badly needed.

Mr Ollerton proved himself a tower of strength. Another man might have disliked Trudie haunting the Emporium for lack of anything better to do. He had more than enough confidence in his own abilities not to have to worry where she chose to poke her nose. Indeed, he encouraged her to wander through the different departments, returning to him at intervals with the ideas pouring off her blunt tongue in a way which delighted him, but which he could see would have driven poor Septimus mad at being asked to think in half a dozen directions at one and the same time.

'I have the business in Wales in hand,' he greeted her one morning. 'The returns may not be quite what you expect, but I think I may safely promise you won't actually lose any money on the deal.'

'As long as it can pay for itself,' she answered. 'Will the Rhys family be able to manage it between themselves, or will I have to put in a manager?'

He sat behind his desk, watching her for a few moments. Not by word or deed had she betrayed any interest in the lime-kilns other than a business one. Apparently, she expected no thanks for her generosity to this family. She had offered no explanation as to why she should favour them, not even as to why she should want a copy of a Malaccan rickshaw made and sent right across the country to the other side of Wales. He recognized the name, of course, for he had once had dealings with Caradoc Rhys when Trudie had been staying with her cousins in Singapore. But then he had really known himself to be dealing with the Ki family. Still, something must have made this young woman go running off to Wales with the state of the roads as they were. It was bad enough to go all that way by train, but he had heard tell that it was better to go by sea if one wanted to arrive safely in such a distant place. Yet Mrs Maddock hadn't turned a hair at embarking on such a journey, taking a young child with her, and making no explanations to anyone.

'Do you want to put in a manager?'

She looked surprised that he should ask. Then, surprisingly, she had grinned mischievously at him, the whole aspect of her face changing. 'Poor Mr Ollerton! You realize their accounts will probably be a little – shall we say original? None of them have the least idea how to run a business and their education is probably modest. However, I have often thought that nothing teaches one so quickly as having to take responsibility for something. If you run into any difficulties, have a word with Mrs Eirlys Rhys. She's very intelligent, if unlettered, and will soon put the family back on the right lines. Am I asking too much of you to supervise it all from London?'

'Indeed not!' he assured her. 'I am glad to do anything I can. They sound a most – interesting family.'

'Yes, they are,' she agreed.

As she was obviously not going to tell him anything

more about them, he changed the subject, telling her about his visit to the shipping office and that he had obtained berths for herself and Black Jade on a ship sailing sometime within the next three weeks.

Her whole being lit up in response. 'That's the best news you could have given me!' she exclaimed. 'Black Jade and I are both longing to be home. I can hardly wait!'

He consulted the papers in front of him. 'You'll be bunkering in Simonstown, Cape Town, as always. They say it's a great, natural harbour, set in a beautiful country.'

'It can be cold,' she told him. 'The winds come straight off the South Pole. There's a mountain there, with a flat top, called Table Mountain. The winds come off the sea, hit the mountain and come back again. I've seen people blown right off their feet there.'

'I suppose you have more than enough time to go ashore?' he questioned her.

'Yes, indeed. There are some magnificent homes not far away. I am acquainted with one family there who make wine, just like the French.' A thoughtful expression crossed her face. 'Is it true that not many wines travel well?'

'I'm afraid so. The fortified varieties do better, such as sherry and madeira. There are wines that won't even move out of the village where they've been made without turning into vinegar. A long sea voyage like that could hardly improve the quality, no matter how good the original product.'

She gave up the notion of importing South African wines with reluctance, hardly noticing Mr Ollerton's amusement at the way her mind worked.

'There may be other products from there we can use,' he suggested. 'Why don't you have a look round while you're there?'

'Good idea!' She looked up, caught his eye and laughed.

'You've no idea how boring such a long sea voyage can be,' she explained herself ruefully. 'It's worse for us women because of the stupid superstition sailors have that women on board are bad luck! We're always being asked to stay in our cabins when anything remotely interesting happens!'

'And do you?' he asked, his eyes twinkling more than ever.

'I wouldn't if I were on my own, but life on board is difficult enough for Black Jade. It doesn't seem to matter to most people that her father was as English as they are themselves, she is Chinese as far as they're concerned! I'm afraid she's Chinese in her own eyes as well!'

'I shouldn't have thought you would have any difficulty in understanding that, Mrs Maddock?'

'Not in the least!' she agreed dryly. 'The difficulty is in getting other people to accept her for what she is. To the Chinese, we're foreign devils and uncivilized barbarians, with no manners or understanding, and I regret that we Europeans look on them in exactly the same way!'

'And that annoys you?'

'It shouldn't, but it does! They have more cause to despise us than we do them, don't you think? Wu Chao used to talk of the Middle Kingdom – that's what they call China – and one realized it was true, they were a civilized people long before we even thought of ourselves as a people at all!'

Mr Ollerton looked a bit askance at that. 'Was your friend a Christian, Mrs Maddock?'

'Oh no! I don't know what she would have called herself, but she was very certain that the Goddess of Mercy, Kuan Yin, would always help her in any difficulty. You know, the Chinese believe that when one dies one's soul takes seven weeks to travel through the valley of death, the *yin* world, or other world – but you wouldn't be interested in all that!'

'Indeed, I am! Please go on.'

'The first week the soul reaches the Gate of the Demon, where he has to bribe the keeper. "Other world" money is buried with the dead person for just this purpose – '

'They really believe that?'

'No, not really.' Trudie struggled to explain something she had only sensed herself. 'It's true in its meaning, rather than in fact. Does that make sense to you? In the second week, the soul is sent to the First Court of Justice and set before the Mirror of Retribution, and so on, from one court to another until, in the fifth week he passes over a high bridge from where he can glimpse his loved ones left behind in the world. Black Jade was certain she "felt" her mother with her during the fifth week. Then, by the seventh week, the soul reaches the Tenth Court of Justice, where the Wheel of the Law determines the form of his reincarnation according to all his past actions.'

'The Wheel of what Law? Can you explain it more precisely?'

Trudie picked up his quill pen, dipped it into the ink, and drew a circle. In the hub of the wheel were three animals, the snake, the bird and the pig, representing hatred, lust, and ignorance. From the hub spread out six spokes. The upper three portions depicted the regions of the blessed; the lower three the regions of the sinful. The outer ring was divided into twelve, each one depicting a different facet of the Wheel of Life.

'That's all I know about it,' she confessed. 'Being an ignorant barbarian, I never took much interest in the dead until someone had to give Black Jade some idea of what was happening to her mother. Her aunt explained it to us both but, young as she is, Black Jade understood much better than I did. Swee Neo said I asked the wrong questions, wanting to know things to which there are no answers. The strange thing was that I understood it better after I took up your suggestion and visited the church in Warwick Street down the road.' She finished the drawing with a flourish, leaving a great blot of ink on the paper.

'She came back to you?'

'I felt less bereft,' she nodded. 'Perhaps it was Kuan Yin's doing.'

'A goddess?'

'A Chinese saint, I think you would call her. Wu Chao told me about her.' She gave him a thoughtful look. 'One really can't appreciate Chinese art unless one knows all the superstitions and beliefs of the Chinese, Mr Ollerton,' she added in bracing tones.

'I'm sure you're right,' he agreed.

What a strange mixture she was, he thought, and came to the conclusion he would miss her when she returned to Malacca. With Mrs Maddock one was never bored, though one might long to box her ears when she took one to task for being so bold as to agree with her!

A fortnight later found Mr Ollerton as the sole witness to Trudie's departure back to the Malay Peninsula. Her family were all otherwise engaged, and she didn't seem to have any friends from her childhood who would want to wish her well on her journey. He had never been aboard a passenger vessel before. He strutted about the decks, admiring the neat way the sails were stowed away and the lines of the other ships that lay to either side of them. He was shocked by the minute size of the cabin Mrs Maddock and Black Jade were to share all the way to Singapore. There wasn't room to swing a cat!

'Oh dear, dear!' he clucked. 'I ordered the very best cabin for you! I had no idea!'

'Don't worry, Mr Ollerton. I prefer to spend most of my time on deck, weather permitting.'

Black Jade jumped up and down by her side. 'We're going home! At last we're going home!'

The rotund figure of the manager bent down to the little girl. 'You look more cheerful now than you did when I first saw you!'

Black Jade stared at him. 'Are you sorry we're going?' she demanded.

'Of course he's not!' Trudie said tartly. 'The poor man's looking forward to having a bit of peace without us! It's been nothing but, Mr Ollerton, please do this and please do that, ever since we arrived in London!'

'That's true,' he admitted. 'You throw off ideas as another lady does old clothes when presented with a new wardrobe!'

Black Jade chuckled. It was so long since Trudie had heard her do anything of the kind that she hugged her. 'He likes you!' the child whispered in her ear.

Trudie laughed back at her. 'Do you, Mr Ollerton?'

The little man twinkled from head to toe. 'Yes, ma'am, I think I may safely say that I like you. I've told my wife so much about you that the next time you are in England she will never forgive either of us if you don't make your home with us for as long as you're here.'

Trudie realized without resentment that he had summed up her home background and found it wanting.

'How kind of you and Mrs Ollerton!' she answered.

'But you won't take us up on the offer?'

She turned and faced him. 'On the contrary, I shall stay with no one else in London on my next visit, I promise you. However, that won't be for years and years, if ever! It might be better if you should come and visit me in

Malacca. I promise you a warm welcome, though it may not be quite the way of life you're accustomed to.'

He saw that she never meant to return to England and was sorry for it. 'Perhaps when I retire, Mrs Ollerton and I will take up travelling instead. We may even go so far as the Middle Kingdom – don't you call it?'

Trudie grew excited at the mere thought. 'Shanghai and Nanking, Hong Kong and Macao, wouldn't it be marvellous!'

'Perhaps you should have gone yourself to Yokohama rather than send your brother?' Mr Ollerton suggested.

She smiled. 'I am beginning to think you would have made a better emissary,' she admitted. 'I am hoping Mrs Grant will display a little more imagination than my poor brother is capable of. Have you met her, Mr Ollerton?'

'Once, ma'am.'

'Did you like her?'

He didn't approve of the abrupt question. 'It isn't my place to like or dislike her, ma'am,' he said stiffly.

'Oh stuff!' said Trudie. 'I didn't expect to like her much,' she added, 'but I didn't dislike her when I met her. Watch Mr Walmsley if Septimus does well in Japan, or he'll cream off all the best of the trade for himself. He's a man after my own heart! As sharp as a needle!'

Mr Ollerton smiled quietly to himself. He was thinking that even Mr Walmsley would have to get up very early in the morning to get the better of his Mrs Maddock! 'I'll bear it in mind, ma'am,' he said aloud.

Shortly after that he went ashore. It wasn't until an hour or so later, however, that there was a sudden flurry of activity on deck as the sails were set in time to allow the full tide to carry them out into the Channel on the first leg of their journey home.

Black Jade sniffed the salt in the air with a mixture of

ecstasy and resignation. 'At last, at last, we're finally going home!' she rejoiced and, although Trudie said nothing at all, she, too, was filled with an exultation that in a matter of a few weeks she would be back in the same city as Caradoc Rhys.

Chapter Twenty-three

Trudie blenched at the thought of taking Black Jade to stay with Mrs Eliot in Singapore. Both the Eliots would have done their duty by the little girl, but that would hardly have been comfortable for any of them. Instead, she booked into a small Chinese hotel which was noisy, spotlessly clean, and astonished to receive her custom.

Almost before they had settled in a messenger came from the great Whampoa, inviting the two of them to spend the day at his mansion. If Trudie wondered how he should have found them so easily, Black Jade's delight knew no bounds.

'*My* family comes from the same village as Mr Hoo,' she informed Trudie. Her family was her mother's family. Not once, in all the time they had spent in England, had it occurred to her that her father's country had anything at all to do with her. 'We speak the same dialect,' she added with deep satisfaction. 'He will know my grandparents, maybe even their parents, if he is very old. Is he old?'

Trudie had always found it quite difficult to tell the age of any Chinese but she didn't think Whampoa was old. 'You'll be able to see for yourself, won't you?' she answered.

She had thought to hire a rickshaw to transport them to his famous bungalow, which was situated in gardens which were already famous and which included a small private zoo, a sight which she knew would appeal to Black Jade more than anything else. Whampoa, however, sent his own *syce*, a Malay groom, in his own carriage, with instructions to drive Trudie anywhere she wanted to go in Singapore before bringing her to his address in time for luncheon. Trudie and the little girl had a thoroughly enjoyable morning, calling on Gwennant for a few minutes to find out if Mr Rhys was in Singapore, and then driving round the harbour, looking at all the ships and trying to decide from which part of the world they came.

Gwennant couldn't tell them where Mr Rhys was. 'Ah, Trudie *bach*, he's missed you sorely and that's the truth. I wish I could summon him up out of thin air just for the pleasure of seeing his face when he sees you are home again!'

Trudie savoured the thought. 'He missed me a little?'

'Did he not? Not that he's had an easy time of it, himself. Those cousins of yours are out for his blood because he wouldn't attend some inquest or other. I'm sorry they're your relatives, they give him no peace!'

'What happened at the inquest?' Trudie asked.

'I don't know. You'll have to ask somebody else that. To own the truth, Caradoc told me it would be better if I knew nothing, we being cousins on his mother's side. What I do know is that there was quite a dust-up over the whole affair. The Army was called out to stand by in case there was any real trouble, but they weren't needed in the end. The worst trouble was between the Europeans in the case, or so it was said amongst the troops.'

It all made Trudie the more determined not to see anything of her cousins while she was in Singapore. She did see several of her acquaintance, however, as they drove out in Whampoa's carriage. Much was made of her when they realized she was on her way to see the Chinese for Whampoa was a popular figure, besides being quite extraordinarily rich. Government circles explained his presence amongst them by telling each other that Hoo Ah Kay was a gentleman, whatever the colour of his skin, which one couldn't say about the rest of the yellow people who flooded into the Colony on every junk that came their way. Trudie thought cynically that it was the colour of his money that gave him the entrée which the colour of his skin would have denied to a poorer man.

Black Jade's excitement at meeting Whampoa had nothing to do with money. The child sat on his knee and giggled various confidences into his ear, some of which Trudie suspected were jokes about her barbarian ways and her lack of understanding of the things that really mattered. The child's joy at being given Chinese food lifted her spirits to the skies.

'The English,' she informed Whampoa, 'eat nothing but great slabs of meat and watery vegetables, don't they, Trudie?'

'I'm afraid they mostly do – '

But Whampoa knew better. 'I am told that English provincial cooking is much better than in the capital,' he said solemnly.

Black Jade made a face at him. 'Have you been to England?'

He shook his head. 'You have the advantage of me, young lady.'

'We had horrid food in Lancashire too,' Black Jade told him.

Glad to find a fellow enthusiast, Whampoa admitted his own fondness for the spices and the shrimp paste the Nonya cuisine is famous for. Looking like a solemn Buddha, he fastened the child with one eye, roaring at her, 'You must be very careful never to eat any of the crabs which are common in the Malaccan Straits which carry a cross on their backs. Have you ever seen them?'

Black Jade, eyes wide, shook her head. 'Are they special?'

'Very special. Have you heard of a man called Francis Xavier?'

'Oh yes! He was a Catholic priest. A Jesuit. We met a statue of him in a church in England. Mr Walmsley introduced us.'

'He was once in Malacca – before he was buried there, I mean. But it was when he was travelling by *korakora*, you know, one of those little Indonesian boats, going from Amboina to a neighbouring island, that a terrible storm blew up. Everyone on board thought they were lost, but Father Francis leaned over the side of the boat and dipped the crucifix he always wore into the water. The storm immediately ceased, but the cross slipped from his fingers and disappeared into the sea. The poor man was deeply distressed at its loss, as you may imagine, but at least their lives had been saved.

'Then, some twenty-four hours later, when the party had landed on Baramurah, Father Francis and a friend went for a walk along the sands, when a crab appeared out of the water, the upright crucifix held securely in its claw, and made its way to the saint's feet. Since that time, no one has ever eaten one of those crabs out of respect for the Holy Man. So don't you eat them either!'

'I won't!' Black Jade promised.

'That's right. One must always respect great men – even barbarians!'

'Skirted devils!' Black Jade said with glee. 'Skirted foreign devils!'

Trudie laughed out loud. She told Whampoa that Black Jade had found an ancestor in the Virgin Mary and had lit a whole trayful of candles for her mother.

At the mention of Wu Chao, Whampoa sobered. 'Ah yes, Ki Wu Chao. That was a sad business!'

'A bad business!'

'That, too,' he acknowledged. 'One of the reasons I invited you here today was because I wanted to meet her daughter. Some of her real ancestors are known to me.'

'Yes, Black Jade told me the Ki family came from your village in China?'

'That's true. Are you now the child's legal guardian?'

'I think so.'

He smiled. 'Hence the English visit?'

Trudie lifted her chin. 'I wanted her to know she is Miss Maddock as well as Ki Black Jade.' She heaved a sigh. 'I'm afraid she doesn't see herself as a Maddock, however. Neither of us found what we were looking for in England.'

'No, she would not, of course, but you, Mrs Maddock, why should you feel out of place there?'

'It was cold.'

Whampoa was amused. 'You must be used to cold weather – '

'Yes, but not cold people.' She bit her lip. 'Oh dear, I didn't mean to say that. People are people, after all, but the English are very good at hiding their feelings. You can imagine the rest.'

Whampoa could. 'If you'll forgive my saying so, Mrs Maddock, I think you went to England for quite another reason. Black Jade's family are grateful to you for your care of Wu Chao's daughter. More, I am grateful to you. You have only to command me, Ma'am, and I will do anything in my power to oblige you.'

'You will?' The words were out before she could swallow them down. 'Because you come from the same village, Mr Hoo?'

He sucked in his lips. 'Isn't that reason enough?'

'If you say so.'

'A wise barbarian!' he approved. 'How few of us know when to insist on an answer and when to keep our own counsel. I congratulate you!'

Trudie gave him look for look. 'Ki Wu Chao was my friend. I don't need any other reason to look after Black Jade.'

'Of course not. You are her second mother, are you not? She will always be your eldest daughter, but it's time now for her aunt, Ki Swee Neo, to teach her the things she needs to know as a Nonya. We are agreed that is her future, aren't we?'

'I suppose so,' Trudie admitted. 'I shall be sad to lose her.'

'But, Mrs Maddock, there isn't the least danger of that! I thought you understood how much a part of the child you will always be. Didn't you give her life? Won't you find the courage to give her the life she has chosen now, then, when she is older, her respect and love for you will be a hundred times greater than if she is half a foreign devil and half a despised yellow person.'

Trudie was thoughtful. She knew he was right, but she didn't want to admit it to herself quite yet. 'What I don't see is what it has to do with you?' she said sharply.

Whampoa said nothing at all, only waited.

'I don't understand you!' said Trudie, immediately looking contrite. 'Is there anything else I can do for you?' she enquired sweetly.

'Why yes, Mrs Maddock. Have a care for your own skin in the near future. Your cousin's business is doing badly and I should hate to hear that they are blaming you for their reverses. Is Mr Rhys waiting for you at Malacca?'

'I don't know where he is.'

'Then my advice to you is find him, find him quickly

and don't be too proud to accept his protection. Your danger is almost as great as the child's!'

Trudie sat for a moment in silence, then she said, 'My danger is greater, Mr Hoo. That blade was meant for me, not Wu Chao. I owe her my life.'

'Your cousins must want that plantation very badly?'

'Yes, but I don't think it is for the money that can be made out of it. They've made themselves very much at home there, and they won't accept Black Jade's claim under my husband's will. They seem desperate to hang on to the place more to spite me than for anything else.'

'They used to go there without your knowledge?'

'Frequently. You know why, don't you?' she accused him suddenly.

'I suspect they've been trading opium through there.' He noticed the way she started and his eyes narrowed. 'Well, Mrs Maddock? Do you wish me to save them from the consequences of their folly? Mrs Horton is still your cousin, whatever she has done.'

Trudie sat tight. 'They're not under my protection, Mr Hoo. I've made them no promises, nor shall I ever do so. The Ki family are far closer to me than my own.'

He smiled, looking more like a Chinese Buddha than ever. 'Are you giving me a free hand to revenge Ki Wu Chao?'

'What I am saying is that you must do as you think best, Mr Hoo, as must we all. My cousins would resent any interference from me. I'm sure you understand how they feel. Mr Horton would particularly dislike being beholden to a female, I believe.'

'Very true. I can see Ki Wu Chao was more than your friend, Mrs Maddock. She taught you to think like a Chinese. No wonder she left Black Jade in your capable hands. She would have known that you will always do your best for the child even though the cost may be great to yourself.'

Trudie managed a smile. 'I hope she may have thought that. I'm afraid, most of the time, she thought me as undisciplined as a child myself.'

'I do not see you as a child, Mrs Maddock. I honour you as a great lady, just as our mutual friend Caradoc Rhys said I would!'

A compliment which rendered Trudie totally speechless.

Trudie was watching her fellow guests at the hotel play mahjong. It was a game she enjoyed and she was itching to take somebody's chair and try her own luck with the pretty tiles, when the proprietor came over to her. 'You have a visitor, Mrs Maddock. Will you take him to your room? I don't think the gentleman would be very comfortable down here.'

Trudie looked up and saw Christopher Horton standing in the shadows, looking completely out of place and rather defiant. 'I don't want to be alone with him!'

'I tell him go?'

Mr Horton came over to the corner of the public room where she was sitting. 'What brings you to a place like this, cousin?' he asked, his distaste for his surroundings written clearly all over his face. Trudie smothered a laugh. Had she once been as easy to read as her cousin's husband was now?

'I chose to stay here,' she told him deliberately. 'What are you doing here?'

'We were told you lunched with Whampoa?'

'So?'

'I told you once before he could put a lot of business my way.'

'Yes, I believe you did.'

Christopher Horton drew up a chair beside her. 'My God, you're not still holding the death of that unfortunate native woman against Hermione after all this time, are you? I'd have thought you'd have forgotten all about it by now!'

'As you have?'

'Hermione was beside herself. She wasn't in her right mind. You know where she had been that evening, Gertrude. She was only trying to protect your property for you in her own muddled way!'

The clink of money changing hands marked the end of the game she had been watching.

'Is that the story you've been telling people? I'll try to remember it, but I've never been a good liar, as you know. Now, what have you really come about?'

He dragged his chair closer. 'Your Chinese friends are bankrupting me, Gertrude. I can't make money anywhere.'

'*My* friends, Mr Horton?'

'I'm blocked wherever I go! It's your doing isn't it?'

'My dear Christopher, I've been in London these past months! You flatter my abilities in the world of business out here if you think I could have any influence over their dealings from so far away! What would I use to get my wishes across to them? Pigeon post? Besides, most of them share your dislike for doing business with women, though they are far too tactful to tell me so to my face – as you so often have!'

'Someone was looking after your business while you were away. Who was he?'

Trudie looked blandly back at him. 'He?' she murmured.

'*She*, then! I don't believe it is a woman! No woman could have resisted the bribes I've offered in the last few weeks. I tell you, Gertrude, I'm being slowly bled to death. If I buy at a good price, I cannot sell except at a loss. The opium trade was protected until recently, but now, suddenly, ships are lost at sea, whole consignments are lost entering the Yellow River. I hardly dare tell my agents in Calcutta to buy any more, in case they, too, are spies set to betray me. If this isn't your doing, whose is it?'

Trudie felt the first stirrings of triumph in her breast. 'Acquit me of omniscience, cousin. I am only a woman, after all!'

'Look,' he went on, 'Hermione doesn't know I'm here. It wasn't I who killed your Chinese friend! Surely, you can't want to punish me along with her? I didn't do anything!' He looked at her, hating her. 'There was an inquest – all fair and square! The jury brought in a verdict of accidental death. There *was* no murder, whatever you may like to think!'

'I haven't yet accused you of murder. Hermione is a different matter. If it wasn't murder, Cousin Christopher, neither was it an outpouring of goodwill, was it?'

'She wouldn't really have killed you, Gertrude. You've got to believe that! In a way you might say she did you a favour – you were far too close to that wretched woman for your own good. You're much better off without her! I ask you to remember, too, that Hermione and I have some standing in society out here – no one who matters would listen to such as yourself – not to someone who chooses to live amongst the Straits Chinese, who even adopts your own husband's bastard as your own daughter! No, I came to give you a friendly warning that if you don't call off your friends, there won't be a Christian household in Singapore, or Malacca, who'll receive you, not if your cousin and I were to tell them all we know about you!'

Trudie actually had the audacity to laugh. 'That's scarcely any threat at all, Mr Horton. I am sure I can count the *Christian* households I know of in Singapore on one hand – '

'Gertrude! You go too far!'

'No, it's you who do that, Mr Horton. To the best of my knowledge, I have never done you, or Cousin Hermione, the least harm. So why do you both hate me so much?'

Mr Horton rose to his feet. 'Do we need any other reason than that you choose to stay in a place like this? People look askance at *us* when you behave this way!'

'I see. I'm sorry. I would have stayed with Mrs Eliot, one of the Christian households we were talking about, but I didn't want to embarrass her by taking Black Jade there. Whom do you suggest I should have asked to take us in? Whampoa? At least he wouldn't mind entertaining a small child, whoever she was!'

'Gertrude, I wish I could persuade you that you're not doing the child any favours by making her believe she's something she's not! Why don't you give her back to her own family and allow Hermione to find a suitable husband for yourself?'

'And what about the plantation?' Trudie asked bluntly.

She thought Mr Horton was about to have apoplexy. 'When it comes to a choice between us and that ghastly Chinese brat, you don't care what becomes of Hermione and myself, do you? Your own family! Your father was right when he called you an unnatural daughter!'

'An unnatural daughter of an unnatural father,' Trudie rejoined dryly.

'We owe a duty to our own family, no matter what.'

'Is that your philosophy? I didn't realize. There's nothing I can do about the plantation, however, as I'm sure you have already ascertained for yourself!'

Mr Horton clenched his fists. 'There is something you

can do. You can tell your Chinese friends that if they don't stop interfering in my affairs, I'll have the law on the lot of them! There are still some advantages in being born British, as they'll find out! And don't be too sure that I can't deprive that half-caste child of her inheritance if they continue to obstruct me from bringing my trade through there. They made a mistake when they closed down all I'd built up there. I've held my hand because you're Hermione's cousin, but I live on the poppy, it's the foundation of my whole fortune, and I shan't go down without a fight!'

'I thought the trade to be illegal these days,' Trudie said.

'Officially it is! But that doesn't mean anything! How else are we to buy what we need from China? They don't want anything from us, any more than they did before the Opium Wars! If we want silks and tea, we have to trade with opium. It's easy for the politicians to wring their hands in horror back in London and say it's nothing to do with them, what else can they do? Do you think the British public would stand for the truth? Of course not! So they're told that after the opium leaves Calcutta it's out of the hands of the British authorities. We can't interfere with international trade outside our jurisdiction. But we turn a blind eye to the trade wherever it is to be found! We can't deprive the British of their cup of tea, having taught them to like it!'

'Do you think it very Christian of us to force the opium on to China?' It made her feel sick that her own relations could do such a thing. How strange that making money was considered sufficient excuse for taking advantage of a defenceless nation! She looked at Christopher Horton with revulsion. 'Perhaps it's a pity the Chinese didn't win the Opium Wars,' she said.

'They don't understand modern warfare, fortunately for us. They would have stopped the trade if they could.'

'And people like you and my late husband would have lost their fortunes. I wonder that you can live with so much misery, Mr Horton, I really do. Especially as you have seen what the results of such a trade can be. Do you care so little for your own wife?'

'It wouldn't help her for me to lose my fortune. It wouldn't have helped anyone else either. Addicts always manage to find another source, and, meanwhile, our government has to protect the interests of our Indian subjects.'

'By making the Empire the largest producer, processor, and exporter of opium in the world? Never mind that the Chinese Emperor had forbidden the drug to his subjects for a hundred years!'

'Who cares about the Chinese? They're not part of the Empire!'

'I imagine the Chinese do.'

'Well, our Chinese have nothing to complain about. They're British citizens themselves now. We've given them law and order, and a safe refuge in a violent world. They owe their allegiance to the Queen now, not to anybody else, not even to their ridiculous Emperor!'

'How convenient for you that they do. You wouldn't have a fortune to lose if it weren't for them, and neither would I!'

Mr Horton sank down on to a chair again. 'You have no cause to take that "holier than thou" attitude, Gertrude. You're as much involved in the trade as I am, living on Mr Maddock's money all these years. If you know which side your bread is buttered, you'll warn the Kis of the consequences of taking me on. It'll come about in the end, you'll see! And I won't have any mercy on them then! What can one Chinese family do against the might of the British Raj,

I ask you that? And the British Raj is me in this instance! The Chinese won't think any the less of you for giving them a warning, if that's what you're worried about. After all, the plantation was thought to be yours all the time the trade was passing through there.'

Trudie rose, hoping to hint him away. 'I'll think about it,' she said.'

He stood up also. 'You'd better do more than think, cousin dear! If I go on losing money, I'll know where to come, won't I? That child won't survive my bankruptcy, I promise you that! And nor will you!'

For a long time after Christopher Horton had gone, Trudie sat on, wondering if Black Jade was really vulnerable to his threats. She knew better than to think of the Ki family in isolation: they had the *kongsi* to sustain and protect them and, for all she knew, one of the *hui* stood behind them also, perhaps with the blessing of Whampoa himself. All the same, she thought, there would be no harm in sending a message to Mr Hoo, telling him what her cousin's husband had threatened. If Wu Chao had been alive, she would have contented herself with telling her, knowing she would pass the message on, but she didn't know Swee Neo in the same way. It was quite possible that the younger sister's interests were entirely domestic, leaving all the rest to the Babas of her family, which was as true of the Nonyas as it was of the women of her own society. What concerned her now though, more than anything else, was how to get a message to Whampoa without the whole of the Singapore underworld knowing all about it.

Long after Black Jade had gone to bed, Trudie sat on downstairs in the little hotel. Food was brought for her and served in a small room which belonged to the proprietor. Pleased to see she could handle the chopsticks which were all he could provide, he bobbed about, beaming at her and encouraging her to try a little from the many dishes he had placed on the table.

'Child belong Ki clan?' he asked her.

'Her mother was a Ki.'

He nodded, the smile leaving his face for a few moments. 'She dead, never mind?'

Trudie wondered how he knew. 'I'm taking Black Jade home to Malacca.'

The smile was back. 'Ship go day after tomorrow. Want tickets?' The smile broadened still more as Trudie agreed that she did. 'Velly good. I buy. Velly pleased to have honourable lady in my hotel. I not charge. Velly good advertisement, you understand?'

Trudie understood very well. She understood that he had made it his business to find out all about her. Lunching with Whampoa had given her endless face. Chinese Singapore was hers for the asking.

She ate her rice and prawns with gusto, amused by her own greediness. She was no better than Black Jade, she remonstrated with herself; whilst they had been in England, she had longed for the food she had come to like better than anything she had known as a child. How much she was going to miss Wu Chao's cooking! Somehow or other, she was going to have to learn to manage her household by herself. The idea was not an attractive one. Left to herself, she doubted she would ever be able to make anything fit to eat, certainly not anything as delicious as what she was eating now! Perhaps Swee Neo would take her on as a pupil when she started to teach Black Jade the skills every Nonya possessed as her birthright.

The proprietor brought her a collection of the little cakes

the Nonyas are famous for, hovering over her as she made her choice. 'Rhys man come to see you!' he announced with as much pride as if he had arranged his coming himself. 'You stay here, I bling him!'

There was a moment when Trudie wished herself anywhere else but there. She had been away so long that they both must have changed from the people they had been when she had last seen him. She had been mourning Wu Chao then, and had had no time for anything else except her own grief. She wished now she had spared the time to share some of what she had been feeling with him. Instead, she had shut him out, refusing to let him see how badly hurt she had been. That had always been her defence in times of trouble, but that didn't excuse her from excluding him from her intimate thoughts at any time. He had deserved better from her than that.

She couldn't wait sitting down. Instead, she stood, facing the door he would come through, every muscle stretched almost to breaking point. Then, when she saw him, she wondered why she had worried. He was so like his mother! So big and infinitely dear!

'I'm back – as you see,' she said.

'So you are!'

'Black Jade wanted to come home.'

'And you?'

She blinked. 'England is supposed to mean home for me.'

'And Wales for me. It's beautiful just, of course, but to live there? Never again, my sweet. I belong out here.'

Almost she laughed. Her eyes took in his appearance from head to foot, looking for any small changes in him that would give her a clue as to how he had been without her.

'I went to Wales,' she said. 'What does Eirlys mean?'

'It's the Welsh word for snowdrop.'

'It suits her. Snowdrops flower under the most unlikely circumstances. I've seen them struggling through the snow as early as January.' She waited for him to say something, but he remained silent, giving her time to tell him all about it in her own way.

'I've never seen such appalling poverty,' she hurried on. 'Even so, it was more stimulating than London. I *liked* them all so much! Your father could have been very bitter, but he isn't. I talked with him a great deal. I was honoured, Caradoc, because I could see that, apart from Eirlys, he prefers the society of men around him.'

'All miners belong to the same brotherhood. If you haven't stood up to your waist in cold water, or crawled along a tunnel a foot-and-a-half high, getting the coal out no matter what, you can't understand how those men live – '

'And die?'

'That, too. Sometimes it's a living death, but it's still death!'

'That's what I thought. You didn't tell me how bad it is.' She hesitated, wondering how best to tell him. 'I did as you asked. I bought a business and asked your father to manage it. It won't bring them riches, but at least they'll be more comfortable in the future. Was that what you wanted?'

To her relief he began to laugh. 'Were you angry enough to buy the whole mine? I wouldn't put it past you at that!'

She grinned back at him. She felt she could sit down then and she did so, gesturing him towards the other chair.

'I didn't fancy the opprobrium being a mine-owner would bring me. I bought some lime-kilns close by St David's. I got them remarkably cheap because they were practically falling down. Then your father and Mr Ollerton both said it would make more sense for us to carry the lime in our own boats. Two of your brothers seemed to know a remarkable amount about the sea and they are to take charge of them.'

'Wreckers, are they?'

'Certainly not. Think what your father would have to say to them if they were to be the cause of any man's death! They are excellent fishermen and, if they do a little smuggling from Ireland on the side, nobody would think the worse of them for that.'

Caradoc took her hands in his. The bruising pressure of his fingers told her a lot about the depth of his feelings for his family. She considered pulling away from him, not quite ready to come to terms with his physical presence beside her. She had forgotten how *big* he was!

'And my mother allowed you to do all this?' he demanded, his dark eyes wild and blazing into hers.

'Your father is going to manage the kilns – '

'From his bed? How did you talk him into that? He wouldn't accept charity from his best friend, let alone from a lady like yourself!'

Her indignation was completely genuine. 'It isn't charity! I won't have you calling it that!' she spat at him. 'I wouldn't insult him by offering him employment if he couldn't manage it as well as any other man. I don't throw away my money on lost causes! You should know that by now!'

'So the quicklime industry is going to make your fortune?' he retorted.

'No, it won't make a fortune for any of us. In fact, if it doesn't pay for itself and give your family a better life into the bargain, then Mr Ollerton has my instructions to sell out. I told your father that. We understood each other very well, I think.' Then her expression changed as she thought about the rotund, twinkling man who was now her manager. 'If we had to lose Septimus, we couldn't do better than Mr Ollerton!' she told him happily.

His eyebrows rose a fraction. 'We? You found someone else to go into business with you?'

'No, silly! I was including you. Was that very forward of me?'

'Unwise.'

'Don't you want to be included?' She looked like a chastened small girl who had been found wanting. 'You were so good to me after Wu Chao died, and I wasn't very nice to you. I was so hurt and, you see, I've always been alone at times like that. I didn't mean to freeze you out – that was the last thing I wanted! Only I wasn't thinking very straight – '

'I understood that! It was the only sensible thing to do!'

'Sensible?'

His fingers were bruising hers again. 'You were right to take Black Jade to England. You should have stayed there, that's all. You ought to marry someone of your own kind and be happy! I was hoping Septimus – '

Trudie frowned, wriggling her fingers in his despite herself. 'Septimus doesn't see me as a woman at all. He and Teresa are going to Yokohama, but I had to agree to share the profits with his father-in-law. I suppose it was something not to find him as painfully pious and – and as *unbearable* as I had feared. I talked to a priest – oh, Teresa didn't suggest it, Mr Ollerton did – and he made me see things more clearly. He wasn't at all like Father! He gave me to understand that if we don't use everything that happens to us, good and bad, we never grow into worthwhile human beings. Wu Chao would have agreed with that.'

'I'm glad if it made you feel better. You'd still have done

better to have stayed in London. You shouldn't have taken the trouble to have gone to Wales, either! I know what that journey is like, remember?'

'It wasn't the journey, that was the easy part. It was walking all over Wales when I got there!'

'Did they walk you off your feet, *cariad*?'

'Even Black Jade did better! I'm afraid they thought me a poor sort of female who couldn't cook, or keep a house clean, or walk twenty miles in a day without complaining all the way there and back!'

'Now that I don't believe!'

'I had blisters the size of half-crowns!'

He shook his head at her. 'You shouldn't have gone! I know I asked you to, but I had no right – '

She looked up at him, her heart in her eyes. 'Would you really rather I had stayed away?'

'No,' he admitted. 'How could I when you've given my whole family a new lease of life? But I wish you had stayed in London afterwards. You were safe there. Who would harm Mrs Maddock, formerly Miss Gertrude Grant, *lady*, in London? Out here, your cousins still hate you as much as ever, and I'm not in a position to protect you! It isn't fitting I should ask you to be my wife, and anything else is unthinkable! Besides, I'm away as often as not, and most Europeans would think you had come by no more than your deserts if you were to be murdered in your bed in Malacca, as very well may happen if your cousins have their way!'

'The Ki family will protect me.'

'I wish I could be as certain of that. They know you were a friend of Wu Chao's, of course. For her sake, they'll put a little business your way and not ask too many questions about any other transactions you may care to make. But you're still a barbarian, a foreign devil, and nothing will change that!'

'I suppose not,' she admitted. 'But, do you know, I think they have befriended me all the same. I'm not afraid of anything my cousins may do.'

'Then you're a fool! The Ki family is powerful, but not even they will want to tangle with your cousins' lies and, very likely, the British authorities behind them all the way from here to London. They wouldn't put themselves in such jeopardy for any *yang kwei*!'

'No, not for me, but for Black Jade they will. Her father may have been a foreign devil and I may be one, but she is one of them. She knows it, and so do they!'

His glance was stern. 'How do you know that?'

'Whampoa invited us both to lunch. He warned me to allow Black Jade to live with Swee Neo from now on, so that she can learn all the things she will need when she's older and the time comes to find her a husband.'

Caradoc cupped her face in his hand. 'Poor Trudie! Are they taking even the child away from you now?'

'She'd already made her choice. She was like a fish out of water in England. Even I could see that her father's people are never going to accept her – barbarians every one! I'm thankful there are civilized people in this world who will treat her as one of themselves, and not as something dragged in from the street! My own sisters wouldn't even give me a bed for the night unless I went alone and minded my conversation in case anyone should guess I was keeping company with a Eurasian child!'

'Bad as that?'

'Worse! I'm completely beyond redemption – past even praying for, having already condemned myself in the eyes of everyone who matters! I can't tell you what a relief it was to me to travel to Wales and be treated with common civility by other people who don't seem to matter to anyone but themselves! There's something very wrong with our society now that respectability has become the sole morality! It doesn't suit me at all!'

He laughed, sobering almost immediately. 'That doesn't make you less of a lady, or me more of a gentleman!'

Trudie found she didn't want to make any intimate decisions at that moment, not until she had digested her homecoming and had found out if Caradoc Rhys had really come to mean to her what she thought he had.

She put her head on one side, a glimmer of humour in her eyes. 'Can you get a message to Whampoa without the whole of Singapore knowing about it? Mr Horton was here and he means trouble for Black Jade, any way that he can contrive it. Will you tell Whampoa that?'

'Wouldn't it be better to mention it to the Ki *kongsi*?'

Trudi shook her head. 'The Ki family come originally from Whampoa's village in the Middle Kingdom.'

For a long moment, Caradoc stood, staring down into her face, his eyes dark and mysterious. 'Do they indeed?' he said at last. 'And did the old devil tell you that himself?'

Trudie put her head on one side. 'Amongst other things!' And she smiled the wise smile she had learned from Wu Chao; a smile that gave nothing away, but which promised all things. 'Amongst other things,' she repeated.

Chapter Twenty-four

Malacca welcomed her like a sleepy woman waiting for her lover. A breeze stirred the feathery leaves of the malaccas on the shore; the iguanas plopped in and out of the brown waters of the river; and the streets were resonant with colour and noise, Chinese and Malay, the food stalls gathering in groups, selling *satay*, tiny pieces of meat served on a stick and dipped in a piquant peanut sauce, or noodles, or one of the many rice dishes of the Chinese immigrants.

Trudie sniffed the smell of curry with appreciation, her spirits lifting the nearer she got to home. It was hard to believe now that she had ever wanted to leave, she was so glad to be home again.

Swee Neo was waiting for her in her house. All her previous homecomings had been graced by Wu Chao, who had seen that everything was ready for her when she stepped inside her own front door. It struck Trudie like a physical blow that that would never be again. It was only the requirements of good manners that made her greet Swee Neo with anything approaching pleasure.

'How well you are looking!' she exclaimed.

'I am happy,' Swee Neo answered simply. 'I am happy you are both home again.'

With the same patience that all the Chinese displayed with their children, she watched Black Jade's reverence to herself with a critical eye, determining in her own mind to take the child in hand as quickly as possible. Trudie had always spoilt her, making it more difficult for her to conform to her own customs, but now she was old enough for an end to be put to all that. She must learn to address her elders properly and it was never too early for any little girl to do that.

Black Jade rattled on to her aunt about their adventures while they had been away, frequently interrupting Trudie to do so. Finally, rebuked by the Nonya in no uncertain terms, she went and stood beside Swee Neo, clutching at the skirt of her tunic.

'I am to live with you now!' she told her, smiling.

'Then you'd better learn not to shame me in this graceless way!' Swee Neo retorted.

Black Jade nodded solemnly. 'And have my feet bound?'

'Yes, you must have pletty feet, not huge ugly feet like barbarians with no civilization. You will have Golden Lilies – much admired for your beauty!'

A shadow crossed Trudie's face. That, at least, she had hoped to spare the child. Swee Neo noticed her unhappiness at once.

'You make too much of it, Tludie. You always did. Didn't I tell you, when you decided Black Jade should live, that a girl-child can on'y give a small happiness, for it has always been that one bling her up on'y to give her to 'nother family?'

Trudie didn't answer directly. 'She is more Nonya than English. Neither of us felt at home in England.'

'Better so!' Swee Neo approved. 'Too many girl-children in our family, but as Nonya, Black Jade is somebody; as Engrish, Black Jade nobody! Maybe some famous man far away find good husband for girl after all – if she learn to behave properly!' she added with a scowl at the little girl.

Trudie wandered round her house in a dream. Everything had been made ready for her, a kindness which touched her deeply. 'I don't know how I'm going to manage by myself,' she confessed to Swee Neo. 'I shall have to find a housekeeper. Oh dear, it won't be the same, will it?'

'Yes, same, on'y different. I live in Wu Chao's house now. Her husband have childlen, so must look after, also Black Jade, also honourable husband and expected childlen from him. I do what Wu Chao did. Make your food, too, see about servants, make comfortable.'

'But you can't possibly look after me as well as everything else you have to do!' Trudie protested.

'Yes, I choose, Tludie. No tlouble! I 'member Wu Chao, too. She not liking you have tlouble with servants, tlouble with cooking.' She shook her head, smiling a little. 'You Elder Sister, no?'

'And, besides, I don't cook!' Trudie sighed. 'I was going to ask you to teach me, but that might be more trouble than ordering my servants?'

Swee Neo merely bowed. 'Elder Sister make money, Younger Sister keep house!'

The new arrangements worked very well. Occasionally, Trudie would hear Swee Neo berating the servants to do better and she would marvel at the high-handed tone the Nonyas took to those who served them, then she would remember the gulf that lay between mistress and maid in many houses in England. The difference was that Swee Neo was equally stern with members of her own family. One day a *sinkeh* would be receiving the rough side of her tongue, the next the same individual would be an invited guest having managed to achieve a little more status than a 'newly arrived'. There was no way a member of the lower orders could rise to the level of her mistress in England, or a man his master, either. Perhaps it was because the Chinese immigrants were all dependent on each other as a community in a land not their own, for the class differences were always there as they were in any society, but they seemed to Trudie to be more forgiving of the base-born, just as they would accept Black Jade, despite her Eurasian origins, whereas her own family would not.

She saw almost as much of Black Jade as she ever had. The child came in and out, following her aunt from one house to the other. Anxiously, Trudie would examine her face to see if she were unhappy, but there was no sign that she was. She was proud of her Nonya heritage.

She and Swee Neo were visiting Trudie one day when Mr Rhys came to call. Everyone was pleased to see him, Swee Neo promising a special meal to celebrate his arrival, and Black Jade showing off her new Nonya dress with a satisfaction that made them all want to laugh.

'She's happy with Swee Neo?' Mr Rhys asked after the Chinese had gone back next door.

'Very. Whampoa was quite right to insist on it. She has an aim in life she never had in England.'

'And how about her second mother?'

Trudie gave him look for look. 'I'm happy to see you,' she said.

'And happy to be home?'

'That too.'

'Then what is causing that shadow behind your eyes, *cariad*?'

She could have told him that it was her own indecision that was gnawing away at her contentment, but she chose not to do so. Not yet, she told herself. She couldn't afford to lay her own weakness at his feet quite yet. Perhaps she never would be able to, but that she wouldn't allow herself to believe. Somehow, she would find a way. She just hoped it would be sooner rather than later.

'Swee Neo is to bind Black Jade's feet.'

'If you really object, you could probably put an end to it,' Caradoc answered her implied question.

'I know. I don't think I have the right, however, not if it will really affect her chances of marriage and being a true Nonya. She hated everything that her father might have given her. She's a different child since we came home to Malacca.'

Mr Rhys said nothing more then, but when Swee Neo came back to find out how much they had enjoyed their meal, he said to her, 'Do you have to bind Black Jade's feet? Don't you have a saying in Chinese that a lake of tears is cried over every pair of beautiful feet?'

'It is nothing.' Swee Neo pooh-poohed the idea. 'Who wants ugly feet? Poor Trudie had better hide feet when man comes to her bed, no? He shudder to see such large appendages!' Her mocking eyes rested briefly on Mr Rhys and then on Trudie. 'Perhaps you not noticing her feet? But I see her new boned corset she bling back from England! Velly hot! Velly bad to wear!' She quivered her lashes. 'One suffers much pain to be beautiful, no?'

Mr Rhys shouted with laughter. 'And to think I never noticed! How could you, Mrs Maddock?'

Trudie muttered something about her mother insisting she had a proper foundation, that she was letting herself go and she soon wouldn't have a figure at all! 'I wear it very seldom. It is so very uncomfortable!'

The hot look in Mr Rhys's eyes brought the colour into her face. She had never liked being laughed at and, when mixed with a quite different emotion, she didn't know how to respond.

'My very dear Mrs Maddock – ' Mr Rhys began.

'No!' she exclaimed. 'I won't be disparaged in this way! What I choose to wear, or not to wear, is hardly a fit subject of conversation in mixed company. Kindly change the subject, or I shall be forced to ask you all to leave!'

Swee Neo and Black Jade scuttled away, but Mr Rhys

merely settled himself more comfortably in his chair, grinning at Trudie as if they shared some private joke. It wasn't a joke she appreciated. Instead, she returned his amusement with a sulky glare.

'And I'm not your dear Mrs Maddock!'

'Are you not, *bach*?'

His words brought her dilemma forcibly to mind, a dilemma she wasn't ready to face. Impatience with him boiled over.

'I wish you'd go away!' she murmured irritably.

He made no verbal response at all. Instead, he waited until she rose to her feet to give force to her command, and then fielded her neatly on to his knee. 'You're not wearing that terrible corset now, are you? Poor love, why should you be embarrassed by my knowing a thing like that about you? Don't you know how much it pleasures me to feel you close against me and know that's where you want to be?'

She was struck by the beauty of the planes of his face as seen from above, which she had never been in a position to do before. 'I thought you said I should have stayed in England – *where I belong!*' she needled him.

'But you came back to Malacca – and me.'

She was too honest to deny it. 'It's too soon, Caradoc. Please don't make me admit to more than I want to quite yet. I need time. I have a lot of thinking to do.'

'About us?'

'I don't know.'

She was baffled by her own indecision. She, who never had the least difficulty in making up her mind, or in facing facts, no matter how unpleasant, was afraid that this time she would choose wrongly. She didn't care a button for herself, but the knowledge that she could ruin Caradoc

Rhys's life as well as her own was a responsibility that weighed heavily on her.

'How much time are you going to need?'

She groaned, as upset as he. 'I wish I knew. Wu Chao took me once to the Temple of the Green Clouds, to consult the Goddess of Compassion, Kuan Yin. She told me I had a great deal to suffer before I would achieve happiness. I don't want to bring you unhappiness by wanting too much, too quickly!'

He relaxed his hold on her. 'I love you, Mrs Maddock,' he said sadly. 'I love you too much to use the attraction between us to tempt you into something you don't really want, but that doesn't alter my need for you as a woman, or yours for me as a man.'

To reinforce what he was saying, he kissed her gently on the lips. Shattered, she clung to him, abandoning any reserve she might have had, opening her mouth to him and seeking a deeper embrace than any she had ever known.

Reluctantly, he pushed her away from him. 'We had better ask Swee Neo to chaperon us if you are going to give me my way so easily, sweetest of women!'

To her own amazement, she was able to laugh at that. 'Oh Caradoc! No one else would ever call me *sweet*! You know I'm as prickly as a hedgehog, without any of the charm most women learn at their parents' knees.'

'I know nothing of the kind! What I do know about you is that you are loyal where you give your love, honest even at your own inconvenience, and that I would trust you as I trust no other human being. If you won't marry me, my darling Gertrude, I shall remain a bachelor all my days.'

Trudie blinked, not knowing how much to believe of that. 'I shan't marry anyone else!' she said finally. 'I'm happier as a widow than I ever was as a wife!'

He put a hand on her breast, delighting in the firm flesh

beneath her clothes. 'You were never Jeremy Maddock's wife but, one day, I hope you may be mine.'

Almost she said she hoped it, too, but she was back in the real world again and the horns of the dilemma were still with her. How could she marry him if to do so would only bring them both to social ruin?

Mrs Beresford could not have been more delighted to welcome Trudie home again. She put it down to the lack of other European ladies of quality in Malacca that she should have missed her quite so much. Few, indeed, were the other females with whom she could have a comfortable coze, or who would listen to her worries and triumphs over the upbringing of her daughters, a subject on which she knew herself even able to bore their doting father.

'My dear Gertrude, how I envy you! Was England as lovely as ever?'

Trudie strove to be tactful. 'I haven't an eye for such things, ma'am. I found it decidedly chilly, despite the fact that it was almost summer for most of the time we were there.'

'Ah yes, you had the child with you. Did your family take to the poor little thing?'

'No.'

Hannah Beresford had forgotten her friend's alarming honesty. 'Is that why you're back in Malacca?' she asked shrewdly.

'Malacca is my home,' Trudie told her simply. 'Perhaps I needed to see England again to fully realize that.'

Mrs Beresford, seeing that nothing had happened to change her view of Trudie's upbringing, paused to congratulate her eldest daughter on the drawing she was making of some kind of lily. She turned her attention back to

Trudie, noticing a bloom on her face that, in her opinion, had never been there before. 'And Black Jade?'

'She's living with her aunt. She prefers her mother's heritage to her father's. I don't regret taking her to England, though. She had to choose for herself, young as she is.'

Mrs Beresford said nothing to that, merely sniffed. It was inevitable, she supposed, that Trudie should have become closely involved with the Chinese community, but she could still wish it to have been otherwise.

'Did you see your cousins while you were in Singapore?' she asked.

'Mr Horton called on me at my hotel. He seems to be having business difficulties. Cousin Hermione kept well away.' Trudie looked away across the pleasant, secluded garden of the Stadthuys. 'Mr Horton thinks my Chinese friends are behind his troubles, though not even he can believe they will take on the whole might of the British Raj and win.'

Mrs Beresford, who had listened to her husband long enough to know how dedicated many of the British were to making justice available to all the peoples they ruled, was ruffled that anyone should make such a suggestion.

'Just let him try bribing my husband here in Malacca! He'll soon find out what the might of the British Raj means! The very idea! Mr Beresford doesn't have any favourites in court, and he'd soon put paid to the career of anyone who denied a Chinese, or anyone else, a fair hearing. I'm sorry to say it, my dear, but your cousins have the unhappy knack of being just about everything that I most dislike about our compatriots out here. Do they imagine we exist for their sole benefit? It's against the very principles on which the whole Empire was founded! We are here to bring proper standards of law and justice to all these people, every bit as much as to instruct them in a proper use of the land and to free them from the worst excesses of poverty. It makes me very angry when I hear it said that we are only here to make money, or to give ourselves airs we should not be entitled to at home. It's very much otherwise – and who should know better than I? We are asked to sacrifice our health, and that of our loved ones, and much else besides, in order to live in some of the most distant places in the world, so that these people should be properly governed! And then along comes somebody like your cousin who appears to think our sole concern is to take his side in any quarrel he may have with the natives. He should have kept his wife away from the Chinese and their weaknesses altogether, if he didn't want trouble from them!'

Trudie was at first amused by her vehemence. It was only when her hostess was pouring the tea that she began to wonder how much that good lady knew about the opium trade and Britain's part in it. Very little, Trudie thought, if she thought of addiction to the poppy as being a peculiarly Chinese weakness. She wondered what the poor woman would say if she were to tell her about her own father and the child her cousin had been when he had first seduced her into preparing his pipe for him to smoke in his study.

'Nevertheless,' she said aloud, 'I can still fear what would happen if Mr Horton decided revenge was the source of all his troubles. His threats against Black Jade and the Ki family were quite explicit.'

'Wretched man! Just talking about him is enough to cut up my pleasure in having you amongst us again! The girls have been asking daily when they might expect you and I, too, had almost despaired of your calling without a formal invitation!'

Trudie smiled. 'I had my own household to set up first – '

'You're still living in that quaint Chinese house, are you?'

'Yes. The only difference is that, whereas Ki Wu Chao used to see to everything for me, now her sister has volunteered to do so in her stead. So, my dear Mrs Beresford, you can still be assured of having some delicious Nonya food when you partake of my hospitality! I dread to think what I might have offered you otherwise, as cooking and keeping house are not amongst my discernible talents!'

'In fact,' said Mrs Beresford, 'you're as deeply entangled with that Chinese family as ever you were! I wish you would be more careful of what people will say about you, my dear! It's all very well to say people should not be prejudiced against them, but the fact of the matter is that they are. I am myself!'

'Most prejudice is fear,' Trudie observed.

'Oh dear,' wailed Mrs Beresford, 'I wish you wouldn't say things like that! Nobody wishes to know what causes prejudice, what one does devoutly hope is that people won't take it into their heads to be prejudiced against oneself!'

Trudie shook her head, still smiling. 'No matter what I do, I shall never take in society, ma'am, not even in Malacca, so I may as well go my own way to perdition.'

Mrs Beresford preferred not to take up that particular challenge. 'You must have enjoyed something of your visit to England!' she said, seeking a happier topic. 'Instead of doing your best to annoy me, why don't you recount some of your adventures? I'm sure the girls would be interested too.'

'I enjoyed Wales,' Trudie ventured in a small voice.

'Wales? What on earth were you doing in Wales?'

Trudie's courage deserted her. 'I had business there,' she mumbled.

'And what about the parties you attended? And the latest fashions? And all the latest gossip? Didn't you meet any personable young men, for instance? My dear, I simply don't believe there was *no one* who made your heart beat a little faster?'

'None who could compare with Mr Rhys.'

There was a moment's frozen silence. 'I hope it isn't true, Gertrude, that you have given Mr Rhys the run of your house, as you appear to have done the Ki family? Unless you mean to marry him? There have been several rumours circulating about the two of you and it is becoming very difficult for Mr Beresford and myself to defend you, unless you make some kind of announcement. You really are your own worst enemy! It isn't a suitable match for you, though we all know Mr Rhys to be a charming man – '

'He's proud of being a Welshman and an ex-miner. He went down the mines first when he was twelve years old. He was so tired that night, his father had to carry him home and put him to bed. The mines are frequently flooded and he nearly drowned several times because he was small enough to be sent into the most dangerous places, sometimes down a tunnel barely eighteen inches high. Fortunately, he soon grew too large for them to bully in that particular way!'

This last was said with such satisfaction that Mrs Beresford's dismay turned to deep concern. 'So that's what you were doing in Wales!'

The even comment lulled Trudie into a false sense of security. More than anything else she wanted to talk to someone about Caradoc Rhys. The colour flew into her cheeks and her eyes lit with remembered pleasure.

'There is no other man like him,' she said simply.

'Possibly not. I didn't realize you were seeing so much of him – not since you returned from England – '

'Not nearly enough!'

Mrs Beresford hesitated. She reminded herself for the umpteenth time that Gertrude Maddock was no responsibility of hers. Then she thought again how much she had missed her company while she had been in England and determined to make one last attempt to bring the young woman to her senses.

'You may feel like that about him now,' she said sharply, 'but a marriage between you could well be disastrous if you should ever want to be reconciled to your family. I would be failing in my duty as your friend if I didn't point out to you the disparity between your birth and education, and so many other things that could easily shipwreck any long-term relationship between you. I am as sorry as the next person about the way he was misused as a child – I cannot think it right for *any* child to have to undergo hard labour! – but the fact that he did go down the mines at twelve years old will hardly be a recommendation to his inclusion in the hospitality, or even the acquaintance, of *your* friends and relations!'

Trudie leaned eagerly forward. 'Yes, but don't you see, ma'am, that I'm not a welcome acquaintance, either. Who else receives me here in Malacca besides yourself? And if they do, it being the kind of occasion when they can't easily overlook my existence, it is only because they know they'll bear the brunt of your displeasure if I don't receive an invitation.'

'That's largely your own fault – '

Trudie's eyes flashed. 'Indeed, it is not! It is my Cousin

Hermione's busy tongue, as I soon found out in Singapore! Be that as it may, if I am not welcome as Mrs Maddock, why should I complain at being ignored as Mrs Rhys?'

Mrs Beresford made a helpless gesture with her hands. She knew better than most the damage Hermione Horton had done to her cousin's reputation, despised and disliked as the woman herself was. She could almost welcome Trudie marrying her miner just to spite the horrid creature!

'It's more than that,' she said in softer, more kindly tones, 'I insist on playing devil's advocate for a moment longer, so don't interrupt me! You don't only have your own happiness with such a man to consider. What about the children you'll bring into the world? Are they to be recluses, too? You must consider these things, my dear, because you know, as a widow yourself, that high romance has remarkably little to do with the bread-and-butter business of marriage. Once the first rapture has worn off, what then?'

Trudie's face was still flushed, despite her closed-in expression. 'My first marriage brought me no rapture. My husband was not a – physical man. He married me for other reasons. Oh, don't misunderstand me, I was willing enough! And I gained incomparably by the escape from my childhood life that he afforded me. But Mr Rhys has only to lift his little finger and I would lie down and die for him. If I cannot have him in marriage, then I shall pray daily on my knees that he will take me without, for I don't think I can live without him. As for children, I think I shall envy them having such a man for a father! *They* shall never lack for love, or a kind word, as I did. That's a better start in life than many of us have to face, no matter how highly born!'

Mrs Beresford's chin dropped. She made a valiant effort

to recover herself, failed, and took a trembling sip of tea as a last, desperate remedy.

'My dear!' she said in a failing voice. 'My dear Gertrude!' She caught the interested gaze of her eldest daughter and was recalled to a sense of duty as a mother. 'Catherine! This conversation is not for you. Go and join your sisters at the other end of the garden.'

Catherine jumped to her feet, her eyes wide with curiosity. 'Yes, Mama.' She went reluctantly, dragging her feet, feeling herself to have been very badly served by her mother's remembrance of her existence when she had been doing her best to stay as quiet as a mouse. It wasn't fair!

'I am shocked!' Mrs Beresford went on in firmer tones. Then she saw Trudie's pinched face and her natural kindness overcame her. 'I am so afraid you will be hurt, child! As if I should abandon you, whatever you do!'

Trudie hung her head. 'I am afraid for Mr Rhys,' she confessed. 'I could never forgive myself if I ruined him.'

This seemed so absurd to Mrs Beresford that she was at a loss to know what to say in response. Finally, she decided on the truth. 'It is you who will be committing social suicide, not him! My dear, even if I were not so fond of you, I should think it my duty to point out to you the most obvious consequences of what you have in mind. It is always the woman who suffers in an unequal marriage – ' She saw Trudie's sudden glare and made an impatient sound with her mouth. '*Now* what have I said?' she wailed.

'Nothing. You're being very kind. If I'm angry, it's with myself. I've embarrassed you and that is unforgivable. I had no right to burden you with my personal problems.'

'*Trudie!*'

'I'm sorry!'

Mrs Beresford poked her hard in the ribs. 'Must you be

as prickly as a hedgehog, my girl? It's time you got over feeling that you were put in this world as an Aunt Sally for everyone around you! If you must know, I missed you abominably while you were away! Even my husband refers to you as the most worthwhile of my friends! So what more do you want? And what are friends for, if not to advise and help when they can? Nor am I in the least stupid, I'll have you know! You can tell me until you're blue in the face that you know all about marriage, and I still shan't believe you!'

It was Trudie's turn to be astonished. Then she burst into delighted laughter. 'I have never thought you stupid, ma'am! And I'm very flattered to be your friend, though I think I have much more to gain than you by the acquaintance!' She stopped laughing and heaved a great sigh. 'You are right. I know nothing of marriage. What am I to do?'

'Didn't you talk to your mother about it while you were in England?'

Trudie conjured up a picture of her bent, pathetic, frightened parent and wished she could convey some of the frustrated, almost contemptuous affection she had always felt for her to the other woman. 'No.'

'I suppose that would be too much to hope! Well, my dear, I think you're going to have to tell me all about it instead.'

The suddenly shrewd eyes of her hostess were unexpectedly reassuring, especially when the glimmer of a smile reminded Trudie that, by some good fortune she would never understand, Mrs Beresford actually liked her and wanted to do her best for her.

'I don't know where to begin!' she murmured.

'How about beginning with your marriage to Mr Maddock?'

Trudie nodded. 'Did you know him?'

'A little. One can't help knowing anyone who passes through Malacca. A strange man, I thought. I can't say I approved of him. I'm not as broad-minded as you, I won't pretend to be! He had told me himself he had a wife in England, and then there was all that business of his marrying a Chinese woman – '

'He did. It was quite legal.'

'And you didn't mind?'

'There wouldn't have been much point when I found out about it. He was dead. As a matter of fact his Chinese wife was the best legacy he left me. I loved her dearly.'

Mrs Beresford only nodded. 'She was the woman who was killed in that unfortunate accident your cousins were involved in?'

'She was murdered. Cousin Hermione meant to kill me.'

Mrs Beresford rattled her cup in her saucer. 'But the inquest – '

'Wu Chao was Chinese.'

'Your friend Wu Chao was the woman your husband married?' There was a moment's silence. 'So Black Jade – oh dear! I never imagined! I mean, I always thought her father to be Mr Rhys. It seemed that he must be, out there, alone, on that plantation. I was trying to think how to tell you so that you wouldn't think any the less of him, and all this time it was your own husband!'

'Yes.' Trudie shrugged her shoulders. 'You mustn't think I minded, ma'am. I didn't really know Mr Maddock very well.'

Mrs Beresford stared at her. 'Didn't you feel anything?'

'I was surprised – a little,' Trudie confessed. 'You see, it wasn't like that with me. All he wanted from me was someone to keep an eye on his business interests in London. I thought perhaps he didn't like that sort of thing very much.'

'Oh, my dear!'

Mrs Beresford could understand the attraction of Mr Rhys all too well, and her busy mind was already engaged in trying to see how she could present the marriage in a more favourable light to the British community in the Straits Settlements. How strange it was, she thought, that one could feel one knew all about another person only to find out that one doesn't know them at all!

A rueful smile played about Trudie's lips. 'On the other hand, Mr Maddock taught me a great deal about Oriental art, and buying and selling. I'm quite good at it.'

'And what does your Mr Rhys think about that?'

The smile became a broad grin. 'The best thing I can say about him is that he sees me as a woman long before he sees me as someone who'll make his fortune! I can't tell you how nice it is to be a real person to someone! The only reason Mr Maddock sent for me to join him in Malacca was because my brother asked him to. Septimus will never be as good at buying and selling as I am and I was constantly treading on his toes when we set up the Emporium in London together. He has no imagination – or perhaps it's inspiration that one needs to succeed in finding the right market at just the right moment. I don't know what story Mr Maddock planned on telling me about Wu Chao because he was dead before I got there, but it wasn't me he wanted for a wife – he wanted me as a business partner!'

'I had no idea!' Mrs Beresford exclaimed faintly.

'I should hope not! I went to a great deal of trouble that nobody should know! I'm only telling you now so that you'll see what a bad bargain I am for any man! I haven't much to lose, but Caradoc Rhys could find all Singapore and most of Malacca lined up against him. I don't want to do that to him!'

Hannah Beresford considered saying something reassuring, such as it being well known that men never suffered socially in the same way that women did. Men could fend for themselves. Women had to depend on their husband's friends to have wives that they could befriend in turn. She saw, however, that Trudie was well aware there would always be some who would gossip about her strange first marriage – and who would resent her masculine taste for making money! Even more would they resent her success at it!

'I don't know how to advise you,' she said at last. 'Will Mr Rhys's family accept you as his wife?'

'His mother will. As for the others, Wales is even further away than London. It won't matter to them very much.'

'Then it really boils down to your cousins, doesn't it? I'm not normally a vicious woman, but one really could hope that something dreadful might happen to them that meant they had to return to England!'

Trudie presented an innocent face. 'One of these days something might!'

Mrs Beresford immediately looked worried. 'Do you really think so? I know my husband would like to be rid of them! He doesn't care for the opium trade even if it is perfectly legal, and he's perfectly certain they're heavily involved in its most unsavoury side.'

'Without doubt!' Trudie said dryly.

Mrs Beresford looked first startled and then flustered. 'I shouldn't have said anything about them! If anyone should know how to hold her tongue, it ought to be the wife of the Lieutenant-Governor! I *pride* myself on it!'

'Did you say anything, ma'am?'

Hannah Beresford laughed. She clapped her hands together, throwing away all her doubts. 'I think you deserve your chance of happiness! I hope you do marry the man!'

Trudie walked down the hill feeling truly happy. She wondered why she had ever had any doubts about what she should do. She would marry Caradoc Rhys, and she would love every moment of it! She hugged herself with glee, laughing out loud at nothing at all. The line of waiting rickshaw men watched her impassively, one of them clearing his throat and spitting in the gutter close beside her. She turned on him, about to rake him over the coals, then she changed her mind and stepped into his rickshaw instead.

'Do you know the big foreign devil with black hair and eyes?'

'Rhys man?'

Trudie sat back, content. 'Take me to him!' she commanded in a lordly tone and didn't mind in the least when the Chinaman giggled and waggled his head at her. Indeed, she hardly noticed him at all.

It was late before Trudie was persuaded that everyone was telling her the truth after all, and that Mr Rhys had gone back to the plantation.

Swee Neo regarded Trudie's unhappy face and told her yet again that there were many rumours of trouble amongst the Tamils.

'Couldn't someone else have gone?' Trudie stormed. 'With the whole Ki family – '

'Excuse me. Velly sorry. Thought Rhys man was manager of plantation!'

Trudie hoped she wasn't going to cry with disappointment. 'Oh, Swee Neo, I did want him to be here tonight!'

The Nonya's knowing look mocked her. 'Never mind, Tludie. He come sometime soon, yes?'

'I certainly hope so!' said Trudie. She felt more lost than ever without him, especially now that her mind was made up and she knew which way she wanted to go in the future – to be the one woman who would always be by his side.

Chapter Twenty-five

'Oh my word!'

Mrs Beresford bridled. 'What else was I to do?' She gave her husband an abashed, cautious look. 'I told her we'd do everything we can to help!'

'So, she really means to have him, does she?'

'Yes. You do like him, don't you? I always think men are better judges of other men than we women can hope to be! I did do the right thing to encourage her, didn't I? Not that anyone can stop her! She dotes on him!'

Mr Beresford regarded his flustered wife with amused affection. 'She could do a lot worse than young Rhys in my opinion. He's got his head screwed on the right way – and he's honest. I dare say that attracts her as much as anything. One can hardly say the same for the Hortons, can one?'

'Oh dear!'

'As a matter of fact, I had a word with Caradoc Rhys only yesterday,' her husband continued, his face hardening with recalled displeasure. 'There's been a lot of trouble out at that plantation he manages – stirred up by the Hortons, of course! Not that we ever seem to be able to prove anything against them. The Ki family will make mincemeat of them sooner or later – but not on my territory if I can help it!'

'Is that what you told Mr Rhys?'

'I hinted as much. I'm hoping he will pass on what I said to the Kis, whose employee I suppose he is these days.

Meanwhile, he's going to do what he can to settle the Tamils and keep the Hortons at bay.'

'I wish he were a gentleman – '

'I'm glad he's on my side, whatever he is! Christopher Horton is a gentleman, I suppose, but few people I know would willingly introduce him to their wife and children.'

'Never mind, *we* shall receive the Rhyses – and then everyone else in Malacca will have to follow our example!'

'Quite right, my dear! And as you're not nearly old enough to be the young woman's mother, you can save your fussing until Catherine is old enough to make a fool of herself over some equally unsuitable young man, no doubt!'

Whereupon his wife preened herself happily and remarked, 'No, I'm more of an age to be her elder sister, wouldn't you say? Though I could wish this abominable climate suited me one half so well as it does her! She was positively radiant whilst she was here! Even little Catherine looked pale and drab beside her!'

Trudie had never known time go so slowly. She did her best to put everything out of her mind whilst she went through the motions of resuming control of her business. She was helped in this by a cheerful communication from Mr Ollerton, telling her that her new Welsh business was thriving beyond any of their expectations. Everything else was going well also, he was glad to report. He had discerned an increasing interest in Japanese products – she had been perfectly right about that – and he was awaiting Septimus's first consignments with high expectations that they would make the Emporium the rage of London.

It was more difficult to find out the details of her Malacca business. Wu Chao's brother, a Baba of few words, ran her soothingly through the books and, it was only after he had gone that she realized she was very little the wiser.

What was clear was that they were making a great deal of money, much of which had been placed at her disposal in one of the few European banks, and that they paid remarkably few taxes to anyone. On this point, at least, she had questioned the Baba, threatening to ask the Ki lawyer if he thought to keep anything from her.

Wu Chao's brother had wagged his head at her, whistling through his teeth. 'Velly sorry, Elder Sister. You never mind. We pay tax to Mr Belesford.'

'How about the taxes due to Queen Victoria?' she had goaded him.

'Mr Belesford same as Rani, no?'

Her first reaction had been relief that the Kis were not bribing Mr Beresford, which would have been ridiculous; her second was that the few taxes they were paying were probably a sop to her sensitivities and that she would be ill advised to press the matter any further. She even began to wonder if she could call it her business any more, it seemed to have been taken over entirely by the Kis – even the accounts were being kept in Chinese, impossible for her to read and, she suspected, most other people in the Colony.

When she went through the heavy ledgers again which the Baba had left with her, her spirits rose as she discerned somebody else's fingerprints running through the accounts, somebody who could only be Carodoc Rhys!

Without hesitating, she ran out of the back door and into Swee Neo's house. The eldest Ki brother was still sitting in her kitchen, drinking tea, and picking his teeth with an ivory pick.

'You didn't tell me Mr Rhys has been inspecting the accounts all the time I've been away!' she accused him.

He waggled his head from side to side. 'You Rhys man's woman. If he want you know, he tell you!'

So much for all the work she had put into the business! 'That's ridiculous!' she flared. 'What does he know about running a business?'

The man hunched his shoulders and ignored her. It was Swee Neo who took her by the shoulders and pushed her gently out of the house, accompanying her back to her own dwelling.

'Never mind, you velly much foreign devil today! Velly bad! Why you no learn restraint, Tludie? Even round-eye man not like woman to shout and abuse him!'

'I didn't abuse him!' Trudie claimed indignantly.

Swee Neo ignored her. 'How I teach Black Jade to kowtow, to be patient before speaking, when you set such a bad example?'

Trudie stared at her. 'You mean you expect me to kowtow to your brother?'

'No, no. You Elder Sister. But he man, Tludie, and you woman. Life, no?'

'Surely I'm entitled to ask any questions I like about my own business?'

'Very much yes. Only you woman, you ask with respect, no?'

'If you say so,' Trudie gave way grudgingly.

Swee Neo's smile warmed her, reminding her of Wu Chao. 'Now you almost Nonya!'

Trudie made a face. 'I'll ask Mr Rhys!'

Swee Neo approved of that. 'Yes. Rhys man tell you. And you, Elder Sister, not lose temper, not get madder than silly hen, no? You do as Rhys man say – very gentle woman!'

'I'll try,' Trudie conceded. 'It's still supposed to be my business, though!'

'You tell Rhys man! He coming home today. You see him tonight!'

Trudie didn't ask her how she knew. She had long ago discovered that, whereas Europeans sent letters to one another, or messenger boys with messages, or even exchanged gossip at their parties, the Chinese apparently knew everything by a process of osmosis. Whisper it in Singapore, every Baba and Nonya knew all about it in Malacca the following day. There were the servants, of course, who always knew everything about their employers – far more than those individuals were aware – but few Nonyas left their own homes to take up domestic work amongst strangers. As far as most Europeans were concerned, they were invisible shadows in society, never seen on the streets, preferring to rule their own homes rather than have any kind of public existence. They were the cement that held the wall of their families together, never the bricks who caught the eye of passersby in the streets where most of them lived.

'What happened to stir up the Tamils?' she asked, testing Swee Neo's knowledge.

'Opium! Too much money. Too much bad mens.'

The suddenly lowered eyes and blank expression alerted Trudie that there was more behind this business than she had suspected. 'White devils?' she asked carelessly.

Swee Neo refused to answer. 'I bling lunch now!' she announced.

However, she sat opposite Trudie all the time she was eating her food, for once without bringing Black Jade or any of the other children she had taken into her own family as a matter of course. It was obvious she had something on her mind and was looking for the right opportunity to bring it up.

'Food good? New cook.'

Trudie didn't envy anyone who took on the task of cooking for a Baba household. Their methods of preparing the food took ages and, even on ordinary days, they ate two full meals. It was far worse during festivals and other social occasions. Then the menus were vast and demanding, endless quantities of food to be given away to the merest acquaintances, let alone the vast numbers of critical relations who sampled everything, their judgements the bane of any good housekeeper's life.

This new cook had a hobby. He made the huge Hainanese kites, *layang Hylam*, which were every bit as high as a man. Swee Neo approved of this interest, even while it meant her new cook would be away frequently, often overnight, to take part in the complicated competitions that meant so much to him.

She had learned of his hobby after she had agreed to take this *sinkeh* into her house. He had arrived last night, his few belongings wrapped in a spare breech cloth, his face shiny with his anxiety to please. He had large hands and feet for a Chinese, and he was apparently wedded to his pointed coolie hat which he wore even in the kitchen.

Swee Neo had spent most of the evening trying to find out if he was as good a cook as the recommendation he had brought from his Chinese village said he was. To her surprise, he had managed everything to her satisfaction and he was every bit as clean as she was herself. His failing, he had told her, was gambling. He had already gambled away one fortune in China. Now, he hoped to make another fortune in Malacca.

'He make fortune with kites!' Swee Neo related, laughing. 'Wake up this morning and he had tied many, many kites by string to the gutters on the roof. I t'ink we all fly, house too!'

Trudie laughed with her. 'I should love to see a kite-flying competition!' she admitted.

Swee Neo and Trudie exchanged guilty looks. 'We go one day? Gamble a little? Very pretty to see kites fly and swoop in the sky, no?'

'Let's!' Trudie agreed.

Swee Neo looked down her nose. 'Rhys man take us,' she suggested slyly.

Trudie grinned. 'And Black Jade?'

'And childlen,' Swee Neo promised.

Ah Nyiok, as the new cook was called, was brought to receive Trudie's compliments on his cooking. He kow-towed, banging his forehead on the floor in his eagerness to please, his cheerful countenance unperturbed by the pain. It was true, he said, he had much to do in his new employment, but Trudie wasn't to hesitate to ask him to cut and stack her firewood, to water her many pot plants she had inherited from Wu Chao, and to keep her house altars clean and tidy. He was a little shocked to find the foreign devil had no family altar in her home, though he hid it as best he could, raising a cautious brow in Swee Neo's direction.

Swee Neo explained his difficulty to Trudie. 'I tell him Rhys man explain what you believe when he comes,' she added, and proceeded to do so. As if by magic, the *sinkeh*'s face cleared.

Of course the Rhys man would know! He tapped his forehead significantly, grinning his happy smile. The Rhys man was not fortunate enough to be a civilized person, of course, but was a good, wise man. Now he knew who this barbarian woman was. He pointed at Trudie, his conical hat almost falling off in his excitement. Rat lady!

Swee Neo translated this outpouring as best she could. 'Rat lady?'

'Rat lady gamble, too. Rat lady has very good joss!'

That much Trudie understood herself. She flicked a particle of dust off her sleeve. 'It's true,' she said. 'I have good joss because I gamble very carefully,' she added. 'If I gamble on your kites, will I win?'

He nodded. 'Rat lady always win!'

Laughing, Trudie turned to Swee Neo and told her about the bets she had made with the captain of the small ship that plied between Singapore and Malacca. 'I was born in the year of the Rat,' she added. 'The sign of new beginnings, no?'

Ah Nyiok's enthusiasm knew no bounds. Apart from kites, his chief interest was *Ming Shu*, the art and practice of Chinese astrology. Uninvited, he sat himself down at Trudie's table, drawing pen and paper to him. At intervals he would ask a question of Swee Neo, demanding the exact instant of Trudie's birth and drawing up a whole chart of her life.

It told of her lonely, unhappy childhood, her escape into a false marriage, of the sadness she would have to suffer. Then it told of the one man she would give her whole life to, the riches she would achieve, the children she would bear, girls as well as boys, but she would not regret her daughters for they would have the minds of men and bring their parents honour.

Trudie was intrigued by the signs and drawings he had laid out on the paper. 'The Goddess Kuan Yin – '

'You b'lieve Chinese goddess?' Swee Neo asked her.

Trudie didn't want to admit as much, but she could see for herself how she had clung to Kuan Yin's answer to her question before her altar at the Temple of the Green Clouds for nearly a year, sure in the centre of her being that one day it would all come true. 'Yes, I believe everything she said.'

Ah Nyiok was less surprised than Swee Neo. He made some more signs on the paper, nodding his head with glee.

'Rat first of twelve animals. Sign is *Tzu*, meaning infant. Same sign means the midnight hour, when only rats and mice run about the house. Last night, I see fat, rich rat. I very glad. Think it come to me! What you think?'

Trudie was less than delighted. 'I don't like to think we have rats in the house – yours or mine!' she exclaimed to Swee Neo.

'But, Tludie, if rats live in house, they guard against intluders, like dog. Money lats bling all good fortune! Like you! Characteristic of Rat people that they understand money. Rats scrimp and save, make many plans when poor; spend much money everywhere when rich! Understand all business problems because making such good plans! You very nice "money rat", no?'

Not entirely convinced, Trudie asked, 'What sign were you born under? What sign does Mr Rhys have?'

Swee Neo hid her amusement. 'Rhys man Tiger.'

Oh yes! How could he be anything else than a tiger?

'Combine very well with Rat,' Ah Nyiok chimed in.

At last Swee Neo felt able to make the suggestion she had been intending to put before Trudie all along. 'Why not you go meet Rhys man?'

Trudie forgot all about rats and tigers. A new excitement seized her, wrapping itself about her like a caress of the wind, stirring the air and pulling at her garments. 'I can't go alone!' she exclaimed.

'No. Ah Nyiok go with you. Pity. Good cook, but better guard for barbarian rat travelling to find tiger, no?'

Trudie chewed on her lower lip. 'You're sure he's coming home today?'

'Yes, velly sure.'

She might meet him at the waterfall! Would he be glad

to see her? Trudie hoped it so much, she shut her eyes to keep out any doubts that might occur to her.

'I don't know if I should go,' she prevaricated, knowing perfectly well nothing, but nothing, was going to keep her away.

'You prefer go through accounts yet again?' Swee Neo retorted with some asperity. 'What wrong with Ki accounts?'

Trudie was stuck for an answer. 'There isn't anything wrong with them. I have nothing better to do with my time. That's the trouble, with everything being run so well for me, what am *I* going to do?'

'Oh, Tludie, go away find Rhys man. He tell you what to do!'

At another time Trudie would have laughed at that. The thing she had always liked best about Caradoc Rhys was that he had never told her what to do. She felt strangely unsettled that everyone seemed to have decided for her that he should be the answer to everything where she was concerned! She wasn't sure she liked being taken for granted in that way. Did the whole of Malacca know she was in love with Caradoc Rhys? And, if so, why should she mind so much that they did? Wasn't she, even yet, completely sure of her own feelings?

Swee Neo waited until Ah Nyiok had gone to put up the Ki carriage, then she sat down again, motioning Trudie back into her chair also. 'I have to tell you 'bout cousins, Tludie. I tell you now?'

Trudie nodded. She stiffened imperceptibly, knowing the Nonya could feel her reluctance to drag her mind back from the coming meeting with Caradoc to the icy blank that was all she would allow herself to feel when her Cousin Hermione was mentioned.

'Ki family against opium trade,' Swee Neo said softly.

'But cousin go on using plantation for that. Many times Ki Thian Heow warn him to stay away. But cousin very stupid white devil. He not listen. Ki family already very angry about murder of Wu Chao – '

'The inquest brought it in as an accidental death,' Trudie reminded her. 'The Hortons probably think that was an end of the matter.'

'Never end!'

Trudie shivered. 'No, it'll never end. Mr Horton won't rest until he gets the plantation away from Black Jade. Warn your family, Swee Neo, because he may convince the foreign devils in court that Mr Maddock's will should be put aside in my favour, which means he will resume control of it.'

Swee Neo was unimpressed. 'Unless you marry Rhys man. Much better you do that, then foreign devils not bothered.'

Trudie flushed. 'True,' she murmured. How odd to think of Caradoc having the right to control all her affairs in the future! She could always bury away in the figures anything she didn't want him to know, but would she want to? A sensation of warm delight passed through her as she realized what a joy it would be to share everything, work or not, with someone one could not only admire, but liked more than anyone else in the world.

'All the same, warn them to be careful, for Black Jade's sake. Mr Horton is in difficulties with his business in Singapore. He may get even more desperate than he is now.'

'Yes, many business difficulties,' Swee Neo said with satisfaction.

'Inspired by the Ki family, no doubt?' Trudie asked dryly.

Swee Neo shrugged. 'Not know. What can Ki family do

against foreign devils like cousins? We poor Chinese people. Why blame us for business difficulties?'

Trudie smothered a smile. 'Be that as it may, I'd sooner have the Ki family on my side than all the foreign devils in the world!' she exclaimed. 'Except Mr Rhys,' she added hastily.

'Ah, but you almost civilized person, Tludie – '

'If I learned to be more restrained, *then* I'd be civilized,' Trudie mocked herself.

'You'd still have hideous, barbarian feet!' Swee Neo mourned. 'Never mind. Rhys man not care and too late now!'

Ah Nyiok had brought the carriage as close to the house as he could. They had some difficulty understanding one another without a translator, for, whilst Trudie had one or two Chinese phrases off pat, she found it very difficult to converse in the language. She was better able to manage in the Malay *lingua franca*, but Ah Nyiok was too newly arrived to have mastered much of that. It didn't matter, however. Ah Nyiok had been told it was more than his life was worth to allow anything to happen to his charge. He gathered up the reins and grinned at her.

'All ready!' he said.

They set off at a smart pace down the street until Trudie recognized the back of the Temple of the Green Clouds and an idea came to her. She made signs to Ah Nyiok that she wanted to stop there, jumping down from the carriage almost before they had come to a halt and before she could change her mind.

Near the temple was one of the shops Wu Chao had shown her, where they fashioned all the things of this world in paper to provide for the needs of those in the spirit world. They were marvellously wrought, every detail as perfect as their makers could fashion them. Trudie bought with a profligate hand. She bought houses; carriages; practically every kind of dress they had in the place; and a whole pile of 'spirit' money. It was the dresses Wu Chao had wanted, and it was the dresses she would have – by the dozen!

The whole shop came to a standstill as they watched this foreign devil buy and buy. Once or twice, the proprietor made an extra bow, wondering how to ask her if she knew what she was doing. It was not his experience that barbarian ladies ever came into his shop, let alone to buy anything. He sent someone out into the street to see how she had come to be there, and a reluctant Ah Nyiok was brought back, but he, too, was quite unable to explain why Trudie had come.

Trudie, herself, was unaware of the comment she was causing. She was enchanted by the beauty of the paper objects she was buying. She had been impressed, she remembered, when she had seen them before, but now that she could examine them more closely, she was astonished by the detail that had been lavished on every aspect of these copies.

Then, just as she thought she had done, she caught sight of the card game of *cher kee*. She jumped up and down, pointing towards them. 'And that!' she said in English. 'That's something that Wu Chao would really like!'

A silence fell over the shop. Trudie chewed on her lower lip, wondering if she had offended in some way. She looked anxiously at Ah Nyiok, but he, too, looked as flummoxed as the rest of them.

The proprietor stepped forward, bobbing his head up and down in a series of small respectful bows. 'Ki Wu Chao?' He enunciated each syllable very clearly.

Trudie inclined her head. She tried to remember how

much stillness was appreciated in the Oriental woman, so she stood quietly where she was, determined not to fidget in her nervousness. Carefully, she tried out some of the Cantonese she had learned from Wu Chao.

'I could not send proper gifts to the funeral because I was on a ship going to England. I wish to rectify this omission now. I wish to show respect to the spirit of Wu Chao.'

A small calculation of the amount she had already spent showed her respect for the dead woman was considerable. The Chinese discussed the matter between themselves, awed that a foreign devil should go to such lengths to show her appreciation of a Nonya.

'What will you do with these things?' the proprietor tested her.

'I shall burn them inside the temple.'

Trudie didn't know if that were the correct thing to do or not. She had an idea that it was already too late for such a gesture, that it had to be at the funeral or not at all, but she could see no difficulty herself in annihilating time in the face of eternity. Surely, it could never be too late to show them all the loving respect she had for Wu Chao.

Ah Nyiok was appealed to again. The *sinkeh* was at first too embarrassed to speak. Finally he muttered that he had been told by Ki Swee Neo that Trudie had been Wu Chao's Elder Sister. He, himself, had been given the task of driving her in the direction of the Ki plantation. He went on to explain the details of the household arrangements he had observed since landing in Malacca and being taken on by the Ki family as their cook. It was true, he insisted, that Trudie was treated as one of the family. She was Wu Chao's daughter's second mother, and even the Babas of the family held her in respect.

The 'ahs' and the 'ohs' that accompanied this recital

brought home to Trudie how ridiculous she must seem to them all. She wished now she had never come.

'Please forgive this stupid barbarian if I have offended against your customs,' she began.

The proprietor suddenly discovered he was able to speak a little English. 'We are honoured, madam. Perhaps I may help you carry your gifts into the temple, yes?'

Trudie thanked him with as much dignity as she could manage. She led the way out of the shop, pausing at the entrance of the temple to greet 'Fo' lion and lioness, as Wu Chao had taught her. She bowed low to the altar as she stepped over the board that lay across the entrance, moving slowly to where she had seen the furnace the last time she had visited the temple.

A great crowd of interested spectators had gathered to watch. They stood in a solemn semi-circle, watching as the proprietor of the shop handed her the 'spirit' goods she had bought, one by one, and she fed them to the flames. Even the children, at first noisily intrigued to see a foreign devil doing such a thing, fell silent.

It took a long time to burn everything. When she had finished, Trudie stood in front of the furnace watching the burning coals, blackened with the ashes of the beautiful paper replicas she had fed into the fire. Had she done the right thing? She thought she would probably never know, unless one day Swee Neo were to refer to the incident in oblique approval, or disapproval, as the case might be.

It didn't matter. She had done what she had done for Wu Chao and for nobody else. It was between the two of them. She could hear Wu Chao saying on that last day of her life the things she would want most in the next world. Trudie remembered the laughter and Wu Chao's insistence on the number of garments she would want. Well, she had sent her all the dresses she could lay her hands on and everything else that she thought might appeal to her. It didn't matter if she hadn't done everything with the right meticulous ritual, she was warmed and strengthened to feel she had done what she could, in her own way, to carry out the wishes of someone she had loved. She could not have done it before. She had been too shocked, too absorbed in her own grief, to have made such a gesture before she had gone to England. Now, it was the happy times she remembered more than the misery of her loss. Now, she could be grateful that she had survived, that life would go on, full of good things for her. Now, she had the strength to give up Wu Chao to her own future and reach out for her own – with Caradoc Rhys!

So intent was she on her own thoughts, that it took a moment before she realized that the custodian of the temple, he who had translated Kuan Yin's message to her, had recognized her and had come to exchange a few words with her.

She apologized for turning the whole temple into a peepshow, knowing even as she did so that he wouldn't see it that way. She followed him gladly when he suggested she might like to see the ancestral altar in a room behind the hall that contained the main altar. He pointed out the various ancestral tablets, elaborately carved in wood and painted gold, with the name of the deceased written also in gold on a scarlet background. Smiling, he pointed to one of the newest, as beautiful as any of the others there.

'Ki Wu Chao. Her name. When others come from the Middle Kingdom, from Penang, or Singapore, to seek their ancestors, they will find her name written here.'

So, Wu Chao had achieved her ambition. She had become an ancestor, after all.

* * *

Ah Nyiok looked sideways at the foreign devil who had been put in his charge for the journey to the waterfall. He had been afraid at first that she would ruin his chances of staking a claim to an existence in Malacca, that he would be laughed at for his association with such a strange barbarian. But the woman had gained great face by her actions, after all. Her face was huge, and, standing in her shadow, his own had grown in her reflection, in a way he never would have believed. Joss. His joss had been very good ever since he had arrived in Malacca. He felt luckier than he had felt for many days. If he was home in time, he would find a game later on that night and test his joss still further. He whistled happily through his teeth and thought of the piles of coins that would be attracted to his side of the table! Who knew what might happen? Today, he might be only a *sinkeh* cook; tomorrow, he might own a considerable piece of whatever action was going on in sleepy Malacca!

He had never been as close to a barbarian woman as he was to this lady. Those he had seen in the streets, he had avoided like the plague, never catching their eyes, or giving them the chance to put the 'evil eye' on him. He had heard once that all round-eyes were unpredictable people who would praise you for your work, only to dismiss you the next moment; that the more polite and distant they were, the more dangerous they became. He didn't believe Trudie to be like that. Her thoughts were written clearly all over her face so that even he could read them – what a terrible gambler she would make! Yet, if all he had heard told in the Ki household was true, everything she touched turned to gold. Joss!

He decided to go round the Malay village instead of through it. Now they were well away from the city, he was afraid of the jungle. It wasn't like any countryside he had ever known. It was dark and impenetrable, full of shadows and strange noises.

He felt Trudie's hand on his arm and jerked himself away from her. 'We go this way!' he insisted.

'No. Mr Rhys always goes through the village. He had friends there. We might miss him!'

He couldn't understand what she was talking about. To his intense annoyance, she snatched the reins away from him and pulled the horse's head round to the direction she wanted to go. He wondered if he should assert himself, or if she would pay him any attention. She was a devil after all, insisting on her own way when any other female he knew would have been glad to follow the lead of the man she was with, even if he were only a cook! He gave her an indignant look, but she wasn't even looking at him. His outrage mounted.

'I drive!'

Trudie glared at him. 'Only if you go my way!' She added an imprecation in Chinese that pricked the bubble of his anger. He waggled his head, his normal grin back on his face.

'We go your way,' he agreed.

There was no sign of movement in the village. The same men sat under the same tree exactly as they had before. They might have been sitting there since the last time Trudie had passed that way. Seeing it was a woman in the carriage, they politely averted their eyes from her face, only looking up at the very last moment when the carriage came to a halt beside them.

'Forgive me,' Trudie said in tolerable Malay, 'has Mr Rhys come this way?'

'*Salaam*. He comes later today. He awaits you by the waterfall.'

Trudie's face fell. 'I had hoped to surprise him!' she snapped.

The headman laughed indolently. 'One must get up very early in the morning to surprise the Welshman!'

Trudie grinned. 'And how do you know he's a Welshman?' she asked him.

'I know it as I know you're his woman, *mem*, because he told me so!'

'Did he, indeed!' Trudie said more to herself than to him. 'Let's hope the *tuan* told you truly!'

The headman laughed again. 'Do you doubt it?'

Restraint, Trudie cautioned herself, she must show restraint. She straightened her back and lifted her chin, nodding to Ah Nyiok to whip up the horse and hurry on to the waterfall.

It was exactly as she remembered it. The water fell gently from one shadowed pool to another, the drops of water shimmering into an eternal rainbow. In the great humidity of midday, it seemed pleasantly cool, the sound of the water making the place a paradise. Trudie sank to her knees beside the water, looking into the muddied green depths and finding only her own reflection.

Above her was the Hindu shrine that Black Jade had discovered and visited. There was no sign of its keeper, no sign of any other human being, only the noises of the jungle, the birds calling to one another and the deep growl of a hunting animal.

She looked back again into the pool. There were changes in her face she had not previously noticed. She looked older and perfectly calm. She thought with satisfaction that she looked a perfect lady. Then there was another reflection in the water, and a large hand stirred the surface, flicking some of the water up into her face.

'*I wonder, by my troth, what thou and I Did, till we lov'd?*' Caradoc quoted softly in her ear.

She was completely undone. Where had he, an unlettered Welshman, learned such poetry? She held out her arms to him. 'Indeed, sir, I thought you might have already come and gone. Am I late?'

'Did we have an assignation to meet here?'

She nodded. 'I found it written in my heart.'

The horse shifted between the shafts of the carriage. Trudie whirled round, expecting to see Ah Nyiok's grinning face. There was no one there.

'I sent him back to Malacca on my mount,' Caradoc Rhys told her. 'I'll drive you back in the carriage myself.'

She smiled, very glad to see him. 'I have so many things to tell you,' she began.

'Later,' he said. He held her tightly against him and kissed her. '*For God's sake hold your tongue, and let me love.*'

'Oh, *yes*!' she agreed. She kissed him back and then she chuckled with sheer happiness. 'John Donne is most frightfully improper! Where did you get to know him?'

He tapped her on the cheek with two fingers which were hard and calloused from the physical work he had done all his life long. 'Where did you?' he retorted.

Chapter Twenty-six

While Caradoc was seeing to the horse, Trudie walked up to the little Hindu shrine, wanting to see for herself what it was like. It turned out to be a small cave, draped about with colourful materials. In the centre was a representation of the strangest being Trudie had ever seen. He was coloured blue, had any number of arms, all of which seemed to be engaged in a separate occupation of its own, and the most hideous expression painted on to his face. Beside him was a spike sticking out of a circular platform, the sexual connotations of which were obvious even to her. She wondered what it all meant. The surrounding ground was littered with small offerings of fruit and flowers, some of them set out in patterns. She wished she had thought to bring something herself.

She was unprepared for the sudden materialization of the holy man beside her. His astonishment at seeing a European lady, dressed in one of the new crinolines, which had lost its domed look and now hung straight to a wide hem, was comic to see. Trudie stood in silence, unconsciously giving Caradoc below a very good view of the bow at the waist at the back, and the way the overskirt was scooped up on to either hip. It was not a very suitable dress for the middle of the jungle.

Trudie waited for him to speak, while he stared at her in return. Finally, Trudie inclined her head to him, gathered up her skirts and started down the hill again.

'Satisfied?' Caradoc asked her.

'I'm trying,' she said, her colour mounting alarmingly,

'to learn restraint. I need it,' she added, 'to become a truly civilized person.'

His laughter made her ears burn. 'Restraint? You, *cariad*?'

'Why not?'

'If I told you, you'd blush even more than you are now! Looking up at you, I could see how delightfully pretty you are, and how ridiculous that widow's cap is that you've taken to wearing!'

It was her turn to laugh. 'Pretty, Caradoc? You must be besotted!'

'Would that be so difficult for you to believe?'

Her mouth felt dry and she had difficulty in swallowing. 'I'll never be *pretty*!'

'Well, no,' he admitted. 'Pretty is the wrong word. You've come to be my ideal of what a woman should be though, pretty or not. To me, you're beautiful. Will you try to believe that?'

She was very much moved. She wished she could think of something equally lovely to say to him, but all she said, in fact, was, 'Big feet and all?'

'Golden Lilies can never appeal to anyone not brought up to admire them,' he assured her. 'Still worrying about Black Jade?'

'No, I'm being surprisingly restrained about that! She wants to do it, Caradoc. She's chosen to be a Nonya. I don't understand why that has to be a part of it, but I shan't interfere. It's a hard lesson to learn that we Europeans are not always right about everything, but I think I learned that much from Wu Chao. I'm only Black Jade's second mother.'

'It's a lesson most of us never learn.'

She leaned against him, enjoying the strength in his tall, hard body. When she shut her eyes and imagined herself back in Wales, she could see how well he would fit in there. He had an affinity with the glorious coastline, just as she felt herself to be as restless and as seeking as the sea. She had been jealous of him for a short time, when she had been staying in the *Tŷ un nos* he and his mother had built when he had been but a boy. She had lain awake and wondered what other girls he had known and whether he had loved any of them, as she wanted to be loved by him. Now, it didn't matter to her how many other women had shared his bed, or even stolen some small corner of his heart in the past. Today he was hers.

'Make love to me!' she begged him. 'There's none to see us here!'

'I would, if I could be sure you know what you're doing! Sweetheart, you may be styled a widow – '

'And a lady!' she reminded him, tapping her foot on the ground.

He grinned. 'Restraint, love. Remember?'

'I don't think this is what Swee Neo had in mind!'

'No? But I think she might point out to you how unequal we are in every way that matters, though. It could be disastrous for you to stoop – '

She rounded on him. '*Stoop?* Did you say stoop, Caradoc Rhys? I've heard a great deal of nonsense on this topic recently, but nobody had the audacity to imagine that I might be *stooping* to your level! Great God in heaven, I could box your ears for you!'

'Such restraint!' he mocked.

'Well, I could! Honestly, Caradoc, how anyone as big as you are can think that anyone as small as I am is going to *stoop* to your level, when it's obviously ridiculous – well, isn't it?'

'You can't make a silk purse out of a sow's ear, nor a gentleman out of an ex-miner!'

'I shan't try,' she retorted.

'Have you thought what your friends will say? Your family?'

She looked at him. 'What friends? You'll be telling me next that I have so many! There's only you.'

'Isn't Mrs Beresford your friend?'

She went very white, and then red again. 'Yes. She knows I hope to marry you – '

'Are you going to tell me she *approves* of that?'

She nodded. 'I won't say she did at first, but once we had discussed the alternatives, she quite saw why I should wish to have you as my husband. Both she and her husband will attend our wedding with as much pomp and circumstance as they can devise. She knows you to be a good man, you see. More, she knows that I need you.' Trudie's voice quivered almost out of control. 'I don't think I can manage without you, Caradoc.'

His concern was immediate and entirely for her. 'You, my love? What do you need me for? You have your own business, a money-making machine if ever I saw one – '

She looked down her nose. 'You ought to know. Money isn't everything!'

'Let's talk about you as a businesswoman first. The other can come later.'

She glanced up at him through her lashes, willing to oblige him, though she felt it to be a waste of time. She sighed. 'Did you imagine I wouldn't examine every detail of the accounts of the business while I had been away?'

'And?'

'Of course the Kis wrote everything down – a lot of it in Chinese characters so that foreign devils, like myself, can only guess *all* that they've been up to! But somebody else had checked every entry long before I got back from

England. It didn't take me very long to guess who that someone might be!'

'You didn't say anything. I was afraid you might resent my interest in your affairs. We'd each make our own million, that was the agreement. I was afraid you'd think I was trying to cheat you!'

'I thought nothing of the sort! When did you learn to read Chinese?'

'I don't. Ki Thian Heow has become a friend of mine and we devised the system together. We both thought it better that someone besides the Kis should represent your interests. Did I presume too much?'

'Don't be silly! Don't you realize that when we marry, everything I have will be yours, anyway. If you want to, you can forbid me to take any further interest in the business, the Emporium – all of it!'

Caradoc clenched his teeth. 'I'll make my own million before I do that!' His glance was sober. 'I'll never be jealous of you, Trudie, not for your ability to make money better than I ever shall. I don't think you less of a woman for that, nor myself less of a man!'

She sighed. 'You must be unique in that,' she murmured with ill-concealed bitterness.

His eyes flashed in response to the look in hers. 'Perhaps I know you better than anyone else – the real you! I shan't claim your business from you, Trudie, no matter what the law allows. Will you trust me in that?'

'Trust you with such a small thing? I trust you with my life, *cariad*. Now will you make love to me?'

His arms closed about her. '*Cariad!* Spoken like a Welsh woman! I shall have to teach you some other words of Europe's oldest language – '

'Is Welsh so old?'

'Ask my mother, if you don't believe me. There is one

older language, or so she once told me, spoken by some people called Basques in the north of Spain.'

'How much you know!' she exclaimed. 'Was it really only a dame school you went to? My brothers all went to Harrow – and hated it! – but they know nothing of the sort of things you tell me about.' She stood on tiptoe, intimating that she wished to get closer still to his laughing face. 'John Donne! None of them would quote such a man to me, I assure you!'

'Why not? He was a clergyman, like your father – '

She turned away, her face closing down before his very eyes. 'Not at all like my father!'

He withdrew also. 'Why do you say that?'

'John Donne loved his wife. He was put in prison for marrying her and, after she died, he mourned her for the rest of his life.'

'And how do you know so much about him? Don't tell me your governess ever read his love poetry to you?'

'No. I "met" him, as Black Jade would say, in St Paul's. His tomb was the only one that survived the Great Fire when Old St Paul's was burned down. He stands in a corner, wearing a shroud, and looking as sad as I used to feel. I always thought we had a great deal in common. I bought a book of his sermons and poems with my very own money and used to read him by the hour when I was confined to my room.'

'And did that happen often?' he asked stiffly.

'Yes.'

'Your father?'

'Yes,' she said again.

'It will not be like that for your children!' he said at last. 'I can't bear to think of you locked away from the sun and the fresh air!'

She thought she would burst for love of him. 'My

bedroom was more comfortable than your Welsh mines. The whole of your "overnight house" would have fitted easily into it.'

He looked at her with an intensity that made her wonder if she had said too much. 'What did you really think of Wales?' he asked her.

'I thought it beautiful.'

'My mother wrote that you lived like one of the family the whole time you were there – '

She took his hands in hers. 'I hope to *be* one of the family.'

She watched his doubts slip away from him and was glad. There were so many things she wanted to tell him, point out to him, things that would have explained her side of the argument so that he would never have those doubts about her again, but, as usual, the right words eluded her and she was afraid her blunt tongue would do more damage than if she were to say nothing and hope he would know, as he seemed to know so much else about her, without her needing to tell him at all.

He frowned. 'We are good together, aren't we?'

She touched his cheek with the side of her finger, enjoying the rough feel of his beard. 'Very good.' She made a face at him. 'We read the same poets, do we not?'

There was none of the answering laughter she expected. Instead, he reached into the carriage and lifted out the rug that had been folded away on one corner of the seat. In silence, he spread it on the ground, sitting down in the middle of it and gesturing to her to take her place beside him.

Now that the moment had come, Trudie wondered if she had been wise to throw herself at him. It was not conduct of which anyone she knew could approve. What if she had over-persuaded him? What if he didn't really want her? What if he were to despise her because she didn't know what he expected of her?

She lowered herself to the ground beside him, her limbs as stiff as if they had been carved out of wood. 'Caradoc,' she whispered, 'should we wait until we're married, after all?'

'Is that what you want to do?'

'I don't know,' she said with her customary frankness. 'I don't know what I want. I don't know very much about it.'

She was grateful to him that he didn't laugh at her. He was as solemn as a judge. Nor did he say anything.

She glared at him. 'I suppose you're an expert!' she challenged him.

He laughed then. He pulled her down against him and kissed her until she forgot her nerves and began to relax. This was Caradoc Rhys, not some monster of her imagination. Caradoc Rhys, the chosen love of her life.

'I love you!'

Saying it out loud was oddly reassuring. She had loved Caradoc for so very long, deceiving herself at first that she thought of him not as a man but as a different species of person altogether. She knew now there had never been a time when she had not been comforted to know him there, the man she would have chosen for herself, no matter what the circumstances. Telling herself it was an impossible marriage had been no more than a game she had played, like the child she still frequently was.

'Trudie, does it bother you that if I become your husband, I can control both you and your possessions?'

'I think it unjust,' she answered seriously. 'That it is you doesn't bother me at all. I shall never want to have any secrets from you. I love you! That the law allows any man to own his wife's possessions as if she were a slave is still unjust, though. As the Chinese say, it's the women who hold up half the sky, but what reward do they ever see for it?'

'I shall never want to take what is yours away from you.'

'You don't have to tell me that! But men do marry women for the basest of reasons. My father married my mother for her West Indian possessions – her sugar and her slaves. He wouldn't have looked at her, otherwise. Do you think Jack Taviton wanted to marry me for my gentle manners and my good nature?'

'There are no slaves in Wales!' he said thoughtfully. 'The English would make slaves of us, but the Welsh have never given a button for the differences between gentlemen and other folk. To be Welsh is enough for any man!'

Trudie thought that was probably true. Caradoc's parents had treated each other as equals, and it had probably been no different when Levi Rhys had been a whole man and had been the breadwinner of his family.

He began undoing the buttons of her bodice. It took a long time and, after a while, she started to help him, her fingers more nimble than his as she slipped the tiny pieces of bone through their embroidered fasteners. Her clothes had not been designed with making love *al fresco* in mind. Her amusement at their plight put the last of her nervousness to flight.

'Why don't you take off your own clothes?' she suggested finally. 'It'll take me ages to deal with these knots. I have to remove my crinoline yet – '

'It's a cage!' he discovered. 'What on earth is it made of?'

'Watch-spring steels.'

'What an incredible thing fashion is! I always thought of you wearing at least a dozen skirts!'

She was touched that he should have thought of her in that way. 'In this heat?' she teased him.

He mastered the last of the buttons, revealing her chemise underneath. Frustrated, he began to kiss her again, the embrace becoming more hectic as he tried to reach her breasts and failed.

'Very well, I'll take a shower in the waterfall, while you remove your plated armour!' he agreed.

She stroked his hair, marvelling at the tough, vibrant feel of it beneath her fingers. 'I think it would be better. If I'd known you wanted to undress me I would have worn something simpler. It was vanity that made me put on my prettiest dress, wanting to please you.' She smiled a small, ironic smile. 'My lack of experience! I don't know how I imagined it would be – I didn't know.'

'Of course you didn't know!' he lay flat on his back, grinning. 'Why don't you cut those strings?'

He grasped her by the arms, forgetting to be gentle, reversing their positions on the rug with one, easy movement. His weight excited her body, interfering with her breathing. She looked up into his dark eyes, seeing herself in miniature in his pupils. She felt herself blushing, but she made no move to look away. He deserved his triumph, she thought.

'With Jeremy it would have been without love. I am grateful to him, Caradoc, as I always must be, but it was you who taught me to love. I never knew love before I knew you, not even affection, except of the most dutiful kind. I'm more of a virgin than you can ever know!'

He buried his face between her breasts. Then he said something in Welsh with such passion that she didn't dare ask for a translation. She felt singed by the heat in his voice, but not damaged. On the contrary, she was the stronger for it, forged in the flames of his love.

'Go and have your shower!' she urged him.

It was easier with him gone to undress more quickly. Even so, it took courage to step out of the last of her clothes. Embarrassed by the sight of her own nakedness, she draped the rug around her shoulders and set herself to wait for Caradoc to come back to her. When she had accustomed herself a little bit to her new state, she forgot her self-consciousness sufficiently to look round to see where he had got to. He was standing, stark naked, in the waterfall, looking so beautiful that she was breathless for a moment, just drinking in the sight of him.

His nakedness didn't shock her as much as it might have done if he had been a less splendid animal. When he turned and came towards her, she never gave a thought to her own emotions, so intent was she on the discoveries she was making about him.

He took the rug from around her shoulders, looking at her with the same appreciation as that with which she had looked at him. 'You're beautiful!' he exclaimed.

She was more embarrassed by his words than she had been by their mutual nakedness. 'Not like you!' she burst out.

His laughter warmed her. She stood to one side while he spread the rug again, not allowing herself to make too much of the glances he threw her over his shoulder, nor even when he stood beside her, putting his arms about her and running his hands down the smooth slopes of her back down to her buttocks and back up over her hips to her breasts.

'I wish I were beautiful!' she exclaimed. 'Oh, Caradoc, you deserve better than such an inadequate woman – '

He lifted her off her feet, lying her gently on the rug and settling himself down beside her. 'If there ever comes a time when I should meet your father, he will be lucky to survive the encounter!' he growled. 'How could any man prefer your Cousin Hermione?'

Trudie made a last effort to be just. 'She is golden and blue-eyed and I have always understood she is everything most men want!'

'She wouldn't do for me!'

He tried to be gentle. He teased her nipples into peaks and spoke the most wonderful words to her, but her first experience of his loving was not a success. She forced herself to accept his invasion of her body, even to welcome him, but when he had done she felt battered and bruised, and even tearful.

Caradoc held her very close. 'It'll be different next time,' he promised her.

She cursed the fact that he could read her so exactly. With another man she might have been able to pretend. 'I failed you, didn't I?' she moaned. 'I ruined it for you, too?'

He waited until he had her full attention, exploring the planes of her body with gentle fingers. 'My dearest one, I hope to have and share your body for the rest of our lives. Just as it took me hours to work out exactly how you keep your accounts, it will take us a little while to match each other's skill in making love, to learn each other, if you like. For me, this was a glorious beginning because I love you. My only regret is that I wasn't able to make it perfect for you. Perhaps I didn't expect as much as you did, because I know we have to grow into each other.'

She sighed, only a little mollified. 'I wish I had one half your wisdom, Mr Rhys!'

'Mine?' She had startled him again. 'I'm not a learned man – '

'I know. You're only an ex-miner. Caradoc, please teach me to please you better. Give me another chance to be more what you want?'

He kissed her lips. 'Your pleasure is important to me, too,' he told her. 'It'll come in time, *cariad*. Don't expect too much too quickly. Get dressed now and we'll go to the plantation. We can try again tonight.'

She tried to rise, astonished by the weakness that had grasped her knees. 'I think you may have to help me!' she said in an accusing voice. And then, when he broke into delighted laughter, 'It isn't funny, you great beast! I may never be the same again!'

'I hope you never will be,' he answered her. 'I hope you'll never be unloved again.'

It could have been no more than the Welsh way with words, but she thought she would keep them close in her heart for ever. How much she loved him, but words didn't come easily to her as they did to him. She hoped that as she learned to love him, she would learn also the words to tell him so.

The jungle had never been more beautiful as they covered the miles to the boundary of where what was now Black Jade's land began. Trudie was astonished by the changes that had been made since she had last seen it. An army of men must have been employed to tidy up the land, push back the encroaching jungle, and plant it. Great tracts had been flooded for the growing of rice, the brightness of the green hurting the eye in the late afternoon sun. There were groves of palm trees, useful for the oil they produced, and areas given over to the production of the tropical fruits that grew everywhere on the peninsula. Apart from the bananas, papayas, mangoes and all the others, pineapples had been planted out in long lines. Better still, to Trudie's eye, was to see that the house where she had lived had been completely restored and realigned in accordance with the principles of *Feng Shui*. Whereas, before, it had had a lopsided look to it, it now stood foursquare and proud, as welcoming as before it had been a disappointment to her.

'What's happened to Wu Chao's house?' she asked Caradoc.

'The Kis had it razed to the ground. There have been many changes since you were last here. One of the most significant is the guards who keep watch at night across the plantation. The opium trail has to go another way these days.'

'The Kis are very much against the poppy,' Trudie agreed. 'Yet the trade is quite legal.'

Caradoc looked grim. 'One day we'll pay for encouraging that trade,' he said.

Trudie was thoughtful. 'I was surprised by the number of people who seem to smoke opium in England now. It's the cure-all for everything from toothache to a fit of the miseries. Perhaps that's why I can't quite hate Cousin Hermione, not as I did at first. It was my own father who taught her to smoke, and other things as well, I dare say. He can see nothing wrong in it.'

Caradoc nodded. 'Is that how it was?'

'One day I'll tell you what it was like to live in that house,' she said with a mirthless laugh. She was silent for the space of a second, then she went on, 'I hated Septimus becoming a Catholic. It seemed a betrayal. Father hates the new "ritualists" and all that – at least, he preaches against them all the time.' She paused again. 'Hell is a very cold place. Don't believe them when they tell you of the fires of hell. There aren't any flames at all. It's cold and grey and without love. Poor Black Jade couldn't understand why anyone should prefer death to life, but people do. My father does.' She shivered. 'Wu Chao was the first person I ever knew who surrounded herself with colour and laughter and said that *living* was what it was all about. God is life. Do you believe that?'

Caradoc shrugged. 'I believe God is greater than any thoughts I may have about him. I've always been too busy to worry about Him much. *Alahu akbar!* God is great!'

Her brow creased thoughtfully. 'Isn't that what the Moslems say when they pray?'

'Maybe it isn't what you say, but what you believe inside that counts,' he suggested. 'Some choose life, and some death, both sure that theirs is the only way. I don't think you need worry too much, love!' he added roughly.

He led the way into the newly reconstructed house, lifting her off her feet and carrying her across the threshold.

'Aren't we going to your house?' she asked him.

'This is my house now. I'm told it's a very lucky place. Whatever it is, welcome to it, my love!'

He put her down on the floor, watching her as she looked about her, at the newly polished wood of the floor, the freshly painted walls with their decorations of carved wood representing scenes from Malay life. Obviously, he had gone to some trouble to try to please her, but the results were terrible to her. To begin with, where had all the furniture come from? A few lacquered pieces, inlaid with flowers and leaves, were probably a legacy from the days when Wu Chao had lived on the plantation. The rest could have been picked up at any jumble sale, and there was far too much of it! English stuffed chairs that had seen better days and badly wanted re-covering. And there was a huge four-poster bed, a mosquito net wrapped round it, like paper round a parcel.

'Will it do?' he asked her anxiously.

She thought of her own house in Malacca and the many hours she had spent buying the exact piece of furniture she had wanted for every room. It had taken her years to get it exactly as she wanted it, a mixture of European and

Chinese furnishings that blended and formed the background she wanted for herself. Compared with that, this was chaos. Furniture had been shoved inside and pushed in a straight line round the walls, without any consideration as to how the pieces complemented others in the room.

With a visible effort, Trudie stifled the cry of dismay that came to her lips. There would be all the time in the world to make the changes she wanted to give the house the style he had sought and had failed to find. It had the same feel as the 'overnight house' in Wales, where there had never been any other choice than to pile everything in as best one could.

'You have some lovely pieces of furniture!' she said aloud.

'But they don't look right,' he said on a note of exasperation. 'I keep moving everything round, but it doesn't get any better.'

'I'll do it for you,' she said gently. 'But not today.'

'It isn't good enough for you! While you were away in England, I kept looking round your house, wondering how I'd ever pluck up the audacity to ask you to live with me here. I even asked Whampoa to pick me out a few good Chinese pieces, and he did, but they don't look as well as I'd hoped they would.'

She leaned against him, smiling up at him. So, all the nerves hadn't been on her side, she thought. He, too, had had his moments of doubt that they could ever find a place where they could meet as equals.

'I'm not much of a housekeeper, but I can arrange furniture. I've always liked doing it. I turned my old schoolroom into a sitting-room in my father's house and, although I say it myself, it was by far the most fashionable room in the house!'

'I wanted it to be perfect for you!' And he was not only talking about the house.

Worse was to follow when the Malay servant that Caradoc employed reluctantly brought their evening meal. He moved about the room, lighting the lamps, muttering imprecations at Trudie.

'Why does he object to me so much?' Trudie asked, puzzled.

'He knows things will change with a *mem* in charge. I haven't the time to check his kitchen accounts every week. He probably gets away with murder, adding squeeze for all his relatives.'

Trudie tasted the meat dish that had been set down before her. 'He's a terrible cook!' she decided. 'Even if he didn't know we were coming.'

Caradoc merely looked at her. Trudie took another mouthful, found it totally inedible and swallowed it whole.

'You won't live here, will you?' Caradoc muttered.

'Indeed, I will! There will have to be a few changes, that's all!'

'It's hard to find a cook right out here, or any servants, come to that.'

Trudie straightened her back and nodded. 'Well, I'm sorry, Caradoc, but somebody will have to be found! I can make your house comfortable, and beautiful, too, but I never learned to cook and I can't think the results would be much better than this muck if I were to try! Swee Neo keeps my house for me in Malacca, which is highly satisfactory because I'm very fond of my food. I refuse to starve – or even to fast for a few days! – so we'll have to make other arrangements!'

'What other arrangements?' he demanded, fascinated.

Trudie thought for a moment, then she said, 'Ah Nyiok!

He's Swee Neo's new cook, a *sinkeh* of only a few days. You met him! He was the one who drove me out to the waterfall and who took your horse home again.' She grinned, delighted with her solution. 'Swee Neo may never forgive me, of course, but she will soon see that my need is greater than hers!'

'But will he come so far from Malacca?' Caradoc wondered.

'I think he may. He makes kites for a hobby. He'll have plenty of room out here to fly them and show them off to his customers. It'll keep him out of the gambling hells of Malacca until he has some money put by, which he won't like at all, but which Swee Neo will approve of, dearly as she loves to gamble, too!'

'I've never known a Chinese who didn't!' Caradoc remarked. 'They even have a god of gambling in one of the temples in Singapore. He tells you which number to back – for a small fee – '

Trudie's eyes lit. 'Is he always right?'

'All gamblers lose in the end,' he retorted piously.

She sat very straight, looking the picture of guilt, for she dearly loved a good gamble herself. Then she saw that he was smiling and she relaxed a little. 'I only gamble at cards,' she said.

'*Cher kee?*'

She nodded, wrinkling her nose. 'Only, I always lose at that!'

The noises of the jungle seemed familiar and reassuring to her when they had finished eating. If it had not been for the mosquitoes and the other insects, she would have suggested they sit on the verandah to drink their coffee and listen to the sounds of the night.

'Has there been any more trouble from the Tamils?' she asked. 'That is why you were sent for, isn't it?'

'It's their living conditions that cause them to revolt. Your husband, God rest him, gave them the minimum of shelter and did his best to destroy their family life. He wasn't interested in the plantation as such, only *bhang* and the money he could make from it – '

'Opium?'

Caradoc nodded. 'If he hadn't died when he had, I was handing in my notice. But then you came along, and nothing would have made me leave after that!'

Trudie looked thoughtful. 'I had an idea that, this time, someone was deliberately stirring up the Tamils. Wasn't that true?'

'Mr Christopher Horton? It could be. He hasn't forgiven me for closing down his enterprises here. None of his businesses have been doing too well recently, but the Kis won't stand for him coming back here.'

'I wondered if the Kis weren't behind most of his troubles?' Trudie suggested.

'Better not to ask,' he answered.

'Much better!' she agreed dryly.

They laughed together, enjoying the easy understanding between them. It was time for bed almost before Trudie was aware.

'You don't have to go through with it, my love,' Caradoc said, very gently. 'I can take you home tomorrow, and wait until you're ready to marry me. You don't have to decide anything now.'

Trudie walked over to the four-poster bed, lifting the mosquito net and staring into its depths. It had been pulled together, rather than made, and the sheets were far from the clean, freshly ironed ones that she always found on her bed in Malacca.

She turned back to Caradoc, wondering how she could tell him how she felt. She had never thought of herself as being over-fastidious, but the way he lived was never going to suit her. Then she caught sight of the anxiety at the back of his eyes and knew she didn't have to tell him anything that he didn't already know.

'It'll do for tonight,' she said, 'but I can't live like this!'

He sighed deeply in relief. 'As long as you think you can make something of the place!'

'Not me! Ah Nyiok! I wouldn't know where to begin!'

'And tonight?' he said.

She put her hand in his. 'I love you, Caradoc Rhys. I always have and, God willing, I always shall. I only want to be a good wife to you – with your help!'

Long hours later, Caradoc lay sleeping beside her, exhausted from their lovemaking as she should have been, too. If their first time had been something of a disaster, he had determined that this time she would know the same ecstasy that he had found in her body. He had laboured long, encouraging her to relax, to forget her fears, and to reach out for that moment when she was one with the whole of creation, and most of all with himself. She had followed his lead, taking the first steps towards a heart-wrenching moment of discovery when she had known exactly why she loved him and why he was the only man in the world for her.

And then he had fallen asleep, leaving her to stare, sleepless, into the darkness, wondering how it was that no one had ever told her of this glorious side of marriage. If this was how children were made, she told herself, she was probably destined to have an exceedingly large family!

But not living as Caradoc seemed to live! She thought back to the life he had known in Wales, the overcrowded little house, filled with smoke and the smell of cooking and human sweat as often as not. That might do for him, but it wouldn't do for her. Before she walked down any aisle and made the vows that would make her into his wife, there was much to be done.

She prodded him in the ribs and he turned on his back, grumbling in his sleep. 'I love you very much, Caradoc Rhys!' she told him.

His arms came around her body, pulling her close against him. 'I love you too!' he said, and slept again.

Chapter Twenty-seven

'*O Nghariad i.*'

She had no idea what it meant. It didn't matter to her. It was the tone of voice in which it was whispered. If he had been wholly awake, he would have addressed her in English: the Welsh was a compliment, a confirmation that she was right for him. *Set me as a seal upon thine heart*, she had said. When she was truly moved, odd phrases of the Bible often drifted into her mind, phrases that reminded her of the happier moments of childhood. And he had answered *O Nghariad i*, and she had known that it was the most beautiful thing he could have said to her.

Her own mention of seals had put something else into her mind. On the day of their marriage, Caradoc would legally own everything that was hers. Nothing either of them could do could change that. Yet, he knew how much it meant to her, how closely she had guarded her business secrets from everyone else. She didn't want to have any secrets from him, though, even if he were not entitled to the information anyway.

She always kept her own seal with her. Called a 'chop', it had her name written in Chinese characters on it and, with it, she could authenticate any of the necessary documents simply by inking up the characters and stamping them on to the relevant documents. She and Wu Chao had had their 'chops' made together, the one completing the other. Since Wu Chao's death, Trudie had held them both. Her own was made of jade, carved with the Rat symbol of her birth. Wu Chao's represented a Temple Lion, a tiny ball of gold in the beast's mouth.

She took the lion chop out of her reticule and set it on the table beside the bed, impatient for the moment when Caradoc finally opened his eyes.

'What are you doing, up and dressed?' he grumbled, when he finally surfaced out of the deep sleep he had been enjoying. 'I was planning on a late morning – a very late morning!'

'Oh, you were, were you? You've slept enough! We have things to do!'

He heard the asperity in her voice and grinned, stretching lazily. 'It wasn't sleeping I had in mind!'

He relished the pink that crept up her face, thinking what a strange mixture she was. She could buy and sell him in the market place, make a nonsense of his most closely reasoned arguments, and yet be as shy as a young bird in bed. Not that that would last long, for the generosity of her passion had already startled him. He believed her, too, when she claimed that only he held the key to all that love she held inside her. Many would condemn him for marrying her, he knew, but he was giving as much as he was taking from her. She would never marry anyone else and it would have been a pity to waste all that she had kept locked away from her family and friends. Only Wu Chao had seen what nobody else had even suspected, that Trudie was starved for love and would repay any loving she received a hundredfold.

Trudie looked down at his recumbent form, her disapproval clear. 'It's time you got up! We must return to Malacca today and, before we go, I want to see the "lines" where the Tamils live for myself – '

'Why must we return to Malacca?'

'I want to get Ah Nyiok out here. I can't live in this

mess, Caradoc, and I'm hungry! I want something decent to eat!'

His shout of laughter should have warned her. Pushing back the bedclothes, he rose to his feet, pulling her against his naked body and kissing her hard on the lips.

'I'm going for a shower!' He smiled down at her. 'Send a message asking Ah Nyiok to come out here to us, bringing some food with him. If you want to see the "lines", I'll take you myself. They're bound to ask you to see their shadow play tonight, though, and they'll be offended if you don't go. Most of them regret the day *Mem* Tludie left the plantation.'

'I never even met any of them!' Trudie objected.

'They get their news from the jungle, like the Malays. Don't be surprised if they openly rejoice that your cousin is in financial difficulties. He used the whip too much to have been popular out here!'

Trudie's eyes rounded in horror. 'The whip?'

Caradoc shrugged. 'Power goes easily to some men's heads. Your cousin invented any number of fiddling rules to keep the Indians under his control, then he cut up really nasty when they refused to obey. One man died. Part of the trouble now is a whisper that he might win ownership of the plantation in court. None of them want to work for him.'

'I'm not surprised. Why are the Indians known as "Klings"?'

'They say here it's because most of them come from Kalingapatman in India. In Singapore, they're less kindly, and say it's the noise the prisoners' chains make, most of the Tamils down there being convicts finishing their sentences, doing hard labour all over the Empire. Ours are mostly free men.'

Trudie sniffed. 'I wonder if it's wise to build the Empire

on such harsh foundations. Such bitterness is seldom forgotten.'

'It's no worse than what they've left behind.'

'Possibly not. Will you ever forgive the mine-owners in Wales?'

She saw the way his fists clenched, though otherwise he was completely in control of himself. 'No,' he said at last.

'And you're one of the rulers here,' she reminded him.

'Me?' The very idea shocked him. 'They may call me *tuan*, but that's as far as it goes!'

She stood up, loving him. 'Nonsense, love! You're my chosen lord and master too, and I couldn't hope for anyone better.' She picked up Wu Chao's chop and held it out to him. 'I want you to have this.' She showed him her own chop and how the two of them fitted together to give complete control over her businesses. 'It was Wu Chao's,' she told him.

She went on to tell him about the 'Fo' lion and lioness that stood on either side of the entrance to every Chinese temple. 'The ball of gold is the sign of the male being the breadwinner. Wu Chao thought it very lucky. May it be very lucky for us! I'm sure it will be – if you want it to be.'

He held the lion chop on the palm of his hand, admiring the intricacy of its carving. 'When did you decide to give me this?' he asked her.

She gurgled with laughter. 'When you fell asleep and I wanted to talk! You sleep far too much!'

He was a long time answering her and, when he did, there was something very like wonder in his voice. 'You trust me, don't you?' he said.

She nodded. 'As I do myself. I love you.'

He was silent again, still staring at the lion chop, then, 'I'll never betray you,' he promised.

'I know that!' She frowned, putting her own chop back

in her reticule. 'What's more, the Kis know that too. They probably knew it before I did, or they wouldn't have allowed you access to all my accounts while I was in England.'

'I'll still never be a gentleman for you,' he said humbly.

Nor was it a recommendation that was likely to appeal to her! 'If we make enough money between us, you'll be accepted by the highest in the land!' she assured him with a cynicism that at another time would have amused him. 'Trade has become quite respectable and is likely to become more so! The Empire depends on it! Far more than on our soldier boys and the boys in blue, if the truth be known.' She smiled then, enjoying his pleasure in her gift to him. 'There's only one thing which is out of bounds to us, Mr Rhys. Opium. I promised Wu Chao I would never deal in the poppy, and never allow Black Jade to smoke, no matter what the temptations. *Bhang* and all its derivatives are out where we're concerned. Will you promise me that?'

'Some opium is needed by the pharmaceutical companies for the manufacture of morphine – '

'There are plenty of others to provide it.'

'Men like your cousin,' he agreed dryly. 'All right, I promise. I don't care for the trade myself.'

'Good,' she said.

No decent farmer would have kept his animals in the conditions the Tamils were expected to live under. Trudie was revolted by the broken-down shacks, the surrounding squalid mud and filth, and the dirty water supply. Back home in England, people were beginning to say that a clean water supply would cure most of the plagues that carried off the poor, and even the rich, every other year in increasing numbers. Cholera, typhoid, diphtheria, all would disappear, the doctors said, if everyone had access to a tap and a proper water supply. The other half of the problem was the drains, they declared. More and more, the open drains that had stunk in the summer and blocked up in winter were disappearing from the towns of England. In their place was being built an underground system of pipes, large enough for a man to walk in, which carried away the 'night dirt', as it was known in the Settlements.

Such thinking had obviously not reached any part of Malaya. The stink of the 'lines', as the shacks where the Tamils lived were called, reached Trudie long before she could even see the *attap* huts themselves, thatched with palm fronds, but so badly that when the rains came the roofs leaked like sieves. It was just as well that the monsoons mostly passed them by on the west side of the peninsula, Trudie thought, or these people might as well have been left to fend for themselves in the open.

White-faced, Trudie turned on Caradoc. 'They're a disgrace to civilization! Why do you allow such places to exist?'

He explained about the materials he had been given to work with; how the Klings were accustomed to such dwellings; how they wasted anything better that was offered to them: none of it altered Trudie's mind by so much as a fraction.

'Your mother would be ashamed of you!' she declared at last. 'She built your "overnight house" with her bare hands, and the help of a boy, so that you wouldn't have to live in complete squalor! What would she have thought of the argument that you weren't accustomed to anything better?'

'It wasn't all that good when it was finished!' he muttered.

'It was better than *this*!'

The children stood about in their rags, their beautiful wide brown eyes following every movement Trudie made.

Their mothers worked on, carrying water from the muddy river, pounding their rations of wheat into flour, or endlessly patting the dough into large flat pancakes ready for cooking. They were never to be seen doing nothing. From the first light of dawn until their cracked lamps ran out of oil, the women worked on in a ceaseless battle against the dirt and the hunger of their families.

'Such quarters can only breed disease and revolution! I shall speak to Mr Beresford about it!'

'The plantation isn't yours any more,' Caradoc reminded her. 'You'd do better to address your complaints to the Ki family.'

'I'll do that too!'

They went on to the nearest Malay *kampong*. By contrast, the compound was neatly swept and the houses well built, all in the Malacca style, on stilts, with the elaborate, tiled steps that led up to the verandah. The Malays were easy to get along with, living simply but well. They knew and understood the jungle in which they lived and made excellent guides and prospectors. They were less keen for the daily round of labour that their new British masters considered so desirable. They would work until they had made sufficient money to buy what they wanted and then they would return home, laughing off the inconvenience they had caused, and refusing to work again until there was something else they wanted to buy for money.

The headman received them with many smiles. His second wife brought tea and served it to them shyly, his first wife looking on to ensure that no mistakes were made.

Caradoc understood more Malay than did Trudie. He accepted the old man's invitation to a shadow play that evening, thinking it would amuse Trudie to see something whose origins disappeared into the mists of time. He, himself, had seen such performances many times, both the

Siamese and the Javanese varieties, and was familiar with the great Hindu epics of the post-Rigvedic period which formed the stories for both.

'We'll come back tonight,' he smiled at her.

'And what will you think up for the night after?'

He wasn't sure if she were serious or not. 'I'll take you home to Malacca tomorrow,' he promised.

Ah Nyiok arrived in the middle of the afternoon. He had his possessions wrapped up in a cloth and his man-sized kites tethered to the back of the cart he had borrowed for the journey. His silly grin already seemed delightfully familiar to Trudie.

She was sitting on the verandah when he arrived. He swept off his conical hat as soon as he saw her, kowtowing madly in the dust. 'The lady Swee Neo say *Nai-nai* has need of my services. I cook for you now, no?'

'Yes,' said Trudie. 'I hope the lady Swee Neo didn't mind your coming?'

He shook his head. 'She say by this time you velly hungry. She say cook good for you!'

'I'm certainly hungry!' Trudie agreed.

His grin grew broader. 'Then I make food right now!'

Ah Nyiok was useful in other ways. As soon as he had installed himself in the kitchen, cleaning everything to his own exacting standards, and chasing away anyone who thought to interfere with him, he willingly helped Trudie move furniture around the house until she was satisfied with the result.

'Better?' she asked him, wiping the sweat from her brow.

He looked about him, carefully changing the position of a vase in which she had placed a single flower. 'Not like home!' he moaned. 'But better, yes.'

As a reward, Trudie suggested the Chinese might go with them to see the Shadow Theatre.

'Anything after that marvellous meal!' Caradoc agreed.

Ah Nyiok bobbed his head, well pleased that his efforts had been appreciated by the *tuan*, no less. Trudie noticed that he was careful to take with him some of his kites *and* that he did good business with the Malays, who were as keen as he was on kite-flying competitions. Their other enthusiasm was bird-singing competitions and many of them had small song-birds tucked away in bamboo cages that they made themselves.

The headman seated his guests opposite the stage, the *panggong*, a twelve-foot platform of bamboos lashed together, made slightly higher at the back than the front. The *Dato' Dalam*, or *To' Dalang*, the Father of the Mysteries, sat himself down on the centre of the stage, with a screen about two feet in front of him. The seven puppets he used for the performance were put in the wings beside him. He used an oil lamp to reflect the shadows of the puppets on the screen.

A small band started to play the peculiar, sliding music of the East, and the performance began. It was simple to follow the basic story, of Rama's marriage to his wife Sita, and how she was stolen away by the evil King of Lanka; how Rama searches for her; how the Haniman, King of the Monkeys, helps him in his quest, the monkeys forming themselves into a living bridge for Rama to cross over to the Isle of Lanka and rescue his bride. The puppets danced and shook, looking unbelievably lifelike in the skilled hands of the Father of the Mysteries. The audience applauded, hissed and marvelled over the story, entering into it with all the zest of children at a pantomime.

'We had a shadow theatre at home,' Trudie remembered, 'but it was nothing like this! I used to invent endless stories for the characters to perform. I'm afraid Septimus was my only audience, however, unless I could coerce the maids to come up to my room and watch.'

She had just finished speaking, when a Chinese came into the *kampong*, circling round the ring of light and stopping only when he came up behind Caradoc's chair. He whispered urgently into his ear, waiting for the Welshman's nod to see that he understood the message. Then, as silently as he had come, he slipped away.

For a moment, Trudie thought he had been a figment of her imagination, in his ragged shirt and short trousers, and with a thin, wispy queue hanging down his back. He had had the half-starved look of some of the mining *sinkehs* before they had earned enough money to set themselves up as real miners, pulling down a real miner's wages.

'Who was that?' Trudie whispered to Caradoc.

'Afterwards,' he answered.

They had Ah Nyiok with them as they walked away from the *kampong* to their own compound. The Chinese went ahead of them, carrying a burning torch to light their way. His hand shook slightly every time an animal in the jungle roared, betraying his city origins. Trudie hoped he would soon get used to living miles from others of his kind. She needed his cooking too much to do without him.

'Who was that extraordinary man?' she asked Caradoc again as they reached their own house.

'He came from Whampoa.' Caradoc looked as grim as his words. 'He came to tell us that the Ki family's revenge is complete.'

Trudie felt as though the bottom had fallen out of her stomach. It was as if all her fears had come into focus in this one, dreadful moment. She saw the world through a haze of guilt, because she couldn't feel any sorrow, or even pity, whatever the fate which had befallen her cousins.

'Are they dead?' she asked, as if from a great distance.

Caradoc took most of her weight as they mounted the steps up to the verandah of their own house.

'Are they dead?' she asked again, as he fastened the blinds against the mosquitoes before he lit the lamps.

'I don't know.'

She thought she would have nightmares for the rest of her life, with strange Chinese coming and going, without sound or difficulty, when she knew that none but the Malays themselves were able to walk about in the jungle without getting lost. It was well known that only the Malays could find their *kampongs*, or know which part of the jungle they were in. Everyone else was lost a few feet from a path they travelled every day. So where had the Chinese come from, and where had he disappeared to after he had delivered his message?

'Who was that man?' she asked Caradoc, not really expecting an answer.

It was a moment before Caradoc answered. 'I've seen him before – up in the mines. I don't know his name.'

'A *sinkeh*?'

'No. Second generation at least. He's Straits Chinese all right. At a guess, I'd say his mother's Malay.'

'Ah, hence his ability to walk round the jungle.'

'He was probably brought up around this place. He's a Moslem, did you notice?'

'How did you know?'

Caradoc touched his forehead. 'He has a mark here. It comes from saying one's prayers five times a day, as only the Moslems do . . .'

'Other people pray!'

'But not with the regular formality of the Moslems.'

'Perhaps not. I didn't know a Baba could be anything else but Chinese in his religion.'

'There are a few Moslems, a few Hindus, even a few Christians. Most of them are the same mixture of Taoist/Confucian/Buddhist as their ancestors.'

Trudie was grateful to think about something other than her cousins. 'It seems hard to remember now that such a tolerant people should have wanted to put an end to Black Jade when she was born! Just because she was a girl – '

Caradoc grinned. 'It would have been different if her father had been Chinese and her mother *fan-poh*. What future did the poor child have with a dead European father?'

'She had Wu Chao for her mother!'

'I think the Kis were ashamed they had married her out of their own people. I hate to think what would have happened if you hadn't come along!'

'Me? What difference did I make?'

'Don't you know?'

She thought perhaps she did. She had acted as guarantor for the child's future – as anyone else would have done in the same circumstances.

'What does *fan-poh* mean?'

'A local native woman.'

She walked into the circle of Caradoc's arms, leaning her head against his shoulder. 'I have so much to learn still about life out here, but we both belong here and nowhere else, don't we?'

'Yes, we belong.'

'No thanks to my cousins!' she said with some asperity.

She thought about telling Caradoc how, even if they were dead, she couldn't grieve for them as a cousin should, but there was no reason for him to share her guilt. All her life long, she had known the same frozen wasteland where there should have been a warm affection for her family. For her sisters and for her youngest brother, she had felt a little, but she had loved Wu Chao far more. If Cousin Hermione was dead, she would try to be sorry, but really she knew she would feel only relief.

'Do you think one has to learn to love when one is very young?' she asked suddenly.

'Maybe some of us do.' He ran a finger over her lips. 'You don't give yourself enough credit. You make me very happy.'

It was so comfortable to be with him, she thought. It was like being by herself, for she didn't have to pretend to something she hadn't yet grasped. He didn't seem to mind her limitations, that she was not invincible. On the contrary, he seemed to love her more for her failings than for her triumphs. It was very reassuring. She tried to imagine anyone else she knew fitting in so well with her every mood and the rough edges of her character. There was no one. Not even Wu Chao would have been so long-suffering of her hesitations and doubts before she had given her heart. Only Caradoc fitted her like her other half.

She tried to tell him so, but Caradoc didn't believe in words when he had action at his disposal. He made love to her more gently and more thoroughly than he ever had before, until her whole world was filled with him and his loving.

It wasn't until the next day that she thought of the fate of her cousins again.

Caradoc drove her home in silence. They rested only briefly at the waterfall and again in the Malay village. The headman served them tea and teased Caradoc gently for not having passed through his village on the day he had been expected. Trudie sat beside Caradoc in silence, for once not minding being ignored, not until the headman motioned towards her and said, 'You have heard the news, *tuan*?'

Caradoc nodded. 'I have heard. Are they dead?'

The headman nodded. 'It was very dreadful. Some intruder managed to get inside their house and murdered them both with a *kris*. The weapon would suggest it was a Malay, don't you think?'

'Is that what the police are saying?'

'It has been said.'

Trudie would have questioned him further but, when she pulled on Caradoc's sleeve to hush up so that she could speak, for once he wasn't prepared to give way to her. Face, she thought. He would lose face if he couldn't control the woman who was with him. It was a man's business to ask the questions, just as it was a man's business to answer him. Very well, she would find the women and put her questions to them!

Caradoc quelled her with a glance. He thanked the headman for his hospitality and helped her back into the carriage, the same stony expression on his face.

'You usually have better manners,' he said at last, when they were already outside the *kampong*.

'They were *my* cousins!'

'And you are my woman now. Please don't forget it again.'

It was not a side of Caradoc she had ever seen before. Mentally, she shrugged her shoulders, grinning to herself. So Caradoc didn't like being crowded any more than did any other man! Truth to tell, she liked him the better for it.

'Do you want me to apologize?' she asked him abruptly.

'That won't be necessary – this time!'

There was a gleam of amusement at the back of his eyes also. She allowed her smile to show. 'Well, I am sorry. I had forgotten your face means as much to you as mine does to me.'

'It's our joint face that's important to me. You would have lost face just as surely as I would have done!'

She flushed, acknowledging the truth of that. 'I've been making my own decisions without reference to anyone else for too long. I am sorry, Caradoc. You will have to teach me better manners for both our sakes!'

'My dearest one, I'm not the sort of man who takes pleasure in beating his wife. I have nothing to teach you that you don't already know.'

'You have much to teach me about loving!'

He stopped the carriage and kissed her. 'The love was always there inside you. What else would have brought a man like me to your feet?'

She put her head on one side, determined to get an answer to a question she had always wanted to ask him. 'Didn't you ever envy Mr Maddock having Wu Chao as a wife?'

'No, I didn't envy him Wu Chao.'

'He had other women?'

'He had you.'

'But you didn't know me then!' She was inclined to be indignant, thinking he was making sport of her.

'I knew about you,' he said simply. 'I saw your picture. I knew Jeremy Maddock didn't deserve a woman like you.'

'You didn't like him much, did you?'

'No.'

'Why not?'

'I have too much pride for a poor man,' Caradoc acknowledged wryly. 'I don't like being made use of. Jeremy Maddock loved money more than friends, much more than he did any woman. He used us all for his own ends.'

Trudie had never resented his use of her. She had used him, too, to make her escape from her dreary childhood, and she had been grateful to him. She had thought his use of Wu Chao rather less admirable, but she had excused that too, for the Kis had benefited from the match as much as he had. She wrinkled her brow. How had he used Caradoc?

'Your cousins weren't the only ones to make money from the poppy trade. What did you see when you looked at your husband? A lover of art? A highly civilized man who could tell the second-rate from the best at a glance?'

'Something like that,' she muttered.

'He preferred the dead to the living and taught others to do likewise. It was as well for you he had died himself by the time you got here. I was glad of that.'

Trudie wriggled a little closer to him. 'I was always more afraid of my cousin.'

'I never thought of you as being afraid of anything!'

'I was afraid of almost everyone until I met you.'

He whipped up the horse and didn't slow down until they reached the outskirts of Malacca. 'Looking forward to being back in our other home?' he asked her.

She hoped he would never know how much. Her house in Malacca was beautiful and the furnishings suited her every mood. They had been chosen with care over the years and each piece reminded her of a past triumph, a satisfactory transaction, part of the profit of which she had invested in something beautiful as a cushion against the lean years. She had put the knowledge Jeremy Maddock had instilled into her to good use. She was glad that she had. He had gone to his grave owing her nothing. She suspected the same wasn't true where Caradoc was concerned, but she would make it up to him and she would enjoy doing it.

Trudie hadn't expected Swee Neo's complete disapproval that Caradoc should live with her in her house until they were married. 'It is not decent!' she told Trudie in no uncertain terms. 'No' good, Tludie. Bad will come of it!'

And so Caradoc went back to his old lodgings in the town until a propitious day could be found for them to marry, which was a sufficiently difficult proposition in itself with the added complications of having to please their European friends as well.

It was Mrs Beresford who told her the details of her cousins' deaths. 'My dear, the last thing I want to do is distress you, but it was almost as if they were expecting it. They had hired two Sikhs to guard their bungalow night and day and had practically barricaded themselves inside it. They hardly ever went out that last week. Mr Horton went to pick up their letters when a ship came in, otherwise they weren't seen by anybody!'

'What is thought to have happened?'

'The Army think they were victims of a burglary.'

Trudie gave her hostess an interested glance. 'But you don't believe that?'

'I don't see how anyone other than a fool can! As far as can be ascertained by anyone, absolutely nothing is missing! Strange kind of burglary, wouldn't you say?'

'Very,' Trudie agreed. 'What do you think really happened?'

'Me? My dear, who would listen to a silly woman like me? Even my husband says nobody but Malay would carry a *kris* on such an expedition. Who else would use that particular kind of knife?'

'Cousin Hermione killed Wu Chao with a *kris*.'

'Fortunately,' Mrs Beresford went on placidly, 'that doesn't seem to have occurred to anyone else – yet.'

'Yet?'

Mrs Beresford met Trudie's wide-eyed stare without so much as a blink. 'How are the Ki family?' she asked.

'Much as usual,' Trudie returned, a shade grimly.

The older woman permitted herself a tight smile. 'We could be wrong,' she said gently.

Trudie wondered how much the British knew about the Chinese *huis*. In Singapore it might be very little, but neither of the Beresfords were stupid. They probably knew as much, or more, than she did. She veiled her eyes with her lashes.

'I'm sorry the Hortons are dead,' she said. 'Of course I am! Cousin Hermione was my cousin! But I shouldn't want anyone else to suffer for her death.'

'You think justice has been done?'

It was Trudie who looked away. 'I don't think I want to know the answer to that,' she said at last.

Caradoc was of the same mind. Patient as always, he listened while Trudie told him of her own doubts. 'It may be just, but it isn't right!' she stormed at him. 'Whatever one thought of the Hortons, they didn't deserve to have their throats cut in their own home! Don't you think we ought to tell the governor all we know about their death?'

'What do we know?'

'We know the *hui* killed them in revenge for Wu Chao's death!'

Caradoc shrugged. 'Do we?'

'Of course we do! Even if we don't tell the authorities, I think we ought to do *something*! It isn't right, Caradoc. I agree that far too many of the British don't bother to learn anything of the customs of the people they are governing, but it doesn't alter the fact that so many immigrants come pouring over the borders every day to escape the debt-slavery of the States where the British don't rule! If one chooses British rule, one has to put up with British justice!

It isn't right for us to condone the *hui* making a mockery of the law!'

Caradoc didn't move a muscle. 'Are you suggesting,' he asked slowly, 'that I should take on one of the most powerful of the Chinese *huis* single-handed on a point of law?'

She was silenced. 'We ought to do something!'

'Why? It may be rough justice, but it seems to me that justice has been done.'

Trudie sat down on the nearest chair and burst into tears. 'I must be a monster!' she wept. 'My father was right! Oh, Caradoc, what am I going to do? I'm *glad* they're dead!'

Caradoc wiped away her tears, pulling her on to his knee. 'There's reasonable you're being now! They were your enemies, even if she was your cousin. Do you think either of them would have mourned your death if it had been the other way round? We never should have had a quiet moment wondering when the blow was going to fall. I'm more thankful than I can say that the Kis have had you in their protection ever since Black Jade was born.'

Trudie managed a shaky smile. 'Death seems so final though,' she said. 'I wish there could have been another way. At least, I hope I do! Thank God for you! I love you so much, so very much, that I shouldn't want to live if anything happened to you! You will stay alive, won't you?'

'I'll do my best,' he promised.

Their shared laughter made her feel better. As long as they were both alive, she thought, life was very much worth the living. How glad, how very glad she was to be alive!

It was late when Caradoc left and she finally went to bed. She didn't notice the small package at first, not until she was about to get into bed did she see it on the pillow. With trembling fingers, she untied the string and opened up the paper. A small, shiny object fell out on to the bed. She picked it up and held it out to the light on the palm of her hand. It was the most enchanting piece of carved black jade she had ever seen. Excitement mounted inside her as she wondered who could have put it on her bed. She saw it had been fashioned into a dragonfly on the point of flight. It was quite beautiful. Then she saw the card that had been enclosed in the package and picked it up, turning it over to find out what was written on it. The legend was in English.

With love, it read, *from Ki Wu Chao*.

Hannah Beresford didn't often visit Trudie in her house in the Chinese quarter. She found it an interesting experience whenever she did so, never knowing quite what to expect, and she did her very best to encourage others from the European community to go with her.

'Considering the circumstances,' she would say darkly, 'Mrs Maddock has done a marvellous job of putting her life together again. My husband and I both admire her very much.' That this admiration was not shared by many others of the small Malacca community did not bother her unduly. She had a touching faith that they would all come round as soon as Trudie was safely married again.

When Mrs Beresford arrived one afternoon without a single daughter in attendance, Trudie suspected she was about to receive a lecture on being more sociable – entirely for her own good, of course! 'How glad I am to find you in!' Mrs Beresford exclaimed, a patent untruth if ever Trudie had heard one.

'My dear Mrs Beresford, come inside and make yourself comfortable. What on earth can have brought you here in a rickshaw and not in your own carriage, and in the full heat of the sun! Please sit down and I'll have some refreshments brought.'

Mrs Beresford paid off the rickshaw and stepped inside, looking about her with appreciation. 'What a haven from the world you've made this place! I confess I know of no more rewarding place to visit in the whole of Malacca. I wish I could find the time to visit with you more often. I always did like you better than any other woman in Malacca!'

Trudie's astonishment at this statement left both women speechless. Finally, the younger woman turned away the compliment with a disbelieving smile. 'I'm glad you should think so, of course,' she said, 'but I'm well aware that few people find me likeable. I have a way with me – '

Mrs Beresford cut her off with a gesture. 'Nonsense! I won't have you disparage yourself so! It isn't true now, and I doubt it ever was! You have many pretty ways and a great deal of generosity, as I and my daughters have reason to know!'

Trudie sat very still. Even her breath was suspended within her. Then she said, 'I've been so afraid, ma'am, that I can't love – as a woman does love a man, that I haven't the feeling – oh dear, you must know what I mean! Supposing I can't give Mr Rhys all he needs to find in his wife?'

Mrs Beresford gave her a long, considering glance. 'I should have thought you would already have discovered the truth of that! Did he have any complaints?'

'N-no.'

'Well, there you are! He doesn't have to marry you, does he?'

Trudie managed a trembling smile. 'No.'

'Thankfully, most men are not like your father, Gertrude. I think you have a lot of love to give, and I'm considered to be a pretty good judge of character, so I think you may believe me. Now – '

The door opened a crack and Black Jade came in, pulling Caradoc by the hand behind her. She stopped dead when she saw Mrs Beresford seated in the best chair. 'Oh!'

Trudie shook her head at her. 'Come and say hello properly to Mrs Beresford!'

The little girl kowtowed, bowing low in front of the strange European woman. Since coming home to Malacca, she had already lost her previous acceptance of Europeans, preferring to merge into the background as most Nonyas did, speaking and being herself only with her own kind.

Mrs Beresford accepted the tribute with her customary elegance. 'What do you think of Mrs Maddock getting married again?' she asked.

Black Jade stared at her. 'I'm going to be the bridesmaid,' she announced.

Alarm signals sped amongst the adults, then Mrs Beresford said, 'Why not? You may as well begin as you mean to go on,' she murmured to Trudie. 'You won't be giving up your Chinese friends, I take it?'

'I doubt I could manage without them!' Trudie answered, hoping the Lieutenant-Governor's lady would never discover the exact truth of that.

'Then what better way to begin than with such a pretty child following you up the aisle?'

Relieved, Trudie watched Caradoc bow over Mrs Beresford's hand in his turn. He did it very well, she thought. Who, looking at him now, would have guessed the poverty of his childhood? She was suddenly very proud of him.

'Could a gentleman do better?' she asked Mrs Beresford in an amused aside.

'Indeed not!' The older woman laughed. 'I make no secret of it, my dear, that if it weren't for Mr Beresford, your young man would throw me into quite a flutter, never mind that I'm years older than both of you!'

'Not so very many years, ma'am!'

'Enough, thankfully, to take this wedding of yours in hand. Now, I won't hear a word against it, so don't waste your breath! I mean to give your marriage a send-off that Malacca will remember as long as there is a British community here to remember! The first thing to arrange will be your dress!'

'Oh but, ma'am – '

Mrs Beresford sighed. 'No, I do not think Nonya dress will be at all suitable!'

Trudie laughed. 'I wasn't going to suggest it! Swee Neo, Wu Chao's sister, did offer to embroider it for me, however, and the slippers I'm wearing as well. I don't think you'll be displeased with the result.'

Having envied Trudie the beautiful detail on her clothes for as long as she had known her, Mrs Beresford was enthusiastic. What was more, when Swee Neo was summoned to discuss exactly how the dress should look, she was surprised to discover herself in complete agreement with the Chinese woman about a great many other things besides the wedding dress, its colour scheme and how it should conform to the very latest look, with no crinoline, but a trailing skirt and possibly just the hint of a bustle. Both ladies were well satisfied with their plans.

'And what will I wear?' Black Jade demanded.

One look from her aunt reduced the little girl to silence. It was Trudie, who never willingly snubbed the child, who hastened to reassure her. 'You shall wear Nonya dress, of course. Perhaps in the same colours as my dress.'

Black Jade nodded, satisfied. 'It must always be as the *Nai-nai* wishes,' she said, with a significant look at her aunt.

Swee Neo looked amused. 'Indeed, we all wish for Elder Sister's happiness, and you, young lady, most of all.' She shook her head at her niece. 'She spoils you, and so you must be all the more careful not to do anything she dislikes – like coming into her house uninvited, hmm?'

'Tludie likes to see me!'

'A married lady likes her privacy also!' Swee Neo informed her with a frown.

Caradoc Rhys would have left the ladies to it if Trudie hadn't taken him to one side. 'Can you wait a minute?' she asked him. 'I have something to show you.'

'Very well.'

Mrs Beresford took her leave shortly after that, well satisfied with her efforts on her friend's behalf. She had almost forgotten her anger of the morning with Mr Jonathan Grant in her interest in having finally met Swee Neo, whom she had liked far better than she had ever imagined she would a Chinese.

'Who would have thought it?' she asked her husband later. 'But she was delightful! I don't know when I've enjoyed myself more!'

'Glad to hear it!' her husband had responded.

With Mrs Beresford gone, Trudie brought out the black jade dragonfly for the others to see. 'I found it on my bed last night, with the label saying it was from Wu Chao. Have you any idea how it got there?'

Swee Neo looked embarrassed, but disclaimed any knowledge of the small package. 'Have you thought, Tludie, it might be *kongsi* who blings dlagonfly from Singapore?'

'*Kongsi* or *hui*?' Trudie enquired dryly.

'Maybe same thing,' Swee Neo answered. 'Best not knowing anything.'

Trudie thought Caradoc would probably agree with that

but, at first, he didn't seem to. He whistled under his breath as he examined the beauty of the carving. 'I don't suppose we shall ever see a more valuable piece!' he exclaimed. 'Will you keep it?'

'Of course I shall!' Belatedly, she remembered he might want a say in that. 'It's your decision,' she added. 'Only, it is exactly what Wu Chao would have sent! A legendary messenger, carved from the black jade she called her daughter after, and coming just at this time! It has to have come from someone who knew her very well!'

Caradoc looked at the Nonya. 'Swee Neo?'

'Much better not knowing!' the Chinese woman maintained. 'Never mind who bling package! Wu Chao velly much liking choice of wedding plesent, never mind!' Her stress showed in her complete loss of control over her 'l's and 'r's. Whether she knew anything or not, Trudie thought, she could guess who had brought it and was afraid. It had to be the *hui*. Probably the same people who had murdered her cousins.

'Very well, never mind,' she said aloud.

Caradoc was still examining the intricacies of the carving when Swee Neo and Black Jade went back to their own house. 'You know,' he said quietly, 'I think Whampoa himself had something to do with this. You're very fortunate to be accepted as an honorary member of the Ki family, my love. Things could have gone very badly for you if they had decided to punish you as well as your cousin. They chose to overlook the fact that you share the same blood. They call you Elder Sister, even *Nai-nai*, which is the highest title a woman ever achieves. I hope you won't lose any of that when you become my wife!'

Trudie took the dragonfly from him. 'I'm very sorry, Caradoc, but I think it's you who will be just another Ki. Can you bear it?'

He grinned at her. 'At least I speak the language. I even understand and approve their notions of justice. It was well done, Trudie. She was your cousin, but it was still well done!'

She wasn't going to argue with that. 'I've done with mourning!' she said. 'I'm just happy that we've both survived to love one another.'

'That's the best of all!' he agreed.

There was a great deal of movement up and down the steps that led between the square in which Christ Church, the Dutch-built Anglican church of Malacca, was situated and the Stadthuys, high on its hill, looking magnificent for the occasion.

It had taken a great deal of effort to dress Trudie to Mrs Beresford's satisfaction. The dress was a magnificent champagne colour, with underskirts of the same colour. Swee Neo had embroidered the bodice in a contrasting shade of pink, and had made the slippers of the same pink silk. Trudie knew she had never looked better. She carried a fan of feathers the colour of a kingfisher and wore a jade necklace and bracelet and a small tiara of silver and jade in her hair.

The European community had sighed with relief when they had heard that Trudie planned to marry in church like a normal person. None of them were prepared to go as far as offending Mrs Beresford by not putting in an appearance, but they had held their collective breath that Trudie would insist on something as bizarre as it was unwise. An ordinary, traditional wedding service was an unlooked-for mercy, though it was only to be expected as Trudie's father was a man of the cloth and, whatever she had turned out to be, she must have been properly brought up in the days of her youth.

Most people, encouraged by the Beresfords, were inclined to be more charitable towards Trudie on this, her wedding day, than they ever had been before. Life hadn't been easy for her, to travel all the way out to the Malay Peninsula only to find her husband dead. And then there had been that dreadful business with her cousin, compounded by the strange murder which had resulted in her death. No one had particularly liked the Hortons, but they supposed there must have been some family feeling between the two young women and now Trudie had nobody of her own in the Colony and that was something they all understood. They felt her loneliness as their own.

Caradoc Rhys was a strange choice for a husband at first sight, but that, too, was understood better than Trudie could have expected. He might be a miner's son, and Welsh into the bargain, but he was a quick learner and most of them were glad to include him on their guest list. They were more pleased still when he put some business their way by allowing them to pick his brains about the tin mines and the customs and temper of the native peoples, and he even gave advice about some sound investments which most men would have kept to themselves. The more astute businessmen among them soon decided that, if Mr Beresford was not above being seen in his company, neither should they be, and they advised their wives accordingly, coming to like Mr Rhys for himself, judging him a shrewd man and an unlooked-for asset to the whole of the Straits Settlements.

Consequently, the church was crowded some half an hour before the appointed time of the wedding, everyone agog to see the most unconventional member of their society safely married. A buzz ran round the congregation when a number of Straits Chinese crept into the back of the church. One glance was enough to judge the quality of the Nonyas' dresses and jewellery, and many looks were exchanged when the Babas herded their wives into a row of pews, stifling their giggles at the width of the pews designed for far wider skirts and more ample Dutch hips than any Nonya possessed.

Meanwhile, Trudie was suffering the joint ministrations of Swee Neo and Mrs Beresford as they pushed and pulled her until her dress sat satisfactorily and Black Jade had mastered the task of carrying the short train without tripping over her recently bound feet. Every time Trudie looked at her, she longed to protest all over again against the crippling ordeal the child was undergoing, but she knew better than to voice her doubts yet again. The die was cast and Black Jade had chosen her own path through life. She might have crippled feet, the much-admired Golden Lilies of the Chinese, but she would also have the warmth and quaint formality of her mother's people. She would be securely anchored in the bosom of her loving family for as long as she lived.

Mrs Beresford fussed over the hemline, wondering aloud whether it was meant to trail in the dust in quite that way. 'I know the crinoline has suddenly gone out of fashion because my sister wrote telling me so, but I can't believe it was intended that one should be able to see a woman's shape quite so clearly!'

'It's a great improvement on the crinoline!' Trudie insisted.

'Do you think so?' Mrs Beresford wailed. 'We'll soon be wearing again those shocking *damp* dresses our grand-mothers wore at Waterloo!'

'Oh, surely not! Not damp?'

'Damp,' said Hannah Beresford in tones that brooked no argument. 'I have it on the very best authority that Caroline Lamb deliberately damped down her dress before the ball on the Eve of the Battle of Waterloo. Of course other silly wenches had to follow her example and got the most terrible colds for their pains! My own grandmother amongst them! She sneezed so heartily, she very nearly blew out the first sparks of romance between herself and my grandfather. No one, absolutely no one, is at their best with a cold in their head!'

Trudie laughed. 'That's something we don't suffer from much out here.'

'No. It's strange how one usually remembers only the best parts about the place where one is not! In England, I am much given to catching cold and frequently have to take to my bed for days together!'

'Thank goodness we're not in England now!'

But that Mrs Beresford would not allow. 'As if things aren't much worse out here! Cholera – '

'There's cholera now in England, too!'

'Don't. It makes one wonder if all we suffer for the sake of the Empire is worth while. I wish I had your clear-sighted view of where we are all going, not for my own sake, but I'd like to know I was doing the right thing by my girls!'

Trudie embraced her, her own problems forgotten. 'Of course you are! They couldn't have a better mother!'

'I hope they may think so when it comes to their wedding day! Do you know, Gertrude, you look quite beautiful in that dress!'

And she did. Even Trudie could see she looked as well as she ever had when she saw herself in the glass.

'Caradoc deserves the best!' she said with a complacence that sat strangely on her. 'I feel the best today!' she added defensively.

Mrs Beresford returned her embrace. 'You are the best! The very best!' she told her.

* * *

She would never forget standing on the top of the steep steps down to the square, her hand on Mr Beresford's arm, waiting for the exact moment to start the descent and her entry into the church. If she turned her head she could see the muddy brown of the river, the Javanese ships moored up by the bridge. Her own godown, discreetly unnamed, stood on the far bank, locked up for the day, for she had given everyone who worked for any of her businesses a day's holiday in honour of her wedding. Behind her was the stately drive of the Stadthuys with the leaves of the malacca trees stirring in the light breeze off the sea.

She took Black Jade firmly by the hand, sweeping up her skirts over her arm. It was painful these days for the child to walk and she hoped to spare her having to stand alone until they reached the entrance to the church. The church, in the Dutch style, had been completed more than a hundred years before, in 1753. The Bible was still inscribed with the first verse of St John's Gospel in Dutch, and on the altar itself was a frieze of Dutch tiles depicting the Last Supper. The British had made their church their own but nothing could obliterate its Dutch Protestant origins. It was Church of England now, familiar and yet unfamiliar, with a sweating young parson standing at the gate to the sanctuary, waiting to bless her union with Caradoc.

She paused at the church door, waiting while Hannah Beresford hurried to her seat. She saw the Ki family, looking strange and uncomfortable in their unfamiliar surroundings. There were other darker faces in the congregation also, most of them unknown to her, so she supposed that Caradoc must have invited them. Beyond them sat the whole European community, their eyes fixed on Black Jade's small form as she hobbled along behind Trudie, carefully carrying the train as she had been taught.

Trudie shut her eyes, calming herself, then she opened

them again and saw only Caradoc Rhys, taller than anyone else there, waiting for her at the altar. How marvellous to be his wife! She could hardly wait!

It was with difficulty that she kept pace with Mr Beresford, she was in such a hurry to stand beside Caradoc in the sight of God and make her vows to him. He turned and saw her and he smiled and, in that moment, it seemed to her that the whole church and her whole world was lit with happiness.

The sun was setting when Mr and Mrs Rhys took their leave of their guests. Caradoc handed Trudie up into the carriage and jumped up beside her. 'We have just one more call to make before we go home – '

'To my house in Malacca?'

'It'll always be one of our homes. The plantation can wait until you've made my house there as comfortable as you've made your own.'

She wondered where he was taking her, content to follow his lead. The sun was an orange ball in the sky when he came to a stop at Bukit China, the Hill of the Chinese, so named because long ago, in 1459, the Sultan Mansur Shah of Malacca had married the Princess Hang Li Po, the daughter of the Chinese Emperor of the Ming Dynasty, Yung Lo. Princess Hang Li Po, together with her five hundred handmaidens, had once lived on the hill which, later on, had been given to the Chinese community for their burial ground, the oldest outside of mainland China.

'I thought you might like to put your bouquet on Wu Chao's grave,' Caradoc said gently. 'You've never visited it before, have you?'

He waited for her by the entrance, leaving her to find the grave for herself. It was easier than she had suspected. She paused here and there at one of the grander, distinctive tombs that she had only ever seen in a Chinese graveyard. Fashioned to resemble a woman's womb, it marked the entry into the next life from this one. It also happened to be a beautiful curving shape that satisfied the eye. Trudie made her way up the hill until she could see the city of the living spread out below her. She would have to hurry up, for the sun was setting fast now.

Yet she still dallied, her mind on the past, as it had been so often since Wu Chao had died. The difference now was that she was able to dwell on the happy times they had spent together.

She remembered the sly look with which Wu Chao had told her about her second marriage. 'You wouldn't know about such things,' she had said. 'It's a nice feeling. Very nice.'

Well, so it was! Trudie knew about that for herself now and she could thank Wu Chao that she hadn't found it sinful to give herself to Caradoc. It had been a disaster that first time, anyway, but how much worse it would have been if she had been eaten up with guilt. She remembered how it had been the second time also and, despite the fact she was alone, the heat in her face made her feel she was suffering from a high fever. There was nobody now that she could tell about that, but she might have found the words to tell Wu Chao how she had felt!

Wu Chao would have understood other things without having to be told. She would know why Trudie had given Caradoc her chop and why, whilst she would have fought the interference of any other man in her business, she welcomed Caradoc's interest and even hoped he would make some of the more difficult decisions for her. She wanted to concentrate on other things these days: things like making a comfortable home for him, bearing and bringing up his children, even welcoming him home in the evenings with a meal of the kind they both delighted in. She would have to take lessons from Swee Neo and pay attention if she were ever to produce anything edible! Meanwhile there was Ah Nyiok – and she thought he might stay, if he could find a market for his kites locally.

Trudie began to look about herself with greater earnestness. She didn't expect Wu Chao's grave to look new any longer. In this climate a few months was enough to give the hardest stone a weathered look, as if it had been there for years.

She tried a new path, hurrying now in case the sun set before she got there. Then she caught sight of the iridescent wings of a dragonfly and was brought to a standstill by its beauty in the reddening sunlight. She followed it a few feet and, as she watched, it seemed to disappear into one of the graves. Trudie wasn't even surprised to find it had brought her to the right grave. *Ki Wu Chao*. That much was written in English characters as well as Chinese. All the rest was in the ancient pictograms of the Chinese language, which only a few people in Malaya could read, there being at least four thousand characters in which to describe the most basic things. It was beautiful though, more beautiful than the Latin script which the English had inherited and adopted as their own.

Trudie stood in front of the grave, remembering Wu Chao as she had been that last day, when they had picnicked by the waterfall where Caradoc had first made love to her. Her emotions jumbled together in chaotic confusion as she stood there, not quite sure how to honour her friend in the way she wanted to do.

She laid her wedding bouquet in the space between the twin arms of the grave. 'Do you already know the news I've brought you, Wu Chao? Do the dead know what is happening to the living, I wonder? Will Goddess Kuan Yin bring me an answer from you? Be happy, dear friend, wherever you are, for I am happy at last, as was promised! So happy, I can't tell you the half of it! See the flowers I have brought you, the flowers of my wedding bouquet!'

A flash of blue glinted at her feet, distracting her. The dragonfly flitted across the tomb, a touch of gossamer in the rapidly fading sunshine. *And dragonflies are the messengers of the dead!* How often had Wu Chao told her that, when she had been trying to turn this foreign devil woman into the semblance of a civilized person?

Trudie laughed out loud, completely unsurprised as the dragonfly appeared to disappear right inside the tomb. She had had her answer. Wu Chao had given her her blessing. She bowed very low, kowtowing as Wu Chao had so often kowtowed to her.

'I love him very much, Wu Chao,' she whispered, 'just as you said I would. Be happy, dear friend, wherever you are, as I am happy!'

Then she turned away, running down the slope to where Caradoc was waiting for her. She didn't look back, there was nothing to look back for. And she walked straight into the arms of her husband, the place she most wanted to be for the rest of her life, and felt the warm comfort of his arms about her. She had come home.